Praise for John Da*

The Mutatus Proceₓₓₓₓ ₓₓₓ ₓₓₓₓ

Suspense Magazine – ☆☆☆☆☆

The Mutatus Procedure *is a blockbuster that takes you by the scruff of the neck and thrusts you forward at breakneck speed until it drops you off exhausted on the last page. Whether you are a believer in all things alien or a skeptic, you too will be highly entertained and swept along with this magnificent tale of David and Goliath proportions.*

"Awesome book, gripping and addictive. It picks up speed fast and keeps you on the edge of your seat."

"Being a science buff, I want science fiction that is well versed in the topics it covers. However, I don't want it to be heavy-handed. I want it to be fun, exciting, thrilling, invigorating, and thought-provoking. *The Mutatus Procedure* provides me the kind of story that is exactly what I crave. We are immersed in government conspiracies, aliens, UFOs, and unexplained scientific anomalies, woven in a tapestry of kidnapping, mystery, the danger of invasions of privacy implicit in Internet usage, and unfettered power granted Homeland Security, juxtaposed against the timeless stories of love and friendship. A Great Read!"

"It won't disappoint. Wonderfully written and well-rounded characters. Awesome, thought-provoking story. Again, as with his other books, Krygelski is able to have you believe the unbelievable. It is excellent (as usual)!"

"*The Mutatus Procedure* is the very best book I have read in the past ten years or so. It ranks right up there with *Amazonia*, by James Rollins. Your way with words in describing a scene is very catching to the imagination, and it is nearly impossible to put the book down."

"What a GREAT READ. I couldn't put the book down. I'm looking forward to the next one. All the characters are soooo cool! Thanks for creating this intriguing adventure."

THE MUTATUS Nullification

Other novels from John David Krygelski

The Mutatus Procedure (Part One)

The Aegis Solution

Time Cursor

The Harvest

THE MUTATUS Nullification

John David Krygelski

For Christopher! Nothing
is as it seems
Remember...

6.15.20

STARSYS PUBLISHING COMPANY

Dedication

This book is for Jean, who never ceases to amaze me with her insights, observations, passion, intensity, and dedication to both me and our books. Without her, this novel would be a pale shadow of what it is.

Acknowledgments

As always, there is my partner in crime, Jean Nolan Krygelski. She is the one person who works harder on our books than I. Another breathtakingly wonderful job!

And, as always, I want to thank gifted artist Michael John Nolan for the absolutely incredible covers.

The Mutatus Procedure (Part One), as well as this conclusion, required a monumental amount of assistance from a variety of areas. For taking the time to patiently talk me through a multitude of issues, politely pretending that my questions were not as ignorant as they actually were, and generally making me feel as though they were happy to help, I would like to thank the following people:

Alisa Lindberg, news director, Tucson, Arizona, for helping me get the broadcast scenes right; Dan Marries, news anchor, Tucson, Arizona, for making it happen – I hope you both have a blast on your fictional adventure; David Hernandez, former Air Force and current commercial pilot, Tucson, Arizona, for being an awesome friend and a great help when Judtson, Kelsey, and the gang needed a quick getaway to Puma Punku – I trust you will enjoy your flight assignments in the story; Matt Harper, Tucson, Arizona, for his invaluable assistance with the medical imaging equipment; Lieutenant Colonel (Ret) Chuck Sherman, for the virtual tour of the C-130; Jim LaGuardia, M.D., VA Medical Center, Marion, Illinois, for his insights and suggestions in his fields of neurology and immunology; Scott Gumble, Tucson, Arizona, my good friend and an amazing computer wizard, for again allowing me to steal his essence for the plot; and those of you who make it all worthwhile – our loyal readers. Thank you for your support and enthusiasm throughout each of our books, particularly *The Mutatus Procedure (Part One)*, and for (not so) patiently clamoring for this conclusion. You are all the best!

And, of course, all that is accurate in the respective areas of the story is to their credit; any errors are solely mine.

Chapter 1

===============

IF THE PRECAST CONCRETE WALLS OF THE SPRAWLING HOME in the Catalina foothills had been somehow imbued with awareness…if the dark and heavy hand-carved doors had possessed a shadow of consciousness…if the discreet components assembled to create the collective construct of this home had, through a fluke of vibration or intent, collaborated to elevate it to sentience…the house would have seen its charge and its master, sitting rigidly before the computer. Her face displaying not a trace of emotion, her hands unwaveringly hovering above the keyboard, Kelsey Batman was as motionless and rigid as if she had been chiseled from the granite indigenous to the bedrock beneath the foundation.

With her eyes fixed upon the screen in front of her, unblinking…her senses heightened, intensified, sensitized, and sharpened by the amalgam of natural chemicals flooding her system…adrenaline and a cocktail of potent endorphins…Kelsey's mind was able to perceive even the subliminal flicker of the refresh rate of the monitor. The muscles and tendons in her fingers flexed and relaxed, initiating a mind-numbingly complex series of motions and actions…resulting in the typing of a single word.

Daddy?

Other than a virtually indiscernible shift forward, a movement unconsciously intended to move her eyes inches closer to the screen, Kelsey waited for a response.

After the passing of approximately two minutes, she typed again.

Daddy, are you there?

A muted whimper of pain, anxiety, and frustration was swallowed into the silence of the cavernous home.

"ANSWER ME, DADDY! PLEASE!"

▽

Chris Ashby realized that he had been staring at the piece of paper before him for more than thirty minutes without moving, his fugue state triggered, no doubt, by the odd phone call from Kelsey. His campus office was blanketed with an oppressive, almost tangible silence, the other members of the faculty and staff having departed to commence their weekends quite some time ago. No students remained on campus to take advantage of his rare accessibility either, all having scurried from their final classes of the day and piled into their cars, bound for the nearest beach or bar.

Exerting a conscious effort, he forced himself to focus on his immediate surroundings. Despite the fact that he had begun grading papers two hours ago, Ashby noted that only three were resting within his out-basket. Irritably, he tossed the red pen down and sat back, vigorously rubbing his face with both hands and thinking back over the several days elapsed since his return from La Paz.

After the frantic and sometimes frightening jumble of events and locales which he referred to as his "experience," he had thought that it would feel wonderful to sleep in his own bed, instead of the bunk at the missile silo, the cot when he had been held prisoner at the FEMA camp, the hotel bed in Bisbee, or the guest bed at Villarreal's home in La Paz. To his astonishment, Ashby discovered that his own bedroom felt foreign to him and oddly devoid of any comforting influence, his bed unfamiliar and unsatisfying. The long, self-indulgent sleep he had promised to himself had not come.

To his further chagrin, he also realized that the mainstays of his life...the familiar and comfortable patterns of his position as a chemistry professor at UC San Diego...his favorite restaurants and bars...his friends...were all imparted with a vague hollowness, as though they were a meal stripped of its flavor. Where, just a few weeks ago, those things had contained a vibrancy, the intensity of reality, they now felt artificial, as if he were moving through a movie set of his life rather than the real thing.

Removing his hands from his face, he stared across the room at the pictures and documents framed and hanging on the opposite wall, and said aloud, "Chris, I hope this doesn't mean that you've become an adrenaline junkie!" The sound of his own voice in the tomb-like quiet of the room felt jarring.

His eyes came to rest on the one family photograph centered on the wall, a professional portrait taken shortly before his mother had displayed the first symptoms of Alzheimer's. She was seated in a high-backed wicker chair, and wore a bright floral-patterned dress and a broad smile which accurately conveyed her personality. Chris was standing to her left, his hand on her shoulder. His sister, Starlight, bracketed her, and the three looked unabashedly happy.

He vividly recalled the day. The portrait had been Starlight's idea, a Mother's Day gift. The photographer was a customer from her healing crystal shop in Venice Beach, and had been doing the shoot in trade for a Bolivian amulet. It was ironic, Ashby reflected, that the amulet, according to the shaman Starlight acquired it from, was intended to convey good health and a long life.

Impatiently, he mentally traveled away from the recollections of the pleasant day, and as his mind wandered, it returned to the same topic it had dwelled upon a thousand times since the end of the "experience." In all the revelations emerging in the press from the Beckleman fiasco, nothing had addressed his personal piece of the jigsaw puzzle, and he was faced with the nagging question...why? Why had *he* been mind-controlled to stop his direction of research? Why would Beckleman even care about his work on monoatomic gold?

"It doesn't make any sense," he muttered.

▽

Lisa Trippiano sat nervously in her brand-new leather swivel chair. Although she had returned to New York as a full producer with the network, this large corner office with the view of Rockefeller Plaza intimidated her, made her feel as if someone would burst in at any moment and demand to know what she was doing here.

Her days and nights back from La Paz were a hectic blur…a frenzied, overlapping series of conference calls, meetings, parties organized for the sole purpose of backslapping – with Lisa's slender back as the target – and a surreal development that she had never dreamed would become a part of her professional life…on-air interviews discussing the details and personalities of the group and the events which had become the number-one news story in the world. And she was the focus, or at least one of them, having made the journey from guns pointed at her, to cameras and microphones.

As she had almost numbly proceeded through the most recent few days, surrounded by colleagues and a personality subtype heretofore foreign to her…sycophants, there had been no time for personal indulgences. Her boss had reminded her several times a day of a fact that she already professionally knew quite well: top news stories, like fame, are fleeting, reliant upon the short and fickle attention span of the public. Over and over again, he would tell her she had to "make hay while the sun shined," an archaic phrase he was far too young to have picked up from his peers and, she deduced, must have been something his parents had often repeated.

One of the personal indulgences she had sacrificed was keeping in touch with the gang, as she thought of them. Certainly, she had seen and spoken with Jimmy Meade, Dean Copeland, Scott Gumble, Bal Singh, and Dylan Falt as they had consented to interview appearances with her. She did have brief phone conversations with Saylor and Doni, Matt, Chris, Ricky, Carlos, and Romeo, pleading with them to come on the show. Regrettably, they had no interest, and nothing she said could change their minds.

"Well," she mused, "at least they didn't go on other programs."

Yet, those conversations, via telephone or in person, had all been business…related to *the story*. Not once had she been able to…just talk…with any of them.

And there were Kelsey and Judtson, who would not return her calls or emails. It was not that they had been rude or unfriendly; they had each sent word to her, through Romeo and Ricky, that they simply were not interested in making, as Kelsey put it, "a public spectacle" of themselves.

In reality, what Lisa craved was basic human interaction with them, hanging out, laughing.

"I guess I just miss them," she murmured wistfully.

Then, unbeckoned and inevitable, the image of Al came to her…poor, sweet, owlish, shy, timid Al Clarkson, unhesitatingly seizing a kitchen knife and charging the two armed killers…to protect *her*. The pain and the overwhelming guilt she felt for what happened that day had not given her even a passing respite, always in the background, always right below the surface, tightening her gut and ensuring that her tear ducts were always filled to capacity, waiting and eager to discharge their contents in a cascade down her cheeks.

The scene, now hard-wired into her psyche, replayed yet again. The men, bursting into the lounge at the silo, guns drawn. Lisa, unable to suppress the same personality trait which had served her so well as an investigative journalist, jumping up from her chair and confronting the men. Al, trying to stop her…trying desperately to warn her. And she, in her arrogance, disregarding his pleas and continuing forward until one of the two men slammed his pistol against her head, knocking her out.

Although she had been unconscious during his final moments, her mind had no trouble constructing a vivid scene of Al as he saw her drop to the floor and reacted, attacking the intruders while armed only with a feeble kitchen utensil. In the movie playing in her head, she heard the boom of the shot, saw the bullet slam into Al, watched as he crumpled to the hard floor…and died.

Arriving at this dramatic point of the mental play, she once again began to cry, the tears and the sobs doing nothing to ameliorate her angst. Lisa neither resisted nor willingly succumbed to the emotional onslaught, resigned to the fact that it was now an integral part of her life.

A small corner of her mind knew what was to come next.

And it did. As it always did. Once the brutal demise of Al Clarkson reached its finale, her mind then shifted to the FEMA camp. To the room with the windows. Lisa, holding a TEC-9 and picking off total strangers across the killing field outside. Doing it calmly, coldly. The deaths of these men did not hold the impact or the intensity of Al Clarkson's killing. Though both of them were living, breathing human beings, they were also *the enemy* and she shot them as easily as if it were an element within a video game.

The dust settling…the umpteenth rerun in her brain coming to the end of the final scene, Lisa recalled a saying: "There are three kinds of people in the world: people who make things happen, people who watch things happen, and people who wonder what happened."

In her own opinion, she had never been a member of the third group; however, she had devoted her entire life to immersing herself in the second, actually rising to the top of the field which pandered to the segment of the population who watched what happened. But now, as a former part of the ensemble who had changed the world, as a woman who had, for at least a few days, made things happen, she was having a tough time going back.

▽

Romeo Jones shifted on the dainty round wooden seat, made more to accommodate the frame and bulk of a man who was much smaller than he. It was late morning and the coffee shop was only partially filled with customers, mostly singles, engrossed in their phones, laptops, tablets, or Surfaces.

It had first been necessary for Romeo to evict a dawdling customer who had been occupying the seat in his preferred location. He accomplished this by settling his imposing, muscular body onto an adjacent chair, only inches from the squatter. The slight and slender customer, with the appearance and ambiance of an ACLU lawyer, wearing wire-framed glasses and sporting a trimmed jawline beard, pretended not to notice his mountainous neighbor at first, although he began squirming in his chair. Predictably, within minutes, the impact of Romeo's powerful presence had its usual effect. The man unplugged his charger from the adjacent outlet, gulped down the half-a-cup remnants of his latte, and hurriedly departed without a word or a glance back.

Not even delaying until the man was five feet away, Romeo moved into the corner seat, his back to the walls, and positioned himself so that he could watch both entrances of the shop. Thus, he began to wait and to repetitively shift his posterior until, twenty minutes later, Kenny

Bowman, the Phoenix bureau chief for the FBI, arrived. The special agent, an old friend of Romeo's from their days together as Army Rangers, was dressed in royal-blue sweats and wearing bright white running shoes. With a quick wave to his friend, Kenny moved to the counter and ordered a large coffee. The girl at the register, not needing the pretentious machinations of the barista, filled the cup herself and took his money.

After Bowman joined him at the table and they exchanged greetings, Romeo pointed at the cup and commented, "Black? Thought you couldn't drink that stuff unless it was half cream with about five spoons of sugar?"

The Fed, who was nearly as tall as his table companion but not nearly as broad, smiled. "I switched to black 'cause it reminds me of you."

Romeo just snorted.

Waiting until Bowman took a sip, he asked, "Anything new?"

As he set the cup down, Kenny responded, "Nope. Beckleman's been squealing like a pig and it's been ugly as hell."

"What do you mean?"

The man shrugged. "It's never any fun to bust fellow agents. Since your fiasco in Bisbee, we have been pretty severely pruning the bushes in the NSA, DHS, NASA...hell, even the CIA and our own agency. We've lost two guys out of our office here. I knew them both fairly well. Thought they were good guys."

Romeo could see his friend's conscious effort to control the emotions this level of betrayal by people he had trusted would elicit.

"But nothing on Luis?"

"Not a damn thing. I've personally interviewed two of the dudes who were on the silo raid. All they could tell me was that Luis had shut down security, lowered the tire slashers, and opened the gate and doors for them. They dropped your man off in Florence before they got to the FEMA camp, and had no idea where he went from there."

"Isn't Florence a DHS office?"

"Yep. That's where they dropped him."

"You talked to the people there?"

Bowman nodded. "Uh-huh. Haven't found anybody yet who remembers anything about that."

Romeo turned away and stared out the window, thinking.

The bureau chief knew his friend well enough to read the signs of frustration and anger in the normally stoic face. "Sorry, brother. I'm not giving up."

A loud sigh came from the big man. "I know."

The conversation, now subdued, continued for half an hour, as Bowman briefed Romeo on the other details of the investigation which had spread over three continents.

A comment triggered a question. "Kenny, have your people figured out how that strap-on gizmo worked?"

The agent's mouth twisted into a grimace. "No! We've brought in scientists from the private sector, universities, NASA, you name it. Nothing. How about you? Didn't you have somebody working on it?"

"Yeah. We did, anyway. Matt Wheeler. He's the one who came up with the fix for it. But we lost the one he was working on when the silo was hit."

"Did he figure it out?"

"No. He said he couldn't even find that it was putting anything out."

"Yeah, that's the same thing our guys are saying."

"Kenny, any chance of getting another one of those from Beckleman? I know Matt's been itching for another crack at it."

"I don't know. I'll see what I can do."

They both fell into a tense silence for a time until Bowman finished off his coffee and stood. "I'd better get going."

Romeo rose and shook his hand. "Thanks, Kenny. You'll let me know...?"

"I promise. If I get as much as a hint where the bastard is, you'll be the first call I make."

"Thanks, again."

"I need to ask you something, though."

"What?"

"Luis *is* someone we want to talk with. Is that...is that going to be an option when you're through with him?"

Romeo's mind involuntarily wandered back to the scenario he had constructed and replayed a thousand times since the killing of Al Clarkson and the abduction of his friends. It was a very clear script of exactly what he would do to the traitor after he caught up to him. Avoiding his friend's eyes, he answered, his voice neutral. "Sure. Of course."

Bowman looked at Romeo for several long seconds, then sighed and muttered, "Didn't think so."

$$\nabla$$

Bal Singh stuffed his spare laptop into the duffel bag, pulled the rope cinch tightly closed and tied it. Between the seemingly endless interviews with the press and his preparations for the trip to the Andes, the major casualty in his life had been sleep. When an open period of time had presented itself, which he could have used for the purpose, Bal found that he was too excited to give in to unconsciousness.

Before the plane from La Paz had touched down in Tucson, he had already decided to reactivate the canceled junket to Peru and Bolivia, the expedition which had been shelved as a result of his conversion at the hands of Beckleman's men. His grad students, previously disappointed in his decision to kill the trip and confused by the comments he made afterward, immediately and enthusiastically leapt upon the opportunity and rallied to help him put it together. Funding was not an issue. Even if the backing had not been secured in the past, the news of Beckleman's treasonous actions, and Bal's part in foiling the plan, would have ensured the university's eager participation. In fact, they did not once bat an eye when he asked for additional money to pay for the completion of Kevin Berry's research.

It was after accompanying Judtson and Kelsey to the disastrous meeting at Fort Irwin which had cost Dr. Kevin Berry his life, as well as seeing Sam Jonassen, Berry's former assistant, and finding out about the massive voids the geophysicist believed to exist inside the range near Puma Punku, that he had decided to expand the scope of his research to conclude the aborted efforts in the area of microgravimetry as it related to the Andes. Fortunately, he was successful in hiring Jonassen to work with him when he and his team were scheduled to arrive at the site. And Jonassen was already lining up the drilling equipment and the sizable labor force needed to perform the exploratory digs. Finishing the deceased scientist's quest was the least he could do for Kevin Berry, Singh thought to himself.

He stood up and surveyed the piles strewn about the floor of his conference room, checking each item off the mental list he had created for the morning departure. Satisfied, he turned to leave and had to step over a watertight chest which blocked his path. Fatigue sneaking up to him, Bal hooked the heel of his boot on the edge of the chest and stumbled, nearly falling. As he caught his balance, a rough chuckle escaped his lips. Continuing carefully, he promised aloud, "There will be sufficient time to sleep on the flight."

∇

"To Coop!"

Jimmy Meade raised his beer glass and clinked it against the glass held by Dean Copeland as they toasted the former astronaut Gordon Cooper.

"To Coop," Copeland chimed in, and they both took a long drink.

The two were on tall stools in a Long Beach bar. This was the first time they had met together since the SNAFU. The bar was mostly empty and they occupied a table in the back for privacy.

"Dean, when you called me to set up this little man-date, you said you had something to tell me."

The retired NASA analyst and author gave him a crooked grin. "Straight to the point, huh?"

Meade shrugged. "What the hell! I'm an old space monkey. Ain't got that much time left. Don't want to waste it on small talk."

"Okay, Jimmy. I'll get right to it. Remember when Beckleman spilled his guts and said that they had duped me by dummying up the photos I was allowed to see in the archives?"

"Sure."

"Well, remember when we were all telling our stories down in that hole in the ground in Arizona and I said I had a stash of a few of the pictures from that first batch I found?"

As he saw where his friend was heading, a wry smile formed on Meade's face. "Course I do."

Copeland took another drink from his beer, slower this time, before continuing, his voice low and determined. "Look, I can handle the truth. Whatever the hell it might be. But I don't like the whole world thinking I'm a fool for being conned into believing in little green men who built stuff on the Moon and Mars if it isn't so."

Meade said nothing, waiting.

"Anyway, I grabbed five of the pictures…the best ones…and had a guy I know, an expert in these things, take a look at them."

"What'd he say?"

"Don't forget, the photographs I'm talking about were out of the NASA archives long before digital cameras, Photoshop, any of that. It was honest-to-God film."

Nodding, Meade urged him to get to the point. "I've got that part, Dean."

"He told me that those structures in the pictures were not…*could not* have been doctored into the scenes!"

"He's sure?"

Copeland's eyes locked on Meade's. "Jimmy, he was so sure, he told me that if he was wrong, he'd kiss my ass in the lobby of the Johnson Space Center in front of a whole busload of nuns on a tour."

Meade chuckled at the image. "You're singin' to the choir, Dean. Don't forget, I'm the guy who saw the saucer land at Edwards and I have my own pictures to prove it. I never did buy the load of bull that spewed out of Beckleman about what I saw *or* about your pictures and all the other things Carlos and Dylan and the rest of them were workin' on."

Copeland eased forward slightly on his stool. "You didn't?"

"Hell, no."

Swiveling to his left, the author shifted his eyes to focus on the length of the bar and stared silently for a minute. Meade waited patiently, taking another drink from his beer. Finally deciding to break the silence, he asked, "Dean, what are you gonna do with this?"

Coming back from wherever he had mentally traveled, Copeland spoke, his voice conveying a sublime weariness. "I don't know, Jimmy. I honestly don't know. Ever since that first day at my desk when I saw something in those pictures and I jumped headfirst into this route I've taken, I knew what it was costing me. I've lost the respect of friends and colleagues. I've lost my family. And the whole time I figured that it'd work out, that I'd be vindicated and they'd all come running back, apologizing for not believing me."

His soliloquy lapsed momentarily. With a shrug, he resumed. "They didn't. Of course they didn't. I was nuts to think they would. But now…now that the press and everybody else believe I was just a gullible patsy for Beckleman and his group, well, there's been a vindication, all right. Except it's a vindication for all of those folks who've been laughing at me for years. Not for me.

"I know that if I try to come forward with this new thing, the expert and what he said about my pictures, I'm not going to convince anyone. All I'm going to do is look…pathetic."

The waitress came to the table and Meade ordered another round. After she returned with the beers and departed again, the astronaut leaned closer to Copeland. "What do you want me to say, Dean? You want me to reassure you that it isn't true? Of course it is. To a lot of folks you'll look like some damn fool who can't give it up…can't turn loose of fame or notoriety or whatever you want to call it. And yeah, somewhere, wherever your wife and daughter live now, they're going to shudder and hope that nobody in their social circle knows they're connected to this ridiculous media sideshow called Dean Copeland."

A halfhearted grin on his face, Copeland retorted, "Boy, you really know how to make a guy feel better."

Meade laughed. "Making a friend feel better is a woman's job. It's my job to kick you in the butt and tell you to quit whining, suck it up, and get over it. Now, if you're interested in what I think, I'll tell you. You go out there and keep telling the truth, at least the way you see it to be the truth, and no matter how much heat you get, you'll never be pathetic in my book. You might get a little sympathy from me for the shitstorm you're in the middle of, but that's it. The only way you're ever gonna look pathetic to me, Dean, is when you act like you're acting right now."

▽

Dylan Falt was sitting at the desk in his home office, watching the steady Seattle rain pelt his window and stream down the glass in zigzagging rivulets as he listened to the canned music tinnily coming from the speakerphone. With a click, the music was cut off and he heard an unfamiliar voice.

"This is Dr. Trandle."

Moving closer to the phone, Falt answered, "Dr. Trandle, my name is Dylan Falt. I was holding for Rosemary Shields."

The man's voice sounded neither friendly nor hostile as he responded. "Dr. Falt, the immunologist. I'm aware of your work, as well as your recent…ahhh, adventure. I'm afraid Rosemary isn't with us any longer. I've taken her position. Is there something I can help you with?"

Falt, realizing that his, as the stranger on the phone phrased it, "adventure" had instilled a level of paranoia he had never possessed in the past, inquired suspiciously, "She is no longer with the CDC? What happened?"

"I can't say for sure. Perhaps the people who worked directly with Rosemary preceding her departure might be able to shed some light, but all I know is that she resigned for personal reasons."

Dylan paused abruptly, irked by the man's imperious attitude. "That's odd."

Trandle, in a clear attempt to return his caller to the point, repeated, "Is there something I can help you with?"

"Oh, *perhaps*. A while back, Rosemary had approached me to work as an outside consultant. I initially accepted and then, for a…variety of reasons, was unable to proceed. My schedule is in order now and I wanted to speak with her about the assignment. I would like to pursue it."

"If I may ask, Dr. Falt, what was the nature of the assignment?"

"Of course. She had shared with me an epidemiological study the CDC had performed on the correlation between some recent vaccine iterations and the onset of autism. The data were quite persuasive. She wished me to approach the question from the direction of my specialty."

"Ahh, yes. *That*." Clear distaste for the topic was communicated in the final word. "As you may have heard, Dr. Shields publicly acknowledged tampering with the data."

Pretending ignorance, Dylan questioned the man. "Did she? I hadn't heard. That wouldn't have been the reason for her departure, would it?"

"As I mentioned before, I'm afraid I can't say."

"Well, I must admit that prior to my refusal, I had done quite a lot of ancillary research on the subject, utilizing data from other studies. Despite her claim that she had tampered with the findings of one specific study, I still believe that there may be a valid correlation. I would like to investigate the possibility…under the auspices of the CDC, of course."

The hesitation from the CDC department head was longer than comfortable before he finally spoke. "In the time since I've taken over Rosemary's department, I have come across this topic in her notes. I've reviewed the subject myself and, to be frank, Dr. Falt, I can't say that I agree with you. I certainly could not justify sponsoring your research."

Dylan Falt was quiet for a moment, staring at the telephone on his desk as if it would somehow provide him with a reflection of Trandle's facial expressions. "I see. Well, I would assume that's the formal position of the center?"

The reply was delivered officiously. "It is."

"In that case, there is no reason to take up any more of your valuable time, Dr. Trandle. Thank you."

He broke the connection without waiting for a response and turned to his computer. Still displayed on the screen was the email he had received yesterday from Rosemary Shields, originating from her address at the CDC. It had been brief, containing only a single line of text and a link to a news article. The article was headlined "CDC Official Admits Tampering" and was accompanied by an interview with Shields. In it, she described how she had deliberately misled Dylan and tampered with the study she had provided to him. When the reporter asked her why she had done it, her answer was a terse "No comment." Alongside the article was a picture of Rosemary. Her face looked drawn and taut.

Falt's eyes then moved back to the one-line message she had sent to him and he reread it for the eighth time. It simply said, "Dr. Falt, I did not do this!"

After he had minimized Rosemary's message, it took only a few seconds to find the email address he wanted and immediately begin typing.

Kelsey,
Hope all is well with you.
I just discovered that the CDC is no longer interested in retaining me to perform the research on immunization I was going to do before our little diversion. :-)
You and I never talked about this, but I was wondering if you might be interested in funding the research. I hope you don't think me presumptuous and I certainly understand if you decline.
Dylan

With a quick glance for errors, he sent the email and turned away from the computer to peruse the latest journal. Having read no more than the first three paragraphs of an article, he heard a soft beep. Returning his attention to the monitor, Falt was surprised to see that Kelsey had already responded. The email opened with a double click.

Dylan,
How much do you need?
Kelsey

Chapter 2

OF ALL THE MEMBERS OF THE NOW FAMOUS, OR PERHAPS INFAMOUS, GROUP, Matt Wheeler found it the most difficult reinserting himself into his life in the aftermath of their adventure. Unlike Lisa Trippiano's network, his employer did not appreciate the acclaim, attention, or notoriety which had been wrapped around him. Rather than basking in the reflected glory, RadTech reacted verging on outrage when the board of directors discovered that he had utilized their facilities and proprietary equipment to fabricate the device which had reversed the mind control forcibly imposed upon Judtson Kent, Carlos Villarreal, and the others. It had not helped that the press had been quite creative in dubbing the hastily designed, head-mounted assembly with such undistinguished appellations as the "gizmo," the "thingamajig," the "zapper," and, most unfortunately from the perspective of the board of directors, the "brain blaster."

In fact, of all his colleagues, the only person who appeared happy to see him upon his return was Robyn Reedy. He had initially been unsure what to expect from her, not certain whether she would somehow blame him for the ordeal she had suffered at the hands of Beckleman's thugs. Back from her captivity in the FEMA camp following an intensive debriefing by the FBI, and reunited with her daughter, Robyn found her first encounter with Matt to be an emotional one, throwing her arms around him and holding him tightly. Her employer was gracious and supportive, giving her a paid leave of absence and holding her position at the radiology lab until she felt up to returning to work. Over a quiet lunch, she and Matt had mutually promised to stay in touch.

He could hardly blame RadTech for their more hostile reaction, since their market niche was high-end medical equipment, and their customers were radiology labs, research facilities, and hospitals – a field which demanded the cultivation of a corporate aura rife with staid conservatism and deliberate, methodical, careful research, not midnight, seat-of-the-pants engineering. In the one and only meeting Matt had with his supervisor upon returning to Tucson from La Paz and after the explosion of media coverage detailing his role in thwarting the government takeover by Samuel Beckleman, his efforts to rescue the people from their mental exile had been unceremoniously summed up with the word *shenanigans*. The outcome of that meeting was suspension without pay.

Sadly, from there it only became worse. As the details of the mental conversion of citizens by Beckleman became widely known, almost instantly RadTech was besieged with thousands of requests from people all over the world. Their inquiries, rapidly escalating into obstreperous demands, could be segregated into two groups. The first group were certain that *they* were being mind-controlled and desperately needed to be zapped as soon as possible. It did not seem to matter to these people that if they were being mind-controlled, the last thing they would be doing was asking to be restored or recovered. The second group were people who wanted RadTech, or more specifically Matt Wheeler, to preemptively, and at times forcibly, restore family members, friends, or in some cases business acquaintances who, they were convinced, were no longer the same people they had been.

Within days of his return, more than a thousand Internet sites offered their versions of the brain blaster, built, the sites promised, directly from the secret specifications provided by Matt Wheeler and/or RadTech. According to the media, most of the devices did absolutely nothing and were harmless, other than the substantial damage to the pocketbooks of the unwitting customers. Scarily, a few headpieces turned up which were actually constructed with x-ray emitters, acquired from China or other offshore sources; and the television news channels, as well as all the web news sources, warned the population of the danger of using one of these devices.

Additionally, and inevitably, the radioactive isotope FDG, the compound needed for PET/CT scans and a necessary injection prior to the use of the brain blaster, began to disappear in large quantities from radiology labs, suppliers, and manufacturers worldwide.

With the evolution of these developments, Matt was not surprised to receive a written notification from RadTech converting his suspension into a dismissal. He was pleasantly surprised by the generous amount of the severance pay, which was contingent upon his execution of a full nondisclosure agreement. The agreement required that he never discuss any of RadTech's proprietary secrets or the fact that he had used their equipment and lab facilities for the creation of the device and, as far as the world would ever know, that his departure from their firm had been a resignation, rather than a termination. Apparently, RadTech recognized that, to the public, Matt was a hero, and they did not wish to suffer the additional bad press of firing him. He signed the paper. By the following morning, Wheeler received an email from Kelsey offering him a job.

Not bothering to inquire how she had become aware of his abrupt change in employment status, he had set up a fantastically well-equipped electronics lab and workshop within the fortress she called home, sharing a large work space with Scott Gumble, Kelsey's computer guru, and, at her request, had immediately begun working on a streamlined and shielded version of his creation. Opting not to use the name "brain blaster," he simply dubbed it "the converter." His other priority was to figure out the strap-on device utilized by Beckleman's men – the device that had so terrified Judtson and the others, turning them into the docile, compliant alter egos from which Wheeler had reclaimed them. The Beckleman mechanism, apparently obtained by Romeo through a friend within the FBI, stubbornly refused to yield its secrets. He was becoming convinced that the device had either been damaged or broken, or that he simply did not know how to turn it on, as he still could not even detect that it had an output of any sort.

In the days since his termination at RadTech and subsequent employment by Kelsey, Matt's contact with the others from the group had been minimal. He, of course, saw Scott on a daily basis and occasionally caught a quick glimpse of Kelsey, looking tired and disheveled as she visited the lab, her demeanor one of intense focus and concentration. But he had not yet seen or spoken with Judtson, Saylor, Doni, Ricky, or most of the others. The only exceptions were phone calls from Lisa, trying to talk him into appearing for an interview, and from Dean Copeland, who had approached him with the suggestion that they travel to Houston and use the converter on Harold Billings, the former photo archivist from NASA. Copeland remained convinced that Beckleman's people had zapped Billings once they discovered he was working with Dean and had kept a stash of pictures taken during the Moon and Mars missions.

Copeland argued that it was the only possible explanation for Billings' sudden reversal and the man's decision to surrender all the evidence back to NASA. Matt had passed the request on to Kelsey, who basically told him to sit tight on it and she would get back to him. This reaction was not consistent with the picture he had painted of Kelsey within his own mind. After their frantic escapade, he had grown accustomed to her being much more proactive and decisive. Shrugging it off, he sent a message to Copeland that they were thinking about it and would let him know soon.

Wheeler was at his workbench when a message box from the intranet appeared on his monitor. It was a question from Scott, who was sitting at his own work station only twenty yards away.

Wanna see something funny?

Shaking his head in silent amusement, Matt rose from his stool and walked to the raised platform where Gumble worked his computer magic.

"This isn't another *South Park* clip, is it?"

Without a word, Scott opened a streaming video and turned up the audio. It was news coverage of a demonstration. The participants were of all ages, and Matt was able to read some of the demands and accusations on the signs they carried: "Free My Brain," "Release the Key," and "RadTech Is a Part of the Conspiracy!"

The coverage was live and the protest was taking place in the parking lot of his former employer, the same parking lot where Romeo and his ex-partner, Luis, had overpowered two of Beckleman's henchmen who had come to capture Matt, or worse – the event which eradicated the lingering doubts Wheeler had been harboring about choosing sides.

Taking in the unruly crowd on the screen, Matt's sympathy for RadTech lasted less than thirty seconds before he said, "Look at the spokesman for the group," indicating a tall, anorexic male who was exhorting the throng with an indecipherable chant.

"That makeup must have taken hours," Scott commented in his normal, almost inaudible voice.

The man had made himself over in the popular guise of a zombie, with pale, peeling latex skin on his face and a blood-soaked shirt.

Matt laughed. "The eyeball hanging out is a nice touch!"

The news coverage of the event ended and Scott muted the sound. Hitching up a leg, Matt perched on the edge of the desk and changed the subject. "Scott, do you have any idea what Kelsey's up to?"

"What do you mean?"

As Scott answered, Wheeler was not able to infer a clue from his friend's expression.

"Well, I'm right here…under the same roof where she lives and I hardly ever see her. And when I do, it's only for a few moments before she runs off. I've been half-expecting her to drop into the lab once in a while, maybe for updates or a chat. But she hasn't. And she's not the same person. She's...I don't know...flat, not the same bundle of nerves and energy I remember. She seems...distracted."

Shrugging noncommittally, Scott told him, "Don't know. She doesn't tell me."

Matt stared at the other man for several long seconds, trying to decide if he did indeed know something and was holding it back or if he, too, was simply in the dark. As was typical, he was completely unsuccessful in getting a read. "You've noticed it, though. Haven't you?"

"I guess."

The terse, uncommunicative responses no longer irritated Wheeler as he had grown accustomed to them from his work companion. "Does she have you working on anything for her? Anything related to our last fiasco?"

Gumble's mouth scrunched into a frown. "I.... Uhh...."

"You can't say?"

Scott merely nodded in reply.

$$\nabla$$

Ricky Ingram sat stiffly at his kitchen table, his posture erect, his fingers rapidly flitting over the keyboard of the laptop. As he typed, his voice softly spoke the words into the empty, silent room:

> Brad Blazek clamped his sweaty hand over the gash from the forty-five slug which had ripped a furrow into his side, in a feeble attempt to stanch the flow of his own lifeblood. Fighting back the blurriness in his vision and the wave of nausea threatening to erupt in his throat, he climbed unsteadily to his feet and faced her. His attacker. His would-be killer. The woman of his dreams. Willow Reed.
>
> Even now, he had to admit, she looked beautiful. Thick, flowing rivers of blond hair framed her delicate face and cascaded around her shoulders, almost seeming to glow in the reflected neon light streaming through the motel window. Ripe, luscious lips, glossed to an obscene shade of red. Her full bosom heaving with each ragged breath she gasped. An impossibly slender waist, inviting round hips, and long supple legs, all not concealed but accentuated by the tightly worn capri pants. In fact, he thought, the only aberration...the only aspect of the delicious vision that she was...which distracted was the ugly Smith and Wesson revolver she held so firmly it might have been her lover. And it was pointed straight at him!
>
> "Willow...why?" Brad uttered, his voice pleading for a reply.
>
> Hearing his question, she tossed her head back, her golden mane swirling, dancing, and flashing in the air around her head, and laughed harshly. Even the muscles rippling her throat

excited him. "Why? WHY, BRAD? Because you're the sonofabitch who sent my father to die in San Quentin!"

Her words unleashed an avalanche...a torrent of puzzle pieces. The facts, clues, and details crashed and tumbled into Blazek's mind at once. All the pieces finally falling into...

The doorbell rang, the invasive sound jarring Ricky from his immersion into the gritty world of his novel. Glancing at the bottom corner of the screen, he saw that it was after ten o'clock at night.

Jumping from the chair, leaving the laptop on and open, he hurried to the door and put his eye to the peephole. With an involuntary gasp of surprise, he seized the doorknob and flung open the door.

"Romeo! Is something wrong?"

The big man was standing on the front stoop, holding a six-pack of Coronas with two bottles missing.

He answered with a shake of his head. "No. Nothing's wrong. Want a beer?"

"Sure...I mean, no, I hate beer!" Ricky's words burst out of his mouth too rapidly. "But come in!"

Romeo smiled. "It's not too late, is it?"

"No! I was just.... I wasn't doing anything." Stepping farther back into the living room, he repeated, "Come on in."

"Thanks."

Romeo walked in and, seeing that the only lights turned on were in the kitchen, crossed the living room, steering straight for the table and the open laptop. Shoving the front door closed, Ricky sprinted around his friend in a tight arc and beat him to the work area, slamming the screen down and nervously asking, "Can I get you anything? Some...crackers?"

His eyes moving from Ricky's face to the laptop and back to Ricky's face, Romeo broke into a broad grin. "Crackers?"

The slender man's nervousness quavered his voice. "Well...I don't know! What do you like with beer?"

"Ricky, relax. Okay? I don't need any crackers and I'm sorry I barged in on you. You're obviously in the middle of...something." With his last comment, Romeo looked meaningfully at the now closed laptop.

Catching his breath and calming his nerves slightly, Ricky was able to manage a weak smile. "No. It's fine. Really. You didn't barge in. I was only doing a little writing."

The two of them were still standing awkwardly at the table.

"Mind if I sit down?"

"Oh! Sure! Please!"

Romeo pulled out one of the chairs and lowered himself into it, handing the beer to Ricky after taking another one out. "Would you mind sticking these in your fridge?"

As Ricky stored the pack in his refrigerator, Romeo asked, "You write?"

"A little," he answered, returning to the table and sitting down. "Just for the fun of it, you know. None of my work has been published."

"Rejections are a bitch."

"Oh no, I wouldn't know. I've never sent it out."

Romeo took a long pull from the drink. "Why not?"

"I'm not good enough."

"No kidding. Can I see it?"

The request startled Ricky. "No! I mean, I've never showed anyone."

"Not even Judtson?"

"Especially Judtson."

"Why not?"

"Because he…and I don't think it's his intention…he can be pretty cruel sometimes."

"He wouldn't do that to you."

A loud sigh gushed from Ricky. "No, he wouldn't. Not to my face. But, you need to remember, over the years I've been with him when other people have given him manuscripts to read. Oh, while they're at the office, he's gracious, all right. Tells them their work is really good and they have talent. Then, the second they walk out the front door, with their precious manuscripts under their arms, Judtson turns to me and lets it all loose. Such nasty, horrible, scathing comments that if the writers heard them, they'd probably kill themselves. I'm sure if he read any of my stuff, he'd be nice. Real nice. All I can visualize is what he'd say to Saylor later. I just can't…deal with that."

Romeo nodded with understanding. "Yeah, I can see that. But why won't you let me read it? I guarantee you I won't be two-faced. I'll tell you exactly what I think." The Army Ranger's face was sincere.

Finally calmed down, Ricky leaned forward. "I'm not sure I want to hear the truth."

"Really? Why not?"

"Because, as long as no one has ever seen my work, in my own mind I'm a writer. It's what I feel and what I believe. It's who I am. But as soon as somebody else reads it and gives me that most dreadful of opinions…the sincere '*It's interesting*'…I think my little bubble would burst. I wouldn't be able to think of myself that way anymore. And I guess I *like* thinking I'm a writer."

Tipping the bottle back and draining it, Romeo shrugged. "It's your call. I was curious, that's all. You might be right. I don't know. On the other hand, it might be a safe way to kind of dip your toe in the water."

"What do you mean?"

"Well, I can see what you're saying about having Judtson read it. He's a monstrously successful author. He's won awards and all that. So his opinion could be pretty damn devastating, I guess. On the other hand, if you received a *positive* opinion from someone like that, it would carry a lot more weight…have a lot more value. Bigger risk but bigger reward."

"True."

"At the other end of the spectrum you've got me. I'm not a writer. I'm not a critic. I'm just a schmo who likes to read. If I like it, no big deal. If I don't like it, also no big deal. Doesn't mean much either way."

Ricky thought about his words for a minute before responding. "I guess. I don't know. You didn't come over here tonight to read my book."

"No, I didn't." Romeo stood and walked to the refrigerator, smiling as he returned with a full bottle. "I came over to see if you wanted to come do something with me."

The comment took Ricky a little aback. "Come do something?"

"Yeah. I think you'd be perfect for it and…I think you'd have a blast."

"This doesn't…do I need my gun?"

Chuckling, Romeo said, "That'd be the last thing you'd need."

"Then what is it? A stakeout?"

The big man shook his head.

"Well...what is it?"

Romeo stood up. "Come on. It's a surprise."

$$\triangledown$$

The muted hum of the jet engines inside the cabin of the Airbus vaguely tickled at the fringes of Carlos Villarreal's consciousness, lulling him gently toward sleep. The lights in the first-class section were dimmed, and his fellow passengers had already succumbed to their fatigue, the man across the aisle snoring sonorously.

Yet, despite the fact that it was the middle of the night, despite the number of flight hours already elapsed and the hours remaining until they reached Atlanta, he refused to close his eyes and surrender. He could not stop the endless loop in his mind, the relentless replaying of his travels during the past few days – first, by car, to Puma Punku and Lake Titicaca, and then to Lebanon and the Baalbek site – where he had carefully acquired the samples now safely ensconced within the steel-sided valise stowed in the overhead compartment above him.

This time, he thought, *there cannot be any doubt, any possibility of error.*

Giving in to the movie in his mind, he walked himself through the minutiae of acquiring the rock samples at Puma Punku – the drilling, the bagging, the labeling, and the sealing of the pouches – before he had moved on to the quarry near the lake, repeating the same painstaking process. On the final leg of the journey, he had returned to his former dig site at Baalbek, and again extracted samples from the ancient wall buried two layers beneath the Temple of Jupiter, which had been built by the Romans.

Since the arrest of the former head of Homeland Security, and the ensuing blizzard of press coverage, Carlos had remained unavailable, essentially hidden from the intrusive microphones and prodding, and the insulting questions of the reporters. From the first moment when he had viewed the videos of Beckleman's "confession," he had known there was something horribly wrong...something which did not add up. In his desperate and excited utterances to Kelsey and Judtson, Beckleman explained to them, and then later to the world, that all of them had been duped. Used. Manipulated into believing untruths to further the bureaucrat's own nefarious agenda.

And the world had believed him...or, at least, much of the world. No doubt driven by the urge to find a comfortable place to park their minds in neutral so that they might continue their superficial and hedonistic lives, the public embraced the scandal with an earnestness which had astounded Carlos. The absolute absence of disbelief among the mainstream media bewildered him, causing him to wonder why skepticism was such a one-way street. It was apparently acceptable to be a harsh, cruel, and nasty skeptic if the ideas or the facts which were portrayed fell into the well-defined category of "fringe." However, provided that it cast either the government or business in an unflattering light, the most egregious, outrageous, and illogical scenario was accepted without examination or question, whether or not there was proof to the contrary.

Even knowing all of this, even accurately foreseeing the rude and vile reception in store for him, Carlos was determined to present his proof.

▽

Saylor Costello instructed Mrs. Barnes to call his office if the severe headaches returned, and stepped from the exam room into the hallway. With a glance in both directions, he was instantly relieved to see that the other exam room doors were open and the chart trays mounted on the wall beside the doors were empty.

Walking to the high counter, he jotted some final notes on Mrs. Barnes' chart, placed it into the inbox, and sighed heavily. Liz, his nurse, who was sitting on a swivel chair at her work station, asked, "Tired?"

He nodded. "Man, I'm glad that was my last one for the day. I was barely able to concentrate on what she said to me in there."

As Liz smiled at him sympathetically, her eyes efficiently swept the week's schedule on her monitor. "Guess what? You are now officially caught up. She was the last of the rescheduled patients."

His eyes widened in disbelief. "You're kidding me."

Although Vance had taken as many of Saylor's patients as he could during his partner's absence, most people detest being handed off to another doctor and insisted upon seeing Saylor when he returned. And, of course, they wanted to reschedule as soon as possible.

The result had been that after returning from La Paz with the others, exhausted, battered, and suffering the effects of the adrenaline crash which comes after the human mind and body experience intense, life-threatening events, he found his work days overfilled with a third more patients on the schedule. Exacerbating the overload, nearly all of his patients had questions about the details of his recent notoriety, unburdening themselves to him with their personal suspicions about what the government was really up to, or wishing to share their own experiences with flying saucers. This had caused his normal fifteen-minute appointments to double or triple in duration, and his eight- to nine-hour days to frequently stretch to ten or eleven hours.

The grueling facet of this was compounded by the fact that he was rarely getting enough sleep. His nights had been plagued with recurring images of the FEMA camp…the commando-style rescue of Doni and the others by Judtson, Kelsey, Romeo, and Saylor himself…and how it very nearly had gone horribly wrong and, in fact, would have, had it not been for the completely unexpected intervention of a small militia group.

Rubbing his face vigorously, Saylor muttered a goodnight to Liz and walked unsteadily back to his office, where he found his inbox overflowing with more work. With a loud groan, he slowly lowered himself into his chair and stared blankly at the wall for a few minutes before finally refocusing his eyes on the computer monitor. The electronic inbox for email was as packed with unread and unanswered items as the physical tray.

Scrolling to the oldest emails, he first winnowed down the list by identifying the spam which had cleverly bypassed his filter, and dispatched it all to the trash. That task completed, Saylor returned to the earliest emails and began scanning the "From" and "Subject" lines, hoping to be able to mentally prioritize the column. Almost immediately, he noticed an email from Dr. McWhorter in New York, the physician who had identified the first patient suffering with the same symptoms Judtson was manifesting when their ordeal had begun. With a double click, he opened the email and read the brief message. It was merely a polite query as to how Judtson was doing, accompanied by a solicitous question about Saylor's health. He typed a hasty reply, informed his acquaintance that both he and Judtson were fine, and thanked him for asking.

He returned his attention to the inbox and was not surprised to see an email from Lisa. He assumed it was probably another plea for Saylor and Doni to appear on *The Jack Bailey Show*. In deference to their bond from the ordeal, he did not delete the email unread, on the off chance that it was merely a friendly check-in which he would eventually answer.

He scanned the inbox again, specifically searching for something from Judtson…finding nothing. The leather chair creaked as he leaned back and looked up at the acoustic ceiling. His relationship with his lifelong best friend had certainly taken a strange turn since they had returned to Tucson. When the mental breaks first began to happen with Judtson, the episodes which were the precursors of the whirlwind that followed, Saylor had been constantly worried, approaching the point of panic, that he was losing his closest friend. At first he was afraid that Judtson had some untreatable disorder which would escalate over time until he would be essentially vegetative. The escalation took a different turn, producing an altered Judtson, someone Saylor did not know and did not at all like. It had taken a freakish event involving x-rays, radioactive isotopes, and a lightning bolt to bring back the old Judtson.

But now, he thought to himself, *I have no idea what I have.*

The real Judtson was certainly still present; Saylor was not concerned about any possibility that he had been somehow reconverted. No, the recent change was fully attributable to his buddy's promise to Kristen. Ever since they had all disembarked from the Gulfstream IV at the executive terminal and had gone to their own homes, Judtson had been clearly struggling to sublimate, conceal, or maybe go as far as to eradicate his old familiar personality.

He and Judtson were still friends. They still spoke to or saw each other daily. But Saylor was an intrinsic part of the personality Judtson's wife so hated…the personality that Judtson was trying his best to eschew…and it was inevitably taking a toll on their friendship.

So much had changed. There were certainly no more paintball excursions, no more two-man battles against the radar vans and photo enforcement equipment in the city. Of course, that was probably also a result of the fact that he and Judtson had been arrested for their final outing. Although the charges had all been dropped, Saylor was certain that if they resumed their former pastime, even Detective Garrett would be able to figure it out.

Not that there was a need for them to take up that cause any longer. It was ironic, Saylor supposed, since Judtson's hope was that his anonymous civil disobedience would trigger something in the public – because it most certainly had, in spades. Ever since the original video posted by Kelsey had swept the Internet, and before he and Judtson and the others had become public heroes, at first tens, and then hundreds of paintballers all over the country had begun to emulate them, targeting out cameras, strobes, and radar vans on intersections and roadways in every state where the devices were being used. Now, someone on the Internet had dubbed the activity of paintballing the traffic ticket devices "Judtsoning," and the name caught on, all the way to the mainstream press.

Saylor had to admit that Judtson was not the only victim from their ordeal. Both he and Doni were now different, as well. There was no mystery as to the reason for the change in them. It was motivated by nothing more complex than simple fear. Doni's nights were as haunted with nightmares as his…reliving his return to the missile silo with Jimmy Meade and Carlos Villarreal when they were attacked by snipers. She was certain that the only reason Saylor was still alive was serendipity. Had he not unexpectedly reversed the direction of the truck just as the gunman pulled the trigger, the bullet intended for his head would not have struck the front windshield. And during his nearly maniacal charge against the blazing automatic fire when he was obsessed with rescuing her, only luck could explain his survival.

Yes, he admitted, they had both come within a hair's breadth of losing one another. Neither of them bought for a moment that people die when it is their time and that if your time is years off, it does not matter what risks you take. No...he knew...they both knew...there would be no more adventures...no more pushing their luck.

Chapter 3

THE SMALL CAVE FILLED WITH THE AROMA OF HOT BUTTER AND SEARING MEAT, overwhelming the acrid odor of the gas hissing softly from the Coleman stove, as Sam Jonassen deftly slipped the spatula under the frying Spam patty and flipped it over. The light from the gas lantern began to vaguely flicker and the shadows danced jerkily on the rough stone walls of his compact redoubt, the performance accompanied by the percussion of a nearly inaudible sputtering. Sam carefully balanced the metal cooking implement on the edge of the portable appliance and turned to pump up the tank pressure on the base of the lantern, instantly becalming the illumination and halting the terpsichorean illusion.

Disregarding the input from his eyes, Sam adjudged the sizzling meat concoction as done based purely upon the spontaneous triggering of his salivary glands. He twisted the knob on the stove, shutting off the gas supply to the burner and, nestling the piece of fried homemade flatbread in his left hand, he picked up the spatula and scooped the Spam into it, wrapping up his daily ration of meat. He hungrily took a bite, washing it down with a generous swig of water from his jug, grateful that the predetermined time of day for eating his only cooked meal had finally arrived.

For weeks now, his daily pattern had been to confine himself to eating a cold breakfast, usually a protein bar or occasionally a bowl of dry cereal. The midday meal usually consisted of a cold-cut sandwich and a piece of fruit. It was not until the hour preceding sunset when the sun, hovering low in the western sky, directly bathed the recessed entrance to his cave for the first time of the day. The rays heated the rocks as well as the camouflaged door he had fabricated from lashed-together totora – reeds which grew so densely in the lake that its historical inhabitants, the Uros, had constructed pseudo islands upon patches of them. As the warming occurred, any heat signature that his cooking activities might generate was effectively obliterated.

Sam Jonassen was on a personal quest, a pursuit attempted by hundreds, perhaps thousands of others in the past decades. And he was determined to succeed where essentially all of them had failed. It was this goal...as he preferred to view it, rather than an obsession, as his friends called it…which had prompted Sam not to return to the States along with the rest of Kevin Berry's group when the geophysicist's work was completed. Instead, he stayed in the high altitudes of the Andes on the Bolivian side of Lake Titicaca, adjacent to the eastern bank and overlooking the water. He made this cave his home for the time being, at least until he did succeed, as he was certain he would.

Where the others had failed, in his opinion, was by stupidly underestimating the adversary. Granted, they *had* certainly spent the time. According to the locals, some had stayed beside this body of water, the highest navigable lake in the world, for weeks, even months, watching and waiting. Sam did not fault them for a lack of patience. No, he determined, where they had erred was in their basic assumptions. If naturalists wished to observe and study an obscure and notoriously reticent animal in the wild, they would not trek to the forest or jungle and set up a noisy and intrusive base from which to watch.

Sam had learned this lesson early as one of four brothers raised in the mountains of Kentucky. Every year, he, his brothers, and his father would load up his dad's jeep and go deer hunting. He discovered at a very young age that if you wanted to get close to one of these skittish animals, you had to be aware of, and respect, the keenness of their senses. You had to understand the limitations of their eyesight, the sensitivity of their olfactory mechanism, the delicate accuracy of their ears. And only then could you adjust, compensate, mask, distract, obscure your presence…your impact on *their* environment…sufficiently for the ever-vigilant bucks to come to you.

His predecessors at the lake had erected tents, built camp fires, brightly lit the perimeter, run generators, driven motorized boats, and loudly played music along the shores, and then wondered why they failed…were chagrined that their quarry had not once made an appearance for them or their cameras. Did they not realize that their enigmatic target simply *had* to be far superior to the most seasoned multi-point buck in the woods, in terms of detecting intruders?

How could they not be? Not only had they managed to elude conclusive detection for centuries, but it was also a tautology that they were technologically sophisticated, even far beyond the gizmos and devices secretly developed by DARPA within the hangars and laboratories of Dreamland in Area 51. The poor ignorant fools who had occupied the edge of Titicaca, acting as if they were attending a spring break party, would have been as obvious to *them* as a deer hunter marching boldly through the woods while honking a horn and wearing cymbals strapped between his knees.

This was why Sam had ensconced himself within the cave, only exiting rarely and carefully. He assiduously satisfied his bodily functions in a pit he had dug at the rear, treating and neutralizing the waste with a chemical compound purchased from a combination hunting and survivalist store. His longest excursion away from the lair had been to meet with the author Judtson Kent and his associates, at Puma Punku.

He had been loath to make that trip at the time, but now, in retrospect, was glad that he did, as it had resulted in his meeting Bal Singh and in the job offer to work with the geologist on the upcoming scientific junket to finish Dr. Berry's work. Sam was certain that the subterranean voids Dr. Berry had detected were somehow directly related to the focus of his current vigil. If he had not believed that to be the case before, the violent execution of Berry had cinched it for him.

Even though he wanted and needed the money, Jonassen was ambivalent about the prospect of leaving his cave for the weeks, or perhaps months, that would be involved in working with

Singh once he arrived. Obviously, he hoped to achieve at least one solid sighting first. He had spent too much time and effort to now be absent for the one time it might happen. On the other hand, Dr. Singh, after what he and his group had gone through recently, would certainly be more open-minded than Dr. Berry had been when Sam brought up his decision to observe Titicaca.

Jonassen chuckled aloud and thought, *Not only more open-minded but a hell of a lot more famous, as well.* The connection would be a natural and most valuable if Sam was able to secure the proof he sought.

His reverie was interrupted by the rustling, scratching sound of a small animal gnawing at the totora reeds which blocked the entrance to the cave. Sam surmised that it was either one of the ubiquitous rats in the area, or a wild guinea pig, no doubt drawn by the aroma of his dinner. Standing, he snatched up a shovel and moved to the mouth of the cave, loudly slamming the metal spade against the back side of the reeds. The chewing ceased.

Leaning the shovel against the wall, he returned to the stove and removed the now tolerably cooler cast-iron skillet from the burner, thoroughly wiping the bottom by using a second piece of flatbread to sop up the flavored grease. Wolfing down the dense bread, Sam squatted and grabbed a handful of sand, tossing it into the pan. With his bare hands he completed the cleaning process by rubbing the sand around the inside and wiping out the dust with a towel, then stowed the frying pan on the top level of a five-tier wire shelving rack, specifically purchased to safeguard against rodent access.

The sun was now below the horizon and it was time for him to begin his regular evening watch. Taking care to slip into his heavy parka, leaving it unzipped and open, and donning his already loaded backpack, Jonassen tucked the heavy gloves into one of the coat pockets, extinguished the gas lantern, and moved to the cave entrance. Maneuvering in the darkness by memory, he took another whack at the reeds with the shovel to motivate opportunistic rodents loitering nearby to scurry away, seized the hemp handles attached to the blockade and lifted, shifting the tightly bound and thick obstacle to the side.

There was enough lingering twilight outside to allow Sam to step out, replace the makeshift door in its opening, and begin the half-mile walk to his favorite observation post. Following a path in the rocky face, a route probably utilized and worn down by the footsteps of indigenes for centuries, he moved to a higher locale, thinking back on how winded this trek used to make him not that long ago, before he had become acclimated to the 13,000-foot elevation.

He reached his preferred blind in minutes, taking advantage of the last feeble illumination to survey the immediate area for any unwanted company. Finding none, Sam shed the backpack and unzipped it, removing the canvas and aluminum director's chair and snapping it open. He then unpacked the rest of his gear, including night vision goggles, a voice recorder, light-gathering binoculars with coated lenses, and his digital cameras, capable of taking still photos and video with a minimum of ambient light. He arranged everything on the level top of the boulder he used as a screen, mounted the two cameras on stubby tripods, and climbed into the chair he had placed behind the rock, settling in for a long watch.

▽

With the southern hemisphere still in the latter part of winter, following sunset, the temperature dropped precipitously from an afternoon high of sixty degrees. The glowing dial on Sam's watch told him it was a few minutes after midnight and he guessed that it was now well below freezing.

He sat shivering, even with the parka zipped, the fur-lined cowl pulled over his head hours ago, and the drawstrings on it pulled tightly to close the front around his face like an aperture on a camera lens, revealing only his mouth, nose, and eyes.

Climbing out of the chair, he dug into his backpack, finding, by feel, the balaclava. The moment he untied the cowl and dropped it back onto his shoulders, his ears were able to hear a soft panting coming from his left. Jerking his head in the direction of the sound, Sam saw, in the moonlight, the dark, almost black-looking shape of a husky canine standing on the trail perhaps twenty feet away and staring at him. The animal's eyes, capturing the available light, shined red at him, bestowing upon the wild beast a mystical, nearly evil presence as it stood its ground despite being detected by the human.

The two-legged and the four-legged beings stared at each other without moving. Sam took in the details of the creature, noting its size as being half again as large as a full-grown German Shepard. Its ears, now perked and pointed skyward, were perhaps double the length of the pinnae on any dog he had ever seen. His mind recalled the myths and stories he had heard from the locals about the Andean wild wolf, an animal spotted over the years by the occupants of this high and hostile terrain although not granted validity by the scientific community, solely because they had not personally witnessed, captured, and examined the mammal. There was, supposedly, one black wolf pelt hanging on the wall of a local. Yet, this was considered insufficient to persuade the biologists of the wolf's existence.

A part of the lore surrounding the Andean wild wolf was that it would lurk around the fringes of the villages and opportunistically mate with the occasional young female human who was foolish enough to wander too far from her home in the darkness. The rational portion of Sam's brain, of course, had not even fleetingly believed this or the other stories, suspecting that the myth was created by parents to keep their youngsters inside at night. But now that he found himself alone in the moonlight and eye-locked with the brute, if it was indeed the wolf of mountain lore, the irrational, primal portion of his brain was eagerly ready to accept just about any arcane attribute, no matter how outrageous.

The wolf took a step forward. There was nothing tentative in its demeanor as it did so, projecting confidence and a complete lack of fear. Sam's mind instantly visualized the precise location of the pistol which was stowed inside his backpack, and calculated the number of seconds it would take for him to bend over, dig it out, flick off the safety, aim, and fire. Comparing the estimate to his best guess on how long it would take the wolf to reach him at a full run, he found the result dismal. He then mentally inventoried all the objects available for his immediate grasp and evaluated each of them for its potential use as a weapon. His conclusion was again dispiriting.

The wolf moved forward another testing step, maintaining eye contact. Somehow, Sam knew that the most prudent thing he could do was to resist the urge to take a step in retreat and he found complying with this self-imposed directive practically impossible. Despite the frigid temperature, he was sweating profusely beneath the layers of fabric and fur. His heart was racing, producing a cacophonous, tympanic staccato in his ears and he realized that he could not switch off the full-color and full-motion imagery inside his own head, depicting the wolf lunging…ripping…tearing. If the lupine visitor was waiting to catch the scent of fear, Sam was certain he was producing it by the gallon and was helpless to bring it under control.

The space separating them now near fifteen feet, the wolf began another step to further close the gap, when it unexpectedly jerked its head to the side. Something had seized its attention, eliciting an instantaneous response as the beast's black ears flattened against its skull and its fangs were bared. Sam heard the wolf make a low, menacing growl, but could not tear his own eyes away from the mythical canid to see what intruder could have triggered these reactions. A moment later, the wolf whirled and bounded away, its movements preternaturally quick, and disappeared into the craggy terrain.

With a loud gasp bursting from him, Sam found that he had been holding his breath. The avalanche of chemicals within his body, induced by the presence of the mysterious threat, sent tremors through him and he felt shaky. Stretching out with his right hand to steady himself against the screening boulder, Sam clumsily knocked over the binoculars, which tumbled away on the downward slanted surface. As he lunged forward to catch them before they arrived at the front edge and fell to their certain destruction, he reached over the top of the rock with both arms. His fingers snagged the leather loop at the last second and he collapsed against the face of the stone, shuddering with ragged inhalations.

Only then did he remember that there had been something...something bad enough... something threatening enough...to scare off the wolf. Raising his eyes from the rescued binoculars, he surveyed the terrain beyond and below the boulder, seeing nothing unusual. As he looked around, a vague movement in his peripheral vision caught his attention and he shifted his gaze to the lake.

As his focus solidified, all thoughts of his intense fear were gone. Sam's breath caught in his throat. The tremors in his hands and throughout his body calmed. Not sure whether his mind or his eyes were playing a nasty trick, he pulled the binoculars back and lifted them to his face. Prefocused for the distance, the light-gathering lens magnified and sharpened the object of his attention.

"Oh, my God!"

Leaning back from the boulder and letting the binoculars fall heavily against his chest, Sam moved to the video camera, still in standby mode, and pressed the record button. He hastily double-checked the battery status and determined there was more than enough capacity. Confident that the object was centered in the frame, he moved to the other tripod-mounted digital camera and, after adjusting the orientation and zooming all the way to the stop, used the wireless remote to activate the preprogrammed mode of a picture every two seconds.

Satisfied, he quickly seized the night vision goggles, slipped them over his head, and turned them on. There was a brief pause before the vista appeared, displaying all the detail of midday in monochromatic green. As he changed the zoom setting on the goggles, the object resolved in brilliant, graphic relief. Sam was even able to make out the water cascading from the rounded sides of the massive cylindrical form as it continued its gradual, silent rise from the surface of the lake.

Chapter 4

LAUGHING MANIACALLY, JEREMY SNAGGED THE END OF THE NARROW LEATHER STRIP dangling from his sister's neck and pulled it hard, untying the knot which held up her halter top. Shar squealed instantly, drawing attention from the other shoppers in the crowded mall while she clutched the flimsy top to her chest with both hands. The six other members of their group joined in the laughter, relishing her embarrassment, and immediately began taunting her to let it go. The random baiting congealed into a cadence as the half dozen chanted, "TAKE IT OFF! TAKE IT OFF! TAKE IT OFF!"

One of the other teenaged girls in the group lunged forward, trying to snatch the leather top. A high-pitched shriek bursting from Shar, she twisted back and away, dodging the would-be perpetrator and attracting even more looks from the surrounding people.

Jeremy saw that one of the *old fart* merchants, working in a bed store, was on the phone. "We gotta move. They're calling security."

His sister turned to face him, her face still flushed from the excitement of her daring spectacle. "Tie me back up, Jeremy!"

With his mind instantly conjuring a hundred nasty tricks he could pull on her, he nodded, and she turned her back to him, ruining his plans by saying, "And if you do anything other than tying it back up, I'll tell everyone about some of your little secrets."

He took the two leather ends and moved close to her ear. "You'd better not," he threatened, trying to sound as menacing as his shaky voice could muster.

Turning so he could see her face, she grinned. "Then tie the damn thing."

Mad and frustrated, he directed his fingers through an overly tight square knot and stepped away, muttering, "Good luck getting that undone later."

They resumed their prowl through the mall just as a single blue-clad security guard arrived. The group turned a corner before the guard spoke with the mattress salesman who could point them out, and rapidly fanned out among the kiosks to harass the vendors, with Shar making a beeline for the eyebrow threading.

Jeremy found himself walking alone, completely uninterested in the cell phones, sunglasses, and teeth-whitening products for sale along his route. He found that his eyes were darting from one face to another, studying the strangers who moved past him, oblivious to his gaze. As he walked, he noticed a sudden, odd calmness spread pervasively through his body, creating an eerie feeling of detachment, not only from his environment but also from his fellow human beings who surrounded him. The mass of humanity became two-dimensional to him...surreal and without any essence. Gradually, imperceptibly, the initial pool of calmness within Jeremy fermented, roiling and turning bitter and black, until reasserting itself as a mild resentment...the resentment ripening into smoldering anger...the anger igniting to rage... hatred. As he walked, a young man from the cell phone kiosk stepped in front of him and asked him what kind of phone he had. Not breaking his stride, Jeremy continued forward and rammed into the salesman, spinning him.

Monica Suarez slumped on the director's chair at her kiosk, typing a text message to her friend Briana.

> If I have to demo eye shadow to one more old white woman I'm
> going to poke her in the eye with the brush!

As she waited for an answer, she heard her friend Josh shouting "Hey, asshole!" from the adjacent booth, and turned to see the stranger who had obviously just offended him now walking toward her. There was something in his expression, something in his eyes which frightened her, causing her to shrink back into the chair as he went past her stand. She lifted her phone and started to video him.

Lacking even a trace of premeditation, Jeremy was only vaguely aware of what the muscles in his right hand were doing as they clenched into a fist. The action seemed distant, as if it were being performed by someone else. Gripped by an unsubstantiated blind fury, the teen fixed his eyes upon the face of an approaching man in his thirties...smiling as he walked with his wife and two daughters...his arms hanging heavily at his sides, weighted by a burden of packages. Without consciously doing so, Jeremy altered his course slightly and barged directly into the man's path, rearing back his arm and punching the stranger with unrestrained force, his fist connecting cleanly with the tip of the unsuspecting shopper's chin.

The man went down immediately.

The security guard, leaving the mattress store at that moment, heard his name called over the combination microphone and speaker clipped to the epaulet of his shirt. He turned his head to the side and keyed the mic. "Go ahead."

"John, we just had a knockout game in front of Cinnabon. The PD has been called."

Sighing heavily, he acknowledged and took off at a full run.

Excited at having captured it all, Monica opened YouTube and began an upload.

▽

In the sanctuary of his library, Judtson Kent stared at his monitor, his hand working the mouse idly, following one link after another in an external manifestation of stream of consciousness and free association. No doubt, he thought to himself flatly, Kristen believed that he was working. But the truth was that he had not written a single word since his return from La Paz – and not for lack of trying.

He could not even remember how many times he had opened the draft of his book on the findings of Villarreal, the story which had triggered the adventure…ordeal…escapade. What should he call it? He still was not able to determine whether the whirlwind of action, danger, and intrigue had been exciting or horrendous.

Despite his attempts, he had been unable to revise, refine, or rewrite a single sentence in the book. Now that the Beckleman videos were out, embellished by the countless news stories, the world consensus was that Carlos, and indirectly Judtson, had been duped, used, and manipulated to further Beckleman's power-mad agenda. Therefore, everything he had written on the subject was invalidated. The content of the book, if released "as is," would be viewed by the potential audience as the twitterings of a gullible fool. His agent, Mitch, and his publisher, Darrow, smelling the allure of guaranteed sales, had both been aggressively urging him to use the book as a foundation and revise it to tell the story of how effortlessly people can be manipulated and facts can be distorted.

He knew that they both wanted to capitalize on the intense media attention and, since Judtson had been at the epicenter of the scandal, who better to tell the story? Darrow estimated that the sales for the book would be in the hundreds of millions of copies.

Although Judtson had not rudely blown them off, as would have been his preferred reaction in the recent past, a trait he was attempting to ameliorate due to his promise to Kristen, he also could not make himself work on the project. But he was not certain what was causing this block.

Nor had he been able to begin anything new. When his alter ego had been in control, Judtson had started work on a book about the pyramids in Egypt, intended to be another in a long line of tomes savaging those who put forward theories other than the accepted science on the subject. Yet, despite two attempts, he now realized that he could not care less about the topic. As a result, he spent hours each day sitting at his computer, sequestered behind a closed door, and played games or surfed the Internet aimlessly.

His choice of venue was motivated by two factors. The more time he spent locked away in the library, the less time he had to spend struggling to sublimate his personality in front of Kristen. And he had discovered that if he distracted himself with games or the Internet, as opposed to sitting alone, walking, or going for meandering drives, his mind wandered less often to one specific topic.

Dropping his hand from the mouse, he buried his fingers in the thick fur of his canine companion, Rocky, who was sitting patiently beside him. Judtson felt the instantaneous medicinal effect of the contact spread up his arm and through his entire body, as he deliberately allowed his mind to wander to the avoided subject…Kelsey. There had been no contact between them since he had said goodbye to her at the airport. Nothing. Not as much as an email or a text message. He knew exactly how *he* would feel if she reached out to him. Happy, perhaps even excited. Still, he could not talk himself into making the first move…though he had no idea why. He wondered if she felt the same.

As his screen refreshed, a news item caught his attention. Under the heading "Trending Now" was the blurb "Knockout game in Arizona mall puts husband/father in hospital."

Slowly removing his petting hand from the neck of his golden retriever, eliciting a slight following movement from his pal, he clicked on the video and watched as the young man strode purposefully up to the total stranger and cold-cocked him, knocking him to the floor in front of his wife and daughters. Despite the fact that he could only see the perpetrator from behind, there was something in the scene which mesmerized Judtson, something in the set of the teenaged boy's shoulders, something in his demeanor or determination.

The videographer had captured not only the assault but the immediate aftermath as well, and Judtson watched the ensuing pandemonium. The wife dropped her packages and screamed, falling to her knees alongside her husband. The two daughters became instantly hysterical, shouting and wailing, holding each other and backing away from the assailant with looks of terror on their young faces. Some of the other shoppers ran out of the scene. A few joined the wife on the floor, checking on the unconscious man who was sprawled in the midst of the jumble of dropped packages.

Yet, through it all, the perpetrator stood planted...stock-still...as if he had been switched off at the completion of his task. A man in Air Force fatigues promptly stepped into the picture and grabbed the boy roughly, spinning him around and gripping him from behind in a restraining hold.

This first glimpse at the boy's face sent an unforeseen shudder through Judtson. Sensing his master's reaction, Rocky stood and quickly surveyed the room, searching for a threat and finding none. Working the mouse, Judtson paused the video and clicked the image to full screen, leaning closer. The boy's face was completely blank, neutral, emotionless. There were no hints of excitement or anxiety, no traces of the visible reactions one would expect from a person who had just committed a daring public attack.

It was not the visage of the boy which had affected Kent. What captured his attention, what disquieted him so, were the boy's eyes. As he stared at the frozen high-definition image, and his eyes connected with the replication on the screen, Judtson finally identified what aspect of these two orbs he found to be so upsetting...recognition.

$$\triangledown$$

Scott, responding to the curt summoning message from Kelsey, knocked softly on her door. Barely audible through the thick slab of solid wood was a muffled "Come in, Scott."

The tech opened the door to her home office, the room where she had been spending at least ninety percent of her time since their return to Tucson, and saw her slumped forward at her desk, her elbows resting on the surface, her hands cupping her lowered face.

"You wanted to see me, boss?"

She raised her head slowly, as if she were afraid of fracturing her neck, and swiveled in the chair to face him. In all the time he had worked either for or, during the days when Kelsey's father ran the company, with her, he had not once seen her in such a state. Her hair was tangled and matted. Deep, dark bags swelled pendulously beneath her eyes. The baggy mid-thigh–length T-shirt, out of which her bare legs extended down to gunmetal-gray slippers, was stained with a large dark blotch resembling a coffee spill. It was the same attire she had worn the last several times he had seen her and, as far as he knew, her sleep shirt as well.

In a voice lacking almost all of her usual fire and vitality, she said, "Were you able to find out anything about the name I got from Ashby?"

She had remembered a few days ago that shortly after they had converted Chris Ashby and were talking to him on the ride back to Tucson, he had mentioned that a private foundation offered to fund his research into monoatomic gold. Although she knew he was never told the identity of the foundation, Kelsey called him to see if he had the name of the person who had initially contacted him. Fortunately, Ashby had kept the man's card.

Moving to her desk and taking the vacant chair beside her, Scott, his voice its usual muted tone, answered, "A little. As you knew from the card, he's a lawyer. Not based in San Diego. His offices are in Century City, up in L.A."

Her expression was neutral as she listened. "Were you able to obtain a client list?"

He knew what she meant by the question. Once the lawyer had been identified, she wanted Scott to again practice his talent.

He nodded. "I got into their billing system fairly easily. Didn't find the name you were looking for, though. Just a slew of LLCs, trusts, and private foundations."

"Are you…?"

"I'm already working my way through the list, determining ownership and principals. A lot of them are owned by other entities or fronts. Several are held by offshore blind entities. It's been a little tedious and time-consuming, to say the least. But don't worry. I'll get there."

Frustration pushed a loud sigh out of Kelsey. "What about the lawyer's private files? His correspondence? He must have written something or received something from him."

"I know. Been trying to do that."

"Don't tell me *you* can't get in."

Trying for a reassuring smile, Scott explained, "They have a system in their offices which isn't really all that unusual for lawyers. Billing, pleadings, and things like that are on the main server. All the privileged communication is kept on each attorney's computer. His paralegal has access to it, and that's it."

"Can't you get into his computer?"

He nodded again. "Even I can't get into a system that has been unplugged. From what I can find out, he's on vacation until next week. And his paralegal takes her vacation at the same time he does. While they're gone, *both* of their computers are turned off and, I suspect, unplugged. After they get back, I'll get in. In the interim, I'll keep working the list of clients."

She fell back into her chair and rubbed her eyes with her knuckles. Scott thought he heard a soft groan come from his employer and friend. Through the past several days he had kept his questions and opinions to himself but could no longer stand by quietly and watch this self-imposed agony.

"Boss…Kelsey…are you sure it's your father?"

This was the first time he had broached the subject and had no idea what reaction to expect.

He was relieved that she did not lash out at him. Her voice was flat. "Yeah, I'm sure."

"But…."

"*Scott, he knew about 'Frasier'!*" A slight spark of emotion flickered in her retort. "No one else knew my nickname. No one! He never used it around anyone else. Only when it was just the two of us together. And he knew who I was…I never gave my name on the blog. And he knew about what we'd done. And he knew about Judtson."

Steeling himself with a deep, steadying breath, Scott countered, "Come on, Kelsey. Your screen name was 'batgirl.' Your last name is Batman. How hard would that be? And after you asked me to trace all of your interactions with Alchemist on the blog, I found that you *did* mention Judtson's name once when you were trying to get Alchemist to respond."

A harsh breath burst from her. "That's true. I did. I forgot."

"And if he knew that you were involved in the Judtson thing – even if he hadn't made the batgirl/Batman connection – when the Beckleman bust hit the Internet and the news, the fact that you were tied to Kent was all over the place."

She stared at him silently, taking in his words as he continued, "And all of your posts on the blog were about mind control. Not exactly a big leap of deductive reasoning."

"But that doesn't explain the Frasier thing."

"No. It doesn't. Seriously, Kelsey, who knows how long they...Beckleman's people or any others, for that matter...had been monitoring you and your father before his accident? You know they were focused on him because of his invention."

"You're saying they bugged the house? They couldn't have. There's no way they could have pulled that off under my father's nose."

He shook his head. "Nope. You're right. Think about it, though. They could have been surveilling the two of you when you were out in public...parabolic microphones, or God knows what else. In the months before...while you two were together, did he ever call you Frasier in public? At a restaurant or a mall...or someplace?"

Kelsey lowered her head into the soft leather of the high-backed chair and closed her eyes, replaying that recent history in her own mind. After several minutes passed, she slowly looked up and answered, "I'm not sure. He might have. Scott, it really doesn't make any sense. If it isn't my father...if this is some deception, why are they doing it? Beckleman rolled over. The whole world is accepting his story. What do *they* have to gain by telling me Beckleman was only a red herring and the real culprits are still out there?"

He responded with a shrug. "Don't know. Maybe there are two opposing factions. Maybe there's just a single person deep inside their organization who doesn't like the way things are unfolding and wants you to keep poking around. Maybe I'm just full of crap. I don't know."

Pausing for a moment, he sighed and murmured, "I can't figure out why you haven't heard from him...Alchemist...since that night."

"Me neither. And the way it all went dead right after he called me Frasier. He was gone! The IM connection was terminated. And when I tried to go back to the site where we had the connection, the *whole site* was offline! By the way, did you ever...?"

"I checked. The IP address he directed you to so you could chat with him was on an offshore server. I poked around a little more and, the way it looks, that server was part of a redirect network and the actual site was somewhere else. Now, with the first site down, I can't pick up the trail and follow it. I have a program running to check it every second of every day. If it comes back on, even for a minute, I'll know and I should be able to find out more about it."

Kelsey forced a halfhearted smile. "I know you're busting your butt on this, Scott. Thanks."

"No problem. In the meantime, you need to get some sleep. And some food."

She started to answer. He interrupted, "And a shower."

Kelsey smirked. "You're telling me I stink?"

He grinned at her. "Let's just say that you've smelled better."

Her eyes shifted to stare upward at the ceiling. "Okay. I will."

"All three?"

"Yes."

"Promise?"

"*Yes.*"

"By the way, have you talked to Romeo about this? He knew your dad, too."

Without looking back down, she slowly shook her head. "Not yet."

"Why not? You know you can trust him."

"Oh, I know that. No, he's focused on finding Luis and I don't want to sidetrack him from that. At least, not now."

"Makes sense. But you need somebody else to talk to about this."

She finally returned her gaze to him. "I've got you."

He reacted with a soft chuckle. "You know, talking to people is not my strong point."

Not able to help herself, she joined him in a smile. "You're doing fine today."

"Kelsey, this is the longest conversation I've had in years. When I leave, I'm going to need a nap."

That made her laugh. It was the first time in quite a while. "Then who?"

Sheepishly, he suggested, "Judtson?"

His single word provoked a brusque, definitive shake of her head. "No. Not Judtson."

"Why not?"

"He's..." – her voice softened – "he's trying to sort out his life now. The best thing I can do for him is stay away...leave him alone."

The computer tech stared intently at his friend, then commented quietly, "That's too bad."

She responded wordlessly with a tight nod.

Sensing that the conversation had run its course, Scott stood and moved to the door. "Okay, well, I'll be working on all of these things. Right after that nap. We'll catch something."

"Thanks, Scott."

"No problem. And don't forget your promise."

Innocently, she asked, "What promise?"

Rather than speaking, he reached up and pinched his nose before stepping hastily out the door.

Chapter 5

ACCOMPANIED BY FOUR OF HIS GRADUATE STUDENTS, BAL, lugging a heavy duffel bag, trudged down the narrow jetway into El Alto airport. Despite his promise to himself that he would sleep on the flight, he had not and was exhausted to the point where he feared he would collapse. Through the fatigue-induced fog, it took him a moment to recognize Sam Jonassen, who was waiting at the gate. Kevin Berry's former assistant was pacing energetically, broadcasting an unmistakable aura of excitement. As soon as he spotted the geologist, he ran forward.

"Dr. Singh! It's great to see you!"

Bal was instantly struck with the dissonance between this currently exhibited personality and the calm, understated, and laid-back character he had witnessed during their meeting at Puma Punku.

"It's good to see you too, Sam. Is everything all right?"

"*All right?* Yes! Everything is awesome!"

He quickly relieved Bal of his duffel, shouldering it easily as the students shuffled past, still stiff and tired from the long flight.

Despite overwhelming weariness, his curiosity now piqued, Bal pressed, "What is awesome? Were you able to obtain permission to drill on the island so soon?"

"No. That's not it. But I do have something to show you. Something amazing."

"What is it?"

Jonassen's eyes darted quickly around the room, as he apparently noticed for the first time how crowded the gate area was. "Not here. Not now."

After studying the man's face for a while, Bal shrugged and decided to drop the subject and wait. The two followed the students through baggage collection and customs before emerging from the airport and climbing into the oversized van Sam had rented for the group.

Sitting in the front passenger seat beside Jonassen, who showed no desire to share his news in front of the students in the rear seats, Bal laid his head back against the rest and closed his eyes. In what seemed like only a heartbeat later, he was startled by Sam who was roughly shaking him.

"Professor Singh, we're there."

The balance of the group had already disembarked from the van, grateful for the bellboys who scurried out to meet them and immediately began loading all the luggage and gear onto wheeled carts. Bal handled the check-in procedure for everyone, and the students, armed with plastic key cards, tiredly dragged themselves to the elevators as he finally turned to face Jonassen.

"Sam, where do you want to talk? The bar? The lobby?"

The lanky young man seemed to be on the verge of bursting from the effort of holding in his revelation. "Your room. I think we should be someplace private."

They rode the elevator to Bal's floor and found the room, swiped the card, and entered to find that the bellboy had already left his bag and suitcases. The intensely colored floral-patterned drapes at the balcony door were partially open. Sam hurried across the suite and pulled them closed, darkening the room, before slipping out of his backpack and retrieving a laptop from it.

Bal wearily sat down at the small dining table where Sam was setting up, and waited quietly. It did not take long. The older man noticed that, despite his almost mind-numbing fatigue, his companion's excitement was contagious, and he could feel his own pulse quicken slightly in anticipation.

"Okay. Professor Singh, I guess I should give you some background."

"By all means."

"Over the years, actually centuries if you include the local lore, people have spotted strange lights around and above Lake Titicaca."

"I've heard that."

Sam nodded jerkily. "People have also sworn that they witnessed crafts of some sort emerge from the lake. The evidence is horribly skimpy. A few blurry photographs. A couple of grainy videos where you aren't even sure what you're seeing. And lots and lots of eyewitnesses, but hardly any with decent credentials."

Bal acknowledged the statements, wondering where this was leading.

"I was told all the stories when I came down here to work for Dr. Berry. I heard them from the locals…and at night, at the end of the day, our group would sit around the campfires, drink beers, and talk, and the other grad students would tell about the things they'd found on the Internet."

His gaze connected with Singh's. "I'm kind of a skeptic. I didn't really buy into it at all. Thought it was stupid. That is…until one night."

"What happened?"

"I had been hooking up with one of the girls in the group. It was pretty good and I thought it was serious until late one evening when I found her in another guy's tent. I was furious and stomped off. I needed to get away. Be alone. We were camped right outside Tiahuanaco and I followed the trail to the lake. When I got to the end of the trail…the shore of the lake…I stopped, sat on a boulder, and stewed for a while. All of a sudden, and this is weird because there was no sound to go with it, I saw the lights over the water."

Bal leaned forward, caught up in the intensity of Jonassen's narrative. "What type of lights, Sam?"

"Orange, red, and white. Sort of traveling horizontally. I guess the best way to describe them is like the streaming light effect created by alternating bulbs on a movie marquee…but moving very slowly, not fast at all."

"And you said they were over the lake?"

"Uh-huh. About a quarter of a mile offshore from me. Maybe less. It's hard to judge distance at night."

"What did the lights do?"

"Just hovered for a couple of minutes. Doing that marquee thing. Maybe fifty feet above the water. And then…and then just…took off."

"What do you mean, *took off*?"

"That's it. One second they were hovering. The next second they shot away, like cannonballs. They didn't simply switch off or disappear. I could actually see the movement…the path. It was faster than hell. Faster than a plane or helicopter could go. Way faster. And there was no apparent acceleration. They went from zero to a bat out of hell in the blink of an eye."

"Where did it…or they…go?"

"Diagonally across the sky and upward. It's so clear here that I was able to watch them until they were only a tiny little speck in the sky. The direction was northeast."

The geologist leaned back in his seat, his face impassive, not revealing any reaction to or opinion about what he had heard. "What did you do after that?"

"I told Dr. Berry and the others about it. Most of the kids thought it was funny." Sam grunted in disgust. "Yeah, a real riot. Dr. Berry didn't take it seriously, either. I think he was convinced that I was drunk or something. From that day on I kept going back to the lake…every night…whenever I could. But I didn't see anything like it again for the rest of the project."

Sam waited, expecting a comment or two from the professor and getting none. He quickly resumed, "That was the reason I stayed behind after Dr. Berry and the others went back north. I was convinced that I hadn't been delusional or drunk. I *knew* I'd seen something. I just didn't know what it was. I did more research. Talked to every local I could find who might have something to say on the subject. And decided that I should stick around, pick up some good equipment, and try to get some evidence. That's why I was still down here when you came with Judtson Kent."

"Well? Have you found anything?"

Sam paused dramatically, a slow grin spreading across his face. "Yes! I have!"

Bal's eyes widened, the sincerity of the young man dampening any skepticism.

Tapping a key on the laptop and turning the screen around to face Singh, Jonassen jumped up and circled the table to stand behind him.

"Believe it or not, it was last night. I've been camped out there for *months*, living like a monk in a cave, waiting. I knew it was my last chance…I had to break camp this morning because I had agreed to work with you. The left side of the screen is the video I took from a hill overlooking the lake, using an extremely low-light camera. Cost me an arm and leg to get it. The right side is a slide show of stills, taken every two seconds and synchronized with the video, again with a good low-light camera. There was plenty of moonlight, and up here, even the starlight is pretty damn bright."

Bal Singh leaned closer to the screen and stared, entranced, his eyes flitting back and forth between the video and the still photos. Minutes later, when the images ended, he rubbed his eyes with both hands before gasping, "Oh…my…God!"

▽

Dylan Falt walked stiffly through the Atlanta airport; the cross-country red-eye trip, the narrowness of the coach seat, and his thick frame had conspired to partially cement his hip, knee, and ankle joints to near immobility, and several painful pops and cracks punctuated his movements.

"This is a fool's errand," he grumbled aloud to himself as he approached the car rental counter. To his surprise, the reservation was actually in the system and the checkout proceeded smoothly. In no time at all, he was out the doors, standing at the curb and waiting for the rental company's van to pick him up.

As he stood there, with his nostrils assaulted by the diesel exhaust of the almost countless shuttle buses which serviced the facility, his mind, not for the first time, recapped the facts leading up to this impulsive journey. After speaking with Dr. Trandle at the Center for Disease Control, Dylan's curiosity had gotten the better of him and he logged on to the Internet and began looking for answers on the precipitous departure of Rosemary Shields.

A basic search had found a press release from the CDC announcing the appointment of Trandle to the post. The release's only statement referencing Shields was that she had vacated her position for "personal reasons." Several news articles then appeared, hinting that her departure was related to her admission that she had tampered with the epidemiological study, but none of the reporters were able to confirm their suspicions. From there Dylan had moved on to a popular business-oriented social media site, of which he himself was a member, and quickly found that she, too, had a page. Another dead end, it did not appear to be up to date, still listing her former position.

His next step had been Facebook, which required him to join if he cared to see the details he was seeking. Signing up, he was overwhelmed with the number of people named Rosemary Shields. His inexperience at navigating the popular site had prompted him to enlist help from the teenaged son of his next-door neighbor, in order to find the right person. This page had been updated, and Dylan read several posts from Shields complaining about the shabby treatment she had received from her former employer. According to her own comments, she had been unceremoniously fired by the CDC and given no warning. The date of her most recent post was the day before.

His young accomplice had told him that she was not online and therefore not available for a chat. He had explained that Falt could not post something on her page until she accepted a friend request, and that the only remaining option was to send a message, but a message from a non-friend did not trigger an alert and would be easy for her to miss. Dylan sent a friend request. He also tried a message, keeping the tone of it light and inquiring as to how she was faring.

The next morning he checked the site. There had been no response from Shields, to either the friend request or the message.

At that point Dylan had attempted to find a street address, personal email address, or phone number for the woman and was teased by numerous sites which promised to possess the information and would share it with him for a fee. Applying the charges to his credit card, he had to go through three such services until he found what he wanted. He was gratified when he dialed the phone number promised to be her cell and reached the voice-mail greeting, a female identifying herself as Shields and asking him to leave a message, which he did. He then sent a brief, friendly note to her private, non-CDC email address, which he had also obtained from the same service.

Although much of his day had been filled with preliminary work on the immunization study, his preoccupation with hearing back from Shields never completely left him. By late that evening, after not getting a reply from her via email or phone, and having yet to receive any sort of an acknowledgment from her on Facebook, he had made the decision to come to Georgia.

Dylan's thoughts were abruptly interrupted by the arrival of his shuttle bus, which took him to a remote lot and deposited him at the end of the aisle where his rental car was parked. Only vaguely familiar with Atlanta, he activated the GPS built into the dashboard and verbally entered his destination. As he merged onto I-85 north, Dylan was immediately ensnared by the morning commute. Even after driving for half an hour on what should have been a fifteen-minute trek, he was surprised to see Lisa Trippiano already waiting for him on the sidewalk. Unable to cut over to the curb, he double-parked in the second lane and leaned to open the door for her, ignoring the rude honks from behind. She sprinted around the intervening vehicles and climbed in quickly, tossing an overnight bag into the backseat.

"You're early," he commented as he surged forward in the lane. "I thought your train didn't get in till eight-fifteen."

She nodded, puffing from the exertion. "We got here a little ahead of schedule. You know, the more I mulled over what you told me on the phone, the more curious I got."

He smiled at her. "Thanks for coming. This is probably nothing."

"Hey," she said, smiling back, "I like riding the *Crescent*. And I was getting bored up there, anyway."

Falt laughed. "Sure you were. I've been watching. You're still in the eye of the media storm on this whole story. Actually, I think you *are* the eye."

She leaned back in her seat. "God, I know! I've been feeling like the belle of the ball. The problem is...we really don't have anything new. All we're doing is rehashing and rehashing, trying to figure out clever new ways to tell the same damn story. Besides, from what you told me, this sounds fishy as hell. Do you think they've gotten to her?"

He shrugged. "Don't know. They already had her out of the CDC, apparently right after she sent me the email. I just need to talk to her. By the way, there really isn't *anything* new coming out on the story?"

"One thing, I guess. A little weird, actually."

"What's that?"

"You know that the FBI is spearheading the investigation. They've been pretty damn miserly with info. I've been cultivating a good contact inside and he's been feeding me stuff I can't use directly 'cause it would bust him, but it gives me good directions to follow. Anyway...he told me yesterday that Beckleman is adamant that only a total of ten people were zapped."

"Zapped? You mean converted?"

"Uh-huh. The two of us, Judtson, Carlos, Al..." – her voice softened as she spoke Clarkson's name – "Jimmy, Dean, Chris, Bal, and Kevin Berry. He swears that was it."

The GPS, working from the second destination Falt had entered, instructed, "*Turn right at the next intersection.*"

Slowing and executing the turn, Dylan asked, "You don't believe him?"

She shook her head. "No. Well, maybe. I don't know. Dean is absolutely certain that Harold Billings, the retired NASA photo archivist, was flipped by them. I guess he's been pushing Matt to go do a rescue."

"That's right. I remember he mentioned it back in the silo the night we were all telling our stories."

"Yeah! Anyway, remember…that night *I* also mentioned that my old boss and his boss… who's now my boss…suddenly pulled the old personality switcheroo. *That's* why I thought they zapped me – to stop me from finding out about the conversions. I noticed the change in both of them, and was digging pretty hard."

"That's true."

"So, no, I don't really buy it."

"*Merge onto the on-ramp for I-85 north, one hundred yards ahead.*"

Falt changed lanes to comply with the directions from the synthetic female voice, as Lisa changed the subject. "And where are we going now?"

"To Rosemary's house."

"Direct approach! I like that."

▽

The former CDC department head's address was mid-block in a relatively new development on the outskirts of the city, the neighborhood upscale. The homes were well set back from the tree-lined street; the desired leafy arbor effect over the two-lane road was still a few years away from completion. The front yards were neatly maintained, the grass a nearly impossible shade of green.

As he parked, Dylan turned to Lisa. "Do you know what they call this style of two-story house?"

"Nope."

"Five, four, and a door."

She glanced at the front of the building. "Oh, I get it. Five windows upstairs, four on the ground floor, with a front door in the middle."

"Yep."

As the two walked up the driveway toward the house, Lisa remarked offhandedly, "You didn't mention this before…is she married?"

"Not as far as I can tell. But that's just going by social media sites."

"Yeah, and everybody lies on those."

They reached the front stoop. The door was a standard wood six-panel, painted with a bright red enamel. Centered below the peephole was a brass plaque with the name "Shields" engraved in an elaborate script.

"Looks like the right address."

Dylan nodded and pressed the doorbell. They could hear the Westminster chimes from inside, followed by silence. He pressed again. No response.

"Not home?" Lisa asked, a vague undercurrent of worry creeping into her voice.

Rather than ringing the doorbell again, Dylan knocked loudly, only to be answered by continued silence.

"Let's walk around the house," he urged, speaking softly for no apparent reason.

They stepped back from the stoop and crossed the thick lawn to the driveway, circling the front corner of the structure, neither of them speaking. The home had a detached two-car garage, the breezeway connecting the two buildings covered with a shingled canopy.

"That's weird," Lisa muttered, pointing toward the house door.

Falt stepped around her and saw that it was slightly ajar. An undeniable tension twisted the muscles in his back and neck as he gently placed his elbow against one of the curtained glass panes and pushed. The door swung fully open on quiet hinges, revealing a wide mudroom. A second door at the other end of the mudroom was also open, and through it, they could see into the kitchen where several full paper grocery bags were lined up on the island counter.

"ROSEMARY!" Dylan shouted. "ROSEMARY, ARE YOU HERE?"

Lisa moved closer and whispered, "Something's wrong."

He nodded and murmured back, "Wish we had some kind of a weapon."

"Are you kidding? Since our adventure I always do. Be right back."

"I'll wait here."

She turned and ran back to the rental car while he stood silently in the open doorway, his ears straining to pick up any sound of a threat. Lisa returned in less than a minute, holding a 9mm Glock.

Speaking again in a muted voice, Dylan asked her, "Do you want to give that to me or do you want to lead?"

She stepped past him, making her answer obvious, and he followed her through the mudroom and into the kitchen. The stillness of the home was nerve-jangling as they rounded the island counter and found that one of the grocery bags had fallen on its side, dumping its contents onto the hardwood floor. A glass bottle of orange juice had shattered, splattering and spreading a quart of the sticky liquid.

They avoided the mess and continued, moving slowly through the dining room, living room, and a downstairs office, encountering no one. After checking the bathroom, Lisa led Dylan up the stairs to the second floor where they silently made a room-by-room search, still finding no one and seeing nothing else out of order.

Lisa's voice broke the silence, her voice anxious. "Where is she?"

"Don't know. Let's go down and walk the backyard."

Again, Lisa took the point position and the two returned to the kitchen, passed through the mudroom, and exited the house. As she turned toward the rear, Dylan lightly touched her shoulder, stopping her.

"Maybe we should look in here first."

Before she could question him, he stepped to the side door of the garage and gripped the handle.

"It's locked," he grunted. "Let's check the backyard."

They cautiously walked the rear perimeter of the house. Everything appeared perfectly normal.

Returning to the breezeway, Dylan trotted around to the front of the garage and, cupping both of his hands around his face and standing on his toes, peered through the small glass inserts in the top panel of the roll-up door. Lisa had followed him closely and asked, "Anything?"

"It's dark in there, but I can see a car."

He turned away from the door and faced her, his expression knitted with lines of worry. "Doesn't add up...a car here...house door open...groceries on the counter and a mess on the floor."

"But where is *she*?"

"Maybe some neighbor had an emergency. Came here to get help."

"I guess that makes sen…." Lisa stopped in mid-sentence. "What was that?"

"What?" Dylan replied, sensing nothing unusual.

"Ssshhhh!" She placed her ear against the white metal of the garage door for a moment. "It's a cell phone ringing!"

He pressed his own ear against the door. "I can't hear it."

"It stopped."

"Are you sure that's what you heard?"

"Pretty sure."

Falt pulled out his phone, searched for Shields' number, found it, and tapped to make the connection. Listening again, they both heard the distinctive ring from inside.

"She's in there!" The exclamation came from Lisa.

The two rushed back to the side and Dylan kicked against the door, aiming for the spot adjacent to the handle. The door held. He kicked again. And then a third time. Loudly splintering, the slab door crashed open. Off-balance from the final kick, he half-fell, half-staggered into the garage and instantly shouted, "Lisa, call 9-1-1."

"What is it?"

Slamming the palm of his hand against the garage door opener mounted on the wall, Dylan looked back at his friend. "Car exhaust!"

Pulling out her phone and entering the emergency number, Lisa stepped beside him and saw, in the bright light now pouring in from the rising overhead door, a female figure inside the car, slumped in the driver's seat, her head against the steering wheel.

▽

Lisa and Dylan were standing together in the shade under the boughs of a mature sycamore tree in the front yard of Rosemary Shields' home, watching the paramedics and police officers at work. Shortly after the first responders had arrived, one of the uniformed officers briefly questioned the two. Dylan told the cop that he knew Rosemary from her position at the CDC and had heard about her termination. Wanting to console her, he became concerned when she did not answer either phone calls or emails, thus the reason for his visit to her home this morning. The policeman seemed to accept that explanation, jotting it down in his notepad, instructing them to wait until a detective arrived.

The activity had attracted several neighbors who stood in clusters across the street, keenly observing the scene. At one point curiosity got the better of the group, who sent their most assertive member across the street to ask Lisa what had happened.

"Thas just horr'ble!" the neighbor, an older woman with an almost unintelligible southern accent, exclaimed.

Lisa took advantage of the opportunity to question the woman, hoping to find out something helpful about Rosemary Shields.

"Ma'am, do you think Miss Shields would have committed suicide?"

"Soo-cide! Lawd no! Rose wuz powerful mad 'bout a-losin' her job, but thas the end ta the story. She wuz mad as hell, not d'pressed. 'Sides, she wuz a God-fearin' woman. No way she'd be a-takin' her own life."

Lisa spent a few more minutes asking whether she had seen any strangers or unusual vehicles around the house, and found out that the woman had been in her kitchen making pies all morning and would not have noticed. After obtaining a promise that she would ask the other neighbors if they had seen anything suspicious, Lisa thanked her, and the woman hurried back to her friends, eager to share the news and complete her assignment.

It was close to noon when the unmarked car, clearly a police vehicle, arrived and parked on the driveway behind the ambulance. A short, stocky female, wearing a white long-sleeved mens' shirt tucked into black slacks, a large semi-automatic pistol hanging on her wide belt, climbed out from behind the wheel and, with barely a glance at Dylan and Lisa, proceeded directly into the garage. From their vantage, Dylan could see her talk briefly with the uniformed officer who had questioned him earlier. Twice during the conversation, the woman, whom he assumed to be a detective, turned her bulldog head and looked quickly in their direction before turning back. The officer then led her inside the house.

They waited quietly. The day had heated to a stifling level and the Georgia humidity was nearly unbearable. After no more than twenty minutes inside, the woman emerged and marched straight to them, extending her hand.

"I'm Detective Cahane." Her deep, gravelly voice, although hard and professional, was not unfriendly.

Dylan and Lisa introduced themselves, and Lisa noticed that the detective was not holding the de rigueur notepad.

"My officer inside, the one who talked to you both, ran your names. You two are part of that group who busted Beckleman, aren't you?"

Lisa spoke first, smiling. "Guilty."

"Well, I say *good job*. But if you want my opinion, you've only scratched the surface as far as cleaning up the scum in D.C."

Chuckling at her candor, Dylan remarked, "I think we'll let somebody else take it from here on out. One adventure is enough for me."

The beefy woman shook her head. "Too bad. Now, what brought the two of *you* to Atlanta and to this house this morning?"

Falt repeated the story he had told to the uniformed officer.

"So you and she were friends?"

"Not friends, really. More like professional acquaintances."

The detective, maintaining her friendly visage, allowed a trace of skepticism to creep into her voice as she asked, "Professional acquaintances, huh? But close enough for you to hop on a plane and fly all the way from…Seattle, wasn't it…to knock on her door?"

"That's correct. And yes. I'd grown to like Rosemary, and when I couldn't connect with her, I became worried. I didn't know her well enough to have met her friends or family, so I didn't have anyone I could call, so…yes…I hopped on a place, as you put it, and came here." By the end of his answer, he had made a point of sounding slightly testy.

Cahane pretended not to notice. "And you also decided Miss Trippiano here needed to come all the way down from New York, just to help you knock on the door of your *professional acquaintance*?"

He refused to be baited. "Yes. That's correct, as well."

The detective raised her hand and scratched her close-cropped brown hair thoughtfully. Watching this, Lisa wondered if Cahane was a fan of the old *Columbo* series. "I don't know. Sounds kind of weird to me, Dr. Falt."

Again refusing to be drawn in by her technique, Dylan smiled broadly and said, "Fortunately, Detective Cahane, I've reached the point where living my life in such a way as to not appear weird to you…is not one of my priorities."

A curious blend of irritation, frustration, and amusement flashed across her face before she laughed softly. "Okay, got it. You've been questioned by folks a lot better at it than me."

Letting out a loud sigh, she continued, "*Anywho*, this is an obvious suicide, so there isn't much point in letting this little chat escalate to the point where it includes phone books to the backs of your heads and pistol-whipping."

"*Suicide?*" The single barked word came from Lisa.

"Yes. That's right."

"That's ridiculous."

Turning her body to face Lisa full-on, Cahane asked, "Why is that?"

Unintimidated, Lisa took a step closer to the woman. "As we told your officer, when we got here, the door to the house was ajar. The kitchen counter was loaded with groceries. One of the bags had tipped on its side and a bottle of orange juice had fallen and broken, making a mess." As she spoke, Lisa's voice rose in intensity. "Who, Detective, if she is going to kill herself, goes to the Kroger and buys a couple of hundred dollars' worth of food first? *Oh, wait, I get it.* Your theory is that it *must have been the orange juice*. She was so devastated when the bottle broke, spilling her favorite drink all over her nice clean floor, that she left everything the way it was, exited her house, leaving the door unlocked and ajar, went back out to the garage, locked herself in there, started the car, and waited to die!"

Both Dylan and Lisa could see the muscles around the corners of the woman's mouth tighten for a moment. Taking a deep breath, she finally said, "Look, Miss Trippiano, I'm not done here. I still need to talk to friends, family, neighbors, former co-workers. And I am going to do all of that before I make up my mind. All I'm saying is that now, without any evidence of foul play, suicide is the most likely explanation. She did just recently lose her job, right after the public humiliation from that study-tampering scandal. People have done it for less of a reason than that."

Cahane paused, eyeing them both, then continued suspiciously. "Unless…unless there's something the two of you aren't telling me. Could this be related to the Beckleman thing? Is *that* why both of you are here?"

Falt glanced questioningly at Lisa, who responded with an almost imperceptible nod.

"Detective Cahane, exactly how much do you know about our recent…ahhh…adventure?"

Her eyes widening, she answered him, "I know that several of you were getting too close to something, something the government, or at least Beckleman, didn't want you to find. So they strapped some kind of gizmo on your heads and turned you into obedient zombies."

He nodded. "But do you remember specifically what it was that I was about to do before they zapped me?"

Her eyes drifted off to the side as she thought. "No. Can't say that I do."

"I had been contacted by Rosemary to do a study of the current universal vaccines. She had serious worries about a side effect, with a study to back up her concerns. She tried to get her bosses at the CDC to investigate. When they refused, she came to me and hired me…off the books, so to speak."

"That was the study she dummied up?"

"I'll get to that in a minute. Before I could even begin the work, I got my visit from the men in black and I dropped it, my alter ego blowing off Rosemary rather harshly in the process. After the Beckleman confession and Rosemary's public statement that the study was bogus, I was ready to move on and forget all about it. Then this came."

He grabbed his folded printout of the email and handed it to the detective. He and Lisa stood silently, sweating in the heat as she read. It became obvious by her expression when she arrived at the single line written by Shields.

Handing the paper back, Cahane only huffed.

"I tried to call her after I received that email. That's when I found out she'd been fired. I spoke with her replacement about doing the research anyway, and he told me that the agency officially had no interest in pursuing it. So I dug up her personal email address, Facebook page, and personal cell number. I left messages on all of them...before today...before this happened." With his last comment, he gestured toward the garage. "She did not answer any of them. I don't know how long she's been dead in there. If it's been a while, that could explain why she didn't answer me. But it couldn't have been too long because the orange juice on the floor of the kitchen was still wet."

Cahane took in a deep breath and let it out loudly. "And you think this might have something to do with the other thing?"

"Don't know. To use your word, it definitely looks weird."

He and Lisa watched as the detective reached around to her back pocket, pulled out a round tin of tobacco, opened it, and nabbed a pinch, tucking the brown wad between her bottom lip and gum. Closing the tin and putting it away, her bottom lip bulging forward, she rasped, "Damn! You two might be right."

As she spoke, a second unmarked vehicle was allowed through the cordon and parked behind Cahane's. She turned and glanced at it before doing a double take and grunting, "What the hell...?"

Without a word to either of them, she pivoted and walked brusquely toward the new arrival.

"Is something wrong?" Lisa shouted to her retreating back. The detective, striding purposefully across the lawn, twisted her head to the side and spit on the grass, saying nothing.

"Dylan, that was strange. What do you think the deal is?"

He squinted in the bright sunlight, scrutinizing the details of the car. "Lisa, check out the plate."

She stared at the green sedan as two men wearing suits climbed out to meet Cahane.

"So? All cops drive cars with government plates."

He turned to face her. "Cahane's are Georgia. That one has U.S. government plates."

Chapter 6

RICKY SIGNED FOR THE DELIVERY AND REENTERED THE OFFICE. Kicking the front door closed with his heel, he hurried to his desk and dropped the package on the blotter. With the blade of his scissors, he sliced the sealing tape on the lid and pulled the box open, revealing salmon-colored foam peanuts. Plunging his hands into the packing material, causing several errant pieces to spill out and scatter across the top of his desk and the floor, Ricky blindly found the rectangular box within and pulled it up and out, causing even more of the peanuts to cascade out. He then balanced the smaller carton on its end and moved the shipping box to the floor, clearing space on his desk. Lowering himself lightly into his seat, he excitedly opened the inner box and folded back the white wrapping paper inside.

Before he could remove the contents, the front door swung open and he saw Judtson coming into the room.

"Good morning, chief!" he blurted, instantly recognizing how over-the-top his voice sounded, as he quickly slammed the lid back on, picked up the box, and shoved it into the knee space of his desk.

Judtson, reacting to the overly effusive greeting and catching the furtive movements, asked, "What's that?"

Ricky raised his eyebrows innocently. "What's what?"

Crossing the room until he was standing in front of his assistant's desk, Kent chuckled. "The package. The one I saw you hide under your desk."

"Oh, that! Nothing! Just something I ordered."

Judtson gleaned a sadistic pleasure from watching his friend squirm. "What did you get? Show me?"

Having no idea what else to say to this, Ricky simply shook his head and replied, "Huh-uh."

His boss grinned, jumping to a hasty conclusion. "You bought something for me, didn't you?"

Ricky seized the offered lifeline. "Yes! That's it. And it's going to be a surprise. So you can't see it yet."

Spotting the larger box on the floor, still half-filled with foam pieces, Judtson moved around the desk toward it. "I'll bet there's a label telling where it came from."

With a breaking voice, his office mate shouted, "JUDTSON, STOP!"

Sensing that the fun had irrevocably gone out of the interaction, Kent paused halfway to the target and sighed loudly. "Okay. Fine. Have your little secret. Whatever it is."

"Thank you."

After his failed attempt at espionage, he looked away from the suspect box and immediately shifted gears to business. "So, what do we have today?"

Hopping up from his chair, Ricky began briefing his boss, his delivery rapid-fire. "Oh, the usual ten million requests for interviews. And Mitch *and* Darrow both called today. I'm sure they want to pester you again about that book they want you to write – the one where you admit to the whole world what fools you and Carlos are."

Judtson laughed.

"There were only two requests for book signings. Nobody you want to talk with. Your new cable show producer, Kari Levinson, called. She wants to talk to you about taping an upcoming episode."

"I suppose she wants it to be about the Beckleman thing, too."

"Yep."

"Anyone else?"

"Yes. I don't know if you remember him...William Chatterley."

It took a moment for the name to click in Judtson's mind. "The man in England. I interviewed him for the show debunking crop circles. He's the one, with a friend, who made them."

"One and the same."

"Been there, done that."

"I know. I told him. But he said that since all the news came out about the guys in black suits and everything, he really needed to talk to you."

"Okay" – he shrugged – "I'll see what he wants. Anyone else?"

"No. That's it."

"You sure?"

Ricky looked at his employer quizzically. "Yes. I'm positi.... Oh!" A sympathetic expression coloring his features, he softened his voice. "Boss, if she had called, I would have told you first thing."

Kent's shoulders seemed to sag slightly. Turning abruptly, he moved to his office. "Chatterley's number on my computer?"

Feeling sorry for his friend as he watched his retreating back, Ricky reminded him, "You know I stopped doing that after what happened. Good old-fashioned phone slip. Waiting on your desk."

Plodding around to the far side of the desk and dropping heavily into his chair, Judtson found the slip and dialed the number. A man's voice answered on the second ring, and they exchanged perfunctory greetings.

"What was it you had to tell me, Mr. Chatterley?"

"Right to the point, mate. I like that. After watching all the news about what happened to you and the other blokes and your nasty visits from the buggers in black, I figured I should make a clean breast of things with you."

Judtson's curiosity was piqued. "How so?"

"Well, afraid I was less than forthright when I approached you in the past…when I told you that my mate and I were responsible for all of those bloody crop circles in the countryside."

"You weren't?"

"Nossir. My indulging in making pretty pictures in the wheat was a one-off."

"I don't understand, Mr. Chatterley. Why would you tell me that you were behind so many of them? For the publicity?"

"Publicity? Gawd no! Ever since I fed you that cock-and-bull story, I've been as popular down at the pub as an infected rat. No, I did it for two reasons…money and, let's just say, I met the local version of the bullies you encountered. They were quite persuasive, they were."

Bolting upright in his office chair, Judtson asked the man to explain. Apparently, in the midst of what was growing into a serious media frenzy on the topic, two men had approached Chatterley and offered him a sum equal to a month's pay if he agreed to enlist the aid of a friend, go out to a location designated by the men and, using the simple implement of two ropes and a board, stamp a design in the wheat field. Then, a second payment would be made after he specifically contacted Judtson Kent and "confessed," taking credit not only for the one crop circle he made but also for hundreds of others over the last few years. Chatterley had declined, telling the two that he did not care to make himself the object of public ridicule.

"That was when they put the screws to me."

"What do you mean? They threatened you?"

"Oh boyo, they did more than threaten." The man paused. As he began to speak, he sounded emphatic and agitated, vividly reliving his panic as if he had been thrust back in time. "After I tell them to pound salt, the next day when I go to work at the postal office, my supervisor calls me in and tells me I'm suspended. Without pay! When I ask why, he says that they're investigating me for postal theft. Stealing out of the mail! Imagine that! And that I am to go and sit in my flat without drawing a quid until the investigation is complete."

"You're kidding!"

"Wish I was. I stop at the Bull and Rooster on my way home for a pint or two. No sooner do I walk through the front door than I see the two buggers, waiting for me at the bar, calm as can be and smiling at me like a pair of farm jackasses. I take a stool and they get me a pint. As soon as the proprietor sets it in front of me and moves away, they tell me that if I want the investigation and the suspension to just go away, I need to do their little favor."

"And if you didn't?"

"Oh, they make that clear as a bell, they do. If I don't play, I pay the piper. I lose my job *and* my pension."

Judtson took a minute to absorb the story, then asked, "Why tell me now? Aren't you worried they'll came back?"

The transcontinental connection hissed softly in the background before the man responded, his voice now calmer, his emotions more removed from the fear. "You know, when they first came to me with their little proposition, I asked them why they wanted the deed done. They never told me. At the time, I speculated that it might be anything from a private wager to a red herring they'd thought up to throw the coppers off somebody else's scent. Doing what they did to me, at my job with the government no less, I figured it must be something pretty big and they were well hooked up and all, but I never dreamed it was something as big and ugly as the mess you uncovered on your side of the pond."

Chatterley paused. Judtson waited patiently.

"My grandfather fought the Kaiser in World War One…in those vile trenches. My father and my uncle fought Hitler. My uncle never came back. My mother and my two dear aunties worked in the hospital during the bombings…one of them catching dysentery and expiring. On the other hand, my whole life couldn't have been any easier if I'd been plopped on a thick, fluffy down pillow at birth and kept there every day from then on. I've never caught a glimmer of what they went through. My idea of a bad day is if a fountain pen leaks in my shirt pocket, and I've always wondered, if something was going on, something bad, something…evil, whether I'd have half the gumption that my grandfather, my father, my uncle, my mother, and my aunts had."

The man's voice deepened. "Reading about your ordeal and watching the videos of that monster Beckleman, I realized that you and your mates all *did* the deed. Put it all on the line. Rose to the occasion. And all of your little group, including you, Mr. Kent, had a whole lot more to lose than my paltry pension. And every one of you could have been killed. Blazes, one of you was. Yet you did it. And as I'm sitting here right now, I can't tell you how my tiny little piece of the pie fits in. I just know it does. It must. So if you're asking me if I'm scared, hell yes, I am. But if you're asking me whether I'll back down a single step from telling this story to anybody you want to parade in front of me, Mr. Kent, you have my word of honor, sir…I will not."

$$\nabla$$

"Damn, I miss Al," Copeland groaned to himself as he struggled with the phrasing of a sentence on his computer. His peripheral vision caught a movement outside the study window of his home in Sugarland, Texas, and he swung his gaze around in time to see the blue and white truck pull away from his mailbox.

Saving the draft of his work, he stood up and stretched gingerly, trying to loosen the kinks in his back, accumulated from sitting in one position for far too long. He then left the room and walked to his front door, opened it, and stepped out, the oppressive combination of heat and humidity almost physically slapping him the moment he exited from the air conditioning.

In the thirty seconds it took to reach the mailbox, his shirt was already plastered uncomfortably to his skin. Quickly opening the hinged flap, Copeland removed the handful of mail and hurried back to the cool refuge of his home, not even glancing to see what had arrived. Once back inside, he dropped the stack on the kitchen table and opened the refrigerator. Grabbing a longneck and closing the door, he stopped after a single pace and turned back, snagging a second bottle before returning to the table.

With two swallows of the chilled brew down and wending their way through his body's core, he perused the mail. The third envelope from the top was from the photo expert who had reviewed his pictures.

"This must be the affidavit," he said aloud and tore it open.

The cover letter was short and simply stated that enclosed was the requested sworn statement pertaining to photographic materials provided by him. Dropping the top sheet to the side, he scanned the document beneath. The opening lines were the usual boilerplate, swearing under oath that the contents were true and accurate. The following paragraph included a detailed inventory of the materials and their source. The next described the standard and accepted methods and practices used to determine authenticity, and outlined the purported contents of each picture.

Copeland jumped ahead to the final comments:

> In conclusion, it is my professional opinion
> that the five prints listed above were authentic
> and genuine reproductions of their original
> negatives, said negatives which had not been
> made available to me for examination, and that
> the prints had not been manipulated and altered
> prior to my receiving them for the analysis.

He grunted in satisfaction and continued reading:

> However, it was obvious from my study of the
> prints that the source negatives from which the
> prints had been created had, in fact, been
> altered prior to the generation of the prints.
> Multiple artifacts were evident, indicating that
> the techniques of airbrushing and masking had
> been utilized to substantially alter the
> contents of the negatives and, therefore, the
> final prints.

"Sonofa…," Copeland uttered, rereading the final lines to make certain he had not misunderstood them.

▽

Dylan and Lisa were sitting together in the airport lounge, discussing the day's events and waiting for the departure of Falt's flight. Soon after the arrival of the government vehicle at the Shields' residence, the uniformed police officer they had first spoken with told them they could leave, and despite several requests, they did not have another opportunity to talk with Detective Cahane, who had entered the garage with the two men.

As Dylan drove, Lisa had spent much of the drive to the airport talking on her cell phone, giving instructions to her staff in New York to begin digging up everything they could find on Rosemary Shields as well as Dr. Trandle at the CDC. She also told them to try to find the rosters of agents with the FBI and Homeland Security who were assigned to the Atlanta offices, hopeful that she or Dylan might be able to identify the two men from the photos.

Now, after settling down in the lounge, Lisa had another idea and called her assistant again, telling her where she was and instructing her to call the two government offices and ask whether they were actively involved in the Rosemary Shields case. Right as she was about to finish the call, a rapid double beep sounded. Focusing on the screen, she complained, "Damn. Battery's dead. And I didn't bring a charger. Do you have one?"

"Sure," Dylan answered, "in the bag that I just checked in."

"Great!"

With a wry grin, he offered, "If you need to make a *fifteenth* call to your staff, you can use mine."

She smirked. "Thanks."

Now that he had her attention, he asked, "You don't think Detective Cahane might conclude that Rosemary killed herself?"

Lisa shrugged. "Don't think she will. She was obviously heading that way at first, but after we talked to her, I got the impression we might have changed her mind."

"I hope so."

Before she could say anything else, a voice came over the airport public-address system. "Passenger Lisa Trippiano, please pick up a white courtesy phone. Repeat, passenger Lisa Trippiano, please pick up a white courtesy phone. You have a call waiting."

As she turned to swivel off her stool, Falt laughed. "Seems that your people are already having withdrawals."

Lisa turned her head back as she walked away. "Maybe they found something."

He watched her cross the room and ask the young man behind the counter for the location of the courtesy phones. Following his directions, she hurried to a corner of the lounge, into a small privacy alcove, and disappeared from his view.

Resting his elbows on the small round table, Dylan let his mind wander, losing himself in his own thoughts for several minutes, when he suddenly felt a hand firmly grasp his shoulder and heard a voice call his name.

Whirling, he was surprised to see Carlos Villarreal standing beside him.

"Carlos! My God, man, what are you doing here?"

Gesturing at one of the vacant stools, his visitor smiled. "May I?"

Falt answered hastily, "Of course, of course. Sit down. I can't believe we ran into you. This is a huge airport. What are you doing in Atlanta?"

He noticed that the Bolivian scientist was carrying a large, apparently hefty squared valise. Villarreal placed it on the floor and slipped onto the adjacent seat. "This is my last stop in a very long, circuitous journey before I return to La Paz. Running into you was quite simple. I was waiting at the gate when I heard the page for Lisa. This was the second lounge I checked, and I spotted you. I'm afraid I haven't found her yet."

"Oh, she's here. She's on the phone to her office."

"I see. May I ask what brings the two of you to Atlanta...together?"

"CARLOS?"

The exclamation came from Lisa who was on her way back to the table. She ran the rest of the distance and hugged him, then slid onto the third stool. "What...how?"

Dylan interrupted her. "Our friend was just telling me that he happened to be at the airport and heard the announcement for you. But, Carlos, you haven't said why you're here."

"As I stated, this is my last stop. The journey began at Puma Punku where I personally took samples from several of the cut stones, as well as from the nearby quarry at Lake Titicaca. From there I traveled to Lebanon and extracted samples from several sections of the lower wall I had excavated in the past."

Lisa leaned forward. "So you're redoing your earlier work?"

He nodded. "I am. Only this time there will be no doubt – no possibility of error, mishandling, or misunderstanding – since I am personally performing each step."

"But why Atlanta?" Dylan inquired.

"This is the city where one of the best metallurgy labs in the world does business. I brought the samples here for testing."

"Well?" Lisa prodded, excitement clearly etched in her voice.

Carlos smiled at her. "I don't know yet."

"They aren't finished testing?"

"Oh, they are quite finished. I remained in Atlanta until they were done. I have the results and my samples with me." His face assumed a boyish, almost vulnerable expression. "I simply haven't had the courage to open the envelope yet. By the way, you two still have not told me why you are both here *together* in Atlanta."

Dylan detailed the events of the last few days, sharing his concerns and suspicions. After his narrative paused at the discovery of Rosemary Shields' body in the garage, Lisa took over and told Carlos about their conversation with the detective and the arrival of the mysterious agents.

The moment she arrived at the end of the story, Dylan asked her anxiously, "Was that your office on the phone? Did they find out anything yet?"

She shook her head, a sly smile appearing on her face. "Why yes, it *was* my office, but they didn't have anything new on Shields." She stopped, relishing the suspense.

"Lisa!" Dylan nearly barked. "I know that look. What did they want?"

With a soft laugh, she admitted, "You're right...this is fun. They wanted to tell me that Dean had called for me."

"Copeland? Did you call him back? What did he say?"

"I did. And you are not going to believe this." She explained about Copeland's desire to continue with the direction of the work he had done prior to the conversion, as well as the five pictures he had recently taken to the analyst.

When she described the contents of the affidavit, Dylan practically shouted, "They're still at it! They got to the man."

"I'm curious," Carlos began thoughtfully, "whether they put pressure on the analyst to reverse his opinion or whether he has been...."

"Zapped!" Lisa interjected.

"Precisely."

"I don't know. Neither does Dean. All he knows is that the man had been one-hundred-percent certain that the photographs were the real deal and that the negatives they were developed from had not been altered – and *now* he's saying they were."

The three cohorts fell into a brief silence, digesting this latest bit of news, when Dylan leaned back and stared down at Villarreal's valise meaningfully. "Carlos, what if they've also put pressure on the metallurgy lab?"

The archaeologist slid off his stool and picked up the valise, hefting it onto the table and snapping it open. "One way to find out."

He reached inside and removed a legal-sized manila envelope. Standing resolutely, he bent back the metal tabs and inserted his finger at the edge, tearing the envelope open. Dylan and Lisa watched and waited quietly as he read the lab's finding. After he looked up, his countenance neutral, he retook his seat and handed the stapled two-page summary to Dylan.

Lisa, unable to restrain her curiosity a second longer, blurted, "What does it say?"

With an even tone, Carlos told her, "According to the lab, the samples identified as collected from the wall at Baalbek are a granite native to that area. The samples identified as collected from Puma Punku are, of course, andesite and native to that region, and perfectly match the samples identified as from the quarry at Lake Titicaca."

"That...that can't be!" She hesitated, and then added tentatively, "Could it?"

Before Villarreal could respond, Falt protested, "I thought you were certain that the wall stones at Baalbek came from Puma Punku."

As Lisa stared expectantly at her friend, she realized that he did not appear to be as disturbed by the lab results as were she and Dylan. "Carlos...what...I was sure you'd be upset or something."

The slender man shrugged expressively. "Why should I be upset? I have learned two very important things from this report."

"I'm confused. Two things?"

"Why yes, Dylan. I have confirmed beyond a shadow of a doubt that the milled stones used to construct a wall in Lebanon tens of thousands of years ago were obtained from a quarry two continents away and at an elevation of 13,000 feet."

"But...."

Looking intently at Falt, Villarreal held up his hand and continued, "And the second thing I have learned, which also confirms my recent suspicions, is that the machinations we thought would conclude with the denouement of Samuel Beckleman have continued unabated." With this comment, he leaned back slightly and smiled.

"I don't get it, Carlos. The report said...." Dylan read the look on his friend's face, and realization staggered him. "You sonofagun, you switched the samples, didn't you?"

The smile broadened. "Yes. I saw this as an opportunity to confirm my earlier findings. However, I also wished to discover whether our nemesis had truly been routed."

"Let me see if I have this right," Lisa interrupted urgently. "The samples you told the lab were from Baalbek really weren't?"

"Oh, no. They were. But they were taken from the top section – the portion of the building known as the Temple of Jupiter, built by the Romans only a couple of thousand years ago. They would, of course, be constructed with native granite. And the samples I identified to the lab as having come from *Puma Punku* were actually extracted from the lowest wall at Baalbek, only recently excavated by me personally."

"And the samples you told them were from the quarry at Lake Titicaca...?"

"Actually were from that location."

Dylan and Lisa glanced at each other for a moment before she spoke, her voice lower and ominous. "So it isn't over."

Chapter 7

After striding purposefully through the kitchen and dining area, Romeo trotted down the hallway, his features taut with determination, and stopped at the door to Kelsey's office. Prepared to see her hunkered down in her chair at the computer, he was surprised to find the room empty. Knowing she would never leave her home without informing him, he backtracked to the separate ell where the living quarters were segregated, and walked briskly to the last door…her bedroom. The door was closed and he hesitated circumspectly, concerned that she might be getting some much-needed sleep.

Just as he was about to turn away, his ears caught the subtle sound of water running. For a minute, his actions were blocked by indecision, when the soft squeak of water valves being turned reached him and the sound of the shower stopped.

Counting slowly to sixty, he knocked, rewarded by her voice shouting from inside. "Just a second!"

Patiently waiting, Romeo began to indulge himself in the oft-repeated fantasy of revenge he had quietly nurtured since La Paz, since the trip he had made accompanying Kelsey, Judtson, Saylor, and the others to visit Sam Jonassen, only to return to their hotel after the meeting and watch the uploaded video showing the abduction of his charges…his friends…from the silo. And the evidence of the betrayal by Luis.

His thoughts were truncated abruptly as the bedroom door flung open. Kelsey was standing there quizzically, wearing a thick terry-cloth robe and sporting a lopsided towel she had wrapped hastily around her hair.

"Hey, Romeo. What's up?" she asked, knowing he would not have knocked without a reason, and backing up so he could enter the room.

Taking a single step inside, he grunted, "Kenny called. He's got Luis."

Her eyes sprang wide. "They found him?"

The big Army Ranger shook his head. "No. That's the thing. According to Kenny, the bastard turned himself in."

He could see her mind working furiously, attempting to make sense of this. Motioning to him distractedly, she turned and walked toward the small desk in the corner of the bedroom, taking one of the seats. He followed her and took the other.

"Have they questioned him? What has he said?"

"Nothing. He told the FBI he won't talk to anyone but me."

"YOU! He's gotta know *you* want to rip him to pieces! I'd have thought you'd be the last person he'd want to see."

Romeo nodded. "I'm guessing that's why he went to the FBI. He probably figures that if he's with them when I talk to him, he'll live through the discussion."

She giggled briefly at the imparted imagery. "You're going, aren't you?"

"Uh-huh. I'm leaving as soon as we're done talking. They're bringing him down to the Tucson office now. He should be there by the time I arrive."

"I still don't get it, Romeo. Why wouldn't he just disappear? Something doesn't feel right."

"I know. My first reaction was verging on ecstacy that I could finally get my hands on the sonofabitch, and then I started thinking that…somebody…would know how much it meant to me. And they're using it."

"For what?"

"*That* I am not sure about."

"Could it be some kind of a trap?"

"Considered the possibility. But a trap for *me*…or for you, Scott, and Matt while I'm gone?"

"You'll be careful, won't you?" Worry creased her face.

"I'm always careful, Kelsey."

She snorted rudely, vividly recalling the moment at the FEMA camp when Romeo charged the passel of armed guards while screaming like a banshee. "Yeah, sure! Each time I'm putting together an inventory of your personality traits, *careful* is right at the top of the list."

He grinned. "Okay. Maybe not careful. How about…ready? But it's the three of you I'm supposed to be worried about. I called Chili," he said, referring to the man he had personally hired to replace Luis. "He'll be here in about ten minutes to stay with you until I get back. Just make sure that none of you go anywhere in the meantime."

She nodded. "Got it."

He stood to leave.

"Romeo…?"

Stopping, he looked back. "This isn't going to be one of those speeches where you tell me to keep my cool and not do anything that'll cause the Feds to throw me in jail, is it?"

His question triggered another muted laugh. "No. I was going tell you that after you find out what the hell happened, I hope you can figure out a way to…square things."

The two held eye contact, sharing a mutual understanding, before he softly responded, "Don't worry. I will."

▽

Saylor Costello heard a light knock on his office door and glanced up from the toxicology summary he had been reading in an attempt to resolve a particularly confounding set of symptoms one of his patients was presenting.

"Come in."

The door opened a few inches and Liz Ganz, his nurse, poked her head through the opening. "You have a visitor."

His eyes quickly swung back to his schedule and saw that it was clear. "Judtson?"

She shook her head. "No. He said he's a friend of yours. Chris Ashby."

Saylor sprang up. "Chris! Bring him back."

She left the door ajar and headed to the outer office, as he checked the surface of his desk for open patient files. Seeing one, he flipped it closed and, in order to free up the only visitor chair, he removed a stack of neurological papers Melanie had printed for his reading, and found a temporary home for the pile just as Liz returned with Ashby and showed him in.

Meeting him at the door, Saylor reached out for a handshake. "Chris! How are you?"

The tall, slender, blond-haired man smiled broadly. "Excellent, Saylor. You?"

Saylor backed up and gestured for Ashby to sit, returning to his own chair.

"Been busy as hell since I came back to work, trying to catch up. God, it seems like months since I've seen you."

Ashby chuckled. "Yes. I think our little escapade has permanently distorted our sense of time. It seems as though every minute of a *normal* life lasts an hour. How's Doni?"

"She's well. Enjoying the peace and quiet."

"I've noticed that she hasn't been making the talk show circuit like Dean and Jimmy."

"No. I think she wants to forget the whole thing."

"What about you? You trying to forget it, too?"

Saylor paused pensively before answering. "In a way, I guess. Part of it scared the hell out of me."

Leaning back in the leather chair, Ashby crossed one leg over the other. "True. But part of it was…."

"You're not going to say it was fun, are you?"

He responded with a sardonic grin. "No. I don't think *fun* is exactly the right word. Especially remembering how close we all came to getting killed at the FEMA camp." He sighed audibly and continued, "Still, I have to admit I've had a bit of trouble settling back into my old routines. Not you?"

"No. Not in the least. First of all, by the time it was over and I returned to my practice, I was so far behind that I've been working from sunup till sundown every day to get current, so I haven't exactly found out what it feels like to settle into a routine yet. Even when I do, I don't think I'll be missing the adrenaline rush."

"Why?"

"You were there alone, Chris. It's a little different if you're only playing with your own life. Hell, we all did it when we were young. But when I thought I'd lost Doni…. No. I don't miss it. Any of it. The most excitement I want now is if she finds a scorpion in the shower."

Ashby accurately read the expression on his friend's face and changed the subject. "I understand. What about Judtson? How's he?"

Saylor shrugged. "He's fine."

The dismissiveness of Saylor's response made it clear that he had no desire to proceed down this conversational path, either.

"Chris, what brings you to Tucson? You didn't make the six-hour drive just to see me."

"Actually, I did."

The answer surprised Saylor, and a momentary jolt of apprehension shot up his spine. Cautiously, he asked, "Is there anything wrong?"

"No. Not at all. It's just that something has come up in my research and I wanted to talk to you about it."

"Does it have to do with the connection that you were working on before, between Alzheimer's and monoatomic gold?"

"Alzheimer's, no. The gold aspect, yes. Obviously, Saylor, I know you're a neurologist, but do you deal with a lot of autism in your practice?"

The topic was not the direction Saylor had expected. "Some, of course. More and more, lately. It's primarily a field for the pediatric neuro guys."

"Well, I'm trying to get myself up to speed on it. All I know about it is what's on the 'net. My understanding is that it now affects one in sixty-eight children, boys are five times as likely to have it than girls are, the number of cases each year is on the upswing and, in fact, it is the fastest-growing developmental disability in the country, and you have no way to detect it, diagnose it, or cure it."

"That's all mostly true. It is an inferred diagnosis based on behavioral issues."

"Sound familiar?"

"What do you...oh, you mean like Alzheimer's?"

"Yes."

Saylor could tell that his visitor was attempting to hook him; however, he ignored the conversational bait and continued, "And there has been a recent study where...in approximately ten out of eleven autism patients...they've found clusters of disorganized brain cells in tissue samples from brain regions that regulate social functioning, emotions, and communication. They aren't certain yet but think that it may be the smoking gun."

"That's interesting."

"It is. Still preliminary, though. A lot more work has to be done on it before we can draw any real conclusions. Chris, if all you were looking for was an overview of autism, you surely wouldn't have had to drive here. We could have done it over the phone."

The slender chemist shrugged. "I know. It's just...something has come up and it's a little weird. So...."

Amused, Saylor quipped, "So I'm the first person who crossed your mind?"

"I didn't mean it to sound like that, but...yes." Ashby's voice was serious.

Saylor focused on him intently, all levity gone from his voice. "Go ahead, Chris."

He took a minute to organize his thoughts. "You remember when I told you about my sister?"

"Yes. Starlight, isn't it?"

"It is. Ever since our mother had her miraculous recovery from Alzheimer's, Starlight has been touting the monoatomic gold to the customers who come into her crystal shop."

Saylor's mouth twisted in a subtle show of displeasure.

"I know, I know. I've tried to stop her. I keep telling her that there is a right way to do it and that the phase of my research involving human trials isn't too far off. The thing is that she's adamant people need help now and shouldn't have to wait."

"She hasn't hurt anyone, has she?"

Ashby shook his head. "No. Nothing like that. As a matter of fact, possibly the opposite."

"The opposite? She has reversed another Alzheimer's victim?"

"Another cure, or *reversal* I guess would be a better word. But not Alzheimer's."

"Autism?"

He nodded.

Saylor was silent, the seriousness of what his friend was telling him triggering an avalanche of thoughts. When he found his voice, he asked, "Have you personally observed the improvement?"

"I have. It happens to be a well-documented case. At least, the severity of his autism is well documented. No one else really knows about his...improvement. Yet. Except his mother, of course."

The expression on Ashby's face was grave.

"Chris, if what you're saying turns out to be verifiable and there aren't any deleterious effects, you should be ecstatic. You look anything but."

The chemist turned his gaze to the window, staring out at the Catalina Mountains before he replied. "That's true. I should be. I suppose I am. Only, you see, we...my group...haven't obtained permission for human trials yet. I'm worried that this will jeopardize our work."

"This is something your sister did on her own. You didn't do it, Chris. You even tried to talk her out of pursuing it. And the material, as I recall, is available off the shelf. I don't see why it would come back to bite you."

Turning back to face Saylor, his voice soft, Chris explained, "I helped her."

"Oh."

"I'm not sure how much you remember about my prior research, but the off-the-shelf monoatomic gold did nothing to the lab rats I was working with."

"That's right. You had to process it in some way."

"I did. I had to use a scrubbing protocol before it became effective on the rats. I...I allowed myself to be talked into running a batch of Starlight's gold through the routine."

Understanding the man's concern, Saylor leaned forward. "You didn't know she was going to...."

"Of course I did. Why else would she want it? To sprinkle on her rose bushes?"

Sensing that shifting gears might be appropriate, Saylor prodded, "Why don't you tell me about the autism case."

A hint of the former animation returned to the chemist's face. "He's a boy, maybe thirteen or fourteen now. Not one suffering from the more subtle forms of autism. Fairly extreme, from what I understand."

"You mentioned that it was a well-documented case."

Ashby nodded. "He was part of a study group. Since first diagnosed, he's been measured, tested, videoed, photographed...he's had MRIs, CAT scans, PET scans. The file on him is a foot thick."

"So there can be no doubt as to the authenticity of the history?"

"Right. His parents, his mother really, came to Starlight's shop in Venice Beach. Not making a special trip to see her, just doing the tourist thing, you know. Looking at all the shops."

"Uh-huh."

"She had Micah...that's the boy's name...with her. And while the mother was shopping, Micah acted out. I understand it's a normal trait among the autistic."

Saylor agreed, "It is."

"The mother explained Micah's behavior by telling my sister that he was autistic. Starlight's a good listener and incredibly sympathetic. Two genetic traits I was short-shrifted on." Ashby paused, a slight smile playing across his face before he continued. "The mother opened up to my sister, telling her everything. I think she had been bottling it up for a long time. She felt that complaining about her son was somehow, I don't know, being a bad mother or something. Anyway, she found a good ear in Starlight and really let it all out. By the end, she was in tears."

"It can take quite a toll."

"I know. Well, Starlight told her about our mother. I think it was, at first, only to commiserate, share the pain of what she went through when Mom had Alzheimer's. Of course, then she told her about the monoatomic gold…and the cure."

The direction of the course of events was obvious and Saylor sighed. "So she gave her some."

"Yeah. She gave the woman a dose matching what we had given our mother. At first the woman was skeptical. As you know, I can relate to that. Afterward, she went home and basically did the same research I had done, discovering that there were a lot of flaky claims about the substance but that no one could find it dangerous."

"She gave it to her son?"

"Yes."

"And?"

Ashby could not repress a broad smile as he said, "It caused a complete…I don't know what the correct term would be…remission, cure, cessation of symptoms. Whatever you call it, the boy is a perfectly normal teenager. Normal in every way."

▽

Sean Collins took one final look around his bedroom, his face expressionless. His eyes were flat and dull as they scanned the Xbox on which he had spent countless hours, his movie posters, and his computer. Shoving earbuds in, he cranked up the iPod, slid his backpack loosely onto his shoulders, and turned to leave, closing the door quietly.

His mother, sitting at the kitchen table and talking to someone on her cell, using the speakerphone and laughing loudly, did not notice him as he walked past. Neither did his father, who was leaning halfway out of his recliner, and shouting hysterically at the football game on the large flat-screen. Sean did not take a single moment to focus on either of them as he slipped out the front door, pulling his keys from the pocket of his hoodie.

During the short drive, Sean's mind was blank, open and receptive…a sponge cultivated to suck in every vibration of the overwhelming, throbbing rhythm of the music in his ears, his head jerking forward repetitively, synchronized to the beat. The only physical object he consciously registered in his environment as he pulled into the parking lot was the pole-mounted metal sign informing Sean that he was entering a gun-free zone, the message eliciting a tight smile.

The grassy mall area of the campus was bustling with young students. It was move-in weekend and the overall impression was one of confusion, intimidation, and awe as they wandered in search of their dormitories.

Selecting a location where a large number of the students were grouped in clusters on the grass, drinking, eating, and talking on their cell phones, Sean scanned the faces of those around him dispassionately as he pulled off his backpack and placed it on a low wall, unsnapping the cover. Reaching in, he pulled out the H&K G36C gas-driven 5.56mm automatic pistol.

▽

Romeo left Matt Wheeler and strode briskly to the kitchen, where he found Scott sitting on a stool at the counter, holding a half-eaten sandwich absentmindedly with one hand, and tapping the screen of his pad with the other.

"There you are."

Without glancing up, Scott gently murmured, "What's up?"

Romeo slid onto an adjacent stool. "Just wanted to let you know I'm on my way to see Luis."

The comment caught the tech's attention. "No kidding? Where is he?"

"He turned himself in to the FBI. They're bringing him to the Tucson office."

"And they're going to let *you* in to see him?"

Romeo chuckled. "They don't have a choice. He won't talk to anyone but me. Kenny Bowman is going to be in with us."

Gumble was perplexed by the revelation. "That's odd. I assumed you'd be the last guy he'd want to see."

"I guess not."

"Anything you need from me?"

"No. Just thought you'd want to know."

"Should I let any of the others know?"

Romeo paused. "Not yet. Wait until I talk to him."

The big man stood up from the stool and started to leave. Scott had already returned his attention to the pad when Romeo stopped and turned back. "Scott, I have a question."

Sensing the sudden change in his friend's mood, he answered gently. "What?"

"I've been beating myself up over this since it happened and…."

"The FEMA camp?"

"Yes. Ever since that day. Since I almost got all of us killed, I've been replaying it in my mind."

"I know."

"When the four of us were making our charge, you were back at Billy Burke's ranch, on the Internet."

"I was."

"Could you have…? I mean, the only reason we nearly got cut to pieces was thanks to the motion sensors. They didn't have a single guard posted. I was thinking…."

Scott helped him get to the point. "You've been wondering if you could have called me and I could have hacked into their system, disabled the motion sensors, and put the cameras on a continuous loop so the four of you could have waltzed right in."

"Uh-huh."

Studying the Army Ranger, Scott could see that his friend's eyes still held the shadow of a haunted look behind them. His voice flat and matter-of-fact, the tech answered, "So you think I could hack into a DOD system and override their top-tier security? Nope. No chance."

Romeo sighed heavily, as Scott immediately turned his attention back to the pad on the counter.

He stared at Gumble for a full minute before turning and slowly walking away. Over his shoulder, he remarked, "Thanks for lying."

"Not a problem," Scott responded without looking up.

Chapter 8

BAL SINGH AWOKE WITH A START, SITTING UP IN HIS COT, breathing heavily and coated with a patina of sweat. His head rapidly twisted from side to side, his eyes darting…surveying the confines of his tent for threats, residual from his dream. His ears attempted to filter the clamorous rumble of the wind oscillating the canvas, for the telltale thud of a footfall from an intruder. It was the same dream he had suffered countless times since his trip to see Kevin Berry in the Mojave. The jarring, smacking rounds of the bullets slamming into the outside metal skin of the field office, the splattered blood from Luis' injury, the deafening reports from Kelsey's gun as she lay by the door and returned fire, and the choking, mind-numbing gas rapidly filling the small space…all these elements played out in a repeating loop in his mind, every night as he tried to sleep.

The most disturbing aspect of the scene, for Bal, was not the imminent threat to his life, but rather the unameliorable image he had of himself, cowering in the corner as Judtson, Kelsey, and Luis fought back.

In the minutes, hours, and days following the horrifying event, none of the three had even once mentioned his actions…or lack thereof.

Strange, he thought, reflecting dolefully. *I was worried about what they would say to me afterward, how they would express their utter contempt for my inexcusable cowardice. But their silence…the absence of any comments, questions, or accusations…was far, far worse than anything they could have said.*

Unzipping himself from the sleeping bag, Singh pulled on his boots and parka, and hastily ducked through the tent flap. He squinted against the wind which was ferociously whipping through their camp, and saw two of his students huddled with Sam around the table set up under the impromptu lean-to on the leeward side of a boulder, where the cook was preparing breakfast.

▽

Romeo's pace quickened as he approached the federal building on Congress. When he walked into the shadow of the building, his eyes adjusted and he saw Kenny Bowman loitering near the front doors. His former Army buddy crossed the sidewalk to intercept him.

"Thought I'd better meet you out front and escort you in."

"I know my way," Jones insisted.

Bowman laughed. "I know. But the men at the security checkpoints all have wives and kids. And some of those guys are friends of mine."

The two entered the chilly, air-conditioned lobby as Romeo asked, "Has he said anything yet?"

The FBI agent shook his head. "He's waiting for you."

They swiftly passed through two guarded entrances before arriving at the elevator. Bowman's presence clearly expedited the process, although Romeo had to relinquish his pistol, and soon both men were on the upper floor where Luis was being held.

Two additional agents were standing outside an unmarked door. Bowman stepped between them and began to turn the knob.

"Kenny?"

The agent stopped and turned back to face Romeo.

"Let me go in alone."

With a rueful smile and a shake of his head, Bowman responded, "Not a chance, pal. Don't worry. I'll stay back in the corner."

Not giving Jones an opportunity to argue, he opened the door and stepped in, followed immediately by the former Army Ranger. Romeo's eyes instantly fixed on Luis, who was sitting at a small table in the center of the otherwise bare room.

The moment their gazes connected, Romeo felt the powerful flush of emotions he had been attempting to keep at bay, and took a series of lightning-fast steps to the man, reaching out and grabbing the front of his shirt, bunching it in his fist, and lifting him up from his seat.

Jones was vaguely aware that the FBI agent was barking his name, yet his attention was fixed upon the man who had betrayed him and cost Al Clarkson his life. Surprisingly, Luis stood with his arms hanging loosely at his sides, his eyes never wavering from Romeo's.

The big man felt the grip of two hands on his shoulders. It was strong, forceful. From close to his ear came Kenny's voice. "Come on, man. Let him go. Sit down. Don't make me bring in the two from outside."

Exerting a monumental mental effort, Romeo relaxed the hold on Luis' shirt and took a step to the side, lowering himself slowly into a steel chair as his erstwhile comrade sank into the other.

Releasing a deep breath, Romeo spoke a single word. "Why?"

Luis, whose face was neither afraid nor defiant, answered, "I didn't do it."

"Don't lie to me, you sonofabitch! It's on the video. We all saw you walking out with the bad guys. You weren't hooded. You weren't cuffed."

The man's eyes pinched tightly closed, as if attempting to block out a memory. "It was me, but it wasn't. They made me do it."

The answer gave Romeo pause. "You trying to tell me they mind-controlled you? Don't feed me that, Luis. That's nuts! We both know that didn't happen. They never had access to you to strap on the gizmo."

Shaking his head strenuously, Luis explained, "They didn't use the gizmo."

Frustration began to build in him and Romeo unconsciously started to rise from his chair, when he felt the persistent hand of Bowman, who was standing close behind, again grab his shoulder and push him firmly back down.

"Luis, I don't know what game you're playing and, frankly, I don't give a damn. You were down in the silo with everyone else. The vault was closed. No one was there except our people and the hostage. And he was secure. How could they have gotten to you? And quit giving me one-phrase answers and just tell me your story."

Luis leaned back in his chair and for the first time looked away, staring at the ceiling thoughtfully before he began. As he spoke, his voice was steady. "I'm not sure exactly what happened or how they did it. But there's only one way I can figure it to work – the Devil's Breath we had down there for the hostage."

Obviously surprised by this piece of information, Kenny Bowman started to speak, stopping himself quickly.

Luis continued, "I was at my station. Alone. Watching the monitors. And everything was fine. The tire teeth were up and in place. The inner gate was closed. The next thing I knew, I was locked in a small room I later found out was at the Department of Homeland Security in Florence."

He stopped and Romeo stared at him for a long minute. "That's it? You want me to believe that you just…blacked out?" His voice was laden with contempt.

"That's the deal, man. That's all I've got in my head. If there's some way to break through and find the rest, I'm game. Hypnosis? Drugs? Whatever. I'll do it. Hell, Romeo, if you can talk your buddy here into leaving us alone, I'll sign off on that. Then you can try to beat it out of me. You know how that stuff works. You give it to someone, and he's your slave. He'll do whatever you want. Even commit a crime. Kill somebody, maybe. I don't know. And you know he won't remember a minute of it later."

Romeo thought over the man's words, evaluating them carefully, and finally shaking his head dismissively. "Still doesn't wash, Luis. And you know it."

"Why? It's the only thing that makes sense."

"To you, maybe, in your convoluted attempt to crawl out of the hole you're in. But they'd have to get the Devil's Breath to you. And then give you the orders. How could they do that if you were down in the hole, locked in?"

Slumping against the back of his chair, Luis sighed resignedly. "You know how, Romeo. You just don't want to admit it. You'd rather make me the bad guy. Simpler that way?"

Feeling his anger swell again, Romeo leaned forward and gripped the edge of the table with both hands, squeezing the metal tightly. "You're saying someone down there was a traitor…an agent?"

Luis slowly raised his head and remained silent.

"WHO? Couldn't have been Clarkson. He died trying to fight them. Wasn't Scott. If it hadn't been for him, we never would have found the group. Are you saying it was one of the people we rescued?"

Shifting his gaze downward, Luis stared at the top of the table without responding for a time. When he did reply, his voice was muted. "Like I said, once you get the stuff inside you, you don't remember anything. But…the last thing I *do* remember…. You're not gonna like this."

"DAMMIT, LUIS!"

"Okay! Okay! The last thing I remember before I blacked out was somebody bringing me a glass of iced tea. You remember we used tea when we tried to get Bob to talk."

His jaw muscles were clamped so rigidly that Romeo was forced to ask his question through his teeth. "*Luis, who brought the tea?*"

Bringing his eyes back up to lock on Romeo's, Luis answered, "Mrs. Costello."

$$\triangledown$$

Entering through the garage, Judtson found Kristen in the kitchen, putting away groceries. Hearing him arrive, she crossed the room and hugged him.

"Hi, sweetheart. How was the day?"

"Not bad," he replied offhandedly, returning the hug and dropping into one of the chairs around the table. "Yours?"

He watched as she gracefully moved back to the counter and resumed unpacking food. "It was good. I have a surprise."

His curiosity was piqued. "What?"

"Tell you later, when I'm finished with this and sitting down with you. You look a little distracted."

Judtson knew he did not actually care to discuss the topic with Kristen, yet he plunged ahead anyway. "I guess. Remember I told you about Chatterley?"

"Uh-huh. The man who made all the crop circles."

Feeling a split-second flash of irritation, which he quelled, Judtson explained, "Actually, no. If you'll remember, he called to tell me that he was paid to take the credit or blame or responsibility for them. And when he had refused, they threatened him. But he hadn't actually made them. Other than one."

Loudly stacking several cans on a shelf, Kristen replied without glancing toward him. "Whatever. So what happened today?"

"I asked him earlier if he'd mind taking a polygraph. He said he wouldn't mind at all, and I arranged it for him. The results came back."

Finishing with the canned goods, Kristen closed the cabinet doors and moved to the refrigerator, opening the vegetable crisper drawer. "So? What happened?"

"He's telling the truth."

With the same vocal inflection she would have used to acknowledge the lack of any mail that day, she uttered, "Huh."

He stared at her intently, a trace of annoyance creeping into his voice. "That's it, Kristen? 'Huh'?"

She paused in her process of putting away asparagus and turned to face him. "Judtson, what's the big deal?"

"Kristen, the man told me that mysterious men approached him and threatened him if he didn't go along with an outright hoax on the public. The polygraph proves he's telling the truth about it."

Her face a mask of patient tolerance, she asked, "So what? Some guys pay him to make a crop circle and take credit for the others. What's the harm in that?"

"The harm? People are being misled…deceived. You think that's just fine?"

Subtly shaking her head, she sighed and picked up a head of broccoli, turning away from him. "What possible difference does it make? It isn't as if it's something, you know, important. Frankly, I could care less."

Feeling his pulse quicken, Judtson snapped, "'*I could care less'* makes no sense. I believe the phrase is '*I couldn't care less'* if you want it to accurately convey what you mean. And it does matter when we are being deceived. Didn't the thing I went through with Beckleman prove that?"

Choosing to ignore his correction of her choice of idiom, Kristen responded, her voice conciliatory, "You're right. But you fixed it. You found the Beckleman conspiracy, or whatever it was, and exposed it. It's over and he's in jail. It could be that the guys who approached Chatterley were a part of that, a part of the Beckleman plot. And all you're doing is finding out more evidence about a settled issue."

He looked down at the floor, taking a moment to think. "Maybe."

"No 'maybe' about it. It is. I'm sure of it. So what are you going to do about this Chatterley thing?"

He glanced back up at her. "A cable show."

"What?"

"A cable show. We did a show a while back, using the misrepresentation as fact. We need to set the record straight."

Kristen closed the refrigerator firmly and took the seat beside Judtson. Reaching out, she held his hands in hers. "Judtson, sweetheart, please don't start up again."

His voice flat, he asked her, "What are you saying?"

Frustration lightly distorting her delicate features, Kristen shifted her eyes away from him and glanced out the window before taking a deep breath and releasing it slowly. "For years you wrote book after book debunking everything from UFOs to the Illuminati. And sold millions and millions of copies. Your cable show did the same thing, and look at how big an audience you've built. Judtson, you came close to throwing it all away over that Villarreal scam. It was a put-up job and you nearly fell for it. That would have been humiliating."

He started to speak, when she lifted her hand and gently touched his lips with her fingertip. "Thank God, it worked out. You found out it was a big con job. A huge hoax. And you did exactly what you've always done – you exposed it for the whole world to see. Judtson Kent once again pulled back the curtain so everyone could see the man behind. I am so proud of you for that. Now…now I'm afraid you're starting to fall for another scam…another hoax."

"But this is the truth."

She shrugged. "So what? I don't care. It doesn't matter. The point is that it doesn't need to be *you* telling the story. Let Alex Jones do it. That's *his* role. That's what *his* audience expects. Not yours."

His mind spun through all of the possible arguments, all of the reasonable rebuttals he could make. Yet, studying Kristen's eyes, Judtson became acutely aware that it would be a complete waste of time and breath.

Changing the subject, he prompted, "What is the surprise?"

Her hands, still holding his, squeezed tightly, and a broad smile spread across her face. "I am so excited. You are going to be ecstatic!"

She took one of her hands from his and reached into her purse, which was lying on the table, and pulled out an envelope, handing it to him. In the upper left corner was the logo of a travel agency.

"What is this?"

As he opened the envelope, she gushed, "After the past few…I don't know…months, I thought we could use a break! Some real time together. Just the two of us. Those…are tickets."

He pulled out two stiff card-stock forms, filled with almost unintelligible printing.

"Tickets? For what?"

"It's a cruise!" Her voice was high in pitch, her excitement palpable. "A four-week trip to the Greek Isles. And you won't believe my luck! I was able to get the reservations on such short notice. We leave in only four days! Judtson, darling, isn't it wonderful?"

Judtson's eyes remained fixed upon the two tickets in his hands. He was not quite ready to look up and see her face. Swallowing once to clear his throat, he muttered, "It's great, Kristen."

▽

"DONI COSTELLO?" The nearly shrieked question came from Kelsey as Romeo disclosed what Luis had told him.

"That's what he said."

"Do you believe him?"

"No. Well, I'm not sure."

"What do you mean?"

"Luis did take a bullet, trying to hold off the bogus Army guys at Ft. Irwin. If he was on their side, why didn't he just stand down and let them take you, Kent, Singh, and Berry? Or even help them?"

"True, Romeo, but it was also Luis who took the pistol with the tracker in it back to the silo."

"I know. He did tell us about that, though…when he figured it out."

Kelsey fell silent, thinking. Romeo waited a moment and then continued. "He has offered to submit to hypnosis, a polygraph, a drug test, whatever I want."

"Would the Devil's Breath show up in a test after all this time?"

Romeo shrugged. "Don't know. What was to stop him from ingesting some before he turned himself in? Just to pass the test."

"True."

"Boss, I don't know how we can be certain about this. No one else was around. No inside video. We can't even look for the glass of tea with the drug in it."

"Because the whole place was blown up."

"Exactly. So, yes, it is possible that Mrs. Costello brought Luis a glass of tea laced with Devil's Breath, waited a few minutes for the stuff to take effect…."

"Did Luis say she stayed with him after he drank it?"

"No. He said she gave it to him and left to go work out in the gym with Jimmy Meade. I'm planning on talking to Meade to see if there's a way to nail down the exact time frame."

"Be careful with that. I don't think we should do anything that would get back to Saylor."

Romeo grunted. "I know. At least, not yet. Besides, she could have left Luis and come back fifteen or twenty minutes later and instructed him to lower the tire teeth and open the gate and the vault door."

"She could have. Or someone else in the silo could have slipped the Devil's Breath into the tea without her knowledge, and that person could have given the orders to Luis after she left."

"In which case, we'd need to ask Mrs. Costello if anyone was around the break room when she got the tea for Luis."

"And that," Kelsey added, "would be hard to broach without telling her why we're asking. The deal is...we know we had a traitor in the silo while we were gone. We know it wasn't either one of us, or Judtson, Saylor, Bal, or Carlos because we were all in Bolivia. That leaves the rest of the converted group, Luis, Scott, and Doni."

"Right."

"Up until today, we were convinced it was Luis. Now I'm not so sure."

"It probably still was."

"Maybe. Maybe not. We have to keep our minds open on this, Romeo. Since we assumed it was Luis, we never really spent the time to double-check his background."

"True."

"Let's have Scott start digging on that. And...and on Doni's background, as well. But quietly."

"What about the others? Kelsey, it's possible that one of the converted group we brought in wasn't actually converted. Or had a relapse."

She thought for a full minute before replying. "Okay. Let's look at all of them. And if Scott needs some help on this, tell him he can hire a private investigator."

"Will do."

Her face darkened.

"Boss, what's wrong?"

Pursing her lips, Kelsey answered in a muted voice, "I'm thinking about Saylor. If this is true.... It's so sad, that's all. And..." – her voice softened further – "in the meantime, I guess I should probably tell Judtson."

"So soon? Before we know anything else?"

Nodding, she explained, "I think we might be able to clear this up if we could talk to Doni. But I don't think we can pop in to see her and ask her point-blank. And if we go to Saylor, he'll go ballistic on us. No, I think our best avenue is through Judtson."

The big man carefully considered her words. "You're probably right. Okay, I'll get with Scott and get him rolling on this."

He was rising to leave, when Kelsey reached out and touched his arm.

"Romeo, wait a minute. There's something else I've been holding off telling you."

His face instantly overcome with an expression of concern, he lowered himself back down. "Something...?"

"Nothing's wrong. It's, well, it's just that...."

Kelsey took a deep breath and plunged ahead, telling him about the claim from Alchemist that he was her father. Other than a slight widening of his eyes as he listened, Romeo contained his reaction until she finished.

"And you haven't heard from him since?"

She shook her head.

"Scott hasn't had any luck tracing it back?"

"No."

"Why did you wait so long to tell me?"

Kelsey was clearly uncomfortable with what she was about to say, as she began, "You knew my father. You were hired by him before…before the accident. When I first started thinking that maybe he was alive, that the accident was staged, I assumed he would have had you help stage it. That would mean you would have known all the time I've been grieving that he really was still alive. I just didn't want to think you could know and not tell me."

Romeo's voice was even deeper than its usual timbre. "What do you think now?"

She stared hard into his eyes, trying to read them. "I…I don't…I'm not…."

"Boss, I didn't know. I didn't help him fake his death. I haven't heard from your father once since the accident. If he staged it for your benefit, he fooled me as well."

With a harsh sigh, she almost whispered, "All right."

Chapter 9

DETECTIVE EUNICE CAHANE ANGRILY SLAMMED THE PHONE RECEIVER into its cradle, spit into the trash can beside her desk, and leapt out of her chair. Fury painted indelicately on her face, she marched rapidly across the bullpen and barged into the captain's office without knocking. Preempting any comment, she barked, "Those motherless sons at the FBI are calling the Shields case a suicide!"

The captain, a thirty-year veteran of the Atlanta Police Department and Cahane's immediate supervisor for the past decade, was well accustomed to her fiery temperament. "How do you know?"

Still standing and shifting her weight back and forth from one widely planted foot to the other, repetitively clenching and unclenching her beefy fists, her deep voice much too loud, she answered, "I called 'em. They promised to keep me in the loop, but I hadn't heard a peep since they took over the case. So I rang up the *special agent* in charge...Birdsall's his name...and asked the little jerk point-blank."

"How did they explain the evidence to the contrary...the groceries, the email to Falt, the rest of it?"

"That's just it. They didn't. I guess those almighty folks at the Federal Bureau of Investigation don't think they need to explain themselves to us poor local hicks!"

The captain allowed a slight grin onto his face. "Eunice, I'm guessing you want my blessing to pursue this, even though we've been officially removed from the case."

Her face beet-red, her breathing rapid, Cahane forced herself to take a long, slow breath, letting it out gradually. Finally wresting a modicum of control, she mirrored his smile. "I sure am glad you aren't one of those television stereotype captains who'd bark at me and order me not to get within a hundred miles of the case."

His grin broadened. "Who said I wouldn't *like* to do exactly that?"

She started to argue, when he held up a hand. "But I already know that if I did, I could kiss off getting a night's sleep. I'd be plagued with nightmares of you comin' at me with that bulldog chin to take a bite out of my keister. *All right*. Dig around. Just don't create any problems with our Yankee friends that I can't handle."

▽

Chris Ashby, sucking on the wide-barrel straw and relishing the chocolate shake he had purchased from the truck stop in Gila Bend, accelerated back onto I-8, driving west toward San Diego. There were no vehicles either behind or in front of him, so he took his time working up to his personal speed limit of eighty-seven miles per hour, and thought back over his conversation with Saylor.

The cloud cover had blotted out the brutal glare of the sun from the highway and desert, providing some relief for his eyes, and he noticed that another vehicle, what appeared to be a passenger truck or van, was also exiting the same ramp he had used and was falling in line behind him, about a mile back.

"Utilizing me," he said aloud, "to catch any radar ahead," and chuckled, knowing he had practiced the same technique many times himself.

Three miles whipped under his wheels, this lonely portion of the freeway straight, empty, and flat, save for the occasional hump in the split four lanes to accommodate an underpass. Clearing one of these, Ashby was shocked to see an eighteen-wheeler with its trailer partially on the right shoulder, the balance encroaching onto the outside lane. The tractor itself was severely angled to the left, blocking the inside lane and the left shoulder.

"Great!" he grunted. His eyes hastily scanned the wide concave median, as he hoped to see a cleared path to enable a crossing to the eastbound side of the freeway, and found none.

Hitting his brakes, he quickly checked the rearview mirror to be certain the truck behind him had not moved nearer and would have enough room and enough time to brake behind him. As he slowed to a halt, he saw that the driver of the big rig blocking his way was putting out triangular red reflectors, and walking toward his car. Once again looking to the rear, Ashby noticed that the vehicle had now crested the overpass and was coming to a full stop directly behind him.

The truck was close enough for him to recognize as a black Tahoe.

▽

Jimmy Meade, working with free weights in his small home gym, heard the shrill ring of his cell phone, which he had placed on the seat of the bench press beside him.

"Meade," he answered gruffly, panting slightly from the workout.

"Jimmy, Romeo."

"Well, hell, if it ain't my Ranger buddy. How are you, pal?"

As he talked, Jimmy moved to the side wall and, using his other hand, snatched up a white towel, wiping his face and neck and deftly draping the cloth around his neck.

"Not bad. You?"

"Great for an old man."

He heard a soft laugh over the connection, followed by "I hope I'm in half the shape you are when I hit your age. You need to tell me your secret."

It was Meade's turn to laugh. "No secret. Doesn't matter what you eat, what you smoke, what you drink. It's all genetics. Either you have the good ones or you don't. Look, you didn't call to talk about my impressive vitality. What's up?"

There was a momentary pause before Romeo spoke. "Jimmy, I need to ask you something, but I don't want it to go any further at this point."

Meade sat down on the bench. "Count on it."

"You remember the day all of you were taken at the silo, right?"

A kaleidoscope of images immediately filled the older man's mind, dominated by his residual frustration at not being able to act when the men burst into the gym, surprising him and Doni. "All too clearly. Why?"

After another slight pause, which Meade correctly assumed was caused by some discomfort on the Ranger's part, Romeo began tentatively. "I need you to think back earlier in that day. I was hoping you could remember the time when Mrs. Costello arrived to meet you in the gym. And whether there was anything...unusual."

"By 'unusual,' what do you mean?"

"Don't know, Jimmy. Just fishing at this point."

"Well...I do happen to recall the time that she arrived. We had a date to meet there at ten. She didn't arrive until twelve after."

"You're positive?"

"Damn right, I am. Always been that way. You tell somebody you're going to be someplace at a certain time, you do it. And I can't stand it if somebody keeps me waiting. She breezed in at twelve minutes after ten, and I razzed her about it. Good-natured stuff, of course. And she gave me some cock-and-bull malarkey that my watch was wrong."

Several seconds of silence passed while Jones assimilated the fact, finally proceeding. "Was there anything...uh...different...about the way she was acting?"

Meade's curiosity, mild to this point, flared. "Romeo, what's this about?" All the joviality was gone from his tone as he asked the question.

He heard the unmistakable sound as the Army Ranger sucked in a deep breath. "Jimmy, I talked to Luis."

Before Meade could react to this revelation, Romeo continued, briefing his friend on the interview and the accusation.

"That's outrageous!"

"That was my first reaction."

"First? You've changed your mind?"

"Don't know. I talked to Kelsey about it and she thinks it's worth checking out. That's why I'm calling."

The astronaut closed his eyes and thought back to Doni's arrival. "As far as anything screwy, it's hard to say. You know Doni. Always pretty steady. Not a firecracker like your boss or Lisa."

"True."

"But when she got there, she *was* a little hyped up – kind of talking faster, and her eyes darting around the room. Nothing extreme. If it had been, I would have asked her about it. I didn't. Chalked it off to her being late and rushing to meet me."

"Would you say she was anxious...or nervous about something?"

"I guess she coulda been. She reminded me of the way the men I went up into space with acted right as we were strapping our asses to the top of the big rocket. Normally calm, steady, rock-solid guys, who'd been that way all through training and the simulators, would suddenly start acting like they were getting ready for their first big date. Have you talked to her about this yet?"

"No. Just gathering up what we can first."

"What's your gut telling you?"

"I'm really not sure, Jimmy. Yours?"

He took a minute before answering. "I don't know. I'll tell you one thing. When everybody was saying that Luis turned on us, *my gut* was talking to me pretty loudly then. I didn't buy it."

"No? Why didn't you say something?"

"Hell, Romeo, we had him on video. And afterward, he went invisible on us. All the facts seemed to be pointing straight at him. But it never did feel right to me. I don't know why. You two working together and all…did it feel right to you?"

"I…I never actually gave my gut a chance. The minute I heard what happened and saw the video, that was it."

"What about now?"

"As I said, I'm not sure. I'm not sure at all."

▽

Saylor was steering his pickup out of the parking lot, when his cell phone rang. It was very late in the day and the summer sun was low, almost touching the peaks of the Tucson Mountains. Diverting to the shoulder of the road, he pulled the phone out and checked the screen, not recognizing the incoming number but noticing that the area code was from California. He answered as if it might be a patient. "This is Dr. Costello."

He heard a faltering female voice. "Uh…Doctor…I mean, is this Saylor?"

Picking up the tension in his caller's voice, he replied, "Yes. This is Saylor Costello. Who's calling?"

"This is Starlight Ashby. I'm Chris Ashby's…."

"You're his sister!"

"Yes. Yes. I found this phone number for you in his office. That's where I am now. I hope it's okay that I called you."

"Of course it is, Starlight. Is something wrong?"

Her voice came at him rapid-fire. "I don't know. I don't think so. But I'm freaked out. Chris should have been back from his trip to see you. He told me he was going to Tucson today to talk with you and he should have been back by now. He isn't still there, is he? With you?"

"No. I saw him earlier today. He left…" – Saylor pulled the phone away from his ear and checked the time – "before lunch. More than six hours ago. Maybe he decided to see someone else while he was here. He could have gone to Kelsey's."

She sighed loudly. "Possibly. It's just that he told me he was going to see only you. And then he was going to come straight back. I rode the train down to San Diego. He was supposed to pick me up at the station. We were going to have dinner together tonight to discuss what you had to say. When he didn't show up at the station, I took a cab to his office. If he *had* changed his plans, he would have called."

"He hasn't?"

"No. And I've called his cell about thirty times. All I get is voice mail. I'm…I'm worried."

Saylor leaned back, his head touching the window behind his seat, and closed his eyes for a moment, not at all enjoying the creeping tension spreading through his body. "Starlight, it's probably nothing, but I think you should call the police. Actually, the California Highway Patrol."

"You think so?"

"I do. Only to be cautious. When you call them, make sure you talk to a supervisor, a sergeant, I guess, and make sure you mention that Chris was one of our…group. One of the people in the news lately."

"Why should I say that?"

"If you don't, they won't do anything for twenty-four hours. That's normal protocol. But if you tell them about that, they'll jump right on it."

"Okay." Ashby's sister sounded even more nervous and upset than she had at the beginning of the call, and Saylor found himself wondering if he should have been more reassuring.

"Starlight, let me know the minute you hear from Chris. This is my personal cell phone and I'll have it with me all the time."

"I will."

▽

Lisa Trippiano was alone in her Manhattan apartment, her hair damp from a shower. Wearing a New York Jets jersey, she sat cross-legged on her couch, watching the news and expertly utilizing chopsticks to eat delivered chow mein from a small white cardboard box, when her cell rang. Without looking at the screen to see who it was, she answered, "Lisa!"

She recognized the gruff voice instantly. "Uh, Miss Trippiano, this is Detective Cahane."

Quickly dropping the carton with the half-eaten meal onto the cushion beside her and unwinding her legs, she sat up straight. "Detective Cahane! Hello."

"I had promised you I would keep you in the loop on this, so I thought I'd call. It's not too late, is it?"

"No. Not at all. What's happening?"

The Atlanta detective described the course of events relating to the Rosemary Shields case, beginning with the arrival of the FBI agents and ending with their conclusion that it was a suicide.

"Suicide! That's crazy! You don't buy that, do you?"

There was a marked hesitation on the line before the detective replied, "No. I don't. Too many indications the other way."

"Are you going to…? Well, I guess that once the Feds take over, you can't investigate, can you?"

Her answer preceded by a throaty laugh, Cahane said, "Last time I checked, Georgia was still an independent state. Yep, I can and will. And now that they've declared it a suicide, their case is closed, so they can't say I'm interfering with a federal investigation."

Lisa giggled girlishly. "In other words, they can pound salt."

"Right."

"I'm glad you're not letting it drop, Detective."

"So I might need both you and Dr. Falt at some point."

"Not a problem. I'll let him know."

There was another pause. When Cahane spoke again, her voice was different, muted, cautious. "Of course, now that the Feds have taken this position in spite of the evidence, I can't help but wonder…."

Alarm bells instantly went off in Lisa's mind. "Uh, Detective, hold that thought."

She immediately jumped up and ran to her bedroom, while clutching the phone. One-handedly, Lisa rummaged through the drawer of her nightstand until she found what she was seeking, glad that she had held on to the cell phone provided by Romeo and sanitized by Scott.

Powering it up and seeing that it still held a decent charge, she asked Cahane, "Detective, are you calling me from a land line?"

The question surprised the detective. "A land line? No. I'm calling from my cell. Why…? Oh."

"Are you near a hard-wired phone?"

"Not right now. I'm driving. Wait…I'll be damned. There's an actual pay phone in front of the check cashing place up ahead. Just a sec. I'll pull in."

The conversation stopped for slightly more than a minute until Cahane came back on the line. "Okay. I'm there. I'm feeling a tad silly. Are you sure this is necessary, Miss Trippiano?"

"It's Lisa, and no, I'm not sure, but…. What's the phone number on the pay phone, Detective?"

"It's Eunice, and they don't display it. Stopped doing that on pay phones cuz drug dealers were using 'em. At least before burn phones came around."

"Do you have any change?"

"It'll take a credit card."

"No! Don't. You don't have any money?"

"It takes bills, and yes, I've got some cash."

Lisa gave her the phone number to the safe cell phone and waited while Cahane dialed. When the second phone rang, she disconnected the first. "Okay, now be careful to turn off your other phone."

She heard a momentary sound of fumbling, then "It's off and in my back pocket. You sure this is an okay way to talk?"

"No. I'm not *sure*, but it should be better than what we were using. I'll have somebody send you a phone you can use to talk to us."

There was a loud snort from the other end of the connection before Cahane blurted, "Alrighty-fine. Now I feel about as spooky-weird as I can."

Lisa laughed. "Tell me about it. It's quite a transition mentally."

"So you think if I follow up on this case, it's gonna lead me to the Feds?"

"Don't you?"

The subdued response came after yet another long pause. "Don't know, Lisa. It all sorta feels wrong."

"Look, Detect…Eunice, Rosemary Shields was a part of the huge fiasco which just blew up. She, without the knowledge of her supervisor, first approached Dylan because she was suspicious about vaccines. After everything hit the fan, she came out and said that she had dummied up the epidemiological study. Then she sent Dylan a message that said she hadn't. And after she sent that message to him, she died."

"I know. I know all that. And maybe I'm naive, but I'm still having a problem digesting that the bad guys are our government."

"Really? Even after the details of the Beckleman conspiracy came out? He had a lot of people in a lot of high places working with him."

"Yeah. I guess."

"You know, I have an idea. Why don't you talk to the detective in Tucson? His name is Ben Hart. He was the one who was working the case there when Matt Wheeler first disappeared. The FBI took *him* off the case. He has some pretty good insights into things, and at least you'll be talking to a colleague."

"That works for me. Do you have his number?"

$$\nabla$$

Kelsey perched on the edge of her bed, staring into the open closet and trying to decide what to wear. For the past days she had only been seen in the long, baggy T-shirt, which was now finally in the hamper. Standing with a sigh, she moved to the closet, pulled another super-long shirt from a hanger, and was about to pull it over her tousled hair, when her phone rang. Dropping the shirt on a chair, she padded across the room, glanced at the screen and, surprised by the name, answered, "Saylor!"

"Hi, Kelsey."

"We haven't talked since I saw you at the airport. How are you?"

"Oh, I'm fine. Been busy as hell. Trying to catch up on my practice. I'm not calling at a bad time, am I?"

"No! Of course not!"

"This...this isn't really a social call."

Kelsey felt her stomach muscles tightening, afraid that Romeo had somehow slipped up and Saylor had found out they were looking at Doni as a possible traitor. Guardedly, she asked, "No? Is something wrong?"

"I don't know. I had a visit earlier today from Chris."

He went on to relate the visit and Ashby's revelations about monoatomic gold and autism.

"Saylor, that's terrific!" A major contributor to her gushing response was relief at the direction of the conversation. "So what's wrong?"

"I was hoping that he was with you or that you had seen him after my meeting."

"No. I haven't. Why?"

Saylor sighed. "It's probably nothing, but I got a call from his sister. Apparently, he was going to drive straight back to San Diego after seeing me and meet her for dinner. He didn't show up. Didn't call her and isn't answering his phone."

She was gripped by the tension she had not felt since Bisbee. "Did she call the police?"

"I told her she should call the Highway Patrol. She's going to let me know when she sees him or hears from him."

"How late is he?"

"Right now, only a couple of hours."

"Still could be nothing," she reassured, not believing her own words.

"I know. He might have run out of gas or had car problems west of Ocotillo, in the mountains. There's no cell service in that area."

"True. And if that's the case, CHP should find him."

"Anyway, Kelsey, sorry to bother you. I wondered if he might have stopped to see you. That's why I called."

"Don't be silly, Saylor. No bother at all. You'll let me know when you've heard from her?"

"Yes. I will."

"Okay. Well, take care. And don't be a stranger."

He chuckled. "I won't."

They ended the call. Kelsey, her mind lost in thought, walked back to the chair and picked up the baggy shirt. Before she could pull it on, she paused and stood motionless for a full minute. Suddenly animated, she tossed the shirt on the floor, purposefully crossed to the master bathroom, and opened the lid on her makeup case.

$$\nabla$$

"Carlos, you're certain?" Judtson spoke excitedly into the phone.

"I am, Judtson. I myself took the samples at all of the locations. They were never once out of my sight. I personally delivered them to the metallurgy lab in Atlanta, and I remained there until the results were complete. I even reversed the labeling on the samples, in the event that the lab would tamper with the findings."

"What do you mean?"

Villarreal explained his ploy.

Thinking about this, Kent grunted in surprise. "So they actually did fiddle with the results."

"Yes! They did."

Letting out a heavy sigh in response, he muttered, "I really thought it was over."

"Did you?" Carlos retorted skeptically.

"I…I guess not. I should probably say I was hoping it was."

"Well, mi amigo, if you have any additional doubts, I believe I can dispel them further."

Sensing a more serious tone, Judtson sat upright in his chair. "What is it?"

"While I was in Atlanta, preparing to come home, serendipity smiled upon me and I had a chance meeting with Dylan and Lisa."

"They were in Atlanta? Together? Why?"

In his methodical, careful way, Carlos described the Rosemary Shields incident as it had been related to him by their two friends. As Judtson listened, an avalanche of thoughts and emotions overtook him.

At the end of the narrative, his voice faltered as he asked Villarreal, "Good God, they killed her?"

"It would appear so. And the federales removed the local detective from the case and took it over."

Kent was speechless. As silence filled the connection, he opened a search engine on his computer and typed in a string, including the keywords "Rosemary Shields," "Atlanta," and "CDC." Within less than a second, his screen was populated with hits. Selecting the first, which was only a few minutes old, he hastily scanned the story, then summarized it flatly. "It seems that the FBI just held a press conference. They're saying Rosemary Shields was so despondent over her disgrace that she committed suicide."

"Dylan…and, in fact, Lisa…are certain that it was not the case."

Before Judtson could comment, Carlos added, "And, while I met with them at the Atlanta airport, they relayed another item to me."

"What's that?"

"When I found Dylan in the lounge, Lisa was on the telephone with Dean." He continued, detailing the total reversal of opinion from the photo analyst.

As Judtson listened, he felt his temperature rising, his heartbeat quickening. "This does not look good." The panoply of competing emotions within him gelled into a singularity: anger.

"No, mi amigo. It does not."

$$\triangledown$$

His conversation with Villarreal terminated, his fury undiminished and exacerbated by his inability to focus it on a target, Judtson paced anxiously from room to room within his small office building. The Chatterley incident now pushed back in his mind, the three revelations from Carlos were creating an urgent, unignorable need to talk it all through with someone. His first attempt had been Ricky, but his assistant was not answering his cell phone and Judtson did not wish to leave a voice mail. He then considered Saylor, dismissing this option as quickly as it arrived, knowing that his friend was not yet receptive to the drama and intrigue this news would evoke. Kristen was out of the question.

Despite his conscious efforts to the contrary, Judtson was not able to divert himself from the path leading directly to Kelsey, knowing all the while that he had made a deliberate point of not seeing her or speaking with her since their poignant farewell at the impound lot...for a reason. He was struggling, desperately, to keep his promise to Kristen, to somehow become the Judtson Kent she believed she had married. And he knew that reintroducing Kelsey into his days, into his life, would make that struggle doubly difficult.

"Dammit!" he shouted impotently to the empty rooms.

Something was obviously still happening. He felt it. He knew it. The Beckleman confession had not even come close to answering many of the questions; and yet, he had been trying with all his might to accept it, to feel confident that their battle was over and that they had won.

But now, with the apparently indisputable facts Carlos presented pertaining to Baalbek and Puma Punku...facts diametrically opposed to the Beckleman line...he was losing his internal battle. *If...*, he thought to himself, *if Carlos was right, then everything else was a house of cards*. The Baalbek/Puma Punku connection was, in actuality, where it had all begun. It was the trigger which resulted in his being reprogrammed. And now it had been confirmed as true.

Feeling as if he were about to explode, ignoring the small voice in his head warning him to refrain, Judtson ran back to his desk and picked up the phone, punching the speed-dial button for Kelsey and then immediately slamming down the receiver before the call could be completed.

"No," he said aloud, his voice sounding harsh to his own ears, "not on the phone. I need to talk to her face to face."

Forgetting all about turning off his computer or lights, Judtson dashed for the front door, digging his keys from his pocket as he ran. Wrenching the handle and flinging the door wide, he hurried through while glancing down to find the correct key on his ring so he could lock up, when he slammed into someone, the abrupt impact causing a high-pitched yelp from the other person.

He slammed against the door frame and, dropping the keys, looked up to see Kelsey, who was reeling backward on the front porch.

Chapter 10

B REATHLESSLY, HIS BODILY SYSTEMS STILL OVERSTIMULATED FROM THE TORRENTS of anger and adrenaline, compounded by the shock of colliding with her, Judtson stuttered, "K...Kel...Kelsey!" He jumped forward as she floundered, and grabbed her left arm, a detached part of his mind instantly registering how good it felt to be touching her.

Counterpoised, she gasped and took a step closer to him, moving within inches as they stood in the threshold of the doorway, and lifted her right hand, placing it gently on his shoulder. Within intimate proximity, Kelsey stared boldly into his eyes. "Wow! Hello." Her voice, steadier than his, was husky, her eyes sparkling with surprise...and something else.

The visual linkage between them was a tunnel excluding the rest of the world, a conduit, its surface glimmering as would an out-of-focus mother-of-pearl lining. The whole of his visual field was the view of her deep-blue eyes, the pupils perceptibly opening wider as he watched, as if to take in more of him. Her breath, shallow and rapid, fanned his face warmly. Her scent, sweet and with a trace of spice, enveloped him.

Neither spoke. As the pointer on a Ouija board, touched by the hands of two, moves without the conscious or deliberate intent of either, Kelsey and Judtson slowly drew nearer. Her head tilted slightly back. Her lips parted. Her right hand, traveling of its own volition, slipped from his shoulder and moved around to the back of his neck, seeking and finding the conductive stimuli of bare skin to bare skin.

Judtson's right hand released its grip on her arm and moved to her back, feeling the tautness of Kelsey's muscles. His left hand and arm rose from his side and wrapped around her slender waist, pulling her to him. As two magnets, brought gradually closer until reaching the critical point of attraction, jump the final distance, their lips rushed the last inches to meet, connecting fiercely and closing a circuit.

Their bodies, willing and eager prey of the attractive force, joined, and he felt the soft and firm front of her pressed against him boldly, at first with a subtle writhing, matched by his, which rapidly escalated to convey an insistency...a need. Her hands moved up and buried her fingers in his hair, pulling him ever more tightly into the passion of the kiss.

In a primal, choreographed dance, the two moved as one over the threshold and inside, without once giving up as much as a centimeter of contact. Judtson freed one hand and slammed the door, a moment later pushing Kelsey almost savagely against the inside face, trapping her body between himself and the immovable object.

As his hands urgently swept down to grasp the bottom hem of the T-shirt she was wearing, not a single corner of his mind held a thought of Baalbek, Rosemary Shields, photographs of the moon, or…Kristen.

$$\triangledown$$

Kelsey, tucked under Judtson's arm as they lay nestled on the couch, stared intently down at his hand, which dangled from over her shoulder; she took in the intimate details of the texture of his skin, the lines, his knuckles, all of it, as if attempting to memorize the minutiae of its topography. With her ear against his bare rib cage, she listened to the steady pattern of his breathing. He shifted gently and pressed his lips to the top of her head, the tender gesture triggering an urge in her to burrow even more deeply against him.

Since their first kiss, not an intelligible phrase had yet been spoken by either of them. Judtson broke the silence by quietly murmuring into her hair, "My…God!"

Her reaction was to almost purr, wordlessly conveying her own feelings to him.

Lightly lifting his arm from around her, he turned on his side to face her. "Kelsey, I can't…I can't believe…."

She touched her finger to his lips, shushing him and following the motion by kissing him tenderly. As their lips parted, she spoke, her voice muted and conveying a subtle vulnerability. "When I came here this evening…I didn't plan this. Honestly. I really wanted to…."

A quick smile broke onto his face. "I know. I think…." He hesitated briefly, wanting to be certain of his wording before he proceeded. "I think this is why both of us were trying to keep our distance. I know that I was sure I wouldn't have a chance if I was near you."

Her eyes danced with a twinkle of happiness at the comment and she giggled. "Uh…yeah! Same here. I did think I could keep it together long enough to…you know…just talk to you."

His smile widened. "*Right!* That worked out well."

Kelsey wrapped her arms around him and pulled him close, burying her face in his neck, while whispering, "*I* think it did."

Savoring the sensations of her yet quite warm, bare skin against his, and her lips delicately and repeatedly kissing the side of his neck, Judtson, feeling himself again stirring, pulled back to face her. She gazed at him with naked anticipation, and he was certain he saw a glimmer of understanding as he found his voice. "We…I shouldn't have."

With an all but imperceptible nod, she responded wistfully, "I know."

Unable to ignore the scarcely concealed disappointment on her face, he hurried to continue, "I'm still…I'm trying to…."

Impetuously, she darted forward and kissed him lightly to, again, stop his words. "Judtson, quit torturing yourself. I knew that. I knew it before I came here. And I understand."

He caressed the side of her face, reveling in the sensation of her raven-black hair tickling the back of his hand. "But Kelsey, that…has nothing to do with the fact that it was…absolutely, mind-blowingly amazing."

Reacting to his words, her mood shifted to one of puckish playfulness. "Well, now when you try to decide between us, you'll have a better...*feel*...for all of the pluses and minuses."

Unexpectedly, he found himself laughing. With the tone of the conversation transitioning to a lighter level, he took some time to look around the room and noticed that the front door to the office was unlocked. Disentangling himself, he stood and awkwardly stepped into the legs of his jeans, nearly falling back onto the couch, then crossing to the entry and locking the bottom knob and deadbolt. As he turned back, he saw that Kelsey was just pulling her T-shirt over her head, and he could not help but pause in mid-step to watch. Tugging the cotton fabric slowly along her torso and firmly down at her waist, she reached for her jeans and grinned at him mischievously. "Did I time that well enough?"

Amused, he asked, "How long did you hold it over your face until I turned back?"

She shrugged. "Not long. Just a couple of seconds."

"It was perfect."

"Glad to do it. Anytime."

Promptly needing to swallow, Judtson resumed dressing, as did Kelsey. Untying his running shoes and slipping his feet into them, he asked her as he retied the laces, "Hungry?"

"Oh God, yes."

"What do you feel...?" His question was interrupted by the rude trilling from his cell phone. Suddenly abashed, he glanced nervously at Kelsey. "That's Kristen's ring."

The corners of her mouth flickered downward almost imperceptibly before she replied, her voice with a forced casualness, "Go ahead. Answer it. She's probably wondering where you are. I don't want you to be self-conscious. I'll...I'll step out front for a minute."

Appearing both saddened and somewhat befuddled by his conflicting emotions, Judtson stammered, "Kel...Kelsey, I...."

Moving quickly toward the front door, she instructed, "Go. Answer it. Hurry up. Let me know when you're done."

She unlocked the door and stepped out into the evening. At the sound of the door shutting behind her, Kelsey slumped heavily against the stucco wall and sighed, consciously sublimating the unnamed negative emotions triggered by the phone call, and focusing instead on the physical, chemical, spiritual, and mental afterglow from the past forty minutes. Closing her eyes, she replayed the details of it, with every moment...every sensation...still fresh in her mind, when her reverie was harshly shattered by the explosive sound of a car backfiring on the street.

Her eyes snapping open, she automatically looked toward the sound, seeing an old pickup truck, overloaded with tree cuttings, rakes, shovels, and picks, smoking its way to the west. Eager to return to the movie in her mind, she began to lower her eyelids again as the landscaping truck passed a white van, parked alongside the curb on the opposite side of Pima.

Her first inclination was to disregard it. *After all*, she thought, *it's a dry cleaning delivery van parked in front of an apartment complex. That's pretty normal.* Then she realized that it was after seven in the evening, late for a pick up or delivery. Her mind considered the probability that the delivery driver lived in the complex and would leave the van there routinely at night, but she summarily dismissed this explanation. The complex had an off-street parking lot, so why would the driver leave the boss's property parked in the bike lane?

Unbeckoned, another memory flashed into her mind. It was the image of the van outside her home weeks ago, as she, Saylor, and Ricky were about to have lunch. It was the same dry cleaning company as this one. And this van was also equipped with a roof-mounted directional parabolic dish, which was now oriented to the front of Judtson's building.

Her senses heightened, Kelsey stood from the wall and began slowly walking toward the street, wishing that she had not instructed Chili to remain at her home with Scott and Matt as she had so hastily departed. This thought prompted a soft chuckle and she said aloud, "Maybe I did subconsciously plan on seducing Judtson when I came here."

Approaching the sidewalk, she was able to discern a large, shiny wet area beneath the van and could hear the engine running. Remembering Romeo's explanation from another day, Kelsey understood that the wet area was a puddle of water...condensation from the long-running air conditioner.

Gripped by indecision, she was unsure whether to cross the street and confront whoever was in the vehicle or retreat back inside, her need to choose eliminated as the van, with a squeal of tires, pulled away from the curb and sped away. Running the few feet to the edge of the pavement, she squinted at the receding truck and was barely able to make out the license plate, memorizing it. She reached into the back pocket of her jeans and was glad to find that her cell phone had not fallen out onto the office floor. With several taps on the screen, a text message was dispatched to Scott, including the license plate number.

Turning around, she saw the front door swing open and Judtson head down the sidewalk, a sheepish look on his face. He noticed her expression. "Is something wrong?"

She told him what she had seen and done.

He whirled and faced in the direction of the departed van. "Those bastards!" he shouted. His voice instantly changed, laced with his worry for her safety. "*Kelsey*, why were you walking toward them? They could have...."

She lifted to her toes and kissed him. "I know. I know. Sorry. It was dumb."

"Isn't Romeo here? I assumed he was always around you."

"He's off tonight. Don't know where."

Before he could say anything else, she added, "He's hired a guy to replace Luis."

Judtson put his arm on her shoulder and they turned to walk back to the office. "And where is that guy?"

"Not here." Casting her eyes downward, she continued, "When I left to see you, I told him to stay at the house with Scott and Matt."

He stopped, his eyes widening, his voice teasing. "Oh, you did, huh? I thought you said you didn't plan...."

She punched him playfully. "I didn't. Really! I just thought...I mean...well, maybe, you know, subconsciously." She paused and tried on a wan smile. "Maybe I was hoping."

As he arrived at the door, Judtson kicked something and heard a metallic tinkle. Looking down, he bent over and picked up the keys he had dropped earlier, and they went inside. Once in, he stepped around to stand in front of her, gripping both of her shoulders. "I have a confession to make. When I was barreling out the door and crashed into you, I was on my way to see you."

"You were?"

"Uh-huh. And, even though I had several good reasons to see you, I'm sure that it wouldn't take a skillful hypnotist to coax out the underlying desire to...ahhhh, the hell with it...to make love with you."

Her face softened and she kissed him once again, this time with more passion than the last, a passion which did not go unreciprocated. As they inched apart, she asked, "Okay. What were those good reasons you had for coming to see me?"

"Not now. I think we need to get out of here."

"Yeah, we'd better."

"You still hungry?"

"Uh, yeah! But don't you need to go…home?" The last word in her question was uttered quietly…sadly.

He shook his head emphatically. "No! She was calling to tell me that she was going to go shopping in Phoenix this evening."

Raising one eyebrow quizzically, Kelsey repeated, "Shopping in Phoenix?"

"Ye…yes." His voice became subdued. "We're going on a trip soon and she wanted some new outfits."

"A trip?" Kelsey made a deliberate effort to keep her voice light. "Where? When?"

Judtson avoided eye contact. "Four days. Well, three now. It's a cruise to Greece."

Nearly inaudibly, she murmured, "Oh."

Forcing a grin, he added, "She's going to be late coming back tonight."

"Cool!"

"So where do you want to go?"

"I don't have anything at my place but frozen burritos and corn dogs."

He grimaced. "That's the stuff you eat?"

"No!" she exclaimed, laughing at his reaction. "At least, not normally. Oh, I forgot…you haven't had one of my meals yet."

"No. I haven't. Something *else* to look forward to."

"Damn right. No, the reason I only have that crap in the freezer is…I've been in…kind of a tailspin since I saw you last."

Her words touched him. "I'm sorry, Kelsey."

She waved her hand quickly. "It wasn't that. Wait. I didn't mean it that way. Well, I guess it wasn't *only* that. There have been some other things. A lot of them, actually. That's why I was coming over." With a salacious smile, she added, "At least that's why I was consciously coming over."

"Other things? Like what?"

"I thought we decided we shouldn't talk about it here."

"True. Okay, I asked before…where do you want to go?"

She shrugged. "You pick."

▽

As soon as Judtson pulled into the empty space in the parking lot, Kelsey climbed out of the Olds convertible and looked across the street. "Greyhound racing? I had forgotten this was here!"

He circled around and joined her. "Come on. I'm hungry."

As they walked toward the restaurant, he took her hand and asked, "Have you ever been to Rigo's?"

Squeezing his hand tighter, she answered, "No. Why did you pick it?"

"Well, the food's great. Plus, it's fairly loud inside. If those folks are tailing us with a long-distance microphone, it won't do them much good once we go in."

"Okay."

He held open the door and she breezed past, turning to flash a smile at him as she did. He saw that her eyes were sparkling; her entire face and her body language were alive with an intense enjoyment of the moment. He hurried to catch up to her and they turned to the right and passed through a second door, which was at the top of a ramp leading down to a lower floor level. As they cleared the second threshold, Judtson heard a shouted greeting. "Mr. Kent! Hola!"

The hostess was beaming at him and scurried up the ramp to meet them halfway. "It's good to see you, señor." She eyed Kelsey and added, "And you brought a friend."

Her exuberance was infectious, causing him to grin broadly as he put his arm around Kelsey's shoulders. "Thank you. It's good to be seen. I hate to ask. I don't know if you can manage this, but we'd like a bit of privacy while we eat."

"Of course, of course," she gushed. "No problema! Come! Follow me!"

The woman turned and marched directly into the dining area. Kelsey leaned closer to Judtson and, chuckling softly, said, "Gee, I guess you're a regular here."

He attempted to downplay the effusiveness of the reception. "You might say that."

As they reached the bottom of the ramp and turned to follow the hostess into the dining area, Kelsey skidded to an unceremonious stop, her gaze locked upon the array of pictures hanging on the wall behind the cashier's stand. "Oh, my God! You're kidding!" she squealed.

Having anticipated the object of her attention, Judtson glanced at the glossy 8x10 head shot of himself. Scrawled slightly below his chin with a Sharpie was the inscription "To my friends at Rigo's. You're the best!" and his autograph.

"Hey! Told you I was a regular."

She snorted loudly, her head swiveling back and forth between him and the photo. "I've never seen anybody look so smug. You're actually resting your chin on your hand!"

"It was a publicity shot!" he explained defensively.

After he firmly pulled her away from the area, they threaded their way through the somewhat crowded dining area, the patrons craning to see who was the object of all the hoopla. The chairs and tables were placed nearly abutting each other, causing the two would-be diners to turn sideways and crab-walk several times in their attempt to catch up with the hostess, who was waiting at a corner booth.

"How is this? Good? I will keep the booths and tables around you empty while you're here."

"Señora, this is perfect. Gracias! Are you sure we aren't a bother? It still looks too busy to keep all of these empty."

She made a dismissive sound by blowing air through her closed lips. "Not so busy we can't take care of you, Mr. Kent. There are plenty of other tables."

He moved aside as Kelsey bounced into the booth, then climbed in to sit next to her. She was still laughing softly at the spectacle their entrance had caused, noticing that several of the other guests were surreptitiously, and in some cases openly, staring at them. She was clearly relishing the experience.

"Yeah, that's you, all right. Just a normal, regular old customer."

"That's all. Really."

Rolling her eyes, she looked down at the laminated place mat, which also served as the menu, and saw that there were featured dishes, accompanied by a photograph of each meal. Moving her eyes across the selections, she came to an exaggerated halt and pointed at one of the pictures. "*The Judtson Kent plate!*"

It was his turn to laugh. "Okay. Maybe a bit more than just a regular customer. Our hostess, the owner, is one of my readers. Besides, mine isn't the only one. See, here's a plate named after a local South Tucson politician."

Her expression changed from outright amusement to something warmer. "Well, sounds good. The Judtson Kent plate, it is."

He cleared his throat. "Did you even read what's in it?"

Keeping her eyes locked on his, she folded her hands primly on the tabletop and wriggled on the seat, snuggling against him. "Nope. Doesn't matter."

Enjoying the tingle suffusing through his body from the contact, he described the meal. "It's, uh, carnitas. Grilled pork, chopped up into small pieces. They season the hell out of it, mix in pico de gallo, and grill it till the outside is crispy. Plus, a side of frijoles and a stack of hot flour tortillas."

Her voice so soft he could barely hear it above the din in the room, she murmured slowly, "Sounds perfect."

The waitress came with chips and salsa and took their orders, with Judtson deciding on his namesake plate, as well. After she departed, Kelsey giggled yet again.

"What's so funny now?"

"It just dawned on me...this is a date. Our *first* date."

He looked at her quizzically. "And that's funny?"

Her voice was playful. "No. I was only focusing on the sequence of things. This isn't the way it's supposed to work."

"I...oh, I get it."

Moving closer to him, she whispered, "I think a good girl is supposed to have at least one date first."

Caught up in the interplay, he assured her, "I think we can salvage your honor and call our trip to D.C. a date."

Her eyes widened. "I don't think...." She was interrupted mid-sentence by the tone of her cell phone, surprisingly audible in the ambient noise. Pulling the phone out of her pocket, she checked the screen.

Judtson was able to see the name. "It's *Saylor*? Why is he...?"

"That's part of why I came to see you tonight. I'll explain in a minute."

She answered. The conversation was brief, punctuated by comments from Kelsey of "Oh, no!" and "Is she sure?" She finished by eliciting his promise to keep her informed of any changes.

Judtson's curiosity piqued, he asked as soon as the connection was broken, "What's happening?"

She put the phone in her back pocket. "Like I said, that was one of the reasons I was coming to see you. Chris Ashby has...."

Cutting off her explanation, his phone rang. Grabbing it quickly, he saw that Saylor was now calling him. Kelsey read the screen. "Before you take that, I don't think you should tell him about...."

He nodded his agreement and tapped the phone to answer.

"Saylor! How are you?"

"Judtson, I thought I'd better tell you about some.... Hey, where are you?"

Realizing too late that Saylor would hear the identical noisy room in the background on both calls, he stammered momentarily. "I'm...I'm...."

"Are you with Kelsey?"

"Uh, yeah. We're grabbing a bite. She told me she had something to tell me. We just got here." Judtson was satisfied with how cleverly he had worded his response to avoid overtly lying to his best friend.

"Oh. Well, she's probably planning on telling you the same thing I called her about."

Out of the corner of his eye, he noticed that Kelsey had received a text message on her phone.

"She hasn't told me anything yet, Saylor. We just got here," he repeated. "What's going on?"

"I don't know what to make of this, but apparently Chris Ashby is missing."

The news hit Kent hard. *"Missing? What? How?"*

Saylor began his narrative with descriptions of the unexpected visit from Ashby, the latest news about monoatomic gold and autism, and then the call from Starlight. He finished briefing his friend by saying, "I called Kelsey earlier today to ask her if she had seen him, in case he had made an unplanned stop at her place. She hadn't, so I promised her I'd let her know if something new came up. Starlight called me back a few minutes ago. I guess CHP contacted the Arizona DPS, and they found Chris' car abandoned alongside I-8, just west of Gila Bend."

The people and the sounds around Judtson receded into the background. "Were there signs of foul play?"

"Starlight didn't say and I didn't ask. It seemed wrong to bring that up to her right now."

"Probably a good idea. Saylor, what do you think this means?"

His question was followed by a long, awkward pause. "I don't know. I hope it doesn't mean, you know, I hope it isn't that things are starting up again."

Saylor's voice sounded flat, worried. Hearing this and understanding, Judtson decided not to tell his friend about the revelations from Carlos, instead stating reassuringly, "I'm sure it's not, pal."

"You think?" The trace of hopefulness in Saylor's tone was clear.

"Yeah, I do. Could be a number of things. He might have run out of gas or broken down. Maybe he's hitchhiking and was dropped off someplace and had to walk from there. We'll hear from him."

Judtson visualized the struggle at the other end of the line as Saylor worked to force himself to believe his friend's scenario, the outcome of the match evident with his eventual response. "Yeah, I bet you're right."

"You'll let me know if she calls you again?"

"Absolutely."

"Okay, man." With an imposed lightness in his voice, he added, "Hey, say 'hi' to Doni for me."

"I will. Bye. Oh, and have fun on your dinner date."

The call was ended as Judtson was opening his mouth to respond. He tucked his phone into his shirt pocket, looking back at Kelsey, who was waiting expectantly.

"Did he buy it?" she asked, clearly referring to his subterfuge at the beginning of the call.

"I think so. Well, maybe not. This Ashby thing is what you wanted to talk to me about?"

"Uh-huh." She nodded. "That and other stuff. By the way, that text was from Scott. The license plate of the bogus dry cleaning van is registered to Homeland Security."

"Really?"

"Yep."

He paused for a moment, his mind reorganizing the influx of details. "Do you think *they* grabbed Chris?"

"Don't you? Especially considering that van outside your office. Let's face it...they snatched him right after he found out that the monoatomic gold works on autism and right after he went to see Saylor. Yeah, I think they're on the offensive again. And you said you had something to tell me, didn't you?"

"I did." Judtson shifted gears and filled her in on the conversation with Carlos, detailing the archaeologist's confirmation of the true genesis of the stone at Baalbek. Before she could say anything, he continued, relating the mysterious death of Rosemary Shields, as well as both Dylan's and Lisa's suspicions that it was murder and that it was being covered up by the government. As he spoke, he saw Kelsey's eyes grow wider at each disclosure, with all vestiges of her earlier mirth now evaporated, but she held her comments until he finished by telling her about the Chatterley confession and Copeland's call to Lisa regarding the faked results of the photo analysis.

He leaned back into the cushion of the booth, suddenly feeling tired.

"Is that it?"

Smirking sardonically, he retorted, "Isn't that enough?"

"That's not what I meant. I didn't want to start telling you about my things until you were done."

"You said you had more than Chris' disappearance?"

"I did. I do. A couple of things."

Kelsey's mood noticeably changed. A new apprehension clouded her features as she started, "After I dropped you off at the impound lot to pick up your car, I drove home and...got on the computer. Remember Alchemist?"

"Of course I do. He's the one who gave us some hints in the right direction before."

"Yeah, well, he was waiting for me to log on so he could chat with me. He knew who I was. I was certain that I had never told him enough for him to figure that out. Scott disagrees and says I was sloppy, but that's not the point." As she spoke, the tempo of her delivery increased. "Anyway, he told me that it wasn't over."

Judtson was about to ask for clarification, when she continued rapidly, "The crisis...the problem...the thing we were all working on...it wasn't over. I guess I kind of lost it with him. Told him I didn't want to hear his mumbo-jumbo and started to log off."

She abruptly stopped speaking, her eyes moving away from his and staring off into the distance. He waited quietly for several seconds.

"That's when he told me that he was...my father."

"WHAT?"

Judtson's barked reaction was so loud, several of the nearby diners stopped eating and turned to look at him.

He lowered his voice. "But your father is dead! You said he died in an accident."

Her voice was bleak, unemotive, as she answered. "He is. He did."

"Then...?"

"Remember I told you his body was destroyed in the explosion and fire?"

"Yeah."

"They could never identify it."

Judtson twisted to face her, seeing the anguish plainly written in her features. "Kelsey, are you saying you believe him?"

"No! Dammit, I...I don't know."

Mentally catching up with this latest revelation, he asked, "Well, I'm confused. Haven't you seen him since the IM chat?"

She shook her head. "The connection was broken. Right after he told me...right after he gave me the proof I demanded. He hasn't communicated with me since."

"Proof?"

Drawing in a shuddering breath, Kelsey told him about her secret nickname and the fact that Alchemist had used it in his final message.

Her pain, her vulnerability were painful for Judtson to watch. He reached forward to hold her. She jerkily leaned away. "Not...now. Give me a minute. Okay?"

"Okay." Dropping his hand down, he asked, "And you haven't been able to reconnect with him, either? Scott hasn't been able to...?"

"No! Nothing. I've had Scott chasing down the IM site. It's offline. Went off right then. And it's never come back on. He's following up on some other things. But nothing yet."

Again leaning back in the booth, Judtson digested what she had told him, slowly turning it over in his mind. "What about Romeo? Your father hired him prior to the accident. Which...if you think about it...sort of reinforces the possibility that he *was* planning the whole thing. So, if your father staged his own death, wouldn't Romeo know about it?"

"I thought of that. Kept Romeo out of it until just recently. He swears he didn't know anything like that about my father...about staging the accident or still being alive."

"You believe him?"

She answered immediately. "Yes. I do."

The tone in her voice did not invite a follow-up. Slightly changing the direction, Judtson asked, "You said Alchemist told you it wasn't over. Did he say anything else? Anything specific?"

Closing her eyes tightly for a second, Kelsey pressed her shoulders against the seat back and lifted her hips so she could dig something out from the front pocket of her jeans. Extracting a folded sheet of paper, she laid it on the place mat and opened it before handing it to him. "I printed the last conversation."

It only took a minute to read the exchange. "He thinks that Beckleman fell on his own sword for the cause."

"Yes. I guess, if we're going to accept what Alchemist says, that's been one of their strategies for a long time."

"You know...there *were* a lot of loose ends after his confession."

As they fell into this direction of the conversation, Kelsey's face restored to a more normal visage. "Yes. There were. A few of them really bugged me. And you know how Carlos, Dylan, and some of the others felt."

Their conversation stopped short as their waitress arrived, placing two sizzling platters of carnitas in front of them with a flourish. Kelsey leaned over the plate and inhaled deeply. "Oh, my God. That smells wonderful!"

A second waitress came to the table with the refried beans and hot flour tortillas. After making certain the guests had everything they needed, the two servers left. Judtson picked up the wicker basket of tortillas, offering one of them to Kelsey. She plucked the top one from the pile and hungrily filled it with the dark brown pork. He did the same and both ate heartily, not broaching the previous topics throughout the meal.

Sopping up the last bit of beans with a corner of tortilla, Kelsey tucked it between her lips and chewed it, swallowed, and flopped heavily against Judtson with a sigh. "That was outrageous!"

With a half grin, he teased, "So you liked the Judtson Kent plate, huh?"

Her hand moved to his, squeezing it. "Uh-huh. I could eat it every day…for the rest of my life."

"Oh, I think you'd eventually get tired of the same old thing and want to taste something different."

She quickly leaned toward him and kissed him, lingering on his lips. When they separated, she spoke softly. "No. Definitely not. It's the Judtson Kent for me."

The two stared into each other's eyes for a time, neither wanting to end the moment.

"How was everything, Mr. Kent?"

He turned to see the hostess standing at their table.

"Incredible!" Kelsey reacted before Judtson could speak.

"Fantastic!" he echoed. "That was the best you've ever made it."

She beamed from the compliments and asked if they wanted dessert or coffee. They both declined the flan and opted for the coffee, which arrived within minutes.

Not attempting to return to the mood from minutes earlier, Judtson sipped his coffee and said, "You mentioned you had something else to tell me."

Kelsey's expressive face once again reflected a new mood, this being sober…anxious. "I do." Her voice was neutral, cautious.

"What is it? Something bad? Is everyone else all right?"

"Everyone's fine." She paused again. "We found Luis."

The news jolted him. "Luis! How did you find him?"

"Actually, he found us. He turned himself in to the FBI."

"That bastard! I've personally wanted to rip him to shreds, but I know I'd have to fight Romeo for that shot. Have you talked to him yet? What's he saying for his sorry ass?"

"I haven't. Romeo did."

A brief bark of a laugh burst from Judtson. "They let Romeo in? Is Luis still breathing?"

She nodded gently. "Yeah, they allowed him in because he was the only person Luis would talk to."

Kent appeared stunned by the turnaround. "That makes no sense. He has to know how Romeo feels. Why would he do that?"

"He said…he swears that he didn't deliberately…or I guess I should say, consciously… betray us. That he was controlled."

"That's total bullshit, Kelsey! He was down in the silo with the others. How could they have gotten to him?"

She twisted on the bench seat of the booth so she was facing him fully, and took his other hand in hers. "That's why I was holding off on this part until after we could finish our dinner together."

Watching her eyes closely, he saw that they were in constant motion, darting from one feature on his face to another, acutely conveying her anxiousness. He felt his stomach muscles tense. "Kelsey, tell me. What did he say?"

Biting her bottom lip briefly, she gathered her strength and blurted, "He swears that one of the people down there was a traitor. Gave him Devil's Breath and ordered him to open up the place."

"WHAT? WHO?"

She began speaking rapidly, almost tripping over the individual words. "Judtson, I want you to know that I don't believe him. I think it's just something he made up to get himself off the hook. And...and I know that you have a long history." Losing her nerve, she stopped and stared almost imploringly at him.

His mind refused to process the input he was receiving. The message was clear, and Kelsey obviously wanted him to decipher it and spare her the ordeal of actually saying the name aloud, but he could not reach the conclusion she wanted.

"A long history...? What are you saying?"

Steeling herself, Kelsey squeezed both of his hands even harder.

"He said it was Doni."

Chapter 11

RETURNING HOME, DYLAN MADE A SANDWICH AND CARRIED IT INTO HIS STUDY, taking a bite while switching on his computer. The top email in his inbox was from Lisa. He clicked on it.

> Dylan, couple of things. Cahane called. She's seriously torqued because the FBI has called the Shields death a suicide. She told me she's not going to drop it. The other thing is a story I saw on the 'net. Since it's kinda up your alley, thought you might be interested. You probably already know about it, anyway. Here's the link.
> By the way, I have an idea for a show about everything that's going on. Just embryonic at this point. I'll keep you posted. Lisa

He clicked on the link and was taken to an article describing recently completed cancer research at the Mayo Clinic and Duke University Medical Center. The paper detailed complete remission by cancer patients suffering from brain cancer or multiple myeloma after being injected with massive doses of polio or measles virus.

Although it was a small sample group and the discovery had yet to be peer-reviewed and validated by others, Falt was fascinated. If this proved to be true, the implications were compelling. The researchers involved were trumpeting the technique as an exciting new therapy. Nevertheless, from the standpoint of immunology, it opened the door to the possibility that scientists, in their zeal to eradicate those two diseases many decades ago, had somehow robbed the human body of a natural defensive mechanism against cancer.

He copied the contact information of the researcher.

▽

Kenny Bowman watched through the one-way glass as the technician administered the polygraph to Luis Tovar. They were performing the test late in the evening to accommodate the schedule of Dr. Vince Thompson, whom they had decided to use instead of the staff polygrapher in the local FBI office. Thompson was considered to be one of the best in the field and happened to be in Phoenix to make a presentation at a seminar earlier that day.

Bowman had contacted the man personally and described the case. It was more than likely a combination of the unusual aspects of Tovar's story, coupled with the high-profile nature of the Beckleman scandal, which appealed to the academician. He had been driven down to Tucson at the conclusion of the day's events by one of Bowman's fellow agents.

So far, the session had lasted nearly an hour, as Thompson progressed, expertly weaving in the control questions with the list he had assembled utilizing Romeo's help. By the end of the test, he had to admit that Tovar had been persuasive, and he was glad to have the impending results to rely upon, rather than simply depending on his own gut. At no point in the interview did Tovar hesitate, falter, stutter, or appear apprehensive. All of his answers were quick, steady, and proved to be consistent when faced with a repeated or rephrased question.

Thompson rose from his chair and walked to the connecting door, leaving Luis at the table. As he joined Bowman, the FBI agent asked, "Well?"

The man stood beside Kenny at the glass and watched his subject. "As you probably know, I will need to run further analysis of the readings through my proprietary software. Even though positive or negative results may appear to be obvious, we do occasionally find microsecond fluctuations which can be quite telling, fluctuations too brief to be properly interpreted by the administrator."

"I get that, Doctor. But, based upon your initial observation...?"

Thompson turned to face him. "Special Agent Bowman, unless my later analysis uncovers truly convincing contradictory interpretations, I would have to say that this man is telling you the truth."

An unidentifiable prickle of emotion swept through Bowman. "You're saying that he *was* drugged and ordered to open up the silo?"

Thompson pursed his lips briefly. "While the actual events following the ingestion of the iced tea are not verifiable, I did not observe indications of deceit *or* honesty as we delved into that portion of his story."

"I don't understand."

"To put it simply, when a subject is telling the truth about an event he has personal knowledge of, that is our baseline for the test. When he lies, we get a distinct variance from the baseline, which reveals that to be the case. On the other hand, if a person is describing an event or series of events he has no *firsthand* knowledge of, but *believes* to be true, the responses are essentially neutral. That was the case with Mr. Tovar as he answered my questions dealing with everything after drinking the tea. However, I believe he was being truthful when he specifically denied any conscious complicity or culpability for the acts of betrayal."

Bowman had listened intently to make certain he had a firm grasp of the results, then asked, "And the tea itself. Did that happen?"

"It did."

"And it was brought to him by Mrs. Costello?"

"It was."

▽

Kelsey had expected an emotional outburst from Judtson. Instead, he absorbed the accusation from Luis silently, not breaking off eye contact with her.

After nearly a minute passed without a word from him, she offered, "For what it's worth, I don't believe him. I don't think Romeo does, either."

Finding his voice, Judtson muttered, "I...it can't be. It doesn't make sense."

"No," she agreed. "It doesn't."

The two were sitting side by side. Although his eyes were still connected to hers, Kelsey could tell that he had disengaged, withdrawn within himself, and was no longer focused on her in the least. She was certain that he was reviewing the countless moments in his life shared with Doni, from their childhood forward. Not inclined to disturb his thoughts, she waited quietly.

At last, he spoke. "I can't make it fit. I can't reconcile this to the Doni I've known. Why would she do something like that? Why would she put everyone in danger? And she did it to herself, too. I mean, she was one of the prisoners. And when we arrived to get them out, she helped! No. It must be wrong. *He* must be wrong."

Kelsey's head bobbed. "I think so, too. I even considered not telling you at all."

The focus of his eyes finally returned to her. "No. You had to. I know."

"I thought so. And there are a couple of aspects of Luis' story that she might be able to help us with. You know, to clear things up. Maybe lead us to the real traitor...assuming Luis isn't lying and one does exist."

"Such as?"

"Well, according to Luis, he was at his station at the security desk right inside the vault door, watching the videos when she brought him a glass of tea. He thinks the Devil's Breath was in the tea because he doesn't remember anything after he drank it."

"So, it's only his word. Someone else could have brought it?"

"Yes. Or she might have mentioned to others that she was going to take him something to drink. Someone else could have doctored it before she went."

Judtson enthusiastically seized upon this possibility. "Yes! That could have happened."

"Obviously, if someone else.... I mean, whoever that person was...isn't going to just tell us if we ask. The one person we can ask is Doni."

"Oh, I get it. And you figured that the best way to broach the subject with her was through me." His tone was not the least bit accusatory as he said this.

"Right. Of course, we'll have to tell her why we're asking. And she's...."

"Going to blow up the minute she hears it."

"Exactly."

Judtson grunted. "And so will Saylor. Believe me, I know him."

"I'm positive he will."

He let out a harsh breath and frowned. "So you want me to talk to them and ask her about the tea."

"Uh-huh." She added hastily, "I'll go with you if you want."

"No. No need. It'd be better if I did it alone. Kelsey, is there anything else? Any other evidence or clues? Was there any video of the inside?"

She shook her head. "The only other thing was that Doni met for a workout with Jimmy Meade at about that time. Romeo was going to talk to him and see if he might remember something, you know, strange that could help us."

"Has he talked to him yet?"

"I think he has. But he hasn't called me yet, so I don't know."

"Can we try him now?"

"Sure." She used her phone and called his number, putting it on speaker mode. After five rings, they both heard it go to voice mail. She left a message for him to call her and disconnected.

Her brow furrowed a little. "That's weird. It's the second time this evening I've called him and it went to voice mail both times."

"Didn't you say he had the night off?"

"Yes. He usually picks up, though. Even when he's off." With a shrug, she put the phone on the table. "Well, for now, I think we should both assume that the Doni thing is a red herring and forget about it. We do have other things to worry about. Like, what do you think we should be doing about Chris?"

Relieved at the opportunity to focus on a different topic, Judtson answered, "I've been thinking about that. I think we should go out to the spot where they found his car. I'm sure all the DPS did was slap an abandoned-vehicle sticker on it and leave it right where it was. I doubt they checked it over very thoroughly."

"That's a good idea. Tonight?"

He took some time to consider the variables. "Don't know. On one hand, the longer it sits, the more risk we have that evidence could be removed or destroyed. On the other hand, it's dark now. It's going to be harder to actually see the...clues, I guess."

"True."

"And there's one more thing. Well, two more, really."

"What?"

"The first is...what do you and I know about gathering evidence? We're not cops. We could look directly at something and miss it."

"I think we'd do fine, but I see your point. And the second thing?"

Judtson's mouth twisted slightly into a smirk. "They...I was hoping I'd never have to say this phrase again...*whoever they are*...are clearly back on the move. And it seems as though they're changing their tactics. Escalating. Instead of covertly attempting to convert people mentally, now they're kidnapping and killing."

"They were before. Don't forget about Emily Benson. They killed her. And Al. And they kidnapped Robin Reedy and the militia guy, Nelson Coburn. Not to mention our group."

He inwardly flinched at the memories. "Either way, as much as you and I both think we're fairly damn formidable, it probably isn't a good idea for the two of us to go out in the middle of the desert alone at night."

"You're right. On both counts. If we went out alone, even if nothing happened, *Romeo* would probably kill me. We need to find him."

Without waiting for agreement, she redialed the last number. The call again went to voice mail. Not bothering to leave another message, Kelsey next called Scott.

"Hi, boss."

"Scott, where's Romeo?"

"Don't know. He went somewhere for the evening. He's been doing that a lot lately."

"You're telling me he has a serious girlfriend?"

"Don't know."

"Are his trackers on?"

"I'll check."

There was silence on the line for less than a minute. "Yeah, both are on."

"Text me the address?"

$$\nabla$$

Judtson parked on the fringe of the lot, and neither made a move to get out. Glancing around first, he said, "You're sure this is the address?"

Kelsey nodded. "This is what he sent. I'll double-check."

She called Scott again. The discussion was brief. After disconnecting, she confirmed, "Yep. And he checked my GPS, too. We're within a hundred yards of Romeo."

"This is a hotel! Do we honestly want to…?"

She grinned and waved off his words. "Bust in on him in one of the rooms? *No*. But let's go in. Maybe he's in the lobby or lounge or something."

They climbed out of the Olds after Judtson took a minute to raise the convertible top and latch it. As they crossed the lot, Kelsey made another call to Scott and asked him to send a real-time map with both Romeo's and her GPS blips displayed. Walking through the glass double doors, Kelsey, holding her phone up and staring at the screen, pointed toward the far side of the lobby. "That way. Looks like I'm right."

On the far wall was an entrance to the hotel lounge. Boisterous laughter and hooting poured out of the opening and filled the lobby. Several patrons were loitering outside the entrance, drinks in hand, and the two were forced to slowly worm their way through the rowdy group, with Judtson leading the way and almost immediately suffering the spill of an entire margarita onto the front of his shirt and jeans.

"Oh, hell," the intoxicated girl, apparently a college student who appeared too young to drink, slurred. "Sorry."

Groaning as the sticky drink soaked through to his skin, he managed to clear the entrance, doggedly followed by Kelsey, who found his discomfort incredibly funny.

Ignoring her and pinching the front of his shirt between his thumb and index finger to hold it away from his body, he yelled to be heard, "Which way?"

Returning her eyes to the lighted screen, she pointed to the far end of the bar. "There! Want to go to the restroom first?"

He shook his head and began to walk forward. "No. Let's get this over with."

Biting back additional guffaws, she nodded and moved alongside him, taking his arm and plunging into the crowd. They had covered less than half the distance, when a spotlight suddenly appeared on the small stage to their left. A moment later, a heavyset man, who was sporting a large handlebar mustache and holding a wireless microphone, jumped up onto the stage and stood in the light.

The crowd quieted somewhat, and the mass of bodies pressed closer to the stage, trapping Judtson and Kelsey in place.

"LADIES AND GENTLEMEN, WELCOME TO THE FINAL NIGHT OF THE BEST OF TUCSON KARAOKE PERFORMERS!"

The throng whooped a raucous response. Kelsey, wedged up against Judtson, her T-shirt sopping some of the syrupy drink from his clothes, shouted, "I never dreamed Romeo would be a karaoke fan."

Within seconds, the MC barked, "WE ARE PLEASED TO HAVE BEEN SELECTED AS THE HOST LOCATION FOR THE FINAL EVENT, ESPECIALLY SINCE THE FIRST OF THE THREE FINALISTS BEGAN THEIR BRIEF BUT SPECTACULAR CAREER RIGHT HERE ON THIS STAGE!"

The audience once again hollered out its agreement wildly.

"AND NOW, WITHOUT ANY FURTHER ADO..."

Judtson leaned close to Kelsey's ear. "Why do so many people say that? They probably don't even know what 'ado' means."

Kelsey snickered at his comment, the sound lost in the din.

"THAT DYNAMIC DUO WHO IN ONLY A FEW DAYS HAS KICKED ASS AND TAKEN NAMES ON THE KARAOKE STAGE...OUR OWN IN-HOUSE FAVORITE SONS...THE PAIR THAT ALWAYS BEATS A FULL HOUSE..."

"This is ridiculous!" Judtson huffed to Kelsey.

"THE TWO-MAN TEAM DESTINED TO BE THE WINNERS TONIGHT..."

"All right, all right, already!"

"**RIGHTEOUS...RICKY...AND...THE...RANGER!**"

Making the connection in a flash, Kelsey squealed loudly as the crowd exploded hysterically into alcohol-fueled applause, shouts, and whistles. Grabbing Judtson's arm so vigorously that her fingers dug into his flesh, she shrieked, "OH, MY GOD! LOOK!"

The spotlight had dramatically swung to the far end of the bar, and a path miraculously cleared. Kent, craning to see over the others, stared in disbelief. Running toward the stage, each carrying his own microphone, and both wearing identical wraparound sunglasses, purple turtleneck sweaters, white slacks, and black zipper boots, were Romeo and Ricky.

Approaching the stage, they split apart and trotted around to the two opposite sides of the platform as the DJ launched the massive sound system into the karaoke version of "Little Latin Lupe Lu," obviously edited to lengthen the hard-pounding drum and guitar introduction.

Judtson was transfixed, speechless as his friend and assistant looked more animated, confident, and alive than he had ever seen him. Their moves choreographed and timed to perfection, the two men leapt onto the platform simultaneously from the opposite ends, turning in midair and landing side by side, facing the audience. Both then spun around a full 360 degrees, completing the turn at the exact instant the vocals began.

Romeo's sonorous bass boomed from the speakers, with Ricky taking the high harmony perfectly, the duo belting out a rousing rendition of the first verse while dancing to the beat as one. As the second verse resounded – "If you want to do the Twist, Lupe Lu can put it down" – Romeo performed a deep squatting version of the famous dance. During the next line – "If you Wah-Watusi, she's the best for miles around" – Ricky broke into an exuberant fist-flinging portrayal of that 1960s classic.

Kelsey, her voice trembling with excitement, yelled to Judtson, "Where did they get those moves?"

"I know! I know!"

"It's great, isn't it?"

"Unbelievable!"

As the song progressed and reached the brief instrumental break, Romeo and Ricky faced one another and gave what began as a high-five, except that Romeo firmly gripped Ricky's hand in midair and, twisting and bending forward, flipped and rolled his partner over his back. Ricky, a huge smile on his face, landed lightly on the other side precisely at the perfect moment to belt out a high, wavering scream. The rambunctious crowd erupted with appreciative yells and whistles, nearly drowning out the music. Both Judtson and Kelsey joined in with the audience as they all spontaneously began clapping in time with the song, the energy urging Ricky and Romeo on.

Both soaked with sweat, the two showmen put everything they had into the final bars of the piece, with Ricky hitting wailing high notes Judtson had never imagined his friend capable of producing, as Romeo repeated the last line in perfect basso profundo – "Little Latin Lupe Lu...Little Latin Lupe Lu...Little Latin Lupe Lu...." As the song faded out, the men each grabbed the other's hand and bowed in unison while the mob clapped, whooped, shouted, whistled, stomped, and screamed its appreciation. Kelsey and Judtson were no exceptions to this outpouring.

Taking three more bows, they stepped aside as the MC returned to the stage. "HOW ABOUT THAT, EVERYONE! RIGHTEOUS RICKY AND THE RANGER!" His words triggered a new avalanche of sound from the audience. From his vantage, Judtson could clearly see Ricky's face. It was bright red, covered with sweat, and beaming broadly.

As the applause continued, they exited stage right and wended their way through the pack of bodies toward the far end of the bar where, Kent guessed, there was probably a dressing room. The fans did not want to let them pass, both the men and the women rushing in to hug the two local stars, pat them on their backs, and shout congratulatory comments.

Judtson felt Kelsey again close to his ear, her breathing ragged from the excitement. "Should we follow them or wait?"

He responded with an exaggerated shrug. "What do you think?"

Turning, he saw that her face was flushed from her enjoyment of the performance. "I say, let's follow them. I want to tell them how awesome they were! I don't want them to go out a back door or anything."

He agreed and they began attempting to work their way through the mass of bodies ahead of them, the number thinning slightly since the conclusion of the first entry in the competition. Now pushing through the crowd, they lost sight of their friends, simply maintaining the same course until reaching the area next to the end of the long bar, currently packed at least three-deep with drinkers, all trying to get the harried bartenders' attention.

Kelsey pointed. "There they are!"

Judtson looked in that direction and saw Romeo and Ricky sitting at a small table against the wall, still wearing their sunglasses, and surrounded by approximately twenty people who were all offering to buy them drinks. He and Kelsey redoubled their efforts to penetrate the human barrier.

▽

"That was *great!*" the young female college student gushed, leaning over the table in front of Ricky to firmly squeeze Romeo's arm.

"Uh, thanks, miss," he grunted, shifting uncomfortably in his chair.

She reluctantly relinquished her grip and straightened. The moment her torso was no longer blocking Ricky's view, he squawked unintelligibly and tapped his singing partner on the shoulder. "Oh, no! Romeo! Look!"

Jones peered into the crowd. "I don't see anything. What?"

By then, Ricky was nearly sputtering. "It's…it's both of our bosses."

Doing a double take, Romeo barked, "WHAT? WHERE?"

Before Ricky could tell him, Kelsey broke through the final line of people around the table and ran up to Romeo, throwing her arms around his neck. "Romeo, that really *was* spectacular! I never knew…."

Kent was right behind her and Ricky sprang up. "Uh, hi, boss."

The grin on Judtson's face was almost ear to ear. "'Righteous Ricky,' huh?" He reached over the table and enthusiastically shook his assistant's hand.

Kelsey had released Romeo from the hug and was standing beside Judtson, when Ricky, sounding self-conscious, suggested, "Why…why don't we go out to the lobby or something? The next act is going to start in a minute."

"Oh, no," Kelsey rebutted. "Didn't you two want to watch the competition?"

Romeo stood. "We don't have any competition."

The three others laughed out loud. "Okay. If you're sure."

In answer to her, Romeo skirted the table and plunged into the crowd. Judtson, Kelsey, and Ricky fell in behind. With the big man running interference, they made substantially better time traversing the length of the lounge and emerging into the nearly abandoned lobby. Finding a grouping of two overstuffed chairs and a couch, the four moved to it, with Romeo taking one of the chairs and removing his sunglasses. Ricky did the same, leaving the couch for Judtson and Kelsey. He immediately noticed how close together they were as they sat.

Kent was the first to speak, practically sputtering. "Ricky…I mean, Righteous, how long…? When did you two…?"

Relaxing some from the euphoria following the performance and the surprise of being discovered by his employer, yet still perched on the front few inches of his seat, Ricky released a loud sigh. "Not that long. Right after we got back from La Paz, Romeo showed up at my place one night and brought me here."

"Romeo, why didn't you ever tell me?" asked Kelsey, her tone a blend of accusation and teasing.

With a conspicuous glance at the contact between her thigh and Judtson's, he stated matter-of-factly, "We are allowed some secrets, aren't we?"

Catching the implication, she tittered nervously and shifted away a few inches. "Yes! We do. I mean, we are. But I would have loved to come see you two perform. It was cool tonight!"

Recapturing the conversation, Judtson persisted. "He *brought* you here? You're saying you came to a karaoke bar with Romeo and just hopped up on the stage that first night and sang? That doesn't sound like you, Righteous."

"Stop that 'Righteous' bit. No. I didn't *just hop up* on the stage and sing. I had to…I was talked into it."

"I got him drunk," Romeo blurted, smirking.

Both Kelsey and Judtson burst out laughing. "You…you got him drunk so he'd sing with you?" Kelsey asked, catching her breath. "Why?"

The Ranger shrugged casually and retorted, "You heard him. He's a great Bobby Hatfield," referring to the high-voiced half of the Righteous Brothers. "I could tell by listening to him talk that it would work. I've been doing the karaoke thing for a while. Since Iraq. To unwind a little. But how many times can a man sing 'Ole Man River'?" Kelsey began chuckling again at his wry remark, as he continued, "I wanted a partner. Figured it was worth a try. As you saw, turned out he was a natural. From his first night in the spotlight."

"What's with the outfits?" blurted Judtson, glancing down. "Zipper boots? Wait a minute. That's what was delivered at the office, wasn't it?"

Ricky's resident smile widened in response. "The outfits, including the boots, were my idea. And, yes, that's what came that day."

Before either had a chance to quiz them further, Romeo interjected, "You didn't come here tonight to catch our show." He could tell by Kelsey's expression that he was right. "What's up?"

She began, speaking rapidly, "That's true. And I'm sorry. If we…if I had known that you were…."

"Boss," he interrupted, his voice firm. "It's fine. What's going on?"

"The first thing we…I want to know is if you talked to Jimmy."

Instead of answering, Romeo cast a meaningful look toward Judtson.

"Romeo, it's not a problem. He knows."

"Okay. Yes, I talked to Jimmy. He was certain that Mrs. Costello was twelve minutes late meeting him. She told him that his watch must have been off. He also said she was acting nervous. Not her usual self."

Kelsey checked Judtson to see how he was taking this bit of news but was unable to read his face, so she continued. "Thanks. The other thing is that Chris Ashby is missing."

"Missing!" The barked word came from Ricky.

She proceeded to tell both of them about Ashby's visit to Saylor and the phone calls from Starlight, ending the narrative by saying, "I'm sure the DPS hasn't done a very thorough job of checking his car for signs of foul play."

Romeo snorted. "I bet they haven't checked it at all. Is it still in the same spot?"

"As far as we know."

"We should get out there. Right away."

"That's what Judtson and I thought. But he didn't think we should go alone."

Giving a sidelong glance to Kent and grinning, Romeo muttered, "At least one of you has some common sense."

"*Romeo!*" she protested. "Anyway, neither one of us knows how to handle a crime scene."

"Neither do I. Luckily, I can call someone who does."

He stood from the chair and slapped the back pocket of his snug white pants. "Uh, Kelsey, can I borrow your phone? Mine's in the dressing room."

Covering her mouth to hide her amusement, she pulled out her phone and handed it to him, saying, "Pants a little too tight for a big old thick phone, huh?"

Curling his lip in a snarl, he took several paces away to make the call.

As they waited, Kelsey and Judtson used the time to fill Ricky in on the other developments. He accepted the various revelations with surprising equanimity.

At the moment Romeo was returning to them, a voice boomed from the doorway. They all turned to see the MC twirling his huge handlebar mustache with one hand, and waving with the other to get their attention. Ricky stood and shouted, "Yes? What is it?"

With a broad smile, the man boomed back, "YOU WON! RIGHTEOUS RICKY AND THE RANGER ARE THE CITY CHAMPS!"

Chapter 12

THE STEADY GROWL OF THE POWERFUL ENGINE, an aural background against the sound of the night air cascading over the top of the windshield, precluded the option of conversation at a normal level between Kelsey and Judtson as he steered the 4-4-2 through the I-10/I-8 junction. As was typical, the westbound San Diego freeway was dark and deserted, a stark contrast to the endless stream of cars and trucks which seemed to perpetually clog the Phoenix-Tucson corridor twenty-four hours a day, seven days a week.

They had decided to lower the top on the classic car and enjoy the night drive across the desert, leaving Romeo and Ricky behind to accept their trophy and change clothes. Kelsey, her head pressed against the top of the bucket seat, was staring straight up, taking in the brilliantly clear display of stars overhead. Romeo had contacted Kenny Bowman, who was going to meet them at Chris Ashby's abandoned car.

The ambient noise drowned out the tones from Kent's phone, still in his shirt pocket, but he felt the vibration against his chest. Holding the steering wheel with one hand, he pulled out the phone, held it up, and tapped the screen. Kelsey twisted sideways to see who was calling.

"It's a text message from Kristen. I guess she wasn't able to find anything suitable at Nordstrom, so she's going to stay in Phoenix tonight and go to Barneys and Neicus tomorrow."

The moon above them was almost full and Judtson could see the amusement play across his companion's face as she burst out, "Barneys! You're kidding! What's she going to buy there...a five-thousand-dollar blouse? I have more money than you do and *I* don't shop at Barneys! And how can anybody not find something *suitable* at Nordstrom?"

He laughed at her comments.

"And what's Neicus? I've never heard of it."

Judtson smirked. "That's what she calls Neiman Marcus."

Kelsey flopped back against the seat rest. "Ohhhh, isn't that cute!" she replied, her voice derisive.

He suddenly felt an uncomfortable twinge. Participating with Kelsey in the act of ridiculing his wife struck him as unseemly, as if he should defend her instead of laughing at her expense. On the other hand, the absurdity of this feeling was not lost on him, considering his actions earlier this evening. Storing away the unsettling sensation, he lapsed into silence. After another mile of highway passed beneath them, Kelsey, either sensing his thoughts or coming to the conclusion on her own, added, "Sorry. That was rude."

He glanced to his right, expecting her to be facing him, but she had returned her gaze skyward; her expression, bathed a ghostly white by the moon, was neutral. Taking advantage of the emptiness of the highway, he pushed the Olds up over ninety, the roar of the slipstream all around them intensifying, and they rode without speaking.

Within thirty minutes, the handful of exits for Gila Bend flashed past. Judtson broke the silence. "Should be about there."

Kelsey, now sitting erect, stared out the front windshield. Three more miles elapsed quickly. As they crested an overpass, she shouted, "Look!"

He had seen it at the same moment. On the right shoulder, two hundred yards ahead, was a Department of Public Safety patrol car, its intense red and blue lights flashing. Judtson decelerated as they approached, and spotted a black SUV also parked on the shoulder and in front of the patrol vehicle. In line ahead of the SUV was a cream-colored Lexus.

Braking, he slowly cruised by the three vehicles and pulled out of the drive lane onto the slightly sloped asphalt shoulder, veering still farther until his right tires crunched on gravel.

His ears ringing from the steady roar of wind on the drive, he leaned closer to Kelsey. "I hope that black SUV belongs to Romeo's friend."

She unbuckled her belt and twisted around, kneeling on the seat and facing rearward. "Yeah. No kidding. Should be."

In the mirror, Judtson could see a man, who was wearing a black windbreaker with "FBI" boldly stenciled on the back, standing alongside the Lexus and talking to the uniformed officer. "Do you know what Bowman looks like?"

"No. Keep the engine running, and I'll call Romeo."

As she tapped her phone, the agent turned away from the cop and began walking their way. "Here he comes. You'd better hurry."

"I am…oh, Romeo. Hi. We're here. Just wanted to make sure of one thing. What does your friend look like?" She attentively listened, readily said, "Okay," and disconnected.

The man was approximately halfway to them. "What did he say?" Judtson asked.

"All he said was…*watch*."

In the midst of her sentence, the agent stopped and unclipped his cell phone from his belt, putting it to his ear. Although the two of them could not hear what he said over the throaty rumble of the engine, they were able to make out that he promptly laughed, glanced toward them and waved, then replaced his phone on his belt, showing no indication that he intended to resume walking. Seconds later, Kelsey's phone rang. She tapped speaker mode.

"Romeo, is that him?"

"You mean, *is that he?*" Judtson mumbled.

Kelsey glared at her car mate and sent a rude hand gesture his way as Romeo answered, "Yes. He waved at you. Now he's standing about fifty feet back, waiting, right?"

"Yep."

"Okay. You're good. We'll be there in a few minutes. By the way, how fast did you drive?" She blithely ignored his question. "We made pretty good time. See you soon."

Judtson switched off the engine, and they climbed out to head toward the man. Seeing this, Bowman met them partway. After the introductions were complete, Kelsey asked, "You knew Romeo in the Army?"

"Yes. We were in the Rangers together. Met in the Sandbox."

"Sandbox?"

"Iraq," Kent explained before the agent could respond.

"That's right. So, Romeo told me about this Dr. Ashby disappearing. I guess he was part of your little group who brought down Beckleman." As he said this, Bowman turned and began walking back toward the Lexus, followed by Judtson and Kelsey. The DPS officer passed them, striding purposefully in the opposite direction, his flashlight methodically sweeping back and forth across the two-lane highway.

Judtson confirmed, "Yes. He was one of the people Beckleman had mind-zapped. We were able to bring him back."

When Bowman arrived at the car, he turned to the two of them, his face serious. "It appears they've taken things to the next level."

"What do you mean?" Kelsey blurted. "Did you find something?"

The agent nodded grimly. "I have a full forensic team on the way, so there may be more – but yes. Here, take a look."

He pulled a high-intensity halogen flashlight from his back pocket and moved around to the passenger door, which was standing open. Shining the light inside, he pointed and said, "See the cup in the holder. It's melted now, but it was a milkshake. And it's almost full."

"What's the significance of the shake?" asked Kelsey, leaning into the car for a better view.

"The gas gauge is on empty. The tank is dry. If you ran out of gas five miles from a truck stop and had to walk back for help during the heat of the day...well over a hundred degrees outside...wouldn't you have taken your nice cold shake with you?"

She backed out of the compartment. "How do you know it happened in the heat of the day?"

"We checked credit card purchases. Ashby had stopped at the last truck stop in Gila Bend, just four or five miles back. Gassed up and got the shake. According to the credit card transaction, that was shortly after two."

"Wait a sec. You said he gassed up. How could he run out of gas in five miles?"

"Right," Bowman grunted. "He didn't. Somebody wanted us to think he did." The man turned and walked toward the rear of the Lexus. "Come on. Let me show you this."

As they followed, the DPS officer, trotting, caught up to them. "Special Agent Bowman. Got something."

The FBI agent paused. "What's that?"

"A little farther ahead, there are fresh tire tracks from an eighteen-wheeler. Some of them are perpendicular to the direction of travel. Tough to say, but it looks like a big rig was stopped across both lanes. Even the shoulders."

Bowman's eyes drifted in the direction the officer indicated. "So they blocked him and boxed him."

"Would you mind explaining?" Judtson asked.

"Pretty simple ambush, really. Ashby comes over the hump and sees that there's an eighteen-wheeler sideways across the road. He slams on his brakes. They probably have a chase vehicle coming up behind him. Trapping him."

Listening to the description of the scenario, Kelsey shivered despite the warm night, visualizing Chris Ashby during the moments he realized what was happening. "They could do it all in broad daylight? I know this highway doesn't get a lot of traffic, but wouldn't they have to worry about *someone* coming along?"

The agent shrugged. "The whole operation takes two, maybe three minutes. They have a third vehicle bring up the rear. That one stops on the crown of the overpass, halting any others who come along. They probably neutralize Ashby quickly, in less than a minute, and then move his car off the road to right here. Once that's done, they can pull the big rig out of the way and let everyone go by. The chase vehicle is parked on the shoulder behind the Lexus at that point. Anyone passing, even a cop, is going to assume it's just somebody with car trouble and someone else has already stopped to help."

He turned to the uniformed officer. "All your units are GPS'd and time-logged, correct?" The man nodded.

"Could you check with dispatch and tell them I need to know if any of your patrol vehicles passed this spot within, let's say, an hour after the time stamp on the truck stop purchase."

"On it," the patrolman answered tersely and jogged to his car.

To his retreating back, the agent shouted, "And let's go ahead and close the highway. It's now a crime scene."

"What good will it do to find out if DPS cars went by?"

Bowman advised Judtson, "Their vehicles are all outfitted with dashboard cameras. If one of them did happen to pass as the grab was going down, we might be able to pull a plate."

"That may or may not do you any good. During our last go-around with these thugs, all of the plates traced back to Homeland Security. But HS denied the existence of the vehicles in their fleet."

"Things are a bit different now. I'm the one handling the investigation of the local HS offices. Thanks to you two, there's a whole new group of folks running things locally and nationally."

Kent stared at the agent. "You think you can trust them?"

Before he could reply, Romeo's black Hummer skirted slowly around the patrol car, which was easing out across the two lanes, preparing to block the highway. Jones cautiously brought his vehicle to a stop beside the group.

With an abrupt shake of his head, Bowman, who had appeared lost in his own thoughts during the arrival of the Hummer, finally spoke. "To answer your question about trusting them, Mr. Kent, all I can really say is that I think we're about to find out."

Romeo, back in his usual garb of a pea-green T-shirt and camouflage pants, and Ricky, also wearing camo pants topped by a black polo shirt, joined them at the roadside. Bowman briefed his friend on what he had found. Romeo took it all in impassively, his eyes scouring the surrounding desert as he listened. Ricky stood silently, worry crossing his face.

When the agent finished, Judtson reminded him, "A minute ago you said you wanted to show us something."

"Right. This way." He moved to the rear of the Lexus and shined his flashlight down at the graveled area adjacent to the shoulder. Reaching down, he scooped up a small handful of the pebbles and held them under Judtson's nose.

The powerful, pungent aroma caused Kent to jerk back his head and rasp, "Gasoline?"

"Yep. I'd say this is where the tank was drained. It's mostly soaked in now."

Kelsey, who had not said anything for the past minutes, whispered quietly to Judtson, "Poor Chris."

Hearing her muted comment, Romeo, his voice deep and determined, promised, "We'll find him."

With an all-business look on his face, he turned back to the agent. "You said on the phone that you had something to tell me about Luis."

Bowman looked toward the east and watched the DPS officer as he lit and placed multiple flares on the highway. "Yeah. I brought in a hotshot polygraph expert. One of the best. He still wants to review the results with some kind of software, but right now, he's pretty sure that Tovar is telling the truth."

▽

Judtson and Kelsey had stayed on the scene until the FBI's forensic team arrived. Feeling as if they were in the way, they climbed back into the Oldsmobile and, with Romeo and Ricky tailing behind, drove back to Tucson. During the first part of the ninety-minute drive, they rehashed the details of Chris Ashby's disappearance, coming to no new conclusions. Exhausting the topic, they fell into silence for the balance of the trip. Judtson noticed that Kelsey was no longer stargazing, but rather was stoically staring straight ahead, not speaking until he pulled his car into the dark driveway of his office. Romeo, now on alert, parked across the street, leaving the engine idling.

Remaining inside the car, Kelsey joked, "Now I know how the President must feel, having the Secret Service around all the time."

"Can't blame Romeo, given Ashby's kidnapping. And don't forget the van you saw outside the office."

The two showed no signs of moving, both staying in their seats, both staring out through the front windshield, neither saying another word. Except for the periods of time his mind had been occupied with the unfolding events, Judtson had grappled all evening with a nagging, unpleasant torment, initiated by the text message from Kristen and the brief exchange afterward.

Awash in his own thoughts, he felt torn between his undeniably powerful feelings for Kelsey and an unshakable disgust for himself. Their earlier spontaneous interlude, which he preferred to think was not premeditated, was not at all consistent with the image he had always held of himself. The pleasure and joy of those moments were blackened by his overriding sense of betrayal of Kristen, a betrayal to his commitment, his word.

Reaching a painful decision, he turned to his right, intending to share his thoughts. Seeing his sudden stirring, Kelsey quickly spun to face him and gently laid her hand on the side of his face. Her voice was fragile...vulnerable. "Judtson, what happened before...was wonderful. It was amazing. And I don't regret any of it. Not for a single second. But...but we shouldn't have. It shouldn't have happened. I know that. I guess I knew it at the time, and I just allowed myself not to care."

Staring at her, wanting to ease the anguish plainly etched on her features, he sucked in a breath to speak.

"Let me finish. Please. This isn't...isn't very damn easy."

He nodded wordlessly.

"I...I *know* you. I think I know who you are...how you think...what you expect from yourself. It's one of the things I...like about you."

As she continued, the tenor of her voice strengthened from a tender frailness to an intense earnestness. "And you need to see this thing through with Kristen. You do. And the last thing *you* need…is for me to make it worse. To make it harder for you."

She hesitated, bolstering her resolve. "I'm sorry I did. Believe me when I tell you…I didn't mean to. So…." Kelsey paused again, and he was certain he caught a glimmer of a tear in her eye before she pulled in a deep breath and whispered, "So…good night, Judtson."

With that, she leaned closer and kissed his cheek fleetingly. He was not able to manage even a word as Kelsey opened the door and hastily jumped out, hurrying down the driveway to her car. Opening his own door, he got out and stood in silence, watching as she started the engine and put the transmission in gear. For an instant he thought she was going to turn the engine off and come back to him, as she gazed through the windshield at his face, hers illuminated with a preternatural green hue from the dashboard. The moment ended and she drove slowly away, with Romeo following.

As Judtson stared at the receding taillights, he murmured aloud, "Good night, Kelsey."

▽

During the drive home, Judtson's body felt leaden. After traveling only a few blocks from his office, he parked briefly in the lot of a business closed for the night, and raised the convertible top, latching it.

Pulling up his driveway, he glanced next door, at Saylor and Doni's home. Their lights were already off, and he remembered his offer to speak with them about the accusation from Luis, dreading the prospect.

With an emotive sigh, he punched the button on the new garage door opener, the replacement for the plastic device broken by Kelsey during a playful episode in the past, and pulled the Olds into the wide garage, lowering the door as soon as the rear bumper was clear of its path. His home, dark and silent, felt more empty than it had ever felt to him before, with the welcome exception of Rocky, who, as always, eagerly greeted his arrival.

Not bothering to turn on any lights, Judtson navigated from memory, crossing the entire length to the library and lowering himself into the leather chair in front of the computer. Toeing the switch on the surge protector and pressing the power button on the face of the computer, he slumped back into the cushion and watched until the boot-up was finished. He then opened the word processor and, in the glow of the monitor, at first slowly, and soon with increasing speed, typed.

▽

At Romeo's insistence, Kelsey followed him to the hotel parking lot where Ricky's car waited. After dropping him off, the two drove to her house. She parked under the porte cochere, with Romeo coming to a stop behind her, and was out of the car and circling around it toward the front door when he caught up with her.

"Hey! Boss!"

She paused and turned, not saying a word. He noticed that her expression was distant, withdrawn; the dark makeup around her eyes, smudged and streaked.

"You okay?"

Rather than making eye contact, she looked down and shrugged, her response barely audible. "Yeah. I guess."

His natural protective tendency was intensified by her obvious vulnerability. "Want to talk about it?"

With her eyes remaining downcast, she shook her head. "No. Not really."

He could not read her well enough to decide whether she was hoping he would push the issue or drop it. Stymied by his own uncertainty, he muttered, "All right. Well, if you do...."

Pulling out her keys, she opened the door and, without turning back, murmured, "Thanks," and hurried inside, leaving him standing in the darkness.

$$\nabla$$

Judtson did not awaken until mid-morning, the result of a fitful night's sleep. Clumsily going through the steps of making coffee, he filled a large mug, doctored it, and left the house, crossing the wide desert area to Saylor's. Although it was Sunday, he paused at their door, not knowing if either or both of them would be home this late in the morning.

As he lifted his hand and arm with the intent of pressing the doorbell, he hesitated again, his mind filling with the vivid memories of the recent past when he had not been able to effectuate even this simple and basic motion to call an elevator. The residual terror from the incident triggering an involuntary shudder, he forced his mind away from the images, the thoughts immediately replaced with the unpleasantness of what he had come here to do.

"Screw it," he barked loudly and jammed his finger against the button. Within half a minute, the door swung open. It was Doni, still wearing a pastel pink summer robe, her long hair pulled back in a ponytail.

"Judtson! Good morning." Her voice was effusive. Clearly she was happy to see him. This only served to deepen his misgivings about his mission as she stepped aside, allowing him in.

"Hi, Doni." Holding the mug of coffee off to the side, he stopped on the threshold and gave her a one-armed hug. She reciprocated warmly, adding a light kiss on his cheek.

"Saylor's in the kitchen," she said, closing the door behind him and turning to lead the way. "Want breakfast?"

"No thanks, Doni. Not hungry this morning."

He followed her to the kitchen where Saylor was sitting at the bar, finishing the last couple of bites from a stack of pancakes. Talking around the mouthful, he greeted his next-door neighbor. "Hey, pal! How are you?"

His voice flatter than he had planned, Judtson simply said, "Fine," and set his mug on the bar near one of the empty stools, sliding onto the seat and facing his almost lifelong friend.

Saylor swallowed the bite. "That didn't sound fine. Anything wrong?"

Doni had taken the stool at her own now empty plate. "Just morning grumpiness?"

Having decided earlier to work his way up to the point of the visit, he answered both of their questions at once. "I'm worried about Chris."

Saylor's brow furrowed slightly. "Something new? Did you hear more about it?"

"Well, yes. Nothing good," he explained, telling them that after talking to Saylor last night, he and Kelsey, as well as Romeo and Kenny Bowman from the FBI, made the drive out to Chris' car, and then detailing what they had found at the scene. He saw, as his narrative spun out, a gradual transformation in the features of his best friend, who cast frequent glances at Doni. By the conclusion, Saylor looked anything but happy, or even neutral.

Seeing this, Judtson added, "Frankly, Saylor, at this point nobody has any idea what it all means. I know the last thing you want is for the drama and intrigue to start up again."

"Neither of us does!" Doni clarified emphatically, her countenance serious.

"Yeah, once was enough, pal," Saylor stated glumly.

"As I said, I know that. And I don't see a reason the two of you would have to get involved, no matter what happened to Chris. The FBI is handling it and…I met the lead agent last night…I think those guys are on the right side this time around."

Saylor's voice was firm. "Either way, we're not going to. Period. Let them do their jobs."

"I agree. I only wanted to let you know about it, since Starlight called you and everything."

"Okay, I guess. But leave us out of it."

"I get it. I will. Honest."

After the exchange, the two friends stared silently at each other for a full minute, when Doni spoke up, changing the subject. "So you were with Kelsey last night, huh?"

Judtson broke eye contact with Saylor and looked at her. "You heard?"

"Of course. Saylor-man told me." A slight smile appeared on her face. "How did *that* happen? I thought you and Kristen were…?"

"We were. I mean, we are. Kelsey called to tell me about a couple of things, including Chris' disappearance. We met for dinner to talk about it."

The smile widened. "Where was Kristen?"

Finding himself irritated by her tone and the implications of her questions, he replied succinctly, "Phoenix. Shopping. She stayed up there last night and will be coming back today."

"Oh, so you were free all…?"

Before Doni could complete her question, Saylor, picking up on Judtson's annoyance, interrupted, "You said she had more than one thing to discuss."

Glad to have Doni sidetracked, yet still tense as he saw himself delivered to the subject he had been dreading, Judtson only nodded, buying a few more seconds prior to plunging in. As he began, he carefully watched Doni. "Luis turned himself in to the FBI."

In his peripheral vision, he saw that Saylor's reaction was instantaneous and visceral.

"HE DID?"

And although Judtson expected, or perhaps hoped for, a similar reaction from Doni, what he witnessed was vaguely unnerving. Her eyes narrowed a fraction. Her brows knitted. Her pupils contracted. The manifestations were ephemeral, passing so quickly that he doubted he had, in fact, witnessed them, before a sincere expression of surprise and astonishment flooded across her face.

"You're kidding!" she exclaimed, her voice an octave higher.

Saylor was almost sputtering. "What has the bastard said? Has he confessed?"

Sitting more erect on the stool, Judtson drew a long breath. "That's just it. Not exactly."

"What are you saying?" Saylor demanded, agitated. "We have him dead to rights. I know I said I wanted to stay out of this, but after what he did to Doni and the others, if I can get my hands on that rotten scum, I'll…."

Judtson held up a hand. "I know. Believe me. He's not actually saying he didn't do it. Only that he was controlled…forced to let them in against his own will."

As he delivered this piece of information, he was again watching Doni. Either she had now achieved full control of her emotions, or the first transitory glimpses had been an illusion or misinterpreted, considering that she now displayed sincere outrage, disbelief, and anger. "That's crazy!" she exclaimed.

"Of course it is," Saylor unequivocally agreed with his wife. "How in the hell could *that* happen? They didn't have access to him down in the silo. You're not buying this load of crap, are you, Judtson?"

Shifting his eyes back and forth between the two people he had known the longest, wondering at that moment how he would react if one of them were to accuse him of a similar heinous act, he began tentatively, "Not really. Well, there are some aspects which are...."

"What?"

A sense of betrayal was a massive wave threatening to engulf him. Clenching his teeth and jerking his head spasmodically side to side, he spat out, "Listen...Saylor...Doni...I don't buy this. Not for a damn second. I wouldn't even be mentioning it except he has been given a polygraph test and passed it. With flying colors, so I understand. Luis *claims* that he was slipped Devil's Breath down there. That someone *made* him open the doors and let Beckleman's men in."

Judtson heard a muted gasp come from Doni. He saw Saylor abruptly look down. The silence hung over the three for several seconds before Saylor looked back up at him and, his voice deep and intense, asked "Who is he saying did this?"

The choice of the question struck Judtson as odd for some undefinable reason. He speculated that Saylor had jumped to a horrible conclusion based not only upon the fact that his trusted ally and confidant was here at their home this morning talking to the two of them about this, but also on the obvious fact that he appeared clearly uncomfortable doing so.

His eyes still connected with those of his best friend, Judtson, speaking softly, his tone flat and lifeless, uttered, "He said Doni gave him the drug in a glass of tea."

Saylor's eyes widened by double, his face visibly reddening, his fists clenching tightly.

Doni was the first to speak. "Squirrel...you don't believe him, do you?"

Shifting his focus to her, Judtson responded clumsily, "Doni, I...no...as I said, I don't believe a word of it."

She smiled at him, her eyes unblinking. "Thank God."

"I'm...I'm only bringing it up because...well, because he passed the polygraph and Kelsey thinks that maybe there's some other explanation."

"Like what, Squirrel?" Her voice was gentle, curious.

He found himself struggling to overcome his discomfort at confronting her, and formulate what he had wanted to say. "She...she thought that...maybe...you did bring him the glass of tea." Speaking more rapidly, he explained, "I mean, that's all he remembers. Sitting at his station and getting the tea from you. At least, that's his story. Kelsey thinks maybe someone knew you were going to take it to him and slipped the Devil's Breath in the tea while you weren't watching."

She shifted her eyes away from him and stared up at the ceiling for a few seconds, apparently replaying the scene from the silo in her mind. Catching his gaze again, she said, "I don't...oh, wait...maybe. I was in the break room with some of the others. Ricky was there. He was on the couch, reading. Lisa, Dylan, Dean, and...Al, the poor man...were playing bridge. I was getting ready to go work out with Jimmy. I thought it would be a good idea to take something to Luis. He was stuck at his station and you guys were all gone, including Romeo. So there wasn't anyone to relieve him.

"And I *might* have mentioned it. Wait! Yes! I did. Because I asked the others if anyone had taken anything to Luis recently. They all told me *no*. I got out a glass. Filled it with ice. I poured it. The tea. And then…and then I *did* leave it on the counter for a minute…because I remembered I needed my workout towel." She laughed softly. "Squirrel, you know how I like to wipe off gym equipment other people use."

He acknowledged her statement with a slight tilt of his head, and she continued, "So… yes…I left the tea there and ran back to our room, grabbed my towel, and came back. Then I…then I took the tea to Luis."

"How long did you stay with Luis?"

"A minute or so. I asked him if he needed to go to the restroom and offered to watch the station for him. He said he was fine. I know I didn't hang around long since I was already late meeting Jimmy and he's such a grouch about people being tardy."

"Doni, was anyone else in the vicinity? Or did you see anyone heading his way when you left him?"

She shook her head. "No. No one. The hallway was empty."

"And Ricky, Lisa, Al, Dean, and Dylan were the only people in the lounge?"

"Uh-huh."

Judtson stole a quick peek at Saylor, who had swiveled on his stool and was watching Doni as she spoke. Again swinging his gaze between the two of them, he said, "Look, Doni, Saylor, I'm sorry I had to be the one to ask about this. Just because I'm the one asking doesn't mean I believe any of it."

Saylor turned back to face him but had still not uttered a word. Doni hurried to respond. "Don't sweat it, Squirrel. I'm sure Kelsey picked you to ask us about it because we're so close."

Allowing himself a brief smile, he added, "Yeah, I think she was fairly certain you'd throw them both out if she and Romeo had come to talk about it."

Then, he shook his head and placed his hand on Saylor's shoulder. "Hey, are we okay?"

Saylor nodded curtly, making a visible effort to relax. Releasing a loud exhale, he finally mumbled, "Yeah, we're fine. Just somewhat of a shock."

Sliding off the stool, Judtson faced them, consciously lightening his tone. "Now that I've ruined both of your mornings, my work here is done. I'd better get going."

Doni and Saylor both stood and followed him to the door as she reassured him, "You didn't. Honestly. I'm glad Luis has popped up. Maybe now we can find out what really happened."

"That'd be good," Judtson agreed, reaching the front door and opening it.

They said their goodbyes and Saylor closed the door, twisting the deadbolt lock. Doni was already walking back to the kitchen when her husband's voice stopped her in mid-step. "Doni."

She turned. "Yes, Saylor, honey?"

His face conveyed turmoil, in constant, subtle motion as a cascade of conflicting emotions assaulted him. With an unsteadiness in his voice, he asked, "Doni, before I left for La Paz with Judtson and the others, why did you ask me about dosages of Devil's Breath?"

Chapter 13

S AYLOR, ROOTED TO THE SPOT INSIDE THE FRONT DOOR, STUDIED HIS WIFE'S FACE, feeling guilty at the same time for doing so. Doni, having stopped ten feet away on her path back to the kitchen, faced him. He noticed that she was absentmindedly, repetitively clutching and releasing the front of her robe, bunching the fabric within her fists.

"The dos...the dosages? Saylor, honey, what are you...?"

As she stammered, he could not help but see that her eyes were rapidly darting around the perimeter of his face, rather than connecting with his direct gaze.

"Donatella, when I was down in the silo packing to leave, you specifically asked me how much of the Devil's Breath we had put in the tea Luis tried to give to the hostage. Are you saying you don't remem...?"

"Oh! Yes! That's right. I did." A nervous laugh burst from her. "I was just wondering at the time.... I was curious what would happen if we increased the dosage. Whether we might get some actual, you know, helpful information out of him."

She stopped talking and quickly covered the ten feet between them, her hands coming up and gripping his upper arms right below his shoulders. "Saylor, honey, you don't think...? You don't really think I let in those horrible men, do you?"

She studied her husband's face, her eyes hastily flitting from one part to another, in an attempt to read his thoughts. Saylor had not yet responded to her question.

Her eyes widened. "My God! You *do*, don't you?"

"Doni...." Saylor's voice was soft, neutral.

Her stare finally settled down and locked upon his eyes. Her face instantly grew stony. Her jaw muscles tightened and knotted. "You...*you bastard!* You think I'm some kind of a... TRAITOR!"

She had screamed the final word and released her grip on his arms. Whirling around, she ran to their bedroom.

Saylor trailed after her, his emotions roiling. Plaintively, he called out, "Doni!"

As he reached the bedroom, the door slammed in his face, and a second later he heard the click of the lock.

"DONI! PLEASE OPEN THE DOOR!"

The intensity muffled by the door, she shouted, "Go to hell!"

He heard sounds coming from inside the room, the sounds of slamming doors and crashing drawers. He knocked loudly and continued beseeching her to open the door, briefly entertaining the image of breaking it down but dismissing the thought as soon as it came. She gave no further verbal reactions to his pleas.

Another two minutes passed and there was an eerie cessation of the banging and clattering from within. Hoping she had calmed down enough to talk to him, he raised his hand to knock again, when the door abruptly flew open and he saw her picking up a stuffed suitcase and an overnight bag. She had dressed in a baggy T-shirt and jeans, and her eye makeup was badly streaked.

Looking at the floor rather than at Saylor, her voice barely audible, she grunted, "Get out of my way," and took a step toward the doorway. He stood his ground, blocking her.

"Doni, please. I'm not accusing you of anything. I just want to...."

She glanced up at him, her eyes blazing with fury. "*I said, get out of my way!*"

She swung the large suitcase forward and Saylor managed to step aside before it could slam into his leg. Following the suitcase, Doni rushed through the doorway and crossed the house at a near run, with him a few paces behind.

"Doni, come on! Please stop."

She dropped the overnight bag on the floor as she arrived at the door to the garage, twisted the handle, scooped up the bag, and went through without bothering to turn on the light. As she opened the back door of her car and tossed the two bags in, Saylor once again came close. "Doni, don't leave! Please don't leave!"

Wordlessly, she slammed the back door and, using her hip, bumped Saylor aside far enough to open the driver's door. She pressed the button on the visor and the metal garage door rumbled upward, flooding the room with sunlight. Climbing in, she started the engine.

Saylor had never seen his wife like this and had no idea how to respond...how to get through to her. He reached for the top edge of the door and she jerked it closed. He was barely able to get his fingers out of the way in time.

Without a glance at him, she put the car in reverse and punched the gas, almost rocketing out of the narrow space and leaving Saylor standing forlornly, watching her depart.

$$\triangledown$$

Judtson parked in the driveway in front of his office. Ricky's yellow Smart car was not present, as was normal on a Sunday. He took a minute to survey his surroundings, looking for the dry cleaning van or anything else suspicious. Satisfied, he unlocked the door and entered, passing through Ricky's area and going straight to his own office.

His mind was still dissecting and analyzing the morning conversation with Doni and Saylor. What she had said made perfect sense. All of it fit with the known facts, even her lateness in meeting Jimmy Meade, which Judtson had specifically made a point of not mentioning.

He was drawn in two opposing directions. His first inclination was that he had known Doni for close to three decades, since she was a small girl, and the idea that she could have double-crossed him or the rest of the group was unthinkable. The pull from the other side, he concluded, was fueled by the same hyper-paranoia he had been so deeply submerged within until only recently, clearly an overly active paranoia which was causing him to see odd reactions and inflections where none existed.

No, he thought to himself, *there's nothing to it. It couldn't have been Doni.*

He picked up the desk phone and then hurriedly replaced the handset on the cradle, worried that *they* had placed a tap on his lines, and simultaneously chuckling aloud at this additional symptom of paranoia. Reaching into his pocket and grabbing the safe cell phone, which he had continued to use since their return from La Paz, he tapped Kelsey's number.

She answered almost immediately, sounding slightly tentative and breathless. "Judtson?"

Hearing the nuance of expectation in her voice, he felt his stomach involuntarily tingle with the unmistakable feeling of butterflies. Stifling his own initial response, he decided it was best to get straight to the point of the call. "Hi, Kelsey." His voice not as steady as he had intended, he plunged forward. "I talked to Doni this morning. Doni and Saylor, actually."

There was only a momentary pause before she reacted with a slight hint of disappointment. "You did? What did she say?"

Judtson described the conversation, deliberately omitting any reference to his personal interpretations. When he finished, she observed, "Saylor's reaction wasn't what I expected."

"Same here. I thought he would throw me out. Instead, he just...I don't know...withdrew."

"Do you believe her?"

Ignoring the small but insistent voice in his mind, he replied quickly, "I do."

"Well, I trust you completely. If *you* think she's being straight up, that works for me."

As Kelsey said this, he had to fight back the urge to qualify his previous endorsement of Doni.

Now all-business, she continued, "So...I really don't think it would have been Al. That leaves Dean, Lisa, Dylan and, I guess, Ricky."

"I don't think Ricky...."

"No, I don't either. But it's a good thing he was in the lounge. That makes him the next obvious person to ask."

"True. Maybe he saw if anyone...I mean, maybe he saw who went anywhere near the tea when Doni left it on the counter."

Kelsey caught the revealing stammer. "Judtson, are you sure you don't have *any* doubts about Doni?"

The directness of her question caught him off guard. He did not want to arrantly lie to her. On the other hand, he realized that he already had. His answer delayed by his quandary longer than he thought, she was prompted to say, "Judtson? Are you still there?"

"Uh, yeah. I'm here. No. No, I don't have any doubts."

"Oh...okay then. Are you going to talk to Ricky today?"

"Yes. I am."

"You'll let me know what he says?"

"Of course I will."

A short silence between them was broken as Kelsey said goodbye.

▽

Sliding the phone into her back packet, Kelsey hopped up from her desk and wandered her home, searching for Romeo and finding him in the kitchen where he was eating a sandwich and watching the array of security camera views on the large flat-screen built into the wall.

"Just talked to Judtson. He saw Doni and Saylor."

He put down the sandwich. "That was fast."

"It was. I think he wanted to get it over with. Anyway, she told him that Lisa, Dylan, Al, Dean, and Ricky were in the lounge when she made the tea. According to her, she asked them if anyone had taken Luis anything and they all told her they hadn't. So they *did* know what she was going to do. She poured the tea and left it on the counter while she went back to her room to get a gym towel. Then came back and took the tea to Luis…asked him if he wanted a bathroom break and he said he didn't. Hurried to the gym to meet Jimmy because she was already late and she knew how much he hated that."

Romeo's face was impassive. "That seems to cover all the bases. Had Judtson mentioned the twelve minutes Jimmy had remembered?"

"No. He said he hadn't."

"One thing doesn't fit."

"What's that?"

"Well, Jimmy is military. Doni knew he'd be ticked off that she was late. The best excuse in the whole world for a guy like Jimmy is that she stopped to drop off something to drink and offer a break to the man standing watch."

"Yeah?"

Romeo looked at her quizzically. "So, why did she tell him that his watch must be off, instead of telling the truth?"

Kelsey considered his words, searching for an explanation. "It's odd. Unless she didn't want anyone to know…no, that doesn't cut it. The people in the lounge knew she was taking the tea. I don't know. You're right. It doesn't make sense."

"So, is he buying her version?"

Thinking, she shifted her weight from one foot to the other and then back before she answered his question. "I'm not sure. I asked him. Point-blank. And he said that he did. But…I have a feeling he might not."

▽

Detective Ben Hart was sitting uncomfortably at his desk, the incessant pain in his hip throbbing, and he was beginning to regret his decision to come to the office today to catch up on his paperwork. Realizing he was half an hour past due for another dose of pain medication, he dug the small pill container from his pocket, snapped it open, and popped one of the capsules into his mouth. Reaching urgently for his mug of coffee and finding it empty, he swore under his breath and grabbed his cane, standing stiffly and moving across the bullpen toward the water cooler, trying to hurry before the outer shell on the capsule dissolved in his mouth.

He had taken no more than three hobbling steps, when the direct line on his phone rang. Momentarily gripped by indecision, his head swiveling back and forth between the trilling phone and the water cooler, he gulped hard to dry-swallow the capsule and turned back, snatching up the receiver.

"Detective Hart."

The voice on the line was a female with an accent Ben recognized as originating from the southeast. "Detective Ben Hart? This is Detective Eunice Cahane with the Atlanta PD."

Struggling to produce enough saliva for another swallow in an attempt to dislodge the capsule now adhered to the wall of his throat, Ben, his voice resembling a croak, managed to say, "Detective, if you would hold for a second. I need some water."

Cahane laughed. "Sounds like you need it pretty bad. Get to it. I'll wait."

Gratefully, Hart dropped the handset with a clatter and finished his trek to the cooler, filling his mug to the top with water and guzzling it all. He had to refill the mug and drain it again before the stubborn pill released its grip and moved through. Finally relieved, he returned to his desk and sat down, picking up the phone.

"Sorry about that, Detective Cahane, was it? I had just taken a pill and it was stuck in my throat."

Sounds of amusement still coming from her end of the connection, she assured him, "That's fine. And it's Eunice. I really didn't expect to catch you today, Detective Hart. Being Sunday and all. I was fixin' to leave a message."

"Please call me Ben. And I came in to catch up on a couple of case files this morning. What can I do for you?"

"I hear you know of two folks I've recently crossed paths with...Lisa Trippiano and Dylan Falt. It was Miss Trippiano who suggested I call you."

"They were two victims of a kidnap case I was working. How did they pop up in your jurisdiction?"

"Well...we had a death here in Atlanta. Mr. Falt was an acquaintance of the deceased, Rosemary Shields with the CDC." Cahane proceeded to tell him the entire story, including the FBI's intervention and their conclusion that it was a suicide.

"It appears you don't think it was, Eunice."

He listened to a brief silence until she answered, "The more I mull over the physical evidence, not to mention the details Mr. Falt added, the only conclusion I can come to is *that dog won't hunt*. What do you think?"

Ben, tickled by her colorful colloquialism, leaned back and twisted in his chair in an effort to take some of the weight off his hip. "Based upon what you've told me, I would tend to agree. But you didn't call me to get my take on your case. It sounds as though you have a good handle on it already."

"No, I didn't. Although I will say that another pair of ears always helps. The reason Miss Trippiano suggested I call you was to get your thoughts on our federal buddies. Since they booted you off your case and all. Don't get me wrong. This isn't the first time they've come in on me with those big clodhopper feet and stomped on my turf. I'm a big girl...a few might say too big...and I can handle it. But what Miss Trippiano said was that they might actually be watching *me*, tapping *my* phone and such. Hell, she even had some techie guy in your neck of the woods overnight me a cell phone that I'm supposed to use when I talk about this case."

As Ben listened to Cahane, he came to the conclusion that he would very much enjoy having her as a partner. "I understand. It can be a bit of an adjustment mentally."

He heard a long, heavy sigh come from the woman. "I guess what I'm asking you is...are *they* good old hound dogs or do ya think they've gotten a touch of rabies?"

This caused him to think back on the day Special Agent Davis Ulrigg took over his case and arrived at police headquarters with the clear intention of detaining Scott Gumble.

"Uh, Eunice? Are you talking to me right now on that new phone?"

There was another pause, followed by a muted expletive from Cahane. "Ben, your question doesn't just speak volumes to me, it speaks a whole damn library. Yes, I am using *that* phone."

▽

Judtson fully intended to call Ricky and ask his assistant if he would mind coming to the office. Instead, he immediately found himself speed-dialing Lisa, who picked up on the second ring.

"Judtson! Hi!"

"Hello, Lisa. How are you?"

She ignored his question and began talking rapid-fire. "Man, have I been wanting to talk to you. I am so glad you called. A lot of stuff is happening. I don't know how much of it you're aware of yet. Have you heard about Rosemary Shields?"

"Yes. I have. I spoke with Carlos and he told me about running into you and Dylan. Filled me in on what happened to her. He also told me about his findings pertaining to Baalbek and Puma Punku. And he relayed your conversation with Dean Copeland about his pictures. But I wanted to see if you've heard about Chris?"

"Chris? Ashby? What?"

"He's missing. We think he has been kidnapped."

"Oh, my God! When? How?"

Judtson told her about Ashby's visit to Saylor, the autism finding, and then the disappearance, describing in detail the middle-of-the-night meeting with Bowman alongside the highway and the evidence they had uncovered. When he finished, she was silent. After listening for her response, he asked uncertainly, "Lisa, are you still on the line?"

"Uh...yeah, I'm here. I'm just blown away by all of this."

"That makes two of us."

No longer speaking animatedly, she ventured, "So...so it's starting again, isn't it, Judtson?"

For a split second, he considered telling her about Alchemist's claim to be Kelsey's father but thought better of it, not certain Kelsey would want that shared at this point. "There is one other thing, Lisa. Luis has surfaced."

She nearly shrieked, "He has?"

"Uh-huh. Turned himself in." Judtson told her the entire story, including Luis' insistence that he had been drugged and forced to do what he did. He ended the narrative by revealing that Luis thought it was Doni who had given him the drug.

"Doni! That's ridiculous! I was with her in the FEMA camp. Why would she have herself kidnapped?"

"I don't know. Doesn't make any sense to me, either. Of course, some other possibilities do exist."

The two brainstormed for a few minutes on all of the possible scenarios which would exonerate Doni, when Lisa abruptly changed the subject. "Judtson, I've been thinking. The whole press coverage of what happened is obviously heading in the wrong direction. It's our own fault. They're simply parroting what you and Kelsey got Beckleman to confess. But now...with all the things that are popping up...I think we're going one hundred and eighty degrees off course from the truth."

"I agree. Print and broadcast have bought the Beckleman story hook, line, and sinker. And now they're repeating it endlessly. What are you thinking?"

"I was thinking about putting together a show, hosted by Jack Bailey. And...here's the kicker...we'd have *everybody* there. Our whole gang. Except Chris obviously. The coverage up to this point has been onesie-twosie stuff, as far as interviews with us. And not even all of us. Nobody has had the entire group on at one time. I think we'd draw a *huge* audience and it would be a chance to get the word out. The right word, not the current line of Beckleman crap."

Judtson thought about her proposal for a minute before responding. "My first instinct was to say *no*. The more I think about it though, the more it makes sense. Carlos could set the record straight on Puma Punku and Baalbek. Dylan could explain what really happened with Rosemary Shields and the CDC. Dean could outline the history of his photos. What about Bal?"

"I've been keeping in touch with him. But since his secure cell phone doesn't work where he is, I haven't mentioned anything about the spooky stuff coming down. He's camped near Puma Punku with Sam Jonassen now. He decided to finish up his original work and also to pursue Kevin Berry's project. By the way, last time I talked to Bal, he told me that Sam showed him something amazing."

"What was it?"

"He wouldn't say. He's going to check it out some and then let me know."

Further considering her proposal, Judtson came up with a likely stumbling block. "Lisa, remember...before it all blew up the first time, your bosses were against Dean and Al coming on Bailey's show with their information. How are they ever going to allow this?"

She snorted. "Not going to tell them. They've been salivating to have all of you guys come on. I've lost count of how many times they've pestered me to use my relationship with everyone to put it together. All of us, *even yours truly*, are hot stuff right now. Big ratings. And if we agree to bring *everybody* on stage, the network will promote the living hell out of it. They think we'll all talk about the party line...you know, the Beckleman load of bull. That's what I'll say we're going to talk about."

"Lisa, that might get us in the studio and in front of the cameras, but how do we know it would actually get aired? You'll recall what happened to my original show with Carlos."

"Already thought of that. There's only one way to make sure they can't kill it before we can put it on the air...we do it live."

▽

Kelsey was working at her computer when an internal message popped onto her screen. It was from Scott, wondering if she had a moment for him. She hopped up and trotted across her home to his work area.

"What's up, Scott?"

"Oh, hi. You asked me to do some digging around on Mrs. Costello."

"Yes?"

"I don't know why I didn't think of this earlier, but I checked the phone logs for the silo on the day of the kidnapping. You know that our cell phones didn't work down there...only the hard lines, and each of those phones had a different number."

"Uh-huh. They were all direct lines. What'd you find?"

If he had any reticence about giving his boss the news, Scott did not show it. "The phone in Mrs. Costello's room received a call an hour and eight minutes before the vault door was opened. The call lasted" – he paused and glanced at his monitor – "about four minutes."

"Could you tell who made the call?"

"Yep. It came from Florence, Arizona. From a number listed as belonging to Homeland Security."

Chapter 14

$\mathbf{B}$AL SINGH, SQUINTING IN THE DIM LIGHT OF THE LED LANTERN hanging from the top of his tent pole, was bent over a topographical map, studying the microgravimetry readings which had been overlaid on the contours. Shadows danced and jumped around the interior of his shelter as the lantern was in constant motion, agitated by a steady wind which buffeted the tent. Almost obscured by the incessant low-frequency rumble from the flapping and shuddering of the canvas sides, a faint female voice called to him from outside.

"Hello, Dr. Singh?"

He picked up three heavy stones from the floor and placed them on the papers, stood, and stepped to the flap, zipping it open and recognizing one of the grad students. "Good evening, Gretchen."

She was bundled in a thick parka, the cowl pulled snugly around her face, her arms wrapped tightly around her torso. Bal ruefully thought that the polite thing to do would be to invite her in from the cold and wind, yet knew that such a simple act of civility would invite unpleasant rumors among others on the team, not to mention the ever-present specter of harassment claims in the future.

A smile was visible from within the fur oval. "We've all gotten pretty sick of eating MREs, so Benny went into town this afternoon. He brought back some stuff and made tacos and burritos for everybody. Well, they're sort of like burritos. The tortillas here are really thick. But they're good. Did you want to join us for an actual meal?"

The thought of tearing open another meal in a bag prompted him to answer immediately. "That sounds fabulous. The main tent?"

She nodded and he told her he would be there shortly. It only took him two minutes to put away his work, don his own parka, and cross the camp. As he entered the community multipurpose tent, the aroma of the ground beef simmering on the stove triggered his salivary glands.

Most of the team members were already assembled, and the enclosed area was overflowing with the raucous laughter and shouted comments typical of the age group. Weaving a route between the numerous students, who were clumped into small groups and eating where they stood, he moved to the impromptu buffet, filled a plate, and unsuccessfully searched the faces for Jonassen. He caught the attention of one of the younger students, whose name he did not recall. "Where is Sam? I cannot imagine he would want to miss this."

The young man shrugged. "Out by the lake, I guess. Like he always is at night."

Bal realized that he had been so engrossed in the day-to-day operations of the field work since his arrival, he had not had an opportunity to spend much time with Sam. Remembering how excited his new friend had been about the video and photos, he felt guilty.

Wolfing down his food, he returned to the buffet and assembled two oversized burritos, wrapping the plate securely with aluminum foil. He slipped his hood back up, snugged the pull strings, snatched up a flashlight, and exited the tent after thanking Gretchen for the invitation.

The night was clear, and a bright moon shone midpoint in its arc across the sky. The wind felt as if it was easing up somewhat. Holding the plate in the crook of his arm to keep the food warm, he followed the path to Lake Titicaca. Reaching a high spot on the route, Bal extinguished the flashlight so that his eyes would adjust, then paused and looked around. It did not take long for him to spot Sam off to his left, perhaps one hundred yards away and perched upon a large boulder. He could not tell whether Jonassen had noticed his approach. He waved and was quickly rewarded with a return wave.

Within two minutes they were sitting together atop the boulder. Jonassen ate hungrily as both men stared forward over the lake toward a small natural island clearly visible in the moonlight. Waiting until the other man swallowed his latest bite, Singh turned to face him and asked, "Have you been out here every night?"

"Yep. Haven't missed one."

"I am sorry I have not followed up with you on the video. I have been so...."

"It's fine. Really. I know you've been swamped trying to get everything set up and everybody trained."

Bal sighed, the subtle sound lost in the wind. "I have...but that is no excuse. You sighted something truly amazing. It must be pursued."

Swinging his gaze away from the vista, Sam smiled. "It *is* being pursued."

"I do not understand. We have all been totally immersed in completing my work, as well as Kevin Berry's. I have not spent a minute with you attempting to understand or document what you witnessed."

"I'm sure it all ties together," he replied with a shrug.

The geologist stared blankly. "What do you mean?"

Jonassen took a final bite from the second burrito, swallowed, and had a swig of water from his canteen before answering. "I think that we are *all* onto something. At this point, I have no idea what it could be. I have a couple of harebrained theories. Nothing I want to share yet. But I am convinced that your tectonic model and the anomaly you discovered in this region of the Andes...Dr. Berry's inexplicable gravity fluctuations...and my sighting of the ship, or whatever it was...are all related. All explained by the same thing. So the more work we do to figure out your tectonics and Dr. Berry's gravity numbers, the closer we come to understanding what is truly going on."

Singh listened to the almost hypnotic cadence of the words and forced his mind to expand to accommodate them. It was daunting for him to integrate the concepts he understood, the science he had been well trained to visualize, with the idea that an extraterrestrial craft might be somehow connected to the orderly, bordering on mundane precepts of geology. The postdoc was silent, allowing his companion the time to process the input.

To help himself concentrate, Bal moved his gaze to the stars in the northeast sky. *I do not need to be a geologist for this. Maybe a cosmologist,* he thought as he picked out a particularly bright star and focused on it. *Good grief, I do not even know what constellation that star is in. It seems as if I should.*

Not for the first time in his life, Bal Singh felt inadequate. His father was a math genius; his mother, a renowned physicist who nearly won the Nobel; his older brother, an electrical engineer who made billions going public with his computer chip company. None of them had once said a word which could objectively be construed as either denigrating or dismissive toward him. None of them had ever compared themselves or one another to him. None had ever overtly competed with him. And that, he had decided long ago, was actually the root of the problem. None of the three felt him to be dynamic enough, competent enough, or sufficiently well-equipped intellectually *to* compete with.

The corner of Bal's mind still dedicated to observing his external environment broke in on his chronic self-flagellation, to capture his attention. Shoving the previous disagreeable thoughts aside, he consciously focused on the spot in the abyss where he had been absentmindedly staring. The same bright star remained centered in his view. Everything around it also appeared unchanged. For a moment he was flummoxed, unable to determine the source of the distraction, until he became aware that the star he had been studying was now brighter. It seemed to be larger as well, although he knew that his perception was certainly an illusion.

He perceived a slight fluctuation in the light coming from the star. It almost appeared to be…pulsating. As he watched, he realized that in the mere seconds since he had begun to pay attention, the star had become noticeably more bright. And the rhythmic, strobe-like light seemed to have incorporated alternating colors.

Maintaining his watch, he said, "Sam, is there not a famous star which actually shifts colors?"

"Yes. Sirius. Why?"

"In what part of the sky is it found?"

"In this hemisphere? Pretty much right overhead."

"Does it not oscillate various colors? Such as red and orange?"

"Not down here. That's true in North America near the horizon, but this far south it's a steady bluish-white color. Why, Dr. Singh?"

He slowly lifted his arm and, with an outstretched finger, pointed at the object. "Then what is that?"

It only took Sam a few seconds to find the suspect light in the sky. Letting out a loud grunt of surprise, he hastily pulled off his heavy backpack and unzipped it. Bal tore his eyes away from the now even-closer object to see that his cohort was unpacking a video camera and small tripod.

Looking back, Singh could now distinguish that the colored lights were distinctly red, orange, and white. He jumped up and stood on the boulder, his metabolism flooded with adrenaline, his eyes locked on the obviously approaching object, his ears picking up the muttering and clatter from his partner who hurried to set up his gear.

"Get down!" Sam barked.

"Can they see us?"

Jonassen finished setting up the low-light video camera and slid awkwardly down the back side of the tall boulder. "I have no clue. But I don't take any chances. I don't want them to spot us and turn away."

Singh sat down hard and slid off the rock to stand beside him. The two crouched so that only their heads were above the top, and watched...silently transfixed...as the object drew nearer. Its final descent was unnervingly fast, abruptly coming to a hovering stop directly above the waters of the lake. In the process the object resolved from a tight cluster of pulsing lights into a cylindrical craft with alternating red, orange, and white lights continuously traversing the shape's perimeter from one end to the other.

No audible sound emanated from it; the massive other-worldly craft floated silently approximately fifty feet above the surface. Sam shifted to his left and checked the screen on the back of the camera, making certain he was capturing the scene, and touched a button to zoom in closer.

Bal whispered, "What is...?"

Jonassen shushed him before he could finish.

They both saw the craft slowly, silently begin to lower itself. When it converged with the surface of the water, there was no hesitation in its downward momentum, continuing steadily until the ribbon of chasing lights submerged, causing a beautiful swirling, flickering, multi-hued glow to come from the water. The light show diminished as the object traveled deeper; and the water meeting at the top of the cylinder as it went under caused a wet, slapping sound which reached all the way to the two men.

Unable to move, Bal watched as Sam grabbed the camera, stopped the recording, and started playback. The final approach of the craft, the seconds of its hovering, and its final descent were all clearly captured in the digital media.

$$\triangledown$$

Kenny Bowman swiped his card through the reader and heard the soft click from the locking mechanism. Opening the door, he saw Luis sitting on the edge of his small bed. The prisoner looked up at him as he entered, and smiled. "Hello, Special Agent Bowman."

The agent closed the door and took one of the two chairs at the small table. Unable to turn it to face his suspect, since it was bolted to the floor, he sat sideways. "Mr. Tovar. How are you doing?"

A sardonic half-smile accompanied his reply. "Oh, just great. Is there any way you could call me Luis?"

"No." He softened the apparent harshness of his answer with a slight grin.

"Didn't think so. But I thought I'd try. How are Romeo and the rest of the group?"

"That's a weird question to ask."

"Why?"

"Most people in your position want to know their own status and the details of the case against them."

Luis shrugged stoically. "I know enough about how that's going...enough to know I'm screwed. But Romeo and the rest of them are...or at least were...my friends."

"I guess that Romeo and the others are having a tough time believing they were betrayed by Mrs. Costello."

"I don't blame them. Hell, I have trouble believing it. She was a nice lady. I feel sorry for Dr. Costello. If he knows about it yet."

"Don't know. I think they planned on talking to both of them fairly soon. As of now, I haven't heard."

"And everyone else?"

Bowman paused for a minute, studying his prisoner. His first impression of this meeting was the absolute normalcy of the conversation. To him, it felt like a casual chat between two acquaintances, rather than what it actually was. Coming to a decision, he shared the current news. "Chris Ashby has apparently been kidnapped."

Tovar's eyes widened, his countenance instantly shifting from a friendly expression to one Bowman could only describe as fearful. He said nothing to the latest revelation.

After waiting several seconds, the agent urged, "What's your take on that?"

Glancing down at his own hands, Luis spoke, his voice coming so softly it was barely audible in the quiet room. "They need help."

"Who needs help, Mr. Tovar?"

He still did not look up. "All of them. Kelsey, Judtson, Saylor…the rest of the group. Even Romeo."

Suddenly, his eyes lifted and connected with Bowman's, his stare intent. "You need to help them. Quickly."

There was something in the intensity of the man which triggered an involuntary tightening of the seasoned investigator's neck and back muscles. "What are you saying?"

"I…I don't know for sure. But I think that grabbing Dr. Ashby is only the beginning."

"Why?"

"From what I've heard, the group were all supposed to buy into Beckleman's story. If they aren't…if they're planning to keep digging…well, they'll be stopped. One way or another."

The room felt suddenly chillier to Bowman. "How do you know this, Luis?"

The man's shoulders lifted slightly and dropped. "I don't, really. Since the silo, I've had time to think. It's just what I believe. I dealt with those two guys outside Matt Wheeler's office that night. They didn't care if they lived or died, man. And the one we captured…Bob. I've never seen anything like it. A prisoner who won't eat or drink. Who will simply let himself die. And the sniper who came to the silo. Snipers! You know what that means. If we hadn't been lucky that day, Dr. Costello and the others in the truck would all be dead."

"Except we're cleaning it up. Rounding them up."

Tovar let out a grunt which was intended to be a harsh laugh. "You think so?"

"I do. We've nailed a lot of them."

"You've only gotten the ones they've served up to you on a platter. They don't care, man! They don't care about their own people. They'll shovel a thousand guys at you to make you *think* you've cleaned it up."

Luis paused soberly before finishing his thought. "And the worst part, Special Agent Bowman, is that if *you* begin to suspect you're being played like a banjo…if you begin to think that there's more to all of this than what you're being fed…they'll just take you out, too."

The course of the conversation unsettled Bowman to a degree he did not care to admit. In an attempt to change the subject, he began, "Can I ask you a question? Why haven't you obtained an attorney?"

The gravity on Tovar's face was replaced with a look of mild pity. "You don't get it, do you?"

"Get what?"

"You still think that the system is real. That all I have to do is get a good lawyer and he'll breeze in with some fancy papers and I'll walk out of here. Or maybe I'll go to trial and a jury of my peers will turn me loose."

"Yes. I do."

Luis shook his head dismissively. "Those days are gone, sir. If they ever were real, either. The truth is that there's no way I'm going to make it into a courtroom. Why do you think I waited in hiding so long before I turned myself in to you?"

"Why?"

"I spent some time watching you. The best I could, anyway. And it seemed like you might be on the up and up. It didn't hurt that Romeo talked about you a couple of times in the past. Told me you were a good guy. I needed to know I wasn't putting myself right in the lion's mouth. This is the only place I'm fairly safe. That's why I don't want a lawyer. That's why I wouldn't post bail if it was set and I could swing it. Special Agent Bowman, I think you've been allowed to clean up this office. To convince you that the rest of the system is also clean. And that makes this the only place on Earth where I'm pretty sure I'm going to wake up the next morning. And there's one more thing. Just because you think this office is clean doesn't mean they don't have a few of their people in here. To watch you."

Kenny Bowman broke eye contact with Luis, turning to stare at the blank white wall to his left. "You're making it harder for me to tell you what I came to say."

"Why? What's that?"

Swinging his gaze back, he flatly stated, "You are being transferred to another facility."

Tovar's entire body seemed to shrink, communicating a bleak resignation. His voice flat and lifeless, he asked, "When?"

"Today. Anytime now."

"Where?"

"The federal detention facility in Florence."

"Are *you* taking me there?"

"No. You're going to be escorted by the U.S. Marshals."

"Who ordered it?"

Bowman shrugged. "All I know is that it came from my boss in D.C."

Luis released a heavy sigh, moving his eyes from the agent's and scanning the small room, as if trying to memorize it before he left. He stood slowly and took two steps forward, extending his hand. "Nice knowing you, Special Agent...."

"Kenny."

A halfhearted smile forced its way onto his face. "It's been nice knowing you, Kenny."

Bowman rose and grasped the man's hand. "Knock this off, Luis. You're only going down the road an hour's drive away. I'll still be seeing you quite a bit. I'm nowhere close to being done with you."

He nodded stiffly. "Sure. Whatever you say."

There was a loud knock on the door. Bowman disengaged from the handshake and saw that Tovar instinctively moved to the far end of the room, the most distant point from the entrance. As the interior knob was not operable, the agent waited for the guard to open the door. When it unlocked, he saw his own man stepping aside to allow two others to move past. The pair were dressed in the normal summertime attire of the U.S. Marshals: long-sleeved white shirts, black slacks, and well-polished black shoes.

One of the two men pulled his ID wallet from his back pocket and flipped it open. "We're here to transport Luis Tovar."

Bowman took a moment longer than he usually did to study the ID, then asked the second marshal to show his. Memorizing both of the names, he moved off to the side.

The two brusquely passed him and directed their orders to Luis. "Turn around and face the wall. Place your hands on the wall above your head."

With a final, almost pleading look at Kenny, he shuffled around and complied with their directions. The taller of the officers stood off to the side as the other gripped one of Tovar's arms at the wrist, pulling it down and around behind his back. He efficiently slipped a handcuff onto the wrist and reached up for the other arm, doing the same. As he snugged the cuffs, Luis let out a short bark of pain.

Stepping nearer, Bowman could see that the steel was deeply buried in the skin of both wrists. "Hey! They don't need to be that tight."

The man who had applied the cuffs knelt behind Luis, unhooked a pair of leg irons from his belt, and glanced back at the agent. "Sir, you need to back off. He's in our custody now."

Bowman stayed in his spot, watching closely. After the irons were firmly attached, the marshal stood and grabbed one of his prisoner's arms, turning him. Luis once again made eye contact with Kenny, and all the FBI agent could find in his eyes was fear tinged with resignation.

The second officer took Luis' other arm and they walked him out of the room slowly, to accommodate the clumsy gait necessitated by the leg irons, and into the hallway. Bowman followed the trio to the elevator, where the doors were being held open by the guard for the detention floor. The marshals walked Tovar into the cab and the three turned to face out. Bowman started to join them, when one of the two raised his hand, palm facing forward, and said, "We'll take it from here, Special Agent. Thanks for your assistance."

Kenny halted and the doors slowly closed.

Pressing the call button for another elevator, he was torn between two conflicting thoughts. His first was that Luis Tovar was simply paranoid and that everything was exactly as it seemed. This was nothing but a routine, mundane prisoner transfer, identical to countless others he had seen in the past, and Luis would safely arrive at the federal detention facility within an hour or two.

The opposing thought, driven primarily by his emotions...his gut, was that Luis was right, and he would never see the man again. Or, if he did, Tovar would no longer be breathing. His disconcerting speculations were interrupted by the soft chime from the elevator, announcing its arrival. He shook off his doubts and stepped through the open doors, tapping the button for his level.

After the quiet of the detention area, the floor where his office was situated seemed noisy, bustling with people in motion. The pace and tempo of the activity immediately drew him in, distracting Bowman from his earlier thoughts, and he weaved through the cubicles, reaching the work station of his assistant, Caitlyn, where he stopped and waited as she finished a phone call.

When she disconnected, he inquired routinely, "What's new?"

She checked the screen of her computer. "Not much, but Dr. Thompson called. He asked me to tell you that he finished his software analysis of Tovar's polygraph, and found no indications of a different conclusion. I guess Tovar told the truth."

He nodded pensively. "All right. Is that it?"

"You had three…no, four other phone calls. The messages are on your computer."

"Anything important?"

"Not really. Well, maybe one. The dispatcher from the U.S. Marshals Service called."

Bowman's pulse quickened. "What? What did they want?"

"Usual personnel issues. One of the two marshals who was supposed to pick up Tovar today called in sick. They rescheduled the transfer to…. Kenny?"

Chapter 15

THE FBI AGENT WAS ALREADY AT A DEAD RUN. As he dodged the people in the aisles, his first impulse was to bark orders to the staff around him...take someone with him as backup...alert the gate guard on the underground garage to stop the van carrying Luis. Yet he did not. Luis' warning that there were people within this office he could not trust stopped him cold.

As he approached the elevator vestibule, Kenny considered taking the stairwell, thinking it would be faster. His decision was made by the emergence of two people from one of the elevators. Squeezing past them, he punched the button for the garage level and, as the doors closed, unholstered his Glock, checking it first and then holding it pointed down at the floor.

Fortunately, the lift did not stop at any of the interim floors, and he pushed through the parting doors before they were fully open, and burst into the underground garage at a full run. Momentarily stalled by indecision, not sure if he should try to go to the guard post at the exit in the hope they had not yet left, or assume they had and get his own vehicle, he chose the latter, glad that his rank warranted a reserved spot almost adjacent to the garage elevator lobby.

With the SUV's tires screeching at each switchback, he skidded to a loud stop at the exit booth. The guard, recognizing Bowman, started to speak but was cut off. "Two U.S. Marshals picked up a prisoner for transport. Did you see them?"

The man nodded. "Yes, sir. They just left a minute ago."

"What are they driving?"

"The usual transport. White van. Metal mesh on the rear windows."

"Which way did they go?"

The guard pointed but again had no time to speak. Kenny punched the gas pedal and the Tahoe squealed up the ramp to the street. Turning west, he flipped on the flashing lights, refraining from using the siren, and veered back and forth among the cars, his eyes frantically searching for the white van.

The federal building was less than a mile from I-10, and the FBI agent swerved to the far right lane, planning on using the westbound on-ramp, which would actually take him north on this leg of the interstate, assuming that it would be their route to Florence. The traffic signal ahead of the freeway was red and he braked hard, falling in line behind several waiting cars and coming to a stop only inches from the one in front of him. His fingers nervously drumming on the steering wheel, he saw that none of the vehicles between him and the turn fit the description. Frustrated that the marshals were increasing their distance from him, Kenny glanced to his left and was surprised and relieved to see the van in the far left lane.

He recognized the man sitting in the passenger seat and looking straight ahead. Through the expanded metal mesh mounted over the side rear windows, he was barely able to discern a figure in one of the backseats and assumed it must be Tovar.

Shutting off the flashing lights on his Tahoe, he flipped his blinker from right to left and, as the traffic signal changed to green and the cars began to move, he waited, triggering a cacophony of blaring horns from the line behind, and allowed the traffic in the middle to pass him before he swung over. Crossing all of the lanes and keeping two cars and a pickup truck between himself and the van, he watched and followed as the marshals proceeded through the underpass and turned left, moving onto the eastbound on-ramp.

"This isn't the way to Florence," he muttered aloud.

He merged into the moderately heavy flow of traffic on the freeway, careful to maintain a buffer of other vehicles to shield his distinctive SUV, and pursued the van. As he drove, his mind methodically ticked through the list of possible agents under his command whom he could call for an assist. He realized that when viewed through the lens of suspicion instilled in him by Luis and the actions of the men he was trailing, there was no one he felt absolutely certain he could trust. Exhausting the roster, he expanded his mental search. The first name which occurred to him was an obvious choice. Pulling out his cell phone and one-handing his way through the list of contacts, he tapped the screen and almost instantly heard "Hey, Kenny. What's up?"

"Romeo! What's your twenty?"

The urgency in Bowman's voice brought Jones to alert. "Doing some shopping at a police supply. Broadway and Kolb."

"That might work. Start rolling south on Kolb. Now!"

"Walking out the door. How fast do you need me? Am I breaking any laws?"

"Every one you can. Once you're rolling, call me back."

"Roger that."

The agent broke the connection, snapped his phone into the hands-free cradle, and waited. The van was in plain sight and the driver was showing no inclination to exceed the speed limit, staying at sixty-five miles per hour. Bowman tracked the marshals past the I-19 junction, grateful that they had not exited, since the only real destination on that piece of freeway was Mexico. Abruptly, his phone chimed and he tapped the screen.

"You on the move?"

"I am. What's coming down?"

Bowman briefly explained what had happened, finishing the narrative by adding, "I'm not one-hundred-percent certain about this. They might be on the up and up. That's why I'm only shadowing right now. But if it turns bad, I might need some backup."

The phone was silent for at least thirty seconds as Romeo mulled over the situation, then finally said, "Doubt they're cool. If they were, they wouldn't be heading the opposite direction from Florence. I don't think the U.S. Marshals Service allows side trips to Colossal Cave while moving a prisoner."

Despite his tension, Bowman chuckled. "No. That's for sure. Actually, protocol prohibits anything other than a direct delivery."

"Well, there you go."

"Anyway, we're on I-10, traveling east. We passed the Nogales turnoff, and we should be getting to Kolb Road in about ten minutes. Where are you now?"

Through the speaker, he heard a loud blare from a car horn, followed by an even louder, closer blast, before Romeo answered, "Running the red light at Golf Links. I think I had my picture taken."

"Just make it here, okay? They're cruising at the speed limit, so chill a little. You can always fall in behind me."

"That's no fun."

As they talked, a worrying thought tickled at the corner of Romeo's mind. Swerving around an eighteen-wheeler as it executed a wide right turn into a truck stop at Valencia Road and took up both southbound lanes in the process, he mentally dug and probed at the idea or concern, trying to bring it to the surface. Clearing the tractor-trailer, he was suddenly confronted with an oncoming motorcycle, and twisted the wheel hard to the right, barely missing both the truck he was passing and the biker as the wide Hummer jinked back into the lane.

Deciding he needed both hands to steer, he grunted, "Hold tight a second. Going to put you on speaker." The road in front was clear. He glanced down quickly and tapped the screen, changing modes, and slipped the phone into his shirt pocket. The simple act released his buried thought, and an additional jolt of adrenaline hit him.

His mind racing, he mentally reviewed the previous contents of the conversation with Kenny, then said, "Hey, Sergeant!"

There was a brief pause until the acknowledgment came. "Uh, yeah, Master Sar."

"This reminds me of Fallujah. Outside the wire. Tracking the deserter. The *only* difference is no dust storm."

Bowman immediately grasped what it was his friend was trying to communicate. The two of them, along with a small squad, Romeo in the lead, had nearly been killed in an ambush. They had lost two men in the action, and Romeo later discovered that their comm gear had been compromised. Al Qaeda had been listening to every word said during their pursuit and approach, and had set a trap.

"I read you five by five," he answered, staring at his own phone hanging on the face of the dashboard as if it had maliciously betrayed him.

Romeo was now pushing the Hummer close to one hundred on the long, straight stretch of road, rocketing up the overpass at the railroad tracks. Clearing the crown, he could see the freeway junction ahead. Keeping his voice calm, he said, "I'm going to have to take you up on that offer to fall in behind and catch up."

"Why's that?" Bowman asked, also sounding utterly normal.

"Some classes are letting out here. School buses got everybody stopped. Traffic's a cluster."

"Damn. Well, don't sweat it. They don't seem to be in any hurry. Catch me soon as you can."

"Will do."

As he climbed the hump over the interstate, slowing down, Romeo twisted his head right and then left, searching for the two vehicles, and spotted Kenny's Tahoe already to the east. He gunned the engine and slalomed the wide-track truck left for the on-ramp, his speedometer passing ninety even before the merge. Traffic was moderate and he maintained his speed. All of the other drivers ahead, seeing the rate at which he approached, pulled quickly to the right to allow him past, until he was blocked by two cars traveling side by side, neither showing the slightest indication of breaking formation.

Through the rear windows of the cars, Romeo could see that both drivers were women talking on their cell phones. He pulled into the left lane, crept forward until his massive grill and bumper were no more than a foot or two from the back of the car, no doubt completely filling her rearview mirror. He simultaneously turned on his brights, as well as the running lights mounted to the grill, and pressed and held down the loud horn of the Hummer.

What happened next was almost comical. As the driver's head jerked to the right to check her mirror, she dropped the phone and, panicking, began to swerve out of his way, oblivious to the fact that she was veering directly toward the pacing car beside her. The second driver, also hearing the racket and seeing the encroachment of the other car into her space, dropped her phone, honked, and swung her car onto the shoulder, braking hard at the same time, her evasive maneuver barely accommodating the first vehicle. Romeo, putting his left tires on the paved shoulder, goosed the Hummer and shot past the two, spotting Bowman's black SUV no more than a quarter of a mile ahead.

Closing the gap, he drew up alongside his friend and waved. Kenny gave a thumbs-up. With hand gestures, Romeo indicated that he would fall back and cover, tapping his brake pedal after receiving an acknowledgment. Once he was several car lengths back, he spoke for the benefit of the phone. "Sorry, man. This just ain't happening. I could bull my way through, I guess. But not without causing some serious distress. How bad do you need me?"

"Any idea how much longer it will take?"

"Maybe another couple of minutes."

"Well, I wanted you here for backup, except right now it looks like a long, boring drive ahead."

As they spoke, the FBI agent eased closer to the van and was barely able to distinguish that the marshal in the passenger seat was on his phone. He then backed off on the accelerator to put more distance between them and, deciding to create a test, added, "I'm still not sure this is the real deal, anyway. I've got someone from my office contacting the dispatcher for the U.S. Marshals Service. Should hear back any second."

Understanding what his Ranger buddy was thinking, Romeo replied, "Oh, okay. I'll get through this mess as soon as I can. And let you know when I do. In the meantime, call me back if anything changes."

"Roger."

The instant the connection was broken, the white van jumped forward, accelerating aggressively. Keeping pace, Kenny watched his speed, seeing that they were both traveling almost a hundred miles per hour. He glanced in his rearview mirror and saw that Romeo was keeping up.

They were well outside the city limits with nothing but desert in all directions. Its brake lights flaring, the van took an off-ramp which serviced a ranching area, and turned hard onto a narrow two-lane, fishtailing dangerously in the process. The driver brought the vehicle under control and gunned the engine again. The road followed a rolling terrain with numerous washes and hills, and as Bowman trailed behind, he lost sight of the van several times, reacquiring it at the next hilltop. Romeo had closed the gap and was no more than fifty yards behind.

Now over a mile from the interstate with no signs of civilization in sight, the FBI agent cleared a particularly tall ridge and immediately slammed on his brakes, coming to a shuddering halt. Romeo, climbing the incline behind him, saw the flash of brake lights as Bowman's truck disappeared on the down slope, and was able to bring his own vehicle to a stop short of the top. In the wide wash ahead, the van was pulled off the road onto a cleared area. None of the vehicle's occupants were in sight.

Opening the glove compartment and retrieving a pair of binoculars, Kenny climbed out of the Tahoe and, continuing to face the white van, back-stepped to the rear of his truck. Leaning against it casually, he put the binoculars to his eyes and listened for Romeo's approach from behind.

"Stay down," he barked without turning.

Understanding the play, Romeo held back so that he was concealed by the bluff. "What's it look like?"

"A trap. The van's parked next to the road. No one in sight. I'm guessing Tovar is still inside. I'll bet one of the two guys jumped out, maybe before they even came to a stop, and is hiding in a blind while the other one sits in the air conditioning, playing bait. If I use the standard training manual approach and just walk up to the van, I'll get popped without coming anywhere close."

"Sounds about right. Got a plan?"

Bowman snickered. "I was sort of hoping you did. You, me, and a couple of handguns.... A little dicey. Two M4s would be nice."

"How's the view from this ridge?"

Lowering the binoculars but continuing to face forward in case he was being watched, the agent muttered, "Wide open. Why?"

"I told you I was shopping when you called. Hang on a sec."

The Ranger trotted back to his Hummer, opened the door, and reached in, pulling out a long case. When he returned, he set it on the hot pavement behind the Tahoe's bumper and snapped it open. Bowman casually glanced back and, seeing what it was, whistled. "Man, you're kidding. That's an L115A3."

"Yep."

"What's it chambered?"

"Point three-three-eight, Lapua."

Kneeling, Romeo quickly assembled the rifle and fastened the scope. "The only problem, it's a new for me. Chet, at the shop, told me he took it out yesterday and sighted it in with the scope at one klick. Said he popped off about fifty rounds and it was dead nuts. But I wish I could've had a chance to put a few through it myself before this."

He snapped the five-round box magazine in, stood, and shouldered the weapon, backing a few feet farther down the slope. "You've got the view. Tell me, which side is better for me to set up?"

Swinging the glasses in a wide panorama, Kenny described the layout. "The road we're on goes straight down and levels off for a wide wash. The van is parked on the right just past the base of the hill and is off the road at a forty-five degree angle. Oriented also to the right. There are a lot of palo verdes, mesquites, you name it, so I can't really pick where the other guy might be." He was silent as he studied the situation for another few seconds. "In his place, I'd probably figure that the dumbshit FBI agent would approach the van on the driver's side, so I'm guessing you should move about fifty, maybe seventy-five yards to the left and find a good blind there. That should keep you in play."

"Will do. By the way, Kenny...."

"Yeah?"

"You need to call for backup."

"Why? I thought.... Oh, you're right. If they're listening to me, that's what they'd expect."

"Bingo."

He slipped the leather strap from the glasses around his neck and rested the optics on his chest. Then, moving forward along the Tahoe, he reached into the open driver's door and retrieved his phone, keying the speed dial. As he made the call, Romeo, running in a crouch, dashed through the rough desert, directly below the ridge. At the point where he estimated he had traveled approximately seventy yards, he spotted a rock outcropping at the top of the hill. The badly fractured granite was bracketed by two medium-sized mesquites, opportunistically rooting to capture the additional moisture from beneath and around the boulders.

Carefully easing his way up, he grunted with satisfaction. The location was about as perfect as he could have hoped for, providing ample space behind the rocks for him to stand, a relatively flat top for the rifle's bipod, and plenty of overhanging branches for head cover. Taking position, he eyeballed the target zone for the first time. His assessment agreed with Bowman's; this was most likely the ideal position. Next, confirming that the sun was behind his back and eliminating the possibility of any lens flare betraying his position, he rested his rifle on top, tweaked the scope, dialed in on the driver's side window of the van, and was able to see one man sitting behind the wheel, talking on a cell phone. Nudging the view a bit to the right, he saw that the passenger seat was empty. Moving farther along the length of the vehicle, Romeo was able to make out a passenger in the rear but, because of the metal mesh, glare, and window tint, could not confirm that the passenger was Luis. Methodically, he used the high-powered scope to look for the second marshal. He kept the search zone close to the van, assuming that the man would only be armed with a pistol and that they had not been carrying a long-range rifle.

"*What do you mean, there's no one close?*" The question was almost shouted by Bowman into the phone. "You're not listening. I have a situation and I need backup immediately."

If there had been any doubts in his mind earlier, they were now erased. Never in his career with the FBI had he been told to stand down as no backup was available.

"Look, I don't care if you call DPS, the county sheriff, *whoever* it is...just get somebody here."

. . . . .

"No! I *don't* know which county. I'm out in the middle of the desert between Tucson and Benson. It's either Pima or Cochise."

. . . . .

"*Yes! I'll stand by.*"

He ended the call knowing with certainty that no one was going to come. The emotions associated with this realization...that his own beloved organization was corrupted...threatened to overwhelm him. He buried the ugly thoughts, promising that he would address them at a later time. Lifting the glasses, Bowman stared down at the van. By now the details of his last call would have been related to the man inside, if, in fact, he was not able to listen in real time. Now the bogus marshal would know that an FBI agent who was not in their pocket was waiting...

hoping...for backup before he would make his move. Kenny knew that they would do something to force his hand.

His theory was confirmed at once as the door of the van opened and the driver emerged. The man circled around the front to the passenger side, and Bowman saw him draw his sidearm before gripping the rear door handle.

Addressing no one but himself, Kenny murmured, "He's making a point of not looking at me. Am I supposed to think he isn't aware that I'm watching?"

Romeo noticed the movement and trained the crosshairs on the driver who opened the passenger door and stepped back. Within seconds, Jones saw Luis emerge, still handcuffed and hobbled. "He's going to execute him out here. Come on, Kenny. Time to move."

The FBI agent was already in motion. Binoculars flapping heavily against his chest, he had jumped into the open door of the Tahoe, dropped it in gear, and floored it. With the aid of the steep slope, the black SUV roared to the bottom of the wash in seconds. As he approached the van, Bowman swerved off the asphalt onto the dirt shoulder and then jerked the wheel to the left while hitting the brakes. The heavy SUV ground to a sideways, sliding stop twenty yards from the van, kicking up a cloud of dust.

He was out before the springs had settled from the violent maneuver, using the vehicle as cover and hoping that the second man was not hidden behind him, at this moment drawing a bead on his back.

"F...B...I! DROP THE GUN!" he shouted, crouched beside the front wheel, and laid his Glock on the hood.

The marshal, standing near Tovar, used his free hand to grab the chain on the handcuffs and pulled his prisoner closer, moving toward the front of the van for cover, simultaneously snapping off a quick shot at Bowman. Luis did not cooperate. As he was yanked backward, instead of resisting, he pushed harder with his powerful legs and slammed into the marshal, driving both of them violently into the side of the van. Seeing that his captor's gun hand was off to the side and not pointing the weapon in his direction, Luis thrust his head back with all the force he could muster, his hard skull smashing the man's nose.

Kenny, not able to clearly see the struggle from his position, circled to the back of his truck. Peering around it, he saw Luis turning awkwardly in his leg irons to face the marshal, who was pressing one hand against his bloody face while bringing his gun hand to bear on his prisoner. Bowman knew that at this range, a shot from his Glock would be iffy at best, but steadied his arm against the side of the SUV and began to squeeze the trigger, when the rear window next to his head suddenly exploded. He dived into the dirt and rolled under the truck, twisting and thrashing his body rapidly to be able to see where the shot had come from and orient himself to that direction.

Luis, about to burst from frustration at his lack of mobility from the ankle cuffs, saw the man continue to lift his pistol. The marshal's urgency dampened somewhat by the intervention of his partner, his arm came up slowly, centering on Tovar's chest. Luis knew that he was out of options and waited stoically for the impact, refusing to look away from his killer's gaze. In a blink, the man's forearm, now fully extended toward his target, severed violently with a splash of blood and flesh. The wrist and the hand, still clutching the pistol, were tossed to the ground several feet away.

Stunned, a pulsing gout of blood geysering from his forearm, the marshal was frozen as the report from Romeo's rifle reached their ears. Luis turned and stumbled as rapidly as he could, falling heavily on top of the pistol. Rolling onto his side, he pulled his legs tightly against his chest and forced his arms forward, dragging the handcuffs over the soles of his shoes, until his hands were in front of his body.

Bowman, prone under the SUV and facing rearward toward the direction of fire, searched the tangle of desert trees and bushes for his attacker. A rapid string of shots kicked up mini-eruptions of sand and pebbles in front of him, one of the slugs ricocheting to the undercarriage and ringing a section of the frame like a bell. He scooted deeper under the truck, adjusting his aim to the spot where he had seen the muzzle flashes, and emptied his clip.

The second marshal, realizing he was positioned too high for a clear shot under the Tahoe, swapped magazines and focused his aim on the rear tires, knowing that his target was lying directly under the axle and differential, and would be instantly crushed when the wheels dropped. The tactic was the last thought his mind would ever produce. His previous volley of shots was all Romeo had needed to locate his blind, and the .338 Lapua Magnum round entered his shoulder at several hundred feet per second.

The sound from Romeo's second shot reached Bowman moments later, but it was not until he heard the high-pitched all-clear whistle from his battle buddy that he knew it was safe to emerge. Shimmying forward, he crawled out from under the truck and rounded it to see that Luis was standing over his former captor, holding him at bay with the pistol.

Still not completely certain who all of the players were, the agent kept his Glock in his hand, pointing it down as he approached. The marshal was sitting on the desert sand, his back leaning against the wheel of the van, his left hand clutching the stump of his right arm in an attempt to stanch the bleeding. Luis, his face covered with sweat and dust, his hands shaking slightly, was pointing the pistol at the reclining figure's head.

Kenny kept his voice steady and gentle. "I got it, Luis. You can put that down now."

Tovar's eyes swung to connect with his, but the aim remained fixed where it was. "Depends."

"On what?"

"What're you going to do with me?"

As they spoke, both heard the roar of the Hummer coming down the hill. Romeo brought the truck to a skidding halt beside the van, climbed out, and came around, holding the rifle. He immediately took in the scene and walked within two feet of his one-time partner, facing him and taking care to not position himself between Luis and the wounded marshal.

He grunted, "Hi, Luis."

"Romeo. Good shooting." As he paid the compliment, he nodded toward the marshal.

"Not exactly. I was aiming for a body shot. Not used to this piece yet."

Glancing down at the rifle, Luis said, "Nice weapon."

Romeo held it toward him. "Here. Take a look at it."

Luis searched the man's eyes quizzically and then chuckled. With a slight shrug, he muttered, "Sure. Why not?" and handed him the marshal's pistol, taking the rifle in exchange.

Romeo popped the clip, emptied the chamber, and jammed the gun into the back of his pants, afterward turning to Bowman. "There's a first-aid kit in the Hummer on the backseat floor. Maybe we should wrap this guy before he bleeds out."

Holstering his Glock, the agent trotted to the truck and brought back the kit, kneeling beside the wounded man, who appeared to be going into shock. As he pulled out a wide roll of gauze, Romeo suggested, "Why don't you see if he has the keys for Luis' irons on him?"

Minutes later, the marshal was lying down on one of the rear prisoner benches inside the van, locked in, and Kenny was cautiously walking up the slope to the spot where the second assailant had been hiding. Luis, his legs and hands freed, was sitting next to Romeo in the dirt, the sniper rifle now stowed on the front seat of the Hummer.

Breaking their long silence, Romeo asked, "You okay?"

The only answer he got was a short, harsh laugh.

Another minute passed until Luis finally spoke. "So what are you going to do now?"

Romeo turned to face him. "About them...or about you?"

"Both. I guess."

"Not sure yet. About them, I mean. Right now, the stuff's hitting the fan. Between this and...did you hear about Dr. Ashby?"

"Uh-huh. Kenny told me. It looks like they're declaring war."

"Yep. And about you...hell, Luis, I don't know. I heard your story. And it kind of makes sense. But...."

"Listen, I understand. If I had a guy right on video letting the bad guys in, I wouldn't be able to trust him one hundred percent, either. Whatever he said."

Romeo did not say anything.

"You know what matters to me, though?"

"What's that?"

"That you, at least partially, believe me."

Staring hard at his former partner, Romeo softly said, "I do."

A half smile formed on Luis' face. "That works for me. What *are* you and Kenny going to do with me? Take me back to the fed building?"

"No. I think he understands that it would be signing your death warrant."

"I know I can't hang out with you. Help you with the coming shitstorm."

"Not really."

"So?"

"What do you think we should do?"

He thought for a minute before answering. "Cut me loose." And then, surveying the desolate surroundings, he looked amused and added, "Not out here. It'd be better to get me closer to someplace. I'll figure out a place to hide."

Noticing that Bowman was returning, Jones answered, "Sit tight. Let me talk to him."

He stood and met the agent halfway. "I think we should turn Luis loose."

Kenny appeared uncomfortable at the suggestion. "I don't know. He was a high-profile prisoner. How in the hell would I explain that?"

Gesturing at the area around them, Romeo quipped, "How in the hell are you going to explain all of this? Two U.S. Marshals, except maybe they weren't really U.S. Marshals, came to transport the prisoner to the federal detention facility in Florence, but instead went the other way and took him out into the desert to execute him, laying a trap for the head FBI guy in the local office at the same time."

Kenny laughed. "And don't forget that the sonofabitches wouldn't send me any backup when I called."

"Oh, don't worry. I haven't. And you'd better not, either."

Chapter 16

AS HE PULLED INTO HIS DRIVEWAY, HIS MIND STILL PREOCCUPIED with the conversation with Lisa, Judtson opened the garage door and saw that Kristen's Audi was parked inside. He eased into the empty space alongside it and got out of his car, standing motionless for a minute and attempting to sort through and analyze his feelings, which were mixed and jumbled and far too fleeting to pin down. He gave up and entered his home. Hearing his arrival, Kristen met him in the kitchen.

"Hi, sweetheart. Where've you been?"

He put a wan smile on his face. "Went to the office. Thought I'd catch up on some things. How did the shopping go?"

Her face lit up with delight and she grabbed his hand. "Come with me and I'll show you." She led him across the house to their bedroom, where several bags bearing Neiman Marcus and Barneys logos were piled.

"Wow," he exclaimed, his voice not as lighthearted as he intended. "Looks as if I need to sell another book just to pay for all of this."

Laughing and not noticing anything amiss in his inflections, she picked up the closest bag and pulled out a blouse, holding it up against her torso. "Isn't this beautiful?"

It was a bright floral print and almost shimmered in the light. "It is. Is that silk?"

Already refolding the top and putting it back in the bag, she nodded. "Yes! And not the fake silk they culture. The real thing."

She moved to the next parcel, and Judtson stood patiently, doing his utmost to provide the appropriate comments throughout the impromptu fashion show. As she was showing him one of the last dresses, the doorbell rang. He crossed the room to a small wall-mounted panel holding an LED screen, and tapped a button, opening a camera view of the front entrance area.

"It's Saylor," he said, swinging his head back to face Kristen, and seeing a subtle flicker of irritation on her face before she smiled.

"Go talk to him. I need a shower, anyway."

"Okay."

Arranging the dress on a hanger, she kissed him lightly on the cheek and turned away. Walking briskly, Judtson crossed into the foyer and opened the front door. He was instantly struck with his friend's appearance.

"Saylor! Come in. What's the matter?"

He could not remember a time in their shared lives when he had seen the man so disconsolate. Rather than answering, Saylor shuffled inside.

"Let's go in the kitchen, pal," he offered, picking the room of the house farthest from the master bedroom where he had left Kristen. He turned and walked, glancing over his shoulder to make certain he was followed, until they reached the kitchen and both sat at the table.

"Can I get you something? Something to drink?"

His friend's posture was best described as collapsed, appearing to have fallen in on itself. His shoulders were stooped; his head hung forward and down. He seemed to occupy half of the space he normally filled.

"Got any scotch?"

The request surprised Judtson. Other than an occasional glass of wine with dinner, Saylor rarely drank, one of the many traits they shared.

"Uh, sure. Rocks?"

"Neat."

Rummaging through the cupboard where he kept alcohol for guests, he pulled down a bottle and half-filled a tumbler, returning to the table.

Setting it down, he repeated, "Popeye, what's wrong?"

Saylor's eyes, which had been downcast, slowly rose to meet Judtson's, and in a soft, raspy voice, he uttered, "Doni left me."

"She...what?"

"She's gone."

Stunned, Judtson found it difficult to form his question. "How...why?"

Before answering, Saylor lifted his glass and downed a third of the scotch, the whiskey triggering a hacking, coughing bout. He caught his breath, set down the tumbler, and broached the subject warily. "After you left...she and I talked about...the Luis thing. I guess she couldn't handle my not trusting her or believing her. I don't blame her. I'd react the same way."

Judtson was still working hard to wrap his mind around something which had always seemed impossible to him...a serious rift between his two best friends. "I don't get it. What are you saying?"

Saylor leaned forward, burying his face in both hands and rubbing it furiously. The distraught action ceased, and he looked up once more, this time his eyes communicating a different emotion. Gone was the anguish from a moment earlier, now replaced with something Judtson could not quite define. "After you walked out the door, I confronted her...." He stopped and drew a deep breath. When he began to speak again, his voice was flat, neutral, emotionless, as if he were testifying. "Before you and I and the others left the silo to go to La Paz...I had finished packing. She was in the room with me. And she asked me...dammit, I don't feel right even saying this!"

"Then don't," he replied, gripping his friend's arm.

Saylor shook his head violently. "I think I have to."

"Okay." Judtson sat back and waited.

His patience was rewarded after several seconds. "It was probably nothing, really. I mean, she explained it to me and I guess it made sense."

"So why didn't you believe her?"

"I...I don't know."

The two again lapsed into silence for a time until finally Saylor spoke. "She asked me about Devil's Breath. She asked me what the normal dosage was for an adult male."

▽

Detective Eunice Cahane stared out the window at the heavy downpour. The weather, she thought, perfectly matched her mood. Since she had pursued the investigation into the Rosemary Shields case, every faint lead had taken her down a blind alley, and the initial frustration she felt was slowly reconstituting itself into a full-blown depression.

Returning her attention to her desk, she surveyed the heaps of folders, files, and notes, trying to convince herself to plunge into them once again, in what she now was beginning to view as a vain attempt to find the missing clue. Without thinking about it, she opened the tobacco tin on the desk and plucked out a large wad, jamming it into her mouth, the bulge it caused enhancing her already present bulldog visage.

With a heavy sigh, she leaned forward in the chair and grabbed the top file, when her desk phone rang. Glad for the distraction, she snatched up the handset. "Cahane!"

"Detective, I hoped you were in today. This is Bessie in the lab."

"Yeah, Bess, what's ya got?"

The technician's normally confident delivery was supplanted with a cautious, uncertain edge. "I...do you have a minute to come down here?"

The detective barked out a harsh guffaw. "Hell, Bess, right now I'm like a lost ball in high weeds. Time is something I've got buckets of. Be down in a sec."

The trip from her office to the crime scene lab was a short one, made even quicker by Cahane's bustling pace. Pushing through the swinging double doors, she spotted Bess Cleveland at her table. The technician, who had noticed her arrival, hastily jumped off the high stool and trotted across the large work area to meet her.

With a furtive glance around the lab, she said, "Detective, I think...would you mind if we went somewhere...?"

Leaning close, Cahane spoke in a voice several decibels lower than her normal bellow. "You want to be alone?"

Bessie nodded and the two exited, climbed the stairs without speaking and, finding an unused interrogation room, entered the observation side. No chairs were present, so they both stood.

"Okay, Bess. Nobody can hear us in here. What's ya got?"

Bessie Cleveland was a heavy, large-boned individual with tightly kinked blondish-brown hair cut short to circle her face like a chrysanthemum. Her hands kneaded each other anxiously. "Well, Detective...."

"If you want me to keep calling you Bess, you'd best start calling me Eunice."

A smile flickered across the woman's face, vanishing as abruptly as it had appeared. "Okay, Eunice. You know I'm the one who processed your scene for the Shields case."

"Uh-huh."

"We were able to get quite a lot from the scene before the FBI took over."

"I know. And I appreciate that." Cahane knew that she had to allow the tech to arrive at the point in her own time.

"Of course the first thing we did was pull prints. And we continued to pull them until those two agents arrived. And after that, for a bit."

"Okay."

"Well, I don't remember if I ever told you about something I found later...when I ran the prints. Maybe I did. Maybe I didn't. I just don't know."

Fighting back her natural impatience, Cahane allowed herself a slight sigh.

"I'm sorry. I'm beating around the bush and I really don't intend to. It's just that when I ran all the prints through the system, I got back some positive IDs. Several belonging to Shields. A few belonging to someone we later figured out was the next-door neighbor, an old lady who was her friend. A few prints from Dylan Falt and Lisa Trippiano in the areas they had touched. And a few prints which we figured as contaminated. *Yes!* That was it! I chalked them off as contamination and never mentioned them to you."

"What do you mean, 'contaminated,' Bess?"

"Oh, you know, like when we work a location and get prints from the first officer on the scene, because he touched some stuff before we arrived."

"Yeah, but how does that apply to this?"

She began speaking rapidly, nearly running her words together. "Well...I just decided from the results that it must be contamination. What other explanation could there have been? And then, during lunch today, I overheard two of the detectives talking in the cafeteria. They were laughing and joking, and one of them said that you had gone 'round the bend so far that you thought maybe the FBI was *in on* the murder."

Cahane instantly became furious. She had made the mistake of conferring confidentially, she thought, with one of her senior colleagues and had hinted at the possibility that the Feds were on the wrong side on this case. She knew he had been around the block a few times, and was hoping he could shed some light. Instead, he was apparently gossiping about her suspicions with the other men in the department. She made a mental note to deal with him later.

She kept her comment to Bessie vague. "Yes, there is a remote possibility. Not the whole FBI, of course. Maybe a bad apple in the barrel."

The explanation seemed to relax the tech somewhat. "Good. Yes. Okay. Well, that might explain things."

"What things, Bess?"

"Two of the results I got back on the prints popped up in the system of course, since the guys work for the FBI."

A jolt of electricity ran down the detective's spine. "What? You're kidding. From the two Feds who showed up and took over the case?"

"No! That's just it. Not from them. That's what confused me. I couldn't understand how we'd get prints from two agents who did not arrive on the scene until I'm certain we had stopped lifting prints. It was so stupid of me to assume it was contamination, when I knew they weren't there. It's just that they were federal agents and all. I assumed...."

To calm her, Cahane assured, "It's fine, Bess. Really. Don't blame you any at all. Usually, I'd of seen it like you did. By the way, about those two print results, I guess the agents could've paid Miss Shields a call prior to the day of her death. Where were the prints?"

The tech pulled out a typed sheet and looked at it. "Several in the kitchen...two on the side door, the door Falt and Trippiano entered...one on the door to the garage...one on the Shields car, adjacent to the door handle. But Detec...I mean, Eunice, there is no way the prints happened during an earlier visit."

"Oh? Why not?"

"Because when I lifted the print on the car in the garage and studied it, I noticed that the normal body oil which causes us to leave prints had an abnormal color."

As Cahane listened, her mind raced ahead.

"I tested the oil residue from the print and it had traces of...."

"Orange juice!"

For the first time in the conversation, a genuine smile spread across Bessie Cleveland's face. "Exactly right."

▽

Seated with Kristen in the formal restaurant at Ventana Canyon Resort, half-listening to the formless solo performed by a tuxedoed man at the grand piano, Judtson mentally snapped back to the conversation with Saylor, as if pulled by a rubber band. In an attempt to push down the thoughts and focus on the surroundings, he complimented his wife. "You look nice in that dress."

She beamed. "Thanks. It's one of the new ones I picked up at Neicus."

The corners of his mouth twitched at the reference, but he was able to restore the bland smile as she continued, "The saleslady...."

Judtson broke in, "What is a saleslady from *Neicus* called...a Neicusite? No, wait, I have it. A Neicuzoid!"

Rather than finding his sidebar amusing, Kristen glared at him as he elaborated on the rant inside his own mind. *Maybe she could be a Neicovite. A Neicusan? Or should that be a Neicusian? Perhaps a Neicusalino! Maybe she's Neicunese? Aha! A Neicukus!*

Finally cracking himself up with the absurdity of the final option, Judtson barked out a loud guffaw, causing nearby diners to turn and peer at him, and embarrassing Kristen, who was still staring at him, stone-faced. Looking at her angry countenance, he suddenly understood that the clear dichotomy between Kristen and Kelsey was almost as extreme as it could possibly be. Nowhere within the woman who now sat before him was the lightness, the playfulness, the aliveness which undeniably sparked something good, something alive, within him. Instead, all he now saw...all he could ever see in her eyes was a never-ending disapproval, disapproval of what he did...what he said...who he was. Her disdain for his fundamental personality had resulted in the unnerving fact that he lived on pins and needles through each minute he was with her, constantly wary of offending or irritating his own wife.

And at the other end of the spectrum was Kelsey, who not only seemed to enjoy his quirks...no matter how outrageous...but also relished them, built upon them, played off of them, and actually encouraged him to *be*. His mind flashed back to the scene during the drive when he and Kelsey had poked fun at Kristen in absentia. At the time he felt he had somehow betrayed his wife, that betrayal fostering guilt. What he realized at this very moment surprised him: *that* conversation had stirred powerful emotions within him precisely because it showcased and contrasted the stark differences between the two women.

With considerable effort, he pulled himself back to the now, cleared his throat, and apologized, "Sorry. That was rude. Go ahead with your story. What did the saleslady from...Neicus say?"

Frowning and shaking her head like a first-grade teacher chastising a misbehaving child, Kristen retorted, "It was nothing, really. She told me you would just love the dress."

Unable to filter out all residual sarcasm, he remarked, "Wow! That's amazing, considering she doesn't even know me."

Her mouth pursed. "Maybe she was assuming you were a normal man."

A single snort came from him. "Yeah, *as if.*"

Okay, that went well, he thought wryly. Deciding to abandon any pretense of small talk, Judtson allowed his mind to return to its prior subject. "I wish Saylor would have come with us."

Kristen, relieved that the conversation had shifted to another topic, replied matter-of-factly, "He needs to be alone, I would think. Besides, he probably wants to be waiting there if she comes back. And I can't say that I blame him. I'm sure he knew that if she came home and found he had gone to dinner with friends, it would make things worse."

"I guess."

"I'm not completely clear on what happened."

Judtson had deliberately been vague on the details when he filled her in after Saylor's departure. "Well, you know what happened in the silo. Somebody let the bad guys in. Al Clarkson was killed and the rest of them were hauled off to the FEMA camp."

She interrupted, "That reminds me. Had I listened to you and gone out to the silo instead of going to my sister's, *I* would have been hauled off to that camp, too. I could have been killed like Clarkson."

He stared at her blankly. "Yes. I guess so. What do you want me to say? That I'm sorry I tried to get you to come with us? I thought it would be safe."

She answered airily, "No. Just pointing out the relative merits of our respective judgment. Anyway, go on."

He bit on his bottom lip for a few seconds before he resumed, "So...we were all certain that Luis had betrayed us. Now, he has resurfaced and is *claiming* to have been drugged by Doni."

"No. I get all that. And, by the way, I can't seriously conceive of Doni as some nefarious double agent. Can you?" Her comment was interrupted by a catty chuckle. "I mean, come on, what is she going to do? Kill someone with a meatball?"

Ignoring her caustic remark, Judtson muttered, "No. I can't either."

"But you still haven't told me how Saylor found out."

This was obviously the entrance to the avenue he wanted to avoid. "From me."

Kristen's eyebrows rose. "From you? How did you find out about it?" There was a new trace of suspicion in her voice as she asked the question.

"Uh...Kelsey told me."

"Kelsey? When?"

He felt his gut tightening with each exchange. "While you were in Phoenix...shopping."

She leaned back in her chair and smoothed the linen napkin on her lap with both hands. With her stare now intent, she pressed him, "Oh.... Did you see her?"

Vivid images of the time with Kelsey tumbled into his mind and he worried that they were somehow also visible to Kristen. "Yes. I did."

He watched the fleeting spasms of her jaw muscles as her eyes narrowed to slits. His guilt since seeing Kelsey had been a monumental weight on him, never completely leaving his conscious thoughts for a single heartbeat; and although he had decided not to volunteer the information about what happened between them, he knew he would not lie if Kristen asked.

She leaned forward and rested her arms on the white tablecloth, her hands clenched into fists. "So it's starting all over again, isn't it?"

The direction of her inquiry, so far off the mark from what he had expected and feared, slightly flummoxed him. "What's starting?"

Her tone biting and accusatory, she spat out the words. "The intrigue. The danger. Joining up with your little posse of fringe lunatics and nutcases and taking on the world. You can't stay away from it, can you?"

His previous dread, tension, and angst were all flushed clean from his system, now replaced with incipient anger. Judtson's voice was low and steady. "Kristen, there are things happening. Very bad things."

She rolled her eyes. "Like what?"

"Just yesterday Chris Ashby was kidnapped. Right off the highway between Tucson and San Diego. In broad daylight."

"So what?" she huffed dismissively. "He probably picked up some cute teenaged female hitchhiker and she rolled him."

Judtson stared at his wife, bewildered. "You're kidding, aren't you? That's absurd."

"*That's* absurd? You think some dark, nasty agency of the government intercepting him and taking him to their secret base inside a mountain in Nevada is the *perfectly reasonable explanation*, I suppose. Oh no, wait! *Maybe this time* a giant flying saucer hovered above his car on the highway and neutralized the electronics as the aliens beamed him up to their ship and whisked him away to their home planet. Is *that* the reasonable explanation this time?" At this, she tilted her head back and rudely laughed.

Judtson wanted to reach over the small table and slap her face, this urge as foreign to him as any impulse he had ever felt in his life. Prior to this instant, the act of hitting a woman, no matter what the reason, was inconceivable. But as he watched her jaw ratcheting with each contempt-laden word, as he recognized the unveiled scorn in her eyes while she spoke, he was barely able to restrain himself from doing exactly that.

At that moment, he could not detect even a vestige of the symmetry...of the grace...of the kindness...of the beauty he had always thought she possessed. It was as if her words had somehow coincidentally mimicked an ancient incantation, breaking a decades-old spell and dissolving a carefully crafted and lovely mask, behind which the real Kristen had always hidden, and revealing, for the first time, what was a true ugliness.

The pointed harshness of her sarcastic dismissal of the abduction of Chris Ashby, a man Judtson had come to see as a good man...a man he had come to like, pierced him to the quick. Through gritted teeth, he growled, "Kristen...stop it."

The laughter ebbed off slowly, but the underlying condescension remained etched on her face.

He took in a deep breath, hoping to modulate the roiling emotions which threatened to consume him. Letting the air out slowly, he stated firmly, "I'm not going with you on the cruise."

Her eyes flashed at him and he immediately sensed that had they not been sitting in one of the most high-end restaurants in the city, she would have started a scene. Instead, visibly exercising all of the self-control that she could muster to keep her voice low, Kristen uttered, "Oh, you're *not*, huh? Well, I guess that now we both know how good *your* word is, Judtson Kent."

"What do you mean?"

"You made a promise to me. Remember? You begged me to stay and promised me that you would try to make it work. You *promised* to be the Judtson I could love, instead of the freak I can't stand. Well...you'd better listen to this, mister...because it's all up to you. Either you forget about this preposterous and *asinine* fantasy right now and go with me on the cruise...or you can just forget about us."

Before he could respond to her, a tall, handsome waiter, dressed in a tailored black suit and white shirt with a ruffled front, appeared at his elbow. "Good evening. My name is Stormy, and I'll be your server tonight. Is there anything you would like?"

Judtson stole a brief glance at Kristen and saw her eyes flare. Allowing a slight smile to play across his face, he turned to look up at the man. "Why, good evening, *Stormy*. A name which is ridiculously affectatious, by the way, and more fitting for a male stripper than a waiter. My name is Judtson, and *I'll* be your customer. And yes, there is something I'd like. A divorce."

Chapter 17

==========

DETECTIVE CAHANE SPEED-DIALED THE ME'S DIRECT LINE.

The senior pathologist answered brusquely, "Shaffer."

"Morning, Doc. This's Eunice."

The man's voice audibly brightened. "Eunice! How are you?"

"Fair to partly cloudy, Doc. You?"

"Bout the same. Hip's killing me. Thanks for calling back right away."

"Course. What's up?"

"As you asked, I sent two of my boys over to the Feds to pick up the Shields body. Guess what? They'd already transported her to the toaster oven."

"*WHAT?*" Her question was louder than it needed to be by three.

"Uh-huh. They said she had no living relatives and since their investigation was done, they were cremating."

Cahane paused for only a second. "Where?"

"Hang on. I'll look."

She heard a soft rustling of paper until he replied, "Cooper's."

"When?"

"My guy called me a few minutes ago. I guess the body just left."

"Thanks, handsome," she grunted and broke the connection before he could respond. Punching a free line and dialing, she heard an answer and barked, "Dispatch, this is Cahane."

"Go ahead, Detective."

"I want a car sent to Cooper's Mortuary, lights and siren. Dispatch somebody close. I want 'em there quick-like. But I don't want it over the radio. Use the phone."

"What's occurring?"

"Destruction of evidence. When you get somebody rolling, have 'em call me. I'll fill 'em in."

"Will do."

▽

Judtson awoke on the couch in the lobby of his office, his face buried in the thick fur of his golden retriever, Rocky, who was snuggled against him. He nudged his pal down, and still wearing his clothes from the evening before, rolled off the makeshift bed himself, and stumbled groggily to the coffee maker in the small galley kitchen and started a pot brewing. As his loyal companion curled up on the floor and went back to sleep, Judtson headed to the bathroom and, after satisfying the basics, splashed some water on his face and stared into the mirror above the basin, examining his face…looking for an external indication of how he felt, thinking that there should be at least a trace of guilt, sadness, remorse or, at the very least, doubt. Instead, he saw that his visage was a faithful reflection of what he felt inside…dispassion.

The coffee noisily brewing, he returned to the couch and, grabbing the remote, turned on the television. The preset channel was one of the cable news stations and he was tuning in, mid-story, to an analysis of the recent Florida campus shooting. The almost painfully thin female reporter was interviewing a middle-aged couple who were identified by the superimposed bar on the bottom of the screen as Edward and Betty Collins, the parents of the shooter. He turned up the sound as the reporter was asking a question.

"So why do you suspect that?"

The mother, attired in a red blazer over a white dress, emphatically contended, "Because he doesn't remember doing it. Any of it! He remembers sitting in his room, playing a video game. And then he remembers riding in the back of a police car. Nothing in between."

"What do the two of you say to the experts who are claiming on many of the news shows that this is a made-up story to set the stage for a possible insanity defense?"

Before the woman could answer, the father leaned into the microphone. "I tell them they can go to hell. Our son isn't a liar and he damn well isn't a killer."

The mother, more controlled than her husband, added, "They can say what they want. And even if that were true, Sean would tell us. He'd tell us it was just a ploy. He'd know he could count on us to keep his secret. But that isn't what he said. He told us flat out that he had absolutely no memory of getting the gun, going to the campus, and shooting those students. And now we're not able to talk to him about it!"

The reporter moved slightly closer. "I'm not clear about what you mean. Are you saying that they won't allow him to see his own parents while he is in custody?"

"Oh, they'll let us see him," she answered. "But they have him so doped up that he only sits and stares. I really don't think he knows we're there. That's why our lawyer is filing this injunction."

"What injunction is that?"

"To get Sean off whatever medications they've put him on. After his first day in custody, the day we talked to him, they turned him into some kind of a zombie."

As she spoke, the director put up a picture of Sean Collins, handcuffed and wearing a bright orange jumpsuit, as he stood beside his attorney in a courtroom. For all intents and purposes, Judtson thought, the young man looked as if he had recently had a lobotomy; and as he stared at the boy's face, concentrating his attention on the eyes, he felt a sudden, inexplicable shiver.

At that moment, Rocky leapt to his feet and barked as a key turned in the lock of the front door and Ricky promptly entered the lobby.

He immediately spotted his employer on the couch and could tell by the condition of the cushions that he had slept there. "Uh, morning, chief. What's wrong?"

Judtson diverted his eyes from the face of Sean Collins and, hearing the coffee maker sputter its final gasp, stood. "Wrong? Nothing. Well, that isn't exactly right. I'll tell you in a minute. You want some coffee?"

Ricky closed the door, locking it, and hastily crossed the room to the kitchen. "I'll get it. Tell me. What has happened now?"

He followed his assistant, his mind wandering back over the events which had transpired since they had last spoken. "Quite a bit, actually. First off…I left Kristen last night."

About to pour the steaming dark roast into a mug, Ricky paused, taken aback by the news. "What did you just say?"

Leaning nonchalantly against one of the cabinets, Judtson smirked. "I said, I left Kristen. Asked her for a divorce."

"Well…," Ricky stammered, "I don't…I'm not sure what to say."

Trying to set his friend at ease, Judtson allowed a broader smile to spread across his face. "How about 'congratulations'? And I'd like to see that coffee actually pouring into the mug, rather than hovering over it teasingly."

Ricky shook his head in mock frustration, huffed softly, returned his attention to the task, and filled the mug before pouring a second cup for himself.

They both doctored their brews to taste and returned to the front room. Judtson dropped heavily on the couch and tapped the remote, turning off the television, as Ricky sat gingerly on one of the visitor's chairs.

"So aren't you going to react?" Kent asked.

Staring at his boss for half a minute first, Ricky responded circumspectly, "Of course. Congratulations. How do *you* feel about it?"

"That's what's weird. After the way I've been beating myself up for so long, I thought I would feel bad. Only I don't."

Ricky nodded in understanding. "Do you feel…anything?"

"Relief, I guess. That's probably the best way to describe it. I don't know if I ever told you this story…."

"One I've missed! That seems impossible."

"Hey, listening to me was in the job description. Anyway, when I was in college, I had a job at a call center."

Ricky's eyebrows shot upward in surprise. "*You* worked at a call center. Actually calling *strangers* and trying to sell them things. I cannot visualize that in my wildest dreams."

Judtson snorted. "I know. Imagine that, huh? It was college and I needed the money."

"Did you ever sell anyone anything?"

"No. At least not much. And I was constantly called into the manager's office because of customer complaints about me."

"That I can visualize!"

"Thanks a lot. My point is that I hated the job. I hated every minute of it. I hated riding to it. I hated the other people who worked there. I'm sure they hated me, too. During the breaks and lunches, they would all cluster in groups and talk and laugh and make plans together. And I'd be sitting off to the side, alone."

He stopped to allow Ricky time for another sarcastic comment. None came and he could see in his friend's face an incipient trace of sympathy. Ignoring it, he continued, "As I said, I needed the money. I needed that job. I also felt that it wasn't good to quit. I just didn't see myself as a quitter."

Ricky nodded again.

"One day, I finally was rude enough with a customer to get fired. What's bizarre is that as I was being told I was fired, I was absolutely certain that I should feel horrible. I guess I halfway convinced myself at the moment that I did. But, Ricky, as I walked out of that building and out to the bus stop…I didn't even have a car then…I started what I can only describe as giggling. I was laughing! By the time I arrived at the bus bench, I was whooping out loud…I was so happy to be free."

Judtson paused in his narrative, his eyes drifting away and focusing on something unseen in the distance. "Last night, after the dinner with Kristen…as I drove here…I whooped."

His young ally looked at him impassively until Kent finally pressed, "Don't you have a comment or two?"

Ricky's shoulders moved in a subtle shrug. His voice muted, he answered, "I never believed she was the right person for you."

"No kidding? Why?"

"She never really…liked *you*. I don't know what she liked…or thought she loved…except it wasn't the real Judtson Kent I've come to know over the last few years. It was some illusion. Unless it's none of my business, can I ask what finally caused you to pull the trigger?"

Judtson described the dinner, embellishing the subtle and not so subtle nuances, and finished by stating matter-of-factly, "She had done worse in the past. Had been worse. I don't know why last night was enough to do it. But it was."

"Well, if you don't mind my saying so, I'm glad you're not moping about it this morning. That whole guilt thing was painful to watch. You were feeling inculpative, basically about the fact that you were not a different person. That was just dumb."

Kent chuckled at his bluntness. "*Inculpative*…nifty word…I like it. Enough about that. I did have something else to talk to you about. Meant to before and got sidetracked."

"What's that?"

He brought him up to date of the topic of Doni, including her explanation about the glass of tea and the fact that she had walked out on Saylor. After he finished, Ricky whistled. "Wow! In one day you and Saylor are both bachelors. It looks pretty bad that Doni questioned Saylor about the dosage."

"Yes. It does. We didn't get a lot of time to talk about it when Saylor was at the house, because Kristen came out and joined us. But he did tell me that her explanation was that she was merely curious. She said she was wondering if we might get more information from the hostage by adjusting the dosage."

With a skeptical grimace, Ricky asked, "You believe that?"

It was Judtson's turn to shrug. "Don't know. In any case…since you were in the lounge with Al, Lisa, Dylan, and Dean when she poured the tea…and, I guess I should say, supposedly…left it there unattended to get her towel, did you see anyone go near it?"

The young man made a show of thinking back to the day, then sighed. "Wish I could say for sure. I remember her coming in and asking us if we had taken Luis anything recently. We all told her we hadn't. She did say she was going to take him a drink. I was lying on the sofa in there, trying to read. None of us had enough time before we went to the silo to grab any books, so I borrowed one from Luis, and all he had were Army TMs...technical manuals. Talk about boring. The one I was reading was how to operate and maintain a howitzer."

Judtson laughed. "You were reading a technical manual about howitzers?"

"Yes! Since all of the action had started, I decided I should get a little more knowledgeable about...you know...weapons and such. And, more to the point, it was all he had. Anyway, I remember that she poured the tea. I think I remember her leaving. I'm not sure if she left the tea on the counter, but I think so. Then...," he finished the thought sheepishly, "I guess I dozed off. I don't remember her coming back for it and I really can't tell you if any of the others approached the glass. Sorry."

"It is what it is." Judtson's inflection and expression were neutral.

"You're hoping she's innocent, aren't you?"

Kent was startled by the question. "Of course I am. I've known Doni forever. I can't imagine her being some evil...traitor. Why? Aren't you?"

Ricky's mouth twisted in ambivalence. "I suppose so. I like her. I haven't actually known her that long...or that well."

"That's true."

"So...hey, chief! If that's all you wanted to talk to me about, can I show you something?"

"What's that?"

Ricky jumped up from his chair excitedly. "Come on!" He moved to the door and opened it. Judtson, still holding his coffee, followed as his friend trotted down the short walk to the driveway, with Rocky trailing behind them. Sitting beside Kent's bright red Oldsmobile was a shining electric-blue Chevrolet with bumble bee striping, massively wide tires, and an elevated rear end.

"You got a '68 Camaro!" Judtson yelped, running around the vehicle, touching it and taking in the details. "Oh, my God...the carburetion stacks. You got the 396!"

Ricky, standing at the front bumper, beamed. "I did indeed. Crossram intake manifold with dual 4-barrel Holley carburetors, competition 4-speed shifter, double sprung with positraction rear end."

Judtson circled the car and peered inside, abruptly letting out what could only be described as a chortle. "Ricky! There's white fur on the dashboard!"

Turning a tad red, Ricky came around to the side and opened the door for him. "I didn't do that! It was already glued on."

Laughing, Judtson climbed in, caressing the small steering wheel, his eyes darting across the instrument panel. Gleefully, he shouted, "And it has the Tick-Tock-Tach! This is beautiful. Where did you find it?"

"Internet. There are a lot of sites offering classics. I bought it and had it shipped here. I have thirty days to check it out until the deal closes. Want to drive it?"

Judtson looked up at him with youthful exuberance shining from his face. "Can I? I mean, do you mind?"

Moving around to the passenger side, Ricky flipped the seat forward, allowing Rocky to scamper into the back, then taking the passenger seat himself. "Of course not. You've let me drive the Olds. Here."

He handed over the keys, and Judtson cranked up the starter, his ears instantly rewarded with an initial roar of the engine, before it settled into a meaty rumble.

▽

Driving with lights but no siren, Cahane was aggressively working her way through the heavy traffic, when her cell phone rang. She backed her foot off the gas pedal slightly and pulled out the phone, answering it in speaker mode without the benefit of seeing who was calling her.

"Cahane."

"Detective, this is Buddy Gleeson. I'm at Cooper's Mortuary. What's up?"

She was relieved that the first officer on the scene was a patrolman she had known for well over a decade; in fact, the young man's family were friends of hers and she had been influential in the department's decision to hire him. "Buddy, glad it's you. I'll be there lickety-split. Right now, you need to go inside and find out if they have cremated the body of Rosemary Shields."

"Ten-four. And if they haven't popped her in the oven yet?"

"Stop 'em."

"Got it."

She ended the call and jammed down the pedal, rocketing through a gap in the traffic. Within five minutes Cahane arrived at Cooper's. Ignoring the painted parking spaces, she skidded to a stop in front of the entrance and jumped out of the unmarked police car, leaving the lights flashing and her door open. She marched toward the glass double doors as fast as her short legs would propel her, and noticed that a second patrol car was also parked in the lot.

Barging through the entrance, she found Gleeson and another officer she did not recognize, standing with a man in a somber gray suit. She walked up to the three of them.

"Buddy, well?"

Gleeson turned to face her. "Got here in the nick of time."

She focused her attention on the man in the suit and stuck out her hand. "I'm Detective Cahane."

He reached out and shook her hand. "Wilburn Cooper. Would you mind telling me what this is all about, Detective?"

"Not at all. I'm investigating the murder of Rosemary Shields and I need our medical examiners to perform an autopsy."

Cooper nodded energetically. "Of course. Of course. We received the body from the FBI with instructions to cremate. But if are ordering me to turn it over to you, I'd be happy to."

"Consider yourself ordered."

"I will go prepare Miss Shields for transport."

He turned and walked away, and she jerked her head toward Gleeson. "Buddy, go with him. Make sure the bag she ends up in ain't a brown-in-bag."

"You bet, Eunice…I mean, Detective."

He trotted after Cooper, and she pulled out her phone, called the ME's office, and was able to get Shaffer on the line within a minute. Informing him of their status, she requested a transport and he agreed to send someone immediately. Before she could break the connection, the second patrolman tapped her on the shoulder. "We got company."

She turned in the direction of the entrance and saw the two FBI agents who had taken the case away from her that first day at the Shields crime scene. The men, wearing matching dark suits, began to head toward her, determined expressions painted on their faces. Twisting back to the patrolman and glancing at his badge, she muttered in a hushed voice, "Terwilliger, stick close and back me. No matter what. You got that?"

As she returned her attention to the Feds, Cahane heard a soft snicker from the cop. "Sounds like fun."

Hastily opening her tin, she crammed a wad of tobacco in her mouth and walked forward, striding straight at the agents until they both came to a halt. Cahane took another small step, placing herself within inches of the two men. "Well, well, well, if it isn't our friendly and always cooperative colleagues from the Federal Bureau of Investigation. To what do I owe the honor of your presence?"

The taller of the agents, whose name she recalled as Blake, fixed her with his dark, nearly black eyes. "We understand that you are countermanding our orders to cremate the Shields body."

She returned his stare, allowing a slight grin to appear on her face. "Officer Terwilliger, would you mind calling Officer Gleeson on his radio. Tell him to ask Mr. Cooper if he or anyone else at this facility has contacted the FBI since his arrival."

"Yes, ma'am." The patrolman briskly stepped away and keyed the microphone clipped to the epaulet of his shirt. As he talked, Cahane stood her ground, glaring at the two agents. He returned in less than a minute. "No, ma'am. No calls."

She grunted out a series of curt huffs meant to resemble a laugh. "Well, Terwilliger, this is indeed a fortunate day for you. It is not often that you get an opportunity to observe the spooky, mysterious, and almost magical abilities of the FBI."

One of the agents, the shorter man, in a move intended to appear casual, reached up and unbuttoned his coat. A second later, Cahane heard the unmistakable sound as the patrolman unsnapped the leather strap on his service pistol. Her grin shifting into a sneer, and her eyes in steady contact with Blake, she lowered the timbre of her voice, losing the earlier bantering tone. "Perhaps you'd care to share the magic trick with us, and tell the poor southern yokels how you pulled the rabbit out of the hat and found out we were coming to get the evidence before you destroyed it."

Blake spoke through gritted teeth. "We are here on federal business and are under no obligation to answer your questions. Now stand aside."

Cahane's eyes widened. "Whooo-weee! '*Stand aside,*' did you say? Let me tell you how it works down here, buster. You do have...how did you put it...an *obligation* to answer my questions."

"You have no jurisdiction over...."

"SHUT YOUR FAT MOUTH!"

The agent stopped speaking, his lips tightly pursed.

"*Anywho,* like I was saying, you have two choices, Mr. Fancy Pants. You answer my questions and you walk out of here on your own power. You don't...and you'll receive, at no additional cost, an exciting ride in the back of one of our local ambulances."

"Are you threatening a federal officer while in the prosecution of his duties?"

"Yep."

She looked down and spat onto the top of one of his polished shoes.

His hand quickly came up, but he was unable to complete whatever move he had planned, as Eunice Cahane's hand whipped forward and grabbed his wrist, squeezing hard, her fingers digging into the flesh and veins on the underside. Simultaneously, her other hand snaked inside his coat and came out an instant later holding his pistol. The second agent took a step to the side and reached under the lapel of his coat, when Cahane heard the squeak of metal on leather and Terwilliger's voice barked, "DON'T!" She knew she did not need to check behind to see her man with his gun drawn and pointed at the agent.

Tucking Blake's gun into her back pocket, she rose onto her toes, bore down harder on the wrist she was gripping, and leaned even closer to his face. "Gonna ask one last time…and I do mean it's the *last* time…how did you know we were coming?"

The Fed's face was a bright red, his voice flat and low. "The radio. Our offices always monitor local police bands."

She let out a loud sigh and shook her head. "Pity. Before you gave me that answer, the only humiliation you were going to have to deal with was when I posted on Facebook that this short, stubby little woman disarmed an FBI agent. *That* you could've probably lived down eventually. *Listen, doughboy!* Nothing went out on the radio. I made sure of that. There's only one way you could have heard about it, and that's if you were listening to our phones. And that, you miserable piece of corrugated horseshit, is not only illegal, but down here in Georgia, it's also considered to be bad-mannered."

With no warning, she jerked up her knee, burying it deeply in his groin. A high-pitched scream burst from the man as he doubled over. Again making a move for his pistol, the second agent was flash-frozen by the sound of Terwilliger's gun as it was cocked. As the quartet was posed in this outlandish tableau, the double doors at the rear of the lobby burst open and Cahane looked to see that Wilburn Cooper was pushing a gurney which carried a zippered black bag. Buddy Gleeson, taking in the scene, drew his Glock and hastily moved to a position where he could cover the detective and his fellow patrolman.

She released her iron grip on Blake's wrist and stepped back. The agent jerked his now free hand to join his other in cupping himself. Moving to the second agent, making certain not to step into the line between him and Terwilliger, she reached inside his coat and disarmed him. Turning away from the two, she noticed a panicked expression on the undertaker's face but ignored it.

"Buddy, cuff 'em both. I'll hold your piece."

He handed the Glock to her and unsnapped a pouch on the back of his belt, removing a set of handcuffs. As he circled around Blake, who was awkwardly bent forward and groaning, Cahane looked through the glass front doors and saw that the transport ambulance from the medical examiner's office was pulling into the parking lot. Over her shoulder, she instructed, "Mr. Cooper, that's the lady's ride. If you would be so kind as to roll her on out there, I'd be pleased as punch."

Cooper mumbled words she could not understand, and pushed the gurney toward the doors at almost a run.

Gleeson, after he finished handcuffing Blake, moved to the second agent, who had not uttered a word during the takedown, until that moment as he haughtily insisted, "You can't arrest us."

Cahane whirled to face him. "Now, that's the problem with you government boys. You get all kinds of fancy training and classes and degrees and such, except they seem to leave something out of your broad education. That little pesky detail called our Constitution."

She moved one step closer to him. "You know what? Coming down here to our fine state and tapping the phones of law enforcement folks doing their jobs is still…last time I checked… against the law. Buddy!"

"Yeah, Eunice?"

"Since they musta missed those classes…you know, the ones on states' rights and civil liberties…Lord knows what other ones they slept through, so you'd better read 'em their rights. And do it nice and slow 'cause I don't think these two boys are the brightest bulbs in the box."

Chapter 18

L<small>ISA CLOSED THE CONFERENCE ROOM DOOR BEHIND HERSELF</small>, fell back against it and, with a single pump of her fist, shouted, "YES!"

She hurried down the hallway, returning to her own office, pulled the safe phone from her purse, and speed-dialed Judtson. He answered on the second ring. "Hey, Trippy."

She suppressed a laugh. They were again using bogus names over the phones, and this was the first time he had used this moniker for her. "Okay. Trippy, it is, JK. I just got out of a production meeting and I pitched the idea for the show…you know, with the whole gang."

"Yes?"

Her voice rose an octave. "*They loved it!* Not only that…they want to do it quickly. While the story is still hot."

"How quickly?"

"Don't know yet. They might reschedule something else. So it could be…days! Not weeks."

Judtson hesitated before speaking. "Well, we need to figure out the logistics of getting everyone together."

"I know. I know. But let's get it going. Make sure everybody is ready to roll."

▽

Carlos Villarreal tore his eyes away from the computer monitor, rubbed them vigorously, and swiveled in his chair to stare at the courtyard and fountain outside the window of his study. One of two multi-hued parrots, which had been purchased by the previous owner, was perched on a branch directly within his line of sight, and he watched it primp for several minutes, while allowing his fatigued eyes and overtaxed mind a brief respite.

Since his return from Atlanta with the lab results, he had been working as a man possessed, attempting to structure the paper he was writing such that it would be unassailable by the inevitable critics and skeptics in the scientific community. In the aftermath of the previous fiasco, he had made the choice to release his findings through the conventional channels of archaeological discoveries...science journals...knowing the travails this move would initiate.

Alone in his sprawling hacienda in La Paz, he tittered softly to himself, thinking, *What has happened to my beloved science?*

The singular aspect of the discipline which had so strongly attracted him in his youth...the precept which had been repeated throughout his education by his numerous professors as if it were a mantra...the principle which was proclaimed a fundamental cornerstone of science... was absolute objectivity: the promise that, in the practice of pure science, discoveries which could be verified, authenticated, and replicated would always be welcomed, accepted, and taken at face value.

Although he had heard whispers to the contrary from some of the seasoned archaeologists under whom he had worked as a postgraduate student and as a postdoctoral aide, he had always assiduously ignored the murmurs, preferring to believe the proclaimed truth. Once established in the field, Villarreal found that his initial work had reinforced this belief. It was not until he had published a very minor discovery, a discovery which dared to contradict the dogma of his chosen specialty...the finding of a large and unexpected cache of ancient pottery...that he witnessed, and suffered firsthand, the bared fangs of his colleagues.

It was in the course of this tempest in a tea kettle, as far as the rest of the world was concerned, that he came to a disquieting and disheartening conclusion. As the avalanche of savage rebuttals engulfed him, he scoured the vicious feedback, searching for the specific indictment which would illuminate for him the error he had made in his methodology. There was none. In the volumes written to debunk and discredit his findings, not a single scientist had commented on an actual flaw in his work. All that was written...all that was said...comprised *personal* attacks, including an accusation Carlos Villarreal absolutely could not tolerate, the suspicion that he had planted the items himself to gain fame in the field.

It had been a very dark time for Carlos. It felt as if the proverbial rug had been pulled from beneath him and, hoping for solace, he sought out a retired professor whom he had always admired. After three aborted treks from his car, Carlos finally worked up the courage to knock on the man's front door. Gabriel Sanchez swung it open and, not at all surprised by the arrival, smiled in a grandfatherly way at his former protégé.

"Carlos, I've been expecting you."

The two sat in the library, drinking sangria and talking for hours, while painstakingly avoiding the main topic, until it was finally reluctantly broached by Villarreal. "Professor Sanchez, why are they doing this to me? I merely did the work. I did it right. And I did it well. Carefully. Methodically. Just as you taught me to do. It is not my fault that I found what I found."

The old man sat back deeply in the wing-back chair and took a sip from his wine before answering. "No, my young friend. You are correct. It is not your fault that you found a cache of pottery that, according to the accepted explanation of prehistoric migrations, should not have been present in all of South America. What *is* your fault is that you dared to share the information with the world."

"But...that is not how science is!"

The professor shook his head dismissively. "Regrettably, you are wrong. That is exactly how it is. And it is exactly how it has always been. In our entire history, there has never been a single time when a scientist, in any of the subfields, could challenge the accepted dogma of the day and be heralded rather than assailed. You can no more upset the apple cart by finding this cache of impossible pottery than an Islamic mullah could share a discovery that Mohammed did not, indeed, rise to heaven. It cannot be tolerated and it will not be allowed."

Carlos, beaten, weary, and half-inebriated from the wine, struggled to grasp the full import of his mentor's words. "Then why did you teach me that this was not so? Why did you pound into my head something which is nothing but an illusion about science?"

He thought that his words would sting Sanchez. They did not. Instead, the man smiled benignly. "Because I hoped, in my lifetime of teaching, that I could break the cast. That I, and others such as myself, could make this *promise* of science…a reality."

Villarreal's retrospective of that distant evening was interrupted by the shrill ringing of his safe phone, which he had never stopped carrying with him. Reading the screen, he smiled and answered, "Hello, Lisa!"

"Carlos! How are you?"

"I am well. And you?"

"Doing okay. Hey, after talking to Judtson about everything going on, I decided it would be a good idea to get everyone together and do a live show. You know…to correct all of the misinformation out there."

He tilted back in his chair, stared blankly at the computer screen displaying the paper he was struggling to write, and thought for a few seconds. "That is actually an excellent idea. When would this program be broadcast?"

"Don't have an air date nailed down yet, but the powers that be want it soon. Very soon!"

"Have you spoken with the others yet? Will they be able to participate?"

"Working my way through the list, Carlos. So far Dean, Jimmy, Judtson, and Dylan are on board. Of course, Chris won't be on the show."

"No? Why not?"

There was a momentary silence. "You haven't heard? I assumed Judtson would let you know. Chris has been kidnapped."

The news stunned Villarreal. "Kidnapped! My God. What happened? When?"

She briefed him on the details obtained from Kent. After they exhausted the topic, he voiced his concern. "It sounds as if we must now all be on guard."

"That's for sure."

"What about Bal? Have you made contact with him yet?"

"Not yet. His phone doesn't work down there and he only has intermittent email service."

"Did you mean that he is down here? Where is he?"

"Sorry, I thought you would know. He's in your neck of the woods. He set up a camp next to the quarry by Lake Titicaca to resume his work."

"No, I did not know that."

"Is that close to you? Maybe you could take a drive out there and let him know I need to speak with him."

"It is not too distant. Perhaps I will do that tomorrow."

They engaged in a few minutes of idle chat, then ended the call with a promise to stay in closer contact, and Carlos put away the cell phone. Before his mind could dwell upon the significance of Chris Ashby's abduction, the telephone on his desk, which did not display the caller's identification, rang.

"Villarreal residence, Dr. Villarreal speaking."

"Uh, hello, Doctor. This is Marty with R & W Labs in Atlanta."

"Yes, Marty. What can I do for you?" Carlos replied, his brow furrowing vaguely.

"I work in the mail room and I wanted to check to see if you got the bound reports we sent."

"I apologize, Marty. I am confused. I remained at your lab in Atlanta until the reports were generated, and left with them. To what reports are you referring?"

There was a brief hesitation and the voice returned. "It was...uuhh...yes, here it is. You ordered a full set of the lab findings and had the package sent to you."

His voice rising slightly in pitch, Carlos declared, "I ordered nothing of the sort. Where were the reports sent? The address, please."

After another pause, Marty provided the number of a post-office box in Chicago. Not recognizing the address, Villarreal felt his back and neck muscles tighten and he unconsciously scanned his surroundings.

After a while, the mail clerk asked, "Dr. Villarreal, are you on the line?"

"Uh, yes. I am sorry. When was the package sent?"

"We overnighted it yesterday. It should have arrived this morning. Is there a problem?"

"No. Not at all. Thank you for following up."

He broke the connection before the clerk could respond, saved his current work both on a flash drive and on the hard drive, and turned off the computer. He began gathering his papers and notes, including the original lab findings, noticed that his passport was still on the stack where he had tossed it upon returning home, and stuffed everything into a metal briefcase. Finishing that, he pulled out the cell phone to call Judtson, replacing it a split second later.

"This is absurd," he muttered aloud. "I am simply being paranoid."

$$\triangledown$$

Carlos finished the light dinner he had prepared for himself and roamed the large house to check the windows and doors, his mind repeatedly drifting to unbidden images...images which frightened him. As the hacienda completely surrounded the center courtyard, with a full array of windows and doors facing inward as well as outward, battening it down was not a minor task. Passing through the master suite, he paused for a moment and engaged in a mental struggle between his rational mind and the instincts triggered by the phone call. The latter winning over, he opened a small built-in cabinet in his closet and removed a 9mm semi-automatic pistol. Making certain the clip was full, he tucked the pistol in his waistband behind his back and continued checking the home.

Satisfying himself that all was secure, Carlos returned to the master bedroom, armed the dual-alarm system, placed the gun on the nightstand, and prepared for bed.

His sleep was rudely interrupted hours later by the insistent buzzing, vibrating signal from the device under his pillow. Instantly, his body was flooded with adrenaline, a reaction to the knowledge that the under-pillow alarm was a secondary system, battery-powered and independent of the house electricity, and tripped solely by motion detectors located inside. The fact that it was alerting him could only mean that an intruder had disabled the primary system and had already entered.

Shutting off the device, he listened carefully for any telltale sounds of the invader. Hearing nothing, he rolled silently out of the bed, snatched up the pistol, flipped off the safety, and jacked a round into the chamber. Holding the gun in his right hand, he grabbed the briefcase with his left and silently crossed the dark bedroom by memory, entering his walk-in closet.

He carefully set the case on the floor and felt the top of a shelf, finding the three-button switch. Working by feel, he pressed each of the buttons in the correct sequence, and a hidden latch in the rear wall of the closet clicked. Lifting the briefcase, he scurried through the concealed opening to a small landing at the top of a descending staircase, pushing the panel closed behind. First making certain the lock was fully engaged, he found the wall switch, turning on the lights and flipping a toggle which deactivated the entry buttons he had just used on the other side. Now the panel could not be opened, even if the person knew the code. With his ear against the door, he listened but heard no sounds coming from his bedroom.

The stairs led down to a narrow room, constructed of gray concrete blocks, and containing only a table, two chairs, a small closet, a flat-screen television, and a single door. Placing the gun and case on the table, Carlos turned on the television, which was actually a security monitor connected to the combination daylight/low-light cameras around and inside his home, and powered by a backup battery system. As he thumbed the remote to scroll through the views, he said a silent "thank you" to the previous owner of the house for his paranoia when he had lived there.

The greenish low-light view of the long hallway outside his bedroom appeared on the screen, and he saw three men completely clad in snug black bodysuits. He watched in detached fascination as the trio methodically worked their way down the hallway, stopping to check and clear each of the rooms along their route. The cameras were equipped with microphones, and he turned up the volume, detecting only silence. Clearly, the men were experienced and worked without speaking.

As they reached the door to his bedroom, he switched views to the interior of the room. From that view, he noticed that only one of the three entered his room and, without saying a single word, raised his arm and pointed a pistol at the bed. From the speaker, Carlos heard the suppressed *pfft…pfft…pfft* of three shots aimed into the jumbled pile of sheets and blankets. His blood ran cold as he grasped that he was witnessing…his own execution…if not for the precautions he had used.

Following the attack, there was a flurry of movement on the screen. The shooter switched on a flashlight and pulled back the covers. Seeing that his target was not in the bed, he shouted this fact to his accomplices, ordering a full search of the house.

Carlos, deciding it was time to move, copied the video to a flash drive, shut off the monitor, and hurried to the small closet where he undressed and donned a black sweatshirt, black slacks, and black running shoes. Jamming his pistol into the waistband at the small of his back, he snatched up a prepacked travel suitcase, retrieved the metal briefcase from the table, and opened the only door in the room. On the other side was a tunnel, which he had only traveled through to the end twice since purchasing the home. At a full trot, his footfalls muffled by the rubber soles of the running shoes, he traversed the length of the passage. Arriving at the end, a full one hundred and twenty meters outside the perimeter wall of his house, he reached the ladder and, dropping the suitcase and valise on the dirt floor, rapidly climbed up to a wooden lid.

The two latches were stiff from rust, and caused him to skin the knuckles on his right hand. After opening the locks, he rose one more rung on the ladder so that he was bent over, and put his shoulder against the wood, pushing upward with his legs, and encountering more resistance than he expected. With a thump and clatter, the lid suddenly flew open. Laying it flat, he returned to the bottom of the ladder and grabbed his briefcase, taking it up and setting it on the floor beside the hatch. He then hurried down for the suitcase and brought it up. Climbing completely out of the hole, he closed the lid.

As he had expected, Carlos found himself in a small shack and thought back to recall the layout. Remembering, he stepped around in a small circle while waving his hands above his head until one of them felt the light brush of a string. Catching it, he pulled down and a naked bulb in a ceramic base illuminated the room. He was inside a maintenance shack which had been built for the adjacent park. Still breathing heavily from the run and his brush with death, Carlos paused to take in his surroundings, noticing a wheelbarrow lying on its side next to the hatch, its load of rakes and shovels spilling onto the floor, and figured out that it had been parked upon the lid.

"Glad they had not stacked bags of concrete on it," he sighed.

He knew that the door to the shack was normally openable from the inside without a key, but his new worry was whether they had, at some point, added a hasp and padlock on the outside. He turned the knob and was relieved when the door opened, revealing the dark, grassy area surrounding the building. He returned for his two pieces of luggage, pulled the string to turn off the light, and departed.

As he began to follow a path in the moonlight, Carlos glanced back in the direction of his home, finding that it was not visible through the dense trees and foliage, and wondered what the three men were now doing. The night was quiet and clear. His senses heightened from the close call earlier, he jumped at each rustle or snap of a branch from the underbrush lining his route. He quickened his pace, albeit not overly concerned that his assailants had found the escape passage in the closet, and wished that he had been able to bring his cell phone.

The park, through which he meandered, was not large, and soon he emerged on the opposite side and immediately spotted a welcome sight…a neighborhood market with pumps for gasoline and, most thankfully, a pay phone. As he crossed to it, he saw that the market was closed for the night. Setting the luggage at his feet, he lifted the handset on the phone and automatically searched in his pocket for money before remembering that his wallet and cash were back at his home.

Replacing the handset in its cradle, he knelt beside the suitcase, laid it down flat, opened it in the circle of light from the phone stand, and chuckled aloud, recalling the day when he had packed the bag. Knowing the previous owner's reasons for the escape tunnel, Carlos had felt silly equipping it for himself, certain he would never have a need for such a setup.

Then, one evening he was giving a friend a tour of the tunnel and she had peppered him with questions: "If you have to sneak out in the middle of the night, what are you going to wear? Won't you need shoes? What about money? And credit cards?"

After they had returned to the house, and sometime between the second and third bottle of wine, she told him she was worried that one of the previous owner's enemies, freshly released from prison, might return with revenge on his mind, not aware that the house now belonged to Carlos. Although he knew that he would typically laugh off such a possibility, the quantity of alcohol coursing through his brain made her concern sound quite reasonable, and he allowed her to talk him into making emergency escape preparations that night. The two, laughing and indulging in spy fantasies, stocked the closet and filled the suitcase with all of the items she determined he might need if he was "on the lam," as she put it.

Slipping the cheap plastic wallet out of the side pouch, he murmured, "Thank you, my dear Leanora."

The phone accepted credit cards and he slid one into the slot, waiting for the preauthorization to appear on the screen and listening for the dial tone. Utilizing directory assistance, he was connected with a taxi service.

▽

Chris Ashby had no idea where he was. After he had been kidnapped from his own car on the interstate, his abductors had kept a hood over his head, then later drugged him. Since regaining consciousness, he had seen little except the four walls of his cell. There was a lone small window, perhaps twelve inches on each side, placed too high on the wall for him to be able to see the surrounding terrain. Other than the sky, all that was visible through it was a portion of what appeared to be a massive white satellite dish.

They questioned him daily. Even for these sessions, he was not allowed to see any other portion of whatever facility he was being held within, since the two men came to him. One asked the questions as the other stood in the hallway outside the doorway, watching.

There had been no roughing up, no torture, no truth-inducing drugs, for which he was grateful. On the other hand, he thought, there had been no reason to withhold the information they sought, at least no reason which made sense to him, so he had been completely forthcoming with his answers. The unexpected side effect of his behavior during these sessions was that the questioner, it seemed, had warmed to him slightly. Chris doubted they were destined to become buddies; however, a trace of cordiality had developed between them. The civility of the interactions did not extend to the point where the man had revealed as much as his first name, despite repeated requests, so Chris had taken to calling him "Freddie."

He had finished his lunch of a prepackaged ham and cheese sandwich, a bag of chips, and a bottled water, and was waiting for the two men, surprised that he was actually looking forward to their arrival, the only real break in his routine. To no avail, he checked the sandwich packaging, hoping to find a hint as to the city or state in which he was being held.

The narrow view slot in the metal door slid open, and his captor peered in before sliding it closed and unlocking the door.

Chris greeted him as he entered. "Hi, Freddie."

With a slight, wry smile, the man answered, "Good afternoon, Dr. Ashby," and took the seat opposite him at the small table. Glancing over Freddie's shoulder, Chris saw the second of the team, whom he had dubbed "Elmo," take his place just outside the open door.

As he was set to begin the interview, Freddie's phone suddenly played the Star Wars theme. He pulled it out and glanced at the screen, tapping it once and dragging the heel of his thumb across it. Whatever message was displayed had clearly displeased him as his brow furrowed briefly. Tapping the screen again to clear it, he set the iPhone down on the tabletop and twisted in his chair to face the door and Elmo.

"That was our southern team…," he began, asking his associate to follow up on something, and being careful to use the vaguest of terms in front of Ashby. He need not have bothered, as the chemist's attention was riveted to the small screen on the phone. The message which had upset his interviewer was gone; however, what caught his eye was the small icon for an app called Compass.

Taking a fleeting look up, he saw that Freddie was turned in his chair and fully facing his partner in the doorway. Luckily, the man's body completely blocked Elmo's view of the phone. Without hesitating, Chris reached forward and tapped the icon. The iPhone immediately displayed a box containing the latitude and longitude of the phone's current location, and he was intensely thankful that over the years he had cultivated an excellent ability to recall seemingly meaningless jumbles of letters and numbers, a trait which came in handy in his field.

After repeating the coordinates back to himself to make certain he had them right, Ashby again tapped the screen, closing the app seconds before the man turned back to him, and then clasping his hands together just in time. Freddie glanced down at his phone and, for a moment, a frown appeared on his face. Noting that the main screen was still displayed, with no sign that his hostage had touched it, he began his questioning, focusing on the scrubbing process Chris had used to purify the monoatomic gold.

For the next hour, as Ashby calmly and honestly answered the questions, a part of his mind repeated and re-repeated the latitude and longitude, in an attempt to burn the location into his brain, when he was startled by an abrupt change of subject.

"Dr. Ashby, I asked you before…have there been any discussions between you and Matt Wheeler or the others in your group as to why our attempt to recondition you at the FEMA camp failed?"

Chris' mind instantly returned to the scene in the small room when the headset had been placed upon him and he had fully expected to be exiled once again to mental oblivion, only to find that the procedure had failed.

"No. Well, I mean, we did speak about it, but Mr. Wheeler and the others had no idea why it hadn't worked. I'm surprised that you don't know."

His captor did not respond to the comment, saying instead, "We've basically exhausted our list of questions for you. The only thing remaining is to solve that issue. I do sincerely hope that you are being candid with us on this topic."

"I am. Why wouldn't I be?"

Freddie shrugged. "Let me put it this way, Dr. Ashby. A possibility always exists that the device we used on you that day was malfunctioning. To rule that out, we are going to attempt it again with a thoroughly tested one. If that fails, we will have no choice other than to take more aggressive measures to determine the problem."

He delivered the statement in a flat, matter-of-fact tone without a hint of threat, yet the words chilled Ashby. "What do you mean by 'aggressive measures'?"

"That's not for me to say. I should tell you that a neurosurgeon has been brought in."

Chris' mind quickly filled with hideous images. "I've already told you that Matt's best guess was that his gizmo, along with the FDG, somehow made us immune to reconversion…or reconditioning, as you called it. Doesn't that make sense? Doesn't it tell you what you need?"

The man again shrugged. "It isn't up to me. As I mentioned, we've asked you all of the questions we had and, from what we can tell, you've been quite direct in answering them."

Ashby, understanding the message, now wished that he had been less compliant, not to the point where they might have hurt him to get the answers, but at least to have bought himself more time.

Freddie stood. "We'll be back tomorrow. I strongly suggest, Dr. Ashby, that if you can think of anything else which might help us, now would be an excellent time to share it."

Chris simply nodded and said nothing. The man left, locking the door behind himself, and Ashby, severely agitated, paced furiously, ending each circuit with a plaintive glance out the small window at the sky, the satellite dish, and freedom. Several minutes elapsed and he tired of the pointless exercise and moved to the cot, flopping down on his back, and stared at the ceiling as his mind raced. *Great! They're going to cut me open and poke around to try to figure out why their damnable machine doesn't work. Well, I guess I'm lucky. That must be the real reason why I was taken alive. The details about my work haven't been exactly revelatory. They need to know what Matt did to us to make us immune.*

Closing his eyes, he fought to calm his rapid, panicked breathing as he once again tried to come up with a way to escape or otherwise get word to the others about where he was. He was certain they knew he had been taken, but was equally certain they had no idea where to look for him.

At least now I have the location! For all the good it does!

It was a shame, he reflected, that Freddie had not actually walked out of the room for a minute, leaving his phone behind. That would have been a perfect opportunity for him to make a quick call to Romeo or one of the others.

A recurring thought returned. *Starlight must be going nuts worrying about me.*

He wondered what she was doing at that moment and decided she was probably at her crystal shop in Venice Beach. To take his mind off his sister and the frightening images his mind was conjuring, Ashby turned his focus back to the string of letters and numbers which represented the exact spot in the world where he was being held prisoner.

▽

Starlight flipped the hanging "open" sign and locked the public door to her shop. As she walked to the rear, Annalee, who was waiting for her, assured, "Don't worry, Starlight. I'm sure he's fine."

Ashby's sister wrung her hands and hurried past her friend to the small table in the back room where two of her other friends were sitting. "God, I hope so. I haven't been able to sleep or eat or…anything!"

She and Annalee took the two remaining seats, completing the circle, and Starlight lit the candle in the center of the table. The four women grasped one another's hands, creating a closed circuit.

"I can't thank all of you enough for coming here. I have been worried sick about Chris."

In a soothing near-whisper, Annalee comforted her, "We know, Starlight. We're all here to help. And our power, driven by the pureness of your love, will be multiplied many times beyond our four."

Almost hypnotically, she continued speaking, thanking spirit for their gifts and asking for help in their search. Finishing the preamble to the seance, Annalee fell quiet and the four bowed their heads in silent meditation, within which they remained for several minutes before Ruth, the oldest of the four, gasped, "I have him! I have Chris!"

Starlight's eyes snapped open and she stared over the candle at her spiritual sister, waiting.

"I have him! I have him! Oh, Starlight, he's fine. He is not hurt. Not in pain of any sort."

"Where is he?" she blurted.

Ruth squeezed her eyes closed and knitted her brows for half a minute. "I…can't…tell. He is alone. Of that I am fairly sure. All I can see is a darkness…wait! It's dark because his eyes aren't open. He is alone in a room where he has been since he disappeared and he is lying down…and his eyes are tightly shut. He is fine, although he is…he is very scared."

Whipsawed by conflicting emotions, with tears filling her eyes and spilling down her cheeks, Starlight whispered urgently, "But where? Where is he?"

Frustration etched deeply on the psychic's face, Ruth shook her head. "I'm sorry. I don't know. I can't tell where he is. I am getting two messages from him. The first is a single word. The word is repeated over and over and over again."

"What is the word, Ruth?" Annalee urged gently.

"I'm getting 'dish.' He keeps saying 'dish...dish...dish.' That's it."

Starlight, her voice more shrill than Annalee's, begged, "Dish? What kind of dish?"

Ruth shook her head, as if to clear it. "I don't know. That is all I get."

Annalee spoke again. "Ruth, you said you were getting two things. What is the other?"

Her frustration nearly overwhelming her, Ruth had tears welling up in her eyes as she sobbed, "I'm so sorry, Starlight. The rest is...gibberish."

"Gibberish? What do you mean? Another language? Chris doesn't...."

"No! It is not another language, just...numbers...and...some letters."

Feeling as if she would explode with anxiety, Starlight prodded, "Can you see them?"

"Y...yes."

"Ruth, can I break the chain to get a pen and paper...or will you lose him?"

"No. It's fine. Go."

Starlight released her grip on the two women beside her, who both quickly reached across the table and took each other's hand to reclose the circle. She jumped up. Grabbing a pad and pen from the counter, she returned and, with pen poised, encouraged her friend to focus. "What are they? Tell me the numbers and letters."

Ruth gulped in a massive breath and clamped her jaw shut, clenching her teeth while pressing her eyes even more tightly closed. In a hoarse whisper, she uttered, "Thirty-four...four...twenty-seven point zero four and then the letter n."

Starlight madly wrote it all down.

Ruth continued, "One hundred and seven...thirty-seven...twenty-nine point twenty-five and then the letter w. Thirty-four...four...twenty-seven point...no, wait, stop. It's just repeating."

"Ruth, are you certain you got it right?"

"Yes. The sequence keeps coming. Over and over."

She opened her eyes and sighed loudly. "That's it. That's all of it. I've...I've lost him."

The three women let go of one another's hands and all leaned forward to stare at the message.

"What could it be?" Starlight asked anxiously.

The four stared at the string, suggesting and discarding various possible explanations, for the majority of an hour before giving up. Finally, Starlight seized her cell phone and speed-dialed a number. When she heard an answer, she let out her breath and began, "Saylor...this is Starlight. I have something. But I'm not sure what it is or what it means."

$$\triangledown$$

The surveillance technician, hearing the audible ping from his system, paused and minimized the active screen and manipulated the mouse to click on the flashing icon labeled "Ashby, S." A transcription file opened. Taking two minutes to read the text first, he chuckled to himself and opened the intranet messaging module, then typed a brief cover note:

Attached is a captured telephone conversation between Starlight Ashby, Dr. Chris Ashby's sister, and Dr. Saylor Costello. In summary, she is relaying a psychic message from her brother. Have fun with this one.

He dispatched the communique up the ladder and returned to the video game he had been playing.

Chapter 19

$\mathbf{T}$HE TAXI BOUNCED OVER THE BADLY RUTTED DIRT ROAD to the edge of the encampment. Carlos was planning on paying the driver to wait until he was certain this was the right place, when he saw Bal and three others crossing the open area toward him. Stuffing a generous handful of bolivianos into the driver's hand, more than enough to cover the long trip from La Paz, he snatched up his briefcase and bag, climbing out just as the small group arrived.

"Carlos!" Bal nearly shouted. "What a surprise!"

Villarreal took a brief glance at the others and said, "My friend, coming here was a surprise to me, as well. Perhaps we could find a place to speak."

Singh looked at him questioningly. "Of course. We can use my tent." He turned to face the others. "This is...."

Carlos reached out and touched Bal's arm, interrupting him. "I would appreciate it if we could perform introductions at a later time."

The geologist's expression changed rapidly from curiosity to concern. "Yes. Yes. At dinner." Clearing his throat, he addressed the students circumspectly. "If you would all be so kind as to excuse us."

The three, staring at Villarreal with unconcealed perturbation at being dismissed, drifted away.

Bal relieved his guest of the suitcase and they began walking toward the camp. "Carlos, what is it? Is something wrong?"

"Yes. Very much so. We have much to discuss." He said nothing further until they were inside and had zipped the entrance flap closed. Singh motioned for his colleague to sit on the only chair, while he perched on the edge of his cot. Speaking softly, Carlos began by telling Bal about the attempt on his life. Singh reacted with a look of shock but remained silent as Villarreal proceeded to brief him on the other events, including Chris Ashby's abduction. When the narrative was concluded, Bal finally spoke. "I was afraid this was not over."

"It appears that you are correct. And as they have killed this Rosemary Shields, kidnapped

Chris, and tried to kill me, none of us, including you, are safe."

"Carlos, we need to warn the others."

"Yes. And we must do it quickly. I decided to come to prepare you. Now I need to return to La Paz and contact Judtson so that he can spread the word."

Singh stood abruptly. Villarreal pretended not to notice that the man's hands were shaking. "I have a truck. I will drive you. But I was thinking...."

"Yes?"

"Should we...should we band together? I know I am vulnerable out here. And you obviously cannot return to your home."

"Are you suggesting that we should return to the States?"

"I am. There might be safety in numbers."

Carlos considered the option for a moment. "Or we might simply be making it easier for them if we are all in one location."

"That is a chance I will take."

Villarreal agreed and Singh immediately began to pack. Hastily filling a single bag, he left Carlos for a few minutes while he sought out Sam, finding him in the community tent. Bal explained that he needed to leave for several days or perhaps even longer, and that Sam would be in charge at the site.

"Do you need me to drive you?"

"That will not be necessary. I will leave my truck at the airport for my return."

The young man accepted the sudden change calmly and asked, "Are you going to take our video with you?"

"Oh, yes. Of course. And, Sam, there is one other thing. I cannot go into great detail, but it would be advisable if you took additional measures for the security of the camp...for the workers and students."

His eyes widened in response. "You can't tell my why? Does this have something to do with your previous...ordeal?"

Bal nodded.

"You can count on me, Professor. I grew up around guns and we have a few here. I'll round up some more in town and see who among our group of sissies knows how to use one. Anything else?"

"Yes. I would like you to proceed with our efforts to find a way into the underground void. That should be your highest priority."

It was the aide's turn to nod, and the two parted.

▽

"You did what? Arrested two FBI agents?"

The barked questions came from Cahane's captain. He stood and circled from behind his desk, closing the door to his office.

"Yep. Sure did."

The man returned to his seat. "I know that even though I am your supervisor, you've always felt it presumptuous of me to question you, but...*why?*"

"They committed a felony."

"A fel.... Which one?"

She grinned at him, clearly enjoying herself. "Wiretapping."

The captain pulled in a huge breath and blew it out loudly, leaning back in his chair. "Eunice, they're the Feds. They are big brother. Wiretapping is what they do."

"Well, I think that might be part of the problem...nobody stands up to 'em. Everybody lets 'em run roughshod over us. Lester, they've been listening in on me, probably you, and Lord knows who else."

His eyebrows shot up. "They tapped you?"

"Damn right they did."

"How do you know?"

She described the sequence of events, emphasizing that none of the communications had occurred over the radio. "Lester, there is no way they could have known so quick that we were going to grab the body, unless they were listening to my phone."

Her boss rested his elbows on the arms of the chair and steepled his fingers in front of his face, closing his eyes as he mentally worked his own way through the events, searching for a loophole in her reasoning. She waited patiently. Reaching a conclusion, he leaned forward. "It looks like you might be onto something. And you know damn well we won't be able to hold them."

She shrugged. "I know. But, man, did it feel good watching the cuffs getting slapped on those arrogant pieces of pond scum."

He shook his head disapprovingly. "I'm glad you enjoyed it, Eunice. Hope you enjoyed it a lot, because now the whole world is gonna come crashing down on us. Hell, the chief has already heard from the DOJ. They're talking about sending a team down here to audit us. They haven't done that since the late sixties. And they want your ass fired...well, suspended."

"So suspend me," she commented flippantly and, as an afterthought added, "with pay, of course."

He could not help grinning at her. "You want me to send you home?"

"Yep."

He stared hard at her. "Eunice...what in blazes is going on?"

She allowed her eyes to sweep around his office meaningfully. "Can't say." She followed her terse comment with a subtle jerk of the head in the direction of the door. "You about done with me?"

Understanding, the captain responded, keeping his voice even and controlled. "I guess. Well, Eunice, you leave me no choice but to suspend you...with pay" – he winked at her – "effective immediately. Turn over your badge and gun."

"Yes, sir."

She stood and began pulling out the two items, when he waved her off from the act, silently. Doing her best to sound dejected, she asked, "Is that all, sir?"

"For now. Stay available. I'm sure we'll be having a disciplinary hearing soon."

Cahane rolled her eyes and had to fight back a guffaw. "No problem, sir."

"Dismissed."

She turned and made a show of stomping out, loudly slamming the door behind herself, and crossed the bullpen area, heading straight for the elevators.

▽

Forty-five minutes later, the captain walked into the dimly lit tavern, his eyes searching the room, and spotted Cahane in a rear booth. Stopping at the bar, he bought a beer and walked toward her. He slid onto the opposite bench and was about to greet her, when Cahane held up a note she had scrawled on a cocktail napkin: "Take the battery out of your phone."

He looked at her and raised one eyebrow quizzically, but pulled out his cell phone and popped out the battery, then asked, "Eunice, what the hell is going on?"

Crumpling the note in her fist and keeping her voice several decibels lower than her usual volume, she said, "Before we get into that, Lester, what's the status on the body?"

"You had it pegged. They showed up at the ME's office almost immediately and already had a writ for the Shields corpse."

She chuckled. "Bet they were madder than a bobtailed horse at a manure plant."

"That they were."

"Did they buy it that we'd misplaced her body?"

"Of course not. Not for a single second. But there wasn't much they could do."

"By the way, Lester, where did Doc Shaffer have them take her?"

Now it was the captain who laughed. "You aren't going to believe this. The VA hospital. He figured they're so fouled up that even if they did catch on to what he was doing, it would take six months until they told the right person. He's doing the autopsy there now."

She suddenly became concerned. "None of this has been discussed over the radio or on any phones, has it?"

"Nope. Just like you told us to do…Gleeson rode with the body to the VA. Once the doc started, Buddy came to the station and told me face to face."

"Not in your…?"

"I'm not stupid, Eunice. No. Not in my office. We had a little conference at the urinals."

She nodded, satisfied.

"Now, will you please tell me what the hell is going on?"

She silently appraised this man, who had been both her boss and close friend for many years. "Lester, I'm not sure you want to hear it. I know you. You're gonna want to jump into it with both feet and you've got your pension and…."

"Dammit, Eunice!"

She held up her hands defensively. "Okay, okay. But hang on to your seat."

▽

The new member of the security team, Chili, answered the door. Judtson, not having met the man yet, looked him over. He was approximately Judtson's height of 6'2", although he probably outweighed him by twenty or thirty pounds, all of which, Kent decided, was pure muscle. His most distinguishing trait was his hair: jet black and impossibly thick, cut longish and shaggy, and piled on the top of his skull in a style verging on a cross between a pompadour and a haystack, adding inches to the impression of his height. His face was accented by wide mutton-chop sideburns, which Judtson had not seen on anyone other than Elvis impersonators.

The man's voice startled him as he had expected it to be deep and resonant, rather than the somewhat thin, reedy-sounding tone which came out as he asked, "Are you Mr. Kent?"

He nodded and extended his hand. "I am. And you must be Chili."

They shook. The guard's grip was gentle, almost offending Judtson as it was probably the lower-intensity version that Chili reserved for old women and children.

"That's me. Come in."

Prudently resisting the urge to point out the grammatical error, Judtson followed. "Is Chili a nickname?"

"Uh-huh. My last name's Keyliss. My sergeant in the Corps was a Hispanic guy. He thought it would be funny. Some Mexican meal with that name. Anyway, it stuck."

As Judtson was beginning to respond, Kelsey burst around a corner at a near run. "Judtson! Hey!"

She came to an awkward, skidding stop on the Italian marble floor, just inches away, and he reached out and took her by the arm to steady her. Chili excused himself and left the two alone in the living room.

"I would have met you at the door, but I was...."

He was surprised at exactly how glad he was to see her. "It's fine, Kelsey."

Rocky ran straight to her and she dropped to one knee to greet him. The golden eagerly rolled onto his back, inviting the inevitable belly rub. She obliged for a minute before saying to Judtson, "Come and sit down."

She motioned toward the burgundy velour sofa, which was accented with a cream-colored fringe trimming the bottom.

"You actually sit on this?" he asked, gently lowering onto the overstuffed cushion.

"Uh-huh. Why?" She sat down beside him, and Rocky positioned himself strategically between their knees.

"It looks too beautiful to sit on, that's all."

"Thanks. So, what's up?"

Knowing that his news would darken the moment, he hesitated, if only briefly. "I received a call from Carlos. Actually from Carlos *and* Bal."

She accurately assessed his expression. "Are they all right?"

"Yes. For now. Men broke into Carlos' house last night and tried to kill him."

"*Kill him?* What happened? How did he...?"

He filled her in on the details, including the call from the metallurgy lab and the unnerving fact that Villarreal actually viewed on the security camera system what would have been his death.

"He said if he hadn't heard about Chris' abduction from Lisa and then the duplicate report which was ordered, he would not have had his guard up. They both want to come up here. They're thinking it might be safer."

She agreed wholeheartedly. "That's true." Kelsey leaned over against Judtson, pulled her phone from her back pocket, and tapped the screen once, triggering a rapid double tone. She spoke into the cell as she would a walkie-talkie. "Romeo? Romeo? Where are you?"

Despite the situation, Judtson was amused by the closeness of what she had said to the famous line. "A tad Shakespearean, aren't we?"

She allowed herself a brief laugh as Romeo's voice boomed out of the small device. "In the lab with Scott and Matt. What's up?"

"I need you to set up a rapid extraction. Bal and Carlos are in La Paz and we need to get them out."

"Roger that. I'll roll right now to the airport and go down there with the new Gulfstream. Get me location details after I'm wheels up."

"Roger."

Kelsey terminated the function. Lifting up from the cushion, she tucked the phone back and turned to Judtson. "I can't believe they'd try to kill him."

"You, of all people, are surprised?"

"Guess you're right. It's just a shock, that's all."

"Yes, it is. Man…I was floored. And believe it or not, Carlos actually sounded a little spooked."

"That is not like him," she commented emphatically. "Nothing ever ruffles him."

"No. It doesn't."

"Judtson, I'm curious. Why did you take the extra time to drive here to tell me this? You have a safe phone."

He stared into her eyes for a few seconds before answering. She sensed, without knowing, what he was about to say, unconsciously lifted her hand, and placed it gently on his. Inhaling deeply, he began, "Kelsey, Kristen and I are…," but was interrupted by a distinctive trilling from his phone. Recognizing the ring he had programmed, he sighed. "It's Saylor. I'd better take it."

Kelsey seemed to flag visibly. "Yeah, I guess. Go ahead."

He answered in speaker mode. "Hi, Saylor."

"Judtson, I got the weirdest call a little while ago. It was so goofy that at first I was going to forget about it, but I convinced myself I should call you."

"Who called? Doni?"

"No." The single word was imbued with remorse. "It was Starlight."

Kent's pulse quickened. "Starlight! Has she heard from Chris?"

"Yes. I mean, no. Well, not exactly."

"What are trying to tell me, Popeye?"

"I understand she…she got together some of her psychic friends and they had a *seance*. You know, hoping to contact him."

Judtson's eyes moved to Kelsey's, expecting to see amusement or disbelief; instead, she was focusing intently on the phone in his hand. "Well?" he prompted. "Did they?"

A loud, long sigh came out of the tiny speaker. "Maybe they *did*. I don't know. And even if they did, I can't see what help it is."

"Saylor, this is Kelsey. I'm with Judtson. What was the message?"

If he was startled that they were together, it was not at all revealed in his voice. "Hello, Kelsey. As I said, it was weird. She told me there were two things. The first was just a word, repeated over and over."

"What word?" she asked.

"It was 'dish.' A little cryptic, to say the least."

"D…i…s…h?"

"Yes. And the rest of the message, if that's what you can call it, was a meaningless string of numbers and letters."

She asked him what they were, and he told her that he had written them down and would send a text message.

"Saylor, send it to Scott. You have his number, don't you?"

"Yeah. Okay, Kelsey. I'll do that."

The line filled with a brief silence, broken by Judtson. "Hey, have you heard from Doni yet?"

"Not a word. Judtson…I don't have a clue where she went."

The despair in his friend's voice, even coming through the puny speaker, tore at his heart.

"She's fine, Popeye. I'm sure she just needs a little time."

Saylor did not respond immediately. "Yeah. I guess. Well, I'd better go. Let me know if this is important. Okay?"

"We will."

At that, Saylor broke the connection.

"Kelsey, you don't really think that a bunch of psychics contacted Chris, do you?"

She stood up, still holding his hand. "Don't know. I don't rule anything out anymore. Let's go see what Scott thinks of the message."

He rose and she turned to lead the way, then abruptly swung back to face him. "Wait a sec! *You* were going to tell me something."

"Uh...it can wait."

She moved closer, raising his hand between them, grasping it with her other hand as well, and holding it against her chest. "Maybe *it* can, but *I* can't. What was it?"

Her blue eyes were boring into his, trying to read his thoughts before he could verbalize them. She wet her lips with a darting motion of her tongue, and her breathing was shallow and rapid. He lifted his free hand and stroked her hair. She tilted her head toward his touch, enhancing the contact, and half-closed her eyelids.

"I left Kristen."

Her eyes flew wide open. She made an audible gasp and released her grip on his hand, flinging both of her arms around him and pulling him against herself tightly. He joined the embrace fiercely and the two stood as one for a time, motionless, until they separated slightly and he kissed her. The contact released a flood of passion, the world around them effaced from their consciousness.

When they eventually parted, Kelsey, after three aborted attempts to utilize her voice, whispered, "Judtson...are you okay...are you sure about...all of it?"

The corners of his mouth curled upward in an unplanned grin. "I'm sure."

Before either could say another word, her phone chirped twice and they heard Scott's voice come out of her back pocket. "Kelsey, what am I supposed to do with this message?"

$$\nabla$$

Kelsey, Judtson, Scott, and Matt were huddled over a small work table, studying the string of figures Scott had printed out from the text message.

"What do you think 'dish' means?" Kelsey asked, flummoxed.

With a subtle snicker, Matt offered, "Madam Ambrosia was probably thinking about what she was going to make for dinner."

Turning to him, she chided, "Matt! Take it seriously."

He shook his bald head. "I'm sorry. I can't. I'm an engineer, not that guy on TV with the crazy hair."

Scott, pointedly glancing at Wheeler's pate, chuckled. "You're just jealous."

"Matt," Judtson jumped in, "why don't you try to make it a hypothetical...a game?"

"All right," he sighed and shifted his eyes back down at the paper.

"Dish...dish...dish," Kelsey repeated as if it were a chant. "It has to be a clue."

"Maybe it's an archaic term for his jailer," Wheeler muttered. "Maybe she's a real babe."

Kelsey made a rude sound with her lips. "Come on! No kidding. What could it be? Scott, any ideas?"

He looked up at her and blinked several times, obviously having been snapped back from contemplation. "I...uh...I haven't been thinking about the word. I've been trying to decipher the string of characters."

"Anything?"

He shook his head. "No. Not really. It seems as though it should mean something, but I...ohhh!" He almost jumped away from the table, hurried back to his computer, sat down and, at a blinding speed, began typing. The other three followed and crowded behind him, watching. He switched from the keyboard to his mouse and opened a program. He then typed the string into a white box, tapped ENTER, and leaned back.

The four saw a picture of the Earth slowly rotate as the view zoomed in.

"*They are coordinates!*" The comment was nearly shouted by Matt.

In his soft voice, Scott said, "I think so."

The zoom process gathered momentum, and the view was zeroing in on the southwestern United States, continuing to move closer and closer, creating the illusion that they were coming in for a landing from outer space. As it further narrowed the range, Judtson murmured, "New Mexico."

The image stabilized. On the screen was an even geometric pattern of bright white objects. They appeared to be mounted on a rail system.

"Where is that?" Kelsey asked impatiently.

Scott was the first to answer. "That is the Very Large Array located outside Socorro, New Mexico."

"Well, I'll be damned," Wheeler grunted.

With a look of amazement on her face, Kelsey stammered, "But that's...that's...."

Judtson finished what she was struggling to say. "Those are radio telescopes. That's where we are listening to the galaxy. Trying to find intelligent life out there."

Leaning closer, Matt tapped the screen. "And I hate to admit it, but those...look like dishes."

Taking a hasty step back, Kelsey again retrieved her phone and tapped it, initiating the two-way mode. "Romeo!"

After a pause of only a few seconds, Jones answered, "Yeah, boss."

"I need you here. Send Chili down to La Paz."

Chapter 20

AS SCOTT AND ROMEO WRUNG EVERY PIECE OF INFORMATION THEY COULD out of the Internet on the VLA, Judtson and Kelsey split the list and called the remaining members of the group, telling them about the attack on Villarreal and suggesting they come to Tucson. Afterward, the two were sitting at the long dining table, snacking on a platter of fresh vegetables and dip. Kelsey was wearing a bright orange T-shirt with the phrase "An apple a day will keep anyone away…if thrown hard enough."

Taking a large bite of celery and speaking between chews, she told Judtson, "Lisa's not coming."

"Why not?" he asked, snagging a piece of broccoli from the platter and reaching down to feed it to Rocky, who was sitting beside him.

"With what's happening, she feels more strongly than ever that we need to do the live show with Jack Bailey. She wants to stay in New York and make sure it doesn't get derailed."

"That worries me. What if they…?"

"I talked to her about it. She told me that the network has been pushing her to allow them to assign security to her. She said she'd let them."

He shook his head. "I'm still not comfortable with that."

"Neither am I. But she wouldn't budge."

"Okay. She's a big girl. What about Dylan?"

"Oh, he's coming. As a matter of fact, he was going to jump on the next flight here, so I told him that Chili would swing by with Carlos and Bal and pick him up. What did Dean have to say?"

"He's with the program. Should we have the Gulfstream make a stop for him?"

"Sure."

"I'll let him know."

"What about Jimmy?"

"Well, let's put it this way. After I told him that it looked as though the bad guys had gone on the offensive, his only comment was 'Hot damn! I'm on my way!'"

Kelsey was in the process of sipping her water and snorted at the comment, spraying liquid out of her nose. Quickly snatching up a handful of napkins, she wiped her face and then the table in front of her, as Judtson sputtered.

After they both caught their breath, Kelsey, turning serious, asked, "What about Saylor?"

Her question had a dampening effect on his mood. "I don't know. I'll talk to him. Since he's waiting for Doni to contact him…or come home…I have no idea what he'll say." He took a deep breath. "On this whole thing…do you think it was she?"

Kelsey's mouth twisted in a grimace, as if she had bitten into a lemon, while expecting a sweet orange. "I don't know, Judtson. I don't think I've told you this yet. Scott checked phone records. He found an incoming call to the direct line in Saylor and Doni's room at the silo, made an hour or so before Luis disarmed all of the security. It lasted around four minutes."

He absorbed the information, scrutinizing it in the hope of finding a reasonable explanation. "Was he able to determine where the call came from?"

She nodded and delivered the final news timidly. "Homeland Security."

Immediately clenching his fists, he muttered, "Dammit."

She reached over and wrapped her hands around his. "Judtson, there could still be a logical explanation."

"I don't know about that. There's something I haven't had a chance to tell you yet, either."

"What?"

His voice was devoid of emotion. "Saylor told me that just as he was leaving the silo with us to go south, Doni asked him what the dosage of Devil's Breath was for an adult male."

One of Kelsey's hands flew up to her mouth and she gasped softly.

"So, I'm not completely certain there can be a logical explanation."

Before she could comment, Romeo entered the room. "Got a minute, boss?"

"Sure thing. Sit down. What did you learn?"

He pulled out a chair and sat across the table from them. "I think we've gleaned all we can from satellite imagery and the other available info. The coordinates we received are down to the square yard, so not only do we know that we're looking at the Very Large Array, but we also know the exact building…assuming the intel is accurate. Now I need to put eyeballs on the target."

"What are we talking about, Romeo, night reconnaissance?"

"No need. They have weekly tours of the place open to the public. Next one is tomorrow."

"I'll go with you."

"I will, too."

"No. You two stay here where it is relatively secure. Ricky and I will go."

"*Ricky?*" Judtson blurted.

"Yeah. He's good for more than hitting the high notes. He has been pestering me for another taste of field work. I've been training him."

Judtson was amazed. "I never dreamed…."

Romeo grinned broadly. "You can't always judge a book by the cover. He's a spunky kid, and remember how he came through for you at your office. Besides, tomorrow will be strictly a look-and-see, to get the lay of the land."

"After what happened…or almost happened to Carlos…we might need to move fast to help Chris," Kelsey warned.

"I know. Depending on what we see, we can take the tour and make our move later that day or the next day, after dark. Already checked the weather charts. It's going to be cloudy. Might rain, but that's not always a bad thing."

The doorbell chimed and the three crossed the house to answer it. Reaching the entrance first, Kelsey checked the peephole and let out a high-pitched giggle before twisting the handle and swinging the door open to find Ricky, wearing a digitally camouflaged boonie cap, wraparound eyepro sunglasses, a pea-green undershirt partially covered with a MOLLE vest, camo pants, and the combat boots given to him by Scott.

He eyed Kelsey, who had her hand over her mouth in a fruitless attempt to hide her amusement; Judtson, who after seeing his assistant, had back-stepped behind Romeo to conceal his laughter; and Romeo, who was grinning at his friend and shaking his head.

His voice breaking, Ricky exclaimed, *"What?"*

$$\nabla$$

Eunice Cahane double-tied the shoestrings on her sneakers, a habit she acquired years ago after she had tripped on her own laces while chasing a man who had robbed a convenience store. He had gotten away. When she finished with her shoes, she hopped up onto the kitchen counter into a sitting position, slid over so that she was partially dropping into her sink, and pressed the side of her face against the window. This enabled her to see farther down her street, and she was rewarded with a view of a white van parked alongside the curb several doors down.

She already knew that the van displayed signage proclaiming that it was nothing but a repair vehicle for a local cable service, a fact she had learned the day before by walking around the block and sneaking up on it.

"Thank the Lord for the inbred incompetence of these folks," she said aloud. "If they'd taken the time to check out that cable company, they'd know it doesn't even come into this neighborhood."

Sliding off the kitchen counter, she trotted to her master bedroom and unlatched the glass patio door leading to the backyard. Whistling "Zip-A-Dee-Doo-Dah," Eunice went to the garage, opened the overhead door, started her car, and drove away, closing the door from the street. After traveling two blocks, she turned right, proceeded to the first intersection and turned again, circling back until she reached the entrance to the alley. With no more than two minutes elapsed since her conspicuous departure, she was parked in the alley directly behind her own home.

Hastily opening the rear gate, she hurried to the patio door and reentered her bedroom. She crossed to the walk-in closet and shouldered her way between the hanging clothes before swinging the door almost shut, leaving it slightly ajar to provide her with a narrow view of her room. Steadying her breathing and settling herself down for a vigil, she waited.

Her wait was not a long one. Within fifteen minutes, she heard a muffled thump, which she guessed was the front door closing. Pulling her pistol out of the holster, she flipped off the safety and held her breath. From the noises created by the intruder or intruders as they opened and closed interior doors, she was able to mentally track their progress through her home, right up to the point where she heard a man's voice coming from very near the threshold of the bedroom. "We've got two more to plant. I'll do the one in here. You hide one in the room that looks like a study."

There was an unintelligible grunt from a second man, and she soon saw the first as he walked across her line of sight. Confident there would be no squeak from the recently oiled hinges, Cahane slowly swung the door wider and saw him on his knees beside her bed. He had pulled the nightstand away from the wall and was working in the area behind it as she crept up to him silently on the thick carpet, and slammed the butt of her .45 against the back of his skull.

He fell forward, his chest landing on the small stand, his shoulder bumping the lamp, which she caught one-handed on its way to hit the floor. Placing it quietly on the bed, Cahane roughly grabbed the man's collar and heaved him to the side, stepping back and aiming her pistol at his face. There was no need. He was obviously unconscious.

First relieving the stranger of his wallet and gun, she used the side of her foot and pushed him flat on his face, pulling out a nylon zip-cuff from a pocket and firmly lashing his wrists. Removing a second, she bound his ankles while keeping a wary eye on the hallway outside.

Satisfied with her work, she rose and crept to the doorway. Checking the hall first, holding her gun with both hands and pointing it at the ceiling, she moved carefully forward, keeping her back almost touching the wall, and repeatedly glancing in the opposite direction, unsure if there were more than two unwelcome guests.

Arriving at the study, she stood with her back firmly against the wall and listened for a moment, hearing the soft rustling sounds of the second man as he did his work. Sucking in a deep breath, she pivoted and centered herself in the opening, bringing the pistol down to point forward, and shouted, "*Well, lookee here!*"

Apparently having completed the planting of the listening device, he had already begun turning toward her as she announced her presence. Dropping a small leather satchel, his hand shot up and under his coat, coming out a split second later with a gun.

Seeing this, Cahane was already barking, "*Don't do...awww, shit!*" when she realized he was not going to stop. Lowering the barrel, she pulled the trigger once. The large-caliber slug slammed into his thigh and violently spun him around, tossing the attacker to the floor. Keeping her weapon trained on him, Eunice quickly covered the distance and kicked the pistol from his outstretched hand before his mind could process the pain and assemble the instructions to scream.

Leaning over him as he howled, she said, "Now see what you made me do. I tried to tell you not to do that. You just wouldn't listen, would you?"

She pulled out another zip-cuff, wrestled his arms behind his back, and secured them together, a difficult task as he desperately tried to hold his bleeding thigh with both hands. Not bothering with his ankles since she decided he would not be hopping up onto that leg anytime soon, she left him on the floor and checked the rest of her home, finding it empty. Next, she grabbed a bath towel, not one of the good ones, but one she had already planned on throwing out, and returned to the injured man. She wrapped the towel tightly around his leg to stanch the blood.

Finishing that, she returned to the master bedroom where she found the first intruder still unconscious and, using the zip-cuff around his ankles, pulled him into the study to join the other bad guy, enjoying the thumping sound his head made as it was dragged over the marble threshold.

Panting from the exertion, she dropped into her desk chair and, using the phone there, dialed her captain's direct line.

"Captain of Detectives," he answered.

"Lester...Eunice."

He heard that she was breathing heavily, and became concerned. "Eunice! You all right?"

"Yeah. I guess. I'm a little out of shape for this stuff."

"What's wrong?"

Keeping her sentences short and to the point, she rapidly filled him in, ending the story by saying, "I'm lookin' at the ID of the first guy. You are not going to like this, Lester."

The line was silent for a short time. "Tell me."

"Naw. I'll just leave it for you to see. You'd better get some uniforms rolling this way quick-like. Otherwise, somebody else'll be popping in to clean up this mess."

"Hold on," he ordered and she knew he was contacting dispatch. When he came back on the line, he told her, "I called it in as an officer in distress. They're hot-shotting their way to you. I'm coming, too."

"Figured you might. I'll stick here to make sure nothing squirrelly happens with these guys or the evidence. But, Lester, as soon as the first uniform rolls up...I'm gonna get outta Dodge."

He thought about what she was saying, then changed the subject. "I got a call from the doc."

Her ears perked up. "You did? Well?"

Another pause. "You want me to tell you on this phone?"

"What the hell! At this point maybe it's better if they know what we know."

"True. I won't go into the details now, but Rosemary Shields was definitely murdered before she was put in her car in that garage."

After disconnecting, she double-checked both men and, satisfied they were not going anywhere, moved to the front of her house, when she heard the first siren approaching. Seconds later, the patrol car skidded to a haphazard stop on her driveway. Unlocking the front door for the officer, she ran back through the house and slipped out the patio door the moment he shouted his announcement. The back gate was still ajar, and Cahane was in her car and rolling in no time.

Clearing the end of the alley and turning away from the direction of the multiple sirens, she drove slowly and dug through her pockets until she found the safe phone Lisa had sent her. She dialed the number of her new friend.

"Eunice?" Lisa's voice came on almost instantly.

"That's me."

"Wow! This has been a crazy few hours. You wouldn't believe the news I've gotten today."

Cahane made a steady chuckling sound and quipped, "You ain't heard the end of it."

She proceeded to brief Lisa on the details of her recent experiences, ending it with a blow-by-blow chronology of the shooting in her home.

"OH...MY...GOD! Are you okay?"

"Yep. Fine as a frog's hair. Can't say the same for Tweedledum bleedin' on my carpet. Oh, by the way, the ME said that Shields was a certain murder."

"*I knew it!* Now...let me tell you some things." Lisa described the murder attempt on Carlos, the execution attempt on Luis, the latest developments on Chris Ashby's whereabouts, the impending live program, and the fact that the entire group was assembling in Arizona.

When she finished the narrative, Cahane let out a long whistle. "So it's hittin' the fan everywhere. You heading to Tucson?"

"No. I need to stay and put together the show."

"You sure that's a good idea, missy?"

"I really need to do it. Once the story is out, they shouldn't have any reason to mess with us."

"Yeah, right," Eunice grunted sarcastically. "And you probably believe that the Barbie doll's proportions are perfectly natural, too."

Her friend ignored the comment. "Besides, the network has provided me with a security detail."

"I don't know, Lisa."

"Either way, I'm staying. I'm only needed here for a couple of days. Then I can probably hightail it to Arizona with everybody else. What are you going to do now?"

"Dunno. Haven't thought that far. I think I'm nothing but a big, fat liability here, though. With the Department of Justice, the FBI, and Lord knows who else breathing down my department's neck, the best thing I can do is skedaddle."

Lisa's voice became more excited. "I have a great idea! Why don't you hook up with the others? I think that would be great."

"This isn't some slumber party, you know."

"Don't be silly. I'll call Kelsey. It'll be cool. Come on…please?"

"Seems like I'd be imposing."

She heard a staccato laugh from Lisa. "You don't know Kelsey. It'll be just fine."

"I'll have to think on it."

They ended the call, promising to keep in touch. Cahane pulled her car into the parking lot of a Piggly Wiggly and killed the engine, opened the car door, leaned out, and spit. She dropped back into the seat, stuffed a fresh wad in her mouth, closed her eyes, and cleared her mind. After several minutes of remaining motionless, she opened her eyes, started the car, and drove.

▽

Matt Wheeler was putting the finishing touches on the converter helmet. Picking it up, he crossed the large work room to Scott's array of desks.

"What do you think?"

Gumble turned away from the endless stream of windows he was always immersed within and focused on the device. A far cry from the bulky and patched-together first-generation headpiece, the new one was sleek and self-contained within the shell of a slightly larger than normal motorcycle helmet.

"Looks cool. I like the red lightning bolts on the sides."

"Came with the helmet I used."

"And it's shielded, right?"

"Uh-huh. After I did some testing, I found that I could use a relatively thin sheet of lead. I removed all of the interior padding and reinforcements and glued the lead to the inside of the plastic shell."

He tilted the device back so Scott was able to see the interior. "Then I mounted the x-ray emitters to that. And I scrounged an adjustable plastic strap getup from the guts of a construction hard hat and installed it."

He slipped the helmet onto his own head.

"As a final precaution, I lined the pull-down visor with lead."

Reaching up, he gripped the formerly clear windscreen, which was now a dull, opaque gray, and rotated it down and over his face.

Scott snorted. "You look like a comic book superhero."

Flipping up the visor and pulling off the helmet, Matt grinned. "Yeah. That's not a bad side benefit."

"Where's the power supply?"

"On the base of the helmet, at the rear, is a small jack I drilled in. The transformer and the controller are all in a compact briefcase. We just plug that into any wall outlet, hook it to the helmet, and that's it."

The tech nodded appreciatively. "Pretty neat. Wonder who we'll use it on."

"Or if."

"Yeah, that's true. Hey, I have something new, too."

"What is it?"

Swiveling in his chair, Scott typed a single word on his screen and pointed at it. "Say that word."

Matt looked at him quizzically for a second but, accustomed to his friend's idiosyncracies, glanced at the monitor and said, "*Criminy?*"

The moment he spoke the word, Gumble held up one finger, then two, then three. As the third finger was raised, a loud burp erupted from the hefty speakers mounted to the wall above their heads, and the tech began laughing. "It…it works!"

Matt swung his eyes from Scott to the word on the screen to the speakers. "What works? What the hell was that?"

Catching his breath, Gumble explained, "I wrote a little app for my phone. Used voice recognition and selected a word not ordinarily spoken. My phone is always listening, so when I say the word, it sends a message through the Internet to my computer which plays a wave file. I can have it trigger any sound I want or a song or the sound track of an old TV show…you name it. I wanted to test it with a voice other than mine."

"So you programmed your phone and computer to burp on command?"

Scott, beginning to laugh again, nodded.

Shaking his head in disgust, Matt turned to go back to his area. "And I thought you were working on something important, like rescuing Chris."

To his retreating back, Scott protested, "I can multitask."

▽

His night's sleep fitful, Chris remained on his cot, staring up at the blank white ceiling, and did not even shift his gaze when he heard the slot open and shut. Assuming his breakfast was being delivered, he said, "You don't need to leave it, Freddie. I'm not hungry."

"Hello, Dr. Ashby." The voice was not Freddie's and caused Chris to abruptly turn his head. Entering the cell was someone he had not seen before. The man was short and heavyset, and carried the now familiar headgear and valise, both of which he carefully placed on the table. Freddie and Elmo were standing behind him, just inside the door.

"I need you to sit here, please." The stranger's voice was flat, almost monotone.

"I'll pass."

"Very cute. I know we explained the necessity of this to you yesterday. I suggest that you cooperate. Otherwise, you will be forced to comply. Which do you prefer?"

Anxiety churning his stomach and tightening every muscle in his body, Ashby slowly sat up and stood, taking a step toward the small table. He considered knocking the equipment against the wall with a sweep of his arm, thinking that perhaps if he broke it, this would delay the inevitable chain of events to follow, at least while they brought another set. The stranger, reading his intent, snatched up the headset and rested his other hand on the top of the valise.

Resignedly, Chris dropped into the hard chair and remained docile as the man slid the device onto his head.

Chapter 21

SAYLOR POURED HIMSELF A CUP OF COFFEE, DOCTORED IT, and sat at the kitchen bar. The silence of his home was oppressive...something he had never noticed in the past, during those times he was alone while Doni was out. His mind churned incessantly with thoughts of where she might be, an activity he had indulged nonstop since the morning she left. Later that day, when he was certain she had not simply driven aimlessly to burn off her anger, he had begun contacting people she knew, hoping to find that she was with them or, at the very least, to determine that she was okay.

The call from Starlight, and the succeeding call he made to Judtson, had not distracted him for long. Nor were his thoughts occupied by the news that Judtson had left his wife, a fact Saylor had discovered when he walked next door the evening before to visit with his friend, only to be met at the door by an angry Kristen.

Every room of the house...every object in each room...was directly attached to a bottomless well filled with memories of his wife. The triggered memories, always so pleasant, comforting, and warming, now threatened to engulf him...plunge him deeper into a pit of depression. And yet he could not make himself leave, could not allow himself to escape from the emotional battering each nook and cranny inflicted. For departing their home...*their* home... felt akin to a betrayal.

"That's a joke," he grunted sourly. "I already betrayed her the minute I doubted her."

He pulled his thoughts away from the self-accusations. After only a brief respite from his mental turmoil, Saylor's mind, unbeckoned, recalled Doni's comments to him after Judtson's mysterious disappearance from his office, the disappearance which was the precursor to the mental transmutation, as she dismissed his concern, insisting that it was typical of Judtson to do strange things and that he had always been "flaky." He remembered his own testiness at her for minimizing his worries when Judtson was in the throes of the mind control.

His brain spinning up into high gear, he begrudgingly realized that nearly every step of the way, she had tried to talk him out of taking the situation seriously, until what was truly occurring had become inarguably obvious. Even the fact that she told him Judtson had kissed her in seventh grade…hitting him with that particular secret which she had kept for all of the years of their friendship, dating, engagement, and marriage…when examined at this juncture, seemed odd. Why would she choose to share it at the point in time he was at his lowest, twisting with worry about his best friend? It was almost as if…almost as if she wanted to pull the two friends apart…drive a wedge between them.

This unpleasant kaleidoscope of vignettes, the spliced-together montage of Doni moments, concluded with her stopping him as he was walking out of their room, suitcase in hand, for his trip to La Paz, and asking him offhandedly, "Saylor, honey, I've been curious about something."

He had paused in the open doorway, eyeing the group impatiently standing in the hallway. "What's that, babe?"

"The…what did you call it…Devil's Breath?"

"Yeah?"

"What's the normal dosage of that stuff for a grown man?"

Already tense from the thought of the impending flight, yet anxious to leave and aware that Judtson, Kelsey, and the others were waiting for him, he had not given her bizarre last-minute question a second thought and told her the quantity.

Suddenly hating where his mind had traveled, Saylor forcibly shoved the images away.

▽

The motel in Socorro, New Mexico, offered a breakfast buffet, which Romeo bypassed, filling two clear plastic cups with orange juice and finding an empty table. He glanced at his watch and decided that if Ricky did not come down within the next ten minutes, he would have the front desk ring his friend's room.

As the arbitrary deadline neared, Romeo drained the second cup and slid back his chair, intending to stand, when he noticed a figure crossing the lobby toward the breakfast area. The man was wearing a wide-brimmed straw hat, a Hawaiian shirt covered with a brightly colored floral pattern, baggy khaki Bemuda shorts, exposing the whitest legs Jones had ever seen, white socks, and black jogging shoes. An SLR camera was slung around the man's neck, and the overall ensemble was capped by a white smear of zinc oxide on his nose.

Romeo scooted back closer to the table, rested his elbows on it, dropped his face into his hands, and his shoulders began shuddering with laughter.

From above, he heard Ricky's voice. "You *said* to dress like a tourist!"

He looked up, tears streaming down his cheeks. "You're…you're right. I…I did."

Frowning, Ricky offered, "I can go back up to my room and change if this is too much."

As he caught his breath, Romeo gestured to the empty chair, fighting back the diaphragm spasms. "No. Sit. You're good."

Ricky lowered himself into the chair. On his face, Romeo could see a mixture of anxiousness, worry, and hurt. "I overdid it, didn't I?"

The Ranger shook his head. "No. Well, yeah. A little."

"I don't know…I've never done…."

"Hey, knock it off. It's okay. Take a gander around the room. I see at least five other guys who look just like you."

Swiveling his head around quickly, Ricky then turned back, a timid snicker pushing out of him. "But *they* look silly!"

The comment unleashed a round of loud snorts from Romeo. When he finally settled down, he said, "Let's hit the breakfast bar. Eat plenty of protein and drink lots of liquids. It's going to be a long day and it's already getting warm."

"What's the plan?"

"The tour doesn't start for three hours. I think we should do a little preliminary recon of the area. Scope out routes, vantage points, things like that. Maybe we can find a hill and watch the actual building where we think...or I guess I should say...*spirit* thinks he's being held. We might get lucky and see the bad guys coming and going."

"Spirit, huh? Do you think this is a wild-goose chase?"

Romeo thought for a moment. "Not sure. Normally, I guess I would. But having a latitude and longitude that points directly at the center of an existing building on a government complex, as opposed to the location being in...I don't know, a Walmart or something...gives it more credibility."

"I agree. And don't forget that message about a dish."

"True. Those radio telescopes out there really do look a lot like big dishes. Anyway, it's worth taking it seriously. Now, let's make ourselves some waffles."

▽

As the train approached Pennsylvania Station, Eunice reviewed the details of her earlier departure from Atlanta. Not wanting to leave a trail with credit cards, she had gone to her bank, cleaned out her checking account, and made a sizable withdrawal from her savings, getting all of the money in bills no larger than twenties. She left her car at the bank and took a bus ride to the Amtrak station, where she purchased the tickets with cash. Cahane had chosen the train because she was certain they would be watching the airports much more closely. Knowing that current transportation security regulations would flag a one-way ticket paid with cash, she bought a round trip, with the return date three weeks off. The ticket agent requested a photo ID but was satisfied with a cursory look at her badge and detective credentials.

She had left the department-issued cell phone in her car and was now only carrying the safe phone. Using it as she headed north, she called the personal phone belonging to Buddy Gleeson, and caught him at home. After giving him a vague explanation that she was traveling on a case undercover, and stressing the importance that he not mention her call to anyone other than Lester, and then only in person, Cahane gave him Lisa's name and asked him to find her home address. He sounded eager to help, and she finished the call by specifying that he get back to her on the phone he was now using. He called back forty-five minutes later with the address.

▽

"Special Agent Bowman, they're ready for you now."

Kenny was sitting in a stiff-backed wooden chair in the hallway outside the hearing room. For the past two days, his immediate supervisor, as well as two special investigators dispatched from the bureau's main offices in Washington, D.C., had been grilling him over the Luis Tovar episode. Now he was waiting for their decision. He stood and followed the clerk into the room, where he walked up the short aisle and through the wooden gate, then took a seat behind one of the two tables facing the front dais.

He tried to read the faces of the three men, deciding they would be excellent at poker since their expressions revealed nothing. As he settled into the chair, his boss, David Dillamon, addressed him. "Special Agent Bowman, as you know, this has not been an easy incident to sort out or digest. It is obviously to your credit that you were able to detect and foil a kidnapping and murder attempt by two men impersonating members of the U.S. Marshals Service. Other agents from this office are now investigating that aspect of the incident. As of now, it appears that the U.S. Marshals Service itself was not compromised, only that two outsiders were able to obtain one of the vans and ascertain that the pickup and transfer of Tovar was delayed, allowing them to make their move."

Kenny disagreed with this conclusion. He doubted that the bad guys simply sat back and hoped one of the marshals would call in sick on that particular day. He said nothing, having made this point to them earlier.

"Unfortunately, that is where your actions became less than exemplary. It would have been a simple matter to return Tovar, a person very high on the federal wanted list, to his cell. Rather, you chose to release him."

Bowman started to object and was silenced by the raising of Dillamon's hand. "I know that you told us he escaped from your custody during the confusion of the firefight with the bogus marshals. However, this is a very difficult aspect of your story for us to accept, due to the fact that the prisoner was handcuffed and wearing leg irons."

"As I said before, the kidnappers took them off him."

Dillamon shook his head sadly. "I know. I know that's what you told us. But, in the subsequent interrogations of the surviving kidnapper, *he* told us that such was not the case."

"And you're going to take his word over mine?"

There appeared to be genuine remorse on the man's face as he answered. "Special Agent Bowman, after we read your preliminary report, and after interrogating the surviving kidnapper, we instructed the lab to check the keys for prints."

Kenny's mind snapped back to the scene, recalling that he had dug the keys out of the kidnapper's pocket and tossed them to Romeo. Seeking support, he looked at the two men bracketing his supervisor. They were unreadable, stone-faced.

"With the exception of a smudged partial, the most recent or topmost identifiable print on the keys was yours. How would that be possible, or even likely, if your story was accurate?"

He only stared at his boss in response, saying nothing until the silence became uncomfortable. Clearing his throat, Dillamon continued, "As a result of these findings, tempered with your excellent record with the bureau, it has been decided that you will receive a written reprimand, which will become a part of your personnel record for a period of five years, and that you will receive a seven-day suspension without pay. The time elapsed since the incident shall count toward the satisfaction of this penalty."

Bowman's mouth dropped. Based upon the clear undercurrent during the questioning, as well as the tone of this meeting, he had been certain he was going to be fired or, at a minimum, put on an indefinite leave of absence without pay.

Standing, he directed his comments to Dillamon. "That is more than fair, sir. If I may ask, will this result in a change of assignment or duties?"

"It will not. When you come back to work in a few days, you will continue to be responsible for the Phoenix bureau and the Tucson office."

"Thank you, sir."

His supervisor smiled at him. "You're welcome, Kenny. You got off lucky." Then, his voice ominous, he added, "This time."

∇

Kelsey and Judtson were outside, watching Rocky run as the golden explored the flat, rock-covered grounds surrounding her home.

"Good God, he's fast! He's almost a blur."

Judtson nodded. "It's a little spooky. And did you know that golden retrievers have one of the strongest bites in the canine world? It's something like a million pounds of pressure."

"Right!"

"Well, I'm exaggerating slightly, but it is powerful."

"How long have you had him?"

"Four years. He belonged to my neighbor, the one on the opposite side of my house from Saylor. That guy and his wife never played with him. Never took him for walks. When I came home, Rocky would be standing at the wrought-iron gate, staring at me...a tennis ball in his mouth."

"Awww, that's sad."

"Yeah. Anyway, I used to take a few minutes each time to play catch with him. Go to the gate and take the ball and throw it. He'd bring it back, stick his head between the rails, and drop the ball right in my hand. He loved it. Enjoyed my little visits so much. I felt horrible leaving him to go into my own home. And I started to look forward to seeing him every day."

"I can understand that."

"One evening I came home and saw a moving van in front of Rocky's house. They were going to leave and I'd never see my new pal again. I felt rotten."

"So what did you do? Go over and knock on the guy's door and ask him if you could have Rocky?"

Staring straight ahead and watching his buddy romp, Judtson answered, his voice growing softer, flatter as he spoke. "I wanted to. I talked to Kristen about it and she said she didn't want a damn dog in the house or in the yard."

Kelsey huffed her disapproval. "You're kidding! But...you ended up with him."

"Uh-huh. The next day, when I came home, the moving van was gone. They had taken the window coverings and I could see inside...the house was completely empty. Man, I was bummed. Then I heard a soft little woof. I walked to the backyard gate and there was Rocky, ball in his mouth."

"I don't understand. Why was he still at the house?"

"They abandoned him! Left him behind in the backyard. Middle of the summer. No food. No water."

"That's...that's horrible!"

"I hopped in my car and drove to the store. Bought two dog dishes and a bag of food. There was a padlock on the gate, so I hopped the wall and fed him. Filled the other bowl with water. I thought that maybe the guy was planning on coming back for him. So I did that every day...in the evening. Filled his water bowl twice a day. On the fifth day I brought bolt cutters with me and cut the padlock and brought him home. He has been with me ever since."

"That bastard! It's a good thing you never saw him again."

"Oh, I did."

"You did? What happened?"

"He showed up three days after I brought my pal home with me, eight days after abandoning him. When he found the padlock cut and Rocky missing, he knocked on my door and asked if I had his dog. I just tore into him. Called him every name in the book. He tried to tell me that he had a friend in Tucson who was supposed to come and feed Rocky daily, but guessed the guy flaked out on him. I told him he was a lying sack of shit. He called me a name, so I hit him."

Kelsey giggled. "You hit him?"

"Yep. Good one, too. Took him down. Told him to get his sorry ass off my property or I'd call the sheriff and report him for abandoning a dog. He got the hint."

"I'm surprised, from what you said a minute ago, that Kristen let you have him."

Judtson turned and looked at Kelsey. "I didn't ask."

The harsh double beep burst from Kelsey's back pocket, and they heard Scott's voice. "Kelsey!"

She pulled the phone out. "Yeah, Scott."

"You'd better come here. Right away!"

His words and his tone conveyed urgency.

"What is it? Something wrong?"

"Uh...no. Well, maybe. You are receiving an IM request from Alchemist."

Chapter 22

KELSEY SAT BOLT UPRIGHT AT THE KEYBOARD, her body as taut as a coiled spring, with Judtson and Scott standing behind and watching the screen over her shoulders. She asked, "Scott, are you tracing this?"

"Yep. I have three separate programs crawling backward toward the source."

Her shoulders dropped with a sigh. "Here goes."

She typed, Daddy! Are you there?

I am, Frasier.

Kelsey frowned for a moment. What happened to you? I've been trying to reach you.

They were tracing our connection. Getting close. I was forced to terminate and shut it all down until I was satisfied it was safe to contact you.

She frowned again, tilting her head and staring at his words.

"Kelsey," Judtson whispered, "is something wrong?"

"I'm not sure. It's probably nothing." She resumed typing. Daddy, I have cell phones. They are Androids that Scott made safe. Can we talk?

Without hesitation, Alchemist answered, No. I want to meet. I missed you. I would love to see you, my darling daughter.

With an angry shake of her head, she typed, Daddy, who are they? Who are the people trying to hurt us?

I can't say. Not through this medium. But I will tell you everything when we meet.

Where?

Gates Pass. The picnic area.

You're in Tucson now?

No. I'll be arriving early tomorrow.

What time do you want to meet?

In the morning. Nine o'clock.

Okay, I'll see you there.

Frasier, I can't wait to see you.

She terminated the chat. Before she could say a word, Scott blurted, "That's not your father."

When she spun in the chair to face them, Judtson could see that her face was flush with fury. "Kelsey, that wasn't your father?"

"NO! Those rotten...."

"How could you tell?"

Still furious, she did not answer him immediately, so Scott explained. "I don't know what else Kelsey picked up, but the Android comment was a dead giveaway."

"What do you mean?"

Kelsey found her voice. "Scott was not the one who modified the cell phones we all use. My father did. I deliberately phrased my question to include the reference to Android phones because he told me they were not practical to run the underlying security software he had written."

"So it was a test?"

"Yeah. It was. And whoever the hell was on the other end of the line flunked it. Big time!"

"How would he know that Scott hadn't overcome the Android issue in the time since he left?"

She shrugged. "He wouldn't. Not for sure. But he sure as hell would have reacted. You don't know my father. The incompatibility issue frustrated him a lot. If he heard that Scott had beaten the problem, he would have made a comment about it. And that isn't all. The way he started, specifically calling me Frasier. That just didn't feel right."

"And then he said 'contact,'" Scott added.

"Exactly."

"You two are losing me."

"Judtson, come on, you're the writer. And my father was a fuddy-duddy about proper English usage."

He glanced at the screen and scanned the dialogue box. "Oh, I get it. He would never have said 'it was safe to contact you.'"

She shook her head. "He would have said 'it was safe to make contact with you.'"

"Right," Scott agreed. "He must have corrected me a hundred times for that when I worked with him."

"That's still not all. There was other stuff, too. 'I missed you' instead of 'I've missed you.' And the whole 'darling daughter' thing was wrong. He didn't talk like that. At least not on instant messaging."

"So," Judtson said, reaching the obvious conclusion, "they co-opted the Alchemist connection and are using it to lure you into a trap."

Kelsey only nodded in response, and he watched her mind process the implications of the conversation. As she did, the fire burning within her was abruptly extinguished. He saw her sag, sinking deeply into the chair. When she spoke, her voice verged on being inaudibly soft. "Which means that either they were able to capture the last conversation between Alchemist and me, or...."

"Or they have him," Judtson finished.

"There's a third possibility," Scott suggested meekly. "That the previous message wasn't your father, either."

$$\nabla$$

Hearing a soft knock on the door to her office, Lisa looked up from her notes to see Brandon Bailey, her boss, standing at the threshold with two men behind him.

"Come in, Brandon."

He entered and took one of the available chairs across from her as the strangers remained standing. "Lisa, I'm glad you finally decided to accept some protection. These are the two men from the agency we've hired, Stu Cutter and Tom Reinhold."

She made quick eye contact with both and nodded.

"They are former NYPD and thoroughly vetted," he added reassuringly.

"I'm sure they'll be great. Thanks."

"Not a problem. Well, I'll be getting along. Again, glad you changed your mind."

"Me too. Like I said, thanks, Brandon."

He left and the man introduced as Stu said, "Normally, ma'am, you'll only have one of us with you at a time. We'll work in alternating shifts. I'll work the days and he'll work nights. Twelve-hour shifts. Since this is our first day with you, you get us both for a little while. At least until you get home and we have a chance to check out your place. Then Tom can catch some shut-eye and relieve me later."

Lisa studied Stu's eyes as he tediously explained their routine to her, and was not able to find anything she considered to be a spark behind them. Almost rotely, she remarked, "I'm about to head home, anyway. So if you two would like to just hang out in my office, I'll be ready in a few minutes."

"That's fine, ma'am. I'll stay in here with you. Tom will wait in the corridor."

She started to argue, feeling self-conscious about having a guard at her office door, but bit it back and muttered, "Fine," as she began shutting down her computer and gathering her notes and files to take home for the evening.

Feeling distracted by the presence of Stu, who was standing off to the side of her office, near the corner of the room, she thought to herself, *I hope he doesn't think he's pulling off unobtrusive*, and chuckled softly. Gathering an armload of manila folders, her large valise, and her purse, she stood and circled around the desk.

"Okay, Stu, let's go."

Lisa felt as if she were on a perp walk through the offices and to the elevator with the two men escorting her. Mildly embarrassed, she hurried to the alcove and pressed the button, relieved that the doors opened virtually at once. The car was occupied by two financial department employees whom she was glad she did not know. Apparently, her arrival intruded on a conversation between them as one of the women slapped her mouth shut almost comically. Lisa and her bodyguards entered and silently rode the elevator down to the underground garage.

As the doors opened into the cavernous space, the women scurried approximately thirty paces away and then stopped to resume their animated chatter as they made plans for a girl's night out, their voices echoing in the concrete structure, the sounds reminding Lisa of the cackling of chickens. She turned to face Stu. "You going to follow me?"

"Actually, ma'am, one of us will ride with you while the other follows. After today, you'll ride with one of us in the morning and we'll take you home at night."

Her mouth twisted in a grimace. "That really necessary? I need my car here during the day. I make a lot of trips."

"Yes, ma'am, it is. Wherever you need to go during the day, we'll take you."

Sighing loudly, Lisa mentally surrendered to this incursion into her life and reminded herself that it would only be for a few days. "Fine. But as far as one of you riding home with me today…not going to happen. My car is a two-seater and the passenger seat is loaded to the gills with stuff." She made a show of eyeing him from head to toe. "And I don't think you'll fit in the trunk."

He started to argue and was summarily cut off. "Sorry," she said curtly. "That's the way it is. Starting tomorrow morning, I'll be a compliant little girl and do what I'm told. Tonight, I drive alone and you follow."

Briefly shifting his eyes toward his partner, Stu nodded. "All right. But don't lose us in the Manhattan traffic. Watch your mirror and if you see us caught in a jam behind you, slow down and wait for us."

"Got it."

Without waiting for further irritating instructions, she turned on her heel to walk away. Glancing back at her bodyguards as she walked, Lisa thought she detected something odd in the way the two men were looking at each other, almost as if it was more than simply frustration at her lack of pliancy. Dismissing it, she trotted to her Miata, which was parked in a reserved spot close to the elevators and adjacent to the two women, who were still arguing over which bar had the best happy hour.

She keyed the alarm and opened the driver's side door, tossing her purse, files, and briefcase on the heap of dirty clothes and old fast-food wrappers already piled upon the passenger seat. Settling in, she started the car and slid the shifter into reverse, when she remembered that she needed one more file, which she had placed on her credenza and then forgotten, distracted by the presence of Stu as he was looming over her. Lisa reached for the key, planning to turn off the engine and go back up for the file. She immediately changed her mind as she visualized herself dashing across the office with Stu and Tom right behind, performing their bad imitation of Secret Service agents.

Pulling out her phone, she remembered that there was no service down in the garage.

"Damn it!" she spat out, took her foot off the brake, and tapped the gas pedal, shooting backward out of the space and startling the two women. As she whipped the Mazda around the hairpin turns at the end of each level, she checked her mirror and saw that Stu and Tom, in a beige Explorer, were struggling to keep up. Finally clearing the exit ramp and rocketing onto the street, she tried her phone again and connected with her assistant.

"Hey, Shannon, Lisa."

"Yes, boss."

"I left a file on my credenza. It's labeled 'Baalbek'…no, wait…'Villarreal.' I'm going to need it tonight. Would you mind grabbing it and meeting me at my place?"

"Just a sec…I'm trying to find…oh, I see it. Sure. I'll bring it to you."

"Thanks. And when you come up, ignore the two dudes at the door. They're my bodyguards."

There was a soft laugh. "I heard about them! Either one cute?"

"No. Not unless you like the dull-eyed Neanderthal types."

"That's Neander*tal*…not *thal*."

"No, it isn't. Changing word pronunciations on us is just their way of checking to see if the programming is working."

"Huh?"

"Never mind. What time can you bring the file?"

"Heading out now. I was getting ready to leave when you called. And on my Vespa, I'll probably beat you home."

"Fat chance of…." Lisa had to slam on her brakes as she encountered a solid backup of cars. "On second thought, you're probably right. Okay. See you soon. I'll owe you a glass of wine."

"That's a deal."

She checked her rearview mirror. The beige SUV was three cars behind, and she was barely able to recognize Stu and Tom through the late afternoon glare on the windshield. The wall of vehicles in front of her, mostly cabs, edged forward and she muttered, "Oh, man. I love New York."

It took her more than twenty minutes to travel the nine blocks to her apartment building and find a parking space. Loaded up with her purse and work materials, she staggered to the entrance to find Shannon conspicuously flirting with the doorman, who was in his mid-twenties and handsome in a 1950s sort of way. Noticing her boss, she rushed over, offering, "Here, let me help you with that," and grasped the stack of files tucked under Lisa's arm.

Stu and Tom came trotting up, obviously not as lucky in their quest for a nearby parking spot, and Lisa introduced them to Shannon and the doorman, whose name she did not remember. As the two women climbed the steps and entered the building, followed closely by the bodyguards, Lisa whispered to her assistant, "You should be ashamed. You're married."

The young woman reached up, casually flipped her blond hair, and laughed. "There's a difference between wife and slave. Besides…in case you haven't noticed…he's gorgeous!"

Lisa rolled her eyes. "Your husband is way better looking."

"You are a buzz killer!"

The quartet rode the elevator to the ninth floor, and the presence of the security men had a definite dampening effect on any conversation during the brief ride. Stu, cutting in front of Lisa at her door, held out his hand. "I need your key."

"I can get it."

"Uh, no. That's not why I need it. One of us has to check out your place before you go in. You and your friend stay out here with Tom."

Letting out a sigh and realizing that this man had elicited more of those from her in the past hour than she had expelled in the previous two weeks, she dug her key out of her purse and dropped it into his waiting palm.

▽

Eunice, disembarking from her train in Pennsylvania Station, and nearly overwhelmed with the sensory input created by the horde of travelers on their exodus from Manhattan, dodged her way against the flow of people and took refuge in a shop filled with snacks, drinks, books, magazines and, thankfully, sundries. Snagging a basket, she found a toothbrush and toothpaste, a travel-sized bottle of her shampoo, and a bar of Ivory soap. Satisfying the necessities, she went on to peruse the snack section and snickered to herself. "Slumber party, it is."

She dropped a large bag of bite-sized dark chocolates and four microwavable extra-butter popcorns into the basket. Then she scanned the shelf filled with Twinkies, Dong Dongs, and individual carrot cakes before stepping to the counter, where a young girl with a nose ring, a silver stud through each eyebrow, and intense purple hair was perched on a tall stool and typing something on her phone. When she finally looked up, Cahane asked, "Excuse me, miss. Where would I find MoonPies?"

"What?"

"Are you asking 'what' because you didn't hear me or because you've never heard of MoonPies?"

The clerk pursed her lips in annoyance. "What's a MoonPie?"

Eunice turned her head for a second and bit her lower lip. "It's covered with chocolate and filled...oh, never mind. How about pork rinds?"

"*Pork rinds?*"

"Yes! Pork rinds. They take the fat off pigs, cut it in strips, deep-fry it, salt it, and put the pieces in a cellophane bag. People eat it."

The girl's eyes opened wider. "Oh! Pork rinds! No, *we* don't have those. But I can tell you where to get them."

"That would be great. Where's that?"

"Get back on a train and go about eight hundred miles south."

Cahane felt the first bubbling of anger inside, which quickly diffused when she noticed that the girl had a trace of a smile on her face. Grinning back, her voice friendly, she said, "Okey-dokey. I got it. I'm in New York now, not Georgia."

The clerk's smile broadened. "I'm sorry. I couldn't help it. I was just teasing."

"Maybe you can help me then. I'm on my way to a...slumber party. You do have those in New York, don't you?"

"Uh-huh. Up here we have our own bedrooms and everything."

Eunice shook her head. "You're cute, but don't push it. *Anywho,* I'm going to kind of a slumber party and I wanted to take some stuff. Already got chocolate and popcorn. What do *New York* girls eat at slumber parties? And don't you dare say sushi."

The girl laughed. "Uck! No. Not sushi. Grab a bag of Doritos, the nacho-flavored kind. And get dip. I like the spinach one."

"That's great. What about something to drink?"

"Jägermeister's my favorite."

Cahane snorted rudely. "I mean soda pop. You have RC Cola?"

"*RC...what?*"

▽

Her apartment passed inspection. Lisa left her security detail outside in the hallway, led Shannon to the kitchen, and poured two glasses of Chablis.

"That Stu guy is creepy," Shannon commented after taking a sip.

"Tell me about it. And Tom isn't much better."

"When I heard you had bodyguards, I was visualizing Kevin Costner."

Lisa snickered. "I'm no Whitney Houston. Hey, I'm going to heat some stew. Would you like a bowl?"

"Are you making that because it's your bodyguard's name?"

"Don't be dumb. You want any?"

"No. I hate stew."

Lisa opened a large can, dumped the contents into a pot, put it on the stove, and lit the burner, setting it to medium.

"How can you hate stew? Everybody likes stew."

Draining her glass and holding it forward for a refill, Shannon answered, "Just do."

Lisa poured more wine for both of them. "But it's the universal food. We all grew up eating stew. It's meat, potatoes, carrots…all in a rich, savory broth. What's not to like? How can you hate that?"

Shannon shrugged. "You sound like a bad commercial! Don't know why. I guess I just hate the texture or the consistency or something. I just like all of those things individually, you know, on a plate, each with its own designated space on that plate. Maybe I just hate the concept of stew."

"You know, you use the word *just* way too much."

The assistant yelped in amusement. Her voice substantially more animated now than minutes earlier, she rejoined, "Oh, really? I do, huh? Well, maybe I shouldn't say this…since you're my boss and all…but you use the word *like* constantly."

"*I do not!*"

"Yes, you do. You're always saying…'it's *like* 12:30'…or…'the show ran *like* three minutes over'…or…'looks *like* rain'…or…."

"Stop it! Stop it! I *like* get it."

"*Just* saying."

The two gave in to high-pitched laughter.

▽

Carrying two overstuffed plastic bags, Cahane, still chortling about the interlude with the shop clerk, glanced up at the large wall clock in the main concourse and hurried through the exit, finding a long line of taxis at the curb. At the front of the line, a man of a national origin she was unable to identify was leaning against the fender. The back door was open and she climbed in, situating the bags on the seat beside her, and pulled out the slip of paper with Lisa's address, giving it to the cabbie as he hopped in behind the wheel without saying a word and dropped the flag on the meter.

The station area was heavily congested, and she settled back in the seat, disregarding the odd aroma which filled the passenger compartment, forcing herself to remain calm as the driver immediately began honking his horn at the sea of yellow cabs jockeying for positions in front of them.

▽

"I really should get going," Shannon remarked, standing from the couch.

Lisa, now slightly tipsy from the wine on an empty stomach, rose unsteadily. "Okay. Thanks for bringing over the file."

"No problem. It was fun. Well, not the 'bringing it over' part. That wasn't any fun at all. But after I got here. You're kind of silly…for a boss and all that."

Lisa snorted at the comment. "Yeah. And you're fun…for a ditsy blonde, I mean." She heard a sizzling, popping sound from the kitchen. "What the…oh! *The stew!*"

Shannon, still giggling, opened the door to reveal Stu, who was standing directly outside. She had completely forgotten about him and, startled, jumped back into Lisa, knocking her boss hard against the arm of the couch and sending her cartwheeling over and onto the cushions. Rushing to help her up, Shannon, who was now hooting hysterically, managed to stammer, "I…I'd really better get out of here now."

Wiping tears from her own eyes, Lisa urged, "Go! Beat it before you kill me or put me in the hospital."

Shannon nodded and backed over the threshold, turning sideways to edge past Stu, and pulled the door closed. Lisa rushed to the kitchen and turned down the burner under the pot, which was now erupting with a thick brown foam cascading down the sides and onto the sputtering stove.

"Oh, what a mess!" she cried and, moving the kettle to the turned-off front burner, spun to get a sponge from the sink, when she rammed into the chest of Stu Cutter. Startled, she demanded, "What the hell are you doing in here?"

$$\triangledown$$

The taxi double-parked in front of Lisa's address, and Eunice paid the driver and got out, bending back into the vehicle for her sacks. Straightening, she slammed the door with her hip, then approached the apartment building and marched purposefully up the steps, where she was stopped by a young man in what appeared to Eunice to be an admiral's uniform. It took her a moment to realize that he was the doorman for the building.

"Can I help you, ma'am?"

"Yes. I'm here to see Lisa Trippiano."

He made a show of examining her before asking, "Is she expecting you?"

Cahane shook her head. "Actually, no, she's not. I was going to surprise her."

"I'm sorry, but I'll have to buzz her and make sure it's okay to let you in."

She heaved a sigh. "Fine. Go ahead."

He turned to a panel mounted on the wall in an alcove, and pressed a button. Her eyes followed his finger and she unconsciously noted the apartment number. After several seconds of silence, he pressed the button again, holding it down longer this time.

"Is she home?"

"Yes, ma'am. She arrived a short time ago with a friend."

"A friend? Maybe they are…."

"No, ma'am. The friend was a young lady from where Miss Trippiano works."

As he spoke, the double doors opened and Shannon, still grinning broadly, burst out. "Hi, Dirk!" Her voice overly spirited, she was fully focused on the doorman and barely noticed Cahane.

"Uh…hello, Shannon. Is Miss Trippiano with you?"

The assistant's eyebrows dropped dramatically at his question, and Eunice thought to herself, *This girl has had a bit too much of the joy juice.*

"No! I left her upstairs just…." Something in what she had said caused Shannon to pause and giggle. *"Just* a minute ago. Why?"

Tilting his head toward Cahane, he explained, "She has a visitor. I buzzed her apartment, but she isn't answering."

Eunice interrupted the conversation. "Was everything okay when you left?"

"Oh, sure! I'm sure she's fine," she gushed redundantly. "Besides...she has those two bodyguards with her."

Hearing the words, Cahane dropped the sacks on the stoop and pushed past the doorman, who shouted after her, "Hey, lady! Wait!"

Stu Cutter did not answer Lisa. Instead, his hand snaked forward and grabbed her arm roughly, his fingers digging painfully into the skin. She tried to pull away and started to scream, but he whirled her around so that her back was against his torso, and covered her mouth with his other hand, stifling the sound. Simultaneously panicked and furious, she lifted her right foot and tried to slam the heel down on his instep. He was expecting this and had shifted his stance, with his feet spread wide on the floor, out of range.

His right arm was across the front of her body, holding Lisa in a vise grip, and when she felt his hot breath on her neck, she reacted instinctively, jerking her head back as hard as she could. Her skull connected cleanly with his chin, loudly snapping his jaw shut and making him bite his tongue. Her move resulted in a momentary loosening of his hold and she was able to lean forward and, with her free hand, seize the handle of the pot filled with still-bubbling stew. Folding her knees and collapsing downward against his body, ducking her head at the same time, she swung the kettle overhand in the direction of his face and felt the satisfying jar as it impacted, discharging the boiling contents.

He screamed and released her, clawing at the steaming, running mixture coating his face. She shoved him aside and ran out of the kitchen to the front door. Halfway there, Lisa saw the knob turn and the door begin to open. Realizing it must be Tom, reacting to his partner's scream and coming in to help finish her off, she did not break her stride and, twisting her upper body on the run, crashed into the partially open door with her shoulder. The impact violently slammed it shut, and a howl of pain erupted from the other side.

Her hands trembling badly, she fumbled the two deadbolts closed and latched the chain only a split second before she felt more than heard the shudder of the door as the other assailant rammed it. With a glance toward the small kitchen, she saw Stu bending forward with his entire head in the sink, running water over his face, and knew she did not have not much time. Unconsciously, she made a breathy shouting sound with each ragged exhale as she ran to the far end of the heavy couch and pushed it against the door, thrusting it into position an instant before another crash reverberated and the wood loudly creaked a protest.

Cahane, panting heavily, cursed the fact that she had not taken elevator. Running at her capacity since leaving Dirk and Shannon behind, she was only up to the sixth floor and could feel the muscles in her legs cramping horribly.

"Come on, Eunice!" She repeatedly coached herself onward and heard the echoing thunder of footsteps from below, assuming that the doorman was giving chase. Deliberately, she conjured an image of what could be happening to Lisa. The gruesome picture did its job and she felt a powerful surge of adrenaline course through her body, quickening her pace.

Indecision paralyzed Lisa for only a few seconds as she tried to decide what to do. There was a gun…a compact .32 caliber pistol in the nightstand drawer next to her bed. Her weapon was unloaded and stored inside a zipped leather pouch, the filled clip lying beside it. The problem with going to get it was that she would have to pass the kitchen, and she decided she definitely did not like the odds.

Springing into action, Lisa dashed away from the kitchen and to her windows, one of which she knew lifted easily and opened to the fire escape. The front door splintered badly from another impact. She wrenched the window latch and slammed the single-hung sash up to the stops. Hoisting one leg into the opening and ducking to pass her body through, she glimpsed back. Tom had managed to shatter one of the door panel inserts and was poking his pistol through the craggy hole in her direction.

She fell out onto the metal landing at the same instant the glass on the upper section of the window exploded from a bullet, showering her with shards. Crouching to remain below the sill, she crossed the small platform to the first set of descending steps. Holding both rusted rails, she scampered down, not looking up until reaching the next landing. Lisa saw Stu begin climbing out the window, his face an ugly bright red and mottled.

Cahane arrived on the ninth floor just as she heard the gunshot. Operating purely on instinct, she straight-armed the panic bar on the fire door and exploded out into the hallway, the steel door crashing loudly against the wall. A man was fifteen yards from her, his arm pushed through a hole in a door. He was already turning to see who had so noisily arrived. Without missing a pace, she surged forward at a full run as he struggled to extricate his arm from the splintered and jagged opening. He jerked it clear and swung his gun toward her.

Stretching her mouth wide, she bellowed an earsplitting wail and, ducking her head down, charged him, colliding with the force of a fullback, sending them both sprawling to the floor, as the pistol skittered across the carpet. They had landed with the stranger on his back and Eunice on top. She scrambled upright to a seated position astride his chest and, without hesitation, began pummeling his face with her fists.

Lisa ran down the steep stairs, tripping twice. The second stumble sent her toppling to her knees, gashing one of them on the steel slats. Gasping for air, she muttered sardonically, "They don't call me *Trippy* for nothing." Above her, Stu stopped and aimed his gun down, firing off a round which ricocheted noisily on the fire escape framework close to her head, creating a blossom of sparks. Fighting off irrational panic, she stole a quick look down and saw what seemed to be an endless latticework of landings and stairs before she could reach the alley.

Again firmly seizing the railing, she jerked her head upward, saw that he had resumed his chase, and shouted, "Hey, Stu, is that the best you got?"

He stopped, aimed, and shot. Again missing.

Dirk, the doorman, came running to Cahane, who was still straddling the now bloody and unconscious man.

His voice cracked as he asked, "What the hell is going on?"

She nodded in a direction down the hallway and, between gulps of air, managed to say, "I'm a detective…with the Atlanta PD. Grab this guy's gun…will ya, Dirk?"

He had the presence of mind to react to her instructions and ran to the gun where it had come to rest, picking it up. She instantly took in how casually he handled it. "I can tell by the way you hold that piece, you ain't afraid of it."

"No, ma'am. Own one myself. Just about everyone in New York does."

"I thought they banned 'em here."

"Yeah, right."

"You got a phone with you?"

"Yes, ma'am."

"Call 9-1-1 and keep...." She heard the boom of a gunshot through the damaged apartment door and jumped up. "Cover him till the cops come. If he tries anything, shoot him."

Without waiting for confirmation from the young man, Eunice spun to face the door and peered through the broken panel, saw the couch jammed against it, and the far window wide open. A second shot, slightly more distant, rang out.

"Is there a fire escape out those inside windows?" she barked loudly at Dirk, who was already dialing his phone.

"Yes, ma'am."

Whirling around, she spotted a window at the end of the hallway and pointed at it. "Is there one outside that, too?"

"Yes, ma'am, there is."

Eunice took off at a full run. Reaching the goal, she twisted the latch and lifted on the sash, which did not budge. Layered coats of paint had, over the years, welded the unit together. She poked the glass with her elbow, shattering the pane, while griping aloud, "Don't they have fire marshals in this town?"

Pulling her pistol, she used the barrel to clear the stubborn shards around the opening, hoping the falling pieces did not hit anyone in the alley below, and climbed through to the metal landing.

Running on autopilot, Lisa moved as fast as she dared...not wanting to fall again, sprinting across the short landings, swinging around to and clambering down each flight of stairs, allowing herself a snap glance up at each turn. Only two flights separated her from Stu, who was charging downward with apparent disregard for his own safety. He was no longer stopping to take any more shots.

Focusing intently on the threat from above, Lisa was astonished when she suddenly set foot on the final landing, which terminated in a vertical retracting ladder. Stepping over the small opening, she grabbed a rung and planted her feet on a lower one, fully expecting her weight to trigger the torsion-controlled drop of the ladder. It did not move.

The crashing, rattling sounds of Stu's frantic descent were getting closer. The asphalt of the alley was too far for a jump. "Come on!" she urged desperately. Flexing her knees and holding on tightly with her hands, she began jumping up and down on the ladder, hoping to break it free. Still nothing.

Beginning to succumb to the panic she had been repressing, she looked up and saw that Stu was now one flight above her on the landing directly over her position, and behind his back appeared the face of an older woman who had pulled her blinds aside to check out the commotion. A wicked grin filling his red and blistered face, he dropped to his knees and poked the barrel of his pistol through the spaced bars. She flailed madly, swinging her body erratically in a futile attempt to dodge the imminent bullet. The desperate movements were the final impetus needed to break the ladder free, and she abruptly dropped a second before he pulled the trigger.

Eunice Cahane heard the gunshot over the clatter of her hasty progress down the fire escape around the corner of the building from where Lisa was struggling to escape. "Dammit!" she shouted and plunged recklessly ahead, afraid she was already too late.

The spring-loaded ladder slammed into the alley floor so violently that Lisa was thrown clear and landed heavily on her back. Due to the sudden, unexpected drop, Stu's shot had missed her, deflecting off a rung above her hands. Holstering his pistol, he ran the length of the final landing.

Lisa, dazed by her impact, took a few seconds to clear her head. Seeing her assailant reach the now descended final ladder, she rolled over and jumped to her feet, taking off at a full run as he raced down to her level. Hitting the pavement running, he chased her, his long legs helping to rapidly close the gap.

The sounds of his shoes slapping on the alley and his loud, wheezing breaths getting nearer, Lisa pushed herself harder. Clearing the corner of her building and crossing an intersection of two alleys, she felt a hand grasp her shoulder and pull her down. Shrieking as she fell, Lisa tumbled, ripping her clothes and tearing open one of her elbows. He was on her in the blink of an eye, pinning her completely with his weight and jamming her face roughly against the ground, as he raised his upper torso and wrapped both of his hands around her neck. A futile sob burst from Lisa as she fully comprehended that she was helpless...that there was absolutely nothing she could do.

Cahane thundered down the metal stairs, shaking the old fire escape, and onto the last landing above the alley. Lisa, running, burst into view to the right, followed a heartbeat later by a large man, who grabbed her and pulled her down. Torn by indecision for only a moment, unsure whether she should try to go down the final ladder to reach the two, Cahane dropped to one knee and pulled out her semi-automatic, gripping it with both hands as the man sat astride Lisa's back and clamped his fingers around her neck. The detective rested her forearms on the railing, lined up the sights and, with monumental discipline, sucked in a massive, calming breath, letting it out slowly and steadying herself. With the breath half-released, she held it and counted to three, gently easing back the trigger on the final digit.

Lisa was teetering on the edge of the abyss, darkness inexorably closing in on her consciousness, allowing nothing other than a chaotic jumble of thoughts and images. At the periphery of her awareness, not certain if it was real or an illusion, she heard the gunshot and, synchronized perfectly, felt the grip on her neck go slack. Spasmodically sucking air into her lungs and not waiting to understand what had happened, she bucked her back upward, throwing off her assailant, and rolled over to see his chest and shoulder drenched with blood; his red and blistered visage, facing her as he lay on his side, a mask of pain; his eyes, not focused on her or anything else, casting a diminishing flicker of life. She stared, unable to divert her gaze, as a seemingly improbable transition erased the animation from within, replacing visible sentience with a dull, glazed, and lifeless mien.

Lisa sat up and scooted backward on her behind, badly shredding her slacks as she put more distance between herself and the now dead man. Panting mightily, with her knees pulled up below her chin and her arms circled around them tightly, she was locked into a fixed stare at this figure who, only moments ago, had been a deadly threat, when she heard a voice say, "You sure know how to throw a slumber party, missy."

The irrationality induced by the previous minutes had not allowed Lisa to connect the sudden death of her attacker with the obvious presence of another person. She was dumbfounded by the voice. Jerking her head to the side, she saw Eunice, still holding her gun, albeit pointing it straight up, and walking toward her with a mixture of relief and concern on her face. She jumped up and ran to the detective, throwing her arms around the burly woman, and...surrendering to the pent-up flood of emotions...sobbed convulsively.

Eunice put her free hand on Lisa's back and patted her comfortingly, while guiding her in a gentle turn, as if she were teaching a dance step, so that she could keep an eye on the fallen man in the alley. "There, there, missy. You're fine now."

Chapter 23

===

NIGHT HAD FALLEN OVER THE ARIZONA DESERT and the sky was crystal clear, revealing an abundance of stars overhead. With Chili in transit, traveling a circuitous route and collecting members of their group, and Romeo in Socorro with Ricky, Scott had assumed the responsibility of monitoring the perimeter cameras and sensors on Kelsey's compound. Judtson, reading that a meteor shower was expected, asked Kelsey if she would like to join him for a dip in her swimming pool to watch it.

The two, reclining on floating lounge chairs, stared skyward and were relaxed in a companionable silence, broken by Kelsey. "I can't believe how lucky Lisa was today."

Judtson chuffed softly. "If you call almost being killed 'lucky,' I guess you're right."

"The operative word is *almost*. Was it Churchill who said, 'Nothing in life is so exhilarating as to be shot at without result'?"

"Something like that. Good thing the detective showed up when she did."

"No kidding. Maybe now Lisa will come along with the rest."

Judtson twisted slightly on the fabric seat to face her. "You're thinking that she *still* might not?"

Expressing frustration, Kelsey sighed. "She's talking about remaining in New York until we do the show. And Detective Cahane is going to stay to keep an eye on her."

"That's a help, I guess. But I'd feel better if she joined us."

"Me too. Hey, I have an idea. Let's see if the show can be done from Tucson instead of New York. Then Jack Bailey would just have to come here to host it, instead of all of us going there."

"I don't see why not. They can use the studio of their affiliate. And the local station has the capacity to broadcast up to the satellite as easily as they can in New York."

"I'll talk to her about it tomorrow. That way, maybe she can join us and put it together from here."

Another silence followed, which lasted for several minutes. Finally, Kelsey asked, "What're you thinking?"

Roused from his reverie, Judtson answered, "Saylor."

"What about him? You wondering what he's doing?"

"No, not exactly. Mainly, I was focusing on how his life has been completely turned upside down in the last few weeks."

Kelsey did not say anything and, after a short pause, he elaborated, "It began before we busted Beckleman. Saylor had this steady, solid, predictable life. He had his medical practice. And he had Doni. It seemed perfect." A few more seconds passed until he continued. "You know…I was always jealous of him."

She turned her head away from the starlit vista. "Jealous? Of What? You mean *you* wanted Doni?" Her voice gently conveyed more than mere idle curiosity.

Sensing the underlying edge to her question, Judtson hastily replied, "No! Well, not really…what I'm trying to say is that for a long time I did. Or thought I did. Going all the way back to elementary school where the three of us first became friends. When we were all together, I was always noticing every time she would laugh at one of Saylor's dumb jokes, every time she casually grabbed his hand instead of mine while we were out rollerblading. Kelsey…this is going to sound silly…or crazy. I actually kept a running tally."

"A running tally?"

"This is so goofy…I hate to admit this to anyone…I never have…but I assigned each of those things a point value. Every time she'd laugh at his comment…or mine…that would be a point for one of us. Holding hands was three points…only if she initiated it. Which one of us she would sit closer to if there weren't three seats in a row…like in a movie theater, because then she always sat between us…five points."

"You're joking. You kept track of all those points?"

He nodded sheepishly. "Yeah. I did. Dorky, huh? And the thing is…Saylor was always just a little bit ahead of me. That's why, I guess, in seventh grade I decided to be more aggressive and even up the score or actually pull ahead."

"Uh-oh, that sounds a little spooky. Like something out of the diary of a stalker."

Chuckling, he explained, "No. Nothing like that. Well, maybe a little. In the initial stages anyway, the only difference between some of the behaviors of a stalker and the actions of a person in love is whether they are welcomed by the object of the attention."

"That's true. So you…loved her?" The last sentence was spoken by Kelsey at a near whisper.

"Thought I did. I'm getting to that."

"And what did you do to rack up more *Doni points*?"

"I kissed her. Wait, let me back up. First I rigged it. I arbitrarily decided that an actual kiss with her would be worth fifty points."

"Wow! That was generous."

"It was. And, of course, it had nothing to do with the fact that, according to the ongoing tally, I was forty-two points behind at that time."

Kelsey laughed. "No, of course not. So?"

"So…what?" he rejoined innocently.

"How was it?"

"How was what?"

She made a rude sound with her lips. "Don't be obtuse. How was it kissing her?"

In the dim light, she saw a slight smile appear on his face. "Why are you so curious?"

The two floating lounges were side by side. Kelsey, while staring unblinkingly into his eyes, abruptly reached out and grabbed the edge of Judtson's chair and jerked it upward, dumping him into the water with a splash. He came up sputtering and laughing, and instead of the expected reaction of dumping her into the water, he grabbed his upended float and towed it to the steps at the far end, where he was able to climb aboard. As he paddled back beside her, she asked, "You going to tell me now?"

Squeegeeing the water from his face with his hands first, he said, "I suppose I'd better. It was blah."

"What?"

"The kiss…it was blah."

"*Blah?*"

"Uh-huh."

"You mean she was bad at it?"

"No. Not that. She did it right. It happened at the tail end of seventh grade and I was a fairly normal thirteen-year-old boy. In other words, fully steeped and marinated in hormones. I was already constantly fantasizing about…."

"I don't want to hear this."

"Okay, okay. Well…I was expecting a hell of a lot more out of it than I got. Which was zero, zip, zilch, the big digit."

"Maybe it was you," Kelsey teased.

"Maybe. But I kissed other girls that same year and, you know, after that. None of *them* had any complaints. In fact, one time I kissed this eighth grader named…."

"Judtson! Stop!"

Tickled by her jealousy, he shifted the topic. "You know how it is when you're around someone attractive. Even if that someone is dating your best friend…or gets engaged…or even gets married…you still, deep down in a secret corner of your mind, can have carnal thoughts about that person."

"Carnal thoughts? I haven't heard that phrase in…ever!"

"I'm trying to be circumspect. Anyway, the point is that all through middle school, high school, and college, I liked Doni. I *really* liked her. In a way, I guess I did love her. Yet, no matter what the three of us did together, or later the four of us after I got together with Kristen, I never thought about her…that way. Not for a second."

"Probably due to how close you and Saylor were…I mean, are."

"I've thought of that. Could be, I suppose."

He lapsed into a thoughtful silence for a time. After giving him a few minutes, Kelsey asked, "What's wrong?"

"I don't know. Yes, I actually do. When I went to their house…to see them both and bring up the Devil's Breath thing, I was surprised by how I felt inside. It wasn't what I expected."

"What do you mean?"

"If you had told me that it was Saylor who was suspected of betraying us, I wouldn't have bought it for a moment. I don't care what kind of evidence you had. I thought I'd feel the same way about Doni. But I didn't."

"Yeah, I sort of picked that up when we talked about it. Why do you think that is?"

He shook his head, spraying her with small droplets flung from his hair. "Don't know. She has always been a good friend. Never given me a reason not to trust her. Since then, it has bothered me…a lot. I feel as if I've betrayed *her*."

Kelsey studied his eyes intently. It bothered her to see him, this man she cared so much about, disconcerted…withdrawn. Hoping to lift him out of his sudden funk by deliberately pressing one of his buttons, she touched his arm and smirked mischievously. "It's not that big a deal, Squirrel. Don't sweat it."

Even in the faint light, she was able to see the desired result. His eyebrows shot up, his eyes widened, and he barked, his voice more harsh than he intended, "Kelsey, I've asked you not to call me that!"

She instantly held up both hands defensively. "Okay, okay. Sorry."

Seeing her reaction, Judtson backpedaled, "No, *I'm* sorry. I didn't mean to snap at you. It's just…I hate that name. Nobody calls me that…except Doni."

"Oh, I didn't mean to infringe on your private little *intimacy*." It was clear by her inflection that she was hurt.

He slid off the floating lounge, pulled Kelsey from hers, and put his arms around her. "Don't. That isn't what I meant. At all. It's only that everyone else knows I hate it and they don't use it."

"Doesn't she know you hate it?"

"Yes. At least I've told her…about a hundred times."

"And she does it anyway?"

"Yes."

"Why?"

He thought for a second before answering. "I don't know. I really don't. She won't let it go, though. I've given up trying to get her to stop. But I didn't want you to start with it."

She kissed him lightly. "I understand. And I won't. Ever. Promise. Are you at least going to tell me where it came from?"

Smiling halfheartedly, he hesitated for a few seconds. "All right. I'll tell you. You'll be the first I've ever told, though."

"Gee, I'm honored."

He ignored her sarcasm, inhaled a deep breath, and tentatively began the story. "It was in elementary school at the end of the year. Saylor and I were already friends with her and we were being our normal competitive selves for her attention."

Kelsey rolled her eyes. "Men!"

"Whatever. Anyway, the school had a spelling bee and all three of us entered it. Saylor got knocked out early. Third round. He has always been a rotten speller. I was already a voracious reader and was kicking butt. Doni was hanging in there, too. As more and more of the other kids fell out, it became obvious that it would come down to either Doni or me."

Judtson paused, lost in his own memories for a moment. His voice was lower and more serious as he continued. "With only five finalists left, I noticed that Doni had changed. She had turned into a different person. Up until then she was having fun, laughing…kidding me and the others. You know, really lighthearted about the whole thing. When it was clear that she could win, she became intense. Unpleasantly so."

"Okay. I think I see where this is going, at least the spelling bee part of it."

"Uh-huh. The structure of the contest was that after each round, the difficulty of the words escalated by one grade level. We had reached tenth-grade difficulty when the other three kids were knocked out. And that left just Doni and me. Her turn was first. The principal gave her the word *amoeba*. She…she almost flubbed it. She panicked, transposed the *o* and *e*. At the last possible second, she corrected it and passed, but as she stepped back, I knew her confidence was gone. My next word was…*squirrel*."

He heard a muted gasp from Kelsey. "So you beat her and she's used that as your nickname ever since to let you know she has never forgiven you."

"No. I wish that was how it went. I told you…I liked her. I wanted her to like me."

Surprise in her voice, Kelsey blurted, "You threw the spelling bee!"

"I did. I knew how to spell *squirrel*. But right before the part where the contestant was supposed to repeat the word to indicate to the judges that it was a final answer, I added a second *l*."

It took Kelsey less than a minute to figure out the rest. "Hold on! You told me that no one knows about this. Do you mean she didn't ever find out that you handed her the contest on a silver platter?"

"She didn't."

"What a bitch! She assumed she had actually beaten you and has, for the rest of your life, rubbed your nose in it! I can't imagine why you didn't eventually set her straight."

"Who'd believe me? It would sound like sour grapes. Besides, what difference does it make?

Judtson suddenly changed the subject. "What about tomorrow? You aren't going to Gates Pass for the meeting, are you?"

She jerked her head in a nod which was almost imperceptible in the starlight. "I have to. What if it is my father?"

"You and Scott have decided it can't be."

"Not *can't be*…just *probably isn't*. I can't take that chance, Judtson. What if it is Daddy? What if he will be waiting out there for me? I can't just not show up!"

"It's not a good idea. I don't like the timing. Do you honestly think it's a coincidence that you are contacted by Alchemist, who wants to have a meeting out in the hills, at the exact time Chili is traipsing around the world and Romeo is in New Mexico? You have no protection."

She leaned her bare shoulder against his. "I have you."

Judtson snorted. "Me? What am I going to do…talk them to death? Disable them with a particularly nasty barb critiquing their grammar?"

Giggling at the image, she snuggled against him.

After briefly considering the options, he asked, "Can't we at least get Chili here in time for the meeting?"

"No. We have our pilot bouncing all around, gathering everyone up. He has exceeded FAA flight hour limits and is on a mandatory sleep break. I could rent another pilot, I suppose. But would you trust him?"

"Absolutely not. That would be a perfect opportunity for the bad guys to insert their own man and grab everyone on the plane."

"Exactly. I had Scott check, and the soonest we can get Chili back, even using alternate transportation, is well after the meeting. And we can't disengage Romeo. If Chris is in Socorro, we need to get him out soon."

"Understood. I really don't like it, though."

"Hey, I don't either. Any other suggestions?"

He thought for a while, coming up blank. "No. We should call Romeo and tell him about it. Maybe he'll have an idea."

"I hate to do that. He's going to forbid me from going. Cancel the mission and run back here. I can't allow that."

"Then don't. You're still his boss."

"I. . .guess."

"Come on, Kelsey. It's not too late. Let's call him now."

▽

Romeo and Ricky were in the black Hummer, driving back to the motel, when Romeo's phone rang. Checking the Caller ID, he answered hands-free, "RJ."

He heard Kelsey's voice. "Hi. It's me. How did it go today?"

"Went well. We had a good recon this morning. After that, both of us took the tour and were able to get nice and close to the building where he is supposedly being held. Spent the rest of the day on a hill, watching the place and learning the patterns, until it got dark."

"Any patrols after dark?"

"Nope."

"Do you think he's in there?"

"I do. We observed a total of three men coming and going from the building at various times. One of the men had a valise and an object which looked a lot like the headpiece they brought to JK's office. On another visit, one of them was carrying a tray of food."

"Sounds right," she remarked, slightly excited. "When are you going to make your move?"

"Not sure yet. My buddy here wants to do it late tonight. Or just before sunrise. We're going to go back and talk about it more and then get some shut-eye, in case that becomes the plan. What's happening with you?"

Kelsey hesitated, not looking forward to the discussion. "We heard from Alchemist."

The news surprised him. "You did? When?"

"Today. I don't want to go into details, safe phones or not. Let's say that confidence is not high that he's a chocolate chip shake."

It did not take long for Romeo to interpret her comment, recalling that one of Kelsey's favorite items was a prepackaged milkshake called F'Real. She enjoyed the company's drinks so much that she had one of their machines installed in her kitchen.

"Got it."

"But, RJ, the deal is. . .he wants to meet me."

The Ranger tensed. "When? Where?"

"Uh. . .tomorrow morning, nine o'clock. Up at Gates Pass."

"*Kelsey*," he barked, uncharacteristically forgetting the protocol of avoiding real names over the phone, his voice firm. "You are not going. It might be a trap."

She attempted to match his firmness. "No, RJ, I am."

"If you are, I'll scrub this mission and get back right now. You are not going in without protection."

Although she had nearly always acceded to his directives, Kelsey took a deep breath and stood her ground. "No. There is a chance he is who he says he is. I have to take that chance. I *am* doing the meeting. You *are* staying and finishing what you went to do."

Romeo pulled his rig off the highway onto the shoulder and slammed on the brakes, skidding to a stop in a cloud of dust and fighting back his anger. Just as the silence on the line had stretched to the point where Kelsey was certain he had hung up on her, she heard a curt "All right."

Letting out her pent-up breath loudly, she said, "Thank you. Now, I know that you and CK are both tied up. I think it would be a good idea to have somebody watching me in the morning. Any suggestions?"

He mulled it over silently. Ricky, who had been quietly listening to both sides of the conversation on the speakerphone, offered, "I have an idea. But we probably shouldn't discuss it on the phone."

Chapter 24

===============

SITTING AT THE SMALL TABLE IN ROMEO'S ROOM, Ricky watched his partner anxiously pace. "You are going to wear a path in the carpet."

The Ranger stopped and faced him. "I don't like it."

"It'll be fine. We have a good plan for covering Kelsey."

Romeo crossed the space and jerked out a chair, spinning it around and sitting in it backward. "I know. The timing has me spooked. It's almost as if they knew Chili and I were gone. How would they know? And she even said she doubted it was her father. The whole thing stinks."

"If they're watching us, they would have seen Chili go to the airport and they would have seen you and me drive out of town. I don't think that's a big mystery. What really has me spooked is *this*."

"What?"

Ricky tried on a grin, hoping to calm the big man. "Since when are you the one nervous and pacing and I'm the one calm?"

Jones steadied his eyes on his slender companion briefly before releasing a single laugh. "That's because you don't know enough to be concerned."

"Thanks a lot! Listen, whatever it is…it is. There is going to be backup. Kelsey isn't stupid. Neither is Judtson and he'll be with her, I'm sure."

"Yeah. I suppose it's fine."

"So let's try to forget about that and focus on getting Chris out. You think the plan is solid?"

Forcing himself to mentally shift gears, Romeo answered. "I do. Nice, clean, and simple. The way it should be. I go in alone. You watch the entrance and let me know if someone comes. What we encounter inside that building is an unknown, but I should be able to handle it." His phone chimed. "There's a message from Scott. He was able to download the building plans."

Ricky scooted his chair around the table, and the two studied the floor plan on the small screen, expanding the view frequently to examine the details.

"It was probably used as a computer building when the facility was first built. Back when they needed a good-sized space to accommodate the processing power required by the radio telescopes," Romeo concluded.

"Now all that processing speed would probably fit in a laptop."

"Pretty much, yeah. So that explains why the place is fairly secure, and why it doesn't have any windows of a decent size. All to protect the equipment. It also explains the monster air-conditioning gear. That would have been needed to keep those old computers cool."

They studied the plans for another few minutes, prompting Ricky to ask, "Do you see anything that could adversely affect the plan?"

"Nope. Everything is about what I expected."

"Which room do you think he's in?"

Romeo slid his thumb across the surface, shifting the view to a small room with a red bull's-eye superimposed over it. "Scott plotted it against the coordinates. This looks like the spot. And, according to him, it makes sense. He said that the tiny window faces in the direction of one of the dishes."

"So that would be the one Chris saw."

"Uh-huh."

"Well…what do you think? When do you want to go in?"

Jones stretched out his back, his eyes appraising his partner. "You ready to do it tonight?"

Throughout the trip to Socorro, reconnaissance, public tour, surveillance, and return to the motel, Ricky had been consciously focused on maintaining his composure and was secretly pleased with how well he had done. He knew that Romeo had been watching him closely for any sign that he might fall apart at some key moment. And he knew that if he gave him that sign, his seasoned buddy would scrub the mission in a heartbeat or, worse yet, go it alone. Ricky did not want to let him down.

Taking extra time to make certain his voice was rock-steady, he replied, "Damn right I'm ready."

$$\triangledown$$

Now that they were out of the pool, Judtson opened the back door of Kelsey's home and let Rocky into the yard. The golden instantly began licking Kent's dripping legs and soon looked up accusingly.

"Judtson, I think he's mad we went in the pool without him. I thought golden retrievers loved water. Why didn't you let him come in with us?"

Moving to a two-person glider, Judtson sat down and Kelsey joined him. Rocky assumed his standard position, seated and pressed against his master's leg.

"He does love water. That's the problem. Between swimming to me and then to you and then back to me, and trying to climb up on the floats with us, he wouldn't have given us a moment's peace."

"Sounds fun!"

"It is. If that's what you want to do. But not if you actually want to quietly watch a meteor shower and converse with another person."

"Yeah. Well, the meteor shower was a big dud!" She reached over Judtson's bare legs and scratched behind the retriever's ear. "Rocky, tomorrow you and I will go in the pool together!

Okay?"

The pooch reacted happily, wagging his tail.

She was leaning across the front of Judtson, and his nostrils filled with the scent of her wet hair, as he haltingly said, "I…just realized something."

"What's that?"

"Well, I…we…."

Sensing his discomfort, she teased, "Go ahead! Spit it out."

His voice conveyed a vulnerability Kelsey did not expect. "I just…showed up today. We haven't talked about…where I should stay. Do you have a spare room?"

She stopped scratching Rocky and turned toward Judtson, her face inches from his. Reading his eyes, she asked, her voice soft, "You're really not kidding, are you?"

"I don't want to assume…."

Cutting him off with a husky laugh, she shook her head before standing up and extending her hand to him. "Come with me. I'll show you the way."

He followed tacitly, being towed into the house, with Rocky trotting behind, the golden's toenails clicking softly on the tile floor. Holding Judtson's hand tightly, she led the way down the length of a long hall, paused to open a door wide, and pulled him inside. Swinging around and stopping in front of him, she wrapped her hands around his bare waist and, looking up at his face, murmured, "Here you go."

He tore his eyes away from hers and took in the surroundings. "Hey, this is *your* room!"

"No kidding, bozo." She smiled and kissed him.

▽

Chili Keyliss was sequestered in a dumpster enclosure, positioning himself behind a large steel receptacle which came up to his shoulders, with his back to the dark green masonry wall, his eyes constantly in motion, his fingers wrapped tightly, but not too tightly, around the stock of an M16A4. So far they had gathered up Carlos Villarreal and Bal Singh from the private airport in La Paz, as well as Dean Copeland from Hobby in Houston, and were now parked in an executive terminal in Dylan Falt's hometown of Seattle.

The small terminal catered to the area's wealthy, who were numerous, and Kelsey's Gulfstream V did not stand out any more than a ten-year-old Chevy pickup would be conspicuous in the parking lot of a Home Depot. The available hangars for this fussy clientele included modest sleeping quarters provided to the pilots and service staff of the customers, and Chili's group now occupied one of them, all bedded down for the night. There would be plenty of time for him to sleep, he had decided, once they were wheels up tomorrow.

From his vantage across the taxiway, he was able to watch the access points of two hangars, catercorner from each other on the tarmac. Both structures were now dark, both locked. The one to his right had been conspicuously rented for the night by Chili upon their arrival, making no attempt at subterfuge in the process. The second hangar had been secured in advance by Scott, utilizing an identification and credit card which were pure fiction. The building rented by Chili was empty.

Keyliss, silent and motionless, stood in the dark alcove, hoping neither for nor against the appearance of the bad guys. Whatever the night had in store for him, tedium or intense action, he would handle.

▽

Lisa emerged from the bathroom of the hotel suite, wearing the provided white terry-cloth robe and a large towel wrapped around her wet hair to resemble a turban. Eunice, sitting on one of the two chairs at a small table and swigging from a bottle of RC Cola Lisa had sent the concierge to hunt down, looked her up and down and pointed at her knee with the neck of the bottle. "You're bleeding again."

Lisa lifted the bottom hem. "Oh, crap. Must have opened up in the shower."

"C'mere and sit down. I'll get the stuff."

She took the other seat as Cahane hurried to the bed, snatching up the plastic bag from the drugstore where they had made a brief stop on their way. Returning, she scooted her chair around in front of Lisa, pulled a pair of latex gloves over her large hands, and patted the top of her thigh. "Put it here."

Obediently, Lisa straightened her leg and rested it on Cahane's. The detective immediately smeared a liberal coat of Neosporin on the wound, tore the cover off the gauze pack, and swiftly wrapped the knee. Watching her practiced movements, Lisa said absently, "I got blood on the robe. They're going to charge us for it."

Eunice merely grunted an acknowledgment as she finished with the gauze and, biting off three strips of adhesive tape, secured the bandage. "Let me see that elbow."

Lisa dropped her leg down and obliged, and Eunice carefully removed the large butterfly bandage they had applied earlier and replaced it with antibiotic cream, gauze, and tape. Completing the task, she repacked the supplies and slid her chair back to its original position, snatching up the cola.

Waiting for her to settle, Lisa softly murmured, "Thank you."

"No biggie. Couple of bandages is all."

"I didn't mean for that. I meant for saving my life."

Her words caught Eunice off guard only fleetingly, until she recovered and replied with a flippant tone. "Yeah. You bet. You gotta admit…that *was* something. Takin' a perp down from a second-floor balcony with a pistol. Man, I wish my range officer back at the academy had seen that shot. He was always ridin' my ass about how I couldn't hit the broad side of…."

"Eunice!" Lisa snapped. "Stop that."

The detective glanced at her innocently. "Stop what?"

"Stop…stop being so damn *Eunice* for a minute, will you? *Can* you just shut up and listen?"

Cahane, her eyes twinkling, made an exaggerated show of squeezing her lips tightly together.

"I was as good as gone. I didn't know if I had a minute more. Maybe only seconds. But when he knocked me facedown…when he was sitting on my back in that filthy alley and strangling me…that was a first for me. The first time *ever*…that I couldn't think of a way out. I…I did something I've never done."

Cahane broke her silence. "You gave up." She could see the beginning of a tear form in the corner of Lisa's eye.

"Yeah," she acknowledged softly. "I did."

"Well, you shouldn't have," Eunice chided, her voice brusque.

The comment brought Lisa back from the dark place she had been slipping into since the attack. "What do you mean, I 'shouldn't have'? What else could I have done?"

The detective's expression softened. "Look, Lisa, in this world we all have our jobs to do. You. Me. Everybody. That's the big plan. Your job was to throw that pot of stew in the bad guy's face, shove the davenport against the door, and skedaddle out the window before his partner in crime could plug you. Then, all you had to do was get down those rickety stairs and make it to the alley in plain sight for me to get my shot. That was *my* job today. You did yours. I did mine. Simple as that."

Skepticism etched itself upon Lisa's face. "Seriously, Eunice, what were the chances that you'd show up right at that moment so you could blow him away just before he killed me?"

"Obviously one hundred percent."

"One hundred...! How...how is *that* possible?"

Eunice sighed softly. "Nowhere in our little chat have you mentioned the Lord. I'm guessin' you don't believe in Him."

Lisa started to speak but was cut off with a wave. "It doesn't matter if you do or if you don't. I, personally, don't believe that He gives a hoot about that. What He does care about are people like you. Good people. People who try to do the right things...not the popular things, not the expedient things, not the things those pinheaded morons in Washington tell us are the politically correct things. People who try to live their lives the way He taught us we should. You know what? You nailed it, Lisa. What *were* the chances that I'd decide to hop on a specific train and come to New York? Meet that goofy purple-haired girl at the station. Get exactly the cab ride I got. Happen to be jawing at the front door with Dirk while we both waited for you to *not* answer your buzzer, right as your friend Shannon came out and told me you were home and had two bodyguards with you. And what were the chances of me running up those stairs and charging out into the hallway right as Tom had his arm stuck in the hole in your door, givin' me barely enough time to knock him flat? And then, remember I couldn't get into your room. Good thing too, 'cause I'd probably have followed Stu down the fire escape and either he could've shot me as I came out the window or, at the least, I would've not been in a great position to help you when you needed it."

She stopped her rapid-fire summation and gulped a breath, allowing a grin to fill her wide face. "But, guess what, Lisa? It all *did* happen. Just right. Just the way it needed to. So now...it's up to you. You can decide that all of those little things were only an *amazing* string of coincidences, or you can figure out...that they were meant to be. Either way you decide...just so you know...is fine with me. But if you're inclined to be dishing out any thank-yous, don't thank the tool. Thank the Man who used it."

▽

Five hours into his self-assigned detail, still anchored in place and concealed behind the dumpster, Chili thought he saw a shadow flit along the wall of the hangar on the right. Two hours earlier, it had begun to rain lightly and the precipitation had reduced both visibility and audibility, so he was not certain of what he had seen, and knew he had not heard anything. His training told him that focusing all of one's attention on a specific spot during a guard detail was a good way to get blindsided. Knowing this, he maintained his grid-by-grid survey of the surroundings. The only concession he made to the shadow was a more frequent check of the hangar.

Because of the dense cloud cover, there was no moonlight. The sole sources of illumination were widely spaced, pole-mounted, low-pressure sodium lights, which cast a sickly yellow glow from extremely high perches. Fortunately, the ribbed metal perimeter walls of the hangars were white, making the four black-clad men, slowly circling the building toward the entrance door, pop out visually for Chili. Moving with exquisite slowness, he lifted his M16A4 and rested it on the lid, using the rifle's night vision scope to observe the advance.

One of the four donned earbuds and affixed a small object, obviously a highly sensitive microphone, to the skin of the building. After listening for approximately three minutes, he gave a hand signal to his team, removed the buds, and stowed the microphone. Chili remained stock-still as they made their final approach.

The standard design of the hangars was basic. The side and rear walls contained no penetrations of any sort, no windows, no doors. The front, which faced the broad taxiway, had a large sectional door centered on the wall. This motorized retractable door rolled to the right with the keying-in of a code, a code changed for each new renter. To the left of the aircraft door was a man door. That entrance point was the target for the team.

In the drizzle, one of the men dropped to his knees and went to work on the doorknob, using a lock-picking gun. It took less than thirty seconds for it to open. Three of the team members, carrying what appeared to be TEC-9 automatics, entered with choreographed movements, while the fourth remained behind. A wry grin softening Chili's intense countenance, he visualized the men as they swept into the cavernous hangar, not finding the Gulfstream V parked within. He knew that since they were inside, they would proceed to the sleeping quarters on the mezzanine level, and wondered whether they were professional enough not to indulge in temper outbursts when they found the beds empty.

As he waited for the team to emerge, he kept the crosshairs of his scope trained on the head of the fourth man, his finger resting lightly on the bottom of the trigger guard, and briefly considered preemptively taking him out, discarding the entertained thought as abruptly as it had arrived. A full seven minutes passed before the trio reappeared. While prior to entering the building, the men had moved in a calm, cold, and controlled regimen, now their actions were jerky and sloppy. They were clearly angry and frustrated by the bad intel they had been given.

"Now comes the moment of truth," he whispered.

The four had been given either both hangars as possible targets, or only one. By their demeanor, Chili guessed the latter to be the case, but he watched them closely nonetheless. His answer came quickly as the team retraced their steps around the perimeter, leaving in the same direction from which they had arrived, rather than crossing the tarmac to the second building.

After he was certain they were gone and would not return, he slowly lowered his rifle to his side, pulled out his phone, typed a brief text message to Romeo, and continued his patient vigilance.

Chapter 25

Romeo, ONLY MINUTES EARLIER COMPLETING HIS PREP CHECKLIST for the extraction, read the incoming message from Chili, added this detail to the overall strategic picture assembling in his mind, and tossed the fully loaded duffel into the rear compartment of the Hummer. He heard Ricky's approach in the parking lot and turned to him. His partner for the evening was again suited up, garbed almost identically as he had been when he appeared at Kelsey's front door the day before yesterday, his attire now appropriate.

The two men climbed into the black vehicle wordlessly. Romeo started the engine and pulled out of the motel lot, then said matter-of-factly, "Chili called. He had visitors at the hangar in Seattle."

Ricky's head jerked around. "Everyone okay?"

"Yeah. The decoy hangar was all they checked out."

"Cool!"

The big man briefly took his eyes off the relatively deserted highway and glanced at his buddy. "You ready for this?"

"Oh, sure." The answer had come too quickly.

"Ricky...it's okay to be nervous, you know."

The younger man sucked in a loud breath, blew it out slowly, and responded, "I think I do a better job nipping off the nervousness at the bud. If I indulge myself in a little of it, I'm afraid it'll escalate all the way to a pants-wetting panic."

His candid comment brought a loud laugh from Jones.

"Look, Romeo, I don't have any illusions about who I am or what I'm capable of. You've given me some training...but not much and you know it."

"True."

"And I know that my part tonight is easy. You'll be doing all of the hard, dangerous stuff. My job is to park my butt in a ditch, maintain my cool, and keep my eyes open. A trained German shepherd could do it."

"Also true."

"I know you're rolling the dice with me. And I appreciate that. So…as far as my role tonight, you don't have to worry about me. I'll do what you need. I won't let you down."

Romeo looked away from the road again. "I have no doubt you won't. And so you know, I'm *not* worried about you."

Ricky was quiet for a moment before he sighed and said, "That just makes it worse."

With a grin, the Ranger grunted, "Yep. It was supposed to."

The two rode through the dark New Mexico night without another word.

▽

Hunched down in the drainage channel they had selected as an ideal spot during their tour and recon, a black balaclava pulled over his head, Ricky watched Romeo methodically working his way close to the building, surprised at how lithe and agile the large-framed, muscular man could be. As they had witnessed earlier, there was no sentry visible. The night was unusually still, the moonlight dimmed by cloud cover. The white rail-mounted rows of radio telescopes, radiating away from his location, appeared vaguely surreal on the flat landscape, each enormous dish topped with a small red beacon. He returned his attention to Romeo and saw that his partner had reached the door to the building.

Romeo circled to the rear of the structure, moving from Ricky's line of sight, and located the electrical service. Using nippers, he cut the low-voltage wire coming out of the wall, uncertain if it was an old-fashioned telephone line or whether it was connected to a security system. He then cut two coaxial cables which emerged from the wall through a small grommeted hole and disappeared down into the ground. Severing the lines was probably overkill, he thought.

Jones was not unduly concerned about a security system. He had learned his lesson, from the near disastrous raid on the FEMA camp, to utilize the talents of Scott Gumble, who had hacked into the LAN security and neutralized it prior to their arrival tonight. Romeo completed his final task at this stop by pulling down the handle on the electric disconnect, killing the power. At the opposite end of the building, the air-conditioning system fell silent.

During the tour, they had decided to bypass the entrance door, as it appeared to be relatively stout steel, secured with an older-model mechanical keypad. Scott had snooped around on the local network of the facility, but was unable to locate the code. The Ranger moved swiftly along the rear wall until he reached the amply oversized mechanical equipment, which was making residual popping and ticking noises in the quiet night. It was a large-tonnage package unit with capacious ducts mounted to its side and penetrating the wall of the building.

Speaking into the radio for the first time, Romeo asked in a muted voice, "All clear?"

Ricky whispered back, "All clear."

"Cutting metal now."

There was a single acknowledging click in Jones' earpiece.

This was to be the noisiest part of the mission. Romeo had felt that it was worth the risk since no patrols on the grounds had been evident during their late evening recon of the site. He pulled a highly sharpened pair of sheet metal shears from his pack and plunged the tip into the face of the ductwork. Now with a starter hole, he pulled the tool back slightly and used the cutting blades to create a large oval opening.

Chris Ashby was awakened by a strange hollow thump. Unable to identify it or its source, he lay still and listened. Throughout his few days of captivity, there had been nothing but silence throughout the night. Since he had no idea how large the building was, Chris was not sure whether Freddie and Elmo departed at the end of each day or were quartered in some distant wing.

The sound which had initially roused him had been loud and definitive, as if someone had struck a metal garbage can with a hammer. Now, through the air register in the ceiling, he could hear a vague, repetitive cutting.

At first flummoxed, Ashby suddenly jumped up from the cot and grinned.

With the opening cut, Romeo set the sharp-edged sheet metal oval aside and whispered, "Going in," heard the click in his ear, ducked his head, and stepped up and through the jagged opening. The sudden addition of weight caused the ductwork to flex and buckle, creating a muffled thunder-like rumble inside the insulation-lined channel. He switched on his head-mounted light and, in a crouch, duck-walked forward. Within five paces he was inside the perimeter wall of the building and encountered a wide-radius elbow directing the air flow upward.

Digging his fingers into the layer of insulation, he pulled it aside and, again deploying the shears, cut another opening, this time only slicing three sides, and then bent back the thin metal, his headlight revealing a small mechanical room. Romeo stepped out of the duct and glanced around, spotting the door. Replacing the shears in his hand with an M9 pistol, he whispered, "I'm in," heard the click, moved to the door and opened it, treading silently into the dark hall.

Ricky's eyes flitted back and forth, surveying the open area around the building entrance. He knew Romeo was now searching for Chris. In his mind's eye, he conjured an image of his partner working his way patiently through the floor plan, from the mechanical space to the small room Scott had identified on the plan as the probable holding cell. The internally generated movie had distracted him more than he thought it would, as he suddenly noticed a pair of men crossing the grounds and walking directly toward the building.

"*Two men are coming!*"

Romeo reacted to the intense whisper as urgently as if it had been a shout, breaking stride from a slow, cautious walk into a full run. Rapidly traversing the length of the hallway and rounding the corner, he visualized the structure's floor plan. The corridor encircled the wide and long center room, which had been the home for the banks of servers in the past. The ring between the corridor and the outside wall was lined with small offices, meeting rooms, and miscellaneous utility spaces. The likely holding cell for Ashby was two doors away. He reached it in seconds and spotted the narrow view slot on the door. Grabbing the knob, he slid the cover and peered in, cocking his head sideways so that his headlight shone through the hole. On the other side, inches from the door, was Chris Ashby's face. The chemist squinted in the flare of the light.

"Dr. Ashby, it's Romeo."

"Romeo! Am I glad to see you! Get me out of here."

"That's the plan, sir. Step back, please."

Not waiting to see if the chemist complied, he slammed the heavy deadbolt open and twisted the knob.

One of the men punched in the code and they both entered. Ricky whispered, "They're inside!" Without even a moment's hesitation, he scrambled up the slope of the drainage ditch, flinging dirt and rocks behind, and sprinted forward, his arms pumping ferociously. The pneumatic door closer was slowly, inexorably performing its function. He dashed toward the opening at the fastest pace he had ever run, calculating the timing while muttering, "Oh, shit! Oh, shit! Oh, shit!" cadenced with each exhale of breath...barely managing to slide his gloved fingers into the slight gap before the door closed and locked.

He paused on the stoop, taking a second to catch his breath and unsling the AK-47 from his back. Widening the gap carefully, Ricky peeked inside. The men were no longer in the small lobby. Using his knee to hold the door ajar, he charged his weapon, flipped off the safety, took a deep breath, and went in.

Romeo assumed that the two men, upon discovering that the power was off, had probably split up and were on alert. Certainly, one would immediately head to their prisoner's cell while the other would most predictably circle around from the other direction. The Ranger led Chris along and hurriedly retraced the route to the mechanical room. With the door to their escape not quite six feet ahead, he saw a man duck his head around the corner at the end of the corridor. Not waiting, Jones snapped off a shot as the stranger wrapped his arm around the corner and fired at them. He and Ashby dived straight for the deck.

The second man, the kidnapper Chris dubbed Freddie, had checked the holding cell to find it empty and was just backing out of the room when he heard the two shots. At a full run, he reached the intersection and chanced a quick glance. He saw Ashby and another man flat on the floor, facing away from him. From his vantage point, Freddie could only see one weapon, in the hands of the interloper. He dared not take a shot at the armed man for fear of hitting his prisoner.

Taking refuge behind the corner, he warned, "Dr. Ashby, you are in a corridor with only two exits. I'm obviously at one end and my partner is covering the other. You can't get out. I suggest you tell your rescuer to drop his weapon and give up before you are both killed."

Without hesitation, Romeo answered, "All right. You win." He placed his pistol on the floor and slowly climbed to his feet, moved forward a bit, raised his hands, and put them behind his head. Ashby followed, staying close.

The same voice from behind them boomed, "They're secured!" and the man's partner emerged from the far corner, pointing his pistol directly at Romeo's head.

Counting on the fact that the two men were professionals and would not want to be on opposing sides of a target and risk hitting each other, Jones took two steps back, positioning himself in front of the closed door to the mechanical room. Ashby moved with him, putting his back against the wall next to the jamb as Freddie and Elmo converged on them.

Freddie glared at Ashby. "This was stupid, Doctor. You could have gotten yourself killed trying to escape."

Glaring back at him, Chris snarled, "So what? You were going to start cutting my head open today, anyway."

The man turned to his cohort. "Kill the hero. We don't need him."

Elmo nodded an acknowledgment at the same moment Romeo heard a single click from the receiver in his ear. Jones dropped his arm and gripped Ashby's a split second before a shout blared from the end of the hall.

"FREEZE, JERKBALLS!"

In a blur of movements, Jones, using his free hand, reached behind and twisted the knob, flinging the door open as he jerked Ashby sideways. Elmo, his pistol already elevated, instinctively turned to the direction of the shout and found himself aiming at Freddie, whose gun remained down at his side. Jones and Ashby fell into the mechanical room. Romeo turned back to see Elmo sidestepping to find a clear shot as his partner whirled and raised his own pistol.

Romeo was geared to charge Elmo, when the harsh stutter of the AK-47 roared and he saw the man's body jerk spasmodically and crash messily to the floor. Cautiously, he leaned partially out and saw that both men were down.

"It's me! Coming out!" he signaled loudly and eased into the killing zone. Ricky was standing motionless at the end of the corridor, enveloped in a wispy cloud of gunpowder, the barrel of his rifle still pointed in Romeo's direction.

"Ricky…partner…lower your weapon."

The young man's eyes seemed to come back from somewhere and snapped into focus on the Ranger. With a slight jerk of his head, Ricky lowered the AK-47.

▽

Dylan felt his back press into the soft cushion as the twin-enhanced Rolls-Royce BR710 turbofan engines of the Gulfstream V accelerated on the runway. He was sitting alone, toward the front of the cabin, at one of a pair of four-person tables. Carlos and Bal were huddled together near the back. Copeland was at the other table, already setting up his laptop. As they had boarded this morning, Chili had calmly informed the group of the failed attack during the night, and was now fully reclined in a seat, his eyes closed.

The powerful jet rocketed skyward, and Falt waited until it leveled off before he opened the leather satchel on the adjacent seat, pulling out the thick wad of mail he had grabbed from his post-office box during the hasty departure. He thumbed through the stack idly, his mind wandering first to the news they had received from Scott of the assault on Lisa and then to the attempt on his own group overnight, and found himself wondering what was to come next.

As he set aside yet another piece of junk mail, the envelope below it caught his eye and suddenly riveted his attention. Both his address and the return address were handwritten in a flowing, feminine cursive. What caused his hands to tremble was the fact that the letter was from Rosemary Shields. Fumbling three times, he finally tore the envelope open, removed and unfolded the powder-blue stationery inside, and began to read.

Dear Dr. Falt,

I'm not certain that you are the one I should be contacting. In fact, after my fiasco at the CDC and the way it affected you, I'm not sure you want to hear from me.

But I really don't know where else to turn. People I thought were my friends at work...aren't. Even old acquaintances going back to college days seem to have turned on me. And I don't know why.

Hopefully, you received the brief email I sent. You didn't respond immediately, so I'm worried that either your spam filter diverted it, you saw it and didn't want to answer, or someone else stopped it from reaching you.

I just wanted you to know that backpedaling on the research I originally wanted you to do was not my idea. I was forced to say the things I said. I hope you believe me. That avenue must still be explored, and I trust that you can find a way to do it.

However, that isn't my main purpose for this letter. Before I can tell you what is, I must give you some background. Two years ago, I was promoted to my last position at the CDC, replacing Herbert Simms when he retired. I don't know if you ever knew Dr. Simms. He was the stereotypical researcher — an owlish, soft-spoken man who shunned the social events. But he had a jewel of a mind. His grasp of biology and pathology was phenomenal, and I admired him greatly. They retired him due to a stroke. He survived it although he was never the same.

When I moved into his office, it was left to me to pack up his personal belongings for shipment to a sister. During that process, I found an old newspaper clipping buried at the bottom of one of his desk drawers. The clipping was the only item in his office which seemed out of place to me. He wasn't a pack rat and didn't keep any mementos, so the article piqued my interest.

I apologize for taking so long to get to the point. I'll try to speed this up. The article described a flu vaccine which had been released for public use in 1986. Apparently, there was a shortage of vaccine and one of the drug companies had substituted a synthetic ingredient in the manufacturing process without FDA approval. More than fifty thousand doses were made and distributed before this was caught and stopped. The FDA, in cooperation with the drug company and working with the CDC, assembled a fairly complete list of the people who had received the vaccine. They wanted to track this group to make sure none of them exhibited any problems in the future.

I read the article that day and was about to throw it away, when I saw that Dr. Simms had written on the back of it. I recognized his handwriting. All it said was — "This may be where it began!"

Obviously, I had no idea what he meant and he was in no condition to ask. So I did an Internet search. There was no mention of any issues or problems in the years since that one vaccine release. I was, again, ready to forget about it, when I noticed something strange. The article itself did not come up in the search. I then checked the specific archives of the newspaper in which the article had appeared. According to their in-house database, no such article had ever been published. I was holding the original of it in my hand.

At the time I thought this was indeed odd. But the exigencies of my new position quickly distracted me and I put my questions aside, fully intending, at some point, to dig a little deeper. It wasn't until your much publicized adventure with your friends that Dr. Simms' article rose to the surface.

Dylan felt a creeping sense of foreboding as he continued to read.

After Dr. McWhorter in New York submitted the eight cases to us, along with the one "unknown," who was later identified in the press coverage as Judtson Kent, and our computer system was running the group through the standard epidemiological analyses, the old follow-up tracking list from the flu vaccine popped up on one of my routine reports as something the nine patients all had in common.

This, of course, got my mind spinning. The first thing I did was check the list to see if I was on it. I was! Then I tried to contact the drug company which had made the vaccines back in the '80s, and found out they had been absorbed by a European conglomerate. Their human resources department told me that the lead chemist and his entire team were no longer with the company. The lead chemist died in an automobile accident two years after the vaccine release. I was able to track down his assistant, Walter Bain, and spoke with him by phone.

Dr. Falt, I don't know what to make of what he

told me. He said that the entire incident never happened, that no substitution of the synthetic had ever occurred, and that he had no idea what in the world I was talking about. I have no idea why I did this, maybe to shake him loose from his story or jog his memory, but I scanned in the old newspaper story and emailed it to him. The next day I was fired.

Since then I've started to notice strange things, as though people have been following me…watching me. I thought I was getting paranoid, until I came home today from a visit with Dr. Simms. Someone had been in my house while I was out. It wasn't burglarized. Everything seemed to be there. I was aware of small things, little differences in each room, as if the intruder had searched the place. I'm now certain of it because I had three printouts of the scanned copy of the article in the desk drawer of my home office. I made them in case something happened to the original. When I looked, they were gone.

Thankfully, I still had the original. I had taken it with me for the visit I made to Dr. Simms, hoping he might remember something if he saw it. Unfortunately, he wasn't able to help.

After the break-in, I decided to write this letter to you. Enclosed is the original article. I wanted to get it out of my hands before they could take it from me. Also enclosed is a flash drive with the altered formula for the 1986 vaccine. I found it on Dr. Simms' computer. Apparently, he was studying it.

If this makes any sense to you...or is helpful in any way...please let me know. I'd really hate to think I'll go to my grave with this mystery unsolved.

Sincerely,
Rosemary Shields

Chapter 26

IT WAS A PLEASANTLY COOL MORNING IN THE TUCSON MOUNTAINS, diminished only by a gusty wind coming over the pass, as the cyclist, clad in brightly colored spandex and wearing an expensive wedge-shaped helmet, shifted to a lower gear and rose off the seat, bearing down on the pedals to climb the steep grade in the road. After the crest, the tight two-lane road swerved sharply to the left and then immediately transitioned into a hairpin turn to the right, following the rugged contours of the hillside. The rider gracefully banked through the turns, leaning hard, and bore down for the final climb approaching Gates Pass.

Ignoring the narrow blasted notch at the top, he angled toward the blacktop lane on the right and coasted down into the county-maintained picnic area, feathering his brakes as he neared the third concrete table. One bench was occupied by a lone man wearing a fishing hat pulled low on his head to protect his face from the sunlight. Squeezing the brakes, the rider skidded to a stop fifteen yards from the stranger and took a moment to hydrate before dismounting and making a show of examining his bike.

Barking out a loud curse, he walked the bike to the closest vacant table. Leaning the apparently damaged cycle against the concrete edge, he unsnapped a small tool pouch from the frame, unrolled it and laid it out on the ground, selected a crescent wrench, knelt, and set to work on the gear assembly. Without looking up from his work, he spoke in a voice barely loud enough to be heard at the other table. "Are you Kelsey's father?"

The man, who had watched the bicyclist's arrival with interest, answered, "Who is asking?"

"My name's Kenny Bowman. I'm a friend of Romeo Jones."

Grunting with surprise, the stranger countered, "You served with him?"

"Yes, sir."

"So you were a Navy Seal?"

Bowman allowed himself a short laugh. "No, sir. Nice test question, though. We were Rangers together. Assuming I passed, would you answer my question?"

He had situated his bike and work position so that he could see the other man through the spokes of his front wheel. Even with the face shrouded in the penumbra of the floppy brim of the hat, there was a resemblance to William Batman.

"I am he. And I am surmising that my daughter sent you for some reason."

Kenny set the wrench down and pulled out a screwdriver, shifting his attention to the center of the bike.

"Yes, sir. She's worried that this is a trap."

He heard a sharp intake of breath from the man. "*She's* worried that this…oh…this is not good, Mr. Bowman!"

The FBI agent felt a prickle of sweat pop up on his back. Casually, he unsnapped the flap on a vinyl pouch mounted on the center frame, revealing the butt of his Glock. Keeping his voice soft and neutral, he asked, "Why's that, sir?"

"I've been in hiding since my staged death. Quite successfully, actually. It now appears that I was reckless and made a serious, perhaps fatal error in judgment as I disclosed my true identity to my daughter."

"Sir, I'm sure she wouldn't…."

"No. I am certain she would not. However, it is clear I underestimated my foes when I chose a mode of communication in order to make contact with her."

"I don't completely follow you, sir."

The man glanced around apprehensively. "Your ruse is excellent, by the way; nevertheless, I have no doubt we have limited time, so I will explain quickly. Since the night I made the disclosure, she and Scott attempted to reconnect with me repeatedly, attempts I deliberately ignored for fear that our medium had been compromised. Yesterday I received another message I assumed was from my daughter. However, this message I could not ignore. She told me that she was in mortal danger and needed my assistance; that, if I did not meet with her and provide help, she would surely be killed."

Bowman, who had been briefed by Kelsey on the details of her IM conversation, corrected him. "She did not send that. Yesterday she received a message from you, or I should say from Alchemist, requesting this meeting. I guess there were some details in the way Alchemist phrased things that made her suspicious it was a trap."

Sighing loudly, the man appeared patently disgusted with himself. "So…the other side was able to co-opt the previous channel of communication, a channel I handed to them on a silver platter, and then use it to deceive us both. I'm sorry to admit that I did not pay attention to her syntax as closely as she obviously did to mine. I honestly believed that it was she and that it was imperative for me to come out of hiding to save her. Sadly, she is correct. This is a trap…and, I must add, a quite clever one, only not merely for her…for both of us."

Kenny stowed the screwdriver and picked up the crescent wrench, making it appear as though he had finished with his repairs and was preparing to leave. "How did you get here?"

"A car, which I parked in a turnoff a mile down the hill. I hiked the balance of the distance."

"Kelsey, are you getting all of this?" As William heard the words, he straightened visibly and leaned forward.

Her voice came through the integrated speaker in the agent's helmet a full octave higher than he remembered it being. "*Yes! His voice was a little hard to hear, but that's Daddy! Is he okay?*"

"She's asking if you're okay."

He nodded in reply. Kenny could not be certain but thought he detected a shimmer under the man's eyes in the shadow of the brim. "Tell her I'm well. And...and...is she...?"

Bowman's heart went out to him. "I just left her, sir. She's fine."

"Kenny, we need to get him out of there!"

He did not directly respond to her urgent statement; instead, swinging his leg over the bike and bouncing on the seat, to all appearances testing his repair, he said, "Sir, it's about seven minutes till nine. If they're watching us...."

"Which they obviously are."

"Yes, sir. They're waiting for your daughter to show up. They won't do anything until then."

"True. You don't suspect they are listening to us with a parabolic microphone right now?"

Kenny shrugged and nonchalantly surveyed the surrounding scenery, as if this were his first visit to the area. "They probably have one with them. In this wind it'd be worthless."

He again dismounted and removed a plastic sack from another pouch, sat down at the end of the picnic table, remaining close to the bike and his Glock, and took out a sandwich and a small bag of carrots. Taking a bite of sandwich, he said between chews, "If you try to walk away from here, they'll forget about her and grab you."

"I know."

"What we don't know...and I hate to say this...is whether they want you both here to kidnap you or...."

"Kill us."

"Right. If the plan is to grab you both, they'll have a decent-sized team nearby. They could be hiding anywhere in this terrain. If the latter is their goal, they probably have two snipers, positioned on high blinds."

He checked his watch. Five minutes until nine.

"Kenny," Kelsey's voice burst from the speaker. "What if I come in?"

"No. Absolutely not. I'm not risking both of you."

"She wants to come here, doesn't she?" The question came from William.

Without looking in his direction, Bowman answered, "Yes."

"Please don't let her do that." The simple plea was heartrending.

"I told her *no*."

"Kenny, I need to come!"

"Kelsey, I said...."

"Listen to me! You're on a bike. You can't drive him out. My father doesn't have his car there. You need an escape vehicle. I'll drive up in the Hummer. The bad guys know my vehicles. They'll see I've arrived. I won't get out. I'll stay in the truck so they can't get a decent shot. Maybe you and my father can get in real fast and I can drive away. If we're lucky, we can surprise them."

The FBI agent was considering her plan, when his thoughts were interrupted by William, who was becoming agitated. "She's talking you into it, isn't she? She can't help herself."

Before he could respond, Kelsey, who was barely able to hear her father's words over the microphone, stressed, "Tell him we don't have any choice. It's the only way."

"She said it's the only way. She might be right."

The man stood. Speaking more loudly, his voice firm, he addressed his daughter personally. "No, Kelsey. It is not the only way. I will not allow you to fall into their hands."

With that, he turned and began walking briskly toward the main road, his path leading him next to Kenny.

"Shit!" Bowman hissed.

Kelsey's voice reverberated in his ear. *"What's happening?"*

The agent snatched the Glock out of the open case and jumped up, grabbing the man by the arm and spinning him around and down. The two fell together beside the concrete seat just as a geyser of dirt exploded from the trail a few feet away, the ensuing report of the shot reaching them moments later. The interlaced ravines and cliff faces echoed the sound harshly, making it difficult to determine the location of the sniper. Bowman pushed William under the seat and table, following him under the cover and mentally calculating the approximate direction of the sniper.

A second shot ricocheted off the concrete apron surrounding their refuge, pelting them with shards.

"Kenny! What's going on?"

"We're pinned down. There's a sniper above us. Maybe two."

"Oh, my God!"

Another shot slammed into the thick edge of one of the benches, shattering the concrete and breaking loose a chunk.

"We're coming!"

"Kelsey...no!"

She did not respond.

Less than a mile from the picnic area where her father and Bowman were trapped, Kelsey, sitting beside Judtson in her Hummer, the radio on the seat between them, immediately dropped the truck in gear. He reached across and forcibly slammed the shifter back into park. "Kelsey, get out. I'll go."

She whirled to face him, at the same time trying to wrestle away control of the lever. *"NO! It's my father out there!"*

"I know. But they obviously want you, too. You need to stay out."

"DAMMIT, JUDTSON! NO!"

She jabbed her elbow hard into his side, the pain making him release the shifter. Shoving it back in gear, Kelsey floored the gas pedal. The truck fishtailed and screeched onto the pavement, leaving behind an acrid stench of burned rubber.

Kenny, huddled under the table with William, quickly ran through his options. It did not take long as there were none. The Glock would not be a help unless the shooter was stupid enough to leave his blind and approach. Whether they would face two snipers or only one, he was not optimistic about making a run for it. Another shot arrived, tearing into the gear assembly on the bicycle, shredding the metal and scattering shrapnel under the bench.

There was a sharp yelp of pain from William. Kenny turned to see that the side of the man's face was bleeding.

"Keep your head down," he ordered. "And protect it with your arms."

William complied silently.

The tumult of the wind was suddenly drowned out by an engine's roar. Bowman twisted his neck and saw the bright yellow Hummer bounce off the road onto the lane leading to the picnic area.

"Get the rifle!" Kelsey called out, and Judtson turned to the back seat and grabbed the AK-47 they had brought with them. Moving much too fast for the conditions and struggling to keep control, she saw the two men underneath the table. Veering toward them, she wrenched the wheel and hit the brakes, pulling the wide-track vehicle into a sloppy arcing slide. As the Hummer turned its side to the direction of travel, it rose precariously on the two outside wheels before coming to a stop, dropping back down with a bone-jarring crash.

No sooner had they halted than the window beside Judtson exploded inward, spraying him with small glass pebbles. Without looking first, he stuck the rifle out, flipped the selector from safety to full automatic, and sprayed a wide burst in the general direction, as Kelsey reached behind herself and jerked open the back door, yelling, "GET IN!"

Bowman was already in motion, gripping William's sleeve and crawling out from under the table. A shot struck the Hummer's side panel loudly, followed a second later by another.

"Come on! Move!"

William Batman, the side of his face covered with blood, peered over the top of the bench and his eyes connected with Kelsey's. The moment they did, she wailed, *"DADDY!"*

Violently jerking his arm free, he protested to Kenny, *"You go! Get her out of here! I'll draw their fire."*

"DON'T!"

Before Bowman could say another word, Kelsey's father rolled out from under the opposite side of the table, scrambled to his feet, and ran down the slope toward a ravine.

Kelsey, seeing this, screamed, "NO! COME BACK!" and, without thinking, opened her door and jumped out just as Kenny got to his feet. Her run was stopped by the agent, who wrapped his arms around her in a bear hug and, lifting her off her feet, pulled her back toward the Hummer.

"LET ME GO! LET ME GO!" she shrieked, pummeling him with her fists and kicking at his shins as she helplessly watched her father's receding form. William's plan was working. The dense cacti around him exploded with the impact of rounds from the sniper.

As they watched, temporarily frozen by the drama, their suspicion of a second sniper was confirmed when a round caught Kenny in his left biceps, grazing him. Ignoring the flash of pain, he kept his grip on the wildly flailing Kelsey and pushed her ahead of himself into the back seat of the truck. He yelled to Judtson, "DRIVE! GET US OUT OF HERE!"

Judtson emptied the clip of his rifle, tossed it on the floorboard, and jumped to the driver's side. The engine, stalled from Kelsey's earlier maneuver, fired up instantly. He dropped the truck in gear and mashed the pedal to the floor, cranking the steering wheel to the stop and spinning the Hummer off the pavement and back toward the main road, sending a dense spray of dust and gravel in the radius of his wake. A loud smack filled the cabin as yet another shot plowed into the roof-mounted rack.

The truck, its engine screaming, climbed the slope away from the picnic area and careened wildly onto the asphalt, heading east. Kelsey, fighting her way from under Bowman, scrambled to the side window and, taking advantage of their elevated position alongside the canyon, searched the steep washes below for her father.

"I SEE HIM! THERE HE IS!"

"WHERE?" Judtson shouted over his shoulder.

"Slow down! He made it to the ravine and he's circling this way. Maybe we can...."

Judtson moved his foot off the pedal and allowed the big Hummer to coast down the serpentine road. He was about to ask the status, just as she gasped, "No! Oh, please. No!" Her desperate pleas broke into racking sobs.

Negotiating a series of sharp turns and switchbacks, he did not dare look away. "Kelsey? *Kelsey, what is it?*"

It was Bowman who answered, his tone flat and defeated. "He was running this way. About a hundred yards from the road. When…when they got him."

"GOT HIM? THEY KILLED HIM?"

"No. They caught him. Two guys ran him down. They took him."

$$\triangledown$$

The majority of the return drive was a quiet one. Judtson drove as Kelsey, using a stowed first-aid kit, wordlessly cleaned, sanitized, and bandaged Bowman's arm. After finishing the job, she slid to the far side of the rear seat, tucked her feet beneath herself, and sullenly stared out the window. As they neared her home, Kenny broke the silence. "I'm sorry, Kelsey. I really blew it."

Without turning, she replied, sounding distant and dispirited. "No. You didn't. We were worried that it was a trap set for me. For that purpose, your plan was fine. We never thought it might be a double trap. If we had, I'm sure you would have done it differently."

They cleared the gate and approached the front of the house, where Scott stood, expecting their return. Kelsey, not even waiting until the Hummer was at a full stop, opened her door and, brushing past the tech, ran through the open doorway and disappeared inside.

As Judtson and Kenny climbed out, Scott circled around and met them, his face creased with concern. "What happened?"

The two filled him in on the disastrous events. As they finished, he asked, "So they took him? They didn't…?"

"No," Bowman answered, "they didn't kill him. The two men tackled her father at the bottom of the ravine, and the last I saw, they were picking him up and cuffing him."

"I don't understand. What did they actually want? To capture Kelsey and her father or kill them?"

The agent shrugged. "That's the way it usually works, Scott. They probably had orders to capture. But only if possible. Kill, if not. When they first saw him get up to leave before Kelsey arrived, they figured that something had gone wrong and that I wasn't merely an innocent cyclist stopping to fix his bike. So they started shooting. Then, when her old man ran into the brush and the three of us were escaping, they went back to Plan A and grabbed the available target."

"You know what I'm worried about?" Judtson interjected, a tense look on his face. "Now that they have him…."

Kenny finished the sentence. "They're going to use him as bait to get Kelsey."

"Exactly. Well…" – Judtson glanced toward the still-open front door – "I'm going to go see if she's all right."

Leaving the two behind, he crossed through the foyer into the massive living room and found Kelsey lying facedown on the sofa. He knelt on the floor in front of her and lightly touched her shoulder. At the moment of contact, she spun toward him and threw her arms around his neck, pulling him tightly to her and giving in to a racking torrent of sobs.

Chapter 27

KELSEY ASKED JUDTSON IF SHE COULD BE ALONE FOR A WHILE. After seeing her to the bedroom and watching as she lay down, he went to Scott's work area and composed a detailed email to Saylor, bringing him up to speed on all of the disturbing events. Running it past the tech, he made certain that it could be transmitted securely. After dispatching it, he waited for half an hour. No response or acknowledgment from his friend appeared.

Throughout the rest of the day, the expected members of the group converged at Kelsey's home. Driving in from a speaking engagement in Colorado Springs, Jimmy Meade was the first to make an appearance, followed somewhat later by Chili, Carlos, Bal, Dean, and Dylan. The final arrivals were Romeo, Ricky...and Chris, who looked none the worse for wear after his ordeal. The travelers, joined by Scott, Matt, Kenny, Judtson, and a subdued and red-eyed Kelsey, were assembled around the large dining table. It seemed that each person had a new piece of the puzzle, and the conversation for the first hour was a jumble of voices competing to make their contributions.

Romeo was clearly upset after he heard the description of the aborted attempt to meet with Kelsey's father and how close she had come to being shot by the sniper, but he judiciously kept his disapproval to himself and curtly thanked Bowman.

When the pace settled, Bal raised his voice to address the group. "I have brought something with me that I have not shared as of yet with any of you."

"What is it?" asked Judtson, his curiosity piqued by the undercurrent in the man's voice.

"I would rather not say precisely what it is or what my interpretation may be. I would prefer to provide the background and then let you see it for yourselves and draw your own conclusions."

Without waiting for an acknowledgment, he proceeded, "Some of you have met Sam Jonassen. For those who have not, he was Kevin Berry's assistant when the geophysicist was in the Andes studying gravity anomalies. It is Dr. Berry's work, along with efforts on my own prior tectonic model, which I have resumed. I was most grateful to find that Sam was available to assist me with the projects.

"What I did not learn until I arrived there was that he, while working for Dr. Berry, had witnessed something truly astounding over Lake Titicaca one night. So astounding, in fact, that even after Dr. Berry departed, Sam remained in Bolivia at his own expense, living in a cave and watching."

The others around the table were silent, captivated by the narrative.

"Quite serendipitously, on his final night before my arrival, his patience was rewarded and he was able to capture the phenomenon on both video and synchronized still photographs, which he showed to me almost immediately after I landed. This evidence was amazing enough. However, just a few days ago, the two of us...Sam and I...witnessed a repeat of the event. We were successful in making a video of this occurrence, as well."

Jimmy Meade's impatience got the better of him. "Dammit, man. What the blazes was it?"

A slight smile appeared on Singh's face. "I will show you. I have the photographs and both videos on my laptop. Scott, do you have a method for displaying my files on a larger screen?"

Gumble nodded. "If your laptop has Wi-Fi."

"It does."

The tech hopped up from his seat and circled the table to Bal, who was sitting with his computer at hand. After several rapid key clicks, Scott moved to the nearby wall of the kitchen and opened a panel which concealed a large flat-screen monitor. Using the mouse beneath it, he started a program and looked back. "Whenever you're ready."

He returned to his seat as Bal began the playback. The moment the first picture appeared, Kelsey gasped, "Oh, my God!"

Ricky muttered an unidentifiable sound.

Bal enthusiastically provided a commentary for the images. "The first is a split screen that Sam created for me. On the left side is the series of photographs he took, overlooking a specific island in Lake Titicaca. On the right is the video taken simultaneously."

Not one person spoke throughout the length of the video. As it completed, Bal resumed, "The video commencing now is the one we captured together. As you can see, we are even closer to the object than Sam had been for the first recorded observation. And the ambient light is slightly stronger."

Bal paused the video at the end, leaving the final image to linger on the screen. The people around the table mesmerized, the first to speak was Judtson. "Throughout the years, in the course of debunking UFO sightings, I have studied hundreds, maybe thousands, of pictures and videos. Nothing I have ever seen approximates this. Not in clarity. Not in steadiness of the camera. Not in the visible details. And it is made all the more persuasive by the fact that the events were witnessed by two people whom I know. Bal, this is absolutely incredible. You and Sam have recorded a...spaceship."

His words triggered an avalanche of comments and expressions of wonder, which abounded for well over half an hour. As the intensity of the discussion diminished somewhat, Judtson again addressed the others. "What Sam...and Bal...have captured in these two incidents is clearly a massive UFO emerging from and descending into Lake Titicaca. Or, if it isn't that, it is the most elaborate hoax ever created. Not only could we see the ship rise out of the lake near that island, but we could also see details...such as the water sheeting and streaming off the object and splashing down into the lake."

"And we could see the marquee-like effect of the lights traveling along the side of the craft,"

Copeland added excitedly.

"And the speed it departed…!" Meade exclaimed, shaking his head. "That's not possible. Not with any known technology."

Judtson glanced at Kelsey, who was beside him. Rocky, forsaking his normal position glued to his master, was sitting on her opposite side, his head resting on her knees. She petted him idly while still staring at the frozen image on the screen. Other than her first gasp of surprise, she had not yet spoken, even throughout the conversational free-for-all. Resting his hand lightly on her leg, Judtson shifted in her direction. "You all right?"

She turned to him, placed her hand on his, and forced a feeble smile. "I guess. I'll be fine. I'm…just…."

"I know," he murmured and gently squeezed her thigh. Returning his attention to the assemblage, he proposed, "The conspicuous question here, at least for me, is what this phenomenon has to do with everything that has happened to us."

Jimmy snorted loudly. "We were getting too damn close!"

"Too close to what, Jimmy?"

The astronaut had to lean forward in his chair to face Judtson. "Carlos obviously found something that pointed a big red arrow straight at Puma Punku. So he was zapped. You were going to go public with it. So they took you over. Hell, Kevin Berry found a giant-sized void inside the Andes directly under that spot."

"I understand all of that. But what, *specifically*, were we getting close to finding? What do *you* think is there, Jimmy?"

"It's obvious! A base!"

Dean chimed in, "I think Jimmy's right. I think that Puma Punku or Lake Titicaca…somewhere in that vicinity…is the spot where they come and go. It might or might not be their only way in and out. But it certainly appears to be one of them."

"Who?" blurted Matt. "Who comes and goes?"

The question hung in the air, none of the group wanting to speak aloud what was in their minds. Breaking the silence, a voice came from the doorway. "Aliens."

Heads turned at the sound. Disheveled, with heavy bags under his eyes, Saylor stood at the threshold. Judtson jumped up. "*Popeye!*" He quickly crossed the space between them and grabbed his friend's arm. "Oh, man! Am I glad you came!"

When Saylor's eyes met his, Judtson thought he detected within them a flicker of their old spark.

"Got your email this morning. The way it sounded, this is the place to be."

Kelsey joined the two. "Saylor, I was hoping you'd be here. Are you…doing all right?"

The man shrugged. "I'll manage. How about you, Kelsey? Judtson told me what happened this morning."

The muscles around her mouth tightened fleetingly. "I've gone from thinking I'd lost my father to thinking he *might* be alive to finding out he actually is. So…overall, it's a good thing."

Judtson wanted to hold her and promise her they would get her father back, yet somehow knew that the last thing she wanted to hear was an empty promise. He kept his silence.

Loudly letting out a breath, she took both of their hands and said, "Come on. Let's get back to the others."

For Saylor's benefit, the videos were replayed. After the second conclusion, Ricky asked, "Saylor, why did you say they're aliens?"

"Why not? Isn't that what you think?"

"It is. I've always been kind of a fringe type, though. You haven't. I'm just surprised."

"You're right. I've always been hard-nosed…a man of science, pure and simple. I actually enjoyed Judtson's books as he tore people like all of you apart."

Muted laughter rippled through the group. He continued tentatively, "Except…in the last couple of days…I've…" – he paused and made a brief chuffing sound – "I've had a lot of time to think. The old explanations…the old answers…frankly don't fit anymore."

His softly spoken words were followed by a thoughtful silence, not broken until Carlos spoke up. "Saylor, your words reflect what many of us have felt for some time. If they are extraterrestrials, so be it. Perhaps that is a fact we must accept. And what we have discussed thus far binds together Judtson, Bal, and me. Possibly Jimmy and Dean. But how do we incorporate Dylan and Chris? What is the linkage which includes the two of them and their work?"

"I may be able to answer that." The comment came from Dylan. "There *is* something which connects us. And it isn't our work."

Having captured their attention, he began to explain. "On the flight here, I found among my unopened mail a letter from Rosemary Shields. I'll pass it around in a minute. The gist of it is that back in the latter part of the 1980s, a pharmaceutical company, struggling to keep up with demand for a flu vaccine, made an unauthorized ingredient substitution. A synthetic. Approximately fifty thousand people received this iteration before the substitution was discovered and the remaining doses recalled. The CDC set up a tracking list of the recipients of this vaccine in the event that the formula caused a problem in the future. The list lay dormant within the epidemiological databases on their computer, forgotten until Dr. McWhorter in New York submitted nine cases of a new neurological anomaly to them. As is the standard practice, the CDC entered eight of the names…one was not available at that time…into their system with the hope of finding a commonality."

Saylor, mentally leaping ahead of Dylan, leaned forward with interest, listening intently.

"One was found. And the ninth name, as it was later learned, also shared the singular distinction."

"Everyone who had been converted had received the vaccine, correct?"

"Yes, Saylor. Judtson, Chris, Bal, Carlos, Jimmy, Lisa, Dean, Al, and I all received the vaccine. According to the letter from Rosemary, she, too, was vaccinated from the same altered batch."

"What about the rest of us?" Ricky asked. "Kelsey, Saylor, Matt…the others in our group who were never converted?"

"I don't know. Rosemary didn't say in her letter. It would certainly be interesting to check the list and see."

"Can we get our hands on it?" Saylor pressed.

"That I don't know, either. When she became curious and began making inquiries, her home was burglarized and her copies of an article related to the original vaccine incident were stolen from her desk. She was fired soon thereafter and then…killed. What she did say in the letter was that the drug company had been merged into a larger European conglomerate and that the head chemist who had been responsible for the vaccine had died in an automobile accident."

"Huh! What a coincidence," Kelsey scoffed quietly.

Falt removed something from his pocket. "When she contacted the drug company, she got the names of others on the team. Rosemary spoke with the number-two chemist, but he denied that the incident ever occurred. The newspaper in question, the one which had originally released the story, no longer had this article" – he held up the aged clipping – "in their archives. Nor could she find it elsewhere on the Internet."

"Maybe I can find it on the CDC system," Scott offered.

"I think you should try," concurred Kelsey.

Gumble left the room, taking with him the newspaper clipping.

As the tech left, Judtson commented, "I think it's interesting that all of us who were converted received this vaccine years ago. And it will be more bizarre if all of the rest of you did, as well. But what does this really mean? Saylor, what do you think?"

The neurologist took a minute before responding. "Hard to say. Could be nothing. Could be some sort of a bad thing. I would give it a lot less weight if someone had not gone to so much effort to obliterate any trace that it happened."

"True."

Kelsey's phone rang. "It's Lisa!" She answered it on speakerphone and laid it in the center of the table.

"Lisa...Kelsey. You're on speaker. Everyone's here. How are you?"

Her voice was animated. "Hi, Kelsey. Hi, gang. It's gonna take more than a couple of goons trying to kill me to ruin my mood. Anyway...glad you're all together. Since my little incident, the network is even more excited to get this story on the air. They've agreed to do it in Tucson and they want to air it day after tomorrow. And...we are going to do it live!"

▽

Kenny Bowman and Romeo Jones walked slowly along the wall surrounding Kelsey's expansive estate, despite the fact that, with the array of cameras and motion sensors installed to monitor the wall and grounds inside, there was no reason for foot patrols.

Neither had spoken a word for several minutes, when the FBI agent broke the silence. "Sorry, Master Sar."

Romeo replied without breaking stride. "For what?"

"I blew it. I let them get her dad."

"Don't sweat it, Bowman. You did what you were sent in to do. Bring her back from the meet alive. That was the mission."

"That's bravo sierra, Master Sar, and you know it! I should have set it up for the possibility that he was the real deal, and planned for an extraction instead of going in on a damn ridiculous bicycle! That was stupid!"

Romeo stopped and faced his former teammate. "You're right. It was stupid. *You* were stupid for not thinking of it. *I* was stupid for not thinking of it before you went in. And both of us were unforgivably stupid for not leaving our primary back about ten klicks so she couldn't come riding into the middle of the live fire. Okay. We've proved to the world that we're stupid. So what?"

Bowman, one of the few men who could stare directly into Jones' eyes without looking up, shook his head in disgust. "*So what?* 'So what' is now they've got him. *And* they've got him alive. *And* she knows he's alive. And that only means one thing."

Jones nodded. "Yep. They're going to dangle him in front of her."

The agent had no comeback. The two resumed their walk. Changing the subject, Romeo smirked. "So, other than that, how are you enjoying your time off?"

The question forced a short laugh from Bowman. "What's the old line... 'So, Mrs. Kennedy, other than that, how was your trip to Dallas?'"

His companion grunted.

"You know, Romeo, I really can't wrap my mind around the fact that I wasn't dismissed. Or, at the very least, demoted and reassigned. Seriously, a seven-day suspension for allowing a federal prisoner to walk away!"

"Kenny, you are still looking at it from the normal perspective. Once you get tangled up with these guys, all the rules change. They have a reason. They have a purpose for wanting you to stay right where you are and to keep doing the same things you have been doing. Or it wouldn't have come down the way it did."

"I get that. But what *is* the reason?"

Jones shrugged. "Don't know. Maybe they can keep an eye on you this way. Maybe they can keep you distracted with other problems...other cases...so you can't focus on the underlying acts. Not sure."

"Or..." – Bowman hesitated – "maybe they're planning on setting up a bad bust or something. Something which results in a line-of-duty fatality. With me as the star."

"Could be. You need to keep your eyes open. What's first on your agenda when you go back to work?"

"I was thinking about taking another whack at Beckleman."

"They've got him in Phoenix? I thought you guys moved him to a federal penitentiary."

"Nope. That was only the word we put out. He's locked down tight up north so all of us working the case have access."

"And what are you going to talk to him about? Haven't you squeezed that lemon dry already?"

"In light of what's happened lately, my perspective is...a little different now. I want to go over some of the same territory with him from that angle. Speaking of which, I've been meaning to ask you an obvious question."

"What's that?"

"Romeo, you and your merry band were jetting all around, zapping people with that helmet and bringing them back to their real selves. Why didn't Judtson and Kelsey strap the gizmo on Beckleman when you had him in Bisbee?"

"Why? Do you think he's not really a bad guy? Just controlled?"

It was Bowman's turn to shrug. "Hell if I know. Probably not. It seemed like a natural to at least give it a shot."

"We thought about it. Problem was that we were pressed for time...his men traveling with him and the backup ops team flying in and all. You've got to shoot the zappee with FDG an hour before the process can be done. We didn't have the extra hour to spare."

"Yeah. Makes sense. I was wondering, that's all."

▽

As he drove north on I-10, his mind wandered back over the past hours, replaying how his morning had begun. It had been clear that something was happening when he saw Kelsey drive her yellow Hummer out of the gate of her compound, with Judtson Kent and a second man he could not see well enough to recognize. He had trailed the distinctive vehicle to the road leading to Gates Pass and watched as it parked in a wide pull-off. Stopping a discreet distance back, he saw the third occupant, whom he then identified as Bowman, climb out and pull a mountain bike from the back of the Hummer.

Once determining the direction Bowman was traveling, he had left the pickup where it was and trotted up the canyon beside the road, following a well-beaten path uphill and arriving at a ridge top overlooking the picnic area, just as the agent was apparently repairing a mechanical problem with the bike. He had nearly fallen for the ruse, until he spotted a man not more than seventy yards from him, lying on the rocky ground and partially concealed by a creosote bush. The man was camouflaged and pointing a rifle toward Bowman, so focused on his quarry that he had not noticed the new guest at the party.

He had backtracked briefly and was cautiously circling around behind the sniper, attempting to form a clear picture of what was going down, when the man opened fire. Seconds later, the screaming roar of Kelsey's Hummer echoed within the narrow canyon walls. From his position, he was able to discern the presence of a second sniper but could not locate his blind.

Cursing his timing, he had accelerated his pace as much as he dared, only to be momentarily stunned by the high-pitched scream from Kelsey. Even in the sound-jumbling acoustics of the canyon, her one-word exclamation was unmistakable. *"DADDY!"* The implications instantly clear, he clawed forward for a better view. By the time he scrambled to the crest of the ridge, the shooting had ceased and the man was gone.

From this vantage, he had seen that the picnic area was empty, except for Bowman's bike, which lay abandoned next to a bench. Motion to his left caught his attention, and he saw a lone man desperately fighting his way through the dense brush, chased by two others, who were rapidly closing the gap. He had watched as the man was tackled, handcuffed, and led away.

Abruptly, his mind snapped back to the present as the black Excursion swung off the freeway at the Pinal Air Park exit. Losing the two-car buffer he had maintained during the tail, he fell in behind, holding back as far as practical. The lead vehicle turned left and proceeded under the overpass.

"They're going out to Evergreen!" he surmised aloud, referring to the aircraft maintenance facility and restricted airfield long suspected by the local residents of being a covert CIA installation. Decelerating slightly, he put more distance between himself and the SUV. His suspicion soon proved to be correct as the truck turned in to the main entrance. Continuing straight, he kept on his course for a mile, then doubled back.

Beyond the entrance, there was a narrow lane to the east of the complex, and he drove it several hundred yards before leaving the pavement for a dirt trail. The stolen pickup bounced and jittered over the rough, rutted path, rattling badly. Guessing he was close enough, he stopped the truck and killed the engine.

The desert around him was fairly dense with palo verde trees, mesquites, and creosotes, effectively screening him and the truck from view. Prior to climbing out, he pulled on a wide-brimmed canvas hat and tucked the nine-millimeter Beretta into the back of his waistband.

A shallow, dry ditch nearby weaved its way west toward the Santa Cruz. The man hiked the meandering wash, moving slowly closer to the perimeter of the airpark until he came to a tall fence, which was menacingly topped with concertina wire. The level of visible security for the facility had diminished drastically over the years, prompting many of the longtime locals to speculate that if it had ever been a base for covert operations, those days were gone.

The fence, where it traversed the wash, was badly battered by torrential flows from past storms, and looked as if it had not been repaired in quite some time. The fence pole in the center of the wash, a victim of severe erosion, was dangling approximately a foot above the sand, supported by the chain-link fencing material, the bottom of the metal stake coated with a thick chunk of concrete.

Lying down in the sand, the man easily rolled under the fence, climbed to his feet, made certain he had not lost the pistol, and resumed his walk. The arroyo led him to an area adjacent to one of the runways. Crouching below the lip of the wash, he removed his hat and surveyed the area. Parked on the tarmac, not more than forty yards away, stood a massive C-130 cargo plane, its large loading door at the rear in the process of being lowered, and a manned forklift standing off to its side, the diesel engine idling. The Excursion was parked well back from the plane, waiting.

The moment the door reached a level orientation, the operator scooted the lift behind it and slid the forks under a fully loaded pallet, carrying oil, spares, and miscellaneous items for the big cargo plane, and stored near the edge of the door. Lifting the pallet jerkily, he backed away and spun the steering wheel, moving off to the side.

No sooner had the pallet been off-loaded than a crew member inside the plane lowered the door the rest of the way, trotted down the incline, kicked the hinged wheel ramps over with a loud clang, and gave the Excursion an all-clear hand signal.

The driver reacted immediately, pulling the SUV up the ramp and into the cargo bay. The inside crew member unhurriedly walked down and flipped the hinged ramps into their stowed positions, moved back inside the bay, and raised the door, pausing again when it was level. As he did this, the operator was already jockeying into position, suspending the pallet of materials above the ramp and lowering the fork as soon as the movement stopped.

Backing away, the forklift operator gave a nonchalant wave to the crew member and sped away, disappearing around the corner of a hangar in seconds.

Making a snap decision, the man hiding in the ditch muttered, "Awww, what the hell!" and jumped up from his position, running in a crouch toward the rear of the plane, waiting for an alerting shout or, worse yet, a slug tearing into him. Neither came and he reached the cargo door and peered inside. The black SUV was pulled to the farthest point forward in the spacious belly of the transport, the lone crew member busily engaged in securing the vehicle with heavy-duty webbing.

Somewhere a switch was thrown and the door shuddered and began to close. Operating purely by impulse, the man hopped up and rolled onto the ascending ramp, keeping the loaded pallet between himself and the crewman as a screen. Peeking around, he first confirmed that the worker was busy wrestling the S-clip on the webbing onto a wall-mounted cleat; then crawled down the now slanted cargo door and moved to his right toward the jump door, which was recessed almost two feet, creating a shadowy alcove. At some point, the crew had shoved extra tarps and webbing into the niche to make a clear path for vehicles to enter.

Burrowing into the heap, he arranged the coverings so that he could watch. As the monstrous turboprop engines cranked up and the plane began to roll, the crewman finished and walked forward and to his left, stepping down two steps and then turning right, climbing onto the flight deck and out of sight. Apparently, the men inside the SUV either had decided or had been ordered to remain within the comfort of the vehicle during the flight.

Settling in, the stowaway moved the stiff roll of strap which was poking him in the back, sighed loudly, the noise drowned out by the now roaring engines, and grumbled, "Luis, you are one dumb pendejo!"

Chapter 28

Kelsey, Judtson, Saylor, and Romeo were clustered tightly in a semicircle behind Scott's chair as the tech's fingers flew over the keyboard, and he narrated as he worked. "There. You see. Shields was right. All nine of the people converted are on the list."

"I'm surprised you were able to get in and find it," Kelsey noted, shaking her head.

"Surprised by which part?" he asked, feigning offense. "That I could get into the CDC system...or that I could find the list?"

With a slight giggle, she clarified, "Not the 'getting in' part. I knew you could do that. I mean I'm surprised they've left it on there."

Shrugging, Scott explained, "They probably forgot about it. It was buried among about a thousand other groups with different commonalities. Getting to it was easy. The CDC makes the epidemiological groups available to the health care industry."

"Okay, so everyone we converted is on it. What about the rest of us?" The question came from Saylor.

"It's a huge database. More than fifty thousand names. But it's searchable. I have to run each name as a query. With common names it helps that you've given me social security numbers." He typed. "Here we go. Saylor, you're on it." Tapping the keys after every answer, he continued, "So am I...Kelsey, you're there...you, too, Romeo."

The big man grunted.

"There's Matt...and Ricky."

"What about Doni?"

"I'll look, Saylor. Do you know her social?"

"Not off the top of my head. It's an unusual name, though. Let's see if any at all come up."

"Okay. Doni is short for Donatella, right?"

"Yes."

Scott typed the name and waited. "Nothing under Costello, but she would have gotten the vaccine before you were married. What's her maiden name?"

"Bosoni." He spelled it.

Kelsey snorted softly. "*Doni Bosoni!*" Saylor glared at her, and she quickly wiped the smirk from her face, holding up her hands defensively. "Sorry. Really."

"No, Saylor. No one under that name, either."

Kelsey whispered in Judtson's ear, "At least it wasn't *Baloney*!"

Fighting back his amusement at her remark, he suggested, "Try Kristen," a quizzical look beginning to form on his face.

Checking first under Kristen Kent, Scott asked, "What's her maiden name?"

"K-a-p-l-u-n-d-e-r."

"Ka-PLUNDER!" Kelsey blurted.

With a withering gaze, Judtson corrected her. "It's pronounced KAP-lunder."

She ignored him and derisively muttered, "Ka-PLUNDER and Bosoni! What's the deal with you two?"

"Put a lid on it, *Batman*!" he snapped back.

After a moment, Scott murmured, "Nope. She isn't there, either."

Kelsey, noticing Judtson's absorbed expression, pried, "What? What are you thinking?"

"Not sure yet. Let's see…try my agent, Mitchell Murray."

After a brief wait, the tech reported, "Yeah. About twenty with that name. Do you have a social?"

"No. His middle name is Thaddeus. Does that help?"

"Uh-huh. All the names in the database have the middle. Uhhh…nope. He's not one of them."

"Try Darrow Shugrew." He spelled it.

"Nope."

"Huh! That's odd."

"Come on, Judtson. Share. What is it? What are you thinking?"

He faced Kelsey. "I'm still not sure. This vaccine connection is a bizarre twist. When Dylan first mentioned it, I didn't know what it meant. Or even if it meant anything. Other than the fact that it provided us…the converted ones…with an epidemiological connection. But now we know that you, Romeo, Scott, Ricky, Saylor, Matt, everybody…well, practically everybody…who was a part of the original group is on the list. And the two people who were fighting me tooth and nail on the book about Carlos' discovery in Puma Punku and Baalbek *aren't* on the list…which all indicates that maybe…."

Kelsey's interest in his theory waxing, she prompted, "Maybe what?"

Glancing surreptitiously at Saylor, he stammered, "I don't…I'm not…."

"Just go ahead and say it," Saylor interjected bluntly. "You think everyone who got the vaccine is a good guy and everyone who didn't is a bad guy."

"Saylor, I…."

Kelsey interrupted Judtson. "Is that what you think?"

He was unable to read his best friend's face as Saylor refused to meet his eyes. "I don't know. How can I be certain? We haven't exactly performed a broad enough sampling to determine anything conclusively."

Romeo's attention was on the list. "Try Chili," he prodded, and gave Scott the man's full name. "You should already have his social since he's an employee."

Fifteen seconds later, Scott confirmed, "Yep. He got the shot, too."

"Now…try Luis."

The tension level in the group elevated slightly at the name.

Scott mumbled something no one could hear.

"What was that?"

The tech swiveled to face Jones. "He's on the list."

Romeo stepped away and sent a brief text message as Kelsey, somewhat timidly, asked, "Could you put in my father?"

More typing. "Yes. He's there."

Romeo returned and handed Scott a slip of paper. "That's Kenny's social. Run him."

Scott complied. "Yes. He's on it."

Saylor sighed loudly. "For only fifty thousand doses nationwide…out of millions…it seems as if almost everyone is on the list."

"It would help if we had more names of people we're sure were on the other side," suggested Scott.

"What about that horrible FBI guy?" blurted Kelsey. "Oh…what's his name? It was odd enough so we shouldn't need his social."

"Ulrigg," Judtson provided. "Davis Ulrigg."

They waited.

"Nope. He's not there."

"Beckleman." The single name was grunted disparagingly by Romeo.

"Of course! Scott, put him in!" Kelsey urged.

Gumble was typing the name of the former Secretary of Homeland Security, when he suddenly barked, "*Hey!*"

"What?" Kelsey asked, concerned by the sudden alarm in the normally imperturbable tech. Scott's fingers worked the keyboard so quickly that they were a blur. "They…I can't…just a sec…. *Oh, no!*"

The group stared at the monitor, trying to make sense out of the meaningless stream. The tech stopped typing and dropped his hands loosely to his lap, releasing a pent-up breath.

"Scott? What happened?"

He made eye contact with Kelsey. "They must have finally figured out that the list was there."

She gasped softly. "They caught you?"

"No. They didn't. Or didn't bother to try. They shredded the database."

Kelsey nearly shouted, "*Shredded it?*" She abruptly turned to walk away from the group and began pacing, obviously agitated.

Judtson looked perplexed. "Can it be recovered? I thought you told us in the past…I remember when you were getting the copy of the cable show for me from the network server…you said you could recover it even if it had been deleted."

Scott's explanation was devoid of emotion. "Yeah, I can do that. But this wasn't deleted. It was shredded."

"I don't understand. What's the difference?"

From several feet away, Kelsey, clearly frustrated, responded as she walked, "It's the positive way to truly lose something stored digitally. You actually go into the file and replace everything in it with random ones and zeros."

She returned to the group and, speaking rapidly, addressed Scott. "A copy might still exist on a backup somewhere. Or on one of the desktops in the CDC. Maybe on an off-site source. They could have shared it with the World Health Organization or some other group doing research."

"I thought of that. I'll start sniffing. With the strings I acquired in the last few minutes, it might work. But I'd better move fast. If they *are* trying to wipe out their tracks...."

"Which they obviously are," Saylor interposed.

"They'll be shredding every copy," Kelsey finished.

"They will. And they have a head start on me because they might already know where the copies are. I need to jump right on it if I have a chance at all."

"Go! Do it. We'll get out of here."

▽

Matt Wheeler, sitting at the patio table, the ceiling fan spinning on high directly over his head, did not hear the french door behind him open and close. He was startled when Chris Ashby, innocuously carrying a tall glass of water, spoke. "Mind if I join you?"

The engineer jumped. "Oh! Hi. No. Sit down. Glad to have the company."

As Ashby sat, Matt inquired, "Have you let your sister know you're okay?"

"Yes. I was going to call her, but Scott insisted I let him send the message via some email format he cooked up to use until we can get a safe phone to her."

"Did you tell her it was her seance that led us straight to you?"

Ashby chuckled. "I did. Boy, have I come a long way since I used to fight with her about her crazy beliefs! You know what? I have to admit she has been quite a bit classier than I would have been if the situation were reversed."

Wheeler, amused, commented, "You mean she hasn't said 'I told you so'?"

"Nope! Not once."

"From the little I heard, that must have been quite an ordeal you went through. How are you doing?"

The chemist took a long drink, then answered, "Actually, it wasn't that bad. It's obviously no fun being kidnapped and locked in a cell. But, at least up until I tried to leave, they were treating me fairly well. It's a good thing Romeo and Ricky came when they did, though."

"Why's that?"

Shrugging, his voice remarkably impassive, he explained, "They were bringing in a neurosurgeon to start cutting me open."

"*Why?*"

"Matt, it appears the whole point of kidnapping me and keeping me alive was that they're desperate to find out how your gizmo operates and why their 'conditioner'...that's what they call it...no longer works on us."

Wheeler grunted in frustration. "That makes it unanimous. I've been pulling my hair out..." – he ran a hand over his smooth pate – "figuratively, that is...trying to determine the same thing."

"You still don't know?"

"No. No clue. I don't know how my equipment undoes the conditioning or why it makes a person immune from then on. And I never did scope out how their device even works."

Chris leaned back in the chair and drained his glass before speaking. "They brought in another headset and tried that on me. They wanted to be absolutely certain that the previous attempt hadn't failed due to a defective one."

"Obviously, the new device didn't work either."

A sly smirk appeared on the chemist's face. "Either that or it did and I'm now a double agent."

Wheeler stared hard at the man for a full minute, studying him. "That wasn't funny, Chris."

The smile disappeared. "You're right. It wasn't. All I can tell you, Matt, is that solving the conundrum of what you've done and what's in your head is one of their highest priorities. From here on out, you need to be extra careful."

$$\nabla$$

Since the overt attempt on Lisa's life...and after the ordeal with the New York Police Department, which had been substantially truncated from its routine length by the security camera footage from the hallway of the apartment building, as well as the presence and participation of Detective Cahane...the two women had avoided Lisa's apartment and had yet to go to her office. They were occupying a corner table at a popular deli two blocks from where she worked, waiting.

Tearing a huge bite out of a dripping Reuben sandwich and talking around the mouthful, Eunice asked, "Ya think he'll show?"

"I do. In fact..." – she pointed through the window at Brandon Bailey, who was checking the time on his phone and hurriedly threading his way through the crowd on the sidewalk – "there he is now."

Her boss pushed his way in, surveyed the room and spotted them, bypassed the counter, and came straight to their table.

"Lisa! How are you?" he gushed too effusively, eyeing the bandage wrapped around her elbow.

"Hi, Brandon. Told you on the phone...I'm fine. Way better than the other guys. This is Detective Eunice Cahane from Atlanta."

"You're the guardian angel who saved our Lisa! It's a pleasure to meet you, Detective." He shook her hand as he dropped into a chair.

Cahane responded with a loud snort. "If heaven's filled with angels looking like me...then all those old painters sure got it wrong."

Bailey stared at her blankly, having no idea how to respond. Lisa took advantage to ask, "Brandon, why did you hire two men who tried to kill me?"

The light and friendly expression of someone who was meeting a good friend for lunch had instantly collapsed. "What? Lisa...I didn't...."

"You didn't hire them?"

Flustered, he stammered, "I...I did. I mean...Candy, my aide, did."

Cahane joined in. "You're really gonna throw your secretary under the bus?"

"No! I...."

Lisa reached across the table and gently gripped his arm. "Brandon, calm down or you're going to have a heart attack or something right here. Listen, the deal is...ever since I came back to work, you've been pestering me to have security. When I finally agreed to it, their first day on the job, the two guys you hired tried to kill me. Of course that would prompt a question or two."

He began to speak.

She stopped him. "Don't answer yet. Let me finish."

He nodded, a bit of the reddish hue in his face lessening.

"I'm not saying that you specifically hired two killers to take me out...."

"Maybe *she's* not!" Cahane's voice intervened.

Lisa continued, "But the facts remain. And there are only two possible explanations. Either you did put a contract out on me, or you sincerely thought you were hiring two good guys to watch my back, and some very evil people slipped in their own killers. Now...I'm giving you the benefit of the doubt. I don't think you want me dead."

"Lisa, of course I don't! I swear!"

"Okay. Okay. So that leaves the second scenario. We need to know details about the company you went through to hire these guys: how they came to you; who recommended them; who gave you references on them. Everything."

"Yes! Of course. It really was Candy who found them. I'll get with her right away and get all those questions answered."

She released her soft grip. "Good. Thanks. So, about the show. Are we all set to do it in Arizona?"

Happy to be back on comfortable ground, he replied quickly. "Yes. The local affiliate has cleared the studio time for the live broadcast. Dad...I mean...Jack is ready to go. He wants some pre-air time with the group. You know the routine...to block out the topics and segments."

She shook her head emphatically. "Not this time, Brandon. I know these people and I know what they have to say. Believe me, the content is going to be pure dynamite. But I want Jack's reactions to be natural and spontaneous. I think that's a big part of what's going to make it awesome."

"I don't know, Lisa. We like to know in advance what's going to...."

"Am I the producer or not?"

"Of course you are. But this is going to be live!"

"Look, he's done it before. He went in totally cold for a live interview with Arafat, and that one won him an Emmy *and* the Edward R. Murrow Award."

The young man hesitated. Lisa waited patiently, aware that she held the cards.

"Well...I guess...on one condition."

She had been expecting this, knowing that a minor concession was inevitable, if only to salve his ego. "What condition, Brandon?"

His eyes shifted from her to Cahane. "That Detective Cahane is on the program with you."

"WHAT?" Eunice bellowed, attracting attention even in the noisy deli. "That dog won't hunt!"

"It'd be perfect," he said reassuringly, attempting to mollify her. "Lisa is going to be on the show. You just saved her life. It's a great part of the overall story."

Lisa, seeing her new friend gulp a large breath, began speaking rapidly. "Brandon, I'm certain that's doable. I'll talk to her later. But either way, we have a *go*, correct?"

Reluctantly, he nodded his assent. Giving him no time to reconsider, she rushed on, "Okay then, I'll be leaving right away for Tucson."

"*Lisa*," he whined childishly, "I need you here."

"No, you don't, Brandon. I should be there. I need to make sure that all the players are in place and ready. And that the affiliate doesn't have us set up in some old broom closet. Want to make sure the uplink is a good one. You know the drill."

He sighed theatrically. "Fine. Go." His face brightened. "By the way, the promo rotation started today. Talk about a heavy saturation. We have it running four times an hour every broadcast hour of the day. And marketing made a spot buy on several cable channels. There's going to be a blizzard of Internet spots. Jack is tweeting about it, too. Within twenty-four hours, the only people who won't know about this show must be living in a cave."

▽

Exhausted from a frenetic hour in the pool with Rocky, Kelsey climbed out of the water, followed a moment later by the golden, who scampishly stayed close as she toweled off, and then violently shook the water from his long, dense fur, the sudden drenching causing her to squeal with almost childlike glee. Judtson, reclining in a chaise longue twenty feet away, roared with laughter. "I warned you!"

Taking the time first to deliberately dry her body once again, she casually crossed the textured deck in his direction, Rocky at her heels. Judtson could not take his eyes away from her lithe form as she gracefully approached, aware she was the object of his attention and playing to it, her slow stride fluid and verging on feline. The one-piece black bathing suit shimmered in the soft luminescence of the landscape lighting as she shifted the towel to her head and massaged the water from her thick black hair. Finishing as she neared him, Kelsey tossed the damp towel onto the adjacent chaise and, with an insouciant swing of her leg over Judtson, settled down to straddle him, the water from her suit seeping into his pants.

"You should have come in. It was fun."

"Nope. I wanted to watch."

She arched an eyebrow. "Really? Wanted to see if Rocky liked me?" Her hand reached out and caressed the side of his face. "Did I pass the test?"

He responded with a throaty chuckle and took her hand, moving it to his lips and kissing it tenderly. "Yeah. You passed."

Feigning relief, she slowly bent closer, her wet hair cascading forward and pleasantly tickling his face, as she whispered, "I'm...so glad." Their lips touched. The contact instantly ignited a passion and he seized her bare shoulders, pulling her against him.

Chapter 29

JUDTSON WAS IN THE SAWMILL. It was bitterly cold and he was lying flat on his back, being carried forward on the rubber conveyor belt. He tried to get up, but could not. He was able to raise his head enough to check his body, expecting to see restraints holding him down, but saw none. He tried to sit up again, but failed. He tried to roll off the moving belt, but was frozen in place. All he could do was move his head and his eyes.

There was a shout from above, piercing the raucous din of the mill. It was someone calling his name. He turned toward the sound. Saylor, his face panicked, was alone on a catwalk high above, yelling feverishly and pointing in the direction of the belt's travel as he ran along the walkway. Judtson lifted his head and looked the way his friend was pointing. Less than thirty feet away spun a massive circular blade at the end of the conveyor.

With renewed urgency, he tried again to get himself off the belt, to no avail. He desperately watched Saylor, who was madly scrambling to reach a ladder at the far end of the catwalk. In a somewhat detached manner, his mind calculated his rescuer's speed and the distance he needed to travel, compared it to the rate the belt was moving forward, and knew that there was not enough time. The screaming whine of the blade was rising to a crescendo as it drew nearer. He stole another glance in its direction, when he spotted something which made his blood run colder still. Just above and to the side of the spinning blur of a blade, there was a small glass enclosure, obviously the operator's booth. Inside the booth, its gloved hand firmly gripping the control handle of the machinery, stood a dark, cloaked figure.

He shouted to it, having no idea if his voice could be heard inside the glass booth. He begged it to stop the belt. He frantically beseeched it to halt the spinning blade. The unseeable figure's only reaction to his pleas was to pull back harder on the handle. Judtson felt the speed of the belt increase beneath him.

Now only yards from the front edge of the blade, he could smell the ozone from the electric motor which drove the saw. He could feel the draft created by the jagged teeth of the blade hungrily ripping through the air at several thousand revolutions per minute. His mind was frenzied, attempting to force his body to respond…to roll off the belt before it was too late. But the only reaction to his mental pleadings was a wild thrashing of his head. As he traveled feetfirst toward a gruesome death, his legs were spread and he was now even closer to the cruel blade.

Stark fear and an overwhelming despair engulfed him, urging him to surrender…to resign himself to the fate of a savage bifurcation. Knowing that he was helpless to escape, and knowing that Saylor would not arrive in time, Judtson squeezed his eyes closed and waited for the horrendous pain…when a sudden pressure pinched his shoulder, accompanied by the sound of his name shouted over the whine of the machinery. Jerking his eyes wide open, he saw Kelsey beside him and climbing onto the belt.

Disbelief and astonishment, followed a split second later by dread, choked his voice. "KEL…KELSEY! WHAT ARE…WHAT ARE YOU DOING? GO…AWAY! YOU'LL BE KILLED!"

He wrenched his head to the side to see the hungry, wicked blade spinning menacingly right behind her.

She forcefully cupped her hands on the sides of his face. Her eyes wild, her voice frantic, she pleaded, "JUDTSON! YOU *CAN* MOVE! YOU *CAN*! DO IT!"

"NO!" he shrieked plaintively. "I CAN'T. I'VE TRIED. GO AWAY! YOU'LL BE KILLED, TOO!"

She shook her head violently and fell onto him, covering his body with hers.

"NO! PLEASE, KELSEY, NO!"

With her mouth jammed against his ear, her words penetrated to his very soul. "*You can do it. You're fine. You're fine*," she reassured him as she pressed her body next to his.

The turbulent wind buffeting his ankles as the teeth of the blade advanced toward the space between his feet, he looked up, past her shoulder, at the glass booth. Although the evil, shrouded figure remained indistinct, his blood froze as he saw a pair of glowing red eyes within the cowl of the cloak, the orbs shining out from under a prominent brow vaguely glinting with scales.

The glimpse igniting an atavistic terror, he wrapped his arms around Kelsey and twisted her violently to the side. The two fell from the conveyor belt and tumbled to the bedroom floor in a heap.

Judtson was still panting mightily from the overpowering horror of the nightmare as Kelsey, holding him tightly, her face tucked into the crook of his neck, repeated soothingly, "You're fine…you're fine, baby…you're fine."

The incapacitating flood of emotions begrudgingly ebbed. He slowly, almost delicately, shifted into a sitting position, not relinquishing contact with Kelsey for as much as a moment in the process. She snuggled against his side, and they sat quietly on the floor for minutes until the ragged pattern of his breathing fully stabilized. When he finally spoke, his voice was uneven. "How…did you know?"

"Know what?" she asked, her tone compassionate.

"That I could get off the conveyor?"

A breathy, muted laugh burst from her. "I don't know what you're talking about. You were having a nightmare. Yelling…thrashing. I was trying to calm you down. I never dreamed you'd throw me on the floor."

Staring at her in the faint lambency of the window-shaped rectangle of moonlight, her face cameoed with wildly tousled hair, he saw her lips curl in a half smile as she remarked, "I had no idea sleeping with you could be such an adventure."

He kissed her lightly.

"I should probably explain." He described the recurring sawmill dream and how he had suffered from it for much of his life. "What's interesting is that, up until relatively recently, the dream was exactly the same. Saylor and Doni always made it to me in the nick of time. Saylor would pull me off the conveyor. Every time. And there was never anyone running the controls of the mill. The glass booth was empty. Then…weeks ago, when I was bouncing in and out of those catatonic states before they fully converted…or conditioned me, I guess…Kristen was in the booth. It was her hand on the lever. And when I begged her to stop, she laughed like a berserk maniac and pushed it harder, speeding up the belt."

"Whew! That is eerie. So…did Saylor still make it in time?"

Judtson reached up and brushed a curled wisp of hair as it traced the outline of her bottom lip. "Uh…actually, no. it wasn't he who saved me."

"It was Doni?"

He shook his head.

"Who?"

"You."

Her eyes widened. "Me!"

"Uh-huh. As the blade was inches from my body, you burst into the control booth and clobbered her with a two-by-four."

A high, girlish giggle burst from her. "I clubbed Kristen?"

He grinned broadly. "Yep."

Kelsey's expression abruptly changed from amused to guileful. "So…you knew back then…."

"Why…I guess I did."

She kissed him. "I know *I* did." Her voice became more serious as she continued, "Judtson, I hate to change the subject…."

"So do I."

"Hush. Don't you think this is weird? They've been trying to mind-control you. There was this other Judtson, all ready to go, who came out to live your life after you were zapped. And you were stuck inside, watching. And all the while, you've been having this symbolic dream where a giant-sized saw is going to split you in two."

He nodded. "You're right. It is a little strange. But the dream started a long time before my first episode."

"When exactly did you have the first sawmill dream?"

"It has been a long time. Since I was…." He paused and leaned his head back against the side of the bed. "Let's see…I was…wait, I remember it was the same year that Halley's Comet came the closest to Earth, so that was 1986."

She bolted upright and turned to face him. "*1986?*"

"Yeah, why? *Oh…my…God.* That…."

Excitedly, she finished his thought. "That was the same year you got the vaccine!"

▽

Romeo, taking a bite from a breakfast burrito, dropped into the swivel chair in front of the bank of security monitors, his eyes quickly scanning the various views until he satisfied himself that all was clear and normal. The system was augmented with motion sensors and a compliment of concealed laser trips, all tied into an alert module which actuated a loud tone in both his and

Chili's phones. Although there was no need for continuous physical monitoring, he preferred to personally lay eyes on the perimeter as often as possible.

The wall in his office was filled with a mounted array of high-resolution screens, surrounding a single massive display. The system, designed by Scott, was programmed to automatically switch any of the individual views to the large screen if activity was detected. The center view now covered an area inside the perimeter wall where Judtson and Kelsey were strolling the grounds with the golden retriever.

He was idly watching them as he ate, when the view abruptly switched to the driveway outside the gate. A sedan he did not recognize stopped at the pedestal-mounted intercom. The view automatically switching to the camera built into the device, he could see that the driver was Lisa Trippiano, which was confirmed within seconds as an orange shadow box flashed on the screen, bracketing her face, and the system's facial recognition identified her. She was reaching out the window toward the button. Sitting beside her on the front seat was a stranger Romeo assumed must be Detective Cahane. The recognition program was still working to ID her.

Standing, he jammed the last of the burrito into his mouth and hurried from the room, pulling out his phone, which had beeped as Lisa pressed the button. Trotting down the hallway toward the entrance, he tapped the small screen and said, "Hello, Lisa. Is that Detective Cahane with you?"

Her animated voice came back. "Romeo! Hey, how are you? Yes, it is."

With another tap on an icon, he activated the gate opener and then rapidly scrolled to the view from a camera mounted high above the gate and oriented toward the approach to the entrance. He checked it and made certain no one was behind her.

"I am well, Lisa. Come on in."

▽

As Lisa drove through the gate and followed the long driveway, Eunice Cahane gaped at the impressive building with amazement. "Missy, what is this place? Some kind of resort hotel?"

Amused, Lisa answered, "No, Eunice. This is Kelsey's place."

Cahane whistled loudly. "We've got some rich folks in Atlanta, mostly old tobacco money and some of the original Coca-Cola family, but I've never seen anything this size."

"It's pretty big, all right. Oh, cool! There's Kelsey...and Judtson."

She pulled the rental under the porte cochere, parking next to Judtson's red 4-4-2, and they got out just as Kelsey ran up to them and squealed, "Lisa! God, I'm glad to see you!"

The two women hugged. Cahane, circling around the front of the car, saw a tall man in his thirties, standing off to the side and extending his arm down to pet a dog. She stuck out her hand. "You must be Mr. Kent."

He came over to her and smiled broadly as they shook hands, the golden retriever scampering close and sniffing her leg. "Yes, ma'am, and that would be Judtson. And this is Rocky. No doubt you are *the* Detective Cahane who saved our friend's life."

She made a loud sputtering sound with her lips and squatted to rub both sides of the canine's head. "That's what everybody keeps on tellin' me. Like I've been sayin', she did the hard part and paraded the guy right in front of me. Hell's bells, even *I* couldn't of missed him."

Lisa, bubbling with energy as always, whirled to face Judtson, her arms spread wide. "Judtson, come here you!"

He took one small step in her direction and she rushed the rest of the way, encircling his neck with her arms. Holding him close and standing on her tiptoes, she whispered, "I've heard about you and Kelsey. Were you the only two who *didn't* realize it?"

Ignoring her comments, he uttered, "It's good to see you, Lisa."

Kelsey, now focusing on Lisa's attire of a narrow tube top and snug shorts, positioned herself to keep one eye on the hug as she smiled brightly at Eunice. "Detective Cahane, I'm Kelsey. I can't tell you how happy I am to have you in our little band."

Cahane snorted loudly as she read the vivid yellow phrase on the front of Kelsey's red T-shirt – "I dream of a society where a chicken can cross the road without its motives being questioned" – and was about to respond to her host's greeting, when the front door opened and she turned to see a massive black man with a shining bald head. The new arrival, wearing camo pants and a green T-shirt stretched tightly over his impressively muscled arms and chest, stepped out and moved toward them. She was struck by the agility of his step as he approached.

From behind, she heard Kelsey's voice. "Detective Cahane, this is my friend and my protector, Romeo Jones."

He stopped in front of her, a neutral expression on his face, and she had to crane her neck to see it. Letting out a low, appreciative whistle, she remarked, "Whew-wee, I never knew they stacked it this high. You're so tall, if you fell down, you'd be halfway home. If I ever need to smack you upside the head, I'm gonna need a ladder."

He looked down at her and, unable to resist, his face creased into a smile. "Ma'am, I'd be willing to wager that at some point in your life you were as tall as I am. That is, before that safe fell on your head."

Her shoulders beginning to shudder with laughter, Cahane eyed Lisa and confided, "You were right, missy. I *do* like this guy." At the same time, she poked Romeo ineffectually in the abdomen with her elbow.

He tilted his head bemusedly and reached out. "Pleasure to meet you, ma'am."

She buried her hand inside his grip. "You, too, big fellah. And all of you folks stifle this *ma'am* and *Detective* bullpucky, will you? My name's Eunice."

"Eunice," Kelsey, tickled by her new guest's interplay with Romeo, responded, "unless you're hungry or thirsty from the trip, why don't we go inside and make sure we're all caught up on everything?"

Cahane glanced at Lisa first, then shrugged. "It don't make me no never mind."

The group, chatting amicably, moved toward the door. Kelsey, noticing that Judtson was still frozen in place beside his car, went back and heard him muttering softly to himself.

"It...*DON'T*...make...me...no...never mind."

He sighed.

"It...don't...make...me...*NO*...never mind."

He sighed again.

"It...don't...make...me...no...*NEVER* mind."

With apparent bewilderment, he stammered, "What...what the *hell* does that *mean*?"

Shaking her head and laughing, she hooked her arm in his. "Come on. Let's go in."

▽

Bal's concentration, as he worked to correlate the data gleaned from the ongoing operations in

Bolivia, was broken by the distinct trilling of his phone. It was Sam, calling on the safe phone Scott had overnighted to him.

"Hello, Sam. How is it proceeding down there?"

"Great, sir. Had to go into town for some supplies, so I thought I'd give you an update while I was in cell range."

"The satellite uplink has not yet arrived?"

"Arrived today. I have one of the geeks setting it up now."

"Excellent. So what is the status?"

"We're about twenty percent ahead of schedule. It's helped that we've had some slightly warmer weather. And the slant drill arrived yesterday. We've already made three bores under Puma Punku. Speaking of that, a local archaeologist and his students showed up and began some additional excavating around the terrace. They've already exposed quite a bit more of the platform."

"That is excellent, Sam."

"*And* I got the approval to begin excavations on the island. We've started digging at one of the old drill sites."

"That is better still. I am quite anxious to find out what obstructed the drilling attempts that you and Dr. Berry made."

"Me too. But the reason I'm calling is the slant-drill bores. Dr. Singh...I think we might be getting close to an entrance."

The postdoc's words electrified the geologist. "Are you serious?"

Clearly exerting an effort to keep his voice even, Jonassen explained, "I am. As you suggested, we've established a pattern of bores which triangulate on the void under the platform at Puma Punku. With the bores we've been able to do so far, adding that data to what Dr. Berry and I found, a pretty clear map is developing. It is remarkably uniform. Not at all what you'd expect from a cavern or pocket naturally created by tectonic forces or eons of water penetration. And...I'm not certain yet...we need to poke several more holes to really nail it down...but it sure looks like we're mapping the top of a smooth, truncated dome."

Singh was silent, mentally absorbing what his assistant had said, when Sam, obviously struggling to keep his narrative cautious and scientific, added, "And...from what we can tell at this point, it appears as if...dammit, Dr. Singh, the exact top of the dome is perfectly centered under the Puma Punku platform. And not just centered under it...I think it *is* it."

Bal loudly sucked in a breath, his mind reeling. "I need to make certain that I understand you, Sam. Are you telling me that the subterranean void approaches the stone terrace at Puma Punku?"

Giving in to his excitement, Jonassen clarified, "No, sir. I'm not saying it approaches it. I'm not saying it is near it. What I'm saying is that the cut stones which make up the floor of the platform, or terrace, are the actual roof of the dome."

Consciously reining in his emotions, Singh countered, "Sam, I most definitely do not intend to be insulting. However, slant drilling has its limitations. I do not see how you could draw this conclusion merely from your borings."

"No offense taken. I should have told you this before. The bores gave us enough info to map the void, all right. And then the mapping led us to extrapolate the shape and precise location and depth of the dome. But the real clincher was the GPR."

With his mouth twisted in an expression of frustration, Bal chided, "Now, Sam, you know that ground-penetrating radar would not be effective on the large andesite blocks used in the terrace."

"I know that, sir. Of course I didn't expect any sort of a reading or image when we fired off some shots in the GPR while it was positioned on the platform. That's not what I'm saying."

"Then what *are* you saying?"

"That each of the four shots we made with the GPR caused the massive stones in the platform…to ring like a bell."

Chapter 30

FINDING CHILI IN THE SECURITY ROOM, KELSEY APPEARED CONCERNED. "Where's Judtson? I've been searching all around for him."

The Marine checked the bank of monitors. "He and Romeo are headed back here now."

She followed his eyes and saw the two men crossing the grounds toward the rear of the house.

"Thanks."

"No problem, ma'am."

Clutching a box under her arm, she trotted down the long hall and passed through the living room, where Lisa was curled up on the couch, reading. She hurried past and headed to the kitchen, arriving at the french doors leading to the patio just as the men were entering.

"Hey, guys! Where've you been?"

"The shooting range," the big man replied, continuing to walk as Judtson stopped at her side.

"I really appreciate it, Romeo," he directed to Jones' retreating back.

Without looking behind, the Ranger complimented him. "You did fairly well today."

Judtson beamed. "Thanks!"

"Shooting range? What for?"

He focused on Kelsey, a bit of a sheepish expression on his face. "After we did our little raid on the FEMA camp, I thought I could use some pointers."

"What do you mean? You did fine!"

"*Kelsey!* Romeo took down the majority of the bad guys. You and Saylor both got your share. All I did was make a lot of noise, waste a lot of ammunition, and hit absolutely nothing. I would have been more effective armed with water balloons."

Trying to change the subject, he pointed at the package she was holding. "What's in the box?"

"A present for you!" she bubbled, her eyes twinkling, and handed it to him.

He tore it open. Inside was a dark blue T-shirt emblazoned with reflective silver type, which read, "GRAMMAR POLICE – To Correct and To Serve."

Pinching his lips together to stifle his amusement, he pulled the shirt out and held it against his torso.

"Do you like it?" Her unabashed eagerness melted Judtson and he kissed her.

As they parted, he mumbled, "It's…it's…yes, I love it. Thanks."

"Put it on. *Please*."

Unable to resist her if he wished, he unbuttoned his shirt and removed it. He was wrestling the stubborn undershirt from the top of his head, when Kelsey seized on his moment of vulnerability to tickle him under the arms, sparking an instantaneous high-pitched shriek as his arms jerked down reflexively, ripping the cotton fabric apart and prompting her to dissolve into a near-hysterical laughter.

Romeo charged into the room at a full run. *"Everyone all r…?"* Stopping in mid-sentence, he skidded to a stop as he took in the scene: Kelsey bending forward and hooting loudly as Judtson stood bare-chested, clutching a tattered undershirt, his arms pressed protectively against his sides.

"You guys!" the big man grunted with disgust. Shaking his head, he turned back and exited.

This finally pushed Judtson over the edge and he, too, burst out with raucous, snorting guffaws.

Lisa, hearing the commotion, casually ambled in and eyed them both. "Can I play?"

$$\triangledown$$

Forty-five minutes later Kelsey and Judtson were in the Hummer, cruising on Skyline Drive, enjoying the view overlooking Tucson, and still chuckling intermittently from the earlier scene. They had decided that none of the food in the house sounded good, and that going out to breakfast was definitely in order. Romeo had opposed the idea at first, then insisted upon coming with them, finally conceding with the caveat that they drive Kelsey's Hummer rather than the Olds convertible and that they both carry weapons.

"I thought we'd never be able to get out of there," Judtson commented, with a smile.

"Romeo can be a real wet nurse sometimes."

"I don't think that's what you mean."

Kelsey was driving and took her eyes away from the road for a second. "Why?"

"A wet nurse is an old term for women hired by the wealthy to breast-feed their babies for them."

"Ha! You're right. Applied to Romeo, that's a funny image."

She glanced at him again. He was wearing the new shirt, untucked to conceal the holster on his belt. "Are you sure you like that tee? If not, you don't have to wear it just for me, you know."

"Actually, I do. Honestly. But you haven't told me how you get them."

She shrugged innocently. "I buy them on the Internet."

"No, you don't! When I opened the box, it still had the silk-screen smell. It's your turn, anyway. I told you about Squirrel."

"Okay. Let's wait until we get back home."

"Promise?"

"Promise. Where do you want to eat?"

"I want pancakes."

She smiled. "I know just the place."

Fifteen minutes later, as she pulled into the parking lot of the Bisbee Breakfast Club, he remarked, "This place is great. I didn't know they had one in Tucson."

"Hasn't been open very long. When we were in Bisbee, you promised me that we'd go back for a pleasant day. Since we haven't had time for that yet, I thought this would be the next best thing."

They entered and immediately encountered a small posted sign telling them to wait to be seated. No host or hostess was in sight. Surveying the room, Judtson saw a young blond-haired child skipping up and down the aisle, stopping at each occupied table and staring at the customers before moving on, loudly singing, "La-la-la-la-la," as she bobbed away.

He grumbled, "I hate this. More than half the tables are empty and we're supposed to stand here like morons until some airhead...."

"Hello! Welcome to the Bisbee Breakfast Club!" The overly effusive greeting came from a college-aged girl who had approached from the side. "Will there be two of you today?"

Judtson whirled to face her. "I hope not. There should only be one of me. And, as far as I know, one of my friend."

The hostess, momentarily baffled, glanced down and read his shirt. Breaking into a grin, she said, "Oh, I get it. You're correcting me. Isn't that cute! Uh...how many in your party?"

"Actually...."

Before he could continue, Kelsey hooked her arm around his and answered, "Yes, please. Two for breakfast."

"Table or booth?"

Kelsey heard him suck in a breath to speak. She again answered quickly. "A booth."

Snatching two menus from a slot, the hostess began to lead them across the dining room, talking rapidly over her shoulder as she walked. "I notice stupid stuff like that all the time, you know. Like on a pill bottle, when it says to 'take one pill three times daily.' How are you supposed to do that? You can't take the same pill three times! Or like when you are going to heat up a microwave corn dog and the instructions tell you to remove the plastic wrapper before eating. I mean...duh!"

Chuckling, Judtson added, "Why would you want to eat the plastic, anyway?"

The girl giggled. "*Yeah!* I didn't even think about that part." She motioned toward the second booth from the end, a shallow two-seater. "How is this one?"

He grinned. "How would I know? I haven't tried it yet."

She let out a rapid-fire series of high-pitched squeaks which he guessed must have been her laugh. "*You're funny!* Uhhh, is this booth all right?"

"It's fine," Kelsey replied, her answer terse, and slid onto the bench near the large corner table. Since there was no room next to her, he sat on the opposite side.

Flipping open the menus and laying them on the paper place mats, the hostess announced, "Lauren will be with you in a minute."

"I don't think," Judtson retorted puckishly, "there's enough room left for her in this booth."

With another ear-stabbing staccato laugh, the girl walked away. Still smirking, he shifted his gaze to Kelsey and saw that she was not amused, her expression unreadable. His first thought was that she was acting like Kristen. "What's wrong? Don't tell me you are embarrassed by me."

"Isn't she a little young for you?"

"A little...what? *Oh, my God, you're jealous!*"

Her unblinking gaze confirmed his accusation. She mimicked his voice mockingly. "*How would I know? I haven't tried it yet. I don't think there's enough room for her in this booth.*" She finished with a sarcastic "Aren't you just cute as a button!"

He flopped back against the cushion. "She's...she's not much more than half my age!"

"So?"

Clinically studying the restrained tension in her body, the fire flashing in her blue eyes, the tightness in the set of her jaw, he found that a smile crept slowly across his face. "This...is *so* cool!"

Kelsey's eyes flared. Her voice came out low and steady. "*Cool?* What's so *cool* about it...Judtson?"

He leaned forward across the table. "You're ready to fight over me, aren't you? You're ready to tear her eyes out."

Only the outermost corners of her lips turned upward slightly. "Is that what you'd like, *baby*? Do you want to watch me kick that little twit's skinny ass?"

The rest of the world disappeared as he lost himself in the intensity of her gaze. He softly uttered, "*Oh...yeah!*"

Her tongue made a brief appearance to moisten her lips. With a husky whisper, she cautioned, "You'd better be careful what you wish for."

"Hi, folks. Do you know what you want yet?"

The trance abruptly broken, Judtson turned to see Lauren standing beside them. She was no more than twenty with extremely long blond hair, gathered in a loose ponytail, draped artfully across the front of her left shoulder, and cascading down to a low-cut top. Jerking his eyes back to Kelsey, he said hastily, "You order for me."

The Mona Lisa smile blossoming, she reached across the table, taking his hands in hers and tilted her head up to face the server. "Haven't looked at the menus yet, miss. Do you have a breakfast with pancakes, eggs, and bacon?"

"Sure do."

"That's what we'll both have. And some coffee and orange juice."

"Okay. And, ma'am, how do you want your eggs?"

"Over hard."

Lauren jotted the request and turned to Judtson. "And you, hon?"

Before he could answer, Kelsey, her voice somewhat louder, said, "*Hon* will have his the same way."

She left and the two, holding hands, gave in to muted laughter. They passed the time with idle chat until their meal arrived.

"Here you go, folks." As the waitress slid the plates of food in front of them, the hostess escorted a family with five small children into the corner booth behind Kelsey's back. The entire section was suddenly overwhelmed with loud, clamorous talking, as though the whole group was speaking at once. The din was almost deafening.

Judtson saw Kelsey say something. Because of the noise level, he was unable to make out the words. "*What did you say?*" He had to nearly shout to be heard.

She shook her head. "*Never mind. Later.*"

He nodded his acknowledgment, irked by the intrusive new arrivals, and began to eat. Within less than a minute, the mother's voice boomed, *"Joey, Joey, Joey, Joey, do you want some jelly? Here's some jelly! Joey, have some jelly!"*

From where he sat, Judtson could see a small boy, no more than five years old, standing on the seat behind Kelsey, his back defiantly to his mother as she shoved a torn open packet of jelly toward him. The child reached over the top of the bench and harshly tapped Kelsey's shoulder, causing her to jump.

"Joey, Joey, Joey, here's some jelly."

Disregarding his mother, the brat cackled maniacally with laughter and poked Kelsey again, harder this time, while staring directly at Judtson, who made an ugly face in his direction. The boy immediately pointed an accusing finger straight at him and, with his mouth inches from Kelsey's ear, began shrilly bombarding the two of them with loud, exaggerated shrieks. *"Mama! Mama! Mama! Mama! Look! Look! Look!"*

Not only finding it impossible to talk, Judtson also found it virtually impossible to think coherently. His mind flashed to an eerily similar assault during a book tour in Denver. He had stopped to grab a bite, when a nasty little red-haired girl leaned over the back of his booth, repetitively yawping, *"Mr. Ma-aan! Mr. Ma-aan! Mr. Ma-aan!"* right into his ear and slamming a purple stuffed Barney the Dinosaur onto his head. Even though he had desperately yearned to shout back, he just sat there, quietly fuming. To this day he had always wondered what would have happened if he had actually....

Kelsey, who had been trying to tune out all of the ruckus and eat, suddenly slammed down her fork, grinned tightly at Judtson, and said loudly, *"Excuse me for a moment, would you?"*

She then turned on her seat and climbed up onto her knees, facing the family, who were oblivious to the young boy's behavior. She leaned as far forward over the booth as she could and began shouting in the same punctuated tone of voice. *"Mama! Mama! Mama! Mama! Look! Look! Look! Joey, Joey, Joey, Joey, do you want some jelly? Here's some jelly! Joey, have some jelly!"*

Abruptly halting her rant, she glared silently at the mother, whose face instantly transmogrified into a mask of fury. Grabbing one of her daughters around the waist, the woman barked, *"Sissy, move! Move, Sissy! Let Mama out!"*

Mimicking the mother's voice, Kelsey railed, *"Sissy, move! Move, Sissy! Let Mama out!"*

Judtson, while struggling mightily to contain his laughter, glanced at the beleaguered father, who seemed to be wishing he could disappear. Mixed in with expressions of shock and dismay at Kelsey's outburst, there was a smattering of applause from other diners at adjacent tables, which further inflamed the mother. She roughly shoved the daughter ahead, clambered out of the curved booth, and marched past Kelsey and Judtson's table purposefully, aiming straight for the hostess station.

The offending boy, stunned by the unexpected actions, had fallen blessedly mute, as had the rest of the family, who were all staring down at the table. Kelsey spun back around and slid down in her seat, bounced once, picked up her fork, and took a bite of pancake. Tears now streaming down his face, Judtson lifted a strip of bacon from his plate and was about to take a bite, just as the mother returned with a stranger who was apparently in charge.

Pointing at Kelsey, she blared, "THAT'S HER!"

"Actually, that's *she*," Mr. Grammar Police corrected.

Kelsey, ignoring the arrival of the two, heard Judtson's aside and snorted. He then innocently remarked to his uninvited callers, "Is there a problem?"

The manager, a middle-aged man wearing a black hairnet and sporting a respectably sized potbelly, answered, "Sir, this customer has complained that you and your guest are creating a disturbance."

Kelsey, who was in the midst of taking a sip of orange juice, suddenly blew the juice out from between her lips and back into the glass. She was whirling around, ready for a confrontation, when Judtson calmly asked, "And what disturbance might that be, sir?"

"Well...I...I...." The manager sputtered to a stop as if he were a leaf blower which had run out of gas.

The mother, who was looming directly above Kelsey, barked, "*This woman...this woman was scaring my Joey. She was up on her bench, facing straight at us and bending right over him and screaming!*"

Before anyone could say a word in response, Kelsey picked up her plate and, with a forced smile, handed it to the man. "Sir, this woman is standing right above me and spraying spittle all over my food. I felt it drizzle on my arm. Could I get another meal, please?"

Out of habit, he automatically took the plate of food from her, as Judtson, his voice level, inquired, "I want to be absolutely certain I understand, sir. Do you view the actions this woman described as being disruptive?"

Clearly uncomfortable, he answered, "Uh, yes, sir."

"So therefore, if those exact actions were performed by her son, directed at *our* table, *he* would be creating a disturbance? Correct?"

"Well...."

As he faltered in his answer, the mother bellowed, "*My Joey was just being a little boy! He was....*"

In an effort to take control and end the scene in the middle of his restaurant, the man interrupted. "Sir, I'm going to have to ask you and your friend to leave."

Lifting one eyebrow, Judtson pressed, "So if a rotten little terror does something to bother other customers, it's fine. But if an adult does it, you ask the person to leave?"

The manager furtively glanced at the apoplectic mother before returning his attention. "I'm very sorry, sir. I'll have to ask you to please leave. Perhaps we could package your meals to go."

"Not that meal," Kelsey retorted impishly. "It has her spit all over it."

"*Sir...,*" Judtson began, raising his voice. At that moment he felt Kelsey's hand on his.

She reassured him, "It's okay. Come on. Let's go," then stood brusquely. Smiling broadly at the mother, she said, "Excuse me," forcing the woman to step back two paces.

Judtson and Kelsey joined the manager, who now had a profound expression of relief on his face as he led them across the restaurant.

When they reached the door, the man turned to face them, asking, "Give me one second, please," and opened a drawer at the hostess station, pulling out a small pad. He scribbled on the top sheet, tore it off, and handed it to them. "I am very sorry about all of this. Please take this and come back again."

Judtson read the slip. It was a gift certificate made out for $50.00 in future meals. He grinned at the still-nervous supervisor. "Thank you, sir. We will. And good luck with..." – he jerked his head in the direction of the corner – "her."

The man rolled his eyes and said nothing.

Walking across the parking lot, Kelsey barked out, "Damn, I wanted to strangle that kid!"

"And his mother," Judtson agreed. With that, the two climbed back into the Hummer and drove east until they came to a fast-food restaurant which served breakfast. As Kelsey was about to park, a bus pulled up to the front door and unloaded a large group of children wearing soccer uniforms.

Shaking her head and chuckling, she suggested, "Drive-thru?"

"Absolutely."

Their breakfast sandwiches in hand, they ate parked under the shade of a large mesquite.

Chapter 31

LISA AND EUNICE ENTERED THE LOBBY OF THE LOCAL AFFILIATE. Life-sized cardboard images of the stars of current network shows were positioned at the four corners of the spacious area, creating the fleeting illusion that the room was populated with impossibly attractive, flawlessly groomed, inexplicably smiling people.

A smile matching those on the cutouts appeared on the face of the woman behind the wide laminated desk. "You must be Lisa Trippiano."

"Yep. And this is Eunice Cahane. We're here to see...."

"Mrs. Lindberg. I know. She told me you were coming. I'll let her know you've arrived."

"Thank you."

As the receptionist made the call, Eunice spoke softly to Lisa. "Don't TV stations usually have better security?"

Lisa answered, duplicating the muted level, "I know! Of course it's way extreme at the network, but I've been to other affiliates where the outside door to the lobby has an electronic lock with a camera and intercom before you even get in. And the receptionist is behind bulletproof glass with one of those drive-thru teller trays for stuff you're dropping off. Why? Are you worried?"

As Cahane was about to answer, the door opened and a woman came out carrying a notepad. She smiled brightly and extended her hand. "Ms. Trippiano, I'm Alisa Lindberg."

The local director appeared slightly disheveled without seeming harried. Her hair had been hastily pulled back, a few wispy strands escaping from the band and dangling along the sides of her face. Lisa's impression was that her new acquaintance had just the right balance of sincere friendliness and clear-eyed professionalism. She liked her instantly and they shook hands. "Please, call me Lisa. Although the whole Lisa/Alisa thing is probably going to be fun. Anyway, this is my friend Eunice Cahane."

Lindberg's eyes widened. "The detective who saved your life! This is awesome."

"You've already heard about it?"

"Oh God, yes! In all its glorious detail. Your assistant, Shannon, told me about it during one of the fifty phone calls we've had, trying to set up this broadcast."

With an understanding laugh, Lisa commiserated, "That's Shannon. If it's any consolation, she drives me nuts, too."

The woman shook Cahane's hand. "It's a real pleasure to meet you, Detective."

"Right now it's just Eunice. And at the rate I'm going, I might never be Detective again."

Alisa eyed her curiously for a moment until Lisa asked, "Do you have time to show me your facilities?"

"Of course. This way." She turned and led them while saying over her shoulder, "You need to excuse the way I look. Since we received the call to put together your show from here, I think I've had maybe four hours of sleep."

"I'm really sorry about that, Alisa. We didn't have much notice at our end."

"No. I'm not complaining. Fire drills get the blood pumping."

Cahane paused at the door leading from the lobby to the studio and checked it for a lock, electronic or otherwise, and found neither. Shaking her head, she caught up to Lisa as their host was explaining, "I've been with the station twenty-two years, and in all that time we've never originated a full broadcast for the network. Obviously, we've done short news bits when a big story happened locally, but for those New York grabbed our feed. So this has been a major deal for us. Especially since we're going live."

"I can't tell you how much Mr. Bailey appreciates all your hard work," Lisa commented, verbally stroking the director.

Lindberg hesitated outside a door marked "Master Control," and briefed her. "I'm sure you want to meet the engineers. The chief is Zack. He's the one with glasses, kinky hair, and the Star Wars T-shirt."

Lisa, chortling under her breath, remarked, "Yeah, that's a unique look for an engineer."

Alisa knocked and immediately pushed the door open without waiting to get a response. The next ten minutes were spent reviewing unnecessary technical issues, as Lisa's sole purpose for talking to the engineers was to develop a comfort level with their skill and competence. Cahane, sensing that Lisa was nearing the end of the discussion, interjected, "Y'all mind if I ask a stupid question?"

Zack, focusing on her for the first time since she walked in, answered, "No. Of course not. What do you want to know?"

"Well, there must be a thousand buttons in this room. I tell ya, I'm glad I don't have to be the one to know which ones need to be pushed and which ones order the pizza." The three techs all gave her a patronizing laugh. "But if the live broadcast is going on…and, let's say, I want to stop it from going anywhere…which one of these buttons is the one I'd push?"

One of the engineers, the oldest of the three and sitting near her left side, pointed at the board beside him and indicated, "The red ones."

"The red ones? There's more than one?"

"Well, yes. This red one would kill the uplink to the satellite. And this one, the red button labeled 'black,' would kill the feed and put up a black screen."

Zack cut in, "And I wish they'd put some kind of a cover on that one. It gets hit accidentally way too many times." The other two men murmured their agreement.

Cahane nodded. "I see. Okay. So if I'm standing here during the broadcast and somebody sneaky-like hits one of the two red buttons, how can I tell he did it?"

"That's easy," Zack replied, pointing at one of the several video monitors filling the wall. "That screen is the air monitor. If somebody kills the uplink, that screen goes to snow. If somebody hits the 'black,' that screen goes black. Do you mind telling me why you're asking these questions?"

Alisa interceded, "Normal stuff, Zack. Remember, this will be going out live to the whole network. They worry about these things."

The man seemed to accept the explanation, and the three women thanked them all and left. Lindberg moved to the next door and stopped before opening it. "I gave them that answer because I didn't want to freak them out. I don't need the entire crew gossiping about people trying to kill some of the guests we're going to have on the set tomorrow."

Lisa sighed. "Good idea."

"Ma'am, I have one more question."

The director turned back to face Cahane. "Sure."

"Once the signal goes out of here, do you know any way someone can stop it?"

She thought for a minute, finally answering, "No. I don't think so. It'll be going straight up to a satellite and then rebroadcast down from there."

"Okey-doke. Thanks."

The next room was the actual control room where Lindberg was usually stationed during the broadcasts. Lisa affectionately patted the control board. "A Kahuna. Love it. First board I ever worked."

Alisa caught the detective's eye. "And, Eunice, to further answer your question from earlier, that large monitor right in front of my console will have a red outline around it during the broadcast. That tells me we are going out."

"No red outline…it's been killed. Got it. I hate to bother you, but where's the little girls' room?"

"Oh, of course. Just out the door and turn left. It's on the right."

As Cahane departed, Alisa urged, "Well, come on, Lisa! Let me show you my biggest source of stress since your office first called."

"What's that?"

"The set we've been building. This isn't New York. We don't have set designers and builders on staff. If we need one, we hire outside contractors. When I got the call telling me that Jack Bailey was coming to do his show from here and we only had a couple of days to get ready, I called my two usual contractors. Both of them were tied up on other jobs and not able to do it. I thought I was going to have a nervous breakdown. Then, out of the blue, this company basically fell into my lap. They had experience. They had crews available. They were ready to go and could work around the clock and hit the deadline. I couldn't believe my luck."

Neither could Lisa. She deemed it best to conceal her suspicion. "That is amazing. How did you find them?"

"They found me. Well, not exactly. One of my regular contractors ran into the estimator for the new outfit at a plan room. I guess the two were talking about how business was. My guy complained that he had to turn down my job and the other guy said he was wide open right then. That's when my guy gave him my number."

"So they know each other?"

"I guess. Why?"

She mulled it over for a moment before responding, "No reason. Curious, that's all.

Anyway, let's go see this set."

The two women crossed the control room toward the studio.

"Lisa, if you're expecting any critical calls or text messages, you might miss them once we go inside the studio. The cellular service in there is hit or miss. Mostly miss."

"No. I'm good. Thanks."

They descended two steps from the elevated flooring system of the control room and walked through the doorway. Gasping, Lisa grabbed Lindberg's arm, blurting, "Alisa! Who is that *hunk*?" and pointing at a tall man with thick, wavy dark hair and broad shoulders, who was engaged in a conversation with someone across the room.

Chuckling knowingly, she answered, "He's one of the news anchors, Dan. And, Lisa, forget about it. He is *so* married. Wife looks like a Miss Universe *and* they have a baby on the way."

"*Damn!*"

The object of their attention noticed the two and briskly crossed the room, smiling broadly. "You must be the producer from New York. I heard you were coming. I'm Dan Marries."

Lisa took his offered hand. "Lisa Trippiano. Great to meet you, Dan."

"The excitement level around here in the last couple of days has been palpable, and tomorrow will be even worse. Hopefully, there's an opportunity to meet Jack Bailey. I've been a fan of his for years."

The man's inflection and expression were both without guile, and Lisa, accustomed to local anchors unabashedly vying, lobbying, and jockeying for a network position, found him charming. "I'll make sure you get some face time with him, Dan."

"That would be great. But only if it isn't an intrusion. I know it's going to be a zoo."

With a sincere smile, she reassured him, "I'll make it happen. Don't worry."

After exchanging another minute or two of pleasantries, he excused himself and walked away. Lisa turned to her host. "My God, handsome *and* not a jerk. Unreal!"

"It's a rarity." The director pivoted and, with a sweep of her arm, announced, "There it is! How do you like it?"

Lisa followed the motion and surveyed the set. The desk, behind which Bailey and the members of Lisa's group would be sitting, was covered with a textured blond plastic laminate, built in the shape of a boomerang, with a short, straight section in the center for the host. The backdrop, fabricated using the same laminate material, was a segmented arc of sizable picture frames, each rectangle filled with an enlarged, sequenced, backlit transparency of a panoramic view of the Tucson skyline, creating the illusion of a series of windows overlooking the city.

"Wow! Alisa, that's beautiful!"

Lindberg smiled proudly. "Yeah! It's great, isn't it?"

"I'm impressed. Considering the tight time frame, I assumed you'd just green-wall us and super something behind."

"Thought about it, especially when I was afraid I didn't have a contractor. But you know, that's tacky. I didn't want you to come here and think we were Podunk."

"Well, anyway, this is amazing. Great job!"

Beaming from the compliments, Alisa suggested, "Let's go see the assignment editor. You can double-check the coordinates for the uplink."

▽

Chris Ashby unpacked the final box from the shipment, the centrifuge, and placed it carefully on the bench. Jimmy Meade, who had helped him carry the delivery back to the impromptu lab in Kelsey's sprawling home, was more than slightly curious about the project. "So when are you going to start making the monoatomic gold?"

Shaking his head, Chris explained, "I don't make the monoatomic gold, Jimmy. My sister found a fairly good source for the material. Of the several vendors who sell it, theirs is, by far, the most pure. All I do is put it through a final scrubbing process I devised to remove the last of the impurities."

"Oh, that's right. I remember that you said the gold didn't work on your lab rats until you scrubbed it. So that's what you're going to be doing with all this gear?"

"It is."

Meade glanced around. "Where's the gold?"

"Over here," Ashby indicated and moved to a stack of three large plastic totes, each secured and labeled with the distinctive "Biological Samples" stickers. Using a box cutter, he sliced through the adhesive label covering the interlocking lid on the top tote, flipped the hinged halves open, and pulled out a sealed plastic bag filled with powder, holding it up.

The astronaut stared at the bag intently. "That's the stuff, huh? Doesn't look...golden."

"The light reflectivity of the gold changes in this form."

Peering into the top bin, Meade whistled. "Man, that's a lot of gold. And you've got three totes full of it?"

"It is quite a bit. I was worried that the lab making it would change their procedures or go out of business, so I negotiated a bulk price. Bought their entire inventory."

"Still must have cost a bundle."

"Oh, it did, believe me. I had a decent chunk of grant money...before they pulled it. That paid for most of it. I bought the rest out of my own pocket. Almost cleaned me out."

Tapping the sticker, Jimmy asked, "Why the 'Biological Samples' labels?"

"People are afraid of bio materials. They won't mess with them. What do you think would have happened in transit if I'd labeled them as gold?"

He chuckled in reply. "They never would have made it here. I'll bet I'm driving you crazy with questions, but why are you going to scrub all this gold? You don't need that much for your research, do you?"

"No. When I've run it all through the process, I'll have about ten thousand times the quantity I'd ever need. I don't know, Jimmy. In any case, until we figure out what the hell's going on, I'm stuck here with the rest of you. I need to do something to keep busy."

▽

Ricky knocked lightly on the bedroom door and heard a muffled voice call out, "Just a minute." He waited patiently in the hallway until Saylor pulled the door open and, seeing his visitor, smiled. "Hey! What's up?"

"I...I hadn't seen you around yet today. Thought I'd stop by. Make sure you were okay."

He had expected to see the same "rough around the edges" look which had been so apparent yesterday, but was surprised that Saylor was freshly showered and shaved, his hair still plastered to his scalp.

"I'm all right. Come in."

Ricky followed him and sat in a reading chair beside the bed as Saylor perched on the edge of the mattress.

"Heard about your commando raid in Socorro. You're turning into a regular Rambo."

The younger man snorted dismissively in response. "Romeo did the hard part."

"That's not what I heard. They had him trapped in a hallway with Chris, and you charged in with guns blazing, and whooping a war cry."

"'Freeze, Jerkballs' is hardly a war cry."

His comment elicited a laugh from his friend, and it did his heart good to see this. Only a heartbeat later, the mirth disappeared from Saylor's face, and as he spoke, his tone was more somber. "I guess a lot of people aren't what they appear to be."

Ricky, anxious to change the subject, quickly asked, "Are you going into your office today?"

Returning to the moment, the neurologist answered, "For a little while. I had Melanie reschedule my morning appointments, but in about an hour I have a patient I really should see. Why?"

"Just curious. You think it's safe to go out?"

He shrugged. "Yeah. I can't imagine why *I'd* be one of their targets. Other than being some comic-relief sidekick, I haven't done anything...no big discoveries or breakthroughs...or anything."

"I wish you'd take Romeo or Chili with you, to be cautious."

"I don't think so, Ricky. That's a waste of manpower. They need to watch the group."

"Well then...I'll come with you."

The smile returned to Saylor's face. "Now there you go...Commando Ricky at my side."

"Saylor!"

"Okay, you win. Let's head over there."

$$\triangledown$$

Dylan stood behind Scott as the tech visually scanned a bewilderingly rapid series of screens.

"Scott, are you sure it's okay pulling you off your search for the CDC list to do this?"

"It's fine. I wrote a worm. Right now, it's working its way through the web on its own, looking for the name strings I identified."

"Do you think you'll be able to find research into the altered vaccine? I checked, and it seemed as if they'd done a fairly good job of wiping out any record of it."

"Oh, probably. There are always nooks and crannies people forget about if they try to wipe out somethi...bingo!"

"You found something? Already!"

Sending the current screen to a printer, the tech replied, "Wasn't that hard, with a little digging. It appears that when the publicity first came out, four university research labs grabbed the formula to study what effect it might have on the population. Their systems *were* wiped recently...probably by whoever is trying to eradicate this. Luckily, several of the faculty and some of the students had loaded the research on their own laptops and home computers to work on it. That's why secure installations never want people to do that. You can zap it from the main data banks, but never even know where else it might be. All I had to do was find one of those PCs turned on, and voilà!"

Falt snatched up the printout. "You are amazing."

"So I've heard," he answered with a self-satisfied smirk.

▽

Kelsey led Judtson down a long hallway, bedrooms lining both sides. This was the portion of her home where all of her guests quartered, a separate wing from her personal area. Reaching the end, they turned left and followed a shorter corridor, which terminated with a door. Knocking, she waited for a moment, until Romeo's voice sounded from within. "Come in."

She opened the door and they both walked through. The first room was the security center, the location where the exterior cameras displayed their views on dedicated screens. The big man, sitting at the console, turned as the two of them entered. "What's up, boss?"

"Just giving my friend here a tour. Do you mind if I show him…your lair?"

A wide grin spread across Jones' face. "You're finally going to share my little secret, huh?"

"He won't stop pestering me until I do. Do you mind?"

Romeo looked him up and down as if he had never seen him before. "I suppose it'll be okay. Go ahead."

Judtson started to ask, "What is…?"

"Ssshhhh," Kelsey stopped him. "Just come with me." She took his hand and led him across the room to three doors, then paused dramatically at the middle one. Facing him and, with the inflection of an announcer leading the viewers into a haunted den, she declared, "You are about to enter the inner sanctum of Romeo Jones," and flung open the door.

The large space was a stark contrast to the security room. Two of the walls were covered with floor-to-ceiling bookshelves, made from mahogany and nearly filled to the limit with hardbound volumes, many of their covers leather. With his attention fully captured, Judtson crossed to the shelves and began scanning the titles and authors. "Plato, Dante, Shakespeare, Bacon, Darwin, Epictetus, Virgil…." His gaze shifted to a lower shelf. "Tennyson, Whitman, Chaucer…! My God, Romeo, this is awesome."

The Ranger had joined Kelsey in the doorway. "Thanks. I even have some of the cheesy pop-culture books on the bottom shelf."

Judtson's eyes moved down and, squatting, he read the spines, "Harper Lee, Jack London, J. D. Salinger, Orwell, Rand…." He gasped softly. "Romeo, you have…you have my books?"

"Uh-huh! And they're not bad, either."

Gripping the edge of one of the bookshelves to steady himself, Judtson stood. "This is amazing! What a superb collection."

Kelsey hurried to him and grasped his arm, steering him. "I know! Isn't it fantastic? But his library's not all. Come here."

She led him to the center of the room, where a massive leather wing-back chair was positioned to face a wide and tall blank wall across the room from the bookshelves. "Sit," she ordered and he complied. Plucking up a small handheld remote from a side table next to the chair, she murmured softly, "Now…watch this."

Romeo stepped farther in and closed the door as she tapped a button on the remote. The room lights were instantly extinguished and the wall, no longer blank, was filled with a sparkling, glittering realistic depiction of the Milky Way.

Dropping to her knees beside Judtson, Kelsey explained in a near whisper, "When they upgraded and replaced the projector system at the Flandrau Planetarium, I bought the old one for Romeo as a gift…for saving my life. It came with the entire library of stars, galaxies, everything."

Judtson was speechless. He looked up and saw the ball-shaped projector suspended from the ceiling.

"We had to reconfigure it some to work on a wall instead of a domed ceiling, so we lost a little accuracy...but I think he likes it anyway."

Romeo grunted in the darkness.

She apparently tapped the remote again. The projected show disappeared and the lights returned. Standing, she held out her hand. "Still and all, everyone needs a hobby. I'll show you his."

Judtson took her hand and dazedly followed her to an alcove bracketed with two doors, Romeo trailing behind. On the left was a bedroom; on the right, a closed door rimmed with a rubber seal. As she opened it, Kelsey stepped to the side and revealed, "You've been wondering where I get my never-ending supply of T-shirts. Now you know."

He walked past her and glanced around the compact work area in astonishment before turning back to Romeo, amusement in his voice. "You like to *silk screen?*"

Chapter 32

SAM JONASSEN SLOWLY MOTORED ACROSS THE SURFACE OF LAKE TITICACA, enjoying the first temperate day of the season. As he neared the shore of the island, he could see that Gretchen was waiting for him, waving her arm excitedly. Beaching the small boat, he stood unsteadily, and carefully made his way to the bow. Too agitated to hold back until he had disembarked, she gushed, "Sam, you are not going to believe what we found!" He allowed her to steady him as he stepped over the rail and onto the small spit of sand.

"What is it?"

"We don't know. But it's…. You just need to see it! Come on!"

She whirled around and led him up a trail, almost running. His long legs allowed him to pace her easily. "Gretchen, at what depth did you hit the obstacle?"

"Eleven-point-two meters," she answered over her shoulder, breathlessly. "Right at the depth where you and Dr. Berry hit a barrier with the drill."

He could feel the first tingles of adrenaline seep into his system, and his stride lengthened. They arrived at the dig within ten minutes. The site was a beehive of activity with a combination of American students and the local laborers hired by Bal. He trotted to the large pit and peered over the edge. A number of the students were clustered around something at the very bottom.

Espying the first in a series of three ladders descending into the pit, Sam moved toward it at once. "Gretchen, it's amazing how deep you've been able to dig so quickly."

She was at his heels. "One of the equipment operators said this was the easiest dig he's ever done in his life. No rocks. Nothing hard at all. The dirt just comes out as fast as they can shovel it."

Jonassen followed the system of ladders and dirt benches, which had been cut into the walls of the pit to stabilize them. When he reached the bottom, several of the students noticed his arrival and moved aside to allow him access. As he approached, he noticed a distinct lack of animation in the demeanor of the typically chattering, boisterous youths. The eerie hush made the hairs on the back of his neck stand.

He walked toward the focus of the attention and dropped to his knees. Gretchen, who was directly behind him, detailed the discovery in a muted, verging on reverent tone. "The Bobcat operator alerted me that he had hit something. I told him to stop and three...no, four of us...came down. When we got here, it was still covered with loose dirt. So we started clawing and brushing the soil away with our hands. Till we found...that." She lapsed into silence.

Sam's mind could not comprehend what he was seeing. At the bottom of the hand-scratched hole, approximately one meter in diameter, was a perfectly flat, unblemished, gleaming metal.

▽

Bal and Carlos were seated in front of the webcam, with Judtson and Kelsey off to the side. On the screen, via a secure Skype connection, was the visage of Sam Jonassen, unconcealed excitement coloring his normally stoic features.

Bal was engrossed in the conversation. "Sam, have you had a metallurgist examine it yet?"

"Not yet. Trying to find one now."

"What do you think it is?" Carlos pressed.

"We have no idea. Since we found it in that first spot, we've pot-holed several locations at the bottom of the pit. Everywhere we dig, we find it. And it's always at the same level."

"That matches what you encountered when you were drilling there with Dr. Berry."

"Exactly."

Off-camera, Kelsey spoke. "Sam, do you think it might be some kind of buried spaceship?"

The slightly jerky image on the screen changed to show a sudden grin on the man's face. "Not too long ago, I would have had a very different answer for you, Kelsey. Except now, after what I've seen down here lately...sure, I guess...sky's the limit."

"Sam, this is Judtson. I know you haven't found a metallurgist yet, but do you have a clue as to what type of metal it is?"

"No. I can tell you that we beat it with sledgehammers, chisels, and then grabbed one of the diamond-tipped bits from the drilling operation and hit it with that. Nothing. Not a scratch. One of the equipment operators took an acetylene torch to it. Couldn't even discolor it."

"That's odd."

"Tell me about it. What's really weird is that he kept the tip of the flame on one spot...that's thousands of degrees...and the metal didn't even glow! And it gets weirder. It was hot down in the pit, using the torch. He was sweating. After about ten minutes of heating the metal in one spot, he killed the torch. I was watching and I saw a drop of sweat fall from his face straight onto the spot where the torch had been directed. It just...beaded and sat on the surface. It didn't boil off instantly as it should have."

"Wow!" Judtson exclaimed.

"No kidding. The metal somehow is able to dissipate the heat almost instantly."

"That would be a great property for the skin of a spaceship."

"Yes, Kelsey. I suppose that's true."

"What is the current plan?" Carlos inquired.

"Well, that's part of the reason I'm calling. For direction. I have as many people working at the bottom of the pit as I can spare, clearing it completely and by hand. And we're nibbling at the sides of the pit, enlarging it. I want to expose as much of this thing as I can. Maybe we'll find an edge…a boundary."

"Maybe a hatch," interjected Kelsey.

The smile returned. "We might. Other than exposing it and waiting for the metallurgist, I don't know what else we can do with it at this stage."

"And your work at the terrace…where you think there might be an opening…what are you doing on that?"

"We're proceeding with the slant drilling, Dr. Singh. I'm still trying to get permission from the Bolivian government to dig on that site. In the meantime, I've split our camp. Left a small camp by the lake and moved everyone else to Dr. Berry's old campsite next to Puma Punku."

"So, no luck at all on the permission yet?"

"No, sir. Can you think of more I should be doing?"

Singh glanced first at Carlos, who gave a subtle shrug. He next looked at Kelsey and Judtson before answering, "None of us have suggestions at the moment. It sounds as if you are doing all that can be expected. I am glad we now have a satellite uplink at the site. It will be easier to stay in touch with you and convey anything which might occur to us."

After addressing some routine matters, they terminated the connection. Judtson resolutely slapped his palms on his knees. "I think we need to get down there. Right after Lisa's broadcast tomorrow."

▽

"Why am I always just a passenger in these 1960s muscle cars?" Saylor complained to Ricky above the loud roar of the 396 cubic-inch engine.

The two had decided to stop for an Orange Julius after Saylor had seen his patient. Grinning like a young boy on a roller coaster ride, Ricky downshifted with another gratuitous rev of the power plant and pulled into an empty parking space in back of Park Place Mall. "You can drive Charlie back if you want."

"Charlie?"

"Yeah. That's what I named him…Charlie Camaro."

Saylor chuffed. "I wouldn't mind, actually."

They crossed the lot and entered the food court, their ears assaulted by the echoing din of overly animated chatter in the crowded open area. Threading their way between the tables to the kiosk, they ordered large cups of the frothy drink and found two seats near the children's play area.

Speaking loudly to be heard, Ricky remarked, "I'm still blown away that Judtson left Kristen and hooked up with Kelsey."

Saylor sucked a mouthful of the sweet frozen concoction up the straw, immediately getting a shooting pain at the front of his head. He groaned and massaged his forehead. "I haven't really noticed. Are they getting serious?"

Ricky made a loud sputtering noise with his lips. "You're kidding, right? Yeah! They're together every minute and they can't keep their hands off each other."

"Huh! Well, he has to be happier with Kelsey than he was with Kristen. This is crazy."

"What is?"

"Listen to us. We sound like two teenaged girls gossiping about our fellow classmates."

Ricky started to comment, when movement across the room caught his attention. Noticing,

Saylor asked, "What? Something wrong?"

Before his friend could say a word, there was a piercing shriek from a girl in the crowd of people lined up to order food at one of the restaurants, followed a split second later by a second scream. Both men jumped up and ran toward the disturbance, fighting their way upstream through the river of bodies moving in the opposite direction, clearly running away from whatever was happening.

The first to arrive, Ricky broke through the last of the fleeing people to see four bodies lying prone on the floor amid a spreading pool of blood with several shoe tracks leading away, and a young male, clad in now bloody jeans and a black T-shirt, and wielding a knife. Skidding to a stop, Ricky reached behind his back and under his shirt as the youth charged him, pointing the large hunting knife forward like a sword.

He whipped his semi-automatic pistol around, pointed it at the attacker, and shouted, "STOP!"

The young man showed no inclination to comply, and Ricky shifted his aim downward toward the stranger's legs and pulled on the trigger. The double action kicked in and the hammer rose and fell, making a distinct click. He realized instantly that he had neglected to jack a round into the chamber and moved to grasp the slide, knowing as he did so that it was too late. A heartbeat before the blood-coated blade plunged into Ricky's chest, Saylor, at a full run, streaked past him and slammed into their adversary with his full weight and inertia, taking him down.

The two crashed to the floor. The wicked knife, jarred from the youth's grip, skittered away. Driven by an almost maniacal energy, the aggressor flailed and kicked wildly, until he was on top and wrapping his hands around Saylor's neck as Ricky, reholstering his pistol, ran to his friend's aid. Coming from behind, he bent down, slid his arms under the armpits of the attacker and, pulling up forcefully, laced his fingers together behind the thug's neck, breaking the stranglehold on Saylor.

Pulling upward and to the side, he was able to manhandle the thrashing assailant off Saylor, who climbed unsteadily to his feet. The young man outweighed Ricky and, although unable to break the grip behind his neck, jerked and twisted violently, causing the two to topple to the floor. Ricky rode the attacker down, landing atop him, and kept his grip as the perpetrator's face collided with the hard floor.

Twisting to Saylor, Ricky shouted, *"I've got him! Call the police!"*

His friend had already pulled out his cell phone and dialed, instructing the dispatcher that multiple ambulances and paramedics were needed at the scene.

Having fully recovered, Saylor quickly moved on to one of the four victims and, seeing that she was alive, alerted the crowd who encircled the tableau, "I need some help here!" Two men in Air Force fatigues broke from the group and ran forward. As they assisted Saylor, two uniformed police officers arrived, breathing hard, their pistols drawn.

Ricky, still pinning his adversary, who was flopping under him like a marlin on the deck of a fishing boat, barked, "He stabbed these people!"

The taller of the two officers holstered his pistol and pulled handcuffs from his belt, snapping them on the flailing youth and allowing Ricky to extricate himself and stand shakily. Practically staggering, Ricky moved to the nearest table and dropped heavily onto a seat. From his side, he heard a young, timid voice. "Sir?"

He turned to see a boy of no more than nine years old standing with the two cups of Orange Julius. With clear admiration in his eyes, the boy said, "You left these at your table."

Panting mightily, Ricky managed a broad smile for the youngster. Between breaths, he uttered, "Thank you very much," and took the drinks from him.

The paramedics arrived. All four of the victims were still alive, although Saylor was pessimistic about one of them, a girl of approximately thirteen who had an apparently severed artery.

He wanted to accompany her to the emergency room but was prevented from doing so by the police, who stated matter-of-factly that she was in good hands, and insisted that he remain for questioning. Resentfully, he complied, and he and Ricky were detained for over an hour, endlessly answering the same questions. Several other witnesses in the crowd, as well as the video from the multiple cameras deployed throughout the food court, corroborated their version of the event.

The two, exhausted, staggered to the restroom and cleaned off as much of the blood as they could with the absurdly dismal trickle of water available from the motion-activated sink faucets, before making their way back out to the parking lot. They reached the Camaro, and Ricky wordlessly offered the keys to Saylor, who only shook his head and climbed into the passenger seat as his friend got behind the wheel but did not start the engine.

His voice troubled, Ricky finally broke the silence. "Saylor...did you see his face?"

"Whose? The kid with the knife?"

"Yeah."

"No. I was coming up behind you. I couldn't. Why?"

"He...he had just violently stabbed four people! Then he was charging right at me...wanting to kill me, too. And his face...his expression...was...."

"What?"

"Saylor, how should someone look while doing something like that?"

Releasing a long sigh, he replied, "I don't know. Wild...crazy...furious, maybe."

"It was none of those. As he ran straight at me with a knife...he looked...calm. Detached. As if he had been standing in line waiting to order a sandwich."

▽

Matt Wheeler left his bench and ambled casually across the large work space. As he passed Scott's area, which was unoccupied at the moment, he remembered to say "Criminy," and was rewarded with the exaggerated, booming voice of Jim Carrey shouting, *"Somebody stop me!"* Chuckling under his breath, he continued to the far corner where Chris Ashby was in the process of calibrating a piece of equipment.

"Hey, Chris. Whatcha doing?"

Ashby slowly raised his eyes from the project. "Oh, just some final checks before I start scrubbing the gold." As he answered, he motioned toward the stacked bins.

Wheeler whistled. "Man, that's a lot of material. How much can you scrub in each batch?"

"Ten grams."

"That's it, huh? And how long does it take each time?"

Ashby smirked. "You can't help it, can you?"

Innocently, he responded, "What do you mean?"

"Matt, you're like Tim 'The Tool Man' Taylor on *Home Improvement*."

"What can I say? I'm an engineer. Besides, I'm done with the new headset. I'm bored. I was thinking maybe we could automate the scrubbing procedures."

The chemist shifted his gaze to the huge stock of monoatomic gold and shrugged. "Sure. Do you think you can do it?"

Wheeler snorted. "Of course I can do it. Talk me through the process."

$$\nabla$$

With the exception of Chili, who did not fully trust the automatic alarm relay to his phone and was monitoring the security system directly, the group all gathered at the long dining table. The mood was subdued as they ate, the only steady conversation prompted by Saylor and Ricky's experience at the mall. It was as if everyone had sensed that this meal was to be the last modicum of normalcy in their immediate lives.

Even Lisa was not her typical effervescent self as she prepared them for the next day's scheduled broadcast. When she finished, Judtson abruptly asked, "Does anyone think that going on television to tell the real story is going to affect anything?"

Lisa was mildly surprised by his question. "Why? Don't you?"

Laying down his fork and leaning back in the chair, he sighed. "I'm probably the wrong person to ask, actually. Saylor, Ricky, and Kelsey, you know me the best. The three of you know I have this problem. I guess it's a general contempt for the vast majority of humanity. It seems to me that just about all of the people in our society have willingly abdicated their roles as sentient, questioning, challenging beings and voluntarily surrendered themselves to a near zombie-like state. I first recognized it in school. Not college or high school. Before that. A visceral disdain for knowledge...for learning...for understanding. Replaced with an obsession for who was dating whom and who was getting and giving sex."

"Don't you think that's simply a hormone thing at that age?"

"No, Jimmy, I don't. I was as hormone-driven as anyone at that time. Had it bad. And yet, every single second that the fog of yearning cleared, my mind automatically reverted back to its normal state of inquisitiveness. An ever-present desire to...understand. And even if I had given the other kids the benefit of the doubt and chalked it off to hormones, that allowance for their behavior would have been shattered by the time I got to college. There, we were all surrounded by a wealth of knowledge, information, resources...all of it. And everyone around me" – he glanced at Saylor – "well, almost everyone was still obsessed with the same shallow, hedonistic things.

"And it didn't end with that. If it had, there would have been the damage of lost opportunities, but that would be repairable. All of you have seen it. Leno used to make a routine out of it. He called it 'Jaywalking.' He'd go out on the street and ask people of different ages questions we all should be able to answer. The responses were embarrassing. O'Reilly does it on his show, too. Same result."

"That's true," Wheeler agreed. "We are an ignorant culture."

Judtson shook his head emphatically. "It isn't that we're ignorant. That is not what bothers me when I encounter it. It's the attitude of ignorance. The celebration of it. The pride they take in *being* ignorant. And the pride they take not only in not knowing...but also in not *wanting* to know. And this desire...forgive the split infinitive...to not learn...not understand...not comprehend extends as well to how they are being managed, handled, led, and governed. It is the relentless dripping of Chinese water torture. It is the frog in the pot of water. There has been a steady, systematic, inexorable, incremental erosion of... I don't know what... our freedom? Our rights? Our ability to merely live as we see fit? And no one cares! If you were able to pluck a relatively intelligent, virile, able man out from the 1950s and transport him into today's society, he wouldn't make it through the first day without becoming outraged... without revolting against the hundreds of subtle restraints imposed upon him. Restraints which were not present in the time he came from. Jimmy, I'm certain you knew some of the old fighter aces from World War II."

"Oh, yeah. They were quite a bunch."

"Imagine taking one of those guys, in his prime, and dropping him into the middle of... let's say, Goodfellow Air Force Base. How would he react if he lit up a cigarette while standing *outside*, in a parking lot, and one of the Security Police told him he wasn't allowed to smoke anywhere on the base other than a small fenced area a mile away?"

Meade laughed heartily. "He'd end up in the brig for clocking the guy."

"Exactly. And what would happen if that same man chanced to be going through the airport and a stranger started to frisk his wife?"

"Oh Lord, I wouldn't even want to visualize that."

"Precisely. And my point isn't about smoking or TSA pat-downs per se. I'm trying to illustrate what we've lost. We, as a society, no longer have the ability to react. To become truly outraged. We've reached the point where our leaders no longer need to concern themselves with whether we, as citizens, will *take it* when they issue a new order. That's why I did the paintball attacks on traffic radar. That's why I confront the people at airports who want to x-ray me and my belongings and frisk me. That's why I'm always challenging strangers about the seemingly minor things they do... just because they've been told to do them... without ever really giving it a thought. People don't act in opposition anymore. They don't get indignant when something new is imposed upon them. Oh sure, a few get on the Internet and complain about it, but nobody *does anything*. No matter how outrageous the new thing might be. So... no... I don't have much faith that they – the general public – are going to watch us tomorrow and suddenly grow a backbone."

"You're right," Jimmy Meade grunted. "They're all just a bunch of damn sheep."

Scott, his voice softer than usual, commented, "You know, at the time the Internet took off, I was excited about it. I anticipated that it would transfer the power from the few who controlled the information, and place it into the hands of the masses. I believed that, with unfettered access to the Internet, we could... would... transcend the reality of the past to a level where the people actually controlled their own lives... their own society."

"That's not the way it worked out." The somber, monotone observation came from Dean.

"I think it actually worked the opposite."

All heads turned back to Judtson.

"What are you saying, my friend?" Carlos asked.

"Well, I hinted at it a moment ago. What the Internet has done is give everyone a voice. Or maybe I should say the illusion of having a voice. Before it existed, as oppressive edicts affected a citizen, the absence of a medium for venting discontent led inevitably to frustration. The frustration grew until it prompted the person into action. Now, people can go on Facebook, Twitter, Instagram, or any one of thousands of blogs and spout off. Rack up a larger and larger number of followers. They can vent and rant and rave, reinforcing one another and giving all of those involved the *feeling* that they are building a posse, a movement... and also creating the impression that they are having an impact by what they are doing."

"I hadn't considered that angle," murmured Scott.

"I don't know if that was the deliberate intent or if it just worked out that way, but no, most people wouldn't have. We no longer *need* to go out and protest…or demonstrate…or boycott… or even engage in an act of civil disobedience…because, after all, last night we sent out twelve tweets letting our audience know exactly what we thought; posted a scathing comment on Facebook, on which more than two hundred 'likes' appeared; and put up a really nasty poster on Instagram expressing how we felt, and gained seventeen new followers. *Boy, did we tell them!* I guess what I'm saying is that maybe the Internet was originally intended to be a conduit for distributing the power to the people. Or maybe the net result, no pun intended, was the original intent. Either way, what has happened is that the web has inserted a billion safety valves…one into each person. And those valves prevent the pressure, which in the past resulted in genuine change, from ever building up to the necessary, critical point."

A soft gasp of understanding was heard from Lisa.

Judtson continued, "And look at what has happened. Whether it is a scandal in the White House, a crisis in the Middle East, or whatever…we now have an avalanche of events overwhelming us. Back in the seventies when Watergate eventually took Nixon down, that was the one big story discussed in the news. I wasn't alive then, but I did the research. The front page of every newspaper in the country had a Watergate headline. Every day. For months! The lead stories of the three broadcast news channels were Watergate related. It was all there was. And…the public reacted. Things changed. Nixon resigned. As the power people watched this happen, they learned a lesson. Unfortunately, the lesson learned was not an ethic to be good, proper, lawful, and respectful of the wishes of the public. No, the lesson they learned was that if they had even more crises…a Watergate-sized crisis every week or at least every month…we, the people, would never be able to get it together enough, to martial enough organized opposition to force any change, any punishment, any result."

"They learned to beat us down," added Meade.

"Yes! They beat us down, all right. They deluge us. They overload us. And the countless cable news channels breathlessly report how many millions of tweets went out overnight outraged about the latest fiasco, as if that matters. But…I repeat…nothing actually happens."

Chapter 33

THE LIVE BROADCAST OF *THE JACK BAILEY SHOW* WAS SCHEDULED for seven in the evening. The group was to assemble at the studio no later than five, and the members were preparing in their different ways. Carlos and Bal spent the majority of the day together, comparing notes and planning their individual statements. The two had provided Lisa with copies of the videos they planned to use.

Matt, expecting to only answer technical questions, if any, from Bailey, devoted all of his time to automating the scrubbing procedures for Chris Ashby, who had sequestered himself in his room, handwriting his statement about the effect the processed material had on Alzheimer's and autism. Dylan was also rarely seen through the day, delving into the vaccine research provided by Scott. Jimmy, planning on a presentation of his story similar to countless other tellings, assisted Dean as the former NASA analyst nervously assembled his documentation.

Shannon, Lisa's assistant, had arrived with the show's entourage and was shuttling back and forth between Kelsey's home and the studio, transporting the still photographs and other graphics to Alisa Lindberg for pre-show prep.

Lisa found Kelsey and Judtson together on the back patio. Compared to the others, she thought the two appeared remarkably calm.

"Hi, guys! Do you have a sec?"

"Of course," Kelsey answered. "What's up?"

"Normally, I would turn over all the videos in advance. It's the right thing to do from a courtesy and production standpoint. Allow the director to copy them in and make sure there aren't any technical tweaks needed. But I don't want even one person in the booth or on the set to know where we're heading with this. Remember, as far as Jack and everybody else are concerned, we're all with the program as far as buying the Beckleman line of crap. Obviously, a video of a flying saucer coming out of the lake would blow that angle wide open. Judtson, what do you think?"

"I agree. Makes sense. Handing the videos to them at the last minute won't cause a problem technically, will it?"

The producer shook her head. "Naw. It happens. Like I said, it isn't the preferred way to do things, especially on a live broadcast. It'll work, though."

"Okay then. Let's keep the cat inside the bag."

"Will do. One other question. This one's for you, Kelsey. Is there a chance of talking Romeo into coming on?"

"None! I've tried. Trust me."

"He's such a big part of the story. And I'd love the way he'd come across on the screen."

"I know. But he's freaked out that this is the first time, out in public at least, when all of us will be together. He's afraid that we're presenting too good a target for the bad guys. One they won't be able to resist."

Lisa's eyes widened. "Does he think they're going to try something while the program is actually on the air?"

"No. Yes. I don't know. He's just being Romeo. Did you talk Eunice into going on?"

"Believe it or not, I did."

"How did you manage that?"

With a nervous giggle, Lisa clarified, "It wasn't really that I talked her into it. She gave in without a fight."

"That's weird. Everything else on track?"

"Yeah, we're good. Gotta run. Bye, guys."

She whirled around and hurried back into the house without waiting for a response.

"She is *so* high-energy!" exclaimed Judtson.

"I know! She makes me seem like someone on Valium."

"Yeah, right!"

▽

Romeo and Chili were practicing at the indoor shooting range. The Ranger had finished emptying a clip into the paper target, when he felt a tap on his shoulder. Turning, he saw Cahane, already wearing noise-cancelling headphones. He slipped his own earpieces down around his neck as he motioned to Chili that they had company.

"Mind another?" she asked, tilting her head far back to look up at his face.

"Not at all. What do you shoot?"

Removing her weapon, she pulled back the slide, and handed the pistol to him. He whistled appreciatively. "Chrome Desert Eagle fifty cal with the muzzle brake...nice piece."

She shrugged. "Ammo's expensive. Don't need as much with this. It's my personal weapon, anyway. Department makes me carry a Glock. I see you shoot a forty-five."

"Uh-huh."

With a glance at Chili, who was standing slightly behind the two, she said, "Heard you're a Marine."

"Yes, ma'am," he answered in his unnaturally thin, bird-like voice.

"What outfit?"

"MCSOCOM Detachment One first, then MARSOC, ma'am."

"Heirs to the Raiders. Y'all were my heroes."

He arched a single eyebrow. "Were, ma'am?"

Cahane laughed. "Don't get a twist in your strap, Marine. Still are. Alls I was trying to say was that I wanted to get in that outfit. But they weren't takin' womenfolk."

Romeo eyed Eunice top to bottom and commented puckishly, "Seems they would have made an exception for you."

"Watch it, sweet cheeks," she shot back. "So how'd you two meet?"

"In the sandbox, ma'am," chirped Chili. "The powers that be were sorting out the whole SOCOM thing and I was rotated through several of the sister services' special ops teams. They were trying to integrate us. It was a good tour. We did some damage. That's when they figured out that there was an Army unit who needed a little help finding their way from their DFACs to their latrines, so they attached me to Master Sergeant Jones' outfit."

Chortling at his explanation, she quipped, "That musta been fun to watch. How long did it take the two of you to mix it up?"

"Almost the first day," grunted Romeo. "But we really tangled after about three months."

"Who won?"

The men answered in unison.

"He did."

"He did."

Romeo cleared his throat. As he spoke, his voice was subdued. "Gunny's being charitable. He mopped the floor with me."

"Is that the way it was, Chili?"

The Gunnery Sergeant reached up and casually scratched the mutton-chop sideburn on the side of his chin for a moment, then moved his hand to the front of his throat and unconsciously touched it lightly before he dropped his hand back down. "Maybe so. But I'm the only one of us who walked away with a souvenir."

The man hung his ear protection on a peg and holstered his M9A1. "I need to get back to the security station. If you would excuse me. Ma'am, pleasure to meet you."

After the door shut behind Chili, Eunice turned to Romeo quizzically and waited. It did not take long for him to begin speaking, his eyes still focused on the closed door. "As I said, it started the first day. We'd been out in that stinking desert for months, pulling recon, sweating ourselves to dehydration in ghillie suits waiting for targets, doing a pretty decent job of routing the bad guys out of their hiding places. Then Gunnery Sergeant Keyliss shows like he's the Second Coming. Wasn't so much what he said as it was the way he looked at me and my men. And the tone in his voice. Got under my skin, you know." He chuckled softly. "I wasn't quite as restrained as I am now."

"Love to have seen that!"

"So one day...after sundown...there were twelve of my soldiers gathered around. We were eating our MREs and blowing off steam, when Gunny sat down with us. In all fairness, he was on his good behavior. Until one of my guys cracked wise about the poor Marine being outnumbered by thirteen Rangers. Chili smiled that smart-aleck smile of his and said that he liked to keep the odds *even*. Wasn't really that nasty a comment, but on top of all of the little jibes over the three months...rubbing me raw...I tore into him. Man, that dude could fight. I wasn't used to being on that side of the fence. He had me down at one point, just wailing on me."

Romeo's deep voice stopped. Eunice waited silently. As he resumed the narrative, his tone was muted. "I was getting my butt kicked and that never happened before. It drove me a little crazy, I guess. I lost it and stepped over the line. He gave me an opening and I took it. I buried my fist...into his neck. Crushed his larynx."

"Good Lord," whispered Cahane.

Shifting his eyes from the door, his voice closer to its normal timbre, Romeo finished. "We rushed him to the doc. He put a tube in Chili and had to medevac him to the nearest hospital. They patched him up in surgery as well as they could, but his souvenir...is that voice. And I didn't only take away his voice that day, I ended his career in MARSOC. The Corps reassigned him to a regular unit."

Several seconds had passed, when she finally spoke. "I'm surprised he's your friend. I woulda wanted to...I don't know...something...after that."

The pain induced by the recollection disappearing from the big man's face, he glanced down at her. "What would *you* do? Bite my ankles?"

Uncharacteristically, she let the barb slide. "Well, I didn't come here just to flirt. Let's shred some paper."

He handed back the pistol he was still holding, slapped a fresh magazine into his, and the pair donned their ear protection and ran two clean targets out to fifty feet.

With both guns emptied, they hit their buttons and the mechanism pulled the targets back. Romeo and Eunice checked each other's target before glancing at their own.

"Not too shabby, big boy. Good group. You almost kept them inside the third ring."

He could not help smiling at her, as he noticed that she had an even tighter cluster around the center of the target. "You're all right yourself, considering you're shooting uphill at the target."

"Dumb luck. Again?"

They repeated the process. This round was a close draw. A third attempt had Romeo edging her out slightly.

She rested the hot pistol on the deck and removed her ear protection completely. Romeo did the same.

"Jones, you got any idea who in blazes these folks are?"

"Are you calling me Jones because you were Army?"

"I was, but nope. I can't make my mouth say your first name. Just too goofy."

He shook his head and snickered. "Fair enough, *Eunice*. By 'these folks,' are you referring to our little group or the bad guys?"

"The bad guys. The two who went after Lisa in New York were rent-a-cops, former NYPD. And the FBI's big fat footprints were all over the Rosemary Shields murder. From what I hear, you were up against private military at the FEMA camp. The boys who went after Kent in his own office were HS. I mean, come on! I have no idea which rock I'm supposed to peek under."

He hitched up a leg and sat on the edge of the counter. "Don't know. On the other hand, there are a few good guys inside the same organizations...like Kenny Bowman. And he seems to think he can trust a handful of others."

"Maybe...and I might be battier than a tick-ridden hound dog...maybe it's some kind of...I don't know...infection or something."

She expected him to be amused by her suggestion. He was not. "I've thought about that. I've also thought about that old movie...*Invasion of the Body Snatchers*. The infection idea isn't so far fetched since it seems as if just about everyone on our side received that vaccine back in '86."

▽

Lisa had returned to the affiliate's station and established an impromptu command post in a small office vacated by one of the ad reps. The afternoon was a whirlwind of activity as the staff from New York had arrived, taking over the premises like a conquering army, causing her to devote much of her time to settling disputes and soothing egos in their wake. Collapsing in the temporarily empty break room and nursing a tepid cup of coffee, she was happy to see Alisa Lindberg enter.

The local director joined Lisa at the table, pouring a cup of her own and taking a quick sip.

Brushing an errant lock of hair back from the side of her face, she asked her visiting colleague, "How can you stand this? I thought our pace was hectic, but this is nuts!"

"It's not anywhere near this bad on our home ground. My cohorts are all freaked out because they're in a strange environment. Except they can't let themselves show that in front of the locals. After all, they're hotshots from New York, so they bluster and bully and generally just act like jerks."

Lindberg allowed herself a wan smile. "Makes sense. Mr. Bailey seems nice."

"Actually, he is. Helps that he's been in the business forever. He doesn't get shaken at all or even excited most of the time. Alisa, I'm glad you stopped in. Been wanting to get with you. Of course we brought our own director down with us, but would you mind pulling TD?"

The woman's eyes widened. "Technical director? Me? Sure. That'd be great. I'm a little surprised, though."

Lisa shrugged. "It makes sense if you think about it. You know the equipment. You're comfortable running the board. And the engineers are used to working with you. Plus...I've been to a lot of affiliates and you're the first local director I've met who has her head together enough for me to trust."

"Thanks, Lisa."

"It's nothing. Think of it as your reward for pulling that cool set out of your keister."

There was a soft knock at the entrance, and Lisa looked up to see Cahane.

"Eunice, come in."

"I didn't want to jump in while you two were gabbing."

"No. It's fine. Sit down."

The detective lowered into a chair at the table.

"Did you need anything? A snack or something to drink?"

"I'll pass. But I'm glad I caught you both. Alisa, when I was here yesterday and said I was trotting off to the little girls' room, I actually wanted to check out the security."

"Security? Ha! That's a joke."

Cahane sucked in a breath through her teeth. "I saw that. I waltzed from room to room...everywhere. Nobody stopped me. Nobody asked what I was up to. I finally had one guy ask me if he could help me, and I think he was one of the salesmen."

"Yep. That's about it. I've been here more than twenty years and have complained about it constantly. We finally had those cameras installed in the lobby and hallways last year. And half the time nobody is in the security room watching them, anyway."

"Figured. That was one of the rooms I just pranced into. It was as empty as church on a Saturday night. What really concerns me is that the perimeter doors don't have decent locks. And that back door! The one smack in the big room where the sets are…where you guys actually do the shows. Heck, that leads straight out to the big satellite dish and then nothin' but desert. Anybody could pull right up to it."

The director nodded slowly. "I know."

"Eunice, what are you thinking?"

"Well, Lisa, I'm trying to figure out how we can cover this whole place during the broadcast. Especially since we've only got Romeo and Chili, seeing as I'm supposed to be up on that set with you guys. There's too many holes in the dyke and not enough fingers to plug 'em all."

▽

Judtson joined Kelsey in front of the garage and eyed the four large white passenger vans with their heavily tinted windows on all sides.

Sidling closer, he held her hand. "This should work. Whose idea was it?"

"Romeo and Eunice cooked it up. I guess it's a variation on the old Hope Diamond trick."

"What was that?"

"They had to transport the diamond to a special shop to clean it. Obviously worried about a heist, the head guy set up an elaborate plan using several transport vehicles with armed guards and police escorts. After they all left, taking different routes across New York, he dropped the world's most expensive diamond in his pocket and took a cab, delivering it personally."

Judtson chuckled at the image. "Not bad. Problem is…something like that only works once."

"True, but Romeo thought it would be our best shot to get everyone to the TV station."

"How do we know the drivers haven't been planted on us and won't tip someone off?"

"Romeo drove down to Fort Huachuca and hung out at a bar outside the gate last night. Chummed it up with four E-3s who just rotated back from Afghanistan. Offered each of them a pretty good chunk of cash to drive a van for one trip."

As she spoke, four young men, still wearing yesterday's clothes, emerged from the garage, rubbing their eyes in the bright sunlight. Judtson and Kelsey watched across the driveway as Romeo briefed them and handed out separate maps. The four split up and climbed into their assigned vans, starting the engines. The first in line slowly pulled away, circling the perimeter of Kelsey's home and continuing toward the distant gate.

"I have them leaving at five-minute intervals," Romeo explained, moving to the garage. "Each one on a different route to the TV station."

"Maybe I'm paranoid," Judtson pressed, "but how do we know somebody didn't get to them between the time you recruited them yesterday and this afternoon?"

A wide grin spread across the Ranger's face. "I met them at a bar. After we made our deal, I bought rounds. A lot of rounds. Didn't take long until I could pour all four of them into the back of my Hummer and drive them here. They've been sleeping it off until an hour ago."

Romeo checked his watch and waved at the second van, which instantly lurched forward.

"When does our ride arrive?" Kelsey asked him.

"Chili should be coming with it about twenty minutes after the last van leaves."

▽

Chili sat inside the Carl's Jr. and sipped his root beer. Through the window, he saw the small bus, decorated with a team of galloping horses, pull in front of the building. He stopped at the fountain, topped off his drink, and walked out just as the driver opened the side door and stepped down.

"Are you my fare to the airport?"

Chili nodded. "Yes, sir. There's been a little change in plans."

"What kind of change?"

"Well, my party was supposed to congregate here for the ride, but things got fouled up. They're all up the hill at one of their homes. We need to swing by and pick them up."

The driver appeared less than happy about the change. "Guess so. It's going to cost extra."

"That's not a problem, sir."

"And I need to call my dispatcher and let her know."

Chili, trying his best to look friendly and unimposing and failing miserably, set his soft drink on the curb, smiled, and pulled out a wad of bills. "Sir, *that* might be a bit of a problem." He began peeling off fifties. "How many of these would it take, sir, for you to skip that part of the process?"

The man glimpsed down at the cash, then returned his eyes to Chili's. "I think we can work something out."

▽

The shuttle bus driver pulled into the employee lot of the television station and parked near the side entrance. Romeo was the first out and quickly scrutinized the area. The building was one of several in an industrial park, all constructed with sturdy tilt-up concrete panels. He trotted to the soldiers who were sitting on the pavement in the shade of one of the four vans.

"Any problems on the way over?"

The young men traded glances for a moment before one of them answered, "You mean like you told us to watch out for? Uh, no, sir. Nothing."

A worried frown appeared on the Ranger's face. "You're sure? No black SUVs shadowing you?"

All of them shook their heads.

Letting out a soft grunt, Romeo instructed, "Okay. As soon as we disembark, that shuttle bus is your ride back to Huachuca. It's already been paid for and the driver's been tipped, so don't let him tell you otherwise."

He returned to the bus and punched in a number on his cell as the four slowly climbed to their feet. The call was picked up after one ring. "Hey, sweet cheeks."

Romeo shook his head. "We're here."

"I'm turnin' the knob."

Eunice stepped out of the building and, holding the door wide open with her back, scanned the proximate area and the adjacent rooftops. Romeo waved Chili out. Keyliss immediately ran to the street entrance of the parking lot, posted himself at the curb, and watched the road.

Satisfied, the big man hopped up the three steps of the bus and stood beside the driver. "All right, everybody, you know the drill. Off the bus one at a time...straight to the building and inside...double time. No stopping for anything. Let's go!"

Matt, sitting in the front seat, moved first as Romeo hustled back out to stand alongside the bus. One by one, the entourage left the vehicle and trotted past Eunice, with Kelsey the last to leave. With a sharp whistle to Chili, Romeo headed in after her. He passed Cahane at the door and waited for the Marine, who entered seconds later, followed by Eunice, pulling the door closed behind herself. The entire group was bunched in the wide hallway, waiting.

"Eunice, any issues so far?" Romeo asked, his eyes surveying the area.

"Other than the place is like a town square on a Fourth of July picnic, nope."

"What does that mean in English?"

She snorted at him. "Too many people. They're in the middle of their evening newscast now, and the joint is crawling with them. And the fact that Lisa's boss is on the premises made a lot of 'em who normally stay out in the field decide to show up so they can play 'lookit me' in front of the big-time network folks."

"They all work here?"

"Far as I can tell."

"Where do they have us?"

"Conference room." She anticipated his next question. "Clean as best I could see."

"Go ahead and take our people there."

"Got it. Come along, gang."

As she led the rest of them away, Judtson and Kelsey held back with Romeo. "So far, so good," Judtson remarked.

"Yeah, a little too good."

Kelsey's brow furrowed. "Why? Is something wrong?"

"Doesn't make sense. For a group of bad guys who have been actively trying to take us out, why would they pass up on a chance to get us when we were all together and out in the open? According to the kids who drove the vans, they weren't even followed. Nothing!"

The doubt clear in his own voice, Judtson hopefully offered, "Maybe they aren't going to make a move on us."

Romeo's face twisted in a scowl. "Right. Or maybe it just hasn't happened...yet."

Chapter 34

TRUE TO LISA'S DECISION, THE GROUP WERE ALL KEPT IN A LARGE CONFERENCE ROOM, separated from Jack Bailey prior to the broadcast. Each of them was escorted to another area where makeup was applied. Jimmy Meade attempted to refuse, until Shannon showed him a brief video clip of a man who had also demurred.

"Captain Meade...."

"Miss, it's Jimmy."

"Okay, Jimmy. Since we've gone to HD, the cameras capture all the minute details, and the high-def screens at home are horribly unforgiving. The public will be able to see every pore on your face. Here...take a gander at this."

"My God! That man's face looks like the surface of the moon!"

She laughed. "Actually, his complexion is pretty normal."

Tearing his eyes away from the screen, he sighed. "All right. Putty me up."

The balance of the group submitted without protest.

As they filed onto the set, Matt, Bal, and Chris rubbernecked at the array of intense lighting suspended from black overhead racks. The maze of cabling was taped down to the floor in wide circuitous arcs to allow for free movement of the wheel-mounted cameras as well as the adjacent sets, which were utilized for the local newscasts and positioned around the perimeter of the large room.

Following the seating chart created by Lisa, Shannon showed the group to their positions on the two wings of the long desk. Judtson noticed that she had placed him in the first chair to the right of Bailey, with Kelsey seated beside him.

Alisa was introduced and stood in front of the platform, giving them all a short lesson on how they should ignore the microphone clipped to their shirts or blouses and speak normally...how they could tell which camera was on...and admonishing them not to tap their feet, drum their fingers or hands on the desk, or create other distracting noises. She then pointed out the two monitors which displayed the image being broadcast. She finished her speech by saying, "Now I know all of you are professionals and most of you have been on television in the past. I do need to remind you, though, that we will be going out live to millions of homes. There won't be any opportunities for redos. So please make sure what you say is what you want to say. Oh, and one more thing…" – she grinned – "watch your language. I don't think you want to cost us our FCC license."

As she finished her final caution, Jack Bailey strode onto the set. Judtson could not help but be impressed by the man's bearing and appearance. Central Casting could not have found a more perfect actor to portray a wise, seasoned newsman, a designation Bailey had always insisted upon, rather than journalist. Tall and firmly built, his hair a dark brown with a liberal sprinkling of gray at the temples, and sporting black horn-rimmed glasses which served to slightly enlarge piercing brown eyes, he clearly possessed the attribute known as gravitas, so prized in the industry. He thanked Alisa and, beginning at one end of the desk, introduced himself to the group, glibly demonstrating that he had done his homework, not only calling them all by name but also including a brief personal tidbit about each of them, carefully phrased to sound casual.

When he reached Judtson and extended his hand, he remarked, "Mr. Kent, I've been looking forward to meeting you for a long time. I'm a huge fan and perhaps a kindred soul. I've loved every one of your books, particularly *Shining the Light*. Your debunking of the Illuminati myths and lore was breathtaking, and I must confess I've stolen bits of your more…acerbic rebukes." With an almost bashful smile, he added, "I've even been referred to as the Judtson Kent of the airwaves, an appellation I do not deserve."

Judtson shook his outstretched hand and returned the smile. "And I've been called the Jack Bailey of books, a compliment I've treasured. You wouldn't be the first to borrow some of my nastier lines. Although, in the interest of accuracy, you may want to hold off on referencing any of my other books from now on."

The comment caused the man to cock his head to the side quizzically. "I'm not sure what you…."

In the midst of the host's sentence, one of the camera operators shouted, "TWO MINUTES!"

Reacting, Bailey quickly nodded at Judtson and promised, "We'll talk later," then hastened through the rest of the group, circled the desk, and slipped into his seat, attaching the microphone to his tie.

▽

Romeo, having stationed himself in the back corner of the control room, waited until Jack Bailey was on the set and seated, before approaching Alisa, who was now in her chair at the board. Bending close, he said, "Lisa asked me to give this to you."

He handed her a flash drive.

"What is it?"

"It has some video you're going to need during Dr. Singh's and Dr. Villarreal's presentations."

▽

"Good evening, ladies and gentlemen, and welcome to what I believe is to be a very special live broadcast of our show. Unless you have been living under a rock for the past several weeks, you have seen and heard countless reports and stories revolving around the notorious Samuel Beckleman videos. By some, they are referred to as confessions by a treasonous government official; by others, as revelatory in that they expose the depth of the corruption within the halls of power. There are those who claim that the statements were made under extreme duress and cannot be relied upon and that the perpetrators should be prosecuted, while a great many others believe that those same people are heroes. No matter where you stand on this issue, there can be no doubt that it has dominated the public debate since the dramatic images first appeared on the Internet.

"As a result, Samuel Beckleman, a longtime bureaucrat and, until recently, the head of the Department of Homeland Security, is now being held in custody, as are several of his administrators and officers. Serious discussions are now taking place in Washington, D.C., to defund, deactivate, and disassemble this department. The investigations triggered by the videos remain ongoing, and no one can predict where they may eventually lead.

"Several of the people responsible for the…unconventional…obtaining of the confession have become household names overnight. These include medical equipment technologist Matt Wheeler, computer wizard Scott Gumble, archaeologist Carlos Villarreal, chemist Chris Ashby…."

Judtson noticed that the prompter was blank; their host was working unscripted. Slowly, he surveyed the panel on the opposite side of Bailey. All of them appeared calm, with the exception of Cahane, whose eyes were in constant motion, studying and examining every person and every movement in the studio. He then focused to his right and saw Lisa, who had positioned herself at the last seat so she could slip away from the set if she was needed. The producer was fidgeting, obviously wishing she were behind the scenes, overseeing the details of the broadcast. Passing over the others, his gaze centered on Kelsey, who had been watching him. He winked at her with his right eye, out of the view of the camera. Each position had been supplied with a pad and pen. Using them, pretending to make a casual note to himself, he wrote, "You look beautiful!"

Reaching under the desk, he placed his hand on her knee. She instantly grabbed it and squeezed, giving him a brief flicker of a smile before turning back to face forward just as Bailey was saying, "And of course, Judtson Kent, the host of his own cable program and a *New York Times* best-selling author of several books debunking fanciful myths, lore, and conspiracy theories.

"Tonight, for the first time anywhere, the entire group is assembled. The members will be relating their own stories, including some individuals who have, up to this point, refused interviews in any medium. We have a lot of ground to cover this evening and, once we begin, I would like to keep the interruptions to a minimum. So, we will now take a commercial break."

The red light on the camera blinked off and Bailey swiveled in his chair to Judtson. "Sorry for the long-winded intro. It seems that no matter how much coverage a story gets, many of our viewers need the background."

"No. I thought it was good."

"Appreciate that. Anyway, I know Lisa has given me a sequence for the interviews and you're about halfway down the list, but maybe we could begin with a brief overview from you. To set up the others. I wasn't allowed to pre-interview, and I have no issue with that. Done it many times. However, I would feel more comfortable if you could lay out a road map, so to speak, that I could use as we go."

"Of course. In other words, be your co-host."

The comment brought a grin. "In a way, yes. Thank you. Do you mind if I ask a few questions while we're at break?"

He shook his head. "Let's hold off, Jack. It'll be more fun that way."

The newsman tried to read his guest, but finally shrugged. "Okay. More spontaneous. Better television and all that." He was clearly unaccustomed to being handled.

Pretending not to notice, Judtson simply said, "Thanks," and twisted away to face Kelsey.

She whispered, "What was that all about?"

"He wants me to brief him on what we're going to talk about."

"Too bad."

$$\triangledown$$

Dan Marries, following the six o'clock newscast, had sequestered himself in his office and called his pregnant wife, receiving a blow-by-blow update of the baby's turns and kicks since the anchor had left to go to work. Hanging on every detail, he had not noticed that it was after seven.

"Honey, I need to go. The Bailey show just started and I wanted to...."

"I know. Go ahead."

"Thanks, babe."

He hung up and dashed out of the office toward the control room, almost colliding with Jan, one of the field reporters.

"Hey! Dan, how's Jennifer?"

He filled her in on the latest minutiae and was about to say goodbye, when he happened to glance down.

"Is that a new look, Jan?"

"What do you...?" She followed his stare and saw that her dark skirt was covered with light-colored hairs. Huffing loudly and brushing madly at the fur, she explained, "Must have been the dog."

"Didn't know you had one."

"I don't. You know that bust today at the checkpoint in Nogales?"

"Yeah. Border Patrol caught two guys transporting the raw materials to make an IED."

"Right. The officers came up here today. I taped an interview on the set between your six o'clock and the Bailey broadcast. You'll have it for the ten."

"Still don't see how you got covered with dog hair."

"They caught the guys by using a bomb-sniffing dog. Adorable German shepherd. I asked them to bring the dog for the interview. Big mistake."

"Why? The audience loves dog segments."

"I know. That's why I did it. But the mutt was going crazy. Wouldn't sit quietly. He was jumping on his handler...jumping on me. Yelping all the way through the interview. It took forever to get three usable minutes."

"That's not like them."

"That's what the handler kept saying. The dog even nearly got away. I could've been fired."

"Why?"

"He was running straight for the Bailey set that Alisa busted her buns to get built. That whole side was roped off. Big-time off-limits. Imagine twenty minutes before going live on the entire network, some dog tears up their set."

He laughed at the image. "How'd they stop him?"

"The other Border Patrol agent just dived and grabbed him. I thought I was going to have a heart attack."

"Well, I don't think you would have been fired over it, Jan."

Plucking at more wads of fur, she huffed again. "At least I don't have to find out."

Checking his watch, Dan excused himself and hurried to the control room.

$$\nabla$$

A woman counted down to zero silently, using her fingers, and pointed at Bailey. Almost as if his facial muscles were hard-wired to the same circuit which actuated the red light, a sincere smile twitched onto his face.

"We're back. I would like to begin with Judtson Kent."

He swiveled a few inches to his right. "Judtson, thank you for joining us this evening."

"My pleasure, Jack."

"First, let's get to the question on the minds of many around the country. Why did you and Kelsey Batman and the others in your group feel that it was necessary to entrap and, some might say, torture Secretary Beckleman?"

Judtson shrugged casually. "Why…obviously to get the truth. We were under siege. Beckleman's people had killed Al Clarkson and Dr. Kevin Berry and kidnapped members of our group, not to mention other attempts to do us harm. And, of course, the entire affair began because of their desire to mind-control several of us. He had declared war upon us and we fought back. This has all been recounted to the public and rehashed countless times. Frankly, retelling that story was not our motivation for coming here tonight."

If Bailey was miffed by this deflection, he did not show it. "Then why did all of you come?"

Hearing this question, Judtson made a brief glance back at Kelsey. She smiled at him and nodded slightly. With an expression which seemed to say "here goes," he began, "As I said a moment ago, Jack, we want to get to the truth. At the time, we believed, or at least some of us believed, that Samuel Beckleman was the mastermind behind what had happened to us. And when he confessed…and that confession was disseminated around the world…it *seemed* as though we had found our answers. Or perhaps I should say, we were *hoping* it was over. Considering that we had been through a horrible ordeal, the prospect of identifying such a high-profile official as the perpetrator and vanquishing him was quite appealing. And a suitable villain was handed to us…on a silver platter. However, now that all of us have had some time and some distance put between us and the, as you put it, 'notorious' videos, we have discovered that many, most, or perhaps all of our questions have not truly been answered."

"Judtson, I'm afraid I don't understand."

"No one does yet. Not fully, in any case. We have a mountain of information to share tonight, so I will try to be brief. To remind everyone of the background, I was visited by Beckleman's people and mentally altered…or, as I understand they refer to it, *conditioned*… because I was going to release a book and broadcast a program unveiling the discoveries made by Carlos Villarreal, discoveries relating to Puma Punku and Baalbek. Carlos was *conditioned* for the same reason. Bal Singh was *conditioned* as he was on the verge of investigating tectonic anomalies in the same area of the Andes. Dylan Falt was *conditioned* shortly after he was hired by Rosemary Shields with the CDC to investigate disturbing connections between vaccines and autism. Jimmy Meade was *conditioned* because he had photographs never before seen of a UFO which landed at Edwards Air Force Base in the 1950s. Dean Copeland and Al Clarkson were *conditioned* before they could release their second book, revealing the presence of unexplainable structures on Mars and the Moon. Chris Ashby was *conditioned* to halt his work with monoatomic gold before he could proceed into human trials. We discovered later that Dr. Kevin Berry was *conditioned* to stop him from pursuing gravity anomalies in the Andes. And your own producer, Lisa Trippiano, was *conditioned* because she was suspicious about the sudden changes in personality she witnessed within your own staff."

Jack Bailey's face was frozen in an attentive half-smile.

Judtson, receiving no reaction to his last comment, began again quickly. "The problem, Jack, is that the so-called confession we obtained from Beckleman leaves far too many holes. Doesn't actually address or account for several of these issues. And the explanations he did provide, in the time we've had to mull them over since that day in Bisbee, simply do not hold up to objective scrutiny."

Recovered, Bailey, his voice steady and professional, maintained, "They certainly appeared to. Beckleman's story described how the bulk of the material and information all of you were pursuing had been planted or even manufactured by him and his people. The metallurgy analysis of Dr. Villarreal's stones…photos Dean Copeland used in his books…the CDC study. In fact, didn't the woman who had hired Dylan Falt admit publicly that it was a hoax and that she had altered the data?"

Judtson glanced down the dais at Dylan and Eunice, then returned his gaze. "You're right. She did. What you are not privy to, Jack, is that subsequent to said public admission, she contacted Dylan Falt and told him she had been forced to say it. The CDC fired her. When she persisted in sending information to Dylan, she was murdered and it was staged to be a suicide."

The host's eyebrows rose skeptically. "A staged suicide? From what I understand, the FBI investigated her…suicide and ruled it such."

Smirking sardonically, Judtson rejoined, "Oh, indeed they did. And Detective Cahane will be happy to share the details of what she uncovered in the course of her investigation. To summarize…those FBI agents were, at the worst, responsible for her death or, at the very least, responsible for covering it up and staging the suicide."

"Oh, come now. You can't be serious that our Federal Bureau of Investigation would perpetrate such a thing?"

Eunice snorted loudly. Before she could speak out, Judtson hurriedly resumed his narrative. "I am. And you will find Detective Cahane's evidence quite persuasive. But we shouldn't get sidetracked at this point. To continue, Carlos Villarreal, alone at his home in La Paz, was working late on his proof that Samuel Beckleman had, in fact, lied and that the carved Baalbek stones actually *were* quarried near Lake Titicaca. Later that night two assassins broke into his house and, thinking he was asleep, entered his bedroom and fired several slugs into the pile of covers on his bed. Fortunately, he had an elaborate alarm system and had already escaped. We have that attack on a security video, by the way."

His practiced expression slipping, Bailey muttered, "Unbelievable."

"As you may recall, the Secretary never even addressed the 'why' of Chris Ashby's *conditioning*."

"I suppose that is true."

"There is nothing in the confession which could possibly explain why it happened then or why Beckleman would have wanted to stop his work in the first place. What you probably are not aware of, Jack, is that in the past few days Chris Ashby was kidnapped from his car as he was driving home to San Diego after a meeting with one of our group. He was taken against his will to a government facility in New Mexico where he was questioned. Had we not rescued him, they were planning on cutting open his brain to find out why they were no longer able to *condition* him."

Bailey's eyes swung away from Kent to glance at Ashby, who was leaning forward, listening attentively and nodding, a neutral look on his face.

"Judtson...this...you're right. We were not aware of these things."

"I know. However, you are aware of the attempt on the life of your producer."

"Yes. Of course I am. We were all devastated by...."

"And Lisa has been the catalyst and driving force behind this broadcast. The point is, Jack...if Samuel Beckleman had truly been the alpha and the omega of his nefarious plot...and he is now safely locked up and incommunicado...why are these things still happening? I'll answer that for you. It's because Samuel Beckleman was a red herring. He was tossed to us as a way to stop us when we were getting too close...to take us off their trail. Furthermore, it had the added benefit of diminishing our credibility in the future, should we attempt to release what we know, by providing the media and the public with a dramatic, sensational, satisfactory answer. And now that they have figured out that we are not all simply forgetting about everything and going back to our normal lives, they are trying to stop us any way they can."

Unconsciously, Jack Bailey leaned away from Judtson, as if trying to distance himself from the man. The last trace of the former collegiality was now absent from his voice. "So...just to make certain I understand...you are saying that there is some shadowy, secret Machiavellian conspiracy against all of you?"

"Actually, Jack, calling it a secret conspiracy is a tad redundant. But...yes. The true culprits have not been caught. They have not been taken down. They are still in place and now want us either silenced or killed."

Not fully successful in concealing his irritation, Bailey retorted, "*They* want you killed? Who is *they*?"

"Who *are* they? We don't know...yet. However, we do have a clue."

"What clue might that be?" he asked with a hint of sarcasm.

"Bal Singh has provided your people with videos which he and a postdoctoral student by the name of Sam Jonassen took at Lake Titicaca."

"Videos? Of what?"

Before answering, Judtson made eye contact with Bal, who silently nodded his assent. "We have clear photographic and video evidence of a..." – he paused, took a deep breath, and plunged onward – "a spaceship rising from the lake."

The loud, abrupt sound which burst from the host's lips was a blend of a harsh laugh and an astonished grunt. "Judtson...Mr. Kent...this is...absurd! I'm surprised at you. Throughout your long and distinguished career, you've always been reasonable...intelligent...skeptical!"

"So?"

Appearing to be truly flummoxed by the casual response, Bailey confronted him. "What do you mean, *so?*"

"Exactly that. I don't understand your reaction."

Even a pretense of the erstwhile friendliness completely evaporating and a new hardness emerging, Bailey parried, "That is disingenuous. Of course you understand. You have made it your life's work to address the idiotic fringe lunatics and expose them for what they are. How can you now sit here and tell me that all of this..." – he seemed on the verge of sputtering – "all of the problems and intrigue and assaults are being perpetrated by *space aliens*?"

Not rising to the bait, he calmly replied, "That appears to be where the facts lead me."

Bailey was momentarily at a loss, and Judtson took the opportunity to glance back at Kelsey, who was smiling broadly at him. He grinned back, returned his attention to the host, and assumed the familiar tone and cadence she had heard him employ with the manager at the restaurant. "Jack, I have been accused of being something my entire career. In fact, you employed the term a while ago. And, I'll be honest, until recently I've never actually examined what it meant. Maybe you could help me. What exactly is a skeptic?"

Surprised by the question, the newsman stammered initially. "Why...a...skeptic is a person who doesn't fall for every cockamamie theory, story, superstition, or myth."

"A skeptic is defined by what he or she is not?"

"No. Of course not. A skeptic requires proof before accepting something."

"Proof? I see. Are you a skeptic?"

"I most certainly am!"

"So you always demand to personally review the proof that a medication your doctor prescribes is safe before you will take it?"

"Of course not."

"Why not? I thought you didn't deign to just take someone's word for something. Especially something which could harm or kill you."

"She's a professional. Her judgment can be trusted."

"I see. Well then, I suppose you do demand proof that all required maintenance has been properly performed every time you are about to set foot on an airplane. And I'm certain you demand proof that sanitation techniques have not been compromised, before taking every sip of water or every bite of food."

Rolling his eyes, he responded derisively, "Of course not. That's beyond ridiculous."

"Oh? And why is that?"

"Obviously, we accept those things...." The man paused.

Judtson finished the sentence for him. "Because everyone else does."

"Well...yes. If that were not the case, society would collapse."

"All right. And you only require this proof you mentioned earlier for the things everyone else hasn't already blessed."

Bailey did not answer, simply glaring at him.

"When Copernicus posited that Earth revolved around the sun, would you say that the skeptics or the lunatics of the day were the ones who dismissed his assertion?"

"It was the church."

"Not entirely accurate. Nor does it answer my question. Which group was it...the lunatics, who are eagerly willing to embrace every crackpot theory that pops up, or the skeptics, who vehemently deny any idea which challenges the status quo?"

Bailey's lips were tightly pursed.

Judtson forged ahead. "Another question. If a commercial or military pilot witnesses a flying saucer, would he or she not be considered a professional and therefore trustworthy?"

"Well...people can become confused...deceived."

"So it wouldn't matter that the pilot is a professional with thousands of hours of training and experience and rigorous certification requirements?"

"Not…necessarily."

"But the doctor you mentioned…the professional who prescribes a medication for you…the professional whom you trust and therefore require no proof…is immune to confusion or deception?"

"That's different." The man rallied to regain control of the interview. "All of this is beside the point. We have quite a bit to cover tonight, and I'd like to proceed with the interviews of my other guests."

"I'm sure you would. And just as you are a self-proclaimed skeptic, I am certain that the majority of your audience will be, as well. That is why it is critical that we address this topic before presenting the information my friends possess. Otherwise, we are wasting our time."

Without waiting for Bailey to respond, Judtson elaborated, "Let me give you an example of what we are talking about. If individuals…such as a pilot, an air traffic controller, a police officer, an astronaut, an astronomer, or members of any other groups normally considered to be reliable observers…report that they have seen a spaceship, their observation is promptly dismissed by skeptics, out of hand. Clearly, they were…per your description…confused or deceived. And clearly, we cannot simply take their word for what they saw…right?"

"Without some pr…evidence, that is correct."

"And what would their motive be for doing this?"

"Why, obviously for the notoriety…attention."

"Notoriety? Attention? That is preposterous, Jack. These people know for a fact that coming forward with what they have seen will destroy their careers and, in many cases, make a shambles of their personal lives. However, to further examine this, I'm going to ask you to bear with me while we do a little thought experiment. You come home unexpectedly and find a strange car in your driveway, the backseat piled high with items. You recognize some of the items as being yours. You mentally note the make, model, and even the license plate of the vehicle. Entering your house, you walk into a burglary in progress where you plainly see the man making his final trip, carrying out your laptop and other belongings. You attempt to stop him and there is a scuffle. He escapes. You call the police and tell them your story. You efficiently provide them with the make, model, and license plate number of the car in the driveway.

"Now here's where the thought experiment comes in. Instead of the police immediately beginning a search for the man and putting out an alert for that vehicle, based upon your description of the events, they ask you if you happen to have a piece of the car…maybe the license plate itself. And they ask you if you happened to obtain…I don't know…the intruder's jacket…or maybe his ear? Did you happen to snap some pictures of him…on film, not digitally because everyone knows that those can be altered…as he was actually stealing your things? When you tell them you do not have any of these pieces of evidence, they sigh, flip closed their little notepads, and begin to leave. You, of course, are outraged. You confront them. You ask them why they aren't rushing out to arrest the perpetrator. And they tell you that there is no real proof the burglary happened. You point out that your things are missing. They tell you that it can easily be explained by the fact that you could have removed those items yourself and taken them elsewhere. You show them the physical evidence of the scuffle, both on your person and in your living room, and they tell you that all of it could have been physically performed by you. You ask them why you would do that, and they tell you why. Obviously, you crave the notoriety…attention. Jack, at that point, how would you feel?"

"That would never happen!"

"But if it did?"

"I imagine I'd be outraged."

"Why?"

"Why? Because my word…."

Judtson smiled kindly. "Wasn't good enough?"

Bailey paused. After a moment, his head nodded slightly.

His voice losing the patronizing and sarcastic edge and returning to a softer, more conciliatory tone, Judtson said, "Jack, skeptics are not clear-eyed rationalists, no matter how vehemently they may insist that this is the case. Skeptics are actually individuals who suffer from a deep-seated pathological fear of being considered by others to be suckers. This is compounded by an intrinsic lack of confidence in their own ability to analyze and evaluate information and draw their own conclusions. The result of this nasty combination is not that skeptics will only accept that which has been *proved*, but rather that skeptics…under any circumstances… regardless of any facts…will *never* be the first to reach a conclusion. They will only accept that the world revolves around the sun after the majority of those around them have endorsed and embraced the new paradigm. They will only accept wisdom once it is recognized as conventional wisdom.

"The people sitting on this set tonight are not crackpots," he asserted, motioning along the dais with his arm. "They are not, to use a phrase I've heard recently, a posse of fringe lunatics and nutcases. They are reputable, respected PhD's, scientists, researchers…and an astronaut. And, as do you, they are people who expect their word to carry some weight. They, too, expect their word to be good enough."

Jack Bailey leaned back in his chair and rubbed his face with both hands, smearing his makeup in the process. He softly cleared his throat. "Judtson, you make some excellent points. And I want to thank you for also reminding me, in the course of your…lecture, I suppose…that it is not my place as a newsman to judge, only to report."

Focusing for the first time in several minutes on the floor manager, who had been frantically gesturing, Bailey faced the camera. "As I promised, we have quite a bit in store for you tonight. After this break, I'd like to take a look at the videos taken by Dr. Singh and his associate."

Chapter 35

ALISA, TURNING AWAY FROM HER BOARD AS THE STRING OF COMMERCIALS BEGAN, saw Dan Marries behind her and allowed a grin on her face. "Wow! That was cool. This is going to be a great show."

"You're not kidding," he agreed. "By the way, Alisa, I've been meaning to compliment you on getting that set done so rapidly. How'd you pull it off? Your contractors have never been that quick."

"Didn't use them. Used a new outfit. Blew me away, actually. They just fell into my lap."

"Well, they did an amazing…." He stopped, a thoughtful expression coloring his face.

She noticed his hesitation. "What's wrong?"

"Uh. Nothing, I guess."

She returned her attention to her board. Dan took a step back, his mind preoccupied with a vague, niggling concern, as he bumped into Romeo who was positioned in the corner of the room. He mumbled, "Sorry. Excuse me. Didn't know you were standing there."

"No problem."

Marries introduced himself. Jones reciprocated.

"Are you with the group on the set?"

"Yes, sir."

"Forgive me. It's probably the journalist in me, but why aren't you up on the dais?"

"I prefer to keep an eye on things."

The news anchor's face abruptly brightened with recognition. "I know you. You were the third person on the Beckleman video."

Romeo only nodded.

"You're their security, aren't you?"

He nodded again.

With an audible sigh of relief, Dan confided, "It's perfect that I ran into you. I…I've noticed a couple of things…probably nothing…but I thought I should…."

Suddenly curious, Romeo interrupted, "What have you noticed?"

Dan first related his meeting with the field reporter whose clothes had been covered with hair from the bomb-sniffing dog which was attempting to break free and get to the Jack Bailey set. As he spoke, he could see the big man's shoulders stiffening. "And Alisa just told me that she used a new crew, a different crew from her normal contractors, to build that set. I remembered that they worked on it all night. Even after everyone else left."

"There wasn't any security with them?"

"No. They were alone."

The Ranger's eyes darted toward the door to the studio. "I need to go in there."

Sensing the urgency, Dan assented at once. "Sure. Come on. I'll take you in."

He led the way and they entered as the break ended and Jack Bailey began, "Welcome back. As we discussed in the last segment, Dr. Bal Singh has provided...."

Romeo spoke softly to Dan. "That desk they're all sitting behind...does it have compartments or anything like that?"

Marries thought for a moment. "I don't think so. I believe it's only a front panel and a top. But stick close to me. We can stay off-camera and take a peek."

He skirted the edge of the set, checking to make certain that the camera was still focused on Bailey, and the two men reached the far side of the backdrop. Lisa, in the last seat at the end, ensured that she was not on-camera and slipped off the platform to join them. Eunice, seeing their arrival, watched them curiously. Ricky, three chairs down from Lisa, caught Romeo's attention and raised an eyebrow quizzically. His friend answered the unspoken offer to help with a subtle shake of his head.

"What's up?" Lisa whispered.

Romeo, from his position, was able to examine the back side of the desk assembly and saw that Dan was right. It was open with no place to conceal anything.

Leaning next to her ear, he murmured, "There might be a bomb."

She visibly reacted to the flat statement, whirling around toward the set. As she was about to speak, he firmly gripped her shoulder, turning her back. "Lisa, I don't know if there is. It might be nothing. But if there is, it could be controlled by a cell phone."

Her face was flushed and he noticed that her hands were shaking. She was barely able to subdue her voice. "That means they'd be watching now."

"Exactly. If we suddenly stop the show or try to evacuate, they'd dial the number."

Cahane, seeing Lisa's change in demeanor, also left her seat and moved to join them. Jack Bailey, aware that two of his guests had suddenly departed, stumbled over his words briefly before introducing the video.

"What's the deal?" Cahane said quietly.

As Lisa repeated what she knew, the big man scrutinized the structure, abruptly asking, "Dan, has that platform always been here?"

"No. It was built for this set."

"I need to get a look under it. How can I do that?"

The two men checked the front edge of the raised floor and saw that it was carpeted. They moved to the rear. "It's only screwed on," Romeo grunted. "Can somebody get me a screwdriver?"

Dan hurried away as Jack Bailey, taking advantage of the on-air video, left his seat and trotted to the group. Before he could ask what was happening, Jones faced him. "Sir, there is a possibility that a bomb might be under this platform."

By this point, the guests along the desk were craning to see what was causing the disturbance. The newsman began to speak. The Ranger cut him off. "I'm sure you'd like to evacuate, but the device may be triggered by a cell phone and this is a live broadcast. No doubt they're watching. If they see everyone suddenly leave, they could detonate it."

"What about a commercial break?" Lisa suggested. "We could all clear out of here within two or three minutes."

Romeo shot down the suggestion. "You just had one. If you go right back into another, that might make them suspicious enough to set it off. You need to at least finish this segment until the next regular break. Then we can make a run for it. In the meantime, I'll take a look under the platform and figure out if we really have a problem."

The floor manager had joined them. Jones turned to him and quickly explained the situation.

When he finished, Lisa intervened, "What's your name?"

"Hal Shieffer."

"Hal, you need to get all nonessential personnel out of the building."

"No. Wait!" Romeo barked. "They might have a man posted outside watching. He could trigger the bomb the second he sees people leaving. Just move them back. Opposite end of the building."

"We have an old walk-in fireproof vault. Used it for tape storage back in the day. It's at the south end of the building and pretty solid."

"That should work. Go."

Shieffer hurriedly left.

His jaw muscles flexing and relaxing first, Bailey spoke slowly. "So you need me...all of us...to sit on the dais and keep broadcasting as if nothing is wrong, until you can get to it."

The Ranger's eyes bored into him. "I know it's a lot to ask, but yes, sir."

"Lisa, how long is this flying saucer video that's running right now?"

She checked the monitor. "It's almost over."

With a slight smile, the newsman said, "Come on, ladies. Get back in your seats. We have a show to do."

Dan returned carrying two screwdrivers, handed one to Romeo, and started toward the aisle between the platform and the backdrop. The big man stopped him with a hand to his shoulder. "What are you doing?"

He looked back. "Helping. It'll be twice as fast."

"Get out of here. You won't be missed if they're watching."

With a hard swing of his torso, Dan broke free of the shoulder grip and rushed forward to the midpoint of the structure, behind the host's chair. Romeo followed and the two dropped to their knees. Working quietly on opposite ends of the foot-high rear face, they began removing the closely spaced screws. As Romeo set the fourth one aside, he was painfully aware of the seconds ticking away and was grateful for the news anchor's help.

Hal, having ordered all but two others in the studio to leave, burst into the control room. Ignoring the network director, he ran to Alisa. "They think there might be a bomb under the set."

"What?" Her hand fluttered up to cover her mouth. "Why aren't we evacuating?"

The man continued breathlessly. "They're...they're afraid it might be detonated by a cell phone…and the bomber could be watching the broadcast. They want us to keep the show going…until they can find it or until the next scheduled break."

She shook her head vehemently. "Cell service in there is horrible."

"It does work sometimes. You want to take the chance?"

"No. I guess not."

"So get everyone out of here who isn't absolutely necessary. But they have to stay inside the building. Send them to the old vault. I'd better get back. I'm going to run one of the cameras."

As he hurried to the exit, she scanned the faces of the people in the control room. Because they were hosting the Bailey show, the room was almost filled with curious station employees. "All right. You heard the man. Head to the vault."

Nathan Keller, Jack Bailey's director, put his hand on her shoulder. "You go, Alisa. I'll run the board."

She did not hesitate. "Maybe I'm too big a fan of Linda Hamilton in the *Terminator* movies, but huh-uh, this is my board. I don't want you teaching it bad habits. Beat it."

As the rest of the group filed out, Eva Gonzales, her assistant, firmly declared, "I'm staying with you."

Their eyes connected and Alisa saw the determination in her colleague's face. "Sorry, Eva. You have three little ones at home. Take off. I've got it."

"You can't do the show alone. You know that."

Nathan interrupted, "I'll be her second. Go on, ma'am."

"Eva, you heard him. Leave here now! And tell their other security guy guarding the lobby, the tall dude who looks like Elvis, to keep everyone inside."

The woman hurried to Alisa and hugged her quickly before reluctantly following the others out.

Jack Bailey's voice was rock-steady as the video finished. "Well, Judtson, you were right. That is an astounding…."

As he spoke, Lisa scrawled a short note on her pad, describing the situation and emphasizing the importance of remaining calm. She slid it to Cahane, whispering, "Pass it down."

Bal was the first to get it and, after reading the words, his hands began to shake badly just as Bailey addressed him. "Dr. Singh, perhaps you could describe the circumstances surrounding the encounter."

The tiny red light blinked on as a camera was aimed at Singh. The geologist was frozen stiff. Seeing this, Eunice leaned close to him, gripped his leg inches above the kneecap, and pinched hard as she quietly urged, "Keep your head together and answer the man, and we'll all get to walk outta here."

With a violent jerk of his head, he fought back the tidal wave of fear paralyzing him and managed a weak smile. "I am…I am sorry, Mr. Bailey. It is simply that…." He paused, sucked in a deep breath, and let it out slowly. More in control, he actually produced a stuttering laugh. "I am a trifle embarrassed. I hate to admit that every time I see the video, I am again awestruck."

Jack, allowing himself to relax from his own incipient panic as he had watched Singh recover from a near meltdown, smiled warmly. "That is quite understandable, Doctor. If you wouldn't mind, please describe the scene as you and your associate recorded the…."

The two men on the floor were down to undoing the final four screws, and Romeo had to fight back the urge to grab the edge of the plywood and yank it off. Bearing down, he twisted the tool as fast as possible and removed another screw as Dan did the same.

The final screw out, Dan whispered, "Hope we picked the right spot," and pulled back on the top edge, almost silently laying the panel on the floor. Romeo was grabbing a penlight from his pocket, when he heard a muted expletive. In the darkness, directly in front of them and positioned on the floor against the front edge of the platform, was a single blinking red light and a blue LED countdown timer. The display read *1:36*.

Handing the penlight to his partner, the Ranger thrust his arms ahead and began shimmying his way under the deck, only to be stopped as his thick shoulders reached the opening.

1:22

"Let me go in," Dan whispered urgently.

The big man quickly backed out and slid aside. Marries, taking his place, muttered, "Glad I skipped the weights at the gym," tucked his head under the deck, and clawed forward.

Jones heard "I need a push," promptly grabbed the man's thighs, and roughly shoved him farther under.

"Got it. Get me out."

Still holding Dan's thighs, Romeo pulled him back and to the side to avoid ramming his feet into the backdrop.

0:47

Judtson, having read Lisa's note and aware that the camera was on Bal at the moment, leaned back and glanced down as Dan popped out from beneath the platform, clutching the bomb with both hands. Involuntarily gasping at the sight, he grabbed Kelsey's hand.

0:39

Romeo grunted, "Give it to me."

"No time!"

The news anchor scrambled to get his feet under him while remaining crouched below the view of the cameras, and awkwardly duck-walked forward, keeping an eye on the timer.

0:21

As soon as he reached the end of the backdrop, he rose and ran straight toward what appeared to be the side wall of the studio, with Jones close behind.

0:09

Intently cradling the bomb in his hands, he elbowed a tall curtain aside, revealing a door with a panic bar. Before he could turn around and back into the bar, the big man arrived and hit it with both hands, flinging the door wide, revealing that this was an exit to a cleared vacant area at the rear of the building.

0:04

"THROW IT!" Romeo boomed, no longer concerned about being heard. But Dan had already shifted the device to his right hand, reared it back over his shoulder, and hurled it out in a high, spiraling arc. Grabbing Marries, the Ranger pulled him out of the way with one hand and slammed the door closed with the other, the two men falling in a tangle of limbs to the floor. The crash of the door coincided with the deeper blast of the explosion from outside, and the metal skin of the door was instantly pelted with the hammering sounds of multiple projectiles, a few penetrating and leaving small outward-puckered holes. None of the pellets hit either man, or anyone else inside the studio.

Hal heard Alisa's voice over his headset. "Something's wrong. We're off the air."

He dashed across to the two men, who were both helping each other up from the floor. "Is it safe to check outside?"

Marries glanced questioningly at Jones, who answered, "Should be. I'll go first to make sure no one's out there."

The door still functioned and Romeo, drawing his pistol, stepped out to scan the area before nodding back at Hal, who emerged tentatively, immediately looked to his right, and whistled. "Man, that did a number on the uplink."

Romeo followed his gaze and saw that the large white dish, pointed skyward, had been perforated with hundreds of holes.

As he reentered the building, the entire group had descended from the set and were clustered around Dan, all boisterously laughing and talking loudly, shaking his hand and slapping him on the back, obviously releasing the pent-up tension from moments earlier. He waited patiently as the dazed news anchor was sheepishly receiving an exuberant hug from Lisa. When she freed him from her embrace, Romeo grinned and stuck his hand toward him. "That's a pretty good arm you've got there."

Marries matched the big man's grip and the two made eye contact...and in a split second communicated volumes. As he began to reply to the Ranger, Alisa, who had dashed in from the control room, threw her arms around him. "Dan, that was amazing! Thank you! My God, I still can't believe it!"

Separating from the people crowding around, Romeo stepped back outside alone and, in the rapidly dimming twilight, reached into one of his vest pockets and pulled out a slender metal cylinder, uncapped it, and slid out a Gurkha Special Ops. Carefully clipping the end first, he lit the cigar and leaned against the wall.

Chapter 36

W ITHIN THIRTY MINUTES THE ENTIRE BUILDING WAS INUNDATED with local police and agents from the FBI and the ATF. The broadcast engineers, utilizing the dedicated line from their facilities to their transmitter on Mount Bigelow, had managed to get the station back on the air. Dan Marries and Jack Bailey were co-anchoring a special newscast on the bombing attempt.

Romeo had sequestered his group in the same conference room they had used before the show. The exception was Lisa, in her typical whirlwind of energy, coordinating between the local and network coverage and obediently followed everywhere by Shannon. He had reassigned Chili from his earlier post in the lobby to a station outside the door of the room. Eunice was staying close to Lisa.

The Ranger was on his way back after a round of questions from one of the detectives, when he heard a familiar booming voice. "Hey, Slick, you just can't stay away from trouble, can you?"

Whirling, he recognized Billy Burke, the lanky black cop who had helped them prior to the FEMA camp raid. The man was out of uniform, wearing cowboy boots, blue jeans, a denim shirt, and a large white cowboy hat, making him look even taller than his already substantial height.

"Billy! Man, it's good to see you."

The patrolman grinned broadly. "Ben came, too. He's talking to one of the detectives. He was out at the ranch watching the show on TV with me when everything hit the fan. Thought we'd come check it out. Your little tussle was supposed to be over and done with. What in blazes is going on?"

Glancing around, Romeo spotted an empty office with its door ajar. "Let's go in here. I'll fill you in."

After shutting the door behind them, he brought Burke up to date on what had happened since the Beckleman confession. His new friend silently absorbed the story, occasionally revealing his reaction with a lifted eyebrow or a shake of his head. As the narrative drew to a close, Jones admitted, "I'm really glad you showed up. I'm worried."

"About what? Seems like it's under control for now."

The Ranger shook his head. "Billy, I was opposed to doing this broadcast from the beginning. It's not that we shouldn't get the story out. We should. But they're not trying to convert my people anymore…or condition them…or whatever they call it. Now they're trying to kill them. And I didn't like parading them around in public in a convenient, vulnerable group. Too easy a target."

"You're right there, pal. Putting a nasty fragmentation bomb under your seats kind of indicates they don't just want to talk. But you're surrounded by about a hundred law enforcement men and women at the moment. I don't see what you're…ohhh."

Romeo nodded. "You got it. Two U.S. Marshals, or at least we thought they were, tried to execute Luis. The FBI is up to their ears in the Rosemary Shields killing, and they wouldn't send any backup when Kenny needed it. No…I don't know if I can trust anyone here. Except for you and Ben, of course."

"Of course. So what do you need? You want us to keep an eye on your group?"

"No. I have them in a locked room with a Marine at the door. My problem is logistics. Before the bomb attack I had a plan to get them out…back to Kelsey's. That plan is shot now."

The cop tilted his chair back against the wall in the tight room. Tipping his hat forward over his face and cradling the back of his head in his cupped hands, he uttered, "Well, let me think on it a second."

▽

The two patrol cars parked outside the gate to Kelsey's property as the SWAT van drove through and came to a stop under the porte cochere. Romeo jumped out of the passenger side and grabbed his phone, checking the status of the automated security system, as Billy Burke exited the driver's side and circled around to stand with him.

"Did you leave someone here to watch the joint?"

Jones grunted his displeasure. "That was my plan, but Kelsey insisted that everyone had to be at the station."

"Want me to go through it with you? Make sure it's empty?"

"Look at the size of this place. It'd take about fifteen of us to check it out, and even then somebody could keep moving and avoid us. No. When we left, Scott set the system on high alert. The place is packed with hundreds of motion sensors, IR beams, and who knows what else he's dreamed up, plus the sensors on all of the openings. And that isn't counting the perimeter devices on the grounds. If anyone came anywhere near the place, we'd know it." He held up the phone. "This is linked to the system. I'm checking the status now. The only activity is the room we used to hold Rocky, Judtson's pooch."

He circled to the rear of the van, knocked twice, and the doors were opened by Chili, lowering his pistol when he saw Romeo and Billy. The group, glad to escape the cramped van, disembarked quickly with the majority trudging tiredly to the front door. Kelsey, Saylor, and Judtson held back to stand with Romeo.

"Well, I'd best be getting this rig back to the boys before they miss it."

Kelsey smiled broadly at Burke. "I can't thank you enough for this, Billy. How did you talk them into letting you use it?"

The tall cowboy smirked and shook his head. "They didn't actually let me. But the keys were in it. And those two guys outside the gate who provided the escort are old friends."

She released a muted giggle. "Well, please thank everyone for me. We appreciated the lift."

They all said their goodbyes, and Billy climbed back in and drove away. The four of them watched until the gate shut behind the black truck. Judtson was the first to speak, his voice subdued.

"I'm still getting the chills thinking about the fact that we were seconds away from dying. That was close tonight."

"Too close," Romeo agreed.

"We're in the same situation as we were before we confronted Beckleman," Saylor observed, frustrated. "Reacting instead of acting. We need to change that."

"Or one of these times our luck will run out," the Ranger warned.

"But how can we be proactive?" Judtson countered. "If it wasn't Beckleman behind it all, and obviously that's the case, then who are they? And how do we get to them?"

The others had no answers. The silence was broken by the ringing of Romeo's phone. "It's Kenny. Go ahead inside. I'll see what he wants."

The three of them walked away as he took the call. "Hey! What's up?"

"Can't believe they tried that! Everybody all right?"

"Yeah. We're good."

"I'm on leave for another two days, so I'm out of the loop on the investigation. You can fill me in on the details later. The reason I'm calling is to see if I can borrow your engineer and his new helmet."

Romeo paused. Curious yet wanting to keep the conversation vague on the phone, he asked circumspectly, "If you can tell me, why do you need him?"

"Been thinking about what we talked about the other day. Nothing solid. I think it's worth a shot to try it out on my number-one guest up in Phoenix."

"Don't see why not. When?"

"Right away. Tonight, even."

Jones was quiet for a moment. "I don't want him to drive up there alone."

"Not a problem. I'm down here. I can pick him up."

"I'll see what I can do and call you back."

▽

They made a brief stop at Bowman's apartment so that he could change out of his sweats and into normal work attire. He emerged from the bedroom carrying a gray fedora, which he tossed to Wheeler. "Wear that when we get there. Your face has been plastered all over the media. I don't want anyone to recognize you."

Matt put it on and checked himself in the mirror. "I kind of like it."

The two arrived at the Phoenix bureau and entered with a swipe of the agent's key card, crossed the deserted lobby, and rode the elevator.

"Are very many people working this time of night?"

Kenny shook his head. "At three in the morning...nope. Two...maybe three, tops."

The elevator opened and they hurried through the small vestibule and past the now vacant reception desk. Using his card again on another door, he briskly led Matt across the empty bullpen with its numerous cubicles, down a long hallway, and then turned a corner at an intersection.

"Bowman! You're here late...or early, I guess."

The two stopped. A man in his forties, having shed his suit coat and rolled up the sleeves of his white shirt, was approaching them and carrying a bag of Cheetos and a Diet Dr Pepper.

"Hey, Campbell! Yeah, not by choice."

With no change in countenance, the other agent eyed Wheeler and the large leather valise he was carrying. "Surprised to see you at all. Heard you were on leave and thought you'd be chasing blondes on Coronado Island."

Bowman manufactured a natural-sounding chuckle. "That's where I would be if something hadn't come up. This is Dr. Simon Langejans. He works with Dr. Thompson."

"Thompson? Oh, that was the polygraph expert you brought in on Luis Tovar."

"Right. I wanted to polygraph Beckleman, but Thompson couldn't make it. So he sent his number-two guy. Trouble is that tonight is his only window."

Putting on his best apologetic face, Wheeler embellished, "I'm very sorry to inconvenience all of you. I'm afraid that I need to be in D.C. tomorrow…or I should say…this afternoon, to polygraph some IRS officials."

The man nodded. "Helping out on that mess, huh? Good luck with that!"

"Anyway," Bowman cut in, "we should get started. Catch you later. And, Campbell, try to keep the orange powder off your white shirt this time, okay?"

"Hey, that was an accident! The bag broke."

They walked past him and continued to the holding cell where Bowman pulled out his pistol, removed the magazine, locked the slide fully back, and placed both items into one of the cubby holes built into the wall next to the door. His key card was employed once more. This time he was also required to place his thumb on a scanner before the door clicked open, the sound loud in the silent hall. The room was dark. He flipped the switch and saw Samuel Beckleman asleep on a twin-sized bed in the corner of the room. Closing the door and ensuring that it was locked, he crossed the room and gripped the former Secretary of Homeland Security by the shoulder, shaking him, as Wheeler placed the valise on the table and opened it, extracting a small case.

The prisoner came awake slowly and, after a few seconds of confusion, his eyes focused on Matt, who had snapped open the case and removed a hypodermic needle. The ex-bureaucrat's eyes sprang wide open and he yelled in alarm, "Matt Wheeler! What's *he* doing here? Keep him away from me!"

Thankful that the room was soundproofed, Bowman wrestled Beckleman around and held him in an armlock as Wheeler performed the injection of the FDG. Over the shoulder of the still-squawking man, the agent protested, "Now we have to wait an hour?"

"Yep."

"And listen to an hour of his caterwauling? How did you guys handle this in the past?"

With a wry grin, Matt remarked, "Usually Romeo would just punch them out."

Holding the struggling Beckleman, Kenny grimaced. "I think I'll pass on that. Grab that pillowcase. Let's make a gag."

▽

Saylor stopped Judtson in the hallway. "Hey! Kristen was on television."

"What? Something wrong?"

Shaking his head, a mysterious smirk on his face, Saylor answered, "Uh, no. I think you should probably see this."

Judtson followed his friend into his room where a laptop was open and operating. The screen displayed a popular video site. At the top of the box was the headline "Has Judtson Kent Gone Bonkers?"

Inside the rectangle was a paused frame with a close-up of Kristen. The red graphic at the bottom of the video identified her as Judtson Kent's estranged wife.

He snickered in response. "Boy…it didn't take very long for her to identify herself as estranged!"

"I was linked to this video when I was looking at the coverage of what happened at the TV station. It's from one of the entertainment channels. Wait till you see what she says."

The camera view was a tight headshot. All he could make out in the rest of the frame was the ocean in the background and a man's arm around her shoulders.

He tapped the arm wrapped around her and asked Saylor, "Who is that?"

"You'll see. Just listen."

Dropping into the seat, Judtson clicked the mouse to start the video. Kristen's mouth sprang into motion. He noticed that her face was brightly animated and her eyes seemed to sparkle as she spoke.

"Judtson has been going off the deep end for a long time. I know the public has always thought of him as this steady, orthodox skeptic, but privately…he's been a different person. I mean, look…for quite a while he and his sidekick, Saylor, have been suiting up in silly faux-military outfits, like immature little boys, and going out to vandalize public property."

"Nice of her to throw you in there."

"Yeah, it was great! Don't worry. I'm not the only one."

Kelsey, searching for Judtson, entered. "Here you are. What's going on?"

"Come on over. You need to see this."

She hurried across the room and stood behind him as Kristen continued, "And I can't remember the last time I was able to go out in public with him without being humiliated. So this latest fiasco fits right in. And now" – she rolled her eyes dramatically – "flying saucers! It was mildly amusing before, but now…now I'm worried about him. He needs help."

"Oh, my God! That's Kristen! She's talking about you!"

"Uh-huh."

An off-camera voice asked, "What about the attempt on his life today? And the lives of the rest of his group?"

Judtson recognized that as she answered, she was consciously altering her expression to project a solemn concern. "I hate to say this…I truly do. But…I wouldn't be surprised if he staged that supposed bombing attempt himself."

"Mrs. Kent, that's quite an accusation. Why would he do such a thing?"

She shrugged. "For the attention…to give credibility to his little posse of fringe lunatics, nutcases, and that obvious sociopath Kelsey Batman. I really have no idea."

"Sociopath!" exclaimed Kelsey. "What is she…?"

Saylor chuckled softly. "Just wait. It gets better."

The view expanded. As more of the background was revealed, Judtson immediately recognized not only the setting, a familiar balcony on the beach in Malibu, but also the man whose arm was around his wife's shoulders.

"That's…that's Mitch! What the…?"

"Mitch?" Kelsey sputtered. "Mitch Murray, your agent?" She gasped. "He's already snaking your wife! That's just…smarmy."

As the shot settled into the wider view, the red bar at the bottom identified Murray as Judtson Kent's former agent. The interviewer inquired, "Mr. Murray, you were Kent's agent for years. Had you noticed any odd behaviors?"

The agent laughed derisively and shook his head. "I wouldn't have the foggiest idea where to begin. Keeping his true personality a secret from the book-buying public became more than a full-time job. Of course, I'd rather not go into that right now. The most important thing is the emotional ordeal Mrs. Kent is suffering through. I'm just glad that I have been able to comfort her during her time of need." After his comment, he gave Kristen an affectionate squeeze, and she turned toward him and smiled warmly, leaning tightly against his side.

"I'll bet you are," snorted Kelsey. "What was that sociopath crack about?"

"I'll show you. Let me sit."

Judtson relinquished the chair to Saylor, who quickly worked the touchpad. "Give me a sec to find it. But you wouldn't believe what I've found about most of us. That bottom-of-the-ratings news channel on cable was on campus interviewing faculty who work with Chris. Basically the same story. They're saying that he has not been the same since his mother died. One of the administrators even said that his funding was pulled because he was using it to pursue New Age fantasies at the behest of his crazy sister, Starlight. They've also been running videos from when Dean and Jimmy were conditioned, where they talked about how foolish they had been and how everything was manufactured to get attention. Another network is running an interview with the head of the metallurgy lab which provided the analysis of the Baalbek stones and swore that they were not from Puma Punku."

As he spoke, he typed in a search string and found a long list of hits. He finally located the one he sought. "Here it is."

The window, titled "Kelsey Batman goes off on family in restaurant," opened and the video instantly began. Judtson readily placed the scene. "Oh, no!"

One of the customers at the restaurant where they had the unpleasant experience with the screaming child and mother had obviously used a phone to capture the event.

"Great!" Kelsey growled, furious. "They don't show the earlier part when the kid was screeching in my ear and rapping me on the shoulder. If I saw that video the way it's edited, *I'd* think I was a sociopath."

The video segment ended at the moment she stood and asked the mother to move aside.

Judtson looked at Kelsey, who was seething. As their eyes met, he commented, "They seem to be swinging into high gear."

"What do you mean?"

"Remember, this is what they do. Disrupt…disavow…discredit…destroy."

Saylor sighed loudly. "So they're up to stage three. That only leaves destroy."

▽

With their subject gagged and secured to a chair with handcuffs Bowman had brought, the agent glanced at his watch. "It's been an hour. Let's get this over with."

He positioned himself behind the straight-back chair and firmly grasped the head of the wildly thrashing prisoner. Wheeler then slipped the helmet onto Beckleman and lowered the shielded visor, securing the device with a chin strap.

"It won't take long now," Matt uttered, activating the control program on the laptop. "Assuming we're actually converting him, that is."

"Good," Kenny grunted, fighting to keep the man relatively motionless.

As the sequence proceeded, the only sounds in the room were the muffled grunts and moans from their subject. When the counter on the screen reached sixteen seconds from the end, Beckleman suddenly went still. Sensing the abrupt slackness of the man under his grip, Kenny looked at Matt, loosing a string of rapid-fire questions. "What happened? Is this normal? Did it work?"

The engineer waited until the countdown reached zero before removing the helmet. "I don't know for sure. He definitely has calmed down. We'd better keep the gag handy in case he's faking."

Bowman nodded and Wheeler untied the twisted pillowcase, allowing the gag to fall to the floor. The Secretary's eyes were not frantically darting from point to point around the room, as Matt had witnessed with some of the others when they had been returned. This man's eyes were steady and flat, his face neutral, almost as if he were asleep with his eyes open.

Matt leaned closer. "Beckleman! Samuel Beckleman! Are you all right?"

His eyes shifted languidly until they connected with Wheeler's. The two men stared at each other for well over a minute, neither speaking. The impression Matt received was that he was looking into the eyes of a person drugged, or even comatose.

"Beckleman. Come on. Talk to me."

With deliberate slowness, the prisoner's mouth moved all but imperceptibly, yet no sound came out. After several more seconds, his tongue dragged across the surfaces of his lips and he tried again, this time quietly rasping, "What?"

Concerned at the drastic difference between Beckleman's reaction to the procedure and that of the others, Matt grabbed his shoulders and shook them gently. "I asked you if you were okay."

In response, his eyebrows lifted and a faint, nearly unnoticeable upward curl touched the corners of his mouth. Inhaling deeply, the man whispered, "Oh…my…God. It really works."

$$\triangledown$$

With the laptop now oriented toward the former Secretary of Homeland Security, the webcam focusing on his face, and video software taking everything in, he spoke as Bowman sat in the chair across the table and questioned him. The man's demeanor was a disquieting combination of bewilderment, disbelief, gratitude, and earnestness. Gone was the Pecksniffian imperiousness he had projected in the past. Wheeler, perched on the edge of the bed, added a question of his own. "Beckleman, I performed several conversions before this one. No one else reacted as you did. Do you have any idea why?"

He shrugged in response. "Don't know. Maybe due to the fact that I was *in there* considerably longer than the others. When it first happened to me, I fought it…tried to regain control…struggled constantly. Then, quite a while ago actually, I suppose I gave up. Surrendered to the new reality that I was exiled, never to return. By the time you converted me…I had checked out, I guess."

"When did they condition you?"

His back stiffened. "Please…don't use that word. I detest that word."

"Okay. When did they…zap you?"

"What's the date today?"

"You don't know the date?" Wheeler was surprised. "I thought…Judtson Kent told me that while you're in there, you still observe what's going on."

The man's eyes stared at some unseen point beyond the walls of the cell. As he began, his speech was halting and uncertain. "He's right. At first you do. It's difficult to describe. Because you aren't...connected...to your environment, aren't able to affect it in any way, what's happening around you becomes less and less important...relevant. After only a month or so, I began to feel as if I were a...soul...whose body had died. That's not wholly accurate. It was as if nothing occurring out there touched me. It became more and more difficult to...care, I suppose. As time went on, I also noticed that I was becoming less and less...real to myself. Looking at it now, I think that had you not brought me back, eventually...within, oh, I don't know...a few more months, perhaps another year...I would have simply faded away. Been assimilated by the other. Ceased to exist."

This glimpse caused a shiver to course through Wheeler. He provided the day's date.

"Well, that would make it a little over two years since they did it to me."

"Why did you come to Bisbee and make that absurd confession? You had to know that it would get out."

"First off, and this may sound petty...please don't use the pronoun *you*. It may have been done by the body you see before you, but it was most emphatically not done by *me*."

"Fair enough."

"To answer your question, they most certainly did know that the confession would get out. With their knowledge of the technological capabilities of Kelsey Batman and Scott Gumble, they were counting on it."

"But the story was so full of holes. You...I mean, they must have known that we'd figure it out. That we wouldn't simply accept it and stop."

"Your assumption has a fundamental flaw. I should mention, by the way, that the ostensible confession I was instructed to deliver had been borrowed from the plethora of conspiracy theories which have been bandied about for decades. There were many who already believed that all UFO sightings and abductions were events staged by the government for the purposes I described. It was assumed that the proponents of the theory...a preexisting, willing support group, feeling vindicated, would pick up the theory and run with it. Your erroneous assumption is that they expected Miss Batman and Mr. Kent to survive."

"Oh."

"They did believe that they would prevail and end the lives of those two, as well as Mr. Jones. And Miss Batman and Mr. Kent were clearly the driving force behind the entire group. Without their resources and without the impetus they were providing, it was assumed that the balance of the group would sheepishly return to their previous lives and keep their mouths shut. Of course, on the chance that they did not, they would have been dealt with on a case-by-case basis."

The cold, matter-of-fact details of the plot chilled Matt to the bone.

Bowman resumed his questioning. "Why did they zap you?"

Before he answered, Beckleman crossed one leg over the other and, for a moment, stared down at his leg with a mien of amazement, verging on incredulity. The agent thought to himself that this was how a paralyzed man would react if he could suddenly move again. The former Secretary gently patted the top of his thigh and briefly squeezed it. His face settled into a serene smile. Then, as though suddenly remembering the question, he looked up. "Why did they do it? Quite simple, really. Just as Judtson Kent, Carlos Villarreal, and the others were getting too close...so was I."

"Too close to what?"

His voice as casual as if he were describing the plot of a book he had recently read, Beckleman began, "So many things weren't adding up. Weren't making logical sense. Political decisions. Foreign policy. Domestic issues. So-called immigration. Economics. All of it. It was a pervasive web of incongruities…all of which seemed to be leading us directly into financial ruin, a collapse of the social order, a surrendering of our industrial capabilities, an overt abdication of our role in the world."

The man paused in reflection, and Kenny, to fill the gap, began to say something. Beckleman, not allowing the interruption, continued, "For better or for worse, I've been a politician…a bureaucrat…my entire adult life. Not always popular, but then, who is? Throughout the various shifts in public sentiment and swings in party control, I had always believed that I remained true to my ideals."

His words had the ring of a confession to a parish priest by a man who had completed an arduous, soul-searching journey.

"You know, Special Agent Bowman, the past two years made something I sorely needed…something I've assiduously avoided my entire life…impossible to abstain from any longer…introspection. And not only was introspection the only option open to me within the confines of my exile, but it was also a far more pure self-contemplation than is remotely possible when one is in the midst of the flood of physical self-gratifications, the indulgences of one's ego, and the infinite barrage of distractions – which, all together, make up a normal human life.

"What I learned about myself was that I had *not* remained true to my ideals. I had merely sold them to the highest bidder in my quest for power, tapping into my seemingly inexhaustible supply of rationalizations to justify each incremental decision. Yes, I was certainly guilty of succumbing to the inevitable thirst for power…assuaging this by telling myself that once I had attained that power, I would use it wisely and well.

"As I indicated, despite my meandering from the idealistic path, I had noticed the incongruities which, taken as a whole, appeared to be leading us as a nation…as a people…to an ugly oblivion. I took advantage of my position to question those in power…those who were devising and implementing the almost daily acts of sabotage and treason under the guise of it all being mere political difference of opinion: valid alternatives within the reasonable realm of academic theory. What I discovered was that their answers were not answers at all. They gave no bona fide, tangible explanations for their insidious deeds. There was, in fact, no academic, poly-sci underpinning whatsoever to support the programs. Nor was there an indication of logical, empirical reasoning to justify the edicts and executive orders. They did not even, in any way, relate to some underlying ideology. Instead, there was only an agenda."

Matt muttered from the corner, "That's the truth."

Without acknowledging, Beckleman proceeded, "Now, sadly, I've come to the juncture where I experienced my own denouement. I could have come out against them, as others have. I could have begun speaking out on the Sunday news programs. I could have run for office on the platform of reason and opposed them."

"Why didn't you?" Kenny asked.

"Courage. Or the lack thereof. I could not face the possibility of ridicule, character assassination, and that worst of all political fates, marginalization."

"What did you do?"

"I hunkered down. I began digging deeper. Just as a blackmailer collects evidence for a lucrative payoff in the future, I worked to ferret out as much as I could about the agenda, who was behind it, and why."

Bowman leaned forward. "And?"

Beckleman sighed loudly. "Prior to being zapped, and afterward as well, I was never able to discover the 'why.' To this day, that remains a mystery to me. The 'who,' on the other hand, was eventually discoverable. It was my unearthing the final piece of that puzzle which triggered my...conversion."

"Dammit, Beckleman!" Wheeler barked impatiently. "Who was it?"

The man displayed a melancholy grin. "Forgive me. I must admit I am enjoying this a bit. It's the first pleasure I've had in two years. I'll answer you by relating where it happened. If you are up on your conspiracy theories, you will know the answer. I was invited...no, summoned would be a more appropriate description...to Buckingham Palace. Ostensibly to have an audience with the queen."

A loud gasp burst from Kenny. "That's where they did it to you?"

"It was."

"Then...you're saying it was the Illuminati!"

Chapter 37

LOSING HER WAY TWICE IN THE DARK HALLWAYS, Eunice finally stumbled upon the kitchen to find Kelsey sitting at one end of the long dining table and taking a bite from a bagel slathered with cream cheese.

Startled by the interruption, she jerked her head up from the meal, beaming at her guest. "Eunice! Hi. You're awake, too, huh? Want a bagel? I have some veggie cream cheese I mix myself."

The detective joined her at the table. "Sounds dandy."

Slicing one of the onion-sprinkled rounds and smearing it with spread, she glanced around the room curiously. "Ma'am...."

"Please, it's Kelsey."

"Kelsey, why on earth do you have such a gigantic place? I was about to call for search and rescue, just trying to find the little girls' room."

The earlier smile left Kelsey's face. "I didn't build it. It was...is...my father's." She sighed softly. "You know, at the time, I thought he was paranoid. Actually worried about him." Instantly, she let out a harsh bark of a laugh. "That's nuts, huh? Boy, was I wrong. So, the answer is that he built this place for security."

"Obviously."

"Yeah. Not only for himself, though. We used to have quite a few more employees than just Scott. Several of them were...I guess you'd call them...key personnel who worked on the software my dad dreamed up. Once he started getting close to solving the cloud security issue, he decided to move the core group out here. Back then, they only worked at the house during the day and went to their own homes at night. But he made the place huge enough so that if we were ever, as he put it, under siege, the critical employees, as well as the rest of us, could all live under one roof."

Cahane swallowed the bite of bagel she had been chewing. "Sounds pretty prophetic to me."

"He was."

"Ma'am…I mean, Kelsey…Lisa never did tell me how this whole thing got started. And especially how you got involved. I know about the folks whose brains were fiddled with. You weren't one of those, were you?"

The smile returned. "No. Just one of those things. Serendipity. Coincidence. Fate. Don't know. I was here one night. All alone and more than a little depressed. Missing Daddy. Feeling sorry for myself."

"The kinda night you'd pop a cork or two."

"You're right. If I'd been a drinker, I would have. Probably would have drunk until I passed out on the floor. But then I would have missed out on…" – she paused and chuckled – "all of this. Instead, I thought I could cheer myself up with some new clothes. Maybe some new makeup."

"Don't forget that bubble bath all the women's magazines tell you to take when you're down in the dumps."

"No kidding. Isn't that dumb? Anyway, I decided to go shopping. Go to the mall. Have a little junk food at the food court. Go to Dillard's and get a new top and a totally different shade of eye shadow."

Cahane snorted. "Yeah, that always works for me."

Giggling girlishly, Kelsey resumed the narrative. "I was going to Park Place Mall and I stopped at a red light at Broadway. I was waiting to make a left turn, when I noticed that a guy dressed in black and wearing a black knit mask over his head crawled out of the passenger side window of the car right in front of me. He was holding what looked like an automatic rifle."

"Get out of here!"

"No. Really. I freaked. I was about to back up and drive away. Almost did. But there was something about it. Something about him. I don't know. I stayed. And I pulled out my phone and started to video him."

She went on to describe Judtson and Saylor's assault on the traffic cameras at the intersection, her later editing of the video, posting it on the Internet, and eventually meeting Judtson as he was in the early throes of the mental transmutation.

As she finished, Eunice let out a long whistle. "Well, I've heard a passel of romantic meeting stories in my years, but that one takes the blue ribbon."

The detective made an exaggerated motion with her mouth, tongue, and lips. Kelsey took the hint. "You need something to drink?"

"Wouldn't mind it to wash this bagel down."

"Sit tight. I have a surprise for you."

Eunice watched as her host sprang up from the chair and trotted to the massive refrigerator, chatting as she crossed the room. "Lisa filled me in on what you like. I have this cool service that finds things I order and delivers them." She opened one of the double doors and pulled out a tall glass bottle, whirling around and holding it up.

Cahane's face broke into a wide grin. "RC Cola. Well, I'll be dipped!"

After giving Eunice the bottle and waiting until she popped the cap and swallowed a deep swig of the soda, Kelsey asked, "How did you become a cop? Is your father a police officer?"

The detective wiped her mouth with the back of her hand and emphatically shook her head. "Nope. Probably be a bunch more pleasant at turkey dinner time if he had been. He's a psychiatrist. I'm the big disappointment in the family."

"Oh, I don't believe that. What does your mother do?"

"Rant and rave."

Kelsey's giggle returned. "What do you mean?"

"That's it. That's all she's ever done. Carry on about this and that. I always figured that Daddy must not be much of a psychiatrist if he couldn't even fix Momma."

"Come on, it couldn't have been that bad."

Eunice smiled. "No. It wasn't. Kind of a hoot, truth be told. Both of 'em. Guess an outsider might call 'em *colorful*. Course my daddy did wish I'd of picked something other than carrying a gun for a living. I always told him it was a division of labor. He'd cure the ones he could and I'd lock up the ones he couldn't. Between the two of us, we'd have the situation under control. He never has seen it that way."

"Does he still have a practice?"

"Nope. Pulled the plug a few years ago."

"Why? You aren't that old, Eunice. I assume he isn't, either."

"He's not. Barely into his late fifties now. I don't know. He just said it wasn't any fun anymore." She paused for a moment, her expression becoming contemplative. "You know, strangest thing...the old timers on the force say that, too."

"What are they referring to?"

"Well...the boys who are up in years, you know, at or right past retirement age...all tell it the selfsame way. That when they first started on the streets, almost all the time, people and the crimes they did made some sense. These folks might rob a store or steal a car, beat up somebody...or even when they killed somebody, there was a certain logic to it. They needed the money. Somebody got 'em mad. They caught somebody sneakin' in to pay their wife a visit while they were gone...something. Might not be anything you or I would consider proper justification, but at least they had a reason. Times bein' what they are...it's not like that. Lots of what we see today dudn't have a reason. It's just...mean-spirited, evil."

"Like the knockout game?"

"Like that exactly. That one's become kind of formal. Famous, you know. Nowadays you get sent out on a call and it's an eighty-year-old man just sittin' on his front porch, mindin' his own business, and five young punks come up and pull him off the porch and beat the bejezus out of him. And after you catch the little sonsabitches and ask why they did it, all they say is 'I don't know.' Like a goldarn four-year-old. You know what I mean, don't you? You catch a little rug rat coloring on your living room wall and you ask him why he did it. That's all you get! 'I don't know.' But you shouldn't be gettin' that sorta answer from people old enough to vote, drink, and go to war. Not that they should be doin' any of those things."

"Is that the same complaint your father had?"

"In a way, I suppose. He said that when he first started shrinking people's heads, they had what he called 'real' problems. Serious stuff. Stuff that was in all the textbooks he studied as he was learning the business." Eunice veered off from her train of thought and, remembering something, laughed loudly. "Here you go. This little slice about sums it up, I think. His very last patient – the very last day he set foot in his office – was some young woman. Couldn't of been more than twenty-four or twenty-five. She wanted to take a bunch of pills and end it all. You want to know why?"

Kelsey, entertained by the animated nature of her guest, played along. "Sure."

"I guess she got into it with one of her so-called girlfriends. Had a nasty fight. And the girlfriend up and took all of the private messages between them, the ones where my pappa's patient got real catty about the other girls in their circle. Making fun of their outfits. Criticizing their makeup. Pokin' jabs at who they were dating and the fact that they put on a couple of pounds. And she up and posted all of them on her Facebook page. Exposed her for the biatch that she was. Next thing you know, the girl in question was defriended and then blocked by the whole ruck of them."

"She wanted to commit suicide because of *that*?"

"Yep."

Kelsey shook her head. "What did your father do?"

"What could he do? He wrote her a big fat prescription for some strong sleeping pills, handed it to her, and walked out of his office, never to come back."

"He wrote her a prescript…." Kelsey broke down in laughter.

"He doesn't know to this day whether she ever got the pills and did the deed. But he figured that if she did, it was thinning the herd."

▽

"Illuminati?" barked Wheeler. "They're real?"

Beckleman gave the engineer a pitying gaze. "Of course they're real."

"What…why…?" he sputtered.

"Surely, you're not serious. The 'why' has been the reason for as long as mankind has banded together and formed societies and governments. Power. Wealth. Control over others."

Bowman glanced at his watch. An hour and forty minutes had elapsed since their arrival. It was now approaching five o'clock in the morning. "Beckleman…."

"Please. Sam."

"Sam, you said you were studying them…tracking them…before they took you over."

"True. And I've had an opportunity for the past two years to observe, as well."

"What did you find? How deep does it go?"

"How high is up? How low is down? It would be far easier to tell you where they have not yet gained the control to which they are so addicted."

"Okay."

"Essentially, for all practical purposes…nowhere. Where they have not been able to overtly dictate to the handpicked figurehead leaders of a country, they have insinuated themselves into the functioning bureaucracy, gaining de facto control of that…to all outward appearances… sovereign state. Their influence around the globe is profound and virtually absolute."

"Virtually absolute is an oxymoron."

Beckleman smiled ruefully. "That is true. There are a few weaknesses in their grip, case in point being Mr. Wheeler's band of renegades." A long hesitation was followed by a curt addition. "And others."

Matt leaned forward. "Others?"

He shrugged casually, as if what he was to describe held little import. "They fall into two categories. The first I cannot tell you a thing about. They're out there, all right. But they're hidden, secretive, and a true thorn in the Illuminati's side. I'm basing this only on what I've overheard. Whoever it is…or they are…that group truly has them worried…to the point of obsession. The second category would be the others who have also deduced what is truly transpiring. Some are merely disgruntled individuals with no influence, no ability to do them harm. Others have forums – blogs…websites…radio programs…and a variety of other creative mechanisms to spread the word. For the most part they have been neutralized, marginalized, rendered ineffectual."

"By selling the rest of the public on the belief that those people are merely crackpots."

"Yes. A ploy they have utilized quite facilely since the time the Romans, the Greeks, and others built their empires."

Changing the direction of the questions slightly, Bowman asked, "Why do they do it this way? Work behind the scenes? Why don't they simply make themselves the kings or dictators or…?"

"Presidents? That is easy to answer. Rulers can be overthrown. Dictators can be assassinated. Presidents can be impeached or simply not elected for another term. Machiavelli understood this long ago." He paused briefly. "Think about it, Special Agent. Put yourself in their place for a moment, and imagine craving the control, the power. Once you set yourself up as a leader, you have made yourself a target. On the other hand, if you remain in the shadows… behind the scenes…you can exert all of the control you need over the current figurehead. And when the public turns against the decisions and policies of that leader, you can create the appearance of bowing to the will of the people…that's a joke…and react to that new sentiment, that new paradigm, by offering an alternative leader to mollify the populace. Once your new figurehead is in place, it is back to business as usual.

"In a pesky hodgepodge of governments such as Europe had, you simply disregard all of the individual nationalistic differences and create a governing union, run by committee. In the case of more formidable entities, you can shepherd Russia from a Brezhnev to a Gorbachev. You can guide China from a Mao, through a series of committee-selected leaders to the current Xi Jinping. You can take America from a Clinton to a Bush to an Obama. And none of it matters a whit to you because none of the underlying structures are truly altered and you continue to get what you want."

His words clearly agitated Bowman. "This is nonsense! Are you saying that we don't pick our Presidents? They do? How?"

"Their techniques have changed over the years. In the past, anyone who opposed them was either coerced into backing out of the race or assassinated. Now, they do it by utilizing their willing accomplices in the media. They still assassinate. Only now it is character which is the target. If a potential candidate who poses a real threat to them begins to arise, in most cases the public never has an opportunity to even realize his or her potential. Something comes up. A scandal is all it takes to nip the would-be challenger in the bud. And they've also made it easier for themselves. In this politically correct age, a person no longer needs to have committed a felony or some other atrocious act to lose the chance for public office. A simple, unintentional slip of the lip, resulting in the casual use of what is now considered to be a forbidden word, is all it takes. Failing that, they always have the option of strapping that damnable mind-altering machine on the winner's head and seizing control of him or her in that fashion."

"Still…some can get through."

"True. They can and they have. However, as a rule, the idea is to manipulate the selection process until the field is winnowed down to only two candidates. In many cases, at that stage it matters not who is elected. Both are suitable for their purposes. In the event that only one of the two fits their needs, the next step in the process is what caught my attention, causing me to investigate into areas which finally resulted in my little trip to mental purgatory."

"What was that?"

"To paraphrase Josef Stalin, it is not he who votes that holds the power, it is he who counts the votes."

The bald-faced statement stopped the FBI agent cold. Filling the silence, Wheeler asked, "Sam, I heard you say that they want power, control, and wealth. But...don't they already have more of those things than any group of men and women could possibly use and enjoy?"

Beckleman nodded. "Your question is more insightful than you might know. In the arena of wealth, this group has gone from gathering money to owning the entire monetary system."

"The Fed?"

"The Fed and the consortium of European banks which produce the euro."

"What about the yen?"

"Of course. The point is that the dollar bill in your wallet is not yours...it is theirs. And they are merely allowing you to use it as a mode of exchange. Once any group has reached that point in a global economy, a need for acquiring money no longer truly exists."

"Then it's gold they're after?" The question came from Bowman.

"That is an enigma I have yet to solve. I assume so. That would be logical. Yet I never discovered, before or after my conversion, a trail of gold leading to them. I never heard a whisper of a huge stockpile at some secure location."

"You mean Fort Knox?"

"No, Mr. Wheeler, there is no gold at Fort Knox. There hasn't been for years. Now the only real reason for maintaining the security of the vault and the perimeter of military around the facility is not to protect the gold but to maintain that secret."

"None?"

"None."

"How do you know this?"

Beckleman shrugged once again. "In my capacity I was allowed inside. It became a part of my sphere of responsibility to guard the secret. To do so, it was, of course, necessary for me to review the complex and its procedures. I am afraid that I've seen it with my own eyes. That is why they have not conducted an audit of the inventory for decades. What many people do not realize is that other countries trusted us and the security of Fort Knox, to the point where they chose it to store their own national stockpiles. Several of those countries, for a variety of reasons, have requested that some or all of their gold be returned to them. Those requests have been ignored and refused. There is no gold to return."

"I'd like to get back to the earlier question," Bowman pressed. "I'm assuming they have all that gold. They control the Federal Reserve, the euro, and the yen. And who knows what other resources around the world are inside their web. Mentally converting people, killing people, rigging elections, cleaning out a country's gold depository...these are all activities with enormous risks. Even if they have a large number of the law enforcers in their pocket, there is always the possibility of a national equivalent of an Eliot Ness...an untouchable...who can take them down. With everything they have to lose, why are they still rolling the dice?"

"That, I'm afraid, I cannot answer with any degree of certainty. My guess, and this is only a guess as I was never allowed into the innermost circle and was never privy to these answers, is that they are analogous to a high-profile wealthy man who has the commission of a murder buried in his past. He will do anything...pay any blackmail, wantonly destroy or kill any person to prevent that secret from ever coming out. The Illuminati, over the centuries, have committed unbelievably heinous acts. If their deeds…if their true nature was ever fully revealed, each and every one of them would be mercilessly hunted down and executed. Every asset would be stripped from them and their heirs. The magnitude of the outrage this revelation would cause is, to me, immeasurable and nearly unimaginable. And nothing is more dangerous than an incredibly powerful individual with much to lose."

"Sam, who are they?"

The former Secretary's mouth twisted in chagrin. "Sadly, Special Agent Bowman, I was never allowed into the highest chambers of power and, due to that, cannot tell you who is at the very top. Or even if there is a single person holding that position. My supposition is that it is a group…a committee. However, I have no idea as to the names comprising that assemblage."

"You must have met some of the heavy hitters. Maybe not the top guys, but their lieutenants."

"I did. There were a total of six. All men. All highly placed and influential. None holding an elected office."

"And their names?"

Beckleman glanced at the laptop. "In addition to the video recording, perhaps you might wish to jot them down."

The agent pulled out a pen and small pad and wrote as the man recited the names. Each revealed identity struck Bowman with an almost physical force. Wheeler released an audible gasp in reaction.

Putting the pad back in his pocket and checking his watch again, Kenny abruptly said, "I don't think we should still be here when all the others arrive."

Matt nodded. "By 'we,' do you mean the two of us, or are you thinking about taking Sam out, too?"

Beckleman's eyes flitted back from Wheeler to Bowman. "I am interested in your answer, as well."

The agent made a snap decision. "I don't think we can leave you behind. There are too many unknowns as far as who is in on it and who isn't."

"I'm certain that's the case. Now that I have been brought back by Mr. Wheeler's device, it is no longer possible for them to reconvert me. Without that option, I've no doubt I would not survive the day in this cell."

"Yeah," Matt interjected, "I've been intending to ask about the mechanism you…I mean, they…used on everyone. What exactly does it do, and how does it work?"

Kenny stood. "I know you have a lot of questions. Hell, so do I. But I really think we need to get him out of here first while only a couple of guys are on duty."

"I completely agree," Beckleman added quickly.

Wheeler sighed loudly. "I guess you're right." He turned off the laptop and packed it in the large valise along with the helmet.

Chapter 38

THE INTERCOM BESIDE ROMEO'S BED BUZZED LOUDLY, rousing him. Rolling over, he pressed a button. "Is it my turn?"

Chili's high, thin voice sounded cartoonish through the tiny speaker. "Yes, sir."

"Be right there."

"Roger."

The big man flipped on the light, sat up, and pulled on his socks and pants. He next tucked his feet into the tan-colored combat boots and laced them snugly. Standing, he snatched up his phone and was about to pocket it, when he noticed an alert on the screen that a text message had come in earlier. Moving his thumb over the icon to display the message, he was interrupted by an incoming call. He answered it. "RJ."

"Hey, this is Big Wheel. Thought I'd let you know. Big Fish has been converted."

Still shaking the remnants of sleep from his brain, Romeo took a moment to understand the cryptic message before he asked, "So he had been conditioned?"

"Boy, was he."

"What did he have to say?"

"You won't believe it all. We got it on video. And we decided we'd better bring him home with us."

Jones paused. "That might be a little dicey."

"We know. But your buddy here doesn't think we can leave him out any longer. He's afraid he might spoil."

"What time are you bringing him?"

"Leaving now."

"Okay. Be careful and keep me posted."

"Will do."

Romeo ended the connection and started across the bedroom, when he remembered the text message. As he walked, he opened it and began to read.

▽

Special Agent Campbell, leaning back in his chair with his feet propped up, heard the phone on his desk ring, checked the caller ID, and saw that it was Dillamon. As he pulled his feet down and rapidly tilted forward, the open bag of Cheetos which was balanced on his stomach spilled its contents onto his white shirt. Cursing and brushing the bright orange powder, he answered the phone, "Special Agent Campbell."

"Campbell, Dillamon."

"Morning, sir."

"I wanted to let you know that I'm calling a meeting this morning. Seven-thirty. To go over the preliminary details on the gubernatorial candidate case we've had dumped in our laps."

"Okay. Who should be at it?"

"That's part of what we need to figure out. For now, you and Casey...and Shelton."

"What about Bowman, sir? He'll be back from leave soon and it'll be under his purview."

"Uh...sure. Probably a good idea. I'll call him."

"No need. He's here."

There was a momentary silence. "He's with you? Now? Why?"

"Just a timing thing, I think. He brought in a professor from ASU to perform a polygraph on Beckleman. This was the only slot in the man's schedule."

This time the silence was longer before the senior agent asked, "This other man...the professor...what does he look like?"

Campbell described Wheeler, the details including the fedora. After he finished, Dillamon, clearly suspicious, instructed, "Check the entry cam. See if you have a decent shot of his face and run it through facial recognition."

"Will do. I'll call you back."

"No. I'll wait."

"Hold on."

Wiping the cheese dust from his fingers, the agent brought up the security system on his desktop and found a fairly good image of Wheeler, captured as he had entered. Shadow-boxing the face, he ran the recognition software.

"It's running now, sir. Of course, if the professor isn't in the dat.... Oh, there he.... Uh, sir...I'm sorry. I should have recognized him when Bowman...."

"Who is it?" Dillamon's voice was taut.

"It's one of the group who brought down Beckleman. Matthew Wheeler."

A loud grunt burst from the phone, followed by a torrent of words. "Find the room they're in and stop them. Whatever they're doing...whatever Bowman tells you...stop it. And do not...I repeat, do not let them leave! I'm already on my way."

With Beckleman handcuffed, the three men were clustered at the exit from the cell as Bowman explained, "Okay, here's the plan. Matt, if Campbell or anyone else stops us – which will happen – and asks why we're taking him out of here, we say that your polygraph machine didn't work and that we need to transport him to my offices. I'll do all the talking, but that's the story if we're asked."

Wheeler made a skeptical face. "You sure about that? Wouldn't it make more sense if you told him you were transporting the prisoner to a more secure facility or something like that?"

"No. Any formal prisoner transport would have paperwork. He'd know that no paperwork along those lines came in. As far as he'll be concerned, this is supposed to be a quick in-and-out. Listen, I admit it's weak. I happen to be on leave at the moment, but I am still the guy's boss. I'll just have to baffle him with bullshit. The deal is…if Campbell is the only one there on our way out and he stops us…the second he does, Matt, you keep moving. Get behind him. Even if he gets suspicious about the fact that I'm taking Beckleman out, he won't be thinking about an attack. If things start going sideways…" – Kenny looked down at the heavy valise meaningfully – "hit him with your purse."

"Okay. Whatever you say."

Bowman inserted his keycard and jerked it back out. A second later, the red LED light beside the biometric scanner came on and he placed his thumb on the small screen. The locking mechanism made a satisfying click. He opened the door and swung it wide.

"Here goes." He stepped out first and retrieved his pistol from the storage cubby, released the slide, loaded the clip, chambered a round, flipped off the safety, and holstered it. He motioned Beckleman to come out and seized his arm in the traditional prisoner escort mode, and the two began to walk, with Wheeler bringing up the rear. They made it through the first corridor without incident and turned, walking briskly down the length of the longer hall.

Agent Campbell slammed the door to the formal interview room, which was normally used for interrogations and polygraphs. It had been empty. Concluding that they must have stayed in Beckleman's cell, he took off at a full run, hoping that they had not slipped out of the building.

As the three neared the bullpen area which was filled with now vacant cubicles and only twenty feet from the exit, Campbell's voice boomed at them from behind. "Bowman, hold up."

The three stopped and turned around to face him as he trotted up, panting hard. Matt instantly began to sidle around to position himself behind the agent.

As he faced his immediate supervisor, Campbell realized that Dillamon had not actually provided any detailed instructions. He was not sure if he was to lock the men up or simply keep them there in a friendly fashion. Opting for the latter, he remarked, "Thought you'd be in the interview room."

"No. We were set up in his holding cell." Bowman looked at the man's shirt and shook his head disapprovingly. "Orange powder again," he chided.

Campbell automatically started brushing at his white shirt, only making the condition worse.

"Yeah. Bag broke again. Anyway, Dillamon called a few minutes ago."

Sensing there was something Campbell was not saying, Bowman felt his gut tightening but attempted to keep his tone light. "No way. He's never been up this early in his life."

Campbell chuckled. "No kidding. Surprised me, too. He was calling about some meeting at seven-thirty this morning. I guess he decided that he wanted you to attend."

"That's odd. I'm still on leave."

"I know. He said it was about an ongoing case, one of the politicians running for governor. Seems the candidate was caught with both hands and one foot in the cookie jar. Dillamon said you needed to be up to speed on it so you'd hit the ground running when you came back. I told him you were already here."

Bowman casually swung his gaze to Campbell's cubicle and saw that the man's holstered gun remained draped over the back of his chair. "Okay. I'll try to make it."

The junior agent seemed to focus on Beckleman for the first time. "By the way, what are you doing with our prisoner?"

Kenny laid out the planned story and could see the vague traces of doubt in his subordinate's eyes.

"Afraid you can't go. Dillamon said I should keep you here...."

"Campbell," he interrupted, assuming his best authoritative voice, "it's an in-and-out. Dr. Langejan's office is close...at ASU in Tempe. We'll be back before the meeting."

The agent pursed his lips, displaying his discomfort, and came to a decision. "Come on, Kenny, he isn't a professor from ASU. He's Matthew Wheeler. Now what...UUGGHHH!"

The last sound was a shouted grunt as Campbell's head suddenly jerked forward, slammed by the heavy valise.

$$\nabla$$

Eunice and Kelsey were still at the table when Romeo burst into the room at a run. Both women whirled around, startled. Kelsey was the first to react. "Romeo! What's wrong?"

Not at all breathless, he handed his phone to her. "This came in two hours ago."

She took it and quickly began reading as Eunice grabbed his attention. "Something up?"

"Has anyone told you about Luis Tovar?"

"Yep. Lisa did. Why?"

"Apparently, he sent a text message to me saying...."

"Why 'apparently'?"

The Ranger shrugged. "It's from a strange phone. We don't know who owns it. The message says it's from Luis, and that's all we have...."

Kelsey, absorbed in reading the text, gasped loudly.

He glanced at her, then continued bringing Eunice up to speed. "Anyway, according to the message, he was watching when the bad guys nabbed Kelsey's father. He says he wanted to help but couldn't. So he tracked them to an airfield north of town where they boarded a C-130. He sneaked on board and stowed away."

"Ballsy!"

"Yeah."

"Where'd they go?"

As she finished reading, Kelsey, her voice anxious, uttered, "Bolivia."

"*Bolivia?*"

"Uh-huh," she replied quietly. "They disembarked on a private airstrip outside La Paz, and he was able to follow them out to Lake Titicaca."

Eunice's eyes narrowed. "How'd he do that without a car?"

"He didn't say."

"If this is on the up-and-up, knowing Luis, he would do what it took," Romeo offered. "He probably either stole one or carjacked somebody."

"Well, where did they end up?"

He waited for Kelsey to answer. She did not, so he filled in the details. "They headed to an island. That's where Luis had to stop. He figured that grabbing a boat and following them out would be too risky...too visible...and he wanted to make sure he got word back to us. So he went back to La Paz where there was cell service and sent this. He said he'd wait thirty minutes for me to reply. If I didn't, he'd head back out and watch the island."

Eunice, sensitive to the strained features on Kelsey's face, asked gently, "Did he see your daddy when they were headed to the island?"

"Y...yes."

"And that isn't all he saw," Romeo added.

"What else?" the detective pressed.

"Did Lisa also tell you about Mrs. Costello?"

"She did. From what I gather, she might've been the one who helped the bad guys at the silo. What does she have to do with this now?"

The big man took a deep breath, then stated flatly, "She was with them, too."

Cahane was silent, absorbing the facts and attempting to fit them together. Kelsey painstakingly reread the lengthy text message before she handed the phone back to Romeo.

"There's one other thing," he ventured hesitantly, not knowing how distressed his boss was at the moment.

"What?"

"I just heard from Wheeler. Beckleman had been conditioned. They converted him back, and I guess he's talking his head off."

The news actually got through to Kelsey. The rigid determination on her face softened slightly to accommodate a trace of curiosity. "What did he say?"

"I don't know yet. Matt didn't want to get into it over the phone. They decided to extract him. They're going to bring him here."

She assimilated this complication quickly and abruptly stood. "I'm...I'm going to wake up Judtson...and...the others. Romeo, forward that text to my phone, then call the terminal and our pilot. Have him get the Gulfstream ready."

▽

Bowman moved before Campbell hit the floor, wrapping his arms around the man and dragging him toward the cubicles. "Matt!" he barked. "Grab a pair of cuffs. There should be some in his desk drawer."

Wheeler dropped the valise, rushed around the two toward the cubicle with the jacket draped over the chair, and began opening drawers. Beckleman remained where he was, an anxious expression clouding his features, and watched helplessly. Campbell was stunned by the blow but not fully unconscious, and began groaning loudly as he was wrestled into a vacant chair. Before he could rally enough to resist, Bowman roughly shoved the agent's hands down between the seat and the armrests as Wheeler arrived with the handcuffs.

Kneeling behind the chair and holding both of Campbell's forearms straight down, Kenny directed urgently, "Cuff him under the seat!"

Matt knelt and quickly snapped one of the cuffs on, then, tugging hard to pull the wrists close enough, was able to slap on the other. Right as they were standing up, the front door burst open and Dillamon, accompanied by a person Kenny did not recognize, entered, weapons drawn. Their first sight was Samuel Beckleman, out of his cell and handcuffed, standing in the hallway.

Bowman's superior sneered, "Looks like we got here just in time. Beckleman, your value to us has dropped to zero," and leveled his pistol at the prisoner's chest, thumbing off the safety and plainly preparing to shoot.

His gun already pulled as he stood, Bowman aimed over the top of the four-foot-high cubicles, and ordered, "Freeze, Dillamon! Now!" Wheeler back-stepped two paces, giving his partner room.

The man whirled and saw Kenny with his gun pointing straight at him. Beckleman took advantage of the distraction to dart into the side aisle and duck below the partitions.

The senior agent's face contorted with fury. "Bowman, you'll never get out of here! I've got more men on the way."

"Shut up! Here's the deal. Raise your hands. You, too," he commanded, shifting his aim momentarily toward the second man. The men remained silent and raised their hands above their heads, both agents still holding their pistols.

"Keep standing. If either one of you tries to dive, you'll never make it. Cooperate and no one's hurt. We just want to walk out the door. That's it. Don't make it worse. Now, face that wall behind you and put your hands on it, laying your weapons flat against the wall, barrels pointing straight up. And move your feet back. Way back."

Moving slowly, they complied.

He chanced a fleeting glance back. "Matt, I'll cover them. Get their guns."

Dillamon spoke over his shoulder. "Bowman, you have no idea what you're biting off right now. Put down the gun and we can end this…."

"I told you to shut up! Not another word."

Matt, making a wide arc around his friend to remain out of the line of fire, moved away from Campbell and toward the two. Reaching the end of the warren of cubicles, he saw the heavy valise lying where he had dropped it, and paused to pick it up, intending to add the two pistols to the stash inside.

The handcuffed agent, still somewhat woozy, saw that he was no longer being watched and quietly, using his feet, steered the rolling office chair toward a nearby cubicle. Once there, he spun around so that his back was to Bowman, bent his knees, and lifted both feet, placing them against the edge of the desk. With a powerful shove, he propelled himself backward into his supervisor, shouting as he impacted, the jolt causing Kenny to reflexively pull the trigger on his pistol as he fell forward.

Matt was emerging from the cubicles into the main walkway when the earsplitting boom of the shot rang out. Dillamon reacted instinctively, dropping to the floor, his gun in hand. The other did the same. Wheeler wrapped his arms tightly around his valise and dived back toward cover, colliding with Beckleman, who awkwardly fell to the floor.

Bowman, recovering his footing, spun around to face Campbell, who was desperately scooting the wheeled chair toward him using the heels of his shoes, obviously hoping to get close enough to kick. Rearing back, Kenny kicked first, connecting with the agent in the chest and toppling him over. The agent and chair tumbled with a loud clatter. The fall breaking one of the man's arms with an audible snap, he howled in pain, wildly thrashing on the floor like an overturned beetle.

The cube partitions separating him from the others, Bowman knew, would not be very effective stopping slugs. Keeping low and out of sight, he eyed Campbell's pistol, still dangling on the back of the chair, and seized it, racking a round. Leaving on the safety, he slid the gun across the carpeted floor to Wheeler while shouting, "Matt! Behind you!"

Wheeler jerked his head around and saw the pistol, grabbed it and, firmly clutching the valise with his free arm, crawled forward, close to the edge of the partition, as Dillamon's man opened fire, shooting randomly through the flimsy cube walls, hoping for a fortuitous hit. Beckleman, alongside Wheeler, propelled himself farther up the aisle by using his feet and elbows, and crawled underneath a desk.

Between shots, Matt could hear that Dillamon was on his phone calling for backup. He edged forward and took a guarded look around the corner. The senior agent was sitting on the floor with his back against a partition, finishing the call. The second shooter was crouched past his boss, peering cautiously over the top of the cubes and now holding his fire, waiting for a clear shot at Bowman. With Dillamon offering an easy target, Wheeler brought the pistol around and, aiming for his legs, pulled the trigger. Nothing happened. Realizing that the safety was still engaged, he hastily thumbed the selector but was too late. The senior agent spotted him and dropped his phone, swung his pistol around, and began firing as Matt jerked behind the corner.

The barrage of rounds shredded the cloth-covered partition. Matt, who had frantically scrambled against a steel filing cabinet, was not hit. A sudden yelp of agony came from behind. Beckleman was pulled into a fetal position and whimpering. Wheeler could see blood spurting onto the carpet.

Bowman, crouching low, circled around beyond Campbell's desk, weaving his way through the interconnected maze of cubicles until he was in line with the location of Dillamon and his man, with only a single ineffectual partition separating him from his targets. His aim a wild guess, he pointed his pistol low and began firing through the cube walls, spacing the shots evenly. His third round resulted in a loud wail of pain. Emptying the clip, he ejected it and slammed in another.

Matt, deducing Kenny's strategy, scampered quickly forward again and stuck his gun around the corner, followed by his head. When his eyes cleared the obstacle, he saw that Dillamon was facedown on the floor, clearly trying to avoid the fusillade from Bowman. The second man was crumpled in a heap beside him, motionless and bloody. Matt stood unsteadily and rounded the corner, keeping the muzzle of his pistol centered on the prone figure.

"Push that gun away!" he ordered. "And put your hands behind your head!"

Dillamon looked up at him. Without the slightest change of expression, the senior agent lifted his gun and deliberately swung it toward Wheeler, who began pulling the trigger on his pistol. He continued firing until the magazine was empty.

Chapter 39

W HEELER, SLINGING THE VALISE OVER HIS SHOULDER, helped carry Beckleman out of the federal building and to their SUV. Popping the lock on the rear gate, they gingerly laid the injured man on the carpeted deck. The handcuffs removed upstairs, he was holding his stomach with both hands and groaning with each movement.

"We need to get going," Bowman muttered. "More are on the way."

"I know. I'll ride in back with him and see what I can do to stop the bleeding," Wheeler answered, climbing inside.

Kenny closed the gate, trotted to the front, jumped in, and started the engine. Trying to balance the need to put some distance between them and the building, and the desire to keep the ride as comfortable as possible for their passenger, he exited the lot.

Matt pulled off his shirt, intending to use it as a bandage, leaned over the man, and lowered the front zipper on the orange jumpsuit, exposing the abdomen. He saw that Beckleman's eyes were unfocused and directed at the roof of the vehicle.

"Dammit, I wish Saylor was here!" he groused angrily. "Sam! Sam, stay with us, man!"

As he talked, he gently unlaced the Secretary's clenched fingers and pulled back his hands, examining the wound. Very little blood was coming out now. The abdominal area was horribly distended from massive internal bleeding. He stared at the injury, a feeling of helplessness threatening to overwhelm him, and suddenly felt one of Beckleman's blood-soaked hands grip his…feebly. Shifting his gaze up, their eyes connected and he could see that their former nemesis knew.

Speaking so softly that Matt had to move closer to hear, Beckleman whispered, "Thank you."

The phrase surprised him. "Thanks? For what? We got you shot."

With an almost imperceptible shake of his head, he answered, "It's…better. I…thought I'd never…." His words were interrupted by an intense grimace twisting his features. Fighting back the pain, he continued haltingly, "I was sure…I'd never come out again…I'd be stuck in that sleepless hell forever. I wanted it to end…I wanted to…die…so many times. But I couldn't even…do that. At least…at least you brought me back for a little…."

The words stopped. Matt, pushing down a rising panic, sat upright and implored, "Kenny! We need a hospital!"

Bowman called out from the front seat. "I know. Two miles to go. Be there in a minute."

Leaning back down, he focused on the eyes of Samuel Beckleman. They were dull…flat. His hand shaking slightly, Wheeler slowly reached out and touched the side of the man's neck for a pulse. Urgently sliding his fingers around the area where the carotid pulse should be and finding nothing, he bent forward so that his ear was touching the still figure's lips.

With excruciating unhurriedness, he sat up and, taking a minute to find his voice, spoke. "Never mind."

$$\triangledown$$

With a portion of his attention split…focused on Chili, who was on another telephone with David Hernandez, the Gulfstream pilot…Romeo, sitting with Judtson, had Kenny Bowman on speaker and listened as his friend described their status, using Wheeler's safe cell. Relating the final details, he stated flatly, "Master Sar, we're screwed. We left Campbell behind. By now, the word is going out to every federal agent, every police officer, every sheriff's deputy…hell, every constable…in the state."

"Without giving me specifics, where are you now?"

"Heading your way. Utilizing alternate routes."

"Do you still have…?"

"We do. He's in the back. I need to figure out what to do with…that. And I need to ditch this company truck."

"That's right. It has a tracker in it, doesn't it?"

"Not anymore. Your boy did something to shield it. We're pretty distinctive, though. All of those uniforms are going to be looking for this make, model, and plate."

Chili broke the connection with the pilot and faced Romeo. "He'll be ready in half an hour."

"What was that?" The question came from the speaker.

"Things are heating up here, too," Jones replied. "We're going to be wheels up soon. Family vacation."

"Can we come?"

"I would say that's a sure thing. But we need to get you down here. Can you get another ride?"

"Will do. After what I've done this morning, what's the big deal if I add GTA? What about our…guest? I was thinking about leaving him in the back when we change vehicles."

Judtson, who had been listening quietly, pointed at the icon to mute the phone. Romeo nodded and said, "Hold a sec," tapped the screen, and glanced at him.

"I don't think we should leave Beckleman in the truck for them to find."

"Why not?"

"They don't know he's dead. If they think he's helping us, telling us everything he knows, that may work in our favor."

The Ranger took a moment to mull it over before turning the phone on again. "I think it's better if you keep your guest with you. Or at the very least, that he remains our secret."

There was not an immediate response and Romeo was about to ask Kenny if he was still there, when he heard "I think I understand."

"Is that going to be a problem for you?"

"Shouldn't be. I might I have an idea."

"Okay. Well, hurry home."

"Oh, believe me, we will."

▽

Hurrying down the long hallway to find Kelsey, Judtson encountered Saylor, who was exiting his room, rubbing his eyes.

"Hey, Popeye."

"Judtson! What's going on? Why the fire drill?"

He continued to walk and Saylor fell into step alongside. "Kelsey didn't tell you?"

"No. She buzzed me on the intercom a minute ago and said it was urgent. I guess we're all meeting in the dining room."

"Uh-huh. Actually, all hell's breaking loose. The first thing is that Romeo got a text message from Luis overnight."

His friend became instantly agitated. "Luis? You're kidding? What did *he* want?"

"Well…it wasn't that he wanted anything." Judtson briefed him on the details of the text, saving one detail for last. He came to a halt outside the entrance to the dining room. Saylor stopped with him. "And it wasn't only Kelsey's father they had. Doni was there, too."

He expected a reaction from Saylor akin to the almost ferocious intensity after his wife had been kidnapped from the silo. To his surprise, his friend slowly leaned back against the wall, his brow furrowed. As he spoke, his tone was impassive. "Did he…did the message say she was…a prisoner? Or was she…with them?"

Emphatically shaking his head, Judtson replied, "Didn't say one way or the other. Just that she was there. When we get with the others, I'll show you the message."

The offer was met with a long silence, broken by two words. "No need."

"Come on, Popeye, talk to me. What are you…thinking…feeling?"

Saylor's eyes darted around, alighting nowhere, focusing on nothing, and in constant motion. Judtson kept his silence and waited patiently. After a time, his eyes came to rest and their gazes connected. "I don't know. When I first asked her about the Devil's Breath, I didn't suspect a thing. I was sure she'd have some perfectly logical, reasonable explanation."

"There could still be one."

"I know…I guess. The fact that she received a phone call from Homeland Security down in the silo directly before she took the tea to Luis…looked bad. The fact that Luis passed the polygraph…that looked bad, too. So far, I've been able to conjure up elaborate explanations for all of it, including the little stuff my mind keeps tossing in my face."

Judtson voice was gentle. "Like what?"

"Don't really want to go into it right now."

"Okay."

"Let's just say that as I went back over the time before the Beckleman confession, she didn't seem to be acting the way I thought she should. And yet, I've been able to explain away that stuff, as well. Even this...the fact that she's down at Lake Titicaca with them. My first reaction...my first impulse...was that they had her as a prisoner. That she was still on our side."

"She probably is, Saylor. I don't know what the other things are that have been bothering you, but you need to keep one more fact in mind. Anyone...all of us...will suddenly look guilty as hell if we're scrutinized *too* closely. Our inflections, our eyes, our body language, you name it, can be interpreted one way or the other. And it all gets magnified...becomes even more unnatural if we know that we're under a microscope."

He shrugged. "I guess. But...with all of the little pieces falling into place and creating a very damming picture of Doni, do you know what the one thing is that I haven't been able to justify, rationalize, or explain away?"

"No. What?"

"When I asked her about it...she left me."

"Oh, get off it, Saylor. That should be the easy one. You know she has a monster of a temper."

"She does. She's a hothead. It would have been just like her to tear into me...come at me swinging. It would have fit if she started throwing things at me. And it would have made perfect sense if she stomped out and drove around for an hour...and then came back and laid into me. If someone or something makes her mad, that's what she does. She confronts...she attacks. But she never, ever simply runs away."

Judtson was at a loss for a response.

Saylor looked away again and sighed. "So, I guess we'll fly down there now. I suppose we'll try to find her and Kelsey's father. And maybe we'll finally find out the truth. And that...that's what scares me."

"What do mean?"

"Judtson...as long as we *don't* know...I can go on telling myself all kinds of elaborate stories. I can go on believing she is a victim...believing she is somehow innocent and it can all be explained. Believing...I am not a complete fool...or worse."

"You're not...."

Saylor stopped him with a lift of his hand. "I might be. I hope not. But as long as we don't know, I can live in a fantasy world where everything is still fine...where everything is as I always thought it was. On the other hand, if we uncover the truth...that world...that fragile construct I've created and maintained...could come crashing down."

In the decades he had known him, Judtson had never seen his friend like this. It was almost as if a maleficent troll had sneaked into his bedroom as he slept and sucked his essence, his spark, his very soul out of his body. He seemed weak...broken...vulnerable.

"Saylor...I don't know what to say to you. I know if I give you some empty reassurance that there has to be a reasonable, vindicating explanation and that we will find it, you will see my words for what they are...devoid of any rational substance. However, I can say something with certainty. Ever since this fiasco began with my first mental trip, there has been one constant...one reality. And it is that everything...and I mean absolutely everything we've held as being rock-solid, stable, dependable, immutable...has been turned upside down. Right is wrong. Up is down. Good is bad. What we thought was real...is an illusion. And once we make that step, once we embrace the fact that we have gone down the rabbit hole or through the looking glass, at that point all we can truly rely upon is each other...and the fact that anything is possible. As it is, you are focusing on the external facts and coming to a damning conclusion about someone you love. Well…I haven't told you this yet, but Samuel Beckleman was not a bad guy."

Startled, Saylor jerked his head back to face him. "What are you talking about?"

Judtson, speaking quickly, filled his friend in on the events in Phoenix. He ended the narrative by saying, "If we could have been that wrong about him…." He let the sentence trail off.

▽

Shortly after leaving the metropolitan area and entering the Indian reservation, a jurisdiction he knew to not be particularly cooperative with the federal authorities, Kenny located a large muddy field, a leftover from an earlier rain, and executed a manic series of sloppy fishtails and sideways slides, effectively covering the entire SUV with multiple splattered layers of the tan muck. He then pulled away and stopped at the edge of the bog, waiting as Matt jumped out, ran to the rear, and scooped up a handful of mud, augmenting the splatters on the license plate and rendering it not only unreadable but also unrecognizable as a government plate.

Having lost the reassuring cover of darkness, Wheeler and Bowman, utilizing a combination of Internet maps and their own knowledge, cautiously wended their way generally southward. They were currently jostling along a heavily rutted section-line dirt road, bordered on both sides with monotonous strings of barbed wire strung between four-foot-high creosote-soaked posts, substantially to the west of the interstate.

Matt pointed a finger at the radio mounted above the front of the center console. "Why aren't we getting anything on that? I would have expected a ton of chatter since they're looking for us."

"There's a lockout on federal radios. Instead of everyone hearing what everyone else is saying on the channels, the dispatcher can selectively send a signal to each unit enabling or disabling it. They added that little feature years ago after a perp we were chasing hijacked one of our vehicles. We had a devil of a time catching him because he was listening to us."

"If I had my equipment, I could probably override that."

Kenny smiled and shook his head. "Too bad you don't."

"Right. By the way, are we going anywhere in particular on this piece-of-crap road?"

"Yep. And it's not much farther."

"You gonna tell me?"

"Sure. I grew up in Buckeye, not far from here. My best friend in high school, Travis Jackson, lived on a ranch and I used to spend my summers working it with him and his dad."

"So we're going to see your friend?"

"No." Bowman's voice grew somber. "His father. Travis and I joined the Army together. Both of us went to Iraq. He didn't come back."

"Oh!"

They drove another mile in silence until they reached a break in the barbed-wire fence on the right and a wide, recently bladed lane. There was no gate or marking of any sort identifying where they were. The agent pulled in. Following the meandering road for half a mile, he pointed to the side and indicated, "He's up ahead," veering off to the left and bouncing severely as the truck climbed the ridge of spoils from previous gradings. Avoiding the mesquites, he weaved toward a lone rider on horseback. The man had noticed their arrival and was watching them.

Bowman stopped the SUV twenty yards away, shut off the engine, and climbed out. Wheeler joined him and the two walked forward.

The rider squinted. "Kenny? Zat you?"

He grinned up at the man. "Hello, Mr. Jackson. How are you, sir?"

The lanky figure swung his leg over the neck of the horse and dismounted gracefully, moving closer and clasping Bowman's extended hand.

"Sir, this is my friend Matt Wheeler."

"Pleasure to meet you, sir."

They shook hands, and the sun-bleached gray eyes slowly swept his length, taking him in carefully.

"Any friend of Kenny's is probably a scoundrel," he pronounced, with a wily smirk stamped onto his leathery face.

"That I am, sir."

The older man surveyed the two and then glanced at the mud-covered SUV. "Kenny, the only times I ever see you since Travis stepped on that mine are pity visits. This ain't one of those. It's too early in the day and you would've come alone. So what's the matter?"

"Mr. Jackson, they aren't pity…."

"Don't! You're not gonna try and tell me that you enjoy comin' out here to shoot the breeze with me? We both know that ain't true. I know *I* sure don't enjoy it."

Bowman, clearly affected by the words, asked, "You don't?"

The man's face softened, as did his tone. "When I see you, all I can think about is Travis. Not that I ever forget about him, but the pictures just get too damn vivid if you're around. I know it's the same for you."

Matt could see the effort the agent was exerting to keep his emotions in check. "It is."

"So, we're burnin' daylight here and I've got lots to do. What you need?"

Drawing in a deep breath, Kenny began, "Well, sir, we need something to drive and…a place to bury a body."

He paused for a moment to study the man's reaction, and seeing no change in expression, he started to explain, "There's a situation…," when he was cut off.

"You don't need to tell me your story. My guess is you don't have that much time to tell it right anyway, and I'll prob'ly be able to figure it out after I turn on the TV. You know your way to the barn, so git goin'. That little backhoe is parked inside. You remember where I keep the key?"

"Yes, sir."

"Dig your hole in the little meadow next to the corral. I'll be along shortly."

Kenny stared at his old friend for a long minute, saying nothing. The man returned the stare, his face impassive. Then, without a word, he turned back to his horse and mounted. His two visitors walked to the SUV and drove away.

▽

The entire group was again assembled around the table. Kelsey, leading the discussion, had already shared the contents of the text message from Luis, as well as the startling news from Wheeler and Bowman and their current, approximate position.

"So it's obvious we need to clear out. Even if we hadn't received the message about my father…and Doni…now, because of what's happened with Beckleman, it won't take much time for the FBI to make the connection and descend on this place."

"Right," Judtson concurred. "They've identified Matt. They know he's tied in with us. And I'm sure they know we're all here."

She directed her eyes to Romeo. "What's our status on the plane?"

"Talked to David, the pilot, a few minutes ago. He has the Gulfstream fueled up. He's filed the flight plan...."

Kelsey interrupted. "He didn't file a plan to La Paz, did he?"

"No. I briefed him on what's happening. He understands. The flight plan is for Hermosillo."

"Perfect."

"There's a mandatory one-hour wait after filing it. That'll be elapsed by the time we arrive. So we should be good to go. I suggest that we get out of here as soon as we can."

"We need to wait for Matt and Kenny."

"We can do that at the terminal," he answered firmly. "I'll have them meet us. But it won't take long for the Feds to block our departure in the plane. We should head out."

She chewed on her bottom lip for a moment as she thought. "Okay. I agree. Everybody grab only what you need and do it fast. Let's get ready to blow this pop stand in..." – she glanced at Romeo as she finished – "fifteen minutes."

He nodded.

▽

With the use of the backhoe and the benefit of soil free of large rocks, the dig took less than five minutes. As Bowman operated the hoe, Wheeler found a large plastic-coated tarp in the barn and rolled Beckleman's body in it, then wrapped the bundle with bands of duct tape, spaced a foot apart. The men gently walked the corpse down the sloped end of the hole and were respectfully laying it down as Jackson arrived.

The two climbed out and Matt, kneeling alongside the grave, bowed his head and said a silent prayer, joined by Bowman and Jackson.

Standing, Kenny turned to his longtime friend. "I don't think it will happen, but there is a chance that the FBI might figure out I came here. The last thing I want is to put you in a jam with the government, so if...."

Cutting him off again, the cowboy shook his head. "Don't talk to me about the government. Far as I'm concerned, they're nothin' but a cancer in our body. All the way up to that worthless piece of human debris who pulled us outta Iraq and made what my boy paid less than worthless. So...let 'em come."

Refilling the hole took only half the time and, after using the blunt side of the bucket to pound the surface for compaction, Kenny dropped down from the operator's seat. Jackson tossed him a key ring.

"Here you go. I believe you've had your mitts on the steering wheel of it more'n once."

He opened his hand and saw that attached to the ring, along with the two keys, was a silver stallion, fully reared up on its hind legs.

"Mr. Jackson...I...I can't."

"Horseshit, boy. He won't be needin' it and it tears me to pieces each time I see it. I've been startin' it up every couple weeks or so. It runs. Just checked it. Gassed it up from my tank. That thing wasn't built to sit out the rest of its life inside a stable. It's ready to see some daylight and stretch its legs again."

A single tear broke free from the corner of the FBI agent's eye and trailed down his dusty cheek. Jackson spotted it. "Dammit, son...don't!" He turned on his heel and walked swiftly toward the house.

Chapter 40

CHRIS ASHBY HURRIED INTO THE CORNER OF THE LARGE WORKROOM where he had set up his lab. The rudimentary automated system Matt had quickly assembled from off-the-shelf parts was clicking and humming in its process. The plastic bin positioned under the final chute was over half full. He swapped out the bin for an empty one, capped the container with an airtight lid, packed it in his duffel bag, and left the machine running. The large totes filled with the unscrubbed material had already been stashed somewhere by Romeo and Chili. He hoped that it would all still be here when he returned.

Saylor, standing outside under the porte cochere, speed-dialed the service he and his partner shared. As he listened to the ring, Kelsey emerged from the front door, carrying a small suitcase. She set it down beside him as his call was answered. Identifying himself, he said, "I've been attempting to reach Dr. Abbott. I've tried his cell and...."

As he spoke, Kelsey's head did an exaggerated double take at him, and she covered her mouth and bent over with barely contained laughter. Befuddled, he stared at her questioningly as he waited for the connection to be made. She had taken two steps away and was leaning against a column, now punctuating her laughter with loud, painful-sounding hiccups as Judtson emerged, took in the scene, and moved to her side. Saylor heard Vance's voice and drifted farther away, explaining to his partner that he had to leave unexpectedly and would return as soon as possible.

The moment the call was ended and he tucked the phone in his pocket, Kelsey's somewhat restrained mirth was unleashed with bellowing guffaws. He moved closer and saw tears streaming down her cheeks. "What? What's so funny?"

Judtson, who had his arm around her and was infected with the contagiousness of her near hysteria, shook his head as she, gulping down a huge breath, tried to speak, her words frequently interrupted by loud snorts. "Abb...." *Snort.* "Abb...Abbott!" *Snort.* "I never knew...." *Snort.* "I never knew your partner's name was *Abbott*?"

Saylor rolled his eyes. "Yes. So?"

"Abbott...Abbott and Costello! Ha! *Who's on first?* Ha! Is that...is that why you picked him?"

Saylor, beginning to give in to her hysteria, was about to respond, when Judtson, suppressing his own amusement, embellished mischievously, "Actually, no. His first partner was going to be Filiberto Piña."

An even more sonorous snort burst from her. *"Filbert Pineapple!"* She turned and collapsed against Judtson, her shoulders shaking violently with laughter.

As Chris, the duffel bag slung over his shoulder, hurried to leave the workroom, he passed Scott who was still working at his computer.

"You ready?"

"Almost," the tech answered. He rapidly typed a final command into the system, sniggered softly, stood, and grabbed his already packed suitcase. "Let's go."

The two men were walking away, but Chris suddenly paused and turned back. "I can't help it. One last time. *Criminy!"*

Nothing happened.

"What happened, Scott? Did you turn it off?"

With a wry grin, he replied cryptically, "No. I changed the trigger word."

▽

The FBI agent slammed the handset onto the cradle and called out urgently, "Special Agent Ulrigg!"

The senior agent, his right hand still in a bulky cast from angrily punching the brick and plaster wall, spun around. "Yeah, Truett?"

The younger agent was clearly agitated. "Our phones are down."

"What? All of them?"

"Yes, sir. I checked every line. Our whole system."

Davis Ulrigg shook his head for a few seconds, attempting to clear his mind. He was standing in the middle of the crime scene where Dillamon, and a second man Ulrigg did not know, had been shot to death. Agent Campbell had been taken to the hospital for his broken arm, and the entire office complex was swarming with crime scene techs and fellow agents.

"We do have cell phones," he barked. "Call D.C., and let them know what's going on."

"I already tried that, sir. All I get is a busy signal."

"That's impossible, Truett. They have about a thousand lines. Try again."

The young agent tapped his cell to redial as another of Ulrigg's team arrived at a near run. "Sir, we have a problem!"

"What?"

Accustomed to his boss's abrasive personality, he answered flatly. "Our system is down."

"Our phone system? I already heard."

"No, sir. Everything else."

"What does that mean? I mean, how does that affect us at the moment?"

"Well, sir, we have no Internet, no intranet with the rest of the agency, no access to our tactical communications, nothing."

Taking a minute to assimilate this and forcing calmness into his voice, he inquired levelly, "How could that happen? I thought we had a bulletproof system."

The man shrugged. "I'm not an expert, sir. I spoke with the one and only technician we currently have on premises and asked if it was an equipment issue. He told me it couldn't be, because the things I mentioned plus, obviously, the phone system, emails, radios, text messaging, even our...."

His description was interrupted as they were suddenly plunged into darkness. The change stunned all of the personnel into a quiet stillness. Scattered around the large bullpen, the lights from several cell phone screens came on, casting a jumble of blue-tinged silhouettes, surrounded by the occasional wall-mounted battery backup lights at the periphery of the large area.

Resuming his statement, the man explained, "Even our lighting and the rest of our energy management system – all of it is in the cloud. And it's all been hijacked somehow."

As he finished, the background sound of air hissing through the ducts and registers halted.

In the ensuing uncanny silence, Truett's voice reached Ulrigg. "Sir, I spoke with a friend of mine on his cell. He's assigned to D.C."

"Yes?"

"It appears that what's happening to us here is happening at every bureau in the country. Even the Hoover Building itself. The entire FBI has been...unplugged."

Ulrigg turned to the second agent. "Call Homeland Security. See if their system is still up."

The man stared at his cell phone, hesitating. "Uh, sir?"

His voice harsh, Ulrigg snapped, "What?"

"What's...what's their phone number?"

▽

Lisa tucked the compact video camera into the middle of the clothes she had packed, and slammed the lid of the suitcase closed just as Meade stopped at her door. "Need any help?"

"No. I'm good." She snapped the latches, picked up her suitcase, and followed him across the house to the front, where most of the others were already congregated.

Romeo pulled up in Kelsey's yellow Hummer and hopped out as Eunice arrived, driving another of the same make, this one painted black, and parked behind him. Chili, driving a second black Hummer, came to a stop at the rear of the line and remained in his seat with the engine idling, waiting to pull forward.

"All right," the big man ordered, unlocking and opening the rear gate, "three groups. Load your gear in back. Get in fast and let's roll. And everybody buckle in, just in case it gets a little rough on the way."

Kelsey, Judtson, and Saylor stayed together and climbed into the backseat of Romeo's truck, trailed by Rocky, who hunkered down across their feet. Meade took the front, pulled his pistol and jacked a round into the chamber, left the safety on, and pointed the weapon at the floorboard. Wasting no time, Romeo slammed the hatch, reentered, dropped the big vehicle in gear, and sped down the long driveway, thumbing the phone icon to open the gate and checking the screen, which was displaying the view outside their egress. The others had efficiently followed suit, and Cahane was already rolling as Chili latched his rear gate and jumped back into the driver's seat.

David Hernandez was performing a final walk-around of the Gulfstream as the first of the three Hummers squealed to a stop inside the hangar, and five people hastily piled out. He recognized all of them. Romeo immediately trotted forward and met the man halfway.

Sensing the urgency in the Ranger, he briefed him curtly. "Ready when you are. Fueled up. Checked out. Flight plan okayed."

"Good."

"Go ahead and get everyone and all the gear on board. With the size of the group, I'm not worried about weight or distribution."

"We're waiting on two more."

"No problem. I'd still get everyone in and ready. As soon as your last two arrive, we can load them and roll."

Romeo glanced back and saw that Meade was approaching. "Jimmy, have our people get their gear and themselves aboard."

"Roger." The old astronaut turned around and sauntered back, barking orders as he walked.

Jones scanned the surroundings. "Has anyone been around to bother you?"

The pilot shook his head. "Not a soul. And I checked the new proximity sensors Scott and I installed after the last fiasco. Nothing larger than a cockroach has been anywhere near our plane, or inside the hangar, for that matter."

"Good."

"Romeo, you told me a little on the phone, but I might need to know more. How bad is the situation right now? Is someone going to try to stop us on the ground or even once we're wheels up?"

He took a moment to look at Hernandez. The man, prior to going to work for Kelsey, had been a commercial pilot with a major airline. Before that, he flew KC-135 tankers in combat zones. There was not a trace of nervousness in his voice or demeanor as he asked the question, merely curiosity. His intelligent eyes were clear and alert.

"A definite possibility, David. Right now the FBI and who knows how many others are after us. And publicly, they may maintain that they want us for questioning, but I think they would just as soon make us all part of a debris field."

The pilot assimilated the news with the same equanimity as if he had been informed that there might be a bit of turbulence en route. "We'll try to make sure it doesn't happen."

The two black Hummers had arrived and the troupe, lugging suitcases, duffels, and other gear, were hurrying toward the plane.

"Once you're all on board, should I go ahead and roll out of the hangar or wait inside for the other two?"

Romeo weighed the variables for a second. "Roll out. Can we park it directly outside the doors?"

"We can."

"Do that."

The passengers, after stowing their bags, settled into the spacious cabin of the Gulfstream, clustering into groups. Rocky roamed the space, pausing frequently to sniff. Romeo, Chili, and Cahane remained outside the craft as Hernandez closed the cabin hatch. The three exited the massive hangar and fanned out, evenly dividing the surrounding area and keeping their hands on the butts of their still-holstered pistols.

With engine two fired up, the pilot began the methodical process of his checklist, when Meade came forward and dropped into the second seat.

"Want some company, David?"

The two men had met on previous flights, and the pilot smiled broadly at the Air Force veteran. "You bet, Captain. Are you rated for this bird?"

Meade had attempted during earlier encounters to dissuade the pilot from calling him by rank and failed. He answered with an amused huff. "I've flown fixed wing, rotary wing, and the lunar module with no wings at all. After that, anything with engines, wings, and air under them is a piece of cake."

As Hernandez feathered the powerful engine and expertly steered the plane between the hangar doors and out to the wide tarmac, Meade asked, "What's the plan?"

The pilot pulled back the thrust lever and set the brakes. "Filed a flight plan for Hermosillo. That way we'll be heading the right way after we're up. I'm going to swing to the west and get over the Gulf of California. Once we're out of U.S. airspace, radar becomes spotty. The commercial boys hate to fly in the area."

"I can see that."

"But in this case, it will be to our favor. We'll be popping on and off the radar screens all the way down to Cabo San Lucas."

"What about the transponder? As long as that thing keeps squawking, they'll know who and where we are whether we're on radar or not."

"True. And we need to keep it turned on for that first leg, or the Mexican Air Force will be scrambling jets to intercept. Once we clear Cabo, I drop closer to the deck, vector west over the Pacific, and kill the transponder. From that point, I have a continuous route mapped out where we encounter no radar at all. It's a little zigzaggy, but it works the entire way to our destination."

"Sounds like it's gonna burn a lot of fuel."

Hernandez patted the yoke affectionately. "This baby has way more range than we need. We're good."

"Okay, now that you've fed me dinner and gotten me drunk with all the sweet talk, it's time you took me to the motel. What are we worrying about?"

The pilot chuckled. "The local National Guard wing shares these runways. They're right next door and they fly F-16s. If somebody calls somebody to stop us and we ignore, which I plan to do, they're going to scramble at least one of those."

"That doesn't seem like much to fret about, David. This craft flies not too far under the speed of sound. We're gonna take off with our nose already pointed south and we're only sixty miles from the Mexican border. We'll be out of U.S. airspace in…what…twelve, thirteen minutes? You know how long it takes them to get one of those guys ready and off the ground."

As Hernandez began to respond, through the cockpit window he saw a large black pickup truck speeding in their direction and noticed that Romeo was waving his arm, rather than his gun, at the approaching vehicle. Getting up from his seat to drop the hatch, he answered Meade. "That might be true, Captain. Problem is that about half the time…and they do it randomly… they have a pilot on strip alert. If this is one of those times, that F-16 will be wheels up no later than three minutes behind us. And he'll be fully loaded, including air-to-air missiles."

Meade absorbed this fact and muttered, "Awww, crap!"

Romeo, having been called by Matt earlier and knowing what vehicle to expect, was still surprised as the F-350, jacked up to double its normal height, painted jet black with bright red and orange flames stenciled on the sides, screeched to a stop beside him. He trotted to the driver's side and looked up at Kenny. "Nice ride. Yours?"

"Nope. Belonged to an old friend. You knew him. Travis Jackson."

The appreciative expression on the Ranger's face sagged. "This was…his?"

"Yeah. I stopped on the way to visit his father. He wanted me to take it."

Shaking off the sorrow over a fallen comrade, Romeo pointed toward the yawning doors. "Pull it in there. It'll be safe. And hustle. We need to get out of Dodge."

Matt opened the passenger door, dropped awkwardly to the ground, clutching the bulky valise, and headed for the plane as Kenny gunned the truck's motor and lurched ahead, disappearing around the corner inside the huge metal building. Seconds later he came running out and the three, joined by Eunice and Chili, boarded the Gulfstream. David Hernandez, back in his seat, started engine number one and had the plane rolling forward even before the hatch was fully closed and secured.

"This is Batwing-127 requesting clearance for taxi."

"Batwing-127, you are clear to taxi to runway one-one-left, via alpha-alpha-four. Contact tower on eighteen-three when ready."

He acknowledged and, as he maneuvered the jet onto the taxiway, he switched to the tower frequency and requested clearance for takeoff. His request was immediately acknowledged. "Batwing-127, you are cleared for takeoff on runway one-one-left."

Two men in dark suits burst into the tower, flashed their identification, and demanded to see the supervisor. A painfully thin and frail-looking man in his mid-fifties, wearing wireless headphones and a microphone loop, slid the device down to his neck and eyed the badges. "What can I do for you?"

"We have reason to believe that two men wanted for the murders of federal agents may be planning to depart from this airport on a private jet. We need to ensure that they don't."

"I can't simply stop all private traffic. Do you know what plane?"

The tension from the FBI agents was palpable. "Yes. A Gulfstream-550. Call sign is Batwing-127."

The man stiffened. Jerking the headpiece back into place, he spun around to the view of the landing field and keyed his microphone.

Hernandez was nearing the end of the taxiway and was about to make his turn onto runway one-one-left, when he heard "Batwing-127, this is tower. Line up and wait. Repeat, line up and wait."

Chapter 41

Hernandez acknowledged, pulled back on the thrust levers, and braked. Romeo had come to the front and was squatting between the two pilot seats. "What's the hold-up?"

"The tower gave us a 'line up and wait,'" the pilot replied, only a slight hint of concern in his voice.

"Why would they do that? There's no one in front of us."

"Could be anything. Another plane in the air with engine problems. They would hold us here and bring him in as a priority. I don't really know."

Their question was answered by the abrupt voice of the controller. "Batwing-127, cancel takeoff clearance. Turn left and exit the runway at alpha-four. Hold short of taxiway alpha."

Romeo saw a black SUV racing across the tarmac toward them at high speed. Rapping David on the shoulder, he called out, "They're coming! We need to roll! Now!"

Hernandez reacted instantly, shoving the levers partially forward and muscling the Gulfstream through a leaning turn.

The controller repeated, "Batwing-127, cancel takeoff clearance. Turn left and exit the runway at alpha-four. Hold short of taxiway alpha. How copy?"

On the runway, he took only a second to line up the plane before yanking the thrust levers to the stops. The roar of the twin turbojet engines filled the cabin and the sleek Gulfstream surged forward.

With more urgency, the tower ordered, "Batwing-127, your takeoff clearance has been cancelled! Immediately exit the runway at the next available turnoff and hold short of taxiway alpha. Acknowledge!"

The SUV, seeing the Gulfstream accelerating, veered across the grassy area, bouncing violently, in a feeble attempt to intercept it.

"Romeo, get back and strap in! Now!"

Heeding the pilot's command, Jones, pushing against the side walls for balance as the jet accelerated down the runway, spun and fell into the first empty seat and strapped in.

The tower controller, recognizing the pilot's intent, snatched up the red handset. A loud ringer jarred the duty control officer at the Guard alert facility. He answered at once, "Captain Sheehan," and heard the controller's alert.

"We have an unauthorized departure, one-one-left, Gulfstream Five, call sign Batwing-one-two-seven, turning right, now 300 feet and climbing."

"Copy. Standby." The duty control officer jabbed a button on his console, triggering the repeating blare of a Klaxon, and followed this action by switching on the microphone and announcing over the PA system, "Runway one-one-left, unauthorized departure, Gulfstream Five."

He moved the telephone handset back to his mouth. "Tower, my pilot is scrambling his jet."

"Captain Sheehan, I have FBI in the cab with me. They want to talk to...."

There was a loud clatter as an agent jerked the phone away. "This is Special Agent Brill," he barked. "This is a national security emergency. Order your pilot to bring that aircraft back to Tucson or shoot it down!"

Captain Sheehan took a deep breath before replying. "Special Agent Brill, you *do* realize, that order can only come from the NCA."

Ignoring the continuing, repeated instructions from the tower ordering him to turn back, Hernandez glanced over at Meade. "All right, our 250-knot airspeed limit under 10,000 feet isn't going to happen."

The astronaut, still scanning the sky above and ahead for another plane, nodded. "Sounds like it's time to barber-pole it."

The Gulfstream in the air and climbing fast, Hernandez pushed down the nose, bringing it to a level attitude.

"I'm going to stay lower. It'll give us better airspeed." He kept his eyes glued forward and shifted course ten degrees farther to the west. "Well, Captain, here's where we find out how good our luck is on those fifty-fifty odds."

Meade, also straining his vision, watched for anything in their path. "If there was a lad on strip alert, won't take longer than about ten minutes to find out. By the time he does catch us, we'll be over Mexico."

"That won't matter to him. He'll follow us anyway."

"Then what?"

"He'll try to talk us around. If that doesn't work, he'll need fairly high authorization to take us down."

"Authorization to shoot down a private aircraft over another country's airspace doesn't come quick and easy. What about our neighbors to the south? How are they going to take to this drama going on over their heads?"

"Hard to say, Captain. They might order him to turn around. They might even scramble a couple of their jets to persuade him. I doubt that would happen quickly enough to make a difference."

"I don't remember the fuel load on the F-16. How much time is he gonna have?"

"He'll be carrying enough for about ninety minutes. He's going to be fully loaded up with armaments and will probably use afterburner for takeoff and pursuit. That'll suck up about a third of it."

"So he'll have thirty minutes with us and thirty back."

"Roughly."

"Well...," Meade commented calmly, "it's gonna be tight."

Soon, the international border passed invisibly beneath them. The droning demands from the air traffic controller had ceased. The utter normalcy within the cockpit was providing, for a few minutes, a deceptive sense of security, suddenly shattered by the thundering boom as an F-16 with National Guard markings ripped too closely past their left side, the turbulence from the deliberately intimidating flyby shuddering the Gulfstream.

"That answers that," remarked Meade.

The powerful fighter jet, now well in front, banked dramatically, breaking hard to the left and circling around to fly apace with them, settling into a tight escort position off their left wing, near enough for David to be able to see the visored helmet and oxygen mask on the man's face. He switched the radio to the Guard frequency. Within seconds, a new voice crackled in their ears. "Gulfstream, you are ordered to return immediately to Tucson and land."

"Well, here goes," Hernandez muttered as he keyed his microphone. "F-16, this is Gulfstream. That's a negative. We are not able to return at this time."

"State your reason, Gulfstream. Are you experiencing mechanical difficulties?"

Tempted to take the offered excuse, David hesitated and checked his watch before he responded, "Negative, F-16. We are not experiencing any mechanical difficulties at this time."

"Gulfstream, are you under duress?"

"Negative, F-16, I am not. We are not under any threat from a passenger."

The two men listened to half a minute of silence, their muscles growing more tense with each passing second, until the unknown pilot's voice, now deeper in tone, stated, "If you do not turn around and return to Tucson, I have received orders to engage."

Hernandez responded, "One moment, please."

Romeo had returned to the cockpit and was again crouching behind their seats. "What's he saying?"

Meade answered, "He says if we don't turn this bird around and go home, he's gonna blow us out of the sky."

The big man's eyes widened almost imperceptibly, the only visible betrayal of his tightly contained emotions. "You believe him, Jimmy?"

"Hard to say. It's what he's trained to do."

Hernandez asked, "If we go back, what happens?"

Romeo's response was flat. "They'll kill us."

The pilot's voice interrupted them. "Gulfstream, I need your answer now!"

"Rock and a hard place," grunted Meade.

"We have one shot." Hernandez keyed his microphone. "F-16 pilot, my name is David Hernandez. Retired Air Force, assigned to 355th Tactical Fighter Squadron. We are on a legitimate mission of critical importance."

Another hesitation followed his words until the pilot responded, "State your mission."

Making certain his microphone was off, he turned to Meade. "We need to burn some minutes and I don't know all of the details of what you and your group have been involved in. Romeo, if it's okay with you, I'd prefer that Captain Meade answer him."

Jones shrugged. "Fine with me."

David looked at his copilot. "Captain Meade?"

Jimmy nodded. "Let's do it."

Activating his mic, Hernandez said, "F-16, I am not intimately familiar with the details of the mission. I am going to let my copilot provide the briefing."

Meade, already wearing his headpiece, keyed his microphone. "If I'm going to get turned into a fireball, I'd like to know who pulled the trigger. What's your name, son?"

"Lieutenant Jason Hollowell."

"Huh! I knew a Hollowell. Flew with him years ago. We called him 'Happy.' Happy Hollowell. Any relation, son?"

For the first time, the fighter pilot's voice showed a hint of emotion. "That's my pop."

"He still kicking?"

"Yes. He is. Identify yourself."

"The name's Meade, son. Jimmy Meade."

The only response to this was the sudden upward jink of the F-16 as the pilot climbed above them, broke right, and dropped into an uncomfortably close position off the starboard wing. David tightened his grip on the yoke somewhat, concentrating on maintaining a straight and level flight. The two jets were cruising together at Mach .86, as Meade turned his face to the window. The Guard pilot lifted his visor and stared.

Hollowell's voice on the radio, now half an octave higher, sputtered, "It is…you *are* Captain Meade."

"That I am. For better or worse. Now…they want me to give you the scoop on what we're up to, but I don't think there's enough time to share the whole story, son. So let me just tell you the bottom line. This plane is filled up with folks who have been fighting a little war lately. We've got scientists and an engineer, a couple of authors, a TV producer, an Army Ranger, a Marine, an FBI bureau chief, a police detective, and yours truly. Maybe you heard about our little tussle not too long ago with the former head of Homeland Security."

"Yes, sir."

"Well, we thought that after we took him down, we were done with the whole shebang. But we were wrong. It goes a lot deeper and a lot farther than we even dreamed. Into places that would give you nightmares, son. Including the places…where your orders come from. We hightailed it out of Tucson because some men were coming, hell-bent on killing us. Every single one of us. They already tried it at the TV station. You mighta heard about that, too."

"I did, sir."

"Now that we're wheels up and out of their reach, they want you to finish the job they couldn't get done. If that's fine with you…if that's the kind of detail you signed on for when you volunteered for this outfit, then I suggest you put on your brakes, back a safe distance away…wouldn't want Happy Hollowell's son to get hurt…he'd never forgive me…and punch that pickle, light up one of those Sparrows on the rail, and make all of us nothing but a big white puff of smoke up here in this clear blue sky."

He paused for a moment, then continued, "I'm sure that you shooting down an unarmed plane filled with American civilians will make your daddy proud. Oh…and one more thing…when you get back to base safe and sound, remember to tell him I said 'hi.'"

Meade stopped. The three men in the cockpit waited in tense silence, hearing only the background hum of the engines, as nearly a minute passed before their earphones crackled to life. "Captain Meade, my pop always said you laid it on pretty thick, sir."

Jimmy chuckled into the microphone. "He did, did he?"

The young pilot and the old astronaut locked eyes on each other for a time until, through the plexiglass of the fighter jet, Meade saw him raise his gloved hand to his helmet and salute. Jimmy returned it smartly, and the F-16 abruptly broke hard right and, within mere seconds, had disappeared from sight.

▽

The balance of the long flight was uneventful. Per his plan, Hernandez directed the Gulfstream over the open water of the Pacific Ocean after passing Cabo San Lucas, and switched off the transponder. Following a less than straight route, he avoided the intermittent radar installations along the west coast of Mexico and the rapidly passing smaller states of Central America. Remaining over the ocean, he skirted the coastline of South America.

Inside the cabin of the fleeing craft, Judtson stood next to one of the tables and stared at the disassembled laptop in front of Scott. Two of the other seats were occupied by Bowman and Wheeler.

"What happened?" Judtson asked.

Matt explained, "During the shoot-out, my laptop took a bullet."

"That's where the video is...the one of Beckleman and his revelations?"

"Yeah."

"Is it lost?"

"Don't think so. The slug nicked the housing of the hard drive but didn't shatter the disk itself. Scott thinks he can pull it out and put it in another one."

Without looking up from his delicate work, Scott added, "There's a problem. I need a matching hard drive to be able to do that. Not exactly something I carry around with me."

"Don't we have one in the other laptops that'll work?"

The tech shrugged. "Maybe. Between all of us, we have seven. I'll check them after I've finished removing this."

Walking up the aisle toward the front of the plane, Judtson passed Saylor, who was staring out his window and squeezing the armrests of his seat so tightly that his knuckles were white.

He paused by his best friend. "You okay?"

Tearing his gaze away from what had been a constant vigilance on the wing, Saylor faced him and nodded. "I hate this," he uttered intensely.

"I know. Need anything?"

"Just my feet on the ground."

Trying a reassuring smile, Judtson replied, "Soon, pal."

He had not even moved away, when Saylor turned back to the view outside. Returning to his seat beside Kelsey, he briefed her on the status of the video. Speaking softly, she reflected, "I'm still trying to wrap my mind around what they told us he said. I mean, the Illuminati! And the six names. Not one of them is someone I would have guessed as being at the top of that group."

"I understand. You know, during the time I spent researching the Illuminati for my book, the people I interviewed...the ones I chalked off as crackpots...all said the same thing. That those really calling the shots...the men and women who were the most evil...the most dangerous...without exception were the very last ones you would suspect."

▽

Less than an hour from their destination, Hernandez left the controls in Meade's hands and walked back into the cabin, finding Romeo, Judtson, and Kelsey sitting together at a table. The lanky pilot lowered himself into the fourth seat, obviously with something on his mind. "Do we have any reason to be concerned about landing at El Alto in La Paz?"

Kelsey answered with a question. "What kind of concern?"

"Well...considering the close call we had leaving, I was wondering if the folks you're up against might have a welcoming committee waiting there. I don't particularly want to run into a reverse of what we escaped from in Tucson."

Kelsey shrugged her shoulders. "We left under a bogus flight plan. Plus, we're leaving a few bread crumbs."

"Bread crumbs?" Hernandez puzzled.

Kelsey turned toward Scott, who was across the aisle taking a break from the laptop, stretched back in a reclining seat, his eyes closed. "Scott, where are we right now on the bread crumbs?"

The tech tapped a button and adjusted the seat to full upright, rotated it to face them, and checked his watch. "Uh, about an hour and a half ago, you used your credit card from a hotel Wi-Fi in Hermosillo to purchase two one-way airline tickets to depart late tonight from Mexico City for Beirut, Lebanon. A little over an hour ago, Chris used his credit card from a hotel Wi-Fi in Cabo San Lucas to rent a boat and some scuba gear. And right about now, Lisa is using her credit card at a resort near Cancun to order room service."

Hearing this from her seat, Lisa bubbled, "Cool! What did I order?"

He grinned at her. "Double cheeseburger, well done, a six-pack of Corona on ice, and a bag of limes."

"Perfect!"

Hernandez shook his head in amazement. "Got to love the Internet."

Romeo spoke up. "They might still see through everything, or go to El Alto just to cover the bases, since we've used it in the past. David, any ideas?"

"One. According to my maps, a small unmanned airport is located a mile or so north of Arica, Chile. Not set up with radar. I'm not sure whether they even *have* a tower. It will be dark by then. We could come in low from the west. Their runway heads roughly northwest to southeast and it is long enough for us. We could sneak in and be on the ground before whoever runs the place even spots us."

"How close is it to Lake Titicaca?"

"Straight line, it's less than sixty miles, Romeo. But all uphill into the Andes."

"Is there a road?" Judtson asked.

"Again, according to the maps, yes. A small highway runs from Arica through Tacna and to the lake. I have no idea what shape it's in."

Kelsey glanced at Judtson and Romeo for a moment before concluding, "I think it's a good idea. We'll figure out how to get up the mountain once we're there. Romeo, what do you think?"

The Ranger thought it through aloud. "The choice is a small coastal resort town or the possibility of being locked up in a Bolivian jail. We've been lucky so far. No point in pushing it. Let's do it."

Judtson agreed and Hernandez returned to the cockpit.

Chapter 42

T HE LANDING WENT WITHOUT A PROBLEM, and David Hernandez' prediction proved to be accurate. As he taxied the Gulfstream to the main building in the darkness with the only illumination coming from the craft's lights, a short, round, ruddy-faced man, wearing a wide-brimmed hat, lumbered slowly out of an old pickup truck to greet them. The pilot set the brakes and killed the engines while Romeo lowered the hatch. As prearranged, Carlos was the first to disembark and, with a wide smile on his face and his hand extended, promptly strode up to the man. The two began a rapid-fire exchange in Spanish as the others came down the steps, carrying their luggage and gear.

After less than five minutes, Carlos walked away and returned to the group. "It appears that our luck has held. Our gracious host, Mr. Sambrosa, has invited us to be guests tonight at his home, which is located here at the airport. His son will be returning in their helicopter tomorrow morning with a group of turistas."

"What time?" Romeo queried, a hint of mistrust in his tone.

Villarreal shrugged. "Our host is not certain but believes it will be fairly early."

Kelsey's voice was far less suspicious and much more excited. "A helicopter! That's great! Is it big enough for all of us?"

"No. Well, actually, yes and no. It will hold twelve passengers, but not if it is going as high in altitude as Puma Punku. To make it to the top, he can carry no more than nine at a time. So it will require two, perhaps three trips. However, Lake Titicaca is apparently a very short flight from here."

"Tell him he has a deal" – she paused – "unless anyone can think of a better plan."

No one spoke. Villarreal turned back to the man and gave him the news. His words were greeted warmly, their host's rotund face splitting into a toothy grin. At Sambrosa's instruction, they loaded their gear in the back of the pickup. He gave Carlos directions for them to follow around the building to his home, and wedged himself back behind the wheel as Chili jumped into the passenger seat to ride with him.

∇

Two black SUVs stopped at the closed metal gate. Davis Ulrigg, having raced down from Phoenix with a total of seven agents, all clad in assault armor emblazoned with bright orange FBI lettering, emerged from the vehicle and pressed the button on the intercom. A second later a female voice came from the speaker. "Who is there?"

"FBI. Open the gate immediately!"

"I am sorry. I did not get that name. Could you repeat it, please?"

The senior agent, his face already turning a brilliant red, raised his voice at the device. "FB.... Awww, the hell with it." To his men, he brusquely ordered, "Ram the gate!"

Not one of the seven raised the issue that they did not have an arrest warrant, a search warrant, or probable cause to perform such a precipitous act. The agent closest to the lead vehicle jumped back in, slammed the door, and dropped the big truck into reverse. Backing up forty yards, he slapped the shifter into drive and gunned the engine just as Ulrigg heard from the speaker "Oh, I am very sorry. You are on the list." With that, the reinforced steel double gates began to quickly swing outward.

The driver, unable to react in time and attempting to remain centered on the opening, rammed the front of the truck into the outer edges of the two steel gates, which were at that moment oriented almost exactly at forty-five-degree angles. The inertia of the truck was insufficient to overcome the structurally optimum resistance of the gates, and both front corners of the SUV crumpled inward loudly as the vehicle came to a shuddering halt, deploying the air bag violently into the face of the stunned driver.

Two agents ran to him, flinging his door open to help him out, as Ulrigg heard an admonition from the intercom. "There appears to be an obstruction blocking the gate. Please remove the obstacle now."

The dazed agent was hefted from the seat and placed on the curb. One of the men, using a knife, cut off the now deflated air bag and tossed it aside, hopped in, restarted the stalled engine, and backed up a few feet. The instant the gates were no longer entangled with the vehicle, they began closing rapidly. In the confusion, the only one who noticed this was Ulrigg, who ran to the nearer of the two gates and grabbed the edge with his good hand, leaning back to stop the progress, but the motor on the gate was too powerful. He was pulled along, his leather-soled shoes wildly sliding on the concrete, and the gates came back together, pinching his left hand between them.

The loud wail of pain instantly caught the attention of the agents. One of the men retrieved a crowbar from the rear of their truck and, with the help of two others, was able to extricate Ulrigg's bloody hand. Cradling it against his chest, he squeezed his eyes tightly shut from the agony, and commanded, "Ram it again. Blow it up. I don't give a damn. *Get in there now!*"

Members of the team were certain that the female voice from the intercom was suppressing mirth as it said, "A threat has been detected. Warning...do not attempt to enter the premises. A threat has been detected. Warning...do not attempt to enter the premises. A threat has been...."

The FBI agents heard a blaring Klaxon sounding from somewhere inside the wall. There was a loud hiss of hydraulics, and six evenly spaced cylindrical steel bollards, which had been perfectly flush with the concrete entrance, rose in front of the gate and locked into position at a height of four feet. Rotating red beacons came to life at the top of the walls on either side of the gate.

As one of the other agents wrapped Ulrigg's hand with a bandage, the injured agent barked,

"Get ladders! Go over the gate!"

Two of the men ran to the back of the second truck, opened the rear gate, and pulled out two collapsible aluminum ladders, unfolding and snapping them into fully extended positions. As the first man rushed forward and leaned his ladder against the top of the gate, showers of sparks exploded at the points of contact. Simultaneously, the agent screamed, his body shuddering. One of the other agents, seeing this, ran at him from the side and rammed the jittering man with his shoulder, knocking him free and to the ground. The jolted agent, both of his hands blackened from the contact, lay unconscious on the driveway.

$$\triangledown$$

Judtson, Saylor, Kelsey, Kenny, Romeo, and Scott were relaxing on webbed chairs alongside the large swimming pool behind the Sambrosa home. A young girl of nine, introduced earlier as Lucinda, the man's daughter, carried out a large galvanized-steel bucket overflowing with ice, the necks of several glass bottles sprouting out from the mound. She was holding the wire handle with both hands and, struggling under the weight of the bucket, waddled awkwardly toward them. Bowman, seeing her approaching, jumped up and attempted to relieve her of the load. She smiled at him and shook her head, clumsily twisting her body away from his grasp, and continued to the handmade wooden table where they were gathered.

Everyone watched as she tried twice to lift the bucket to the tabletop, her slender arms straining, failing both times, before Kelsey leaned forward and gripped the sides, helping her.

Kenny, back in his seat, asked the girl in Spanish what she had brought for them, and translated, "Coronas and piña pops."

He thanked her and the girl left.

Kelsey grinned at him. "Kenny, what's a piña pop?"

"Soft drink made with pineapple juice. It's delicious."

"Sounds like it." She dug into the bucket, pulled out a bottle of the yellow-orange drink, and turned to Judtson. "Want one?"

"I do."

Using the bottle opener tied with a string to the handle of the bucket, she pried off the caps, gave one of the bottles to him, and quaffed eagerly from the other. Finishing the swig, she made a loud pop-smack sound with her mouth. "Oh my, that is wonderful!"

As Romeo and Kenny grabbed beers, Saylor helped himself to one of the soft drinks. "Once we get up there, how will we find Luis?"

Romeo took a long draw on the Corona, then replied, "Not sure. I sent him a text message telling him that we were coming and that we'd first go to Bal's camp. And afterward, head to the lake. I never got an answer, and now we're out of service range. I guess we'll have to hope he sees us."

Kelsey looked over at Scott, who, since their arrival, had been staring forlornly at the screen of his phone. "Scott, don't you want something to drink?"

The tech responded only with a subtle shake of his head.

"Is something wrong?"

Still without glancing up, he answered softly, "Just trying to get a signal."

"Hoping to catch a message from Luis?"

"No. I mean, yes, of course. But I'd really like to log on to the game."

Judtson snorted. "Game? Now? You're kidding."

He finally tore his eyes away from the phone and connected with Judtson's. His voice flat and neutral, he explained, "Not that kind of game. I want to watch what's happening at the house."

"I don't understand."

"Well, there's a fairly hefty assortment of security measures installed at Kelsey's, ideas that Romeo and I cooked up. All nonlethal but pretty cool stuff. And all set up so that if we're there when we get attacked, he, Chili, or I can monitor what's happening and activate them. Since we were all leaving, that wasn't an option. I didn't want to use any sort of an automated program. They're still kind of lame. Easy to outwit. So I linked the whole system, all the cameras and the defensive measures, to a popular gaming site. The second the bad guys pull up to the gates, they trip an alert which signals a slew of top players. Beta testers for the big gaming companies. Whoever logs on first gets to manage all the defenses."

Saylor, staring wide-eyed at Gumble, burst out laughing. Catching his breath, he said, "So if the FBI shows up and tries to get in, some geek somewhere who thinks he's only playing a game will be deploying all the defenses against them?"

"Yep," Scott acknowledged, a subtle smirk on his face. "He won't know he's playing against the real FBI. He'll think he's playing against another gamer."

▽

The agent with the badly burned hands had regained consciousness and was sitting up, leaning against the side of the damaged SUV. Ulrigg, his throbbing left hand tightly bandaged, his right in a cast, felt helpless. He had directed his team to carefully place one of the ladders against the tall wall beside the gate, using a short rope tied to one of the rungs. There was apparently a conductive metal cap on the wall, as the ladder sparked on contact. The men pulled the ladder back down and immediately began wrapping the top rails with a blanket to serve as an insulator. Finishing this, they again set the ladder. This time no sparks emanated.

Working efficiently, one man climbed the ladder and carefully arranged another heavy blanket on the top course, draping it partially down both sides. Once this insulator was in place, two men on the ground passed the second lightweight ladder to him and, by pulling it upward one rung at a time, he was able to manhandle it over the wall and lower it down the other side, leaning the rails against the blanket.

Seeing the process completed, Ulrigg directed the five fully ambulatory men to go over and in, leaving both the still-dazed driver who had rammed the gate, and the burned agent behind with him. The now smaller team, carrying assault rifles and a compact battering ram, rapidly scaled the wall, fanned out, and sprinted across the wide, flat gravel-covered expanse toward the house. As they neared the halfway point, several sprinkler heads popped up and began spraying. Two of the men were caught in the fluid onslaught. The liquid drenching them was not water, but a rancid, foul-smelling concoction which triggered instantaneous and involuntary vomiting, blurring their vision and doubling them over in torment.

The three remaining team members, abandoning their uncontrollably retching colleagues, rushed to the front entrance. As the first reached out to check the knob, there was an ominous click, and the entrance opened a few inches. Charging his weapon, he used the barrel to push the door farther open, revealing the gleaming Italian marble floor of the spacious foyer. He moved forward cautiously; his partners charged their own rifles and held back to cover him. As he leaned in over the threshold, his ears, straining to pick up any sounds in the total silence, only heard a slow, steady dripping. Locating the source, he noticed that it was what appeared to be a fire sprinkler head, suspended from the ceiling a few feet from the entrance. Assuming the fixture had developed a slow leak, he glanced at his backup and nodded curtly before stepping inside.

The second man, Special Agent Plotz, moved to the opening and was about to follow, when his partner suddenly shrieked in surprise and began flailing his arms wildly. His rifle, flung from his grip, crashed into a tall, elegant vase, shattering it. The first man's feet and legs were a comical blur as he frantically tried to keep his balance on what had suddenly become an impossibly slick surface. The entire unchoreographed dance lasted less than three seconds until the FBI agent's feet shot out from beneath him and he fell, the back of his head absorbing the majority of the impact onto the rock-hard surface.

The remaining agents, now fighting off a growing sense of panic, stared at their partner, saw the rhythmic rising and falling of his chest, and concluded that he was unconscious. Maintaining a firm grip on the edge of the door, Plotz stepped in and, with extreme care, edged around the perimeter of the foyer, avoiding the thin, clear film of liquid which, with a different angle of lighting, he could now see shimmering in a pool around his inert cohort.

The next man, Special Agent Dimmle, following his path, took a cautious step forward and bent down. Touching the puddle with his gloved fingertip, he sniffed. "Smells like silicone."

▽

Trudy Benkowitz, tears streaming down her cheeks from near hysterical laughter, kept the two still-ambulatory men on one monitor as she quickly checked the three outside the gate and saw that they were no threat. Finally, on a third monitor, she zoomed in tightly on one of the two figures on the grounds. Her motions fluid and expert, she captured a short video, opened another window, and posted the clip on a gamer's blog, commenting, "Check this out! This is the best CG vomit I've EVER seen! Each guy's puke even looks different!"

Returning her hyper-attention to the interior, Trudy saw that the image of an old-fashioned traffic light had switched from green to red. Grunting, she tried the various video feeds and found that she did have control of those. Only the row of icons across the bottom of the screen, now a light gray rather than a solid black, had been disabled. The only exception was a compact image of a radio tower with waves radiating around it. The label read, "Jammer." She clicked it.

On the screen above the traffic signal was a curt message: "Hold for level two."

▽

Plotz keyed his microphone and attempted to contact Ulrigg to inform their superior that they had made it inside. He frowned. "My comm is down. Does yours work?"

Dimmle tried his. "No."

With a shrug, Plotz grunted, "Let's keep going."

The men began methodically searching the sprawling estate. Staying together, they first passed through the ornate living room and then proceeded slowly into the dining room and kitchen. Finding no one, they selected one of the halls and systematically worked their way down the length: one agent taking the rooms on the right, the other taking the left, both shouting "Clear!" after checking each space.

Reaching a junction in the hallway, Dimmle complained, "I feel like I'm checking a maze. This place is huge."

Plotz nodded and pulled a felt-tip marker from his pocket, marking an X on the wall. "At least we'll know we've already done this one."

"So what? Could be a whole group in here, circling around us, playing hide-and-seek."

"True. Well, you saw all the cameras. There has to be a security center with monitors. If we can find it, we might be able to check the whole place."

"Good idea. Let's double-time it down these halls and look for that room instead of clearing one at a time."

Plotz nodded again and the two moved out, walking briskly, only momentarily cautious when opening a closed door, and again splitting the sides. Five minutes of hastily glancing into the rooms paid off.

Swinging a door open wide, Plotz peered inside and shouted, "Found it."

His partner joined him at the entrance. "I'll go in first."

He executed a textbook entrance and worked his way into the large workroom, his ears immediately picking up a faint hum and repetitive clicking sound. After checking all of the empty cubicles and passing Matt Wheeler's work area, he found what he was seeking. To his left, on a raised platform was a sprawling desk filled with a total of six computer monitors, arranged in a semicircle. From where he stood, he could see that each of the screens currently displayed a different view of the grounds and house.

Before moving in that direction, Plotz wanted to make certain that the rest of the room was unoccupied, so he veered in the opposite direction and found Chris Ashby's area. The source of the hum and click became obvious. On top of the worktable was some sort of mechanism. After ensuring that no one was lurking behind the table, he examined the device more closely. Mounted high at one end of it was a large plastic bin, which appeared to be filled with some sort of powder and was feeding the material into a wide-mouthed hopper. The machinery in the middle was a mystery to him. At the opposite end was another plastic container, and he could see the fine powder emerging from a small chute and trickling into the receptacle. His first impulse was to taste a sample of the powder, but he thought better of it.

Finishing his sweep of the room, he moved toward Scott's desk. Having a fairly expensive home theater system himself, he noted with appreciation the array of massive ceiling-mounted speakers surrounding the platform in a wide circle, and the two large black subwoofers bracketing the desk.

Plotz paused, glanced around one more time, and then shouted, "Clear!"

As Dimmle, hearing this, rushed in, Plotz noticed the cell phone on the desk. Two words suddenly appeared on the formerly dark screen: "Message Sent."

He only had a split second to ponder this, when all of the lights in the room abruptly extinguished, as did the six computer monitors. In the pitch darkness of the windowless room, a deep voice from behind him boomed, "Eat lead, G-Man!"

He whirled to the sound just as a barrage of thunderously loud gunfire erupted from multiple locations around him. Plotz dropped to the floor and triggered his rifle in the direction where he thought the voice had originated. Dimmle, already in motion crossing the room toward his partner as the lights went out, heard the shouted voice and the gunfire and, fortunately, hit the deck. His maneuver saved his life as the bullets from Plotz' wild firing swept through the space he had occupied only moments before.

Amid the piercing cacophony, Plotz lifted his finger from the trigger as his mind registered that there were no visible muzzle flashes accompanying the shooting around him. Cupping his hands around his mouth, he yelled over the din, "DIMMLE!" and repeated the shouts several times until he thought he noticed a muffled answer mixed in with the deafening shots.

"DIMMLE! IT'S FAKE!"

He received back a disgusted "I KNOW!"

Plotz stood and switched on his barrel-mounted flashlight, swinging the AK-47 around until he located the bank of three computers in a freestanding rack he had seen earlier. Pulling the trigger, he emptied his clip into the cases. Instantly, the audio assault ceased and the lights came back on. Blinking in the sudden brightness, with his ears still ringing badly, Plotz saw his partner stand unsteadily where he had dived.

$$\triangledown$$

All of the security systems, including the video cameras operated through equipment located outside Scott's work area, were still online. Trudy Benkowitz saw the two CG agents, who had made it all the way to the deep interior, slowly walk toward each other. Checking the perimeter view, she saw that the CG agent who had been dazed from the SUV's impact with the gates was now climbing the ladder to assist his teammates. In the background, she also saw two more black SUVs pull up, disgorging a total of twelve more of the agents.

As the new contingent of CG foes scaled the wall, the traffic light at the corner of her screen changed from red to green and she heard Scott Gumble's prerecorded voice say, "Welcome to level two."

Cackling maniacally, she laced her fingers together, rotated her joined hands, and popped her knuckles. "All right! Let's rock and roll!"

Chapter 43

After overindulging in the sweet and spicy feast prepared by Sambrosa's wife and daughters, the group had been shown to their sleeping quarters, which was when they discovered that, although their host referred to the meandering estate as his home, it was actually a colonial-style inn with thirty guest rooms.

The early morning sun, blocked by the majestic Andes which towered above them to the east, was muted and indirect as it filtered through the curtains. Judtson sat on the edge of the bed and pulled on his socks. He scratched behind Rocky's ear and idly listened through the partially open door to the sound of the shower until it ceased. As he buttoned the flannel shirt, donned in deference to the decidedly chillier weather they were soon to experience, Kelsey emerged from the bathroom, her hair tightly turbaned with a thick brown towel, and a large green towel encircling her body.

With a false pout, he jutted his lower lip. "You're all covered up."

Gracefully traversing the distance between them, she straddled his legs and sat, a lascivious smile on her face. Draping her arms onto his shoulders, she murmured, "Gift wrapping. Happy birthday!"

"But…today isn't my birthday."

In mock surprise, she jerked up her arms, teased, "Oh, darn! Guess you'll have to wait," and began to stand.

He grabbed her shoulders and pushed her back down on his lap.

"Huh-uh. You stay right here."

Kelsey, with a husky chuckle, reached up and grabbed his hands, lifted them away, and stood, moving toward her open suitcase. "No time. We need to get dressed. Sambrosa's son is probably ready to go. And I want breakfast. I bet it's terrific."

Judtson, sighing audibly, acquiesced and watched her turn away. "Hey! That's amazing."

Detecting change in his tone, she stopped and eyed him curiously. "What?"

Pointing, he stuttered, "Your thigh…. Your gunshot wound from the FEMA camp….

It's…wow! You healed fast!"

Her eyebrows arched. She hastily took three steps closer to the window and turned her body, orienting her leg so that the part in question was facing away from him and toward the light. With a nervous giggle, she pushed open the curtain and insisted, "No, I didn't. It's still there. Come look at it by the window."

Judtson walked over beside her, dropped to one knee, and stared. The shiny line of smooth scar tissue was clearly visible. "That's weird. I was sure I couldn't…."

"It was just the light. Or a shadow. Nope. Sorry, I am no longer perfect."

He rose and kissed her before saying, "True. Damaged goods."

She returned the kiss quickly and twisted away. "Well…maybe you'll do better with your next girl."

▽

Breakfast finished, Kelsey and Judtson circled the building to the spot where the helicopter was parked. Dropping her bags on the ground, she grabbed the lapels of his jacket and adjusted them. "You look like a lumberjack in that outfit."

He was dressed in the heavy plaid flannel shirt, brown corduroy jeans, and high laced boots. He slowly appraised her. Abandoning her signature T-shirts in deference to the colder clime, she wore a snug-fitting, long-sleeved black turtleneck sweater; tight black stretch pants, which disappeared into the tops of her black boots; and a tanned calfskin jacket with a fleece lining.

"Well, except for the jacket, you look like one of the X-Men."

"Cool!"

He reached forward and touched a slender gold chain bearing a gold eight-pointed star, which dangled around her neck.

"First time I've seen you wear any jewelry."

"Like it?"

"Yeah. I do."

"My father gave it to me. He told me it would keep me safe."

Their host's badly rusting pickup rattled loudly to a dusty stop in front of them, and Scott and Romeo emerged.

"Good morning, guys. Where were you?"

"Hi, Kelsey…Judtson. Went into Arica," answered Romeo. "Mr. Sambrosa told Carlos that we could get cell service."

"Did you get a message from Luis?"

"Yes. He told us to go to Bal's camp near Puma Punku, and he'd meet us."

"Has he seen anyone come or go since the first message?"

"He didn't say."

"Were you able to find out anything else while you were there?"

Scott grinned broadly. "The FBI moved on your house. Oh, man…you should see the video."

Judtson was amused by the tech's expression. "I'd love to. Didn't you download it?"

"No. The connection speed stank. Would've taken forever. The video is great, though. Ulrigg's going to have a cast on both hands now."

Romeo interrupted, "From what Scott could find on the 'net, just about every person in the country with a badge is searching for us."

"Did the plan work? Do they think we have Beckleman alive?"

"Yes. It worked. But I think it's safe to say that Kenny's career with the FBI is history."

"That'll be the least of his problems if he's in a federal prison," Judtson commented dryly.

Saylor rounded the corner of the building, toting his own bag, and joined them. The first thing his eyes fixed upon was the helicopter parked on the hard-packed dirt field.

"How old is that thing?" he asked, dubious.

Romeo grunted. "Probably World War Two surplus. I don't even recognize it."

David Hernandez suddenly appeared from behind the craft, wiping his greasy hands on a towel and, hearing their remarks, explained, "Actually, it's a Sikorsky UH-19. Several were sold to the Chilean government a long time ago. They used to call it the Chickasaw, and Sambrosa's son has done a fairly good job maintaining it. The way it looks, he's tweaked the engine and transmission and upgraded the rotor blades."

"So, it'll fly?"

The pilot nodded at Saylor. "It's not the Gulfstream and I wouldn't want to take an extended trip in it or fly it in bad weather, but it should take you where you want to go."

Saylor was unconvinced. "David, can't we take the Gulfstream up to the lake or the camp?"

"No place to land it up there. Sorry."

"Saylor," offered Judtson, "you can stay here."

Setting his jaw in determination, his best friend replied, "No. I'm going."

$$\triangledown$$

It had been decided that the first group would be Judtson, Kelsey, Saylor, Chris, Carlos, Bal, Romeo, Lisa, and Eunice. Sambrosa's son, whom everyone called "Gordo," and who did not look older than seventeen, performed a final walk-around of the helicopter, accompanied by Hernandez. The circuit completed, he hopped inside the cabin, turned around, and leaned out, picking up the rigid plastic milk crate used as a step and carrying it to the cockpit as Hernandez closed the hatch. Standing the crate on its end where the pilot's seat should have been, he dropped onto it and buckled in.

Judtson stole a peek at Saylor as their youthful pilot started the engine, and saw that his friend's face was already white as a sheet and they were yet to take off. As the rotors began to turn, Rocky, who had been prowling around the cabin and sniffing, dashed to Judtson's side and sat tightly against him. The engine backfired, the sound louder than a shotgun blast. Saylor reached down to grip the armrests and pulled one of them off in his hand. Snorting loudly, he threw it on the cabin floor and began digging behind his hips for a seat belt. Eunice, in the seat beside him, patted his arm reassuringly and said, "There ain't any."

"There *ain't* any? There *ain't* any?" he snapped, his voice almost an octave higher than normal.

Grinning broadly, she shook her head. "Boy, you're shakin' like a hound dog trying to pass a peach pit. If you don't simmer down, you're gonna burst a blood vessel."

His head and eyes swiveling back and forth between her and the window, he croaked, "I can't!"

"Lookee here, we're gonna be just fine. That boy up front has done this a heap of times and it's only a hop, skip, and jump up that hill. Nothin's gonna go wrong."

The monumental effort he was exerting to bring himself under control was plainly etched upon his face. Focusing all of his attention on Cahane, Saylor took in a huge breath, let it out slowly and, with his voice much steadier, mimicked her accent. "Don't piss on my leg, missy, and tell me it's rainin'."

The comeback surprised her. Rearing back in the seat, triggering a sharp cracking, snapping sound from the frame, she slapped her knees and guffawed loudly. Her mirth subsiding, she slapped him on the thigh hard enough to leave a mark. "You're all right, Doc Costello."

The rotation of the blades jarringly increased. Within seconds, the helicopter violently lurched upward and, still only mere feet from the ground, sickeningly gyrated around until the nose was oriented to the base of the mountains. Saylor lunged forward and madly dug into the back pocket of the seat in front of him.

"Where are the damn airsickness bags?" he whined. "It's regulation! There are *always* supposed to be airsickness bags."

Eunice poked him in his side with her elbow and pointed over at the floor between his knees. "Just toss your cookies down there. You won't be the first."

He leaned slightly and stared at the heavily textured deck, partially lifting up one of his feet and hearing a sound like velcro separating. Disgusted, he grimaced. "My shoes are stuck to the floor!"

She chortled and jammed a pinch of tobacco into her mouth as the craft canted sharply forward, the tips of the blades whipping dangerously close to the ground; and the chopper rapidly accelerated.

▽

As the helicopter clawed its way into the thinner air of the high altitude of the camp, the aging engine, revved to the maximum and laboring mightily, began producing a nerve-racking cacophony of squeaking, rattling, and grinding noises, the entire craft developing a disconcerting shuddering vibration. With each new sound and quiver painfully reflected upon Saylor's face, he unconsciously grabbed Cahane's hand and squeezed it tightly as they barely cleared a ridge, coming so close that the chopping roar of the blades echoed back at the craft and he could make out the individual rocks strewn about the surface. Without a word, she reached across with her free hand and placed it on top of his.

Within minutes Bal's camp came into view, and Gordo brought them in so fast that Saylor was certain they were going to crash rather than land. At what appeared to him to be the last possible moment, they decelerated so abruptly that he felt his stomach slam into his diaphragm, and the chattering, shaking aircraft landed hard, bouncing once on its rails until coming to a stop.

Saylor jerked his hand away, leaped up from his seat and ran to the hatch, twisted the handle, and opened it, jumping out before Gordo could bring the milk-crate step. He was followed immediately by the golden retriever. The rest of the group, taking the time to gather their gear, with Judtson grabbing his friend's forgotten bag, disembarked in a more dignified fashion.

Eunice, Lisa, Kelsey, and Judtson gathered beyond the still-swirling blade and watched

Saylor as he and Rocky both walked in apparently mindless circles farther away from the helicopter, with Rocky satisfying his bodily needs and Saylor simply staring down at the ground beneath his feet and grinning.

"He looks as happy as a dead pig in the sunshine."

Judtson swung to face Eunice. "Happy as a dead...? That doesn't make any.... What does that mean?"

As Lisa giggled at his consternation, the detective explained, "You'd hafta see it to understand. When a pig dies out in the sunshine and starts to desiccate, the skin or somethin' contracts, makes him look like he's got a big ole smile on his chops."

The engine on the helicopter picked up tempo, building to an earsplitting scream as it bit through the thin air, straining to gain sufficient lift. The group edged backward as Gordo, with a broad smile and a wave through the cracked side window of the cockpit, muscled the craft up. Again barely off the ground, it swung ninety degrees and chattered away.

Eunice spit and tucked another wad of tobacco in her mouth. "Well, I'd better see to our boy there." She ambled off toward Saylor, who was now sitting on a small boulder, hugging his knees and rocking back and forth.

As she departed, Kelsey remarked, "She is a real...I have no clue what the word is!"

"I'm sure *she* would have an appropriate phrase for you to use," Judtson quipped, shaking his head. "Lisa, does she always talk that way?"

"No. Actually, she doesn't. I think it's her way of handling stress. Don't you just love it, though?"

"Yes!" Kelsey exclaimed, smiling in Cahane's direction. "I think it's adorable."

"It's certainly colorful," he admitted. "Even if it does demolish every rule of grammar I've ever learned."

The three joined the others as Sam Jonassen approached Bal at a trot.

"Dr. Singh, I didn't know you were coming."

"We found it necessary to leave rather hastily. Sam, you appear to be agitated. Is anything amiss?"

"Yes. Well, everyone is okay and everything, but right after our last conversation, a group of soldiers arrived and made us leave the island."

"Leave the island? For what reason?"

"They didn't say. Only that our permit was revoked. Wouldn't let us pack up our stuff. Just escorted us to the boats."

Growing concern spread over Bal's face. "Did the soldiers threaten you?"

Jonassen shook his head. "No. Not really, anyway. They had rifles and...I think it was pretty clear they'd use them if we argued. Of course none of us did."

Romeo, hearing this, commented under his breath, "Good decision," and turned to Kelsey. "It sounds as if all of them were cleared off the island right before Luis followed those men here with your father and Mrs. Costello."

She agreed. "Seems like it. His text said they went out to an island. I'll bet it's the same one. Obviously, they needed to get our people away first."

"But why?" Judtson asked. "Are they holding them on the island?"

Jonassen, trying to follow the conversation, cut in, "Who? What men? What are you talking about?"

Kelsey took a minute to describe her father's abduction and the text message from Luis.

When she finished, he shook his head emphatically. "If the two of them were taken out to the same island, I can't imagine where they are being kept. It's fairly small and the only structures are in villages the Aymara occupy."

"Unless," she objected, "there's a way into that thing you found buried...and that entrance is on the island. By the way, has Luis come to the camp? We're supposed to meet him here."

"No. At least no one by that name has shown up. And, actually, we haven't had any newcomers or strangers around."

His eyes casually sweeping the craggy perimeter of the camp area, Romeo hazarded a guess. "Have you had things disappearing lately? Last couple of days or so."

The postdoc raised a quizzical eyebrow. "Disappearing? Like what?"

"Food...water...clothing?"

He thought briefly. "Now that you mention it, a couple of the students complained that their private food stashes...you know, stuff their parents sent...had been taken. They were accusing some of the others. And one of the students is even missing a parka."

Romeo nodded.

The group, led by Jonassen, toted their luggage and gear to the cluster of tents, leaving Romeo behind. He stood in the open field for a minute, slowly surveying his surroundings. Locating what he was seeking, he walked directly toward a large rock outcropping a hundred yards away. At the base of it, he stopped, jamming his hands into his pockets, and his loud, clear voice boomed, "If I was going to keep an eye on the camp, this is where I would be."

A few seconds passed, when he heard the sound of loose pebbles skittering down a hard surface, followed by the soft scraping of boots on rock. Emerging from behind one of the larger boulders high in the formation, came Luis, a half-cautious, half-happy expression on his face.

"Man, you look like hell!" Romeo said, as a means of greeting him.

Navigating down the escarpment, his ex-partner was filthy, unshaved, and bedraggled, wrapped in a too-large fur-lined parka. "What do you expect? Before I found this camp and was able to sneak in and steal food, I slept in a cave and ate bugs."

"You could have introduced yourself, you know. They would have let you use a tent."

Luis shrugged. "Didn't know how I'd be received. Besides, you know me...I don't like to impose."

The Ranger slapped him on the shoulder. "Come on. Let's get you cleaned up. You smell horrible."

$$\triangledown$$

Using the portable facilities, Luis showered and shaved. Wearing borrowed clothes, he sat at a long table in the community tent, surrounded by Romeo, Kelsey, Bal, Eunice, Judtson, and Saylor, and eagerly snarfed down a large bowl of chili, speaking between bites.

"Kelsey, I'm sorry I couldn't help back at Gates Pass. I wasn't in a good position and only had a pistol. Wish I had borrowed that rifle from you, Romeo. By the time I closed in on the one guy, he was already on the run, chasing down your dad."

Kelsey's mouth pursed tightly. "It's okay, Luis. Really. At least you followed them. Or we wouldn't have a clue as to their whereabouts. That took a lot of guts."

He chuffed loudly. "Guts or stupidity. Don't know which. I almost got caught on the C-130 after we landed. One of the guys actually stepped right on me under all those tarps. Anyway, Mrs. Costello was already at the airstrip when we landed. She left with them in the SUV."

Saylor interrupted, "How did she look? Was she a prisoner?"

Luis made eye contact. His voice sounded apologetic. "I'm not one-hundred-percent sure, sir. I had slipped out the back of the plane and was hiding behind some crates about fifty yards away when they brought her out. She did have an escort walking with her. She wasn't handcuffed or anything, but she looked...funny, I guess."

"Funny? How so?"

Tovar took a long drink from a bottled water before answering. "I can't say. I mean, she was always so...feisty, you know. Spunky. Had a spring to her step. This time she was...meek, I suppose. Flat. During her walk from the building to the truck she didn't glance around or even speak, that I could tell. She just kind of shuffled...looking down at her feet."

Saylor's brow furrowed deeply. "Was she injured?"

"Not that I saw."

Staring downward silently for a moment, Saylor returned his gaze. "Okay. Go ahead."

"Luis," Romeo took over, "if they drove away, how were you able to follow them at all?"

With a sardonic half-smirk, he sighed with mock wistfulness. "That's where I continued my life of crime. Remember, I came down here with no money and no credit cards. Nothing. The airstrip where we landed was a military base. I don't know which one. I was hiding in the middle of a slew of crates that had been off-loaded from a truck. The keys were still in it. I kinda helped myself."

"Wasn't that a little conspicuous for tracking them?"

"You could say that. I knew I was sticking out like a sore thumb, but those guys didn't seem to be paying a lot of attention to what was behind. Maybe they didn't figure on someone down here shadowing them. Anyhow, they stopped for gas, and I pulled in and made off with somebody's car. Left the truck as payment."

In spite of herself, Kelsey let out a soft giggle.

"Not much to tell after that," he added. "Followed them all the way out to the lake."

"Titicaca?"

"Yes, ma'am. That's where they transferred from the SUV to a boat and went out to the island."

Romeo unrolled a large aerial photograph and pointed. "Is this the island?"

"Yep. That's the one."

Bal leaned closer. "That is the island where my people were digging before being evicted."

"Where they found the spaceship?" Kelsey blurted.

With a slight shake of his head, Bal clarified, "Where they found the buried metal barrier."

"*Spaceship?*" The startled question burst from Luis.

Judtson described what Bal's team had discovered.

"You think it's a spaceship?"

"I don't know," he answered.

"I do! What else could it be?" Kelsey countered excitedly.

His tone droll, Romeo intervened, "If we could get back to what you saw...were you able to follow them to the island?"

"No. I couldn't find a boat to swipe...or, I should say, borrow...and I thought it would be way too obvious if I did go, so I watched from the shore."

"Did you see anyone leave?"

He shook his head and downed the last bite of a thick tortilla. "No. I hung out for about a day. Watching the island from a cave. Nothing. That's when I went back to La Paz and sent my text message. I was waiting there for an answer from you, and I heard some kids coming out of a store, speaking English and talking about working for Dr. Singh. They left, and I followed them to the camp. Stuck around the perimeter, running in during the evening while the kids were gathered in this tent, and grabbing some grub when I could. Then went back to La Paz once to check for a message. Got yours and sent mine. Came back here and been waiting ever since."

Kelsey faced Romeo. "We need to go to the island."

"I know. But I don't think riding out there in broad daylight is a good idea. Especially if those soldiers are still hanging around."

"What are you thinking?"

"A small group. A night recon. No action. We need to see who and what they have, as far as defenses. And we need to find out where your father and Mrs. Costello are being held."

"I'll go."

His voice deepened. "No, Kelsey. You won't."

"But...."

"No 'buts' this time. We've initiated two actions in the past. Neither one went as planned. I almost lost you and the rest of the group at the FEMA camp, and even getting Dr. Ashby out of Socorro was a little dicey. This time we do it right. Nothing hasty. Nothing ill-planned. Period."

Staring directly into his eyes, she bit hard on her lower lip and finally let out a resigned sigh. "If you say so. Who goes?"

"I'll go. And I'll take Chili. That's it."

"No way!" objected Luis. "I'm going, too. If it wasn't for me, you wouldn't have any idea where they were."

The Ranger swung his gaze to him and said nothing in response. Tovar's expression was defiant.

"Unless...unless you still don't trust me." A sly grin spread across his face. "In that case, you'd better take me to keep an eye on what I'm doing, instead of leaving me behind with your unprotected people."

Romeo's impassive features softened. "Okay. You're in."

"I'll make it a foursome." The barked offer came from Eunice.

The big man shook his head. "No, Detective Cahane. You're staying to keep an eye on the group."

She leaned forward and rested her fists on the table. "I told you before to can that *Detective* crap. If you think I'm gonna sit here with my thumb up my ass and my heart in Arkansas, you're nuttier than a fruitcake. You've got Kenny-boy and, from what I hear, your singin' partner is pretty good in a pinch. And I think a few other folks in this bunch know which end of a gun to point. Besides, far as we can tell, nobody knows we're here yet."

"Detecti...I mean, Eunice...."

"And one more thing. If the soldiers are there and you get tangled up with them, four is a bunch better'n three."

Judtson, his shoulders shaking with silent laughter, interjected, "*Sit here with my thumb*.... Romeo, I think she earned a spot on the team just for that."

Cahane winked at him and grinned.

Romeo, making a show of painfully giving in, grunted loudly and acquiesced, "All right. You're in."

Chapter 44

THE BALANCE OF THE GROUP SAFELY DELIVERED FROM SAMBROSA'S, Romeo gathered his three teammates and they began to prepare for the nighttime reconnaissance mission. The smaller camp, which had been left near the quarry at Lake Titicaca, was partially broken down and transported to Puma Punku in a caravan of trucks, the remainder to be brought in later. The members of the group not involved in the planning of Romeo's patrol scattered among the camp's students and workers, sharing stories of their recent experiences and discoveries. Kenny Bowman met with Sam and Ricky, established a perimeter around the camp, and created a patrol schedule. The agent spent half an hour briefing the other two on the proper watch procedures. Jonassen provided handheld walkie-talkies.

Although not yet springtime, the temperature was comfortable and the air was still. Judtson and Kelsey took advantage of the less hostile weather by packing some sandwiches and drinks and taking a long walk, sneaking away from the camp to avoid the inevitable tirade from Romeo for going out alone. Rocky crisscrossed the path lazily in front of them, his nose to the ground, tracking secret scents. In deference to Romeo's concern, both carried pistols. Judtson tucked his into the back of his waistband. Kelsey carried hers in the picnic basket, along with spare magazines.

Following directions obtained from one of the students, they casually meandered along a well-defined trail, holding hands and engaging in light banter, carefully avoiding any of the tension-inducing topics which incessantly swirled within their minds.

After approximately three hours, they stood on a ridgetop. The dramatic view, with Lake Titicaca in the distance a few miles away, was as breathtaking as the altitude. Rocky scampered ahead on an erratically weaving route down the slope, seemingly oblivious to the thinner air. Shielding his eyes with his hand, Judtson gazed out at the vista.

"The sun is so glaring up here. Wish I'd brought a hat."

Kelsey, beside him on the crest, circled around to stand in front of him, slipped off her jacket and, with a muted giggle, draped it over his head and tied the sleeves under his neck.

"There!" she declared, her tone playful. "How's that?"

Patiently submitting, as would a child to an embarrassing Halloween costume, Judtson suppressed a laugh. Kelsey's arms rested on his shoulders. Her mouth was partially open in a mischievous half-smile. Her ardent blue eyes seemed to be sparkling at him in the sunlight. As he stared into them, he felt an intensity, a warmth, a sense of belonging and unconditional acceptance he had never previously known and had unconsciously perpetually craved.

Gently putting his arms around her, he leaned closer and whispered, "You...are...perfect."

Belying her smile, the answer to his three words was evident, as a single glistening tear pooled at the corner of her eye and spilled down her cheek...kissed away before it could reach her chin.

Rising onto her toes and swallowing in search of her voice, she murmured, "So are you."

The distance between them vanished and their lips touched, the tangency igniting a perfervid passion, and the two urgently bound themselves to one another.

▽

At twilight, they arrived at the top of a small rise outside the boundary of the camp. The tents, their interiors illuminated by lanterns, glowed, the view resembling a miniature village. With Rocky in the lead, they stepped cautiously down the darkened trail, the preternatural quiet of the encampment broken by a sudden voice from the shadows.

"Where in the hell have you two been?"

Moving closer, they recognized Kenny.

Keeping her voice light, Kelsey answered, "We went for a walk and a picnic."

Shaking his head disgustedly, Bowman snapped, "A picnic! Romeo and the rest of us have been going crazy all day."

Unclipping a handheld radio from his vest, he keyed it and called, "Big Dog. Come back."

Judtson sought out eye contact with Kelsey in the dimness and grinned at her, sheepishly. She smiled back.

The radio crackled, "This is Big Dog."

Broadcasting his loud sigh through the microphone, the agent reported, "The children are home."

▽

The next twenty minutes were dominated by Romeo as he ranted at them for their irresponsible actions, with Chili, Ricky, and even Eunice chiming in when the Ranger paused for breath. In one of the tents and perched side by side on the edge of a cot, Judtson and Kelsey sat docilely like schoolchildren taken to the principal, and received the angry tirades, taking turns repeating their apologies. His ire finally dissipated, Romeo curtly told them to stay put for the rest of the night and stormed out, followed by the others, to load up for their mission.

At last alone again, Judtson faced her and whispered, "Want to go for another walk?"

Her giggle, now so familiar to him, bubbled up. "I don't think that's a good idea. Maybe we should stay close."

"Yeah. You're probably right. Hey, I know. Puma Punku is inside the perimeter, isn't it?"

She snorted. "Uh…no!"

"Come on. I've never been there at night. I bet it's awesome."

"Well…we should probably tell somebody this time."

"Good idea. I'll go tell Saylor. I wanted to check in on him, anyway."

She stood. "Okay. I'll see if I can mellow Romeo out a bit. Meet you in front of the community tent in, say, half an hour?"

Rising, he asked, "You want me to grab a heavier coat for you? It's getting chilly in Chile."

She rolled her eyes at the comment. "We're in Bolivia, bozo, not Chile. And, no, I won't need it. I don't get cold when I'm with you."

The two kissed before exiting. Kelsey stopped momentarily and watched Judtson as he hurried down the row of tents, a broad smile spreading across her face in the darkness.

He came to a halt outside the tent Saylor was using. "Popeye! Are you in there?"

"Come in."

Swinging open the flap, Judtson stepped in and found his lifelong friend sitting on a wooden-slat folding chair at a small bench, papers spread out on the surface.

"What are you reading?"

"Dylan thinks he's onto something regarding the vaccinations we received in 1986. Well, not just those. He wanted a second pair of eyes to look at his notes."

Judtson sat down on the other chair. "What did he find?"

Saylor leaned back, causing the wooden frame to creak loudly. "If he's right, it's spooky. Let me start with vaccines in general."

"Okay."

"How technical do you want me to get?"

"For now, keep it basic."

"Well, you know that vaccines are a combination of peptide sequences and proteins, or partial proteins. Alternatively, they are made from a deactivated or dead virus, an attenuated or live virus, or a synthesized version of the virus."

"Understood. And when they are put in us, that gives our immune system a sneak peak at the little buggers so we can develop a specific antibody against them."

"That's how it works. What most people don't know is that the largest percentage of a vaccine dosage is inert."

"If the substances are inert, why include them?"

"The supposedly inert ingredients make up a pretty weird soup. Nutrients, proteins, all kinds of stuff. They are there to provide the medium for the active proteins or peptides, but once inside our bodies, they are no longer needed and don't do anything."

"You said 'supposedly.'"

"Well…that's where Dylan thinks he's found something."

"Enough background, Popeye. What has he found?"

Saylor smirked at his friend's impatience. "Just about there. Let me pose a hypothetical." Judtson huffed.

"Let's say that you wanted to insert something extra inside vaccines."

"Like what?"

He shrugged. "Depends on your motives…on your end goal. Fluoride is added to our water because it is claimed to reduce cavities. There's mixed science on whether it actually does. And for now, that's beside the point. Look at all the attention and flak it has gotten since they first started adding it. So, if you wanted to do something for us…or to us…it would need to be less up-front and more circumspect…more surreptitious."

"That's true."

"Not only that, but more and more people never drink publicly supplied water, anyway. Many are only drinking bottled water."

"Also true."

"So, an alternate delivery system is required. If you wanted to slip something to an entire population, what better way to do it than through vaccines? Especially the child vaccines which are essentially mandatory."

"Parents can still refuse."

"They can. The government has made it a tough choice, though. Most school districts around the country will not accept children without immunization records. And now that we have what is essentially a nationalized health care system, coverage could be refused for anyone who doesn't submit to the vaccinations."

Pensively, Judtson paused for a second or two. "So far, I'm with you. That makes a vaccine an effective delivery system."

"It does. And then, if you're the government, you follow up those child vaccines with a slew of others, containing the secret ingredient as well. Most notably, flu vaccines. But also pneumonia and shingles vaccines, and so on. Offering them at every corner drugstore in the country and using the media to frighten people into getting the shots."

Judtson chuckled. "You're sounding like Alex Jones."

"If the shoe fits…."

"Are you any closer to telling me what Dylan found?"

"We're there."

"Thought we'd never make it."

Giving his friend a nasty glare, Saylor continued, "Four universities began studies of the '86 vaccine right after the scandal came out. Dylan, with Scott's help, was able to get his hands on the work they had completed before it was dropped. Now, I am greatly oversimplifying this, but with the old research and the help of several colleagues around the world, he found a synthetic protein which binds to a specific receptor on certain cells in the brain. And it is fairly aggressive. It will even evict another protein already in residence."

"Which receptors?"

"The receptors that, according to what he has been able to uncover as of today, are used by two drugs. Chloral hydrate and fentanyl."

"I don't recognize either of those."

"You probably wouldn't. Needless to say, I sure as hell did. The two are related pharmaceutically, not chemically, and have slightly different effects on us. Chloral hydrate has been used by the medical profession for children getting an EEG. Chills them out without putting them to sleep. Fentanyl has been used on children to make them calm and cooperative for a tricky procedure like a spinal tap. So, basically, both substances make us…docile…compliant."

Judtson suddenly lurched forward in his seat. "They make us zombies?"

Saylor nodded. "Rough term for it, but yeah! To varying degrees, based upon dosage. At a light dose, they would just make a person easy to get along with. At high doses, a basket case."

Taking a deep breath as he absorbed the import of this, Judtson then spoke thoughtfully. "My…understanding of how this works is that if the altered 1986 vaccine had a synthetic protein which bound to those receptors, it would essentially lock them out, make them unavailable for these zombie-creating drugs. It would make us immune."

"Exactly. And keep in mind that if a person had been given one or both of the drugs prior to the vaccine…."

"The 1986 vaccine booted them off the receptors and took their place."

"Yep."

"The obvious question is…are they actually slipping us chloral hydrate or fentanyl in the other vaccines?"

Saylor vigorously rubbed his face with both hands for a moment before responding. "That…is where it gets interesting. And this is all really preliminary. Dylan has not had much time to delve into it, even with the past research and the help he has received."

"I know. I understand."

"To answer your question specifically…no. They wouldn't dare put chloral hydrate or fentanyl directly into the vaccines. And if there were a broad worldwide conspiracy to control all of us, there would still be a biologist, a chemist, a doctor, or a pathologist somewhere who wasn't on the payroll. Just like our little group, not everyone is with the program. Someone somewhere, probably someone who was in one of those professions and also had a child, would notice those ingredients immediately."

"Without a doubt. They'd have to conceal it somehow."

"And did they ever! I have to hand it to them. If Dylan is right, this is unbelievably clever. Remember those inert peptides and proteins I mentioned which are present in all vaccines? And, by the way, I do mean *all* vaccines."

"Yes."

"It is way too early in Dylan's research to identify or understand the exact mechanism. But apparently, what happens is that those inert proteins, once inside the body, combine with an amino acid present in every living person, and interact…change. The protein turns into a little factory – producing a chemical which makes a beeline straight for those receptors."

"The proteins actually make chloral hydrate or fentanyl?"

"No. Not exactly. A variant of sorts. The way receptors work is that each type of receptor has a purpose. These specific receptors are the ones relating to the general area of compliancy and submissiveness. So, whatever those proteins are making would be engineered to trigger something in that realm."

"I don't understand. If a substance binds to a receptor and that activates it, why doesn't the protein in the 1986 vaccine do the same thing? Why doesn't it turn us into zombies?"

"Because the process can work either way, Judtson. When a protein binds to a receptor, it can switch it on or off. The '86 protein turns it off."

"And the protein being churned out inside us…."

"Turns it on."

"So this is why nothing out of line has been found in the vaccines?"

"That's right. As I said, it is clever as hell. Everyone would be looking inside the vaccine for known substances with known effects. No one would be looking for something in the inert medium which was going to turn into a drug-manufacturing plant once inside you."

Judtson flopped back heavily. "This is mind-blowing."

Saylor snorted. "I'm not done."

"There's more?"

"Oh, yeah!" He paused dramatically. "I mentioned that Dylan has had some help. Now that they know specifically what to look for, it was easy to isolate the new drug being produced by the suspect vaccines. A biologist friend of his administered the drug, at different dosage levels, to lab rats."

Feeling the muscles in his back and neck tighten, Judtson leaned forward again, sliding to the front edge of his seat, listening intently.

"Again, this is only the result of a relatively short-term observation. However, the rats at lower doses, again to varying degrees, basically mellowed out. Anywhere from slightly mellower to looking like a rat version of Cheech and Chong."

"Yeah?"

"The rats who received a dosage over a certain level…became agitated…irritable. Nothing too bad. Just noticeable."

Judtson remained silent.

"At the next dosage up, rather than being irritable, they were overtly hostile. Trying to bite the hands of the lab techs and turning on the other rats in the cage. Engaging in repetitive challenging, fighting behavior."

Saylor hesitated, drawing in a deep breath before revealing the final stage. "At an incrementally small dosage increase from *that* level, the rats no longer fought…they killed the other rats in the cage. And continued killing until only one rat remained in each group."

"Oh, my God!"

"Still not…." Saylor's voice broke in mid-sentence. Taking a moment to steady himself, he began again. "I'm still not done. As I said, during the stage with the merely challenging, fighting behavior, the demeanor of the rats was overt, belligerent. But at the final…fatal stage…as the rats with the highest dosage killed…according to the biologist who observed it…they did it while being absolutely calm. He told Dylan that he had not been aware of that ability…the ability to go on a killing rampage…anywhere in the animal kingdom…without exhibiting an extreme emotion such as rage. With, of course, the notable exception of mankind."

Judtson's words were spoken barely above a whisper. "So it turned them not only into killers…but cold-blooded killers, as well."

"Yes. It did. And when I heard those results from Dylan earlier today, the first thing I thought of was the kid Ricky and I encountered at the mall…the one with the knife. Ricky said that as the young man charged at him, knife in hand, ready to kill him, the attacker's face was perfectly serene. He compared it to the expression someone would have while waiting in line to order a meal."

As his mind instantly flashed back to the newscast with the picture of Sean Collins, the campus shooter, Judtson vividly pictured the blank, unemotive visage. He then recalled the video of the youth engaging in the knockout game, and how he had been stunned by both the lack of emotion in the boy's face…and his own unexplained connection to the assailant's eyes. As he reexamined the image, understanding and recognition slammed into him with a gut-wrenching force.

"Saylor…I don't remember if I told you about this. I saw a video of that kid who did the knockout game at the mall recently. Just a few days ago."

"What about it?"

"At the time, I was astounded by how he could do that to someone while showing no emotion whatsoever. Now…it sounds like the way you described the killer rats."

"Uh-huh."

"One other thing, though. When I saw the punk's eyes, they looked so familiar. They freaked me out. But I couldn't place them. Until...now. Saylor, they were the same as the eyes I saw in the mirror while I was conditioned."

"Oh."

The first traces of an incipient fury began to build within Judtson. "We need to replicate the '86 vaccine! We need to get it out there. To everyone!"

"Yes, we do. I mean, after Dylan finishes...."

"No! Now! Right away. Something's happening. It has been building for a long time and now it's approaching critical mass. I don't know if *this* was their plan or if it's a horrible accident, an unintended consequence of their desire to make us manageable...compliant, but these random attacks are escalating, almost daily. People are dying!"

After a few moments of reflection, Saylor concluded, "You have a point. If Dylan's on target and people have had their bodies turned into little factories cranking out those proteins, there wouldn't be a self-regulating mechanism. The levels would just keep escalating until reaching the highest dose Dylan's friend saw in the lab rats. And it *would* manifest first in young people. That's the age when people are most susceptible. It has been suggested that the brain doesn't finish wiring itself until a person is almost thirty years old. Some believe that this explains why mental illnesses such as schizophrenia present when they do. The process of wiring gets disrupted."

"But just because we're seeing it first in those few...."

Saylor finished the thought. "We're getting a glimpse of what is in store for everyone in the near future as the levels in the body increase. I'll talk to Dylan about re-creating the '86 vaccine. Mass-producing it. Maybe he knows people who can start on it immediately. But you have to understand that we're all personae non gratae out there for the time being. I'm surprised he was able to get any of his old friends to even talk to him, much less help him."

"They have to help. Maybe now that they've done the research and have seen it with their own eyes, they'll realize what needs to happen."

"I'll talk to him tonight."

"Okay."

The two best friends fell into a tense silence for over a minute before Judtson broke it. "Kelsey and I are heading off for a little walk. After the commotion we caused today, I thought I'd let you know so people don't start searching for us."

"Judtson, are you sure you want to go outside the perimeter?" he asked, disapproval evident in his voice.

"We won't be far this time. I want to see Puma Punku at night. And we'll both have our guns."

With a slight shake of his head, he sighed. "All right. But be careful, okay?"

"We will." Judtson focused on his friend's face. "Saylor, how are you doing?"

"I'm fine."

"Don't give me that. Doni's being held somewhere around here. All hell's breaking loose in the world. How *are* you?"

Their eyes met. "I'm...I'm keeping my mind focused on other things. After Romeo gets back from the island, we'll have a plan. And then we can find out..." – he broke the eye contact and stared at the fabric wall of the tent – "whatever it is we are going to find out."

He put his hand on Saylor's shoulder. "I don't know why. I don't have a reason other than what my gut is telling me. But I think it's all going to work out."

Saylor's gaze returned and he absorbed the words, digesting them slowly. "Thanks. I think you actually mean that."

"I do, Popeye. I do."

Judtson stood to leave, when his friend said, "Hey, pal?"

He stopped. "Yeah?"

"I'm glad that you found Kelsey. I can't think of a better…."

"Accomplice?" he responded, grinning.

Saylor rose in the confined space, standing inches from his best friend. "Yeah. Accomplice. Partner. Mate? You deserve it."

Judtson's voice caught in his throat for a second before he was able to say, "This isn't one of those horrible male-bonding moments where we're supposed to hug, is it? Because if it is, forget it."

"No. No. Absolutely not."

"Good."

He began to leave, paused, and turned back, spreading his arms. "Aw, what the hell."

The two men gripped each other in an intense bear hug. After they parted, both embarrassed, Judtson muttered, "See ya, Popeye," and left.

Chapter 45

THE CAMP WAS EERILY QUIET, despite the population of the characteristically boisterous students. It was almost as if all present had been imbued with the sense of urgency...the conjunctive substance of anticipation made bitter by an undefined dread, as carried by the band of newcomers to the camp. Although many of the details remained unknown to them, these young men and women, who with exuberant gusto had indulged in the uncovering of archaeological and tectonic secrets long concealed from the human race, were now confronted with a new context. Until today, they had been pursuing answers to age-old questions, comfortably ensconced within the knowledge that the proofs they sought had eluded others for centuries and would certainly wait patiently for another day...another week...another month.

Yet now, thanks to the arrival of the grim-faced men and women who swooped in unannounced on a helicopter, the clues they sought in their quest to break the safe, academic, abstract ancient riddles...were no longer the mere satisfaction of scholarly curiosity. The prize they labored to win was no longer the mere addition of another paragraph in some future textbook, another mundane detail, verging on irrelevant, to be memorized for only as long as the end of the semester. Now they sensed that there was something...something buried under their very feet...something which might forever alter the future of humanity.

Rather than congregating in large assemblages, as was the evening norm, most of the students were sequestered within their own tents in ones and twos, preferring the near darkness of a lantern on its lowest setting to the brightness of the community areas in the compound. Judtson, as always, accompanied by Rocky, traversed the quiet path to the edge of the camp where Romeo and his team were loading their gear for the night's adventure. He espied Kelsey as she helped, tossing a stuffed duffel into the rear of one of the trucks, and he joined her.

As Romeo, Eunice, Luis, and Chili busied themselves, he leaned closer. "Has he calmed down yet?"

She shrugged. "A little. Did you talk to Saylor?"

"I did. And he told me about something that will blow you away."

"What?"

"It's fairly detailed. Let's wait until we see them off and I'll explain it all."

Patience was not one of her strong attributes, but she nodded as Romeo approached, obviously preparing to leave.

"All right. We're out of here."

Kelsey's voice conveyed a tinge of concern as she cautioned, "Please take care."

"Yeah," Judtson added. "Be safe."

The big man's eyes swept back and forth between the two of them. "You, too." He began to step away, paused, and with a new gravity in his deep voice, declared, "I mean it."

"We will. Don't worry," Kelsey assured.

The second truck, operated by Chili, was already idling noisily. Romeo climbed into his, started the engine, and the vehicles disappeared into the night.

"Are you ready?" Judtson asked.

"Uh-huh. Did you tell Saylor what we're doing?"

"I did."

The couple crossed the open area which surrounded the camp. As they were about to exit the arbitrary perimeter established by Romeo, the beam of a flashlight struck their eyes and someone called out. "Where are you guys going?"

Recognizing the voice, Judtson chastened, "Ricky, get that light out of our eyes."

His assistant switched off the light and approached, stepping around a large boulder. They saw that he had a pair of night vision goggles pushed up and riding on the top of his head. "Come on, chief. You aren't really heading out again, are you?"

Judtson raised his hand and pointed across the relatively level plateau. Even in the moonlight, the vague outline of the stone monuments was visible. "Ricky, we're only going to Puma Punku."

"It's not inside the perimeter. Romeo's going to be furious if I let you go."

"Then don't tell him."

He sucked in a breath to speak, when he was cut off by Kelsey. "Seriously, Ricky, nobody knows we're here. And we'll be right over there. The perimeter should probably include the place, anyway. Consider it a patrol. We'll be the early warning if anyone comes."

"No. I can't."

Judtson huffed loudly. "Look, we're going. If you want to call Romeo on his radio and turn him around, that's up to you. We'll be back in an hour or so."

He clasped Kelsey's hand, and they both walked past. As they did, Ricky cautioned, "You two be careful. *Please.*"

Over his shoulder, he answered, "We will."

As they walked slowly toward the shadowy jumble of carved stones, with Rocky trotting ahead of them in a wide-ranging, serpentine pattern, Judtson repeated the details of the discussion with Saylor. Kelsey refrained from interrupting although several of the pivotal points elicited soft gasps. Their arrival at the stone terrace coincided with the completion of his narrative.

"So they are doping everyone up? Turning people into sheep?"

"Looks that way."

"Just the United States?"

"I don't think so. All of the developed countries use the same vaccines."

"But why are they doing it?"

"That, I don't know. What I can say is that the theories I have come up with are all fairly ugly."

"You're right, Judtson. We need to get the '86 vaccine out there."

"I know."

He took Kelsey by the waist and lifted her up to sit on an edge of the recently unearthed platform. Then, gripping the stones, he hopped up beside her, the motion resulting in a loud metallic clatter from behind.

"What was…?" he muttered, reaching back. "Oh, I had forgotten I had my gun tucked in. It fell out."

"That reminds me…I never got mine out of the picnic basket when we went back to camp."

Judtson laughed. "Gee, you think maybe the tirade from Romeo distracted you?"

He placed the pistol on the stone surface next to his leg and put his arm around her shoulders. Rocky, several yards away, sniffing at the base of an H-shaped stone, noticed they were now sitting and ambled to the terrace. Realizing that his master was perched too high for proper petting if he sat at his feet, the golden leapt up and nestled against him, taking a single tentative lick at Judtson's face.

"Rocky! You're sitting on my gun."

His pal stood. Judtson grabbed the pistol and placed it farther away. Rocky immediately reassumed his previous position.

They settled into a comfortable silence, staring out over the dark outlines of the ancient stonework. The reverie was eventually broken by Kelsey. "Do you still get that cool feeling here? The one we talked about last trip."

"I do. I don't know why, but when I'm here, I feel…this is going to sound goofy…I feel serene. As if this is where I am supposed to be. What about you?"

She shook her head. "No. Not anything at all. From this place, anyhow. When I'm with you, I feel wonderful. And that's true wherever I am."

He pulled her tighter and lightly kissed her cheek. As he did, he released a muted chuckle.

She turned to face him. "What? Something funny?"

"Just then, I was remembering how jealous you were over that waitress."

In the moonlight, he could see a meaningful smile spread across her face. She responded in a matter-of-fact tone. "You're mine. You have a problem with that?"

"No. Definitely not. Actually, I like it."

"Good!"

She snuggled closer to him and spoke while facing forward. "I was just wondering…didn't Kristen ever get jealous? Oh, wait. I know she did. I caught the brunt of it at the hospital."

"That was odd. When you told me about what happened that day, I was surprised because she never did."

"Guess it must've just been me."

"Could have been."

Kelsey looked up and stared at the canopy of stars. "Can I ask how you met her?"

"Of course. It was a spring break. Cancun."

"Really? What year?"

"1999."

Her gaze returned to connect with his. "Huh!"

"What?"

Once more, her eyes darted away for a split second before they refocused on him. "Nothing. Go ahead."

"Okay. I never participated in the whole spring break trip thing, but Saylor and Doni talked me into it that year. Now that I'm thinking back...it was Doni who did. She said I'd meet someone. I hated it. The kids were so out of control. It all made me think of what society would be like if twelve-year-olds were suddenly allowed to travel on their own, drink, and have sex. Guess I was some sort of dud."

She reached up and squeezed his hand. "No. You weren't."

"Thanks. Anyway, the last night of the break they had a big party on the beach, with a huge bonfire, a booming sound system, kegs, bottles, drugs...you get the picture." He chuckled at the memory. "To give you an idea of what a dork I was...while everyone was going nuts around the bonfire, I grabbed a book I'd been wanting to read and moved about a hundred yards away. Found a table. And...oh, man...this is not the image I want you to have of me...I had this little battery-powered book light, one that you strap on your forehead. There I was...sitting at a table in the dark, on spring break in Cancun, with a headlight on, reading *The Hitchhiker's Guide to the Galaxy.*"

He expected to see amusement on her face. Whether it was the duskiness in the moonlight or something else, what was there Judtson could not identify.

"So, as I said, I was all alone, hating the trip, hating my life, and reading. Even my effort to read was only mediocre at best. From the party in the distance, the heavy metal song ended and someone put on 'Can't Fight This Feeling,' by REO. I stopped reading and looked up. That's when I spotted her. Halfway between my table and the water, I saw this girl...barefoot...slow-dancing to the song. She was immersed in her own little world...alone. There was some moonlight and a faint, flickering light from the bonfire...and..." – his voice became hushed – "she was beautiful. Like something out of a movie. Wearing some type of short wraparound...I didn't know what it was called."

He felt the grip of Kelsey's hands tighten almost imperceptibly on his. She said nothing, waiting.

"At that instant, I completely forgot about the book. I was *pretending* to read all right, except I found myself transfixed, unable to tear my eyes away from her. She was so into it...I could tell...so engrossed in the moment, listening to the distant music, hearing the surf pounding on the beach, savoring the sensation of the sand on her bare feet. I was certain she hadn't noticed me at all."

He continued the narrative wistfully. "Of all the hundreds of girls I had seen on the break, not one appealed to me. Not for a second! They were all too vacuous...too vapid...too fatuous and too blatantly narcissistic. And I remember thinking at the time...as I stared at this girl who, like me, had also abandoned the party...who preferred losing herself in the sensual elements of her environment, rather than drinking herself stupid and sleeping with someone she didn't even know...that she and I were somehow kindred spirits. It was pathetic, yet from the minuscule input I was perceiving, I manufactured this entire persona for her. Who she was. What she liked. How her voice sounded. Her favorite music. Everything. By the time I was done...I had...fallen in love with her."

Judtson paused briefly, shifting his gaze to the surrounding shadows. "You're probably thinking Kristen was the one out on the beach dancing and that was how we met. You'd be wrong. I sat there desperately trying to make myself take off the imbecilic headlamp, put down the book, and walk over to the girl. Dance with her. Something! Only…I didn't have the guts. She was…or this fantasy I had built in my head…was unattainable…untouchable. I tried and I tried. Gave myself every pep talk I could think of…but I was paralyzed. That's when Kristen, who had seen me leave the party, found me at the table and suddenly plopped down on the bench beside me."

He chuffed under his breath and his tone hardened. "Oh, she told me that she hated the party scene, too. Couldn't stand the typical people who came to these things. I guess she caught me at the exact right moment. I was feeling…I don't know…vulnerable, lonely, like a total loser…I'm not sure. And then, all of a sudden, she just kissed me. I didn't see it coming. When it ended…the girl on the sand was…gone. It was as if she had only been a dream."

With a muffled snicker, he finished, "At the risk of unleashing your jealousy again, I have to tell you…I have never forgotten that girl…woman. A thousand times since that night I have wondered, what if…?"

He looked back at Kelsey. Her earlier cryptic expression had changed. Changed to what? Not the flash of jealousy he expected. Something else. Something he could not define. She started to speak but was interrupted by a sudden sharp bark from Rocky who, a split second later, scrambled to his feet and leapt from the terrace, landing in a full run. In the process, unheard by either of them, the pistol was knocked over the edge and fell to the soft sand.

Jumping down, Judtson followed, shouting, "Rocky! What is it, boy?"

Kelsey, concerned, grabbed for his pistol. Straining in the faint illumination, she saw that the stone platform was bare.

The golden form, gray in the moonlight, dashed away into the shadows in the general direction of the camp.

Calling Rocky's name over and over, Judtson wandered forward, his eyes urgently searching the variegated patterns of black and gray. Kelsey, slipping down to her feet, moved forward to follow him. Navigating only by the ambient light and struck by the surreal shapes and textures of the landscape around him, he was circling one of the large carved stones when, cutting through the silence, from his left came a simultaneous vicious snarl and a startled, pain-filled scream.

Panic in his voice, Judtson moved toward the sounds. *"Rocky!"*

The distinct metallic clacks of an automatic rifle being charged reached him. He froze in his tracks and an instant later was blinded as the beam from a bright flashlight struck his widely dilated eyes.

He raised his hands above his head as the unknown attacker spoke, apparently into a microphone. "I've got someone here."

Judtson, squinting into the glare, was not able to see the man behind the light but heard him order, "Move back."

Obediently, he carefully began stepping backward, his mind swirling with thoughts: the first, a hope that Kelsey had seen what was happening and had hidden; the second, a rueful recollection that his gun was back on the terrace. His first wish was dashed as the man swung his flashlight away. Judtson could now see that it was a barrel-mounted light and, following the beam, saw that it was now centered on Kelsey, who had been only a few feet behind him. Gratefully, he was able to discern that their assailant was alone.

"Both of you, move back!" the man commanded harshly.

In response, Judtson stepped closer to Kelsey, and the two returned to the terrace, his spirits crashing when he did not see the pistol where he had left it, and then lifting as he surmised that Kelsey must have it. Standing together, they listened as the assailant again spoke into his microphone. "I have two here. Kent and Batman. Instructions?"

Judtson thought of nothing that he could do or say. After a pause of only a few seconds, he heard the stranger acknowledge, "Roger." It was immediately clear what the instructions had been, as the aim of the barrel shifted to point directly at Kelsey's chest. With the light now focused on her and out of his eyes, he was able to see the intruder move his finger off the guard and onto the trigger itself. Time became elastic as Judtson, realizing what was to come, felt a flood of adrenaline explode within him.

With no conscious thought, he lunged forward and to the side, vaguely aware of the shouted plea from Kelsey to stop, intending to put his own body in the path of the inevitable slugs, at the same moment that an almost supernatural streak of gold burst into his peripheral sight, slamming into the side of the assassin. The impulse to pull the trigger, already in motion, was not thwarted by the impact from Rocky, and the three-shot burst was dispatched, two of the rounds connecting with Judtson, reversing his motion and tossing him to the ground.

$$\triangledown$$

Ricky keyed the microphone on his radio and shouted, "Shots fired! Shots fired!"

Instinctively, he began running in the direction where he knew Judtson and Kelsey had gone, when Kenny's response came back clearly. "Roger that. Stay on your post! Repeat. Stay on your post!"

Romeo was in the lead truck, driving slowly on the narrow road, less than half the distance to the dock where the boat they were to use was stored. Hearing Ricky's four words over his radio, he jammed down on the brakes, wrestling the truck off the road and onto the shoulder. He twisted in his seat and pulled his pistol, aiming it at Luis who was already reaching for his own gun, and accused, "You rotten bastard! You did it again."

Chili, seeing his partner's maneuver and having also heard Ricky, swerved to avoid Romeo and stopped in the middle of the road beside him. Through his open window, Jones yelled, "Get back to camp!"

Reacting instantly, Chili executed a squealing, bouncing U-turn and raced away. In the dim green light from the dashboard instruments, Romeo could see Luis' face. It showed a mixture of fury, frustration, and…fear.

"Get out!" ordered the Ranger.

Bowman, in his tent when he received the alert, donned his backpack, snatched four AK-47s from a rack, two NVGs, and dashed out, sprinting across the dirt path to Saylor's tent.

$$\triangledown$$

Kelsey, reacting on sheer impulse, dived toward the lone attacker, who was already on the ground, desperately attempting to shield himself from Rocky's slashing teeth with one hand, while swinging the butt of the rifle stock against the wildly snapping, biting head with the other. She grabbed the barrel of his rifle, violently twisted it free, and turned it back on the man, intending to empty the magazine into his body, when she saw the snarling golden retriever clamp his jaws on the assailant's unprotected throat, his head ferociously jerking back and forth, his teeth ripping the flesh and tendons. Within moments, the stranger's body went limp.

Whirling around, she saw Judtson lying faceup on the dirt, his flannel shirt saturated with blood. With a primal wail, Kelsey dropped the rifle and fell beside him, gently lifting his head and cradling it on her lap.

"Judtson! Judtson! Oh God, Judtson. Please, my darling...*please* answer me!"

The flashlight on the dropped rifle reflected off the wall of the terrace and illuminated his face. A wave of relief washed over her as she saw his eyes open. She took in a breath to scream for help, when the night was once again shattered with the sounds of multiple gunshots coming from the direction of the camp. Careful not to jostle him, she shed her fleece-lined jacket and, unbuttoning his shirt, delicately pressed the absorbent wool on his wounds, causing him to flinch and groan with pain.

Stroking the side of his face, she murmured, "Judtson...baby...you're going to be okay."

He nodded almost imperceptibly and she saw a slight smile curl the corners of his mouth. "I...I know."

"Ssshhhh. Ssshhhh. Don't talk," she soothed, as she tenderly brushed an errant shock of hair back from his face.

His licked his lips. "Then...you...talk."

From somewhere near, yet beyond her field of view, Kelsey heard the plaintive howl of a wolf. Rocky, his snout, neck, and chest soaked with blood, slunk pathetically to where his master was lying and, with a muted whimper, lay down on the sand and nuzzled against him. The sporadic gunfire from the camp fading into her perceptual background, Kelsey, with every ounce of will in her possession, forced a smile onto her face and said, "It...it...was called a mini-sarong."

He stared up at her, uncomprehending. With a voice so soft it verged on a whisper, he asked, "What was?"

"The...wraparound...I was wearing on the beach that night."

His eyes widened with disbelief. "That...was...you?"

She leaned closer to his cradled head. A single tear broke free and leapt from her cheek, landing on his lips. "Uh-huh." Disciplining her voice to a semblance of near normalcy, she answered, "That was *I*. Dancing...and parading around in front of you...like a stupid school-girl."

"You were there...for me?" His eyes pinched closed in pain.

Waiting until his eyes reopened, she touched his lips with a fingertip. "Ssshhhh. Yes. You were why I was there...on that beach...dancing. I was part of that horrible mob on spring break." She chuffed faintly. "I hated it, too. I despised the drunken jocks hitting on me. Even my girlfriend, the one who talked me into going, turned into an...I don't know what...the minute we arrived."

Her voice delicate and fragile, her eyes glistening, she stared at him steadily and described the night. "I was so unbelievably miserable...hopeless. Some football-playing clown had tried to grope me at the party. I stormed off, furious. I wanted to be alone. To think, you know. I couldn't understand why everyone else was having so much fun and I was so unhappy. I figured that it had to be me. That it must have been. That something was faulty in my wiring...in my brain. God, I was depressed. So, I was walking along that beautiful beach under the idyllic moonlight...on the last night of what was supposed to be this wonderful trip...and I was all *alone*."

Kelsey's momentum wavered. Taking in a deep, shuddering breath and letting it out slowly, she continued. "In my depression-fueled introspection, it dawned on me that, of all the guys I had met…not only on the trip but in my entire life as well…not one had ever captured my interest, appealed to me, reached me in any way."

She realized that as he had taken in her words, the underlying grimace of pain on Judtson's face had gradually slipped away.

"Then…then…in the middle of my self-pity and despair…like something out of a sappy love story where your fairy godmother grants your wish…I saw someone up the beach. Sitting at a table. He was alone, too. Avoiding the party…avoiding the booze and drugs…avoiding all of the ridiculous girls…all by himself…and *reading*!" A sobbing giggle punctuated her story. "And he had a *goofy* headlight strapped on! I never saw his face clearly. I guess I didn't need to. At that moment…at that precise second…I realized that *he* was exactly what I had always been looking for. He was sitting there…so many yards away…and yet, I already knew his favorite food…movie…song…the sound of his voice, the way his arms would feel around me…how his lips would taste."

The faint smile on his face coalesced…grew more defined.

Believing with all of her heart…every fiber of her being…that her words were somehow helping him…holding him…healing him, she continued, "And boy, did I blow it. I really did. My fairy godmother plopped him *right in front of me*. Sadly, she didn't think to whisper any instructions in my ear. There he was…there *you* were…the person I had decided in a blinding flash was the man of my dreams, and I had no idea what to do. I knew if I approached you… you'd think I was just coming on to you…like those others. I…this is going to sound incredibly stupid…I actually thought about pretending to fall down on the sand and twist my ankle so that you would run to me and help me. Except I didn't want the only real relationship I would ever have in my entire life to begin with a blatant deception. So…so I heard the love song begin, and just started to dance. *Right in front of you*. Boy, did I plan it out, though! I positioned myself not too far away. I wanted you to know that it was directed at you. But not too close. I didn't want you to think I was some artless exhibitionist."

Judtson struggled to speak. "Kelsey, I…."

Again touching his lips with her fingertips, she hushed him, her voice barely above a whisper. "Wait…please, my darling. I need to…." She hesitated and drew in a steadying breath. "I was dancing like a fool, all by myself, feeling like a complete idiot and waiting for you to *get up* and come to me…talk to me…dance with me…*anything*. I wasn't sure that you even noticed me. Or if you did, that you even liked what you saw. Then…I made a decision. I decided that the whole dancing thing was asinine…ludicrous. I knew I needed to simply stop it…I needed to walk over to you and *say* something. Of course that couldn't be easy, either. I needed to come up with just the right thing to say. I…I was too slow. I took too long. While I was trying to think of the perfect line…one of the blondes from the party flounced straight up to you as if it was no big deal, sat down, and…kissed you. Kissed *my* guy! *And he kissed her back!*"

The narrative faltered as she was living, for one fleeting moment, inside that night on the beach in Cancun rather than on this dark, desolate plateau. "I ran. I ran like hell all the way to my room in the hotel. And I didn't come out until it was time to fly home. But…you know what? Ever since…for every day of my life…my mind has flashed back to that night, if only for an instant. I have never stopped wondering how different my life would have been if I had not been so slow...if I had gone to that table before she did. I have never forgotten him...*you*. Not for one...single...day!"

Silence enveloped them, and the two stared into each other's eyes. Tracing the edge of his lips with her fingertip, she whispered, "I have also never forgiven you for kissing her."

Working to force out the words, he uttered. "I'm...I'm sorry."

She shook her head as more tears began to stream from her eyes. "Those words...for all of this time...were all I *thought* I ever wanted to hear. I...I...Judtson Kent...*I love you*."

With a painful effort, he raised his hand and touched the side of her face. "I love you...Kel...."

His hand dropped to the ground.

Chapter 46

SAYLOR WAS COMING OUT OF HIS TENT, when he spotted Kenny running toward him, carrying rifles. "What's wrong?"

The FBI agent handed him two of the AK-47s, a pair of the NVGs, as well as a spare radio. "Ricky reported shots fired."

The words struck Saylor like a hammer blow. "Dammit! Judtson and Kelsey are out there."

"Out where?"

"He told me they were going to Puma Punku."

Anger and concern instantly colored Bowman's face. "We need to move."

The two men took off at a run for the perimeter in the direction of Puma Punku. Sam Jonassen, carrying his own radio and a bolt-action thirty-aught-six, burst from his tent. Slowing but not stopping, Kenny barked, "Sam, get everyone secured. All your people who can shoot, put a gun in their hands. Then go help Meade."

"Got it!"

The postdoc turned and ran down the row, shouting into each tent he passed.

Sprinting, Kenny caught up with Saylor, and both came to a skidding stop at the boulder where Ricky, his NVGs pulled down, had taken cover and was staring out across the plateau.

"Anything?"

Without taking his eyes from the perimeter, Ricky answered the agent, "Nothing else. Just those first three rapid shots. They were tight together. Sounded like an automatic set on a three-shot burst."

"Where?" Saylor asked nervously.

Chancing a quick glimpse back, Ricky muttered, "Puma Punku."

"That's where...."

"I know. I talked to them on their way out."

"They haven't come back?"

"No."

Saylor handed one of the rifles to Kenny, pulled the other from over his shoulder, popped the magazine and checked it, charged the weapon, and slipped the goggles onto his head, leaving them up on his forehead. "I'm going out there." His tone brooked no argument.

"I figured" was all Bowman said. Dropping the backpack, he extracted three spare magazines and handed them over. "You shouldn't go alone."

Determined to not be delayed, Saylor snapped back, "You're needed here. So is Ricky. You stay and watch the camp. I'll be fine."

"I'm coming with you!" The breathless offer came from behind. Saylor whirled to see Lisa, who had dashed to join them when she heard the alert from Sam.

Bowman resisted. "Lisa, I don't think…."

"Dammit, Kenny, we don't have any time!" Saylor almost shouted. "I'm going now. Lisa…grab a gun and let's head out."

Before he could make a move, there was a stutter of gunfire from the opposite side of the camp, answered by the authoritative crack of a heavy rifle. The assault on the camp was clearly a coordinated one as multiple rounds suddenly impacted the boulder they were all clustered behind.

The four were instantly galvanized into motion. Kenny tossed the spare rifle to Lisa, slapped his goggles over his eyes, and dived to the dirt beside the boulder, facing outward. Saylor dropped to the opposite flank of their cover as Lisa crowded next to Ricky, stretching up on her toes to peer over the top.

Scott heard the shots and closed the program he had been using, opening another. Typing frantically, he brought up a software interface connected via USB to an all-band receiver. The black screen was immediately filled with a jumble of light-green tracings, segregated into two frequencies. He already knew the frequencies of the radios his group employed, so using the mouse to encapsulate and select that narrow region, he opened a drop-down box and chose a command which inverted the selection. He then opened another box and clicked on the command to jam all other frequencies. Using the base station of the camp radios, Gumble punched on the microphone and announced, "The bad guys no longer have radios. Repeat. The bad guys are deaf and dumb."

"Who's at the other end of the camp?" shouted Saylor.

"Jimmy and probably Sam by now," Kenny replied and scanned the greenish terrain. Seeing a figure crouched and running, he triggered his rifle, sending a short burst, and saw the man dive to the ground.

His shots were answered by a volley from a spot several yards to the right. Lisa, seeing only the muzzle flash, aimed and drained half her magazine at the target, her effort rewarded by a scream of anguish.

All of their handheld radios crackled with Chili's voice. "What's your status?"

Kenny awkwardly pulled his radio from his pocket. "We're pinned down. Two teams. At least."

"We're coming. How many?"

"Don't know."

Cahane, hearing the exchange, yelled at Chili, "Stop a second!"

"What? No!"

"Just for a second. I want to get in the bed of the truck. You ever spin brodies?"

The Marine considered it and decided. "Good idea. You ready?"

She looped the strap of the AK-47 snugly around her shoulder and arm, grabbed the pair of NVGs, pulled it over her head and down to her neck, letting the bulky device dangle, and checked to make certain that the leather strap on her pistol was secured. "Yep."

He hit the brakes. The nose of the pickup dipped down and the vehicle quickly came to a jarring halt. Even before they were fully stopped, she opened the door, then jumped out and vaulted into the bed. Checking hastily to make sure she had not lost anything, she slammed the palm of her hand on the roof of the cab and shouted, "Go!"

Chili wasted no time, the tires screeching as they clawed for traction. Eunice clung to the front lip so she would not slide the length of the bed and slam against the back gate.

Jimmy was crouched behind a short stacked-stone wall, his eyes incessantly sweeping back and forth across the open area before him, his ears keenly tuned to any new sound. Sam was positioned forty yards to his right. After the first salvo of shots, the men out in the darkness had become still. Meade guessed that it was a result of the jamming of their comm gear. They would take a minute or two to regroup. What he did not know was that the leader of the group attacking their flank, team two, upon losing contact with the team one, had decided that they should circle and join forces rather than risk a blue-on-blue situation.

With Ricky, Lisa, and Saylor maintaining a steady counterfire, Kenny, communicating with Chili, rolled behind the boulder and dug into the backpack until he found two flash-bang grenades. Keeping close behind cover, he rose to his knees and waited. Within twenty seconds the shouted words "Coming in" burst from the small speaker. Yelling at the others to remove their night vision goggles, he pulled a pin on one of the grenades and reared back, throwing it over the boulder and out into the darkness beyond.

Reaching the camp at nearly fifty miles per hour, Chili steered for the area described by Bowman, slowed down, crouched low in the seat, and moved one of his hands to partially shield his eyes. Two rifle shots pinged harmlessly off the sides of the pickup before the flash-bang detonated approximately thirty yards in front of him. Taking that as his cue, he cranked the steering wheel hard to the left and floored the gas, putting the truck into a tight spin on the loose sand of the plateau. With the front wheels remaining in place, as if the bumper were tethered to a spot, and the engine screaming at maximum rpms, the tail of the truck spun in a circle as the drive wheels spewed grit and gravel outward in an arc.

Eunice, having shifted back to the tailgate and jamming herself against a corner, leveled the AK-47. She had no way of knowing that their dramatic entrance coincided with the arrival of team two. She was rewarded with the sight of five men in assault gear, crossing an open area and still upright. Using the rotation of the truck, she calmly lined up with the first of the men and squeezed the trigger, loosing a short burst. Her rounds connected with two of the men cleanly, cutting them down and winging a third, who dropped his rifle and stumbled forward, falling and clutching his side.

As the rear of the truck whipped around for another pass, she saw the other two flat on the ground, lining up for a shot. Ignoring the incoming rounds, she emptied her magazine in a churning straight line across the dirt, the line stitching its way through the two shooters.

One of the slugs from the attackers had plowed into the rear tire of the truck, and within seconds the steel rim was grinding into the rocky, sandy surface, bringing the maneuver to a jittering halt. Killing the lights and the engine, Chili jumped out and, keeping the bulk of the vehicle between himself and the other team, moved to the back and lowered the tailgate. Eunice rolled out and onto the ground and joined him. She dropped the clip out of her rifle and slammed in another as the two lined up against the bed of the truck and opened fire.

Kenny and the others, witnessing their friends' flamboyant arrival, focused their attention on the original assailants who had them pinned down. Following Cahane's disposition of team two, he lobbed his second flash-bang, and all four initiated a relentless barrage, joined by flanking fire from Chili and Eunice. The return fire, initially uncoordinated and sporadic, ceased entirely.

Calling for a stop to the shooting, Kenny used the radio to ask Meade if he was secure. Receiving an affirmative, he ordered the astronaut to hold his position in the event that another party was lurking out there. In the aftermath of the horrendous din, the silence, save for the ringing in their ears, was ominous. Saylor rose slowly and moved to a position beside him. Radioing Chili, asking for cover, Kenny cautiously stepped around the boulder, his AK-47 at the ready, and tentatively inched ahead, when his ears were further battered by the roar of an approaching engine.

Backing up, he heard Romeo's voice from the radio. "Coming in! Status?"

"We appear to be secure. Moving out now to check bodies."

"Hold on. I'll provide some light."

After the truck rumbled past the position held by Chili and Eunice, the headlights were blindingly augmented as Romeo switched on the over-the-cab rack of halogens. The wide arc intensely illuminated the ground where team one had died. Jumping out of the truck, Romeo, holding his rifle forward, moved toward the bodies warily. Kenny trotted to join him as Ricky and Lisa hurried in the direction of the hobbled truck where Cahane and Chili, spread apart by several yards, were cautiously approaching the still figures of team two. Automatically, Saylor took one step in their direction and then abruptly stopped, whirled to his right, and began to run. Toward Puma Punku.

His heart pounding, his breaths coming in harsh gasps which tore at his lungs, Saylor drove himself onward, running beyond the penumbra of the light, his footfalls repeatedly puncturing the obdurate silence, as if each were an act of violence. The stark outlines of the sculpted stones and ravaged remnants of the structures lay strewn before him, exposed and yet concealed by the illuminant moon. In the midst of the monochromous landscape, a single forlorn island of light shone to his right. Veering toward it without breaking stride, consciously willing his pupils to further dilate, he quickened his pace.

As he neared the terrace of Puma Punku...with a mechanistically detached brutality, his eyes absorbed a sight which his mind, upon first grasp of the image, rebelling...refused to accept. Against the stone base, bathed in the counterfeit light of a fallen flashlight, was a scene Saylor involuntarily transposed with the Madonna. Kelsey...her legs sprawled forward, her head deeply bowed, her black hair dangled and draped, cloaking her face...was caressing Judtson's cradled head. Beside them, pressed tightly to his master's side, was Rocky.

His muscles…slack in an instant…brought all motion to a halt and caused the rifle to fall, unnoticed, from his fingers. As he drew…unaware…a deep breath, his obstinate eyes defiantly fixed upon the tableau his heart profoundly wished not to see, and his foot moved a step closer. He did not perceive the scuff of his boot on the stone. With an absence of willful purpose, he took another step.

Reluctantly returning from the world to which she had escaped, Kelsey, with infinite deliberateness, raised her tear-streaked face to Saylor, and their eyes met.

Ricky, having assisted in the process of confirming that the camp was now secure, had separated from the others and was hurrying to follow Saylor, when his soul was pierced by an anguished wail of pain and despair. Staggering to a halt, he fell to his knees. And began to weep.

Chapter 47

As THE WORD SPREAD THROUGH THE CAMP, the members of the original group slowly congregated near the terrace of Puma Punku, no one closely approaching Kelsey...or Saylor, who silently knelt, bent forward, hovering over the body of his friend...each of the assemblage dazed and moving aimlessly, as if in a stupor, and not daring to speak. Ricky, one arm slung over the shoulder of Romeo for support, reached the scene reluctantly and could only take a single fleeting look at his fallen friend before wandering to the extent of the shadows...where he dropped to the ground, hugging his knees, alone. Time inexorably passed, unmeasured and unacknowledged, the silence unbroken.

Kelsey, intently brushing Judtson's cheek with her fingertips, lifted her eyes to rest upon Saylor's devastated countenance. Staring down at the face of his lifelong friend, he sensed this and forced his eyes to rise, meeting hers.

The small erratically flexing muscles around the corners of her mouth rippling the covering skin, her stare interrupted by the cyclic fluttering of her eyelids, Kelsey bit her bottom lip for a time, then spoke. "Saylor...Saylor...I'm sor...." Her neck succumbed to a series of clenching spasms, choking off her words.

Reeling and numb from the horror of this reality, Saylor uttered, "I..." – he stopped, gulped a convulsive breath, and finished – "am too."

Clinging to the tragically forged connection between them, Kelsey swallowed, and swallowed again, finally whispering, "He...he loved me."

With controlled, tight jerks, Saylor nodded at her. "Yes. I know he did." The end of his sentence was bitten off as a sob broke free.

Her voice fragile enough to shatter in the thin air, she repeated, "He loved *me*." Her spoken recognition, making the abstract real, unleashed a new torrent of tears. A high, keening mewl emanated from deep within her, audibly painting a vivid portrait of desperation. Fighting for and winning a few more seconds of control, she added, "And...and...I loved.... No! I *love* him." The sustained whimpering tone returned, stronger than before.

Saylor knew he should say...something, but could not. He again nodded. His reservoir of inner strength had departed with his friend. Watching the naked hurt, the abject anguish etched upon her face, made him feel a voyeur and was more than he could bear. He averted his eyes downward. Saved from the sight, he now only had the pathetic sounds of her suffering penetrate his heart.

Focused again on Judtson and burying his fingers in the thick fur of the golden retriever still pressed firmly, unmoving, against his master's side, Saylor willfully beckoned the thousand, or million, vignettes from their shared life. Rather than pushing them down...rather than avoiding them...he immersed himself into and embraced each and every one of the moments his memory proffered. His consciousness eagerly escaped the dark, dusty plateau. Magically traveling back to their very first meeting as small boys, a loving and respectful editor residing within his mind unarchived and spliced together a story...a movie...an epic...of joy, laughter, drama, suspense and, above all, friendship and trust. A story he had always been certain would not have an end. At least not for a very long time to come.

Distant and lost in the bittersweet reverie, Saylor did not, at first, notice the change come over Kelsey. When he did sense a difference, a tension, almost a potency arising from her, he looked up. Her right hand was clutching an object which hung from a glittering gold necklace. Although her left hand was stroking Judtson's temple and cheek, she was no longer staring at him. There was no trace of a tear streaming down her cheek. No quiver in the muscles of her face. Only firmness. In the haunting chiaroscuro, her features now appeared chiseled, solid, immutable; her eyes now unblinkingly locked upon something unseen...perhaps unseeable.

Turning to Saylor once again, her voice now different as well...stronger, but also tender...she requested, "Would you hold him, please?"

He slipped one hand beneath Judtson's head, the other beneath his back, and lifted gently. She took the leather jacket which had covered his wounds, and rose. Once on her feet, firmly gripping the blood-soaked coat, she strode to the terrace.

Romeo, who had been respectfully keeping his distance, saw Kelsey move, and instantly followed as she tucked the jacket under one arm and used the other as a brace, vaulting onto the stones of the terrace; he, scrambling up behind her. She quickly reached the center of the platform and stopped.

Slowing his pace as he neared her rigid figure silhouetted in profile on the ancient stage, Romeo, his voice solicitous, asked, "Are you all right?"

Kelsey was not looking in his direction. When he spoke, she did not react...but mutely stared up at the stars. Some of the others...Chris, Lisa, Eunice, and Carlos...had climbed atop the stone terrace and quietly, curiously drew together behind the big man, who was watching her uncertainly.

She unfurled the jacket and lifted it over her head...spreading it wide above her, with the lamb's wool lining facing skyward...and remained frozen in the surreal pose. No one spoke. Soon, Kelsey lowered the jacket, clutched it momentarily to her chest, and slowly, reverently knelt, laying it flat upon the stone surface with the blood-soaked fleece down.

Then she stood once more. In the moonlight, Romeo was able to distinguish the gleaming eight-pointed star affixed to the gold chain hanging from her neck. Her hand came up. Her fingers wrapped around the star. Pivoting to the north, aligning her face to the region of the star-filled sky which held the constellation Pegasus, Kelsey began to speak. Her words, if they were words, plainly directed at someone or something other than the five people watching, rang out clearly and powerfully into the night.

The sound, the tone, the cadence, and the structure of her declamation struck a disquietingly familiar chord within Romeo. Before he could make the connection, Carlos gasped, "She is speaking Sumerian."

Within less than one minute, she stopped and fell silent, shifting her gaze from the constellation downward until her eyes were once more upon the calfskin of the jacket. She dropped to her knees, laid the palms of her hands upon the leather, set her teeth, and began to create a soft, unvarying, unwavering monotone hum. Her body was fixed and perfectly still. Following the cessation of her imprecation, supplication, diatribe or prayer, whichever it might have been, an impenetrable silence blanketed the terrace, save for the whisper of a tone produced by Kelsey. The anticipatory quiescence so complete, so absolute, it seemed to nullify even the faint sounds of breathing from the gathered. No one dared to move.

It first began at a level far below their perceptual threshold. A deep, susurrant bass vibration, felt more than heard, was conducted into the soles of their feet, relentlessly escalating in pitch, strength, and intensity until attaining a frequency discernible by the delicate malleus, incus, and stapes of the human ear. The nerves, ducts, and glands of the observers, reacting at an atavistic, primal level to the irrational stimuli, unleashed adrenaline and a nearly intoxicating panoply of endorphins...the purely biological, mindless purport, to prepare the body for a threat...whatever form it might assume. Despite the chill of the air, the skin of the five was uniformly prickled with perspiration. Their breathing quickened. Their senses heightened. Without a trace of conscious intent, the witnesses clustered and withdrew by yards. Stopping. Waiting.

Standing alone and immune to the sensorial onslaught, Kelsey did not, for even a moment, avert her eyes from the massive andesite stone which supported the coat. The physical force that was sound crescendoed to the brink of thunder, reaching and affecting every living being in an ever-expanding radius. The others who had converged, milling beyond the terrace, moved to the edge and froze. Waiting.

As if all were suddenly struck deaf, the trembling, rumbling tumult abruptly ceased, supplanted by a faint buzzing tone notched at a midpoint between a hum and a whine, previously present, yet obscured by the other.

Kelsey, with patient deliberateness, straightened and took a single step back, never shifting the focus of her gaze. The stone upon which her coat, and the blood of her beloved, rested...the dense mass of thousands of pounds...slowly and almost gracefully rose from the midst of the collinear pattern.

Under her breath, Cahane gasped.

Exposing a vertical thickness of many feet, the stone continued its gradual upward progress until, revealing the full extent of its form, it stopped...the humming, whining tone now diminished but not ended...the block impossibly hovering inches above the adjacent floor, with no visible support. Kelsey reached out and placed a single hand on its side and pushed. As effortlessly as if she were guiding a buoyant raft on the surface of a pool, she walked along the edge of the dark pit vacated by the stone, moving the massive block with her. Having repositioned the object beyond the outline of the chthonic opening, she stopped, lowering her hand to her side. The cut stone, now without the provided impetus, continued drifting forward for several inches before attaining a point of impossible stasis.

For the first time acknowledging the presence of the others, Kelsey directed her words to Romeo, who was standing, spellbound. "I need your light."

Eunice poked him in the hip with her elbow and, from the side of her mouth, whispered hoarsely, "I'da thought she could generate her own."

$$\triangledown$$

All of the group, with the exception of Saylor, had assembled near the opening. Matt, Carlos, and Scott repetitively circled the raised stone, lying down and hugging the platform to peer under it, touching it, nudging it to watch it move. Romeo, keeping close to his charge, knelt at the edge and stared into the pit, its intimidating darkness pierced by the stabbing beam of his flashlight. All that was visible, approximately twenty feet below the opening, was a stone platform. He stood to face Kelsey. She had remained on her feet and, although directing her gaze into the opening, had not demonstrated the interest or curiosity he expected.

"Are you planning to go down there?"

She nodded without comment, her attention remaining with what lay below. Her face was rigidly impassive.

With his voice absent the confidence and authority it normally conveyed, he ventured, "Kelsey...what is down there? How did you lift that...?"

Romeo's questions seemed to break her concentration. She looked away from the pit, her eyes meeting his. Reaching out, Kelsey took the flashlight from his hand. "Get a ladder for me." Her tone was neither soft nor harsh. Her words were spoken flatly.

"On its way. Along with the rest of our gear."

"Bring what you wish. All I need is a ladder."

He tried to read what was written within her eyes, but could not. Before he was able to say another word, she abruptly turned away and walked to Chris Ashby, who had joined Matt and the others alongside the floating stone.

Reacting to her arrival, his voice concerned, he began to speak. "Kelsey...I am so sorr...."

Holding up a hand to stop him, she inquired, "Chris, did you bring the gold?"

His eyes widened. "Yes. I did. Why?"

"I need it."

Clearly not understanding, he agreed regardless. "Of course. How much?"

"All of it."

Sensing that this was neither the time nor the place for questions, he told her he would get it and hurried away.

Kelsey then strode to the perimeter of the terrace, jumped down, joining Saylor where he had remained, and squatted down beside him. The man, plainly enduring more than any person should, looked up but said nothing.

"Saylor, I am going below," she explained, her voice soft and gentle. "My father is down there. So is your wife. I'm going to get them."

He absorbed her statements and, with another glance down at his friend's still visage, nodded. "I'm going, too."

"I know." Leaning closer, she wrapped her arms around his shoulders and whispered.

$$\triangledown$$

The rope ladder, secured to the joints of the stone platform with multiple knifeblade pitons, was dropped over the edge. Ashby returned, carrying a bulky plastic container with a snap-on lid, and gave it to Kelsey. She hefted it. "Anyone have a sack?"

Jonassen stepped forward. "Here." He handed her a leather pouch, closed at the top with a woven drawstring. "I picked this up from one of the locals when I was living in the cave. Traded a spare pair of gloves for it."

He tugged at the top, pulled it open and emptied its contents, an assortment of wrapped hard candies, into his hand.

"Thanks." She took it and, with Chris' help, poured in the monoatomic gold, the powder completely filling the pouch. First pulling the drawstrings tight, she tied them to her belt.

Jamming the flashlight into her back pocket, she returned to the entrance and, kneeling beside the ladder, stepped onto the top rung.

"Kelsey," objected Romeo. "I'll go first."

She looked up at him, a half-smile barely bending the corner of her mouth. "Not this time," she answered and quickly descended. The big man leaned out over the pit and, using a borrowed light, illuminated her progress.

A somber Kenny, Jimmy, and Saylor gingerly lifted Judtson's body and placed it upon a blanket, brought by Lisa, at the edge of the terrace.

"Why don't we take him to the camp?" suggested Bowman.

"This is what Kelsey asked" was the only explanation Saylor gave.

"Somebody ought to stay with him," grunted Meade.

As he spoke, Rocky leapt up and lay down beside his master.

Saylor rubbed the golden's neck. "Somebody is."

The moment Kelsey released the last rung, Romeo clambered onto the ladder and started down, going faster than he ever had on the boot camp obstacle course. Concentrating on his foot and hand placements upon the wildly gyrating rungs, he was not able to keep her in sight. Dropping the final few feet, he grabbed his light and whirled around, sweeping his surroundings. He was in a large chamber. It appeared to roughly mirror the surface dimensions of the platform above and was uniformly enclosed on eight sides by perfectly fitted stone blocks rising to the top. Centered in alternating sections, positioned in the cardinal directions, were tall openings, spanned by wide stone lintels. The floor itself sloped away from him in all directions, as if he were standing atop a massive dome.

Kelsey was gone. Frustration welling within him, he cupped his hands around his mouth to yell for her, then stopped, thinking better of it. The ladder flapped against him and he saw that Chili was already on his way down. He steadied it for his partner.

One by one, those who had chosen to join the search stood with Romeo in the octagonal chamber. He assessed his team. Chili, Lisa, Eunice, Kenny, Carlos, Chris, Matt, and Saylor, each armed with a rifle, waited in a semicircle around him, expectantly. Three of them had their flashlights turned on to push back the pressing darkness.

"All right, here's the situation." Even though he spoke barely above a whisper, the space instantly filled with the reverberations from his voice. "We don't know where we are or what we're walking into. Kelsey has already taken off and I don't know where. We have four ways we can go. Each one of those openings leads to a passageway. No dirt on the floor. No dust. No tracks. Nothing that would indicate which way she went."

"Do we split up?"

"That makes the most sense, Matt."

"Our radios won't work down here."

"No, probably not."

Lisa cautioned, "So one of the parties could get lost, killed, or…whatever, and the rest wouldn't even know."

"True."

"I think we should stick together."

Romeo grunted his disagreement. "Then we cut our chances of finding Kelsey, or the others, to a fourth."

For the first time since they had all descended, Saylor spoke. "Let's try something. Everyone, turn off your light."

The flashlights were extinguished, plunging them into an eerie blackness. After a few seconds, as their eyes adjusted, Saylor's voice was heard. "Behind you, Romeo. There is a faint light at that opening."

Romeo spun around. The blackness before him contained a barely discernible dim gray rectangle. Switching his light on, he nodded. "Okay, we stay together."

As he began walking toward the opening, a voice from above stopped him. "Wait."

Awkwardly climbing down the ladder, an AK-47 slung behind his back, was Ricky. Romeo rushed to the bottom and gripped the ropes, pulling down hard and steadying his friend's descent. As his feet touched the floor, he forced a weak smile. "You weren't going without me, were you?"

Romeo, concerned, asked, "You okay?"

The slender blond man thought about his answer for a moment first. "No…I'm not. Don't think I ever will be. You?"

His somber reply was accompanied by a shake of the head. "No."

Bal, on the terrace with the others, was on his knees and bent forward, the side of his face resting on the surface. "Sam! Come look at this."

The postdoc, several yards away and giving instructions to a small gathering of his students, trotted to the still-hovering andesite. He dropped down beside his mentor, also leaning forward. "Yes, sir?"

His voice a blend of scientific curiosity and childlike wonder, the geologist began, "I have been studying this since the others went below."

"Do you have any idea how it became weightless?"

"Ideas? I have no shortage of ideas. Explanations which might be palatable to the scientific community…that is a different matter entirely. Nonetheless, I have noticed something which could give us a clue."

"What's that, sir?"

"In the several minutes since Kelsey raised it, the block has descended. Look!"

Sam focused on the gap between the bottom of the stone and the surface of the terrace. "You're right. It seems lower."

Bal rolled onto his side to face his earnest assistant and handed him a small notepad with a spiral binding at the top edge. It was flipped open to an empty page. "As they were obtaining the rope ladder, I marked the height above the terrace." He directed his penlight and pointed. "There. That was the elevation." The line was nearly to the top of the page, only a fraction away from the row of holes punched for the spiral.

"Its progress was so minuscule that I did not notice it. It was not until I returned and double-checked the measurement that I discovered the difference." He indicated the second hash mark down. "It was less than a quarter of an inch. I assumed that I had made an error initially. Even so, I began monitoring it. The succeeding three lines down the page were distances recorded at five-minute intervals."

"What do think is happening?"

Frowning thoughtfully, Singh finally hypothesized, "It is as if the stone had been imbued with an energy...."

"Or a vibration...a frequency?"

"Possibly. And that force, whatever it might be, rendered the stone...buoyant, allowing it to rise and then be moved. As it floats here, Sam, I am able to move it laterally with the pressure from a single fingertip. But now, with the absence of Kelsey, or whatever it is she employed, the energy...or vibration...is gradually dissipating. Soon...I estimate seventeen more minutes...this several-ton block of andesite will be resting lightly on the terrace. And eventually, it will have regained its former weight."

Sam cautiously touched the stone with the tip of his index finger and pushed. The pressure sufficient to counteract the inertia of the mass, the block began to move. "Dr. Singh, I think what we are witnessing explains so much."

Bal smiled and nodded. "It does. For instance, the mystery of how monuments such as the pyramids were constructed. There is another interesting aspect."

"What's that?"

Pressing the side of his face down against the terrace once more, he indicated, "Look at this."

Sam lowered himself so that he, too, could peer underneath the stone. Unsure of what he was seeing, he pulled a penlight from his pocket and shined it on the underside. The tightly focused halogen beam reflected off the surface brilliantly. With a soft gasp of surprise, Sam blurted, "It's gold!"

The passageway was tall, well above ten feet in height, and wide; and rather than following the slope of the dome, it was level. The floor, walls, and ceiling, all made with snugly fit cut-stone blocks, almost infinitely repeated every scuff and scrape of their shoes, every exhalation. Romeo cautiously led the group forward, with Chili at the rear. More than once they came upon intersections and paused, turning off their lights. The feeble illumination which guided them in their original choice was gradually brightening, leading them onward in a straight line.

To keep his mind distracted from the claustrophobic environs, Ashby dwelled upon the question of why Kelsey had wanted his monoatomic gold. Villarreal stared intently at the passing block work, struggling to incorporate what he was seeing with any known archaeological beliefs.

Wheeler contemplated the depth and breadth of technical expertise needed to design and build the labyrinth through which he walked. The others dealt with the surreal nature of their setting, each in his or her own way.

Acutely alert, Romeo allowed a portion of his mind to ponder the change he had observed in Kelsey after the death of Judtson Kent. In the time he had known her, since that first night in her home when he had saved her from the intruders bent upon killing her, Kelsey had always been intense. That intensity had taken many forms. Happiness, joy, loyalty, anxiety, and anger, as well as the balance of the emotional spectrum, were all experienced by her at a level deemed extreme by most.

Yet now, since the moment she rose from holding Judtson, there was something different. . .something he had never before seen in the set of her jaw, the posture of her frame, or the look in her eyes. Although foreign to Kelsey, it was a transformation familiar to him: a transmogrification which, in his experience, only occurred on the field of battle. . .and even then, only at those most exigent of circumstances when all appeared to have been lost. It was, in his experience, the sparking of that primal fire within some which caused a soldier to rise up. . .to charge the guns. . .to confront impossible odds. And. . .to occasionally emerge alive and victorious. And. . .to occasionally emerge only victorious.

He knew she was somewhere within this underground maze. . .unarmed and unafraid. He also knew that it was his job to find her. To help her. To protect her.

▽

Sam Jonassen briskly crossed the camp, attempting to satisfy himself that the students had been rounded up and were all congregated in the community tent, and that several of them were armed. Jimmy Meade, Dylan Falt, and Dean Copeland were standing watch outside the tent. The astronaut saw him approach and trotted forward. "Sam, one of your damn-fool students, Gretchen, took off."

"Took off? Why?"

"She said she had to go back to the other camp, the one by the lake, and get her field notes. I tried to tell her that we didn't know what other bad types might still be around and we needed to stay together, but she wouldn't listen."

Frustrated, Sam shook his head and grunted. "All right. You stay here with the group. I'll head over there and bring her back."

▽

As they approached a T-intersection, a nearly inaudible undercurrent of sound caught the attention of Romeo's conscious mind. Raising a hand to stop the progress of those behind him, he directed the halo of his light onto his face and held a finger to his lips. They stopped and stood silently, holding their collective breath. Focusing and listening, he found that his mind conjured images of branches colliding in a breeze. . .mingled with the staccato chittering of cicadas. . . punctuated by the atonal, guttural consonants of a roadrunner.

Motioning for the others to hold back, he clutched his rifle at the ready and edged forward. Reaching the intersection, he carefully peered around first one corner and then the other, before stepping out and turning. The stone walkway they had traveled bore both to the right and to the left, incorporated into the top of a descending wall. The ceiling maintained a level plane, extending away from the wall and spanning, without supports, a distance of a thousand yards or more. No longer composed of stones, it shined with a seamless metallic gleam. He stood at the rim of a massive chamber, a cavernous pit. From the distant bottom, he knew his body would appear to be the size of an ant.

The space was filled with light, cast upward by a dense scattering of sources from below. Across the floor, structures filled the available space, divided like a patchwork quilt by narrow walkways, laid out in an orderly pattern. From his vantage, Romeo was able to discern bustling movement on the aisles or paths, but could not clearly identify the residents of this outlandish domain. Shouldering his rifle, he pulled a pair of binoculars from a pouch as Cahane, who had decided to follow, rounded the corner and looked down.

With a sharp intake of breath, she muttered, "Well, butter my butt and call me a biscuit."

Chapter 48

THE GROUP, BEWILDERED AND OVERWHELMED BY THE VISTA BELOW, wordlessly trailed Romeo as he followed the wide ledge around the perimeter of the void. They encountered no one else on the path and, after less than a hundred yards, arrived at a broad, bifurcated set of steps, perpendicular to the ledge and extending down to the floor of the chamber in a continuous, straight run. The material of the stairway matched the ledge, in that it was constructed from cut stones and was composed of two parallel rows. The width and height of the steps on the left side were of conventional dimensions, comfortable for their use. On the right, the risers were much taller, as were the treads longer.

All hesitating at the top, Ricky asked rhetorically, "What is this place?"

"Whatever it might be," answered Carlos almost reverently, "it is impossible."

Surveying the faces of his team, Romeo saw a gamut of emotions from awe to fear, reflected in all with the lone exception of Saylor, who resolutely returned his gaze.

"Let's move." Romeo began his descent. The balance of the party fell in line behind.

As they traveled downward, the details resolved, revealing a complex community. The structures, all built with milled stones varying from megalithic size to that of a brick, were neatly laid out in a grid-like design, abutted by a minimum of one walkway, also of stone. Most of the aisles were relatively narrow. Those fed into secondary, somewhat wider lanes. And those connected with broad avenues.

Yet, despite the astonishing details of this small city within a mountain, the one aspect of their discovery which distracted them from the rest was the physical appearance of the residents, who were casually traveling the interlinked thoroughfares, blithely unconcerned with the new arrivals. As the group drew near the floor level, surveying the bustle of activity on both sides of the stairs, it became clear that the great majority of the occupants were not people...although certainly humanoid in outline with two legs, two arms, a torso, and a head. More striking were the differences. Much taller than even the most extreme of the human race, these beings stood well over nine feet. Their skin shimmered, refracting light in a random mosaic.

Saylor, who was studying the milling throng carefully, noticed that despite the preponderance of the alien forms, there was a small mingling of humans. The shorter, familiar figures moved with the others. Their eyes downcast. Their gait slow and deliberate. Focusing on one in particular, Saylor stopped on the steps for a moment. And stared.

Romeo, who had been scrutinizing the surroundings for threats, returned his eyes to the fore. The stairs terminated in an open courtyard occupied by a stately figure, apparently waiting for them. He, if gender assignment proved appropriate, was accompanied by a person, a very old and frail man who was garbed in a loose-fitting beige jumpsuit and sitting on a small ledge, regarding the visitors blankly.

The Ranger took three steps forward and paused, allowing his team to assemble behind him. The tall being, the entirety of his body covered with a snug red fabric, save for his hands and head, came into sharper focus. The visible skin was scaled and seemed to glimmer with a prismatic mother-of-pearl iridescence. Its eyes, fixed upon Romeo, were large and dominated by vertically split pupils. The mouth, lipless, could have been a horizontal slash cut with a sharp scalpel. On the sides of its head, where humans would have ears, there were subtle single folds of skin.

Eunice sidled close, and from the side of her mouth muttered, "If I had a dog as ugly as that, I'd shave his butt and make him walk backward."

Before Romeo could respond, the old man spoke in a weak and croaking voice. "We have been expecting you."

Saylor separated from the group and brushed past Cahane and Jones, striding directly toward the being. The others moved to close ranks behind their friend who, looking up at the chimerical face, demanded, "Where are my wife and William Batman?"

There was no perceptible change in the being's face in reaction to Saylor's words. The white-haired man to its side made a rapid series of clicking noises with his mouth, tongue, and throat. The being's slit of a mouth, in darting movements, created a somewhat longer string of clicks, after which the man said, "Enlil has no knowledge of this. He does not know where these people are and, in fact, does not know who they are."

Instantly, Saylor's voice rose in intensity. "That's a lie. We know that the two of them were brought here by your people."

The translator completed another exchange. "You are sadly mistaken. Those above...those who have harassed, assaulted, kidnapped, and assassinated your friends...are not of us. They are your enemy. We are not."

Saylor maintained eye contact with the disconcerting split pupils of the tall being the intermediary had called "Enlil," and sternly asked, "Who are you?"

The elderly emissary translated, listened to Enlil's reply, and said, "We are the Anunnaki."

The name was familiar to Saylor. "The Anunnaki of lore. The race described in Egyptian and Sumerian myths as gods?"

After hearing the interpreter, Enlil nodded.

"And who are the people who killed my friend?"

Once more, the old man facilitated the interaction and answered, "The assailants have been our foes...our enemies for thousands of years. They are called the Illuminati."

Saylor pivoted on his heel and glanced back at his friends, his gaze lingering for a time on Ricky before returning. When it did, the hint of a wry grin was on his face. "Okay. I'm sorry. I'm a little fuzzy on all of this. Maybe you can give me some background. And, by the way..." – he shifted his attention to the liaison – "who in the hell are you?"

The aged intercessor cocked his head. His wrinkled skin creased in a fruitless attempt to match the smile. "I am merely a loyal friend to Enlil and his people. My name is Arthur Posnansky."

A loud gasp burst from Carlos, who stepped forward to stand beside Saylor. "You are the explorer who was the first to investigate Puma Punku and theorize that it was built by aliens!"

The man's eyes met Villarreal's. His expression remained neutral. "That is I."

"No, that is preposterous. It would make you one hundred and forty years old!"

"Indeed it would…and does."

"How is such a thing possible?"

"It is possible with the science and medicine of the Anunnaki. As you see, they were not able to reverse the aging process, yet did succeed in slowing it dramatically."

Warily, Villarreal moved to within a foot of the man. "I…I am your grandson."

Arthur's eyes widened and he took in the details of Carlos from toes to face. "That…cannot be."

More confident now, Carlos responded, "Oh, but it is. My grandmother was your personal maid. Her name was…."

"Adelita." As the old man spoke the name, there was an almost indiscernible hint of wistfulness to his voice.

"Yes. She believed…or perhaps I should say that this is what she told my mother…that you left here and returned to Europe, never to make contact with her again."

Posnansky's light gray eyes drifted away, focusing on a distant point. "This is true. It is true that I departed. It is true that I never contacted Adelita again." Reconnecting with his grandson's intent stare, he shakily lifted his arm to encompass his surroundings. "However…it was this place to which I came, not my home country."

Saylor gently cleared his throat. "I'm sorry to interrupt, Carlos. Right now, we need to know what's going on."

"Of course. Yes. There will be time." The archaeologist moved back a step.

Looking at the translator expectantly, Saylor prompted, "Well, Mr. Posnansky?"

The old man appeared to pose a question to Enlil. The tall being nodded once and responded, beginning a long succession of clicks which the man translated as a streaming narrative.

"We are from another world. A world…and a sun…not young as are yours. In the latter part of its cycle, our sun began to inflate. The first effect of this was a gradual, steady erosion…a relentless stripping away of our atmosphere which resulted in a myriad of problems: drastic fluctuations in our weather patterns…life-threatening cancers of our skin…a disruption and breakdown of our bodily organs…and countless others. To survive, we, as a species, moved underground. Admittedly, that was merely a stopgap measure, for we knew that it would only be a matter of time until our entire planet was destined to become completely uninhabitable.

"The mechanisms of the universe operate at a timescale deceptive to living beings. The inexorable progress of our demise was stretched over centuries, and each generation succumbed to the temptation to solve only the immediate, temporal, existential threats, while ignoring the more distant, inevitable extinction. Always one step behind the escalating onslaught, the incremental adjustments we made…the reactionary changes in our lifestyles, food sources, and other aspects of daily life…turned country against country, city against city and, eventually, person against person in the ever more difficult quest for dwindling resources. It was a time of utter chaos. A time of overarching pragmatism. A time bereft of compassion. And, as far as those of us who survived, a time of great shame for what we had become. For the price we had paid to ensure our survival.

"There is no greater provider of impetus than the loud ticking of the doomsday clock. Even though we were a species steeped in a weakness practiced and perfected to an art form… denial…we ultimately realized that there truly was no choice but to escape…abandon our beloved home. Technological research, discovery, invention, and creation were, at last, elevated to the pinnacle of the hierarchy within our priorities, the resources jealously allocated. Until, generations after the effort was begun, we had perfected and constructed a total of twenty-four massive ships, each ship capable of transporting a colony.

"Our astronomers had identified twelve potentially hospitable suns…twelve likely solar systems within the galaxy…twelve of the most salient candidates for our migration. The potential new homes for our race were far-flung and widely separated from one another. Each pair of ships…each band of Anunnaki…randomly chose a destination. We said our farewells and wished the other eleven expeditions the best of luck…and we set out. I…my cohort…had chosen Earth."

Saylor's face betrayed no reaction to the being's story. "Ask him, Arthur, how long ago they arrived."

Posnansky relayed the question and replied, "More than four hundred thousand years ago."

"So, hominids were already present when you arrived," concluded Carlos, his statement also conveyed.

"They were. The debate raged at the time whether we should seek another world rather than disrupt one already occupied. Having left behind the horrors of our brutal acts and deeds, we had no interest, desire, or wish to disrupt, destroy, or as much as affect another species, even one which we viewed at the time as vastly inferior…primitive. After intense discussion and debate, the decision was made, based upon the cold, hard realities of our ships and our diminishing resources, that the odds of finding another habitable planet in time were virtually nil."

"That's hard to believe, Art," commented Saylor. "Considering the millions of solar systems just in our neighborhood."

The old man, his features animated by a slight flicker of irritation at the employing of the diminutive name, again communicated the expressed doubt and received an answer. "You are correct. There are millions of systems nearby. Near, in a relative sense. Yet you might be surprised to discover, as were we, how rare and unique your planet truly is. As we closely passed hundreds of systems and observed thousands more from a distance while traversing our route to you, we found that, in essentially all cases, an elliptical path is the normal configuration for planets to orbit a sun. In this system, your orbits are, for all practical purposes, circular. The difference, in terms of the impact upon the habitability of the planet, is profound. In a circular orbit, with a tilted axis of rotation, you have relatively moderate seasons throughout each trip around your sun. In an elliptical orbit, with the planet drawing much nearer the sun at the perigee of its orbit and falling much farther away at the apogee, the environment annually goes from boiling hot to frozen solid…a variation not conducive to life in almost any form, certainly not ours."

"So, as did the Europeans when they came upon the New World already occupied, you decided to move in."

Enlil, hearing the translated words, shook his head and replied through Posnansky. "That comparison is neither accurate nor fair. We supplanted no one. As a result of centuries of living below ground on our home planet, we had lost our ability to survive on the surface, exposed to the radiation of a sun, even in a benign environment. No, our decision was to inhabit the underworld."

"Surely, you needed food...water."

"We did. And we do. Water is not an issue. There is ample groundwater for our needs. And the lake above us serves well as a reservoir. We are now self-sustaining insofar as food, given that we have adapted the techniques from our home and maintain...inside this mountain and elsewhere...what are essentially farms and, in a sense, ranches which provide for all of our needs."

From behind Saylor, Carlos asked, "Elsewhere? Other than here in the Andes, where do you reside?"

"Our other complex is nestled under the region of the world known as the Levant."

Villarreal uttered a soft gasp. "Baalbek?"

"Baalbek...extending to Jerusalem."

"You said that you are *now* self-sustaining," pressed Carlos. "That was not always the case?"

"No. For quite some time, we required assistance from those above. Merely to gather food and other items for us."

Saylor, listening to the exchange, took the forefront in the questioning and charged, "I've heard that you enslaved people to get them to do your work."

Once again, as Posnansky translated the accusation, Enlil shook his head, more emphatically this time. "No. That was never the case. Nor was it ever needed. We simply established a trading relationship with those primitive people. For their labor, we exchanged basic skills, techniques, the teaching and demonstration of elementary science. This included a variety of methods for fire starting, the creation of rudimentary tools, and other simplistic yet helpful knowledge. Sadly, those early alliances...those first interactions...were the seeds which, over time, created the powerful group you have been battling."

"How?"

"The indigenes became dependent upon us. Intensely so. We began to fear that our benevolently intended, spoon-fed morsels of advanced civilization had the unintended consequence of stilting their own innate curiosity...their own spark to explore, invent, and learn. We also discovered that those individuals to whom we provided glimpses of our knowledge, rather than sharing it openly, hoarded it...subverted it, used it to amass power over their brothers. Capitalizing on the fact that they were the holders of our secrets, the recipients declared themselves to be priests or gods...made themselves despotic rulers...and used what we had taught, not to elevate the plight of their people, but rather as a weapon to be wielded. As we came to understand this, we had simultaneously arrived at a point where self-sufficiency was possible. At that juncture we cut our ties with the people above."

As Posnansky's voice related the narrative, Saylor noticed that the courtyard, if that was what it was, had begun to fill with both the tall beings and a few humans. "What happened then?"

"Sadly, all that occurred was predictable. Even though much of the lore and myth of ancient civilizations will have a trace of truth, the real truth is vastly different. We severed ourselves from these megalomaniacal men, who had already learned that we were pacifistic, obsessively so, and that we abhorred violence in any form. Through their cold-hearted calculation, this weakness within us was exploited. The perpetrators built temples upon the sites of their meetings with us in the past. Temples with altars. And they would bring to the altar the most pure...the most innocent...of their people and offer that life to us."

Saylor heard a muted gasp from Lisa.

"That ingenuous life was offered not to please us or appease us, as was claimed. Instead, it was employed as a means of...blackmail. Either we provided what was sought...more knowledge, tools, and the other elements of our advanced science...or the killings would continue. Those were truly dark days for us. At first, we capitulated. We did provide more...only to observe as our newest offerings were also subverted and made into weapons, strengthening the power of those same heinous men. With great difficulty, we closed our ears to the threats... and then to the pleas...to the screams...to the horror above. Our hope was to wean them. To eliminate dependency upon us so they could advance...evolve...develop into a race with which we could share an enlightened partnership."

"Didn't work out quite that way, did it?"

"It did not. To our acute sorrow, the course chosen by mankind above has been quite the opposite of our hopes for it. We are no closer to that partnership today than when we taught that first grunting primitive man how to build a fire. We have come to understand that we are not without blame for this course. Some of us even believe that we were the primary cause. That had we not intervened...had we never arrived here...mankind would have followed a different path. That it was our very presence...our intent to elevate which provided an easy shortcut to progress. The reality of handing humans a shortcut, instead of forcing them to earn each incremental step, has proved to be that those among them who would have been the thinkers, the inventors, the creators are marginalized...unneeded and unheeded. And those who can most effectively capitalize upon the technologies gifted to them...those who excel at ruthlessly taking advantage of the toil of others...come to the fore and become the dominant, influential, and powerful members of the society. Unfortunately, the latter group does not include the best of the species. We believe that our actions...our very presence...cultivated and nurtured a cult of exploiters. Not only cultivated this subset but also handed it the tools needed to rise to the top of the social hierarchy. It is a cult which has tenaciously clung to the reins of power in the world ever since."

"The Illuminati?"

"Yes. Those original priests, self-proclaimed gods, rulers, and leaders of ancient times, when cut off from us...severed from the bounty they had come to expect...to demand, utilized their wealth and power already amassed, and in a sense went underground as well, figuratively as opposed to literally. We created a beast, and it thrived and grew within the very bowels of your social infrastructure. Its members are bloodline related. Its tendrils extend to every seat of power on Earth. Its appetite for wealth is insatiable and has moved beyond merely acquiring money, to owning the monetary systems themselves."

More and more of the reptoids arrived, accompanied by a handful of their human counterparts, pressing closer to the assemblage in a dense circle.

"And through all of this, it...cannot resist taunting us...baiting us. It dangles messages, symbols, dates, images before our eyes as it promulgates or commits the most flagitious of acts. Where once the villains brought a young child to our portal and spilled her blood, they now instigate the deaths of thousands, millions. Using war, disease, famine, and pestilence."

Saylor grunted. "So the bad guys are still trying to get you to fork over your goodies?"

"Yes. That is true."

"I don't understand how all of this relates to what has happened to my friends."

"Each of you, in your own field, had begun a journey which would ultimately have exposed them for the monsters that they are. That is why they attempted to control you. That is why they attempted to kill all of you."

Taking in a deep breath and adopting a subtle mocking tone, Saylor said, "Okay. Let me make sure I understand, Enlil. You and your fellow lizards are just a bunch of benevolent, easygoing, well-meaning hippie peaceniks. And all you want is to live in your cave and be left alone. Oh, and you're sorry about that nasty group of bad boys above who are now running roughshod over our entire civilization. You're sorry about creating that gang and setting them up in business. You didn't *mean* to do it. *You were just doing the best you could.*" His final sentence was soaked in sarcasm.

He watched the unemotive visage of Enlil as Posnansky translated. When the clicking stopped, Saylor added with a smirk, "Do I have it about right?"

Carlos, who had remained close to his side, gently touched his friend's arm and whispered, "Why are you...?"

Before Villarreal could complete his sentence, the elderly go-between, finishing a brief conversation with the being, spoke. "Enlil has acknowledged that you are correct in your summation. These are now my own words. Why do you take such an offensive tone?"

Swinging his gaze from the beast to the man, Saylor took a step closer. "Tell you why, Artie. I have...had...a friend. His name was Judtson Kent. A lot of people thought he was abrasive...odd...rude...pompous...well, I won't go on. But he was my best friend. And he was the best friend a man could have. Knew him almost my whole life. He had an amazing sense of humor. He was loyal. He was honest. He was smart. Perceptive. Insightful. Well, you get the picture. He also taught me a lot of things. Like how important it is to really live each day...each minute. Or..." – Saylor choked somewhat – "that we don't get another crack at this life, so we should try to get it right the first time. You know what else he taught me? Something he was very good at. Fantastic, in fact."

Pausing, he stared intently at Posnansky. When the old man gave him no reaction, he continued, "He taught me how to smell a load of bullshit from a mile away."

Carlos made a muted sound as he sucked in a short breath.

The translator's voice grew in timbre. "Are you saying that Enlil deceives you?"

Saylor casually reached up and brushed a shock of hair from his forehead. "Well now, logically, there are only two possibilities. One, old Enlil here is a big, tall bullshitter. Or...all the translating you've been doing since we arrived has been about his tasty cockroach casserole recipe. And you're the one making this stuff up. Which one is it, Artie?"

The wrinkles, lines, and folds surrounding the man's eyes bunched together, leaving only narrow slits. With tightly controlled inflection, he answered, "Neither Enlil nor I have deceived. Why do you say that we have?"

His sardonic smirk broadening, Saylor expressively shook his head in wonderment. "Oh, I don't know. Maybe...oh, wait, I remember...as I was coming down those stairs and looking out over this...nest...I saw a few human folks wandering around. And I have to say that this was pretty stupid of you...but one of the guys window-shopping, or whatever the hell he was doing, was somebody I knew. Somebody I recognized. I never knew his name. None of us did. Back then, we called him 'Bob.' He was our guest inside the missile silo. You know the place. The one your goons blew up after kidnapping my friends."

Posnansky was in the midst of responding, when the tall reptoid placed his scaly hand on the man's shoulder to silence him, and in a buzzing, chittering yet understandable voice declared, "Enough!"

Saylor fixed his gaze back on the slitted eyes, but rather than retreat, moved inches closer. Romeo, positioned two paces behind, surreptitiously switched the selector on his AK-47 from safety to full automatic. Chili, noticing this from where he stood, did the same and subtly moved to the side, covering the flank.

With his head tilted well back to squarely face the being, Saylor challenged, "Care to tell us who you really are and what you've really done with my wife and William Batman?"

The two were separated by less than three feet, and he saw diaphanous membranes convulsively blink over the surfaces of the alien eyes. The slitted mouth opened. "No! But *you* will tell me where we can find his daughter."

There was a sudden loud scuffling to the side. The tightly bunched circle of reptoids parted and three humans pushed through. Saylor's heart jumped to his throat when he saw that the first of them was Doni, followed by a man he did not recognize, and then Kelsey, who stared intently at the being as she spoke. "Right here…Draco!"

Chapter 49

SAYLOR RUSHED TO DONI'S SIDE, WRAPPING HIS ARM AROUND HER SHOULDERS. Her face was blank...slack, her eyes dull and expressionless, her demeanor dazed. The two stood beside the seated Posnansky. As her father angled to the side and stopped, Kelsey strode forward with a controlled power and a grace in her form that the others had never seen until that moment, and took position near the reptoid. The being's face, unreadable to the group, canted downward to her.

"Why do you call me...'Draco'?"

Standing before him, her muscles taut, her countenance defiant, she shrugged. "That's who you are."

"You...."

She cut him off with a wave of her hand. "I heard the fairy tale you told to my friends. I listened as you attempted to, once again, deceive. As you have for thousands of years. But I...I...know the truth. You can't deceive me."

"And...what is this *truth* you believe?"

With an exaggerated sigh, Kelsey gave a fleeting glance and nod toward Saylor and began, "As Judtson taught *me*, every good story has a kernel of truth. Your description of the demise of the Anunnaki's home planet was accurate. As was your description of their agonies suffered as a race before the migration, to eventually find this inhabited planet Earth. Your depiction of them as benign...benevolent...peaceful was also true. And upon arriving, true to their eleemosynary spirit, the travelers conducted themselves as good and proper guests of the primitive humans encountered here...freely sharing their knowledge, techniques, and technologies, at a level, of course, comprehensible and viable for the natives."

Her eyes becoming unfocused, she paused as if recalling something. Returning to the present, she resumed, "That's where your spin on history...your version of the saga goes off the rails. In reality, the Anunnaki had no problem living on the surface. After their long, desolate subterranean exile on their own home planet, they relished the benign warmth of this sun. They reveled in it. They rejoiced in it. After their arduous trek, the one-in-a-million long shot of finding a new home had actually paid off...in spades. And the fact that the newcomers were accepted...in reality, welcomed with open arms by the indigenous people...made it all too good to be true. By the way, I should probably mention at this point that their generosity, with regard to knowledge, was not the only reason the humans accepted the new arrivals. It didn't hurt that the Anunnaki, although not identical to mankind, more closely resembled them than would...say, a freakish giant-sized lizard."

The inscrutable face of the being seemed to twitch for a second.

"Too bad, too. Because the Anunnaki soon found out that it wasn't all peaches and cream. As they taught language to the natives, stories surfaced of another group...another race. Not a race like theirs...not benign...not gracious at all. In fact, according to the tales told by their hosts, this second group was pretty rotten. Some of the humans believed that the others were also from another planet. No one knew for sure. What the locals did know was that these vile interlopers came...not as friends...not as guests...but as an unpitying parasite, a malignant infection. The monsters were described, by several of those who had seen them and lived to talk about it, as snakes, lizards, dragons."

The tension was palpable in the group clustered behind Kelsey. She did not look back, keeping her steady gaze upon that of the reptoid. "The native dwellers called the trespassers the 'Ancient Ones.' And said that these repugnant beasts lived in the underworld, only coming to the surface at night and only to kill...to feed. Apparently, they...you...viewed the surface of Earth as your breeding farm. Whether you ate a rat, a bird, a deer, or a human mattered not to you. It was all the same. The people pleaded with their guests, these new and powerful friends, for help. And the Anunnaki gave them help, listening carefully to the stories...to the lore...and discovering a weakness. So, by using the weakness, as well as the technologies and science brought from their home planet, they worked with the people to contain the threat."

Kelsey smiled, her eyes once again briefly drifting to another vista before snapping back, new fire now showing within. The smile erased. "See, the big difference...well, one of them... between you and the Anunnaki was that they really were pacifists and, as such, could not make themselves enter a battle with you and your ilk. All they could find within their hearts to do was devise a way to lock you up. Confine you. Keep you underground. Make all of your kind just go away. And that is exactly what happened! With the humans' knowledge of your habits and your movements, the Anunnaki located your snake holes around the world, then gathered the most skilled artisans...the most proficient stonemasons and, toiling together, blocked your ways up and out. On the Yucatan, on the Giza Plateau, and on top of almost countless other locations around the planet, they built pyramids and other massive structures, such as the one at Baalbek. And with their knowledge of harmonics and gravity, the building was completed in days, not years."

She laughed harshly. "It's ironic, though. The Anunnaki had won. You were contained, imprisoned, trapped forever. Tragically, it was through their own efforts and processes that you were accidentally released. The act of quarrying andesite near Lake Titicaca, to produce stones to be used elsewhere, allowed your escape. Oh, how you must have felt that day as your unbroken darkness was suddenly pierced when they broke through into this chamber. Angry, hungry, and desperate, your horde swarmed out, laying waste to the stone-milling field of Puma Punku and killing all in your path. And, once free, you were determined to never be incarcerated by the Anunnaki again."

Her voice deepened and grew more intense. "Moving at night, under the cloak of darkness, you cold-bloodedly hunted down and killed the Anunnaki, down to the last one, wiping them from the face of the Earth. After all, it was easy. They refused to fight back. There were some…a few who had learned of your weakness…your vulnerability…and shielded themselves from your attack. But you did not allow this to deter you. For those who were invulnerable to you, you enlisted humans…humans who were impervious…to do your work. By pandering to their greed, their thirst for power and control, their hedonism, and the inborn baseness within some, you assembled a willing army. Once the Anunnaki were defeated…eradicated…you stole their knowledge, their science, their technology. And kept it for yourself. Only parceling it out over the succeeding centuries to support and maintain your legion of humans, who, to this very day, do your bidding. They are the ones who, using an ancient technology provided by you and then refining it, have influenced and controlled the minds and the hearts of the people. They are the ones who have greedily captured and hoarded the most critical resources on the planet. They are the ones who have manipulated, directed, and controlled the currencies and the governments."

Abruptly, her voice rose. "You were correct, in a sense. They *are* the Illuminati. Yet they are nothing but your lackeys. The descendants of your original army. And they are the ones who have killed Judtson Kent!"

With her fists clenched at her sides, her face instantly transformed into a tight mask of fury, and her blue eyes locked into an unblinking stare with the slitted pupils of the other. To her right, Posnansky exclaimed, "This is…!"

Without turning, she barked, "Silence!" The authority of her command stopped him in mid-sentence.

Several hushed seconds blanketed the area before the being spoke. "Who are you to say these things?"

Unexpectedly, she relaxed. Her rigid posture almost imperceptibly loosened. "I'm disappointed, Draco. I would have thought you'd recognize me by now. Well, not my face. Not any of my appearance, really. But surely, my words were familiar."

"They were not."

"That's a shame. I was hoping I'd…ring a bell. Maybe my name will help jog your memory. I've had a couple of them, actually. Depending on whom you were to ask over the centuries. To some I was known as…Ishtar. To most, though, I was always Inanna."

The beast's eyes widened. "That cannot…."

"What's that, scale-face? That can't be? Why is that? Because you know I'm dead? Because you had my head delivered to your feet?"

He did not answer.

"Well, if you'd like to hear the story, I'd be happy to tell it."

He only nodded his assent.

"It's understandable that you'd be surprised. Because I did die. I mean, the body of Inanna, the last living Anunnaki among you, died. That's what you thought. That's what you counted on. Wasn't it?"

He still did not answer.

"Your vile minions found me where I was hidden. Living with a pair of humans I had befriended in the course of constructing your cell. The master builder of the pyramids, and his wife, had taken me in. Concealed me at great risk to themselves. Tried to protect me from you and your rampaging horde. Except I knew it wouldn't last. I knew it was only a matter of time until you succeeded in finding a human willing to betray me. I was also painfully aware that I was the last of my people. The last to know the truth about you. And I knew that I couldn't allow that knowledge to disappear forever. So I did the only thing I could do."

Inanna paused, allowing an untainted quiescence to fill the air around them. "You should know it, Draco. You have used it yourself many times. It was one of the things you stole from us. Our method of immortality. The Anunnaki, like all other races, craved it, sought it. In the pursuit of this dream, we never discovered how to turn our bodies into perpetually repairing organisms. What we did learn was that we could each transfer *who we were* into a new, young body. And through the new bodies, *we* would live on. What we learned, as well, was the price to be paid for this. For to take another body, one must replace...evict the singular essence within. Our own respect for the uniqueness of each individual whom we would forcibly eject, the sanctity of each being who would cease to exist, caused us to decide never to use the knowledge merely to indulge our own narcissism. It would be the ultimate pride and arrogance to supersede others so that *we* might continue. It would, de facto, declare that our own essence was somehow superior to that of the persons we would supplant."

She moved inches closer. "An arrogance...a hubris...which you have had no trouble exhibiting. As my clock ticked down, waiting for the inevitable knock on the door, I devoted hours upon hours to sharing all that I knew with my two friends. One of the facts I imparted was this knowledge, this ability to transfer myself to another. As the human soldiers arrived at our town in Sumer and began the systematic trek from dwelling to dwelling, searching for me, it was Sila who suggested that I...that I occupy her...that I hide within her. I refused. I explained that she...the 'she' who was Sila...would be forever lost in the process. She was, however, unrelenting in her arguments, maintaining that all I knew, what I possessed and could not possibly convey in the time remaining, was far more important than her own existence. Not until she threatened to leave her home and confront your men, force them to kill her, did I acquiesce. You were close...your soldiers were but a few doors from where we hid...when the transfer occurred. They arrived and located the sleeping shell of an Anunnaki who had been known as Inanna. And they killed it. Decapitated it so they could take you my head. This was done right before my eyes.

"I lived out my life with Heran, Sila's husband. And we had children, the last being a daughter. Heran and I had many long and agonizing discussions as to when, or even if, I would transfer myself to our daughter. He insisted that I must do it. Otherwise, Sila's sacrifice would have been in vain. So the only remaining question was whether we should allow our daughter to grow as the person she was, until the arrival of the painful day on which I would replace her. Or whether the better plan was to take her then...near her birth...so that she would never know what she had gained and subsequently lost. Together...we decided to do it then. The shell of Sila, the body I had left behind, slept until she quietly, peacefully died. Leaving Heran alone to raise our children."

A subtle smile of remembrance touched her lips. "Of course, he did have help from a very precocious daughter. And so it went. I grew up. And as I did, Heran, my father and once my husband, began to gather together a group of loyal friends, men who had never betrayed the Anunnaki during the genocide. He shared with these men the secrets taught by me. As I reached maturity...physically, that is...my spouse was chosen from this group. He knew what he was getting into and thought it an honor. In fact, that position established the successor for Heran, when he was ready to relinquish his position."

Inanna glanced to the side, her eyes connecting fleetingly with her father's.

"Children were born until a healthy daughter came to be. At which point…well, you get the picture. A couple of things happened over the centuries. Heran's group grew and flourished. All the while preserving and safeguarding my knowledge, and the knowledge of how to defend against you and to defeat you, if the time ever came. In early years, they became a band of knights who took it as their sacred duty to protect mankind from you. As their force became far too effective, you, through the Illuminati, manipulated the pope and the king of France into hunting down the members of the order and killing them. You almost wiped them out. But the few who remained afterward were quite aware that to survive and carry out their primary duty, it had become necessary to change their methods. Laying down the swords and shields of the Templars, they became a seemingly innocuous group. Yet a group with the knowledge…the secrets…my secrets. And this band of men spread across the continents, permeated every culture and government. Until they were finally able to create a new world. A new society. A place they hoped would be immune to the temptations and machinations from below. They created America."

"The Masons!" Romeo grunted, surprise clear in his voice.

Without turning, she nodded. "Yes. And that is why key, prime founders of that country were loyal followers and adherents to that which was taught by Heran to his first band of friends…Masons. That is why the Constitution was essentially based upon Masonic rules. And that is why, for the past two centuries, *you* have targeted that land, that people. At first you attempted simple, straightforward assaults by manipulating other leaders into wars against them. Those failed. You lost. They won. It was not until after the last great war when you realized that the only way to tear down this society, established from its very birth to be the antithesis of you, was from within. If you could not beat them on the battlefield, you would patiently eat away at them on the street corners and in the living rooms…inexorably and incrementally destroying every aspect of their society which made them invulnerable.

"And…the other thing which happened over the centuries, over the succeeding generations, was that I discovered something about the immortality transfer, something my people had never practiced the procedure long enough to learn. With each iteration, with each new baby girl imbued with my essence…my being…I became ever so slightly more detached… more removed. The 'who' which was within the infant was no longer supplanted by me, only pushed aside. This shift, more pronounced with each new generation, resulted in the ongoing diminishment of the impact *my* self had upon the new form…and in time relegated me to continuing forward only as an…observer, allowing the person born to actually live out *her* life. Heran's successors…my husbands…understood what was occurring.

"When the tipping point finally arrived, when I was no longer the dominant, effectuated sentience of the baby daughter, but instead displaced to the background, my father and then my husband were the only ones who could call me forth. And would only do so to ensure that the next transfer took place. We also discovered, at the same time, that my transfer to the new daughter and my departure from the mother…no longer resulted in the sleep and death of the mother. For, once I had been removed, the 'who' which was she, unencumbered, continued and was able to fully blossom. That brings me to today. I suppose a 'thank you' is in order. Prior to today I was buried deep inside this woman you knew only as Kelsey Batman. Cut off. Separated. Exiled. Merely watching."

She turned her gaze to William. "My father knew I was there. It was he who carried the knowledge and the ancient trust. It was he who could bring me forth, but only in time to perform the act of the next transference. It's another irony that I was no threat to you. And it was because of you, through your actions, through your decision to kill Judtson Kent, that I stand before you with not only the knowledge necessary to destroy you and all of your..." – a snarl lifted the corner of her lip – "ilk, but also, for the first time, the ability. Kelsey always felt, more than knew, that I was there as well. Buried within. Impotent. During most of her life, she regarded the hints of my presence within her as a delusional fantasy. We never communicated directly, except in her dreams. Yet she somehow came to grasp the reality of my being...the substance of who or what I am. And when you took away her one true love, *our*...one true love...she...Kelsey... merely stepped aside...allowing *me* to come to the fore."

Inching toward the beast, their bodies practically touching, she looked up into his cold, dark eyes. "Why, Draco? Why did you kill Judtson Kent and rob her...and me...of this love?"

If the gritty, grinding voice was capable of expressing emotion, his response was filled with contempt. "It is as it is, Inanna. The price for your love has always been death. And it shall always be so."

Her muscles tightening...her fury barely contained, she countered, "And so it will be for you."

"And you believe that *you* can destroy us?"

"Yes." Her single word was spoken with an absolute finality.

"You are a fool. You were a fool thousands of years ago and you are one now. You are here...in my domain. It is you who will be destroyed."

She heard from behind the rustle of a rifle being brought to bear and, without even a fleeting glance back, commanded, "Romeo, stop!"

He froze in mid-motion, the barrel of his rifle elevated halfway.

Draco lifted his thick, sinuous arms...his scaled claws reaching for her neck. With the talons rapidly nearing her, she raised her clenched right hand and opened it in front of his face. The gold necklace, with the eight-pointed star, dropped and swung inches from his face. Reflexively, he jerked back, his arms crossing in front, shielding himself.

Taunting him, she swung the necklace closer, relishing his flinching reaction. "You see, Draco, we *did* learn your secret...your fatal weakness. It is gold."

She glanced at Saylor, who was still holding Doni, and directed her words to him, a subtle smile playing across her face. "As I described, we...the Anunnaki...built massive stone monuments upon the gateways of the Ancient Ones, to imprison them in the underworld. We had also learned that they cannot tolerate the slightest contact with gold. I suppose you would call it an allergic reaction. Whatever it is, their bodies react to it violently."

"Anaphylactic shock."

"Yes. But a thousand-fold more potent. Untreatable. Unstoppable. Invariably fatal. The planet they evolved upon and in time were forced to leave did not have a single ounce of gold within its strata. Gold is not a normal, plentiful element generated in the natural processes of the production of solar systems and planets. Rather, it is an extremely rare by-product of the collision of two neutron stars, subsequently producing an intense burst of gamma rays, and its presence on Earth is, to put it mildly, a fluke. Imagine their dismay. After passing by thousands of uninhabitable planets on elliptical orbits before finally finding Earth, they discovered that it was laced, through and through, with this element deadly to them.

"That is the real reason...the true reason...that throughout all of history, gold has been used in the vestments, headdresses, scepters, and icons of the political and religious leaders. Not as a gaudy adornment, but as a shield...as protection. Even many holy places in history were completely lined with gold. My first husband...Heran...and all who came after him made certain that this was so. It is also why gold has been so widely distributed, fashioned, coveted, and worn. The masses were taught to crave gold for its beauty, never aware that its widespread presence kept the Ancient Ones at bay. And it is the reason all of the monuments built by Heran, with the help of my people, to contain and imprison the Ancient Ones at every possible suspect location, were built upon a seamless layer of the element."

She turned back to Draco. "Since the days of the Templars, who had made it their quest to gather all of the gold they could find, with a plan to attack you in your lair and defeat you, you have used the Illuminati to acquire the element. To amass it. To hoard it. To sequester it. To, in fact, eject it from Earth and store it elsewhere, in an attempt to make the surface safe for your eventual emergence. That is why the gold depositories are now empty. Yet, although you were able to manipulate governments to surrender their gold, there was still a problem. Millions upon millions of people were wearing the deadly element. On their wrists...around their necks...on their fingers..." – she reared her head back and laughed – "even in the fillings of their teeth. My husbands, and those who have followed them, made certain that the metal was spread as far and wide as possible. Predictably, your people have attempted to counter that, as well. Which explains why tens of thousands of shopkeepers around the world are offering higher and higher sums if only the people will bring in Grandma's jewelry. Your Illuminati have created an insatiable market for gold, with the intent of removing it from the world. It has been quite a show to watch, really...seeing your forces utilize every devious and cold-blooded trick in the book to capture the gold, while those who followed my husbands ensured the opposite.

"Of late, the scales began to shift. More and more of the lethal metal had been removed from above. You were still far from your goal of eradication, of making the surface safe for your presence, for your free access once more, but the time was drawing enticingly nearer. I cannot imagine how you felt, if you indeed have feelings. Finally, after all these millennia, you saw the end of your subterranean exile within reach. Unfortunately for you, that was when the problems also began. An archaeologist, a geologist, and a geophysicist, all working independently, had identified an anomaly which, you knew, would lead them to your doorstep. An immunologist had begun research which, you knew, would uncover the mechanism your foul accomplices above were using to, at first, keep the public docile, compliant, sheep-like. And step two in that plan was to foster an irrational, unstoppable hostility within people...a hostility which would fester until, like the rats in a lab, they all began mindlessly murdering each other...self-annihilating... wiping out the entire species, and further clearing the land for you. An author was about to expose the infrastructure you were using as a repository for the gold you had removed from the Earth. Worst of all, a chemist had discovered a revolutionary new property, a new use for monoatomic gold. And the others, due to the positions they held, their skills, or simply their credibility with the public, were acting as facilitators and disseminators of these breakthroughs.

"Your rage must have been something to see. This tantalizingly close to the consummation of your carefully orchestrated plans, you had no choice but to set your forces against this small yet dangerous group. First utilizing ancient Anunnaki knowledge to control them. Then implementing more modern techniques. When those failed, you ordered their deaths. What you did not know...what you could not know...was that this assailed group would serendipitously cross the path of your worst nightmare...me. I am now here, Draco. And I am here to finish that which should have been concluded thousands of years ago."

The reptoid, with increased distance between himself and the dangling bauble, showed in his posture more confidence as he said, "There is one problem, Inanna. A singular flaw with what you say."

"Oh? What is that?"

"You *are* Anunnaki. And therefore, you *cannot* find it within yourself to finish it. You cannot kill me or mine. Because…down to the very core of your being…you cannot kill."

She did not immediately answer. The silence following his words was heavy with dread and anticipation. Her countenance neutral and betraying nothing, her voice more muted than moments earlier, Inanna finally replied, "You are correct. I am Anunnaki."

Emotion choked her voice as she added, "And…you are correct that I cannot…kill you."

With a loud sigh, she reluctantly hung the necklace around her neck and pivoted on her heel to face her group, turning her back on Draco. One by one, she made fleeting eye contact with each of them, until settling her gaze on Romeo, who met it fiercely. She could plainly see in him the readiness to fight, the willingness to die.

As he stared at her, this person who had been his friend and who now was someone else, he read the set of her jaw, the intense determination in her eyes, the coiled tightness of every muscle in her body. The two were frozen in time, and nothing else existed. And then, in the blink of an eye, he saw her change. The tautness of her frame dissipated. The tension within her face released. Her eyes once again reverted to the familiar eyes of his friend.

She whirled back to face the Ancient One, a broad sardonic smirk now on her face. With a flippant tone, she again acknowledged his words. "You were right."

Taking a single step closer, Kelsey pulled the leather pouch from her waist. "But *I* sure as hell can!"

Before the beast could even react, she pried open the pouch and whisked out a pinch of Chris Ashby's monoatomic gold. Holding her fingers together in front of her lips, she blew as she opened them, sending the faintly visible cloud into Draco's face.

Chapter 50

AS KELSEY BLEW THE MONOATOMIC GOLD INTO DRACO'S FACE, Arthur Posnansky shouted and leapt up from the bench toward her. Prepared for this, Carlos instantly lunged, knocking the surprisingly strong old man to the stone floor. His head struck with a sickening thunk. Through it all, she stood her ground and watched as the reptoid reeled backward, his arms across his face, and fell. Writhing and thrashing wildly on his back, the beast made a loud clamor, a guttural cacophony of earsplitting clicking, triggering a primal, involuntary neural reaction of revulsion in the group.

Unable to look away, Kelsey, joined by Romeo, stared at the convulsive spasms of the jerking beast, flailing as if he were possessed by warring demons. With the sickening, gut-wrenching sounds of tearing fibrous, chitinous membrane, multiple gouts of foul-smelling yellowish pus erupted from the backs of his hands and from his face, oozing between his clawing fingers. Like paintball splatters, numerous wet blotches stained the red fabric covering the rest of his body.

Others of his breed, those who had been surrounding the group, charged forward, intently focused on the one who had killed their master. Chili took two steps toward the attackers and emptied the clip of his AK-47 into the front of the surging mob...ripping and shredding them... and they fell. Others, from behind, climbed over the bodies of their kin, and as he replaced his magazine, Cahane jumped between Kelsey and the advancing pack, efficiently taking them down. The three who had been off to the side – Doni, assisted by Saylor, and William Batman – darted into the protective circle formed by Eunice and Chili and augmented by Kenny Bowman.

"Kelsey," William called loudly over the stuttering din of automatic fire, "we must leave!"

Tearing her eyes away from the gruesome disintegration of the reptoid, she turned to her father and, with a single step forward, embraced him, letting out a sobbing "Daddy!"

Separating from her, he lifted his hand and caressed his daughter's cheek. As he did, she caught a glimmer in the corner of her eye. On his finger was the ring of the 33rd Degree Mason. Clutching his hand in astonishment, she said, "I didn't...."

"Not now, Kelsey."

She nodded.

Romeo had joined the fray and was defending the area to the fore, as Eunice, Chili, Ricky, and Kenny split into pairs and covered the flanks. The staircase was to their backs as Kelsey shouted, "*Up the steps!* We need to get to the top!"

They retreated as they had arrived, with Lisa and Matt several steps above, rifles at the ready, guarding the course. The throng of scaled attackers, heedless of their losses, surged ahead over the higher and higher mound of bodies. Arthur Posnansky, underfoot, was trampled by them, his scream of pain barely heard or noticed.

As the group backed up the lowest of the steps, several of the frantic beasts climbed the sides in an attempt to catch them or cut off the escape route. Lisa and Matt, facing away from their friends, efficiently brushed off the frenzied pursuers with their assault rifles. One of the reptoids leapt from the roof of an adjacent structure onto the steps, landing amidst the fleeing group and closest to Cahane, who had, a moment earlier, emptied her magazine and had yet to replace it.

The beast lunged forward across the oversized steps, arms outstretched, mouth agape. She dropped the rifle and, in a blur of motion, pulled the .50 caliber Desert Eagle from its holster and, aiming at the attacker's head, pulled the trigger a single time. The brute's skull exploded. The body collapsed backward, toppling off the side and falling to the stone path below. With a quick wink at Ricky, who had pivoted to provide her with backup, she holstered the pistol, retrieved her rifle, and slapped in a new magazine.

Once above the vulnerable elevation, they increased the pace of ascent and reached the towering rim at a near run. Ricky and Eunice remained stationed at the top landing, alternating bursts from their rifles at the scrambling, climbing mob on the stairway below.

The others in the retreating band fanned out on the ledge. Kelsey stood with her father, Romeo, and Chris, looking out over the small city below. The denizens on every avenue and path were all swarming toward the stairs…toward them…the mass of pushing, moving bodies so dense that the lanes resembled dark, turbulently flowing rivers.

"We need to break for the terrace," grunted Romeo.

Kelsey acknowledged, "We will. But I need to finish the job." She glanced at her father, her voice exhibiting a hint of uncertainty. "Don't I?"

Inhaling deeply, he answered, "Yes."

"How?" asked Romeo. "We don't have enough bullets, and you can't exactly go back down there and blow them all little gold-dust kisses!"

Before she could reply, Ashby, who had been silently surveying the cavernous chamber, spoke up. "I don't think that's necessary. Kelsey…the monoatomic gold is essentially as light as air. It remains in suspension and disperses. This is a fairly enclosed environment. They must have a fresh air supply of some sort, but I definitely don't feel any air movement."

A fresh volley of shots from Ricky rattled from their side. At the same time, a broad smile spread across her face as she absorbed Ashby's words. "You're right."

Untying the large leather pouch from her belt, she hefted it. "This is a huge place, Chris. Is this enough?"

Taking only a moment to consider the variables, he began his reply in a metered tone. "Inanna must have thought so. The monoatomic gold has a dispersal rate of…aw, hell, I don't know. Just dump it!"

She gave a final glance to her father and then Romeo, who both nodded solemnly. Pulling the thong, she spread the opening wide and, gripping the bottom of the pouch, swung it out away from the ledge in a wide arc and then shook it, inverted. The grayish powder, at first escaping in an aggregated cloud, scattered and dispersed, spreading horizontally away from them and gradually disappearing.

"I feel like I only put a drop into an ocean," Kelsey wavered, a strong note of doubt in her voice. "Is this going to work?"

"Don't know," hesitated Ashby, his eyes trained upon the rampaging mass of reptoids, coldly pushing the bodies of their dead and wounded cohorts off the sides and surging up the stairs.

Still dubious, Kelsey, gnawing her lower lip, worried aloud, "Chris, the stuff looked like it was staying up high. Is it even going to get down to them?"

Without turning away, he explained, "It mingles with the molecules in the air and is going to be subject to the convection currents inside this...."

His answer was abruptly drowned out by a sudden intensification of the vocalizations coming from the ascending beasts. The uppermost of the pack initially began to stagger, then fall to their knees, and then collapse...some foundering on the treads, others tumbling off the sides and plummeting to certain deaths.

Eunice and Ricky, seeing the change, held their fire and watched, astounded, as the effect expanded downward and outward through the pushing, shoving mob below, converting the mindless attack of an army into a thousand individual agonies. The indescribable sounds first made by Draco as he died, now multiplied exponentially, soon engulfed the entire chamber with a grinding roar of horrific pain and death.

Finding it necessary to shout into her ear to be heard, Romeo bellowed at Kelsey, "Let's get out of here."

She agreed and took steps toward the passage, when she was waylaid by Lisa. "Kelsey," she yelled, "what about the people down there? The...humans?"

Kelsey stopped in her tracks and grabbed the binoculars from Romeo's belt. Focusing hastily, she studied the details of the pandemonium below. Within an ever-expanding circle radiating away from her, the reptoids were staggering, falling, writhing on the ground. They all seemed to be oblivious to the few humans among them, who were crouching in shadows, niches, or alcoves, terrified. Beyond the encroaching boundary of invisible gold dust, the unaffected were madly running north in a desperate attempt to escape it. Kelsey handed back the binoculars and cupped her hands around her mouth, shouting her response above the din. "The lizards are leaving them alone! Once things settle down, if the people want to come out, they can. They know the way."

$$\triangledown$$

Sam, driving northward, was bounced and jostled on the narrow lane to their former camp, pushing the truck to its limits, his rifle and backpack riding to his right as his only passengers. The tires protesting loudly around the final bend, he spotted Gretchen and floored the gas pedal, fishtailing wildly in her direction. Startled, she jerked her head in his direction and watched as he came to a jarring halt and jumped out, toting the rifle.

"Gretchen, what in the hell do you think you're doing?" he barked. "You were supposed to stay with the others."

Her entire body seemed to flinch at his verbal assault. "Sam...I'm...I'm...sorry. I just remembered that all of my field notes were still here and...."

She stopped in mid-sentence, turned away from him, and gasped. "What was that?"

Tightening his grip on the stock of his rifle, he listened. "What?" His answer came before he was able to finish the lone word, as he heard a deep, shuddering rumble from the direction of Lake Titicaca. They were on high ground, at least one hundred yards from the shore, a vantage which afforded a clear vista over the expanse of water. Conspicuously visible in the dim illumination were multiple boats, large and small, seemingly packed to capacity with people, many carrying lights or lanterns.

"They're all leaving the island," she whispered.

She was right. All of the boats were on radial outward courses bound for the nearest shores, away from the island upon which Sam's team had earlier dug, discovering the bizarre metallic layer.

"Why?" he uttered, mainly to himself, and took off toward the bank at a lope. Gretchen followed. The disparate rumblings, as if controlled by a patient hand on a rheostat, steadily accreted. The intense low-frequency sound was pierced by the call of first one wolf, then others, joining in the plaintive chorus. As Sam ran, he felt the hairs on his neck rise, and sweat begin to prickle his skin.

Reaching the shore, he stopped only inches from the water's edge. The island inhabitants, the Aymara, now closer to him, were all speaking excitedly in their ancient language, the individual words indistinguishable. Casting his gaze down, Sam saw something he could not explain. The surface of the water was jittering and dancing with a million tiny overlapping waves, mirroring the vibration he now felt under his boots.

Gretchen, panting from her sprint, stopped beside him. A vague sense of understanding dawning upon Jonassen, he ordered, "Go to my truck. Get my backpack. Run!"

Without acknowledging, she turned and dashed back up the gentle slope. The boats arrived. The Aymara beached the crafts carelessly, hastily, and scrambled out, all clutching bundles against their chests, their few most precious belongings. Muttering and chattering to one another, they scurried past him unaware of his presence. Not one paused to look back as they scattered and ran, putting distance and elevation between themselves and the lake. Worry added itself to the ensemble of emotions coursing through Sam. The muffled thunder louder than before, he took a step backward...then another...and another, distancing himself from the edge of the water and intercepting Gretchen halfway up the slope.

"Here!" she shouted.

Snatching his pack, he opened the top flap and dug inside, extricating his video camera. Checking to ascertain that the battery held a charge, he handed his rifle to her, thoughtlessly dropped the backpack on the ground, and gripped her arm. "I don't know why, but I think we'd better move back some more."

They did, returning to the edge of their abandoned camp. He faced the lake and began to record. The madly oscillating surface of the water captured and reflected the moonlight, casting it toward him from a billion discreet points, creating the illusion of an undulating glittered blanket. The ground was no longer merely vibrating, as it now seemed to be trembling beneath them. The low-frequency rumble had escalated to a growling aural assault upon their ears. As the two stared forward, Gretchen with her own eyes, and Sam through the view screen of the light-enhancing camera, the chorus of wolves, as though on cue, fell abruptly silent, embellishing the moment with a new eeriness.

On the glowing LCD, the island was disassembling, as if it were a time-lapse video capturing eons of erosion. As Sam's camera zoomed in, he was able to discern details. Rocks and boulders, shaken from their ancient points of repose, broke free and tumbled from the mount, soundlessly splashing into the distant roiling water. Trees, their roots losing grip upon the shuddering soil, toppled. The vague dark outlines of the homes and other buildings of the people who had only just fled from those same structures now shook and twisted, tearing themselves apart.

"Oh, my God!" Jonassen swore under his breath. Gretchen pressed close to him, sharing the view on the screen.

The crown of the island itself, resembling a mound of granular sand on a vibration table, seemed to liquify and flow outward and downward to the lake, creating the illusion that the entire island was melting. The rumbling reached an amplitude, becoming a steady, even roar. The lake surface, previously vibrating, now danced with interlocking waves and whitecaps, reminding Sam of a pot of boiling water. All of the forces at play intensified until the last of the island disappeared into the churning, frothing surface.

The tumult grew, expanded, escalated, strengthened to a point where the two humans watching the spectacle could feel it in their teeth, bones, and joints. The tremors in the ground causing them to waver and wobble as they stood, the awestricken witnesses determined to remain upright and hold their ground, consciously overriding the confused jumble of conflicting messages from the semicircular canals of their ears. Jonassen was thankful for the image stabilization technology of the camera. Where the island had been, the plane of the lake's surface unnaturally bulged upward, the mass of water briefly riding atop an unseen vertical conveyor, before surrendering to the force of gravity and cascading down the curved sides in a savage, roaring flood.

The millions of cubic feet of water shed by the now rapidly rising dome impacted the surrounding surface with an explosive crash, displacing the incompressible volume and violently thrusting it outward, birthing a monolithic annular wave. Unable to speak, even if he could have been heard above the deafening onslaught, Sam watched, entranced…and recorded, zooming the scene fully back to capture both the breadth of the rising object, whatever it might be, and the wall of water, tens of feet high and racing toward the shores.

Heedless of the threatening tsunami, he kept his attention upon the object, which he now thought of as a ship, as it continued its inexorable ascent. Having cast off the concealing water, the dome shone in the moonlight. He focused on four incongruous objects, breaking the smooth symmetry of the gracefully arcing outline and fastened to the skin, and recognized the cylindrically shaped crafts he had observed and recorded that night above his cave and on another fateful night with Bal.

The wave engulfed the shore below and thundered up the slope effortlessly. Gretchen wrapped her arms around Sam, holding tightly as the frigid water, its kinetic energy virtually spent, reached the two, washing over their shoes and up their legs, cresting above the knees. Had they not been clutched together and braced, the impact would have swept both from their feet.

Through it all, Jonassen did not waver from his recording of the departure of the ship. The gargantuan sweeping curve of the upper dome descended to a narrow banding edge, now visible above the lake, revealing a perfectly flat bottom. No sooner had this appeared than a higher-pitched, turbulent, sucking sound replaced the prior clamor. The water, which had coursed around Sam and Gretchen and sheeted out over the former camp, was already receding, gaining momentum and force with every passing second of its retreat.

Once again, their feet were almost pulled from beneath them as the water rushed back toward the lake. Struggling to keep their footing on the shifting soils, and still entwined together, they somehow stayed up. As the shimmering craft rose higher, the lake beneath was in turmoil as a nascent eddy sprang into existence. The huge swirling phenomenon, roughly the diameter of the craft, thirstily pulled water into itself from all directions, filling the void left by the departing mass. The initial churning, sucking noise was surmounted by a screaming torrent of sound as the maelstrom fully formed.

Dazed, chilled, buffeted, and overwhelmed, Sam divided his attention between the cataclysm below and the ever-ascending craft above, until the ship, in the blink of an eye, transitioned from the steady climbing rate to a rocketing velocity, not traveling across the sky as had the other small ships he had witnessed in the past, but instead launching straight upward, away from the Earth. Within moments it was gone, no longer visible as even a bright speck in the night sky.

Shifting the captured view of the camera downward, he continued to record as the water of the vast body known as Lake Titicaca was drawn into the insatiable maw of the whirlpool.

$$\nabla$$

Kelsey, followed by the others, scaled the rope ladder wordlessly. Reaching the platform above, she hurried to the still figure on the blanket, guarded and mourned by the golden retriever, and, sobbing, dropped to her knees and then sat beside them. With a single muted whimper, Rocky nestled his head upon her lap.

Chapter 51

SAYLOR TOOK THE STILL-DAZED DONI TO THE COMMUNITY TENT OF THE CAMP, thankful that the area was now occupied by only a handful of people, the rest called out by Jonassen minutes earlier. His arm wrapped tightly around her shoulders, he walked her to the nearest table and helped her sit down. She lowered herself into the chair without speaking. Her face was blank, her eyes bloodshot and vacant, the lower regions limned with bags.

Leaving her at the table, Saylor crossed the room quickly to the coffee urn and filled a cup with the strong black brew. Returning with it, he knelt on the floor in front of her.

"Take a sip, Doni," he urged gently.

Her eyes, not focused on him or the coffee, remained fixed upon some invisible sight. Her hand rose and grasped the cup, moving it to her lips. As he watched, his mind automatically ticked off the presented symptoms. Although she was both stuporous and clearly fatigued, there did not appear to be any physical injuries. She had been barely strong enough to climb the rope ladder out of the sub-terrace. He concluded both that she was severely drugged and that her condition was not life-threatening.

Waiting until she had taken a few small mouthfuls and was holding the cup on her lap with both hands, he reached up and touched the side of her face. "Doni, baby, try to look at me. Please!"

There was a momentary flicker in her frozen gaze. She blinked twice. Then, to his relief, her eyes shifted to meet his.

Letting out a heavy sigh, he caressed her cheek and smiled. "Hi!"

The vaguest hint of animation returned to her features. With what was clearly a difficult mental effort, she curled the corners of her mouth upward ever so minutely and whispered, "Hi, Saylor-man."

Tears of gratitude burst from him. Heedless of the steaming cup in her hands, he leaned forward and hugged her. She awkwardly set it to the side and returned the embrace passionately, murmuring, "I love you."

"I love you, Doni," he responded, his voice breaking on the words.

The two remained locked together for a time, neither speaking, simply relishing the reunion. When at last they parted, she ventured tentatively, "Is…is it over?"

He nodded. "Yes."

"No, I mean…is it really over?"

"It is. Finally."

Her wan smile was abruptly erased as earnest intensity knitted her brow. "Saylor, I…I…it wasn't me back at the silo. I didn't…."

He kissed her lightly, stopping her in mid-sentence. "I know. We all know. Luis was guilty all along. Doni, I'm *so* sorry I doubted you."

Rallying further from the haze she had been in, Doni shook her head. "Please. Don't. I understand. I know how it must have looked." Shaking her head once more to help clear the fog, she glanced around the room expectantly. "Where's Judtson?"

Before he was able to form a single word of response, she read the sudden twist of his features and gasped, "Oh…*God, no!*" Her fragile and tenuous grip on her emotions shattering, she surrendered to wrenching sobs.

▽

Romeo, checking the outlying area with Chili, found the second of the two-man team who had approached the terrace. His neck was savagely torn open.

"Looks like Rocky took him out first," the big man grunted.

The Marine nodded, his frail voice respectful. "Helluva dog."

The two men joined Kenny and Eunice and returned to the truck Romeo had used earlier. Letting the tailgate fall open with a loud clang, he showed the others the trussed-up figure of Luis lying on his side in the bed. The man's eyes shone in the darkness, staring at Romeo with a feral hatred. The Ranger reached in and seized the ropes binding Tovar's wrists behind his back and pulled harshly, roughly sliding the traitor off the gate and letting him fall to the hard ground. He hit with a muted grunt.

Squatting in front of Luis and making eye contact, his voice low and intense, Jones stated flatly, "It's done. Your lizard buddies are finished. Forever."

A defiant snarl twisted Tovar's mouth. "You won't get me to talk."

With a harsh, throaty chuckle, Romeo answered him. "Talk? I don't need you to talk. There's nothing you can say that I either want or need to hear."

Although his face was a mask of bravado, Luis' eyes betrayed him as he asked, "You gonna kill me?"

Romeo glanced up at his three friends standing in a circle around them, then answered, "Kill you. No. As much as I'd like to, that's not who or what we are."

▽

Carlos and Bal stood together in the moonlight, twenty yards from the edge of the platform, both staring at the motionless tableau of Kelsey…Rocky…and Judtson. Villarreal, deeply shaken by the loss of his friend, as well as the events he had endured, found it hard to speak as he haltingly relayed the details. "So…thousands of years ago, this place…Puma Punku…was the last stand for the Anunnaki."

"So it would appear. The history we have learned tonight is far different from what has been disseminated over the centuries. The Anunnaki were, in fact, benign, not the monsters portrayed by the Sumerians and others."

Shrugging, Villarreal muttered, "It always falls to the victors to write the history."

The archaeologist closed his eyes and attempted to visualize the horrendous night, so far in the distant past, as the Ancient Ones emerged from the bottom of the quarry to the north. "Thinking that they were doing something good...something beneficial for mankind...the Anunnaki accidentally opened Pandora's box."

"Perhaps...," Bal uttered in a fervent whisper, "we have closed it forever."

$$\triangledown$$

One by one, the members of the original group, with the exception of Kelsey, made their way into the community tent to join Saylor and Doni. Sensing the connection between those gathering, the students and workers left them alone, congregating into small groups elsewhere. Sam arrived, still wet and clutching his camera as if it were the Holy Grail. Transferring the video to a laptop left behind by one of the students, he showed the others the dramatic departure of the craft.

"That must be their mother ship," Wheeler speculated, his whispered voice filled with awe.

Scott, who had arrived as the video played, reported urgently, "I was on the uplink until just a minute or two ago. There were others leaving, too. It has been dominating the news."

"Others?"

Nodding at Matt, he explained, "All over the world. A province in China, a desolate area in Australia, the Yucatan, and Baalbek."

"Spread across the continents...but not Africa," observed Chris.

"Probably too much gold in the strata there," guessed Bal.

"So they've run like rabbits," Matt remarked with a note of triumph. "You think for good?"

Speaking for the first time, Kelsey's father, idly twisting the ring on his finger, answered, "Yes. I suspect they have. I believe that, after thousands upon thousands of years, we are finally rid of the malignant parasites."

$$\triangledown$$

No one slept during the night, huddling instead in small clusters and speaking in muted tones. The following morning, contact was made with Sambrosa, and Gordo arrived with his helicopter to shuttle the group down the mountain to Arica where they boarded the waiting Gulfstream. The handcuffed and gagged Luis was secured at the rear of the cabin. None of them trusted their emotions enough to speak to him. Silently, solemnly, they loaded the body of Judtson Kent. The jet lifted off from the small airport, winging northward. Sam Jonassen had stayed behind to supervise the process of breaking down the camp and the transport of equipment and personnel to La Paz and, eventually, the United States.

The mood in the plane was somber and subdued. Kelsey sat rigidly, her eyes directed only toward the sky and the clouds outside the window, with Rocky curled up on the seat beside her, resting his head on her lap. Lisa had taken a seat next to William and, in hushed tones, used the opportunity to question him.

"Sir, I've been meaning to ask how Kelsey…or Inanna, I guess, rescued you and Doni. She didn't have a weapon or anything."

The man shrugged. "Mrs. Costello and I were being held together in a small room. The door opened and she was there. A single guard, one of the Ancient Ones, had been stationed outside. But it was gone. I don't know how she got rid of it."

"I've been thinking about the fact that you faked your death, and I'm not sure I understand why you did it. It almost seems as if…and please don't be offended by this…you ran away and left Kelsey to take the heat."

"Not offended at all, Lisa. I can see how it would appear that way. The reality is quite the contrary. My people…."

"The Masons?"

"Yes. We learned of a new device the Illuminati was developing…the *conditioner*. It was to be a truly terrifying device, as you discovered personally. And one with, as far as we knew, no countering mechanism. My group had been the steadfast opponent of the Illuminati for thousands of years…their archenemy. The Illuminati knew I was its head. What they did not know was that I was also the father of the host for Inanna. That was our society's most guarded secret. There was great concern that I would be captured and conditioned. If that were to have happened, all of our secrets would have been revealed and Kelsey's life would have been endangered to a far greater degree."

"That's when you split?"

"Yes."

"And why didn't you at least tell Kelsey? Thinking you were dead devastated her."

"I couldn't tell her why without revealing everything. And that…." He paused for a moment and glanced out the window of the plane before resuming. "That would have violated a long-held promise. One I could not break."

"So you disappeared and left Romeo behind to guard her."

"Yes."

"Did he know the truth?"

"No. He did not."

"One thing that's been driving me crazy is the whole mind-control deal…the conditioning."

"Which part of it, Lisa?"

"Well, all of it, really. Starting with how it was done. I know Matt drove himself nuts looking for the actual mechanism in their headpieces. He never did find anything."

"He was looking in the wrong direction. He was searching for an electromagnetic output or field. The headpiece used sound waves at a frequency far outside the audible range of humans. When the Illuminati discerned that there was a group of people who had received the '86 vaccine and were resistant to their normal methods of population control, they devised a process of unseating the proteins which blocked the neuroreceptors, by using a precise, focused frequency which would resonate with the proteins. The proteins vibrated violently and basically shook themselves off, thus freeing up the receptors for their abominable implanted proteins to attach."

"Then why did Matt's device make us immune when they tried it again?"

"No one has determined the reason. *They* never figured it out. That's why Chris was kidnapped. My guess is that Matt's procedure somehow actually disabled the receptors completely."

Taking a minute to absorb what he had said, she delved more deeply. "The people who haven't gone through the mind control, or conditioning, think that we remained who we were, but somehow were forced to do what the bad guys wanted. That wasn't it at all. It seemed like being locked up inside your own head while an alternate consciousness actually took over. All of us who were converted had this other personality…this alternate entity…inside us. We've all talked about this…a lot. How could they replace me with another *Lisa*? A Lisa who knew everything I knew. But she reacted to the same stimuli differently than I would…the way the Illuminati wanted. Where did they get this other Lisa and is *she* inside me now? Is she feeling trapped, as I felt, and wanting to escape?"

He took in a long breath. "The short answer is *no*. There is no independent, discreet consciousness locked up inside you right now. There is only your own."

"Then…?"

William held up his hand to stop her. "Before I can explain who or what the visiting Lisa was, I need to give you some background."

The producer sat back to listen.

"Over the years scientists have pondered the behavior of several species which seem to think as a group, rather than individually."

"You mean like ants?"

"Ants, bees, flocking birds, various others. They have not had much success understanding the mechanism, chalking off the behavior as being driven by vocal cues, pheromones, and a host of further possibilities, despite physical evidence to the contrary. The one area not granted legitimacy or credence, except by those considered to be on the fringe of science, is the concept of interconnected group thinking. The idea that there is an actual collective consciousness, separate from the individual. And that each insect, each animal is indeed living as an ostensibly independent individual…while, in fact, its consciousness comes from…."

"The cloud!" she exclaimed.

With a sardonic grin, he replied, "As good a term for it as any, I suppose."

"You're saying that everything I am, everything I know and have experienced, is uploaded to the consciousness cloud. Almost like a…a backup."

"In a rough sense, yes."

"So when I was locked up inside my own head, the cloud took me over?"

"Yes. If – and I understand that this is a big *if* – this is the case with ants, birds, and… people, you can see how the problems would begin to arise should an ant or a bee suddenly develop a mind of its own as opposed to simply doing what the collective wants or needs."

Lisa's eyes widened as a new understanding slammed into her. "Oh, my God! You're talking about free will, aren't you?"

"I am."

"Did the Ancient Ones create this cloud as a way to control us?"

He shook his head. "From what has been passed down to me, the answer is that they did not. At the time of their arrival, the hive mentality of the early humans was already in existence."

"I don't understand. Why did it exist?"

"In the process of evolution, humans, or proto-humans, shifted from being lone hunters to belonging to cooperative tribes. This occurred long before the advent of speech, perhaps to the extent that it preceded the evolution of the physical mechanism which enabled verbal communication. The collective consciousness allowed the tribal members to work together and defend one another, and facilitated all of the various aspects of a mini-society, without the benefit of speech."

"How did it actually work?"

"In a sense, like ESP. The minds of the tribe were connected. Not in a way which encompassed what we would consider to be conversation. Much more primal than that. More along the lines of…lets say that a scouting party was out hunting. While they were gone, the village was attacked. They would know…the instant it happened…and rush back. This hive mentality also guided the day-to-day, even minute-by-minute decisions of the individuals, keeping them in line, so to speak, and causing them to only act in the interest of the tribe, in lieu of acting selfishly. Otherwise, the social cohesion would disintegrate."

"So, way back in the past, we were all like worker bees or ants in a colony. And then, at some point, we developed free will?"

Nodding, William elaborated, "No one knows whether the ability to break off from the hive and think freely…independently…came in concordance with the ability to speak, or whether there was some other trigger. What we do know is that the hive mentality, ever expanding as tribes absorbed tribes, was quite effective at maintaining a status quo…yet remarkably ineffective at promoting growth. At least what we would consider to be progress as a species."

"Basically, it made people mindless drones?"

"That may be a tad harsh, but yes. Here, let me give you another example. Going back to the beehive. With a pure hive mentality, when a threat appears, all available bees are ordered to attack the threat. Without this ability, there would be no defenses. And the bees do it unquestioningly. They attack despite the fact that each individual bee, by stinging the intruder, is committing suicide. That is the benefit of the mechanism. On the flip side, if each bee were sentient and had free will, one could *decide* not to attack. Make the selfish decision that it isn't going to die for the hive. The result would essentially be social chaos."

"I see that. How can free will evolve in that setting?"

"Simple. Same scenario. The hive is disturbed and an attack is perceived. The order to defend goes out. An individual bee with free will, flying toward the intruder, will still attack if the hive is truly threatened. After all, the destruction of the hive, and the queen within, spells out his end as well. However, as he approaches, he sees that it is merely a man who is doing nothing more than pruning the tree and is not, in fact, a threat to the hive at all. That bee does not sting the man and lives another day. The ability to reason and decide on its own becomes a survival mechanism for the individual, as opposed to a survival mechanism for the hive."

"That makes sense. Now…something else I don't understand. If the cloud remains out there through today, is there a discreet, separate Lisa kind of floating in the program, waiting to be called into action?"

"That isn't easy to answer. In a way, all of your knowledge and experiences have been shared, put into the pool. The totality of it is there but mingled with the input from all others. Probably the best way to explain this is that the Lisa who took you over is akin to a software program which exists only on the cloud. Once you log in to that program, it defines what can and cannot be done. It follows its own internal rules. It simply *runs* on your computer. Now, within that program, you are allowed to specify and create a wide and very detailed assortment of preferences and settings, essentially establishing the parameters of *how* it runs on your computer. You can, within the predefined boundaries, make it unique…personalize it, after a fashion. But no matter what, the program can still only do what it can do and nothing more."

"What happens to *me* when the cloud program is initiated? Why am I cut out of the loop?"

"Again, sticking with the computer analogy, the cloud program is a resource gobbler. Once it is started, it takes up all of your RAM, random access memory, leaving nothing for your consciousness to utilize. You are still there, in the background. But *you* can't run…as long as that giant-sized program is resident."

"I think I understand now. How…big is this? How many of the people on Earth are living out their lives as part of the…hive, instead of through their own consciousness?"

"Depends on the era. Prior to the twentieth century, several fell victim to it. Yet many did not."

"What changed?"

"Mind-altering drugs. The variable throughout history which they could never control was the strength of the personality. The powerful mind, the strong mental being was able to retain his or her independence. The weaker the individual mentally, the more prone to surrendering to the hive that person was. In the middle of the last century, scientists discovered compounds which induced a more docile, compliant consciousness. And, consequently, a feebler one. These drugs, through various methods and techniques, were foisted upon the public from a very young age. The ensuing passivity or compliance was all that was needed for the collective conscious to prevail. Because there was no strong will internally to resist. Until, that is, 1986."

"The accidental release of the messed-up vaccine."

"It was neither messed-up nor accidental."

"You did it?"

"My group did. We knew they were drugging the public. At first we opposed and resisted the methods of distribution, though we were soon marginalized and discredited by the willing, controlled establishment. Then, a researcher within our group identified a synthetic peptide sequence that would produce a protein and block the receptors which had been hijacked. By feigning incompetence and slipping it into the supplies during a mass flu vaccination, we successfully disseminated more than fifty thousand doses before it was detected."

Lisa pressed her head onto the back of the seat and closed her eyes, assimilating the information for a moment, then faced him and asked, "Up until the vaccine, how were *your* people able to remain immune to the control?"

William shrugged casually. "It was, in truth, not that difficult. We avoided the dispensed drugs. The natural tendency of the human consciousness is to emerge, to prevail. This is true at least in the first third of everyone's life. Throughout the formative years, the teen years, and through the early twenties, each individual goes through an internal battle between his or her own consciousness and the collective mind. The never-ending assault from the cloud takes its toll, especially when assisted by the drugs I mentioned, and people are worn down, eventually surrendering to it."

She suddenly giggled. "Maturity?"

"So-called, yes. The process of giving in and allowing the collective to define the individual and establish what that person will accept, or even be willing to consider, has all the trappings of what society considers to be growing up. Nonetheless, to answer your question, Inanna taught her first husband some very simple techniques for retaining one's identity…one's own mind. Since then, our people have practiced those techniques, pardon the expression…religiously."

"Okay. Assuming that I now have all the background needed, why did the Ancient Ones do all of this?"

He allowed himself a smile. "First, to survive. Then, to exploit mankind as they have over the millennia. They had to ensure that they were never exposed. It was far easier for them, through their accomplices on the surface, to control and direct a single monolithic hive mind, rather than billions of unpredictable, independent individuals. As you and your group have proved them correct."

"What do you mean?"

"It's simple, Lisa. Everyone who has played a part in defeating them received the vaccine. All of you are examples of uncontrolled, unrestrained humans. Your group emerged from the field of fifty thousand. As all of you grew from that day and chose your various fields and careers, an unstoppable confluence of knowledge, power, and ability arose, with the only possible conclusion being the eradication of the Ancient Ones. And in our vigilance, my group spotted these seemingly disparate efforts and facilitated from behind the scenes whenever possible."

"You did? Like what?"

"The most obvious example was Dr. Ashby. After his initial funding for his research into monoatomic gold was pulled, one of our foundations offered alternate funding."

"So that was where the secret offer came from!"

"Yes. Unfortunately, our offer and his impending acceptance triggered their decision to condition him."

Taking a few seconds to absorb what she had heard, Lisa shook her head, confounded. "You know what's weird?"

"What?"

"Fifty thousand doses are not a lot, in the general population. How did so many of us end up together? I know that Judtson and Kelsey assembled the people from the CDC list. What about the others, though? Ricky, Romeo, Saylor, and the rest. How did we all become connected?"

William smiled. "Because you can tell the difference."

"What are you referring to?"

"Simple, Lisa. Anyone not enmeshed in the hive mentality can tell almost immediately when meeting someone who is also not. If you meet a hive member, you are left flat, unengaged. If you meet an independent mind, you instinctively connect."

"I get it. So, for example, during the time Judtson was interviewing for an assistant, he would have talked to a whole slew of applicants. But when Ricky walked in the door, Judtson would have known that this person was…."

"Like him."

"That makes sense. I have another question. Why didn't you and your group ever defeat them, the Ancient Ones, over the years?"

"We most certainly wished to do just that. From the very beginning. But without the knowledge of exactly where they hid, which your group discovered…and the perfected method of refining the monoatomic gold, which your group created…we were impotent."

Doni, who had substantially recovered from the drugging, occupied a seat next to Saylor and across the aisle from Ricky. Romeo emerged from the back area and dropped into the seat beside his friend, who had rarely spoken since Judtson's death.

"Are you all right, buddy?" the big man inquired solicitously.

Ricky answered without turning his head, his voice tightly controlled. "I should have stopped him. I never should have let him go out there. Or I should have gone with him and Kelsey. He'd still be alive."

"Don't blame yourself, Ricky," interjected Saylor before Romeo could respond. "He came to me and told me what he was planning. I could have stopped him. I should have…." Emotion choked off the rest of his sentence.

Carlos, who was with Eunice a few feet forward in the cabin, spoke up. "If anyone is to blame, it is I. The fault is mine. All of the horrible things which happened to Judtson, the mind control and…the rest…befell him after I initiated the first contact, drawing him into my discovery."

Kelsey, overhearing their mea culpas, rose from her seat and stopped in the aisle between them, her stance defiant, her visage drawn into an intense, rigid mask. Her voice was harsh. *"Stop this. All of you."*

"But…," objected Ricky.

She whirled to face him. "But *nothing*, Ricky. Don't you understand? I can't deal with it! With the very idea of Judtson's death being someone's…anyone's…*fault*. Because…whether it really is your fault, or Carlos' fault, or Saylor's, or…whoever's…I'm going to hate that person. I know I am. And I don't want that. I don't want to hate any of you. And I don't particularly want to hate the one other person who is probably more to blame for Judtson's death than *anyone* else. *Me*."

Saylor, desperately wanting to say something to help her, began to speak but was cut off with a sharp wave of her hand. "Don't, Saylor. There isn't anything you can say. I was there. I saw it."

Tears began flooding down her cheeks, unnoticed. "That horrible man was ordered to kill…not Judtson…*me*. And Judtson stepped between…. He only did it for one possible reason…to save *me*."

She stopped speaking and stood frozen for an unbearably long, painful minute. No one else dared to say a word as she surrendered to the tidal wave of emotions which had been pent-up within her since the preceding night, her body involuntarily becoming slack. The first to move was Eunice, who jumped to Kelsey and grabbed her before she crumpled to the floor, holding her firmly as she wept. William, Lisa, and the others, witnessing the raw scene, tentatively moved closer, unsure of exactly why…or what they should do.

The only sounds in the cabin were the hum of the engines and her racking, heartrending sobs.

Chapter 52

THE OBVIOUS AND UNDENIABLE DEPARTURE OF THE ANCIENT ONES around the world predictably created an aftermath of confusion and turmoil. What had been considered by many as indisputable absolutes were overturned. The mainstream dogma that aliens and spacecraft were nothing but figments of fervid imaginations was shattered, destroying the credibility of its vocal claimants in the process. Those who had, in the past, steadfastly insisted, maintaining and defending claims of their existence and presence, were vindicated, and saw themselves elevated to positions of newfound respectability.

As the revelations exposing the identities and the nefarious plot of the Illuminati came to light, those who previously had arrogantly, insultingly, and dismissively derided the proponents of cognominate conspiracy theories, relegating them to the categorical dustbin of crackpots and fringe lunatics, were suddenly shunned and fatally ignored. In fact, those who had theretofore been considered immoderate by even the erstwhile extremists soon became aware that they enjoyed a modest enhancement of their reception and acceptance within the media and society at large.

Kelsey's notorious group itself, over the span of weeks, meteorically flashed from the status of villains to heroes to villains and then, finally and begrudgingly, to heroes once again.

The one facing the most exigent challenges upon his return was Kenny Bowman, wanted for the killing of two federal agents. He was immediately placed into custody upon his arrival. As agents loyal to him doggedly pursued the details he provided, the interconnected web of intrigue unraveled, revealing a hornet's nest of foul motives and repugnant deeds. In due time, this investigation disclosed that the independent polygrapher Bowman had enlisted to interview Luis Tovar was not, in fact, the actual Dr. Vince Thompson, but an imposter sent in to ensure that Tovar passed.

The bogus U.S. Marshal, the survivor of the subsequent shoot-out, began to talk, admitting that the false polygraph results were a part of a plot. He and his partner had been ordered by Dillamon to set a trap for Bowman, to lead him into the desert and kill him, their plan thwarted as neither they nor Luis had expected the intervention by Romeo Jones that day.

As the evidence grew, Bowman was first released from custody and soon elevated to the position of task force leader, charged with pursuing the original list of powerful, secretive men named by Samuel Beckleman, some of whom, discovering the loss of their collusive subterranean allies, had already disappeared, absconding with their concealed fortunes.

In the course of his investigation, Kenny was not exactly shocked that Luis, now in his custody, betrayed his own promise to Romeo and did indeed talk. Tovar explained that in the very beginning, he had simply been in the wrong place at the wrong time. Running from an impending, certain conviction for gun smuggling, he had taken the job with Kelsey as guard and caretaker of the silo, thinking it would be a remote, secluded, and quiet position...an ideal hideout, never expecting his employer to become a lightning rod for attention by the authorities. A short time before the group abandoned Kelsey's home and relocated to the underground facility, he received an unexpected visitor, Davis Ulrigg, who offered him a deal.

In exchange for all charges being dropped, Luis was to inform and cooperate. It was he who notified Ulrigg, in advance, of the planned trip to the Mojave Desert to meet with Kevin Berry, and he who insisted upon accompanying the travelers so that Romeo would not be present to foil the attack. The people he reported to were profoundly disappointed with the outcome of that mission, as not only was Berry to have been killed, but Kelsey, Judtson, and Bal were to have been either captured or killed, as well.

It was also Luis who lowered the silo defenses, allowing unfettered entrance to the kidnappers. After the attack and subsequent demolition of the facility, he fell further from favor with Ulrigg's superiors. Following the raid, they were furious that Kelsey, Judtson, Saylor, Romeo, Bal, and Carlos had not been present. As a result, they blamed Tovar for not informing them of that fact.

After the debacle at the FEMA camp, Luis came up with a plan which would allow him to reinfiltrate the group. He turned himself in to Bowman's bureau. Ulrigg, in fact, provided the counterfeit Dr. Thompson to convince Kenny of Tovar's innocence, knowing that the agent would certainly relay the results to Romeo. Luis remembered that shortly before he had deactivated the various defenses at the silo, Doni Costello brought him something to drink. And, as icing on the cake, he remembered overhearing her innocently ask about the Devil's Breath as Saylor stood in the doorway of their room, preparing to leave. The final embellishment, planting the four-minute call to her room, originating from Homeland Security, was also concocted and implemented by Ulrigg, who had one of his tech people insert the nonexistent call in the phone records.

The scene in the desert had again not gone at all as planned. The intention had been to kill two birds with one stone, as Luis put it. Bowman was to be drawn out to the desolate location where he would observe the marshals as they planned to execute their prisoner. The expectation was that he would intercede and, in the process, be killed in the ensuing shoot-out. Tovar was to have escaped and contacted Jones, attempting to worm his way back into the man's trust by using the execution attempt as proof that he was on the right side. Romeo's unexpected intervention drastically changed the outcome, forcing Luis to improvise.

After Jones and Bowman dropped Luis at a convenience store southeast of Tucson, he called Ulrigg, who picked him up. Ulrigg and his superiors were less than happy with the reversal of yet another plan which had involved Tovar, and blamed him for one more failure. The two stopped at a coffee shop in Tucson and were arguing over their next move. Ulrigg said his people wanted Luis out of the picture. Tovar, sensing that losing his value to these people would result in either a prison term or death, argued that he had established enough credibility with Jones to still be effective. Ulrigg was not buying it.

Their discussion was interrupted by the sudden appearance of a clearly distraught Doni Costello. As she entered the coffee shop, she instantaneously and obviously recognized both Luis and Ulrigg, meeting together. Hastily exiting, she was dialing her phone when the two men grabbed her. The agent arranged for her to be whisked out of the country and, due to the uncertainty regarding what value she might have for them in the days ahead, drugged and held captive in Bolivia.

Ulrigg also cut Tovar loose. On his own, Luis essentially went rogue. He staked out Kelsey's residence and followed her to Gates Pass, doggedly looking for an opportunity to redeem himself with Ulrigg's superiors. When he witnessed her father being taken, he followed the kidnappers and stowed away on the plane.

At the conclusion of his marathon interview session with Luis Tovar, Bowman stepped out and called Romeo, filling in the blanks for his friend. After he finished, Jones remarked, "It sounds as if he wasn't strictly a part of their hive."

"No, he wasn't. Ulrigg found him at the silo and recruited him. It was all purely business for Luis."

The big man grunted. "Man, I hate mercenaries. Guess that explains why he didn't turn his gun on Kelsey and the others while they were trapped inside the field office at Fort Irwin."

"Why is that?"

"In his warped mind, he had to play both sides. That's what those dirtbags do. That's why he acted so freaked out when he realized he had the gun with the tracking chip after we brought Bob back to silo. It genuinely *had* been an honest mistake by him. Hell, Ulrigg already knew where we were. When the pistol turned up in Luis' vest, he couldn't be sure if I already knew about it and was testing him to see if he'd bring it up. Whatever side mercenaries are performing in front of, those turncoats always give it one hundred percent. They're never quite certain who is going to come out on top at the end, so they try to arrange it so that both sides like them."

"Yeah. That's true."

"And it also explains why he made a point of giving Bob the Devil's Breath while I was gone. He had to guarantee that the guy wasn't going to give *him* up. When the dude started blabbering in what Luis thought was gibberish, he went ahead and showed us the recording because he didn't see any reason not to. The only thing that's bugging me is the vaccination list. Luis was on it and Mrs. Costello wasn't."

"That's easy," Bowman responded. "Heard about this from some of the others we've rounded up and interrogated. They were monitoring Rosemary Shields and knew she had come across the connection to the vaccine. Suspecting that she might have communicated it to Dylan, they…."

"Dummied up the list to mislead us."

"Exactly. Mrs. Costello was on the list under her original surname. They deleted her so you would believe she was the culprit."

"Makes sense."

"And they monitored who was accessing the list. When Scott got in the system and began searching, he was allowed to do it until he had the last tidbit they wanted *you* to have…about Doni Costello…and then they shredded the file. Luis' name could have been added at the same time."

"Or...he might have actually received the shot," Romeo speculated.

"How's that?"

"All the vaccine did was allow free will. Didn't necessarily make you a good guy. You could have free will and still choose to be a scumbag."

"True."

Romeo sighed loudly. "It all fits. Kenny, we need to give Saylor a call and paint the rest of the picture for him."

"I'll do it. And after that" – there was a soft chuckle over the phone – "I'm going to do something I've been looking forward to for a while now."

It was with enormous pleasure that Kenny Bowman personally arrested Davis Ulrigg, although he found it difficult to handcuff the man, who now bore casts on both of his hands. After exhaustive interrogations, Ulrigg also talked and was able to fill in the details of multiple issues, both in the immediate vicinity, as well as nationally and even globally. After one particularly long, grueling interview, Bowman left the room and pulled out his phone.

"Cahane," the voice answered.

"Eunice, Kenny."

"Hey, good lookin'. What's up?"

"I just learned something. Thought you should be the first to know."

▽

Special Agent Birdsall was stepping out of the restroom, still in the process of zipping up his fly, when he heard a voice boom, "Hey! Birdsall!"

He whirled around, forgetting completely about his zipper, and saw Eunice Cahane, accompanied by three men, marching toward him.

"That's Special Agent Birdsall to you, Detective."

She came to a stop inches from his chest, a broad grin spreading across her wide face. "Is that so? Well, not for long, boysie. You are under arrest. Buddy, cuff 'im."

"Under...! What...! You can't...!" The man protested loudly as Buddy Gleason circled around behind.

As the agent sputtered, she declared, "You're under arrest for the murder of Rosemary Shields. Terwilliger, read 'im his rights."

Birdsall began to argue. She grabbed his tie and pulled his head downward, closer to her face. "Shut up, you smelly piece of chum. And listen to the man."

The two officers escorted Birdsall to the elevator, ignoring his shouted demands that they zip his fly closed. Cahane and her captain were left standing in the hallway.

"Well, Lester, that's the last of them."

"Four in all, Eunice. That's a pretty good catch."

"Yep. Thanks to Kenny Bowman and, I guess, Davis Ulrigg singing like a canary. Between Ulrigg's testimony and the physical evidence Bessie found, we've got them cold."

He slapped her on the shoulder. "Good work. Now...are you ready to come back yet?"

"Awww! Don't tell me that you miss me," she teased.

"Well, I hate to admit it, but you do liven up the bullpen."

She stared at her friend for a while. "Lester, I hate to admit this, but I kinda miss you, too. Heck, I've known you since before I joined the force."

"We do go back quite a ways."

"That we do. But I'm sorry. I'm going to have to decline. At least for now."

"Why's that, Eunice?"

"I made a few friends out west. You've seen their names on the news."

"Yes, of course."

"They're real good people. All of them. And they've just taken a huge bite out of something that's been ripping this country and even the whole world apart for a long time."

"I know. Can't wrap my mind around it all."

"Neither can a lot of folks, Lester. And that's why their job isn't done. Nowhere near. There's still a boatload of real evil people. Hiding under rocks all over the place. Gone to ground. And things aren't going to be right...until they're all dug out of their hidey-holes and dealt with. And I have a feeling that between now and then...my friends are gonna need my help one or two more times. I know they'll be able to keep me busier than a moth in a mitten. And sure would hate it if I wasn't there to lend a hand."

Her eyes briefly drifted away from his, becoming glazed. Cahane's voice, subdued and choked with an emotion he had never heard in it before, continued, "I've spent my whole adult life being that clown at the end of the circus parade. You know the one...the guy with the shovel and pail, following the horses and elephants. I'm tired of cleaning up the mess after the fact. Lester...these folks actually want to *fix* something. Something that's been broken for longer than anybody can remember. Something that...that desperately *needs* fixing. And...one of 'em...a good man...a kind and gentle soul...well, we lost him. And we lost him on my watch. And I...." She stopped for a moment, struggling to retain control of her voice. "And I *can't* let something like that happen again."

Unable to find the words, Lester nodded. Eunice turned away and he watched her as she slowly walked the length of the corridor to the elevator. She was well out of earshot when he murmured, "Godspeed, Eunice."

▽

Dylan Falt, without delay upon his return, had begun working with a pharmaceutical firm, now under contract with Kelsey and William, to replicate and mass-produce the 1986 vaccine. Initial batches were made available almost immediately.

With the recently granted access to the formerly underground chemists and biologists loyal to William Batman and his organization, including those men and women who had been involved in the vaccine program, he was able to find the answer to what had been a troubling question. Late in the evening, after most of the staff had gone home, he composed an email.

Dear Saylor,

I hope that you and Doni are well. I know you've wanted to understand the cause of the breaks, or fugue states, that Judtson and the rest of us suffered through prior to our conversions, or conditioning. Between working with Kelsey's father and his people, and the information streamed to me by Kenny as he has systematically broken through the barriers of the Illuminati, I think I've been able to piece it together.

Apparently, it was a symptom of the battle for the available receptors inside our brains. The introduction of the Trojan Horse...that's what we've dubbed the nasty little additive they hid in the inert portion of their vaccines...turned our systems into mini-factories producing the compliancy proteins at an ever-increasing level in most people, at least those who hadn't received the 1986 vaccine. What I've found out is that not only did the '86 vaccine hijack the receptors, making them unavailable to the bad proteins, it also disrupted the production itself. Should the receptors somehow again become available, there would be no culprits inside us to capitalize upon the opportunity. So the bad guys knew they had to do two things: unseat the squatters on the receptors *and* resupply us with a substantial dose of their proteins.

In the days prior to our visits from the guys with the headpieces, all of us were pre-doped. Instead of using the Trojan Horse, which slowly and gradually churned out the nasty proteins, they basically flooded our systems with the finished product. The delivery mechanism was different for each of us. They watched us. They observed our habits. And then, whether through something we ate or drank, they got it into us. According to Kenny, in two or three cases, they would bump into us in public and, using an old CIA trick, give us a pinprick injection of the stuff. We'd never as much as feel it. Kenny never did find out the specific method used on Judtson, but it would have been one of those.

I'm being longer-winded here than I intended; however, the bottom line is that the breaks occurred in response to the systems suddenly being inundated, you could even say overwhelmed, with the bad proteins. There was an internal battle between the bad proteins and the good ones from the '86 vaccine, with each side gaining ground in terms of how many receptors it controlled and then losing them again. Back and forth. The '86 dose still in all of us was battling a bio-threat which was a million times or more greater than it had been originally designed to control. The breaks were a by-product of this war being waged inside us.

And, of course, when the boys in black arrived and zapped us with the resonator, or conditioner, as they called it, unseating all of the friendly proteins at once, the hordes of bad ones were ready to seize the receptors, and the final conversions were completed. Until you and Matt undid the process, that is. We'll be learning more details as we go, but that's the gist of it. Hope this clears it up for you.

Let me know if you have any questions. And Saylor, I really want to hear from both of you…when you feel like it, of course.

Kindest Regards, Dylan

Lisa Trippiano organized another live broadcast of *The Jack Bailey Show*. Several of the group returned to complete the presentation which had been aborted by the bombing attempt, as well as to add the details of the final chapter. At Ricky's suggestion, William Chatterley was included to discuss his experience with the men who had coerced him into lying about the crop circles. At the end of the show, which had drawn a historic, record-setting audience, Jack Bailey and his entire production staff, including his son, Brandon, received Falt's vaccinations on the air. The broadcast triggered an avalanche of requests from his viewers for the vaccine.

Romeo emerged from his bedroom and found Chili in his usual spot, watching the security monitors. He dropped into a chair.

"How's it going?"

The Marine softly grunted, "Quiet."

Jones pulled an envelope out of his pocket and tossed it to his number two, who turned it over in his hands for a moment, looking slightly perplexed. "What's this?"

Sighing heavily, Romeo answered, "A pathetic attempt on my part to set things right."

Their eyes connected as Chili tried to read the Ranger's expression. Failing, he opened the envelope and pulled out the folded papers. He took a minute to peruse them. "I don't understand, sir. This looks like an itinerary to Geneva. You have a mission for me?"

Romeo nodded. "In a sense, yes. Scott, with Saylor's help, located a surgeon in Europe who is pioneering a new technique. You're booked to climb up on his table next month."

Chili's eyes widened. "Me? What…?"

"Look, I broke your voice box. This guy can supposedly fix it."

The Marine's hand unconsciously traveled to his own throat, touching it lightly. "Master Sar, I don't…. You don't need to do this."

Romeo stood and gazed down at the man. "It's the least I can do."

He received no reply and started to leave, stopping at the doorway and turning back. "Chili, answer a question for me, will you?"

"Sure," came the response in the thin, high voice.

"I told Cahane about our little dust-up, the one that…caused this. She asked me why you would even want to throw in with me after that. More I thought about it, the more I wondered the same thing. Seems like you'd hate my guts. Certainly not want to work for me."

Chili shrugged. "Not a big mystery, Master Sar. We're pack animals. You. Me. All of us. You know that. We tangled. You won."

He paused for a few seconds before finishing. "We follow the biggest dog."

Matt Wheeler, accompanied by Dean Copeland, traveled to Texas to convert Harold Billings, the photo archivist from NASA. Afterward, the reunion between the two old friends was an emotional one. As more and more of the henchmen were captured and interrogated, the list of those requiring the conversion services grew, necessitating the production of additional helmets. Robin Reedy was hired by Wheeler to oversee the team of technicians trained to perform the actual procedures. Freed up from the hands-on duty, he assumed the top position in the engineering department of Chris Ashby's new organization, the first task being the mass-production of monoatomic gold.

Chapter 53

CHRIS ASHBY, SPEARHEADING THE ORGANIZATION HASTILY CREATED BY KELSEY, had assembled a team of chemists and researchers who began exploring the uses and benefits of monoatomic gold. His first act as the president was to appoint his sister, Starlight, to head the exploratory innovation department.

It was late in the evening, the tail end of a long and exhausting day. He finished reading the last page of a voluminous preliminary report, pushed the pile to the side, and rubbed his eyes in a feeble attempt to ease the pain behind them. Unsettled by the research results, he pulled out his safe phone, which he still carried, and speed-dialed a number.

Dylan Falt answered on the first ring. "You're working late tonight."

Ashby's voice conveyed his fatigue. "Too many in a row."

"Then knock off, Chris. Whatever it is will wait."

"I don't think so."

The immunologist detected the subtle undercurrent of worry in his friend's tone. "What's wrong?"

Before he replied, the chemist released a loud sigh. "Maybe nothing. I don't know. These last several weeks have probably made me paranoid."

He heard Falt chuckle over the connection. "Just because you're paranoid doesn't mean people really aren't out to get you. Come on, Chris, spill it. What's wrong?"

Taking a minute to gather his thoughts first, he began, "Well, you already know what we've learned regarding Alzheimer's and autism, as they are affected by the monoatomic gold, right?"

"Yeah! It's incredible."

"We've been struggling to figure out the 'how' and the 'why' of it. And I think we're getting close."

"Okay...?"

"I won't get into the details of the studies yet, but it appears that the monoatomic gold...the MG...increases the efficiency, or maybe the functionality, of the brain...by as much as a hundred-fold."

Dylan whistled softly, saying nothing. Ashby continued, "So it basically compensates for the effects of those two diseases by cranking up or turbocharging the brain. We're probably going to find the same thing true with other diseases which misdirect or diminish capacity."

"Like senility?"

"Yes. And probably several others, including actual brain traumas and strokes. Things like that."

"So what's the problem? Seems to me you'd be jumping for joy instead of moping."

Following a brief silence, Ashby shared, "I guess I'm worried about the ethics."

"Ethics? I don't get it, Chris. Why?"

"Maybe...maybe I'm nuts. I don't know. It's a feeling I haven't been able to shake. That's why I wanted to talk. Everybody here is on cloud nine. Almost euphoric. Granted, the benefit to people with those problems is obvious. That's not the part I'm worried about."

"Go on."

"Dylan, what about people who don't have a problem? People who are healthy? Fine?"

"I don't...oh, I see. You're saying that a normal, healthy individual who takes the MG is also going to have his functionality, or cognitive abilities, enhanced a hundred-fold."

"We're not certain yet. I mean, we haven't run any human trials, so I can't say for sure. But yeah...that probably will be the case."

This time it was Falt's turn to become silent as he digested what his friend was telling him. Not inclined to wait, Chris added, "One of my people administered a human-level dosage to an orangutan."

"What...what happened?"

"It's weird, Dylan. I can't stand to look in the ape's eyes."

"Why not?"

"They're different now. They're...I can't describe it. Eerie. It just creeps me out. It feels to me as if our roles were suddenly reversed. It's...how he must have felt when humans stared at him."

"You think he's smarter than you?"

"I don't know. Maybe. It's spooky."

"Any other changes in behavior?"

"Don't know yet. This happened yesterday. I'm not saying that he's reading Chaucer already. Just that there's a difference in the way he looks and acts. It's way too early to measure possible changes. What's driving me up the wall is that maybe we have no business sticking our noses here...maybe *we* aren't prepared to make the sort of decision we're faced with."

"Explain."

"If...and for now it's still *if*...we were to disseminate the MG to the general public and it increased everyone's intelligence one hundred times...basically, *we* are trying to understand the incomprehensible. How can we...let's say I have an IQ of 128...and I know that the original IQ structure wasn't designed for this type of scaling...but relatively speaking, how can a person with that IQ even begin to imagine a world where the average IQ isn't merely 100 any longer...it's *10,000*? How much would the world change? And would the changes necessarily be for the better?"

"Wow! Chris, you really know how to bite into a heavy-duty concept, don't you?"

"I guess. My point is...do we have a right to release something which will drastically alter the world in ways we are totally incapable of imagining? In this new world, with everyone's IQ in the 10,000 or more range, you and I would be considered to be imbeciles...idiots...morons. And yet, we imbeciles are supposed to make this decision?"

After another thoughtful pause, Dylan suggested, "What about problem solving? Don't you think a species that much smarter would finally be able to fix some of the things which have plagued us forever? Other diseases? Famine? Energy? Pollution? Seriously, Chris, with that level of brain power, maybe every single one of the thorny problems would topple."

"I have considered that. And that is exactly what everybody here is focused on. The benefits. The benefits! It's always only about the benefits. I'm not so sure we shouldn't also be contemplating the downside."

"Like what?"

"There could be several issues. What if the MG has unintended long-term consequences? As did the protein created by the Illuminati vaccine, which started individuals out as docile and compliant, but was eventually to turn people into cold-blooded killers."

"Kelsey seems to think that was actually their plan. For all of us to kill one another off."

"That's certainly possible. In the case of the MG...it could start out with some huge step-up in intelligence but...I don't know...shorten lives dramatically. Or burn out the brain in a year. Or a month! We simply don't know. What about the balance between intellect and ethics or morality? Pure intellect can take a person in some scary directions."

"True. On the other hand, when we're all that much smarter, maybe the ethics or morals will also be even stronger. There are arguments to support that."

"You're right. It could go either way. My point is...we don't *know*. And what about stimuli?"

"What do you mean?"

"How much daily mental input would a person one hundred times smarter need? And is that level of stimulation at all physically possible? I'm not a psychiatrist, but what if these new, improved humans, starved of sufficient stimuli, just went stark raving mad? Well, as I said a minute ago, maybe we can't imagine what the downsides would be. In and of itself, increased intelligence is no guarantee that bad people will suddenly become good. Think about the group we recently confronted and defeated. And then visualize them a hundred times smarter. Isn't that a scary thought?"

"I suppose it is. But if the rest of us have also moved up the scale, it would balance."

"Maybe," Ashby acknowledged. "Maybe not. Or maybe, with that kind of IQ, the bad people would be able to do things so cleverly, so rapidly that the good guys wouldn't even have a chance to respond. Dylan, there are folks we've always considered fringe who maintain that certain technologies...the atomic bomb, for example, or gene splicing...provide us with an ability we are not smart enough to handle. Perhaps that problem would be amplified, not ameliorated. And the other issue is...no matter how hard we try, we can't guarantee that everybody, and I mean every single person on Earth, would get the MG. Think about a world where you would have two classes of humans...those with super-intelligence and...us. People at what is currently our level. They would be viewed by the former group as unbelievably inferior, the way that we would view...."

"That ape? Before the MG, that is."

"Exactly. Scary thought as well."

"I have to ask...what does your sister think?"

Ashby laughed softly. "Starlight thinks that this is all a huge mistake. She wants me to bury the process. In her opinion, we're basically doing the same thing the Ancient Ones did, arbitrarily tampering with mankind. Short-circuiting nature. And she also thinks that making everyone one hundred times smarter would only be giving the bad people bigger and better weapons to use on all of us."

"At this point, is there any chance of actually keeping it under wraps?"

"Not really. All the members of the team know what it is and have a feel for what it does. I've already had several of the researchers…volunteer…come to me and ask me if they can receive a dose."

"Don't they have access to the finished product?"

"They did. Until the orangutan test. I grabbed all of it and locked it up for now. Although I can't be certain that some of it hasn't already been grabbed and stashed by one of the staff. A single dosage is tiny. And Dylan, right now my scrubbing process is still secret. I'm the only one who knows it. Well, Matt and I. But it isn't that hard to figure out. It's only a matter of time."

"Well, my friend, it appears as if that answers your original question."

"I don't understand."

"You started out by asking me if you should release it. The question implies that you *could* keep it to yourself. It doesn't sound as though you can. I think, with all of the people who are aware of the tempting qualities of the substance, it's going to get out with or without your help. And if it gets out the back door, so to speak, that would certainly be ugly. Then it *will* become selectively used and probably end up on some million-dollar black market. Or, worse yet, certain government types will be deciding who gets it and who doesn't. If you take it out there, at least then the playing field should be kept relatively level."

"That could be. You have to admit the timing is bizarre."

"In what way?"

"My MG coming out, multiplying everyone's brain power beyond all proportion at the same time you are cranking out a vaccine which, for the first time, gives almost every person on the planet free will. We still have no idea how that is going to play out."

There was another pause before Falt, his voice more somber, agreed, "It does promise to be an interesting time."

Ashby huffed once. "Yeah. Interesting, all right. I only hope that we aren't lighting a fuse."

He stared at the wall for a moment, then confided, "I'm scared, Dylan. I'll admit it. Whether all of this results in a phenomenally wonderful new dawn for mankind or blows up in our faces, either way…we are the ones playing God. And I don't particularly enjoy being cast in this role."

They ended the call, promising to talk soon. Shutting down his computer and turning off the light in his office, Chris walked slowly down the corridor of the hastily leased complex until he arrived at the lobby. Expecting it to be dark and deserted, he was surprised to see two men working on a scaffold.

"You two are working late."

One of the men, startled by the sudden voice in the silence, leaned out over the side to answer. "Our boss is paying us triple time for this. I guess somebody wanted it up as soon as possible."

Ashby nodded and moved closer to the exit in order to see what they were doing. As the platform of the scaffold no longer obscured their work, he saw they were attaching polished gold lettering to the high wall, in a position which would be the first thing every visitor would see. He knew that the quote had been a suggestion by Saylor.

Judtson Kent Foundation
To Take Back Everything That We've Lost

Carlos Villarreal teamed up with Bal Singh. In the period following the routing of the reptoids, they had learned that the Ancient Ones, upon their arrival, had injected a reactive compound into the area now known as the Andes. The compound, upon contact with groundwater, expanded exponentially, creating the mammoth cavity which extended from Puma Punku to Lake Titicaca and beyond, substantially inflating the towering mountain range and creating the gargantuan underground lair. This monumental terraforming effort finally explained an ongoing mystery: why fossils of sea creatures had been unearthed at an altitude of twelve thousand feet. Their joint project was to rewrite the history, archaeology, and geology books to reflect this new knowledge, as well as the related details they had gained from their experiences.

Jimmy Meade and Dean Copeland, working as advisors with NASA, put together a proposed plan for expeditions to the Moon and Mars, the two celestial bodies where the Ancient Ones, using relatively short-range spacecrafts with engineered androids as pilots, had transported much of the Earth's gold supply in their efforts to rid the environment of the toxic substance.

As the investigation of the Illuminati progressed, long-held secrets, now finally released, revealed that the Roswell incident, the subsequent cover-up notwithstanding, was indeed a crash landing of one of their ore shuttlecrafts. Remnants of a ship and crew, which had been whisked away to Wright-Patterson and concealed for decades, were brought out and put on public display.

Eunice Cahane arrived from Atlanta and joined Romeo Jones as a part of the security detail around Kelsey and her father. Scott Gumble returned to his computers and his position as head of the technical department of their company, while also working as an independent contractor for Kenny Bowman, assisting him in the search for the shadowy members of the Illuminati still at large.

▽

Ricky Ingram sat alone in his living room, the space dark and quiet. Since his return from Puma Punku, he had immersed himself in the hectic yet mundane details of the aftermath. He discovered, to his surprise, that Judtson had named him the executor of his estate. As Judtson's marriage to Kristen had been intact upon his friend's death, most of the assets reverted to her, so there was little for him to administer.

Thinking of Kristen prompted an ironic chuckle from him. Mitch Murray, in a grandiose public gesture to his former client's memory, had volunteered to receive Dylan's vaccine. In very little time, the proteins had their effect, freeing him from the hive mentality and revealing his true personality, which Kristen had found to be as repugnant as she had found Judtson's. The two were now estranged.

There was a light rap on the door. Not expecting a visitor, he quietly crossed the room and peered through the peephole, seeing that the caller was Romeo. He opened the door and stepped aside to let him in, nodding as a greeting.

"Hey, buddy. How is it going?"

Ricky switched on a single lamp and they sat at his dining table. "I'm fine, I guess."

"Of course you are. Everybody who's fine sits alone in a dark room."

"I...just...didn't see the point of turning on a light."

The big man whistled softly. "You know what that's called, don't you? Depression."

The accusation, if that was what it had been, did not faze him. "I suppose. I mean...I *am* depressed."

"I know."

Both men were silent for nearly a minute before Ricky asked, "How's Kelsey?"

"I'm certain she's depressed, too. But right now I've also noticed that she's in deep denial."

"How so?"

"If she's sleeping more than four or five hours a night, I'd be surprised. And every waking minute, she keeps charging from task to task. Running at full speed. Between the Foundation, getting Dylan's vaccine out to the entire world, and keeping in touch with Jimmy, Dean, and the others, she jam-packs every single second of the day."

"Keeping herself busy."

"Yeah. Exactly. She's trying to keep her mind off of it."

"That can't last."

"Oh, I know. There's a burnout coming. I just don't know of any way to head it off."

Standing, Ricky crossed the room to a small desk, returned with a manila envelope, and handed it to Romeo. When he spoke, his tone was level. "I went to Judtson's house and picked up his computer. Kristen didn't want it. God, it was hard going through his stuff."

"I can imagine."

The younger man sighed gently, pointing at the sealed envelope. "I ran across something and printed it. I'm sure he'd want Kelsey to have it."

"What is it?"

The answer was deliberately vague and a slight tremor now fluttered his voice. "Something he wrote. Let her know that the entry was time-stamped late at night...the same day he and Kelsey came to find us at the karaoke contest."

Romeo, sensing that the contents were private, turned the envelope slowly in his hands and asked no further questions. "I'll get it to her."

"Thanks."

He shifted the topic back to his friend. "What are you going to do now?"

Ricky stared hard at Romeo. "I wish I knew. Judtson was...." He hesitated, his voice failing for a moment before he was able to finish. "He was generous to me in his will. I guess I'm set."

"I have an idea."

"What?"

"Why don't you start writing again?"

Ricky shook his head emphatically. "That does not appeal to me at all."

"Why?"

"I don't know. After all we've been through, the glimpse I've had into what the world is truly like, writing mindless detective novels doesn't interest me anymore."

Romeo chuffed softly. "That isn't what I meant."

"Then what?"

"Listen, Judtson released a total of nine books debunking things, ripping apart the people who espoused the ideas that he trashed. Prior to his death, he found out he was wrong. Maybe not about all of it. But certainly some of it."

"So?"

"Those nine books…do you really think that's the legacy he wants to leave behind?"

Ricky's voice rose slightly in pitch. "What can I do? Rewrite them? That would be coming from me…not Judtson."

"No. That still isn't what I'm saying. You do have his rough draft of what was to be his tenth book – the one on Puma Punku. The book that started everything. You can do whatever he would have done to finish it…polish it…get it ready. And after that, make sure it gets published." Romeo paused. "As he wanted."

Taking the words to heart, Ricky shifted his gaze away and pondered the suggestion for minutes before responding. The Ranger waited patiently. "I guess I could do that. I always worked with him on the rewrites. I know how he would want it."

"Yes. You do."

"But so much has happened since he wrote it. So much more about the story has been learned."

"Ricky…do you honestly think Judtson would have minded if you added an epilogue…to complete the story?"

A tear welled up in his eye and spilled down his cheek. "*Of course* he would have minded! He was a perfectionist."

Romeo stood and looked down at his friend, placing his hand on the slender shoulder. "Then, write it perfectly."

▽

Saylor and Doni pulled away from their garage, on the way to their first dinner out since returning from Puma Punku. As Saylor turned onto the street, he glanced at the "For Sale" sign in front of the dark and desolate house next door, his gut tightening involuntarily at the sight, his foot unconsciously touching the brake pedal. Sharing his sorrow, Doni wordlessly placed her hand upon his, squeezing hard. With a sudden exhalation of breath, he punched the gas, speeding away too quickly.

The trip was completed without conversation and the two crossed the parking lot to the restaurant, to be promptly greeted by an overly effusive host, who led them to a booth in the corner. Handing menus to the couple, he informed them that Josh would be their server, and immediately scurried back to his station. Neither broke the self-imposed silence, both knowing that the only topic they wished to discuss was far too painful to broach.

Their examination of the menus was interrupted as a tall, well-tanned young man, wearing a long-sleeved white shirt and black slacks, suddenly appeared at the table. In a voice which, to Saylor's ear, beckoned the image of a game show host, he enthused, "How are you doing, folks? My name is Josh and I'll be your server this evening."

The menu slid from between Saylor's fingers, unnoticed, as he swung his eyes to connect with Doni's, where he saw a spontaneous upwelling of tears begin to cascade down her cheeks. He could feel the chill tracks upon his own face, as well. Glancing up, he asked with an uncertain voice, "You haven't had the vaccine yet, have you?"

Their server did an almost comical double take at the question. There could be no doubt what Saylor was referring to; the vaccination was in the news and on the Internet incessantly.

"Uh, no, sir. Not yet. I haven't had the time."

Returning his gaze to Doni, the portrait of emotions painted upon his face changed...the first traces of a sardonic smile beginning to crease his face. She noticed this at once. Understanding caused her eyes to widen...followed, moments later, by a broad smile which spread across her face, the first she had allowed since her rescue.

Taking a deep breath and clearing his throat, Saylor again faced the young man. "Josh, my name is Saylor! And this...is my wife, Doni! And we'll be *your* customers this evening!"

The two-thirds of the former longtime trio, holding hands across the table, burst into an uncontrolled, purging laughter.

Chapter 54

KELSEY, WITH ROCKY CURLED UP AT HER FEET, WAS SITTING AT HER DESK and typing rapidly, in the midst of an IM discussion with Dylan on the number of vaccinations administered worldwide. At the same time, she had a phone tucked against the side of her face and was talking to Chris about the details of a new study group who had recently received a dosage of the monoatomic gold, when a hand suddenly reached across her desk and broke the phone connection. She whirled around and saw her father, just as he pressed the power button on her laptop, disconnecting her from Dylan as well.

"Daddy! What are you doing?"

He gently took the phone receiver from its perch on her shoulder and placed it back into the cradle, while pulling a chair close to her and sitting down.

"I'm unplugging you."

She sputtered, "Why? I'm in the middle of…."

He interrupted, barking out, "Stop it."

The expression of concern on his face was obvious. Forcing a long breath into her lungs, Kelsey slouched heavily back in the chair, causing it to tilt dangerously. "I *can't* stop, Daddy. There's too much to…."

"They can handle it. These are intelligent, competent people who know what they're doing. Let them do it."

"But…!"

"No 'buts.' We both know what you're really doing and why. It needs to stop. Now!"

Her breathing rapid, her blue eyes darting furtively from one point to another in the room and remaining nowhere for longer than a second, she argued, "I don't know what you're talking about."

Both of her hands were gripping the leather arms of the chair, digging deeply into the hide. He tenderly placed his hand upon the nearer. "Kelsey…honey…you can't keep running away."

"I…have to."

"Or what?"

"Or…." She stopped, having no explanation she was able to elucidate.

William's tone was gentle. "All you're doing is deferring it. You know that, don't you?"

With a tight jerk of her head, she acknowledged that she did.

"You're doing exactly the same thing I did when I lost your mother."

The reference managed to reach a part of Kelsey. "Daddy…you've *never* talked about that."

"I know. And that was probably a mistake. A big mistake. But it was…too hard."

"Why? I mean, I understand why, believe me. After all these years though, you should have at least talked to *me* about it."

Casting his eyes down for a second, he spoke so softly she barely heard his words. "You were the one person I could never talk to about it."

Stunned, she blurted, "Why?"

Steeling himself, her father broached the subject. "I couldn't allow you to know…to *feel*…the guilt."

"The guilt? For what?"

His eyed bored into hers. "Kelsey, I loved your mother with all my heart and soul. More than I ever thought it was possible to love. Just knowing that she was my wife made me happier than anything I could have imagined. Although, in the earlier days of the transference, the husbands for the women who were to carry Inanna forward were historically chosen by the predecessors, over the centuries that gradually changed. It corresponded with the diminishing prominence of Inanna in each female host. In the succeeding generations, as Inanna faded into the background and the true person inherent in the host was allowed to exist…to survive…the host…. My God! What a cold name for each of the women, isn't it?" He fell silent for a moment and shook his head. "Sorry. To continue, these women who carried and concealed Inanna were allowed greater and greater input into the choice of a mate, albeit the final decision was always retained by the father. Your mother and I met in college. We fell deeply and profoundly in love. She was keenly aware of the responsibility which she had thrust upon her and took it quite seriously. To a fault, perhaps."

"What do you mean?"

"Be patient. I'll explain. You can imagine the shock I experienced when I was told the truth…the incredible history."

He paused and chuckled to himself, reliving the recollection. "I obviously accepted the mantle or burden or privilege, whatever you want to call it, mainly because I loved her so much. Once I was taken into the inner circle…once I was fully taught…the importance of it, the truth of it…it engulfed me fully. And I accepted the duties as the head of the Masons wholeheartedly. During those days, we had a joy-filled marriage, marred only by horrible recurring nightmares, nightmares we later came to understand were Inanna's attempts to communicate with your mother."

Moving forward to the front edge of her seat, Kelsey admitted, "I've had them, too."

"I know."

"Why didn't you ever tell me what they were?"

"I couldn't. I promised."

She started to say something but was cut off.

"I will address it all. Trust me."

Kelsey nodded and waited.

"In time we learned that she was pregnant and that it was to be a girl. I can't begin to tell you how happy we were. The old days when the transfer cost the life of the woman from whom Inanna departed were but a distant fact, something which was no longer the case. We knew that we were on the brink of fulfilling my obligation and her destiny, transferring Inanna to you upon your birth, and that your mother would then be able to continue as she had always been, without, of course, the dreaded nightmares. Our idyllic period quickly ended. Your mother developed a vague numbness on her left side. After several doctors and tests, we discovered that she had a disease called AVM, or arteriovenous malformation, and that the problem was located far too deeply within her brain. There was nothing which could be done to help her...to fix the problem."

He again paused, needing time to regather the courage to finish the story. "She...she and I...were told by her doctor that she should not have you or, for that matter, any other baby in the foreseeable future...unless and until a day arrived, hopefully while she was still within her fertile years, when a surgical procedure to repair the defect would be perfected. The concern was that prolonged labor would increase intracranial pressure...risk rupture...which would be fatal to her."

Kelsey let out a forlorn sigh.

"He, the doctor, expressed his sadness for our plight. He knew how important it was for most young couples to have children. But he assured that all she needed to do was abort the baby...abort you. And that your mother...my wife...as long as she maintained a healthy diet and was cautious with physical exertion...would live a long life. Then he suggested that we consider adoption. Obviously, he did not know the truth...the realities of the almost sacred trust that she carried."

Her father's voice and posture projecting defeat, he continued, "We had no options. It wasn't as if we could simply adopt a girl and perform the transfer. And if that *was* possible, the mechanism for doing it had never been shared with us. Your mother and I decided, together, that you would be born, and that I would be present to ensure the transfer occurred, no matter what happened. And that...is what we did."

"Oh, my God," Kelsey gasped softly.

He lowered his eyes briefly. "Before the birth, we discussed everything. We decided... actually, she insisted...that you would never be told of our decision. She wanted you to believe that we had no warning...no knowledge of the problem. She wanted you to believe that her death following childbirth had been completely unexpected. She did *not* want you to grow up with the knowledge...with the guilt...that your very existence was at the expense of her life."

With a single pathetic cry, Kelsey sprang forward and threw her arms around her father's neck, holding him in an intense embrace, and the two remained motionless for minutes. When they parted, he brushed tears from her cheeks with the heel of his thumb.

"I'm not certain why I've broken my promise to her and told you now. Other than that it seems to be the right thing to do."

Kelsey did not comment, simply nodding.

"We are the last. You...and I. With the defeat and departure of the Ancient Ones, with the knowledge Inanna carried to do this...no longer relevant, there is no further need for my people, the Masons. We have done all which was promised and sworn so long ago. I am the last."

"But...."

"Ssshhhh. Nothing needs to be said to address that truth. I am confident that your mother, looking down upon what has happened…looking down upon you, Kelsey…is proud. As am I. Vindicated that her decision to proceed with your birth was made not in vain. And that it was you, specifically, who were brought forth at *this* critical time…when the long-sought culmination of centuries of prior sacrifices has come to be. You have finally finished what was started by Heran's wife, Sila, in the dim and distant past, as she made that first and ultimate sacrifice for us all, a tradition continued by the selfless actions taken by her many successors. And I am the last link in the unbroken chain forged by Heran. The Illuminati were created and supported by the Ancient Ones to serve three purposes: conceal their presence, transform the world into an environment suitable for them, and provide them with…well, let's simply say, that which they required to live. My predecessors, and the multitude of our adherents over the ages, were chosen to be the countering force. Now…both are irrelevant…no longer needed in this new world."

William lifted his hand and tenderly touched the side of his daughter's face. "We all carry the painful sorrow of this legacy. Your mother's dream, and mine, was that you would be spared this anguish. It has broken my heart that you were not. That one more sacrifice was necessary before the final battle could be waged and won. Kelsey, my beloved daughter, I am sorry beyond words that what we have done, what was set in motion so long ago, cost you…your only real love."

His words removed the last sandbag in the dyke she had hastily constructed to protect herself from the emotional storm within. Collapsing into his arms, she finally surrendered to the unrelenting pain.

▽

Kelsey did not know where she was. Nothing was recognizable. Nothing vaguely familiar. The sky above a brilliant cerulean hue. The air crisp, clean, and almost sweet. Beside her was a wall, unweathered and pristine, as if untouched by the hand of nature, the structure standing double her height and built from flawlessly shaped H-stones. The path she walked was blanketed with a dense, soft mat of grass, which rebounded in the wake of her steps as would a sponge.

Her treads led her to a point where the wall terminated. Beyond was a wide, sweeping meadow, populated with majestic arching trees and flowers blossoming into a staggering array of deep, vibrant colors. In the midst of the glen stood a lone figure. A woman. Tall and stately. Wearing a simple, flowing white robe.

As she approached this person…this being…whom Kelsey did not know but somehow knew, she was first captivated by her eyes. The most strikingly blue eyes she had ever seen. The top of the figure's perfectly smooth, clean head shone in the brilliant sunlight. On her face…a serene smile.

Kelsey stopped a foot from her.

"Do I know you?" As she said the words, she was struck with the sound of her own voice. It seemed as if she had spoken directly into her own ear.

"Of course. I have been a part of you since your birth."

"You are Inanna?"

The woman answered with a single graceful dip of her head.

"I have never known your name. And I have only before seen you in my dreams."

"As you are now."

"This is a dream?"

"It is, Kelsey."

She shook her head in confusion. "All of the other times...the hundreds of other dreams of you...were...hideous, ugly."

The figure's smile broadened. "But now, the ugliness is gone. Forever."

Hearing the words made Kelsey's heart rise, only to quickly fall again. Sensing, or knowing this, Inanna said, "I loved him, too."

"What...how?"

"I have lived not only through your eyes and ears, but also through your heart. How could it be other?"

Kelsey was silent. Comprehending.

Inanna continued, "I have come to you to thank you and say goodbye."

"Goodbye? I don't understand. How can you leave me? Except...."

With a subtle shake of her head, she replied, "I will not be leaving you."

"But...."

"Whether or not you may ever bear a daughter, I will not leave you."

"Why?"

"Because I am done. What I wished to finish is completed. Save for one final task. One gift."

"What is that?"

"As you awaken from this dream, you will know all that I know. All of the remaining secrets, the knowledge of my people. This will be yours to either share or not share, as you may choose. When you may trust enough."

"Then what will happen to you?"

An even more intense expression of serenity and happiness colored Inanna's countenance. "I will, at last, be allowed to remain within you until your final breath. And, at that moment, you and I shall pass together."

"If you aren't leaving me, why did you say goodbye?"

"I have infringed far too long. Harmed far too many. After this...our last meeting...I will permit myself to fade back into the deepest reaches of your mind and soul, never to affect you again. I will...sleep."

"What if I need you? What if...?"

The woman was gone. As were the azure sky and the bountiful trees and the beautiful flowers and the meadow itself. All Kelsey now saw was the faintly lit ceiling above her bed.

$$\triangledown$$

The turbulent air tumbled and cascaded over the top of the windshield. Darkness surrounded the car like a cloak, only pierced by the two probing headlights, revealing the narrow lane ahead. In the mirror, Kelsey saw another set of lights behind her, trailing at a discreet distance, and knew that the driver was Romeo. Her right hand drifted to the passenger seat. Her fingers buried themselves deeply into the soft, thick fur of the golden retriever at her side. At her touch, he shifted closer and turned to stare at his new master, her face illuminated by the faint green light cast from the instruments.

In time, the sign came into view, marking the entrance, and she turned the Oldsmobile into the parking lot of the hotel. Rather than driving to the bright lights of the canopy, she parked at the distant edge and climbed out, snatched up the large canvas tote from the backseat, and began to walk, paced by Rocky. She was vaguely aware that the black Hummer behind her had also entered and parked, but knew that her protector would stay well back.

After leaving behind the boundary of the pavement, she followed a rock-covered path up a gradual incline. Cresting that, she hastened her gait, moving now downward. Using only the light from the moon and the stars, Kelsey navigated the winding trail. Coming to its end, she turned to her right, knowing her route by heart. Five more minutes of walking brought her to her goal.

Sliding onto the bench seat, oblivious to the coldness of the concrete, with Rocky snuggling tightly against her leg, she opened the tote, placed it on the table, facing toward her, and pulled out the head-mounted book light, slipping it over her hair and switching it on.

She reached inside and removed the envelope given to her by Romeo...the one he had received from Ricky...the one containing something from Judtson. He had told her the date it had been written. She knew that it was the night of the first time Judtson and she had made love together. He must have written whatever it turned out to be after their painful, sad parting in front of his office.

Kelsey's hands shook slightly as she placed a fingertip under the edge and tore open the flap. Inside was a single sheet of paper. Anxious and at the same time apprehensive, she gently slid it out and laid it on the table, immediately recognizing that it was a poem.

Stopping herself from reading it for a second, she first closed her eyes and visualized Judtson...sitting at the keyboard with Rocky at his side...as he typed. Writing this. She opened her eyes and read.

Before today...

While stumbling through my bitter haze

An endless stream of jumbled days

Empty vessels, each offered free

Filling nothing, especially me

Resigned, was I, to play it out

Without a worry, nor a doubt

For such was life, I'd come to know

I'd never blossom, merely grow

And giving up, I'd realized

That through it all, I'd compromised

To honor oaths to all but me

I'd settled for facsimile

Till mindless stupor led me here
And crossed my path, and brought me near
A glimpse, a sip, to tempt my soul
A taste, a touch, to make me whole

On her wings, I soared so high
And in her eyes, her gentle sigh
And her caress, her tender kiss
My cup now filled to rim with bliss

I never looked, now knowing why
I never sought, so sure was I
Suspecting not, that it might be
That there could be someone for me

I'll never have another chance
I'll never get another dance
My time is now, my day, today
I'll never let her slip away

With both hands, she held the single sheet to the table, firmly pressing it down in the breeze with the tips of her fingers, fearful it would blow away forever. Her head bowed. She read the poem again. And yet again. Each in the succession triggered a renewed, prolonged wave of sobs from her. When every line, when every word had been etched permanently into her memory, she carefully, as if she were handling a delicate and ancient parchment, placed it back within the envelope, then returned it to the tote.

She next pulled out a larger manila envelope, also as yet unopened, and carefully peeled back the adhesive flap. The contents were a single sheet of paper and a large piece of photographic film. She read the letter. Halfway through taking in the text, she heard a single whimper burst from her lips. Setting the letter aside, she picked up the picture and stared at it in the halogen light for several minutes, tears freely streaming from her eyes.

"Look, Rocky." Holding the film toward him as he gazed at her, she struggled to force out the words, her voice shaking as badly as her hands. "Judtson and I are going to have twins! A boy and…." Kelsey's already quavering voice was torn away completely by the involuntary convulsions in her throat. Tears dripped, splattering upon the sonogram. Swallowing hard and taking a breath, she finished, "A boy and a girl."

He mewled softly, the sound nearly hidden by the incoming surf, and licked the tears from the picture before jumping his front paws onto her lap and licking her cheeks. She dropped the film on the table and hugged him as she wept. Finally releasing him, she slowly, carefully and with trembling hands, slipped the paper and film into the envelope and returned it to the tote. Her hands reemerged with a portable MP3 player.

Kelsey removed the book light from her head and, keeping it switched on, set it gently upon the tabletop. With a single glance down the now deserted beach, her eyes lingering on the spot where a bonfire once burned, she slipped off her shoes, tapped the player, and stood quickly, moving to the familiar location in the sand. At the first notes of "Can't Fight This Feeling," she began dancing slowly, gazed back at the table…focused on the book light…and, forcing a smile onto her face, said, "Hi! I'm Kelsey."

If you would like to purchase any of John David Krygelski's other novels, they are available at *Amazon.com, Barnes&Noble.com,* and many other fine booksellers.

A personalized, inscribed, and signed copy may be obtained at *www.starsyspublishing.com*

From the author –

To all of my many loyal friends and readers…the two-book saga of Judtson, Kelsey, Saylor, and the others became a monumental part of my life, delightfully filling nearly three years. None of my other projects have lasted quite so long, and I cannot begin to describe the impact most of the characters have had upon Jean and me. There were many times, while not in the midst of actual writing, that I caught myself wondering what Romeo and Ricky, for example, were up to at that moment.

As I sit here writing this message to you…now that the story is finished…the editing completed…the cover designed…and the whole package about to be dispatched to the printers, I can tell you that I already miss all of them. Well, almost all. Not Kristen, Mitch, Ulrigg, and a handful of others. But the rest, those who became a part of our circle…who all became very real friends…will be missed.

It was a joy for me to bring back for these two stories my real-life pal and angel – Rocky – whom we lost years ago. Our love for him has not diminished in the slightest.

Now, on to the nuts and bolts…

The two Mutatus stories evolved as they were written, driven by new discoveries in a number of fields, new developments in the world and in our own society, and the inevitable crystallization of theories and explanations as the process played out. As is always the case, my novels are a blend of fact and fiction. The Mutatus Nullification is no exception, although there may be some debate as to whether certain of the plot points are truly fact or merely theory or speculation. I'll leave all of that up to you, my astute readers, to ponder.

I would like to repeat that the aspects and uses of monoatomic gold are purely fictional. The interesting exception to this would be Kelsey's comments near the end of the story, regarding the actual rareness of the element. Apparently, gold is not a regular by-product occurring in the natural production of planets in various solar systems. According to numerous researchers, it is thought to be created as a result of extremely uncommon collisions between two neutron stars, events which are estimated to happen in our galaxy once in every 10,000 to 100,000 years. In other words, the chances of a habitable planet also containing gold are (pun intended) astronomical.

Finally, I wish to thank each of you for your feedback, your intensity, your enthusiasm, and your passion. On my darkest days, when the world seems more unfriendly, I know I can count on you to send an email, post a review, or put up a Facebook comment that instantly dissipates the clouds and brightens the day. And I must, once again, thank you for taking time to share your enjoyment of my books with your friends, relatives, and co-workers. Word of mouth is, and always has been, the most critical nourishment for this beast called publishing.

I hope that you enjoyed this outing.

All the best,
John David Krygelski

If you enjoyed reading *The Mutatus Nullification* by John David Krygelski, you may wish to consider his other novels. You can order a personally inscribed and autographed copy of any of his books by going to *www.starsyspublishing.com*.

The Mutatus Procedure (Part One)

In this taut psychological thriller, the protagonist, Judtson Kent, is a professional skeptic. In fact, he has made millions writing books debunking the myths and ridiculing the proponents of everything from Illuminati conspiracies to alien abductions. Then one day he is confronted with evidence…undeniable proof even he cannot refute. His world and belief system turned upside down, Judtson suddenly finds that his mind is slowly, inexorably losing control.

As Saylor Costello, a neurologist and Judtson's lifelong friend, battles the inexplicable mental transmutation, he discovers that several others around the world…others who are all on the verge of earthshaking discoveries…are suffering from the same symptoms.

Praise for John David Krygelski's fourth novel
The Mutatus Procedure (Part One)

The Mutatus Procedure *is a blockbuster that takes you by the scruff of the neck and thrusts you forward at breakneck speed until it drops you off exhausted on the last page. Whether you are a believer in all things alien or a skeptic, you too will be highly entertained and swept along with this magnificent tale of David and Goliath proportions.*

– Suspense Magazine - ★★★★★

"*The Mutatus Procedure* is the very best book I have read in the past ten years or so. It ranks right up there with *Amazonia*, by James Rollins."

"*The Mutatus Procedure (Part One)* is a compelling story that once again turns conventional wisdom on its ear – and does so in an appealing manner. I certainly never saw the 'big reveal' coming, but surely loved the twist! Love the author's ability to create such engaging characters who are so easy to identify with on a personal level. WARNING: this book is a page-turner!"

"What a fun ride! As always, Krygelski delivered again. What I love most about *The Mutatus Procedure* is that it always had me guessing what was going to happen next. It made me think about things and reevaluate my opinions over and over again. It had a great ending. By far, if you can read…you will love *The Mutatus Procedure*."

"Awesome book, gripping and addictive. It picks up speed fast and keeps you on the edge of your seat."

You can order a personalized and autographed copy of *The Mutatus Procedure (Part One)* in the softcover, audio book, or hardcover edition by going to *www.starsyspublishing.com*.

The Aegis Solution

In this, John David Krygelski's third and perhaps most powerful novel yet, he creates a spine-tingling story of suspense, drama, and intrigue. After the only child of the President – his teenaged daughter, Neve – commits suicide in a violent and senseless act, President Walker proposes an institution where people who have lost all hope may enter.

Impelled by Walker's grief and compassion, Aegis, intended to be a civilized alternative to suicide, is built and opened. There are only two rules in Aegis: no communication is allowed between the outside world and those who enter, and once individuals go in...they can never leave. Without the benefit of any personnel in Aegis, anarchy reigns, forcing those who enter to forge a new society.

Twelve years pass and what began as a noble social experiment has turned into a hideous nightmare, fraught with controversy and public outrage. In response, Elias Charon is selected by the new President to be the first to enter Aegis and be allowed to leave. Ostensibly, he is sent in to investigate the claims of abuse, but a darker and heinous personal motive arises.

With pulse-pounding suspense, *The Aegis Solution* takes the reader through a twisting, turning plot to an explosive and electrifying climax.

Praise for John David Krygelski's third novel
The Aegis Solution

"Once I started *The Aegis Solution*, I could hardly put it down. It was truly captivating, thrilling, and awe-inspiring. Thank you for such an outstanding read. It almost felt like I was there in Aegis with 'Mr. Death' and the lot!"

"I enjoyed it – of course! Again, a fantastic read! I look forward to your next literary entry! Don't make us wait too long!"

"I really enjoyed reading *The Aegis Solution*! Loved it, in fact. The characters were full of life, and I can see how something like this could happen. It gave me goosebumps."

"*The Aegis Solution* not only had me dying to know what happened next, I found myself intrigued by concepts, and deep in thought for most of my experience. I can't seem to find a word to describe how much I loved the book."

"I just finished reading *The Aegis Solution*, and I was totally enthralled from start to end. This book is by far my favorite of the three, with so many changes and points that caught me off-guard. I love the character Tillie. She was so stubborn and had strong opinions about what had happened and what could happen."

"Wow! That was quite good. I had trouble putting it down."

"I finished *The Aegis Solution* on my way home for the holidays. I must say, you have impressed me once again."

"When I am 90, one of my only regrets in life will be waiting until I was done reading my other books before I started reading yours. I did not see the ending coming at all – how a small isolated problem affected the whole world! It had me on the edge of my seat."

"All I can say is…Damn! That was a great story!!!!! It kept me on edge the whole time, and it was hard to put it down. It kept me wanting to know what would happen next. Again, thanks for the great book."

"*The Aegis Solution*, I have to say, was an amazing book. Every time I picked it up, the action kept me on the edge of my seat. The character development, as well as the plot twists, made for an awesome read."

"I wondered what the alternative to suicide was going to be for these folks. Would they be in suspended sleep? Would they go through intensive therapy? Alternate universes? Parallel timelines? One way in, no way out. I was really painting many pictures in my head. Nice layering of who was the baddest bad guy. When I thought I was close to one decision, you would spin me another way. Again, a fantastic read! Cover to cover, I was trying to decide where you were going, and I had many roads open, yet you led me down one I hadn't seen. Thanks for another fun ride."

You can order a personalized and autographed copy of *The Aegis Solution* in the softcover, audio book, or hardcover edition by going to *www.starsyspublishing.com.*

Time Cursor

Jack Augur comes back from thirty years in the future to stop his own wedding. Although warned of the dire consequences if he tampered with any other events, within minutes of meeting his younger self, he is responsible for the accidental death of the man who is to eventually invent the time machine. As the older and younger versions of the same man join forces to undo the damage they've done and get the world back on track, mysterious beings thwart their every attempt. *Time Cursor* is a roller coaster ride of suspense, action, and intrigue with an ending that will not disappoint.

Praise for John David Krygelski's second novel
Time Cursor

"It is amazingly brilliant, right there with some of the best I've read. In terms of science fiction, it's up there with greats like Heinlein; definitely a book I'm going to make sure stays in my possession."

"I couldn't put it down! I really enjoyed it. I truly hope that they make a movie out of it!!! Seriously…it was amazing!!! The ending freaked me out!!! :) I actually was sad when I finished it!!!!"

"The only thing I can say is **WHAT A RIDE!!!!!!!!!!!!!!!!!!!** Far exceeded my expectations. I've been reading SF since Asimov & Bradbury started, and this was a treat and a blast. Thanks again for a great run."

"Finished the book yesterday…WOW! Great story – super plot. Really twisted my mind on the intricacies of time travel, or time segment repositioning, if you prefer."

"I finished it over the weekend…LOVED it!!! Never saw the ending coming."

"Just finished *Time Cursor*, and I loved it! So enjoyable to read a book that wasn't dumbed down!"

"What an incredible read!!! Quite the twist at the end that I wasn't expecting."

You can order a personalized and autographed copy of *Time Cursor* in the softcover, audio book, or hardcover edition by going to *www.starsyspublishing.com.*

The Harvest

John David Krygelski's suspenseful debut novel – *The Harvest* – is a stunning tour de force! Whether tackling the epic battle between good and evil, or answering the subtle and persistent questions which haunt us all, Krygelski writes a compelling and startling story centered around the mysterious arrival of a man who claims to be The Creator.

Clearly not a mortal, Elohim – as the stranger prefers to be known – astounds those he meets with unexplainable miracles and reality-altering answers. All of this is but a prelude to his announcement that he has come to do something…something which will affect every person on Earth…something which will occur in five days.

Against the backdrop of a world reacting to the announcement that God has arrived, a hastily assembled group of interviewers question and test Elohim…while hidden forces emerge to thwart his plans.

The Harvest is a gripping page-turner – a book which will change your view of the world.

Praise for John David Krygelski's first novel – *The Harvest*

In this ground-breaking novel, John Krygelski weaves a story of intrigue and suspense, all the while defining and explaining some of the greatest mysteries of life itself.

– **Janet K. Brennan**, author of *A Dance in the Woods*

If you only have time to read one book this year – make it this one. It's one of the best books I've ever read.

– **Jan Marshall**, author of *A Curious State of Affairs*

This dense and carefully plotted story involves a thoughtful look at religion. Reese Johnson, a professor at the University of Arizona, is teaching "Religion Under Assault" when he suddenly finds himself investigating a man who calls himself "The Creator." For hopefuls everywhere looking for a second chance to create a better world, this is an intriguing novel.

– **J. C. Martin**, *Arizona Daily Star*

"It is, in one word, a masterpiece! The best book I've ever read, and I've read thousands."

"Not only is *The Harvest* the best book I've ever read, it is very likely the best thing I'll ever read!"

"...this book was one of the most extraordinary books I have ever read. It touched me and made me examine my entire life. It is hard to believe that this is anyone's first book. Thank you for writing it."

"*The Harvest* is amazingly written, intriguing, very different and fascinating, deep...highly recommended reading."

"...this book is our lives; we are living it as we read it. Krygelski reached into my most inner thoughts and put them in words. *The Harvest* will have you questioning the very foundations of your beliefs."

"I have been reading nearly all of my 60 years. This is the most profound book I have ever read. I can't believe that this is the first novel by Mr. Krygelski. I plan on re-reading it again, as well as ordering more for my family."

"*The Harvest* had me completely enthralled from beginning to end. I never wanted to put the book down, being one of the most interesting reads I have ever had the pleasure to experience. I have difficulty expressing in words how much I truly loved this book."

"...congratulations on *The Harvest*...I appreciate the way you clarify some of my deepest beliefs. I think your book challenges the reader to look inward and think. Brilliant. I'm telling everyone I know to get *The Harvest*."

"I have really enjoyed *The Harvest*. It has been one of the best books I have read. I was even shocked to have found myself referring to certain passages in the book and looking more into the depth of the history in certain topics, and actually using a dictionary as well; no book lately in the past 5 years has accomplished such. I actually am reading it again for the second time. Thank you."

You can order a personalized and autographed copy of *The Harvest* in the softcover, large print, audio book, or hardcover edition by going to *www.starsyspublishing.com*.

Starsys Publishing Company
is proud to announce the release of
Grabbing the Brass Ring – Michael Earl Nolan
Featuring
An Extraordinary Life: The Biography of Michael Earl Nolan

Grabbing the Brass Ring is an epic Homeric tale of a complex and enigmatic man, Richard Mansan – a front-line fighter, an adventurer, and a natural leader. In a time close to ours...on a world not unlike our own...Mansan is either blessed or cursed with the ability to clearly see the inevitable consequences of mankind's actions, choices, and hubris – a vision shared by no one else.

As a result of serendipity or design, he finds himself inextricably entwined with the major leaders of the day. Yet, despite the benefit of his friendship and counsel, as well as their own valiant efforts, they are unable to stem the tide of events as the world catapults madly to an unavoidable fate.

A story of power, war, greed, ignorance, pride, and redemption, *Grabbing the Brass Ring* will give the reader a glimpse at the worst…and the best within all of us.

About the Author

An Extraordinary Life: The Biography of Michael Earl Nolan, the complete biography of the author, is included at the conclusion of his novel.

After a phenomenal career as a legendary football player, record-setting track and field star, powerhouse wrestler and weightlifter, and multi-titled heavyweight boxing champion – Michael Earl Nolan joined the U.S. Marine Corps in 1941. He fought at Guadalcanal, Bougainville with the famed Raiders, and Iwo Jima, rising from private to captain during the war, and retiring a major.

With an amazing life that spanned hopping freight trains in the 1930s to becoming the highly respected civil engineer responsible for the massive Coronado National Forest, Nolan was a fascinating individual, a sensitive and prophetic novelist, a devoted family man and friend. To this day, he remains an inspiration, a real-life hero in every sense of the word.

Praise for Michael Earl Nolan's
Grabbing the Brass Ring
Featuring
An Extraordinary Life: The Biography of Michael Earl Nolan

★★★★★   "Michael Earl Nolan takes a 'no apologies' approach to *Grabbing the Brass Ring*. The narrative at times reads like a cross between a journal and a memoir which complements the main character's personality. Richard Mansan's description and evaluation of other characters and events come across as if he is engaging in an elaborate chess game rather than living his life. The novel is surprisingly filled with ironies which invite the readers to identify ironies in their own lives. One major irony present throughout the novel is the term 'elusive bauble' used at times in place of 'brass ring.' This mirrors Richard Mansan's calculated measures and obsessive lengths to ensure humanity's future despite his low expectations of human capacity and their lack of invested interest in society.

"The included author's biography is thorough and excellently compiled. There are not many opportunities for insight into the life and character of an incredibly accomplished and well-respected and loved individual. Given the excellence in all aspects of Mr. Nolan's life, it is no surprise that taking the time to put pen to paper would result in an insightful and succinct evaluation of human nature which still holds true today."

★★★★★   "Amazing. Absolutely amazing. It would be difficult to express the enjoyment and thrill I have had from this book. The biography alone was worth the price of the book to me.

"Thank you for doing this. Thank you for putting Earl's writings into the world where they most certainly belong. Thank you for giving such a thorough and honest accounting of his life. His is a story which needed to be told. It is a rich topic handled with a quality that such riches deserve."

★★★★★   "This book is a phenomenal combination of a gripping, visionary novel about a world not unlike our own, facing certain environmental disaster. A lone figure, a front-line fighter, decides that he may know the answer to saving the planet before it is too late. To do so, he must somehow gain the position of leader...leader of all people. He must 'grab the brass ring.' While there is still time. The second half of this book is a biography of the author...a college and professional footballer, a track star who set a record which stood for three decades, a Marine Raider who fought on Iwo Jima, Bougainville, and Guadalcanal, entering the Corps as a private at the beginning of WWII and ending the war as a captain. An amazing man whose story needs to be read to be believed. I highly recommend this book!"

You can order a copy of *Grabbing the Brass Ring* in either the softcover or hardcover edition by going to *www.starsyspublishing.com*.

To learn even more about any of these books, or to order a copy, go to

WWW.STARSYSPUBLISHING.COM